Prai

'Exciting stuff with -
gered up by mystery and intrigue . . . Leather is an intelligent thriller writer' *Daily Mail* on *The Tunnel Rats*

'One of his best . . . ingenious . . . the tension is continuous, increasing in a crescendo as the tale reaches its conclusion'
Oxford Times on *The Tunnel Rats*

'A well-constructed and fast-moving plot . . . stunning . . . another top-notch thriller'
Yorkshire Evening Post on *The Tunnel Rats*

'Impressive' *Glasgow Herald* on *Pay Off*

'As high-tech and as world-class as the thriller genre gets'
Express on Sunday on *The Bombmaker*

'A whirlwind of action, suspense and vivid excitement'
Irish Times on *The Birthday Girl*

'Atmospheric suspense' *Daily Mirror* on *The Eyewitness*

'Stephen Leather should be nestling in your bookshelves alongside Frederick Forsyth and Jack Higgins . . . exciting stuff with plenty of heart palpitating action gingered up by mystery and intrigue . . . Leather is an intelligent thriller writer' *Daily Mail*

Also by Stephen Leather

The Fireman
Hungry Ghost
The Chinaman
The Vets
The Long Shot
The Birthday Girl
The Double Tap
The Solitary Man
The Bombmaker
The Stretch
Tango One
The Eyewitness
Hard Landing
Soft Target
Cold Kill

About the author

Stephen Leather was a journalist for more than ten years on newspapers such as *The Times*, the *Daily Mail* and the *South China Morning Post* in Hong Kong. Before that, he was employed as a biochemist for ICI, shovelled limestone in a quarry, worked as a baker, a petrol pump attendant, a barman, and worked for the Inland Revenue. He began writing full-time in 1992. His best-sellers have been translated into more than ten languages. He has also written for television shows such as *London's Burning*, *The Knock* and the BBC's *Murder in Mind* series. You can find out more from his website www.stephenleather.com.

STEPHEN LEATHER

The Tunnel Rats
Pay Off

HODDER

The Tunnel Rats first published in Great Britain
in 1997 by Hodder & Stoughton
Pay Off first published in Great Britain
in 1987 by Hodder & Stoughton
This omnibus edition first published in 2006 by Hodder and Stoughton
A division of Hodder Headline

A Hodder paperback

2

A CIP catalogue record for this title
is available from the British Library

ISBN 0 340 92216 8

Hodder Headline's policy is to use papers that are natural, renewable
and recyclable products and made from wood grown in sustainable
forests. The logging and manufacturing processes are expected to
conform to the environmental regulations of the country of origin.

Typeset by Hewer Text UK Ltd, Edinburgh
Printed and bound in Great Britain by
Mackays of Chatham Plc, Chatham, Kent

Hodder and Stoughton
A division of Hodder Headline PLC
338 Euston Road
London NW1 3BH

The Tunnel Rats

For Maureen

I am indebted to Alistair Cumming for keeping me on the right track regarding the work of the British Transport Police, and to Mr Hoang, who took me deeper into the Vietnamese tunnels than I really wanted to go. I read and reread the definitive work on the Cu Chi tunnel complext – *The Tunnels of Cu Chi* by Tom Mangold and John Penycate, first published by Hodder & Stoughton in 1985 – and unreservedly recommend it to anyone who wants to known more about one of the most remarkable battlefields of the Vietnam War.

The scorpion's jet-black endoskeleton glistened as it scuttled away from the anvil-shaped rock. It moved quickly, its stinger arched over its back, leaving a trail in the sandy dirt the only record of its passing. The jungle at dusk was usually a noisy place, with birds and insects marking their territory before the final rays of the reddish sun disappeared below the horizon, but for several minutes there had been a heavy silence as if the whole world was holding its breath.

A small indentation appeared in the dirt in front of the rock, as if a ghostly finger had scratched the surface. The indentation formed a straight line and grains of dirt dribbled down into the crease. A second line appeared, eighteen inches away from the first and running parallel to it, then a third line appeared, and a fourth, and the lines slowly grew together until they formed a rectangle in the dirt. There was a gentle scraping sound from somewhere under the ground, then the rectangle of dirt lifted up. Grains of soil spilled around the sides as the rectangle tilted, revealing a bamboo hatchway into which dry leaves had been intertwined. The hatch was thrown to the side, uncovering a square hole.

A soft peaked cap made of camouflage material appeared, and then a face. The face was striped with light and dark green paint and there was no way of knowing where the flesh ended and the cap began. Narrowed eyes scrutinised the surrounding area for several minutes. Only when the man was satisfied that it was safe did he leave the hole, crawling on his belly like a snake, a silenced automatic in his right hand, an unlit flashlight in his left. As he crawled away from the hatch, a second figure appeared, another man wearing identical gear, but with a scarf of camouflage material tied around his head instead of a cap.

The first man knelt in the shade of a thick-trunked tree around which vines wound like the veins in an old woman's arm. He made an 'okay' gesture with the thumb and first finger of his left hand and beckoned for the second man to come out in the open, all the time his eyes scanning the jungle, alert for any sign of danger. The second man joined him, a sawn-off shotgun cradled in his hands like a valuable antique. The second man nodded at the first, then moved off to the right.

A third head emerged from the hole. The third man wasn't wearing a cap, and his short, dark, curly hair was the only sign that he was of a different race to the first two, because every inch of his exposed skin was covered in camouflage paint. He crawled out, an M2 carbine with a paratrooper stock in his right hand, closely followed by a fourth man.

They fanned out until the four men were equally spaced around the hatch, far enough apart so that they couldn't all be taken out with a single hand grenade or a spray of automatic fire. The men were used to working together as a team and communicated only with small hand movements and nods. They remained immobile for a full minute until they were satisfied that they were alone in the jungle, then the man with the flashlight crept back to the hatchway.

A fifth man appeared at the entrance, his face contorted with pain, and the man with the flashlight helped him out. The fifth man could barely walk, and even with the other man's help he stumbled and fell face down into the sandy dirt. The back of his shirt was ripped and torn in more than a dozen places and streaked with still-wet blood. The man with the flashlight knelt down by the side of the injured man and checked his wounds with a professional eye. He patted the man's neck and whispered something in his ear, then went back to the hatchway where a sixth man was already crawling out into the open.

The eyes of the sixth man were wide and staring, the whites exaggerated by the camouflage paint smeared over his flesh. He stumbled to his feet and looked around anxiously as if wondering which way to run.

The man with the flashlight holstered his gun and gripped the shoulder of the sixth man, pulling him close so that their faces were only inches apart. 'It's okay,' he hissed. 'We're out.' The sixth man opened his mouth but no words came. The man with the flashlight glared at him with a fierce intensity. 'It's okay,' he said. 'Tell me it's okay, Rabbit.' He tightened his grip on the man's shoulder.

The sixth man visibly relaxed. 'It's okay,' he whispered.

'Again.'

'It's okay,' said the sixth man, slightly more confident this time. 'I'm sorry, Doc. I lost it.'

The two men stared at each other for several seconds, then the man with the flashlight nodded. 'We all lost it,' he said. He took his hand away from Rabbit's shoulder and stared at his palm. It was red with blood. 'Are you hurt?' Doc asked.

Rabbit shook his head. 'No. It's . . .' He shook his head as if trying to rid himself of a bad memory.

A seventh man climbed through the hatchway, a green headband holding his dirt-encrusted hair flat against his scalp. He had a rope tied around his waist and it tightened as he crawled away from the hole. 'Help me,' he said, through tightly gritted teeth.

Doc and Rabbit grabbed the rope and pulled, grunting with exertion. 'Are you sure he's . . . ?' began Rabbit, but Doc silenced him with a threatening look.

Together they hauled in the rope. Attached to the other end was the body of another soldier. The rope had been looped under his arms and they heaved the body out of the hole. The neck was a mass of torn flesh as if it had been hacked with a dull blade and the shirt was caked with dried blood.

The seventh man took an eighteen-inch-long knife from a scabbard on his leg and used it to cut the rope from around his own waist. As he replaced the knife in its scabbard he saw that the back of his hand was covered with blood. He knelt down and wiped his hand in the dirt. His skin was a dark olive colour and even under the camouflage make-up his high razor-sharp cheekbones hinted at his Latino ancestry. 'Now what?' he said, looking up at Doc. His voice was flat and cold and his eyes were equally emotionless.

'Put the hatch back,' said Doc.

The man in the headband nodded and did as he was told.

Doc went over to the injured man and knelt down beside him again. 'On your feet,' he whispered. 'We can't stay here.'

The injured man murmured something incomprehensible and struggled to stand. Rabbit came over to help and together with Doc he pulled the man upright. In the distance there was a low rumbling growl as if a thunderstorm was approaching. 'I'm all right,' said the injured man.

'Can you walk?' asked Doc.

'Don't worry about me,' he said.

The Latino slotted the hatch into its original position and smoothed dirt over it.

Doc looked over his shoulder. 'Sergio, put the rock over it. Rabbit, give him a hand.'

The two men pushed the rock over the hatchway. Doc looked towards the horizon, smeared blood red by the dying rays of the sun.

'That was bad, Doc,' said the injured man.

'I know.'

'Real bad.'

'Forget it,' said Doc, cocking his head and listening to the approaching thunder.

Rabbit and Sergio joined Doc and the injured man. Doc motioned for the three other men to join the group and they stood in a circle, avoiding each other's gaze as if fearful of what they might see in their eyes. The sun began to slip below the horizon and the shadows of the seven men faded on the sandy ground.

'That goes for all of us,' said Doc. 'We forget it. We forget it ever happened.'

'There'll be questions,' said Sergio.

'And I'll answer them. No one gets blamed. No recriminations.' He looked across at the mutilated corpse. 'What happened down there stays dead and buried.' He looked back at the men. 'Any arguments? If there are, I want to hear them now.' All six men shook their heads. Doc reached towards Rabbit and seized his hand. He wiped his forefinger across Rabbit's bloody palm, then smeared the blood across Sergio's right hand. He did the same to all the men, then held out his own hand, palm down. Sergio put his hand on top of Doc's, and one by one the men followed suit until there were seven hands piled one on top of the other. Below their feet the earth began to vibrate.

'Not worth a rat's ass,' said Doc. 'Let me hear you say it.'

One by one the men repeated the phrase.

Doc took his hand away from the bottom of the stack. 'Let's go,' he said. 'We've got a long walk home.'

The men unlinked their hands.

'Shit,' said the injured man, his hand reaching up to his neck.

'What?' asked Doc.

'My dogtags. They've gone.' His head swivelled around and he stared at the rock and the covered hatch. He took a step towards the rock.

Doc gripped the man's arm. 'Leave it.'

A sudden explosion far off to their right knocked them to the ground. It was followed swiftly by a second and a third.

'B-52s!' shouted Sergio. 'They're dumping their shit!'

Doc got to his feet and helped the injured man up. 'Let's get out of here,' he shouted.

There were more explosions off to their left. The last of the sun disappeared below the horizon as the seven men regrouped. Rabbit helped Doc with the injured man and together they headed south, away from the falling bombs.

The scorpion emerged from underneath a twig torn from a tree by the force of the explosions. Doc raised a booted foot and stamped on it, squashing it flat without breaking stride.

The old lady muttered to herself as she walked along the street pushing a supermarket trolley, and passers-by gave her a wide berth. She had a red woollen scarf tied around her head and a thick tweed coat that reached down almost to her ankles. She was wearing scuffed leather boots with bright yellow shoelaces and from around her ankles protruded pieces of newspaper. One of the wheels on her trolley kept sticking and she had to concentrate hard to keep it moving in a straight line. The trolley contained everything she owned, packed into plastic carrier bags which were stacked on several sheets of cardboard.

She stopped next to a rubbish bin and began searching through it. Her first major find was a copy of the *Daily Telegraph*, rolled up tightly. She unrolled it carefully and flicked through it. She beamed with pleasure as she saw that the crossword hadn't been done, and refolded it, slipping it into one of the carrier bags. Deeper inside the bin she came across a Burger King carton containing a barely touched cheeseburger and a pack of French fries, along with an unopened sachet of tomato ketchup. She giggled and did a little jig around the bin, then packed her treasure into another carrier bag and resumed her journey. There were more than a dozen rubbish bins along the one-mile stretch of road and she checked them twice each day.

Small drops of rain began to patter around her and she glared up at the leaden sky. A raindrop splattered on her spectacles and she took them off and wiped the lenses with a pale blue handkerchief. After she'd put her glasses back on she untied a large golfing umbrella from the side of her trolley, unfurled it, and jammed the handle down among the carrier bags so that she had some shelter as she walked.

The train lurched to a halt, throwing a Japanese tourist off balance. Her husband steadied her by the elbow as the doors opened and half a dozen passengers spilled out on to the platform. The doors closed and the Tube train swiftly accelerated towards the next station. Tommy Reid rested the back of his head against the window and exhaled through clenched teeth. He'd been riding the Circle Line train for more than two hours and he was dog tired. He had a bottle in a brown paper bag, which he raised to his lips, taking a couple of swallows. He narrowed his eyes and stared at the map on the wall of the carriage opposite him. Bayswater was the next station. He sighed mournfully. The muscles in his backside ached and his ears hurt from the near-constant noise. He scratched the two-day growth of beard with the palm of his hand and grinned across at the blind man sitting opposite him, a thirty-something man in blue wrinkled linen jacket and black jeans, holding a white cane between his legs.

The train began to slow as it approached Bayswater. Reid's earpiece crackled. 'We have a possible contact,' said a voice. 'Three white males. Black motorcycle jacket, red baseball jacket with white sleeves, green anorak.' The three muggers had struck four times in the last week.

Reid sniffed and took another swig at the bottle as the train slowed then stopped.

'Fourth carriage,' said the voice in his ear. Reid was in the fifth carriage from the front. He swivelled his head. Through the window in the connecting door he saw the three teenagers board the carriage and huddle together, laughing at something Anorak had said.

The doors closed and the train lurched forward again. Motorcycle Jacket took a stopwatch from the back pocket of his jeans and nodded at Anorak and Baseball Jacket. All three of the teenagers pulled out black objects from inside their jackets, the size of flashlights with small metal prongs on the end, and spread out along the length of the carriage. Baseball Jacket clicked the trigger on his and blue sparks arced across the prongs.

Reid got to his feet and went over to the connecting door. Two schoolgirls moved away uneasily. He slowly buttoned up his thick overcoat, figuring it would offer at least some protection against the stun guns. Reinforcements would be waiting at Paddington, and all Reid had to do was to make sure that no one got hurt.

A businessman handed over his wallet. Anorak took it and put it into a green Harrods carrier bag. A housewife fumbled in her shopping bag while Baseball Jacket stood over her menacingly. An elderly black man was waving his hands and shaking his head, clearly unwilling to give up his money. Anorak walked quickly over to him, thrust the prongs of his stun gun against the man's thigh and pressed the trigger. The man screamed and then stiffened, his whole body shuddering involuntarily.

'Oh shit,' said Reid. The muggers had never actually used their stun guns before – the threat alone had always been enough to frighten their victims into submission. He gripped the metal handle and pulled open the door. The noise of the rolling gear rattling down the rails was deafening. He opened the door leading to the adjoining carriage and stepped across the gap.

The three teenagers looked up. Reid held out the bottle and grinned blankly. 'Wanna drink?' he asked, pretending to lose his balance. Reid figured they were about thirty seconds away from Paddington – all he had to do was to keep them distracted.

Suddenly the door at the far end of the carriage opened and two men in leather jackets and jeans burst in. Reid cursed. They might as well have been wearing uniforms.

'Cops!' yelled Motorcycle Jacket. 'Run for it!'

All three teenagers hurtled down the carriage, towards Reid. Anorak reached him first. Reid stepped to the side and slammed his bottle against the teenager's head. Anorak slumped to the side, falling against two young men in suits who grabbed him and wrestled him to the ground.

Reid tried to bring up the bottle for a second time but Baseball Jacket ran into him, slamming him against the carriage door, then stabbed the stun gun against Reid's shoulder and pressed the trigger. Reid felt as if he'd been kicked by a horse. He tried to breathe but his lungs wouldn't work and the life seemed to drain out of his legs. Baseball Jacket yanked open the door and he and Motorcycle Jacket spilled into the next carriage. Reid heard the brakes begin to bite as the train approached Paddington.

They rushed along the carriage, pushing the two schoolgirls out of the way, the two plainclothes policemen about ten paces behind. Ahead of them the blind man was getting to his feet, one hand gripping his white cane, the other outstretched. The train burst out of the tunnel and the platform flashed by.

'Out of the way!' Baseball Jacket shouted, pushing the blind man to the side as the train came to a halt and the doors opened. Baseball Jacket stepped out, but as he did so, a hand grabbed his hair and yanked him back.

'You're under arrest,' said the blind man, slamming Baseball Jacket against the side of the carriage. The white cane dropped to the floor.

Motorcycle Jacket skidded to a halt and held out his stun gun. 'You're not blind!' he shouted.

'It's a miracle,' grinned the blind man, jerking Baseball Jacket's arm up behind his back until the teenager yelped in pain.

Motorcycle Jacket glared at the blind man, then spat at his face and jumped out of the carriage. The blind man pushed Baseball Jacket towards the two plainclothes policemen, who grabbed his arms, then he tossed his sunglasses away and chased after Motorcycle Jacket.

The uniformed inspector shook his head in frustration as he stared at the closed-circuit television monitor. The teenager in the motorcycle jacket was cannoning down the platform, pushing people out of his way and waving his stun gun in the air. Nick Wright was in pursuit, his arms pumping furiously as he ran. On another monitor Tommy Reid stumbled out on to the platform, still holding his bottle, and was almost bowled over by the fleeing mugger.

'Keystone bloody Cops,' muttered the inspector.

'Sorry, sir?' said the shirtsleeved officer sitting in front of him.

'Where are the reinforcements?' said the inspector, putting his hands on the back of the officer's chair and leaning closer to the rank of monitors.

'Main ticketing area, sir,' said the officer. He pressed a button on the panel in front of him and the image on the central monitor changed to show half a dozen uniformed British Transport Police officers sprinting towards the top of the escalators.

The inspector straightened up and ran a hand through his thinning hair. He watched the mugger run into one of the exits, closely followed by Wright. At least Wright appeared to be gaining on him.

Nick Wright exhaled through clenched teeth as he ran, his lungs burning with each breath. He swung around a corner just in time to see Motorcycle Jacket collide with a guitar-playing busker, scattering a tin can of coins across the tiled floor.

'Stop him!' Wright shouted, but no one moved to help. His quarry sprinted to the escalators and ran up, pushing people out of the way.

'Police!' yelled Wright. 'Move, people, please!' Again his pleas were ignored and he had physically to force his way up the escalator after the teenager.

Motorcycle Jacket was halfway up the escalator when a

group of six uniformed officers appeared at the top and fanned out. The boy snarled at the waiting officers, then leaped off the escalator and on to the concrete stairs. He sped down the steps, taking them five at a time, as the policemen rushed to the down escalator.

Wright vaulted off the escalator and on to the stairs, twisting his leg as he landed. Passengers on both escalators watched in amazement as the teenager cannoned down the steps with Wright in pursuit.

As they neared the bottom of the stairs, Reid appeared around the corner. His jaw dropped as he saw Motorcycle Jacket running towards him, and before he could react, Motorcycle Jacket ran into him, knocking him to the side.

The teenager was a good fifteen years younger than Wright, and Wright cursed the age difference as he ran. He took a quick look over his shoulder, flashing Reid a sympathetic smile. In his earpiece, Wright could hear the inspector giving instructions to his men, but there was no sign of the uniformed officers. Motorcycle Jacket reached a crossroads and dashed off to the left, forcing his way between two students with rucksacks. The tunnel led to a platform which Motorcycle Jacket sprinted along. Closed-circuit television cameras stared down at them as they ran along the platform.

Motorcycle Jacket slowed as he realised that there were no more exits off the platform, and all that lay ahead was the train tunnel.

Wright slowed, too. In his earpiece, the inspector told his men which platform Wright was on. He heard footsteps behind him and he turned to see Tommy Reid jog on to the platform, some distance behind him.

'I've got him, Tommy,' Wright shouted. Reid waved his bottle in acknowledgement.

Motorcycle Jacket turned to face the two men, holding his stun gun in front of him, then jumped down on to the track and began to sprint towards the tunnel mouth.

Wright took a quick look up at the digital display above the platform – the next train wouldn't be along for six minutes. He ran after Motorcycle Jacket, into the blackness of the tunnel, then gradually slowed and stopped.

The teenager was bent double, his hands on his knees, fighting for breath. 'What are you waiting for?' shouted Motorcycle Jacket.

Wright jumped as if he'd been pinched. He swallowed. His mouth was dry yet his whole body felt as if it was drenched in sweat. He tried to step forward, but his legs wouldn't move. Reid had jumped down on to the track and was walking uncertainly towards him.

Motorcycle Jacket grinned. 'What, afraid of the dark, are we? Jesus, are you in the wrong fucking job or what?' Laughing, he turned his back on Wright and began to jog down the track, into the blackness.

Wright closed his eyes, willing himself to follow the teenager, but he simply couldn't move. His legs remained locked. A hand fell on his shoulder.

'What's up, Nick?' asked Reid, and he moved to stand in front of Wright. 'You're soaking wet,' he said.

Wright opened his eyes. 'He got away,' he said.

'Don't worry about it. We'll get the bastard.' Reid held up his bottle. 'How about a drink?'

Wright shook his head. He took one last look into the black depths of the tunnel, then turned and walked towards the platform. Back into the light.

The old lady splashed through a puddle and grimaced. The newspapers lining her leather boots kept her warm but they didn't keep out the water. The rain was pouring down, and even with the golfing umbrella over her head, she was still getting soaked. Ahead of her lay the mouth of the tunnel she knew would provide her with warmth and sanctuary.

She rattled the trolley along the side of the railway line, the rails crusted with dirt and rust from years of disuse. The wheels of her trolley skidded across a patch of gravel and then locked as they bit into damp grass. The old lady whispered soft words of encouragement and coaxed the trolley into the tunnel. It was suddenly quiet. One by one she removed the carrier bags, then she carefully placed her sheets of cardboard and three blankets on the ground and sat down on them with a grunt.

She leaned over to the carrier bag where she'd put the Burger King carton. She opened the carton with an expectant smile on her face, then took out the burger and sniffed it. It couldn't have been more than a couple of hours old; it was still warm. She took a bite and chewed slowly. Something moved at the tunnel entrance, something small and black that kept close to the rail furthest from her. It was a rat, almost two feet long from nose to tail. The old woman watched it go. She had no fear of rats, and no revulsion either. Like her, it was only seeking food and shelter. She tore off a small piece of hamburger and tossed it over to the rat, but it ignored the tidbit and hurried by.

The man woke as the first rays of the morning sun hit the tops of the New York skyscrapers. Down below, the city's garbage trucks growled through the streets and far off in the distance a siren howled like a lovesick dog. As soon as his eyes opened he sat up and swung his legs off the single bed. There was no clock in the small room and no watch on the man's wrist but he knew exactly what the time was. He walked naked to the bathroom, his feet padding across the bare wooden floorboards. He stood under a cold shower and washed methodically from his head down. He rinsed and dried himself before going back into his tiny room and opening the door to the wardrobe. A single grey suit hung there, with three identical long-sleeved white shirts that had been laundered and were still in their polythene wrappings. A tie rack on the back of the wardrobe door held a solitary tie. At the bottom of the wardrobe were two drawers. The man pulled the top one open. It contained a dozen pairs of khaki shorts. He slipped on a pair, then took the sheets, blanket and pillowcase from the bed and put them in the wardrobe.

Behind the bathroom door was a black plastic bucket and a wooden-handled mop. The man filled the bucket with water and swabbed the wooden floor. When he'd finished with the floor, he used a cloth meticulously to clean the toilet, basin and shower.

The cleaning over, he went back into the room and sat down on a wooden chair, his hands on his knees. In an hour's time he would exercise for thirty minutes, then he would go to a local diner and eat breakfast. He would only leave the room twice, both times to eat; the rest of the time he would spend exercising and waiting. Waiting for the call. The man knew the call would come eventually. It always had in the past.

The rat scurried purposefully down the disused rail track, its nose twitching as it scented the air ahead. It could smell something sweet, something nourishing, something that it hadn't smelled in a long time. It was joined by a second rat, a female several inches shorter. A third rat emerged from the darkness to their left, its eyes glinting and its ears forward.

The three rats began to run, their paws crunching on the gravel around the sleepers. Soon they were among more rats. A dozen. Twenty. All heading the same way. Before long the tunnel entrance was nothing more than a small squashed circle behind them. The three rats stopped running: there were too many furry bodies ahead of them to keep up the pace. They slowed to a walk, then they had to push their way through the mass of rodents to make any progress. The sweet smell was stronger, driving them into a frenzy. Food. The food was close by.

Superintendent Richard Newton stirred his tea thoughtfully as he watched the video recording. He looked up as his secretary entered his office and placed a plate of assorted biscuits on his desk. 'Thanks, Nancy,' he said, using the remote control to switch off the recorder. He sighed and leaned back in his executive chair. 'I suppose you'd better send in the clowns,' he said.

Nancy opened the door and ushered in Nick Wright and Tommy Reid. They stood in front of his desk, unsure whether or not to sit. Newton continued to stir his tea, a look of contempt on his face. Reid had changed out of his tramp's disguise, but his brown suit and stained tie weren't much of an improvement. Wright was as usual the better dressed of the two, but there were dark patches under his eyes as if he hadn't slept for a week. Both men studiously avoided Newton's stare, their eyes fixed on a point in the wall behind him.

'Tell me, Tommy, what does the word "assistance" mean to you?' Newton asked.

'Help?' said Reid, hopefully.

Newton nodded. 'Help would do. Support. Aid. All perfectly reasonable alternatives. So when the Moles asked for assistance, what do you think they expected to get?'

'Help, sir?' said Reid, frowning.

'Exactly,' said Newton. 'Help. Not hindrance, not a foul-up, not two of my men making fools of themselves. What happened down there? How did he get away?'

'The guy was fast, sir. That guy could run for England.'

Newton sniffed and wrinkled his nose. 'Maybe if you two spent more time in the gym and less time in the pub you'd have been able to keep up with him.' He picked up his spoon and started to stir his tea again. 'What was in the bottle, Tommy?'

After several seconds of silence, Reid shrugged. 'I was supposed to be an alkie, sir. I could hardly have carted around a bottle of Perrier, could I?'

'Inspector Murray said you'd been drinking on the job. So I'm asking you on the record, what was in the bottle? On the record, Tommy.'

Reid looked across at his partner, then back at the superintendent. 'Ribena, sir.'

Newton put the spoon down and sipped his tea. 'Ribena?' he said, as if it was the first time he'd ever heard the word. 'That would account for the smell on your breath, I suppose,' he said dryly, then opened the top drawer of his desk and took out a pack of Polo mints which he rolled across his desk towards Reid. 'We're going to need an artist's impression of the one that got away. There's nothing usable on the video.' He dismissed them with a tired half-wave, then had a change of mind. 'Nick, stay behind, will you?'

Newton waited until Reid had closed the door before asking Wright to sit down on one of the two steel and leather chairs facing the desk. 'Are you still living with Tommy?' he asked.

Wright nodded. 'Yes, sir.'

'How long's it been now? Three months?'

'Five.'

Newton traced his finger along the edge of his saucer. 'What about getting a place of your own?'

Wright pulled a face as if he was in pain. 'It's a question of money, sir. Things are a bit tight just now.'

'Your divorce came through, right?'

Wright nodded again. 'Yeah, but she's still after more money. There's the house payments, child support, she wanted double-glazing put in.' Wright held his hands out as if warding off an attack. 'I'm sorry, I shouldn't bring my problems into the office.'

'You've nothing to apologise for, Nick. Divorce is becoming the norm these days. Unfortunately.' He stared at the cup with its pattern of roses. 'Five months is a long time to be living with Tommy. He's one of our best detectives, but his personal life leaves a lot to be desired. You've got a lot of potential, Nick. I wouldn't want any of his – how shall I put it? – habits, rubbing off on you.'

'Understood, sir.'

Newton's telephone rang and he waved for Wright to go as he reached for the receiver.

The old woman muttered to herself as she threaded a plastic-covered chain around the shopping trolley and padlocked it to the lamp-post. She checked that it was securely fastened before walking into the police station.

A uniformed sergeant looked up as she approached the counter. He smiled politely. 'Hello, Annie, how are you today?' he asked.

'I've seen Jesus,' said the old woman. 'On the cross.'

'That's nice,' said the sergeant. He was in his early fifties, with greying hair and a tired face from years of dealing with irate members of the public, but the smile he gave the old lady seemed genuine enough. 'How about a nice cup of tea? Two sugars, right?' The sergeant called over a WPC, a slim brunette, and asked her to fetch the old woman a cup of tea from the machine in the reception area. The sergeant reached into his pocket and gave the WPC a few coins. 'Milk, two sugars,' he said. The WPC gave the old woman a quizzical look. 'Annie Lees, she's a regular,' the sergeant explained. He lowered his voice to a conspiratorial whisper. 'She's harmless.'

The old woman stood up straight and glared at him through the thick lenses of her spectacles. 'Young man, I am not harmless,' she said, her voice trembling with indignation.

The doctor unscrewed the cap off the tube of KY Jelly and smeared it over the rubber glove, making sure there was plenty over the first and second fingers.

His patient hitched his gown up around his waist and bent over the examination couch. 'I had hoped that by the time I became Vice President I'd be past the stage where I'd have to let people shove their hands up my backside,' he joked.

The doctor smiled thinly and put down the tube. He knew how concerned his patient was, but he also knew that there was nothing he could say to put him at ease. The examination was purely routine, and neither man was expecting a change in the prognosis. 'Okay, Glenn, you know the drill. Try to relax.'

The patient chuckled dryly and opened his legs wider. 'Relax, says the man. You know when I last relaxed?' He grunted as the doctor inserted two fingers into his rectum.

'Try to push down, Glenn. I know it hurts.'

'Pete, you have no idea.' The patient forced his backside down on to the probing fingers, biting down on his lower lip and closing his eyes. The doctor's fingers moved further in and a long, low groan escaped the patient's mouth. 'I can't believe that some men do this to themselves for pleasure,' he said.

'No accounting for folk,' agreed the doctor. He moved his fingers gently, feeling for the hard mass that the Vice President's prostate had become. The patient tensed and gripped the sides of the couch. The doctor continued to probe the mass for several seconds and then slipped out his fingers. He stripped off his gloves and dropped them into a bin before handing his patient a paper towel to wipe himself with.

'How've you been feeling, Glenn?'

The patient shrugged. 'As well as can be expected, considering I've got terminal cancer.' He forced a smile. 'Sorry, shouldn't let the bitterness creep in, right?' He finished cleaning himself and changed back into his clothes. 'It's the unfairness of it, you know?'

'Yeah, I know. There's nothing fair about prostate cancer, I'm afraid.'

'I can't believe the speed of it all. Six months ago, I was fine. Now . . .' He smiled ruefully. 'Now I'm not so fine, right?'

The doctor made some notes on a clipboard. 'It's bigger.'

'A lot bigger, right?'

The doctor nodded. 'It's just about doubled over the past month.'

'That's what's so unfair,' said the patient. 'Mitterand's cancer took years to kill him. Hell, he even stood for re-election knowing that he had it. But mine . . .'

'There's no predictable pattern, Glenn. I told you that.'

'I know, I know.' The patient adjusted his tie and checked his appearance in the mirror above the washbasin. 'So what do you think?' he said, his voice matter-of-fact but his eyes fixed on the doctor's reflection. 'How long?'

There was no hesitation on the doctor's part. The two men had known each other for many years and had developed a mutual respect that the doctor knew merited complete honesty. 'Months rather than weeks,' he said. 'Nine, possibly.'

'Nine productive months?'

'That would be optimistic. Four would be more realistic.'

The patient nodded. He turned around. 'Enough time to get my affairs in order,' he said. 'Ensure a smooth transition and all that.'

'How's Elaine taking it?'

A sudden sadness flashed across the Vice President's face. 'She's only just gotten over her father,' he said. 'I intend to spend as much time with her as possible before . . .' He left the sentence hanging and gave a small shrug. 'I'll see you next week, then, Pete.' He headed for the door. 'Give my love to Margaret.'

Two Secret Service agents in dark suits were waiting for the Vice President in the reception area. They escorted him to the elevator, one of them whispering into a concealed microphone as they walked.

Tommy Reid carried two plastic cups of coffee over to his desk and sat down heavily. His desk was pushed up against Wright's and they shared three telephones between them. Reid looked over his shoulder and reached into the bottom drawer of his desk. He took out a quarter bottle of vodka and winked at Wright as he poured a slug into his cup. He held up the bottle, offering Wright a shot, but Wright shook his head. Wright was trying to arrange a photofit artist but no one was available. A bored secretary had put him on hold and for the past six minutes he'd been listening to a computerised rendition of something that a child could play with two fingers. He watched Reid sip his laced coffee.

Reid put down his coffee. 'What?' he said.

'What do you mean?' asked Wright.

'You were staring at me like I had something in my teeth.'

'Nah, I was just thinking.'

Reid passed over Wright's cup of coffee. 'Yeah, well, you don't want to be doing too much of that.'

Wright slammed down the receiver. 'It's a plot by British Telecom, that's what it is.'

'What is?'

'The music they play to keep you hanging on. In the old days they'd say that they'd call you back. Now they put you on hold for hours. Who profits, huh? British sodding Telecom, that's who.'

Reid grinned. 'The old days,' he said. 'How old are you, Nick?'

'Old enough.' The middle of their three telephones rang. Wright raised an eyebrow. 'I suppose you want me to get that?' he said.

'Wrong, Wright,' said Reid. He picked up the receiver as he took another sip at his coffee.

Wright began pecking away at his computer keyboard. He was working on a report of the morning's undercover operation and had come to the section where he had to explain what had happened in the tunnel.

Reid replaced the receiver. 'That can wait, Nick. We've got a body on the line.'

Wright stopped typing. 'Jesus. Another? That's three so far this month and we haven't even had a full moon yet.' He picked up his notebook. 'All the pool cars are taken. Can we take your car?'

'Sure. I could do with the mileage.' The detectives were supposed to use pool cars when available, but if they had to use their own vehicles they were paid a substantial mileage allowance.

They went down together to the car park. Reid's car was a four-year-old Honda Civic with forty-three thousand miles on the clock and a back-seat littered with empty fast-food containers.

They drove out on to Tavistock Place, headed south to the River Thames and turned right along the Embankment. It began to rain and Reid switched on the wipers. They smeared greasily across the glass.

Wright flicked open an *A to Z*. 'Where are we going exactly?'

'Nine Elms, not far from New Covent Garden Market.

Nearest road is Haines Street, off Nine Elms Lane. I thought I'd swing across Vauxhall Bridge and double back, the traffic'll be lighter.'

Wright tossed the street map on to the back seat. 'I don't know why you bother having an *A to Z*,' he said. 'You know every bloody road there is.'

'Just one of my many talents, Nick. You hungry?' Wright shook his head. 'Thought we might stop off at a pub or something.'

'Maybe afterwards,' said Wright.

Reid snorted contemptuously. 'What, want to see it on an empty stomach, do you?'

Wright said nothing. It wasn't his stomach he was thinking about: he was more concerned about his partner turning up on a job smelling of drink.

It took them a little under twenty minutes to reach Nine Elms. They saw two police vans and a white saloon parked at the roadside, and Reid pulled in behind them. Wright climbed out of the Honda and peered down an embankment overgrown with nettles. A beaten-down pathway through the vegetation showed where the occupants of the vans had gone down to the tracks. The sky was a dull grey and a fine drizzle gave the scene the feel of a washed-out watercolour painting.

'I thought you said this was a body on the line?' said Wright.

'That's right,' said Reid, opening the boot and taking out a pair of mud-covered Wellington boots. 'What's wrong?'

'See for yourself,' said Wright.

Reid took off his shoes, pulled on the Wellingtons and joined Wright at the edge of the embankment. The two lines down below were crusted with rust and dirt. 'Ghost train?'

said Reid. He popped a mint in his mouth and started down the slope. Wright followed him, his shoes slipping on the muddy path.

At the bottom they looked up and down the tracks, unsure which way to go. To the south, they could see several hundred yards before the lines were swallowed up in the drizzle; to the north, they curved to the left. Wright looked down at his feet. A trail of muddy footprints led north. He nodded in their direction.

Reid grinned amiably. 'You ought to be a detective,' he said.

They followed the trail. Moisture flecked Wright's suit and he put his hands in his pockets and shivered. Reid was wearing a brown raincoat which fluttered around his boots, and from somewhere he'd produced a battered tweed hat. He looked like a farmer setting out to market.

As they walked around the bend they saw a young uniformed policeman in a fluorescent yellow waterproof jacket standing at the entrance to a tunnel. The tunnel entrance was of weathered stone crisscrossed with veins of moss and overgrown with ivy and brambles. The policeman tensed as the two men approached.

'British Transport Police,' said Reid, taking out his warrant card and showing it to the constable. 'Tommy Reid. This is Nick Wright.'

'Reid and Wright?' The constable rubbed his hands together. 'Sounds like a comedy act.'

'Yeah, yeah, yeah, we've heard all the jokes,' said Reid wearily.

'Our guys are already inside,' said the constable.

'Then they're wasting their time, it's a BTP case,' said Wright.

'There hasn't been a train along here for ten years,' said the constable.

Wright shrugged. 'Makes no odds. It's Railtrack property, so it's ours.' He put his head on one side and listened to a rumbling noise from inside the tunnel. 'What's that?' he asked.

'Generator,' said the constable. 'The SOCO boys brought it with them to run the lights.'

Reid stepped into the tunnel. Wright stayed where he was. 'Nick?' said Reid.

Wright swallowed. 'Yeah, coming.' He followed Reid into the tunnel mouth. He shivered involuntarily. Ahead of them they could see white, ghostly figures moving around, and beyond them, a bright wall of light. Wright stopped. He could feel his heart pounding.

'Nick, are you okay?'

Wright took a deep breath. 'Yeah.' He shook his head and started walking briskly down the line, towards the lights. As they got closer, they saw that the ghostly figures were Scene of Crime Officers in white overalls and boots, gathering evidence. Two dark silhouettes carrying flashlights walked towards Reid and Wright, tall men with their hands in the pockets of their raincoats. Wright recognised them immediately and his heart sank. The slightly shorter of the two, Inspector Gerry Hunter of the Metropolitan Police CID, was a good-looking man in his mid-thirties with black curly hair and tanned skin. His sidekick was Detective Sergeant Clive Edmunds, slightly older with receding hair and a thickening waistline.

'What brings you on to our turf, lads?' asked Reid goodnaturedly.

'A uniform found the body and called it in,' said

Hunter. He nodded at Wright. 'Thought we'd have a look-see.'

'What was the uniform doing down here?' asked Wright. 'Having a kip?'

Hunter smiled coldly and ignored Wright's sarcasm. 'A down-and-out name of Annie Lees was sheltering from the rain a couple of days back.'

Edmunds lit a cigarette. 'She's a bit crazy. She kept talking about finding Jesus.' He offered the pack of cigarettes to Reid and Wright but both men shook their heads.

'Jesus?' repeated Reid.

'You'll understand when you've seen the body,' said Hunter. 'No one took her seriously at first.'

'Where is she now?' asked Reid.

'We've got her back at the factory. We'll keep her for you.'

Reid nodded. 'Cause of death?'

Edmunds chuckled. 'Well, it wasn't suicide.'

'The doctor's there now,' said Hunter, 'but I think it's safe to say we've got a murder enquiry.'

'We?' said Wright quickly. 'This is our case.'

'Yeah, handled many murders, have you?' asked Edmunds.

Wright felt Reid's hand on his shoulder. He realised he was glaring at Hunter and he forced himself to relax.

Hunter started to walk away and he motioned with his chin for Edmunds to follow him.

'Don't forget your gloves, lads,' said Edmunds.

Wright was about to reply when Reid squeezed his shoulder. 'Don't let them get to you, Nick. They're just taking the piss.'

They continued along the tracks towards the lights. There

was a flash, then, a second later, another. 'What's that?' asked Wright.

'Photographer,' said Reid. They walked by a small generator. A white cable snaked away towards two large fluorescent lights mounted on tripods.

A woman came down the tracks towards them. She was in her forties with greying blonde hair tied back in a ponytail. She was wearing disposable rubber gloves and carrying a large moulded plastic briefcase.

'Excuse me, are you the doctor?' asked Reid.

'Pathologist, actually,' she said brusquely. 'Anna Littman.'

'Tommy Reid and Nick Wright,' said Reid. 'British Transport Police.'

'I've already spoken to your colleagues,' she said briskly, and stepped to the side to walk past them.

'They're not our colleagues,' snapped Wright.

She raised her eyebrows and stared at Wright with the greenest eyes he'd ever seen. 'I've known Gerry Hunter for three years,' she said. 'I can assure you he's a detective.'

'He's with the Met, Dr Littman,' said Reid. 'We're British Transport Police.'

'Sounds like too many cooks to me,' she said.

'Can you tell us what we've got here?' asked Wright.

'What we've got is a dead white male, late forties, I think, and he's been dead for several days.'

'It's murder?' asked Reid.

'Oh, there's no doubt about that.'

'Murder weapon?' asked Reid.

'A knife, I think.'

'You think?'

'The body's in a bit of a state. The rats have been at it.

I'll know better after the post mortem. Now if you'll excuse me . . .' She brushed past Wright.

The two men turned to watch her go. 'Nice legs,' said Reid.

'I'm off women just now,' said Wright.

Reid sighed and turned up the collar of his raincoat. 'Why would anyone dump a body down here?'

'What do you mean?'

'Bound to be found eventually. If you really wanted to hide a body, you'd bury it, right?'

They walked down the track, their feet crunching on gravel. 'No footprints,' said Reid. 'And none outside if it was two or three days ago.'

'No drag marks either. So how did they get the body in here?'

'Carried it, maybe.'

'Which brings me back to my first point. Why carry it in here? Why not bury it?'

A Scene of Crime Officer stood up and stretched. He was in his fifties with steel-grey hair and thick horn-rimmed glasses. 'Nice day for it,' he said.

'Found anything?' asked Wright.

'Lots of stuff. Problem is knowing what's relevant. Down-and-outs have been sleeping here, kids playing around, dogs, cats, rats. There's litter, used condoms, sweet wrappers, empty bottles, cigarettes. We'll bag it and tag it, but as to what's relevant and what isn't, well, your guess is as good as mine.'

'No sign of a murder weapon?' asked Wright.

The man snorted softly. 'No, and I haven't come across a signed confession. But if I do . . .'

Reid and Wright walked past one of the tripod lights. A

woman in white overalls was kneeling down, examining a wooden sleeper. Wright flinched at a bright flash of light. The photographer was a small, squat man in a dark suit, standing with his back to them. He took a step back, adjusted his focus and took another picture of something against the tunnel wall.

Wright moved to the side to get a better look. 'Jesus Christ,' he whispered.

'Yeah, practically crucified,' said the photographer laconically. 'I don't think they cut Jesus's dick off, though, did they?' He turned his camera side on and took another photograph. 'Who are you guys with?' he asked.

'British Transport Police,' said Reid.

'Don't think he was hit by a train,' said the photographer.

A young man in blue overalls joined them carrying a large metal suitcase. He placed it on a sleeper and opened it to reveal a large video camera and a halogen light. 'Are you going to want the video, then?' he asked, pulling the camera out of its foam rubber packing.

'Yeah,' said Wright, handing him a BTP business card.

The body was naked, spreadeagled against the wall, the hands impaled on thick nails. The man's groin was a mass of blood, and strips of flesh had been ripped from his chest, arms and legs. A knife had been thrust into the chest.

'That's not what I think it is in his mouth, is it?' asked Reid.

Wright lean forward. Between the man's teeth was a piece of bloody flesh. Wright's stomach lurched. He screwed up his face in disgust. 'What sort of sick bastard would do that?' he whispered.

'Black magic?' said Reid. 'Some sort of Satanic ritual?'

Wright shook his head. 'There'd be symbols. Candles. Stuff like that. This guy's been tortured to death.' He took a step closer to the body. There was something impaled on the knife. A playing card. Blood from the man's face had trickled down over the card. Wright reached out his hand.

'Don't even think about touching that!' boomed a voice.

Wright looked around. The grey-haired man in overalls was standing behind Wright holding a polythene evidence bag. 'I wasn't going to touch anything,' said Wright defensively.

'Who are you anyway?' asked the man. 'Gerry Hunter's already been over the crime scene.'

'I'm Nick Wright. This is Tommy Reid. British Transport Police.'

'Been at many crime scenes, have you, Mr Wright?'

'What?'

The man sealed the evidence bag. Inside was a cigarette packet. 'Standard procedure is for detectives to wear gloves and shoe covers before they go trampling over a crime scene.'

'Yeah, well, we'll watch where we put our feet,' said Wright. 'And it's Sergeant Wright. What about the victim's clothes?'

'No sign of them. Assuming he didn't walk in naked, the murderer must have taken them with him.'

Wright put his hands in his pockets and turned to look at the body again. He peered at the playing card. 'Ace of spades,' he said. 'Now what the hell's the significance of that?'

'Bridge game got a bit nasty, do you think?' said Reid.

'It must mean something, Tommy. Someone went to a lot of trouble to stick that on his chest.'

Kristine Ross opened the UPS package, taking care not to damage her blood-red fingernails. Inside was a manila envelope, with the senator's name and 'PRIVATE AND CONFIDENTIAL' typed across it. She picked up the UPS wrapper and looked at the name of the sender. Max Eckhardt. It wasn't a name she recognised. The address was an apartment in London, England. The space for the sender's telephone number had been left blank. She clicked her mouse on the logo for the senator's contacts book and entered the name Eckhardt. Nothing. She scrolled through the Es, just to be on the safe side, but there was no name that was even remotely similar. It wasn't unusual for members of the public to mark their mail private and confidential in the hope of reaching the senator's desk unopened, but it was Kristine's job to make sure that he made the maximum use of his time. Whoever Max Eckhardt was, he wasn't known to the senator and so his envelope was fair game. She slit open the envelope and peered inside. All it contained was a Polaroid photograph. Kristine closed the envelope and tapped it on her desk, a tight feeling in her stomach. She doubted that it was a wedding picture. There was no letter, no card, just the photograph, and the fact that it was a Polaroid meant that it probably wasn't the work of a professional photographer.

People sent strange things to the senator. His mail was

scanned before it reached Kristine's desk, but X-rays couldn't weed out all the nasty surprises. In the twenty-two months she'd been working for Senator Dean Burrow she'd seen pornographic pictures of housewives offering themselves to him, hatemail written in crayon, obscene drawings, and on one occasion a small bottle of urine from a woman who said that the FBI were trying to poison her. Anything threatening was passed on to the Secret Service; anything obscene went into the shredder. Kristine sighed through pursed lips and tilted the envelope so that the Polaroid slid out, face down. She turned it over. For a second or two she stared at the image, unable to believe what she was looking at, then she felt her stomach heave.

'Oh, sweet Jesus,' she whispered.

Tommy Reid dropped Nick Wright at the door to Battersea police station and went looking for a parking space. Wright waited until the grey-haired duty sergeant had finished taking details of a stolen bicycle from a young girl before showing his ID and asking to see Annie Lees.

The sergeant's face creased into a grin. 'What, has she been fare-dodging now, then?' he asked.

Wright smiled coldly. 'She's a witness in a murder investigation,' he said.

The sergeant's grin vanished. 'I know that, son. I was just pulling your leg.'

The door opened behind Wright and Reid joined him at the counter. From somewhere he'd managed to buy a portion of fish and chips. 'Hello, Reg,' said Reid, shoving a chip into his mouth.

'Bloody hell, Tommy Reid,' said the sergeant. 'What've you been doing with yourself?'

Reid offered his fish and chips and the sergeant helped himself to a handful of chips. Reid gestured at the fish and the sergeant broke off a piece. 'Same old rubbish,' said Reid. 'I thought you'd retired.'

'Next year. You on this murder enquiry?'

Reid pushed a chunk of fried cod into his mouth and nodded.

'I'll let you in,' said the sergeant. He disappeared from behind the counter and unlocked a side door. Reid and Wright went inside. 'Second interview room on the right,' said the sergeant.

Annie Lees was sitting at a table, her hands cupped around a mug of weak tea. She looked up as the two detectives walked into the room. 'Where are my things?' she snapped.

Wright stopped in his tracks. 'I'm sorry?'

'My things. They said I could have my things.' She scrutinised Reid with wary eyes. 'What's that you're eating?'

'Fish and chips. Want some?' Reid put what was left of his meal on the table and wiped his hands on his coat.

The old woman picked up a chip between her first finger and thumb and inspected it closely before taking a bite.

'Annie, did you see anyone near the tunnel?' asked Wright.

The old woman's eyes narrowed. 'What tunnel?'

Wright sat down opposite her. 'The tunnel where you found the body.'

She averted her eyes and concentrated on selecting the best chips. She ate several more before speaking. 'I've already told that other detective everything.'

'Other detective? What other detective?'

'Gerry. He's such a nice young man, isn't he?'

'Gerry Hunter?'

'Inspector Gerry Hunter,' she said, stressing the title. 'He's very young to be an inspector, isn't he? Are you an inspector?'

Wright's jaw tensed. 'No,' he said. 'I'm not an inspector.'

Dean Burrow was bored out of his skull, but the three women sitting opposite him would never have known. Burrow had smiled his way through more than a decade of television interviews, rubber chicken dinners and factory openings. He'd perfected the technique with the aid of a style coach, the same woman who'd shown him how to walk with authority, how to shake hands sincerely, how to show concern and sympathy when the occasion warranted. He smiled and from time to time he nodded to show that he agreed with them, giving them all equal eye contact so that none of them would feel slighted. They'd wanted to talk to him about abortion, a subject close to Burrow's heart, and they represented a group of more than five hundred churchgoing middle-aged women from Burrow's home state. Five hundred votes was worth twenty minutes of anybody's time.

Burrow had been consistent on his views on abortion.

In public he was against it; in private he thought it was a necessary evil: his own wife had had an abortion soon after they'd married, and his former secretary had been persuaded to have one three years ago. Both women had agreed to the abortions for financial reasons – his wife because they were struggling to meet the payments on their first house; his secretary because he'd paid her fifty thousand dollars. She wasn't his secretary any more; she'd opened her own beauty salon in Cleveland and Burrow remained convinced that she'd deliberately become pregnant in the first place. Burrow wondered what his three visitors would do if they discovered that their pro-life senator was responsible for two aborted fetuses.

The woman who'd been doing most of the talking, a stick-thin black woman with swept-back hair and tortoiseshell spectacles, stopped speaking and looked at him expectantly.

Burrow nodded urbanely. 'I couldn't agree with you more, Mrs Vine,' he said, even though he hadn't been listening. 'You can rest assured that we are of one mind on this issue.' He stood up and adjusted the sleeves of his jacket. 'It's been a pleasure, ladies. I want to thank you all for the time and trouble you've taken to come and see me.'

The three women stood up and he shook them by the hand. His handshake was as practised as his smile, strong enough to show strength of character and determination, but not too overpowering. He escorted them to the door and opened it, giving each of the women a warm smile as they left.

Kristine Ross was standing in the outer office, holding a manila envelope. Burrow gave her a genuine smile and looked her up and down. With her long tanned legs, full figure and shoulder-length blonde hair, Kristine could have worked as a catwalk model. Not that Burrow would ever do anything more than look – he'd learned his lesson the hard way and he didn't want to throw away another fifty thousand dollars. She looked worried.

'Something wrong, Kristine?' he asked.

She gestured with the UPS package. 'Can I have a word with you, Senator?'

'Of course,' he said, ushering her into his office. He watched her walk over to his desk. She had a sexy, sensual walk, slow and easy as if she knew that men liked to watch her move. Burrow made sure that his gaze was levelled at her face when she turned to face him.

'This came in the morning mail,' she said as Burrow went back behind his side of the large oak desk. 'It was addressed private and confidential, but office policy is to—'

'I know, I know,' he said brusquely, adjusting his cuffs. 'What's the problem?'

'It's a photograph.'

'So?' Burrow was starting to find the secretary's reticence annoying. She gave him the envelope, a look of disgust on her face, then looked away as he opened the envelope and took out a Polaroid photograph. Burrow grimaced. It was a human figure, spreadeagled, dripping with glistening blood, the flesh made ghostly pale by the camera flash. 'Why would anyone . . . ?' he began, then he noticed something impaled in the chest. He held the photograph closer to his face and squinted.

'I wasn't sure whether I should give it to the Secret Service or—'

'How was it delivered?' interrupted Burrow.

'UPS. From London, England.'

Burrow clicked his fingers impatiently. 'Get me the pack it came in. You've still got it, don't you?'

'Yes. Yes, I do.' She backed away from him and then walked quickly out of the office. For the first time ever, Burrow didn't watch her go. He continued to stare at the photograph. His heart was racing and his palms were damp with sweat.

Kristine returned with the UPS pack, and Burrow practically ripped it from her hands. He scanned the label. 'Max Eckhardt,' he whispered.

'I couldn't find his name on the computer,' said Kristine. 'That's why I opened it. I didn't do anything wrong, did I?'

Burrow put the UPS pack down on the desk and leaned back in his chair. He smiled as if he didn't have a care in the world. 'Probably a crank,' said Burrow. 'Nothing to worry about, Kristine.'

'Shall I give it to—?'

'No, it's nothing. There wasn't anything else in the envelope, was there? No note or anything?'

'Just the photograph,' said Kristine.

Burrow shrugged dismissively. 'So it's nothing.'

Kristine brushed a stray lock of hair away from her face. 'You're sure?' she asked.

Burrow crinkled his eyes slightly. It was his serious, sincere look. 'Absolutely,' he said.

Kristine looked as if she wanted to say something else, but she could tell from Burrow's demeanour that the conversation was over. She left the office. This time Burrow watched her leave, but his eyes were cold and hard as if his mind was elsewhere. As soon as the door closed, he picked up the photograph again and stared at it.

Reid and Wright got nothing of value from the twenty minutes they spent with Annie Lees. The old lady was showing all the symptoms of Alzheimer's disease and seemed unable to concentrate for more than a few minutes at a time. Several times during the interview she wasn't even able to recall finding the body, and once she'd burst into tears. They left her with a uniformed policewoman and the remains of the fish and chips.

'She needs to be in a home,' said Wright as they closed the door to the interview room.

'Care in the community,' said Reid. 'Part of the cutbacks.'

Wright shook his head sadly. 'She needs looking after. Her family should be taking care of her.'

Reid snorted. 'Come off it, Nick. Who'd take care of you if you went crazy? Do you think your ex-wife would put you in the spare room? What about your son? He's what, seven? And even if he was older, kids don't take care of their parents any more. Those days went out with the village bobby and free school milk. It's every man for himself nowadays. Little old ladies like Annie Lees fall through the cracks and the cracks just get bigger and bigger.'

'Yeah, well, isn't that a cheery thought?' said Wright.

Reid clapped Wright on the back. 'Come on, old son, you're never going to reach retirement age anyway.'

Wright shrugged him off. He didn't feel like laughing.

They headed down the corridor towards the reception

area. Gerry Hunter came out of an office, a large envelope in one hand, a cup of coffee in the other. 'Any joy?' he asked.

Reid shook his head. 'Nah. She thinks the world of you, though. Said she wanted to adopt you.'

'What can I say? Must be my boyish charm.' He gave the envelope to Reid. 'Pathologist's report. She didn't know where to contact you.'

'Tavistock Place,' said Wright.

Hunter looked pained. 'I know that, but she didn't. She hasn't dealt with BTP before, so she called us to attend the post mortem. It was straightforward, nothing out of the ordinary.' He nodded his head towards the interview room. 'Do you need Annie for anything else?'

'No, we're through with her,' said Reid. He tapped Wright on the shoulder with the envelope. 'Come on, Nick, let's go.'

Hunter disappeared back into his office. Wright and Reid walked towards the door, but before they reached it, someone called out Wright's name. It was Clive Edmunds, his tie loosened and the tail of his shirt flapping over his trousers. He waved a sheet of paper at Wright as he walked towards them.

'Thought this might help with your investigation,' he said, handing the paper to Wright. He walked quickly away and disappeared into a side office.

Wright scanned the sheet. Across the top, in typed capital letters, were the words 'QUESTIONS TO ANSWER'. Underneath, in a single column, was a list of words. 'Who? When? How? Why?' Wright felt a surge of anger.

Reid read the list over Wright's shoulder and snorted. 'Ha bloody ha,' he said.

Wright screwed the sheet of paper into a tight ball and threw it down the corridor. 'I bet Hunter put him up to it,' he said.

'Nah, Edmunds is enough of a twat to have thought of it himself. Come on, forget about it. Do you want a drink?'

Wright shook his head and reached for the envelope. 'You drink too much,' he said.

'Yeah, well, you snore but you don't hear me complaining.'

The duty sergeant unlocked the door for them. 'Where's the nearest pub, Reg?' asked Reid.

'Bull's Head,' said the sergeant. 'Left, then first right.'

The two detectives walked there. It was an old-fashioned public house with a smoke-stained plaster ceiling and a long wooden bar that had been varnished countless times and was now almost black. A shirtsleeved barman was pulling a rack of steaming glasses from a washing machine under the counter and nodded a greeting. 'Be with you in a minute, gents,' he said.

'What do you want?' asked Reid, leaning nonchalantly against the bar.

'I want to go back to the office,' said Wright, looking at his watch.

'Don't be a party-pooper, Nick. We're allowed a lunch hour.'

Wright could see that it was pointless to argue and sighed in resignation. 'Lager shandy,' he said, then went over to an empty table and sat down. He read through the pathologist's report until Reid came over with their drinks. Wright looked at Reid's double vodka and tonic and shook his head admonishingly.

Reid pretended not to notice. 'Wasn't sure if you wanted

ice or lemon. Or a cherry.' He sat down, took a deep pull at his drink and smacked his lips as if deliberately trying to antagonise Wright. Wright looked down at the report again. 'So what does the delightful Dr Littman say?' Reid asked.

'Sixty-three cuts, a dozen of which could have been the fatal one. Three different blades used.'

'Three?' repeated Reid incredulously.

'He was dead when his dick was cut off.'

'That's a relief, then.'

'And his vocal cords had been cut. Presumably so he couldn't scream.' Wright dropped the report down on top of the envelope. 'Who the hell would torture a man in that way, Tommy?'

Reid shrugged and drained his glass. 'Whoever it was, they went to a lot of trouble. Three knives. The nails. Something to bang them in with. Something to put the clothes in. And the playing card. Another?'

Wright looked up sharply. 'What?'

'Another drink?' said Reid, tapping his empty glass. He stood up, grunting from the effort.

Wright refused the offer. He rested his head against the back of his seat while Reid ambled across the carpet to the bar.

Superintendent Richard Newton pushed the photographs with his index finger and grimaced. He'd seen more than his share of mutilated bodies during his twenty-year career, usually suicides who'd decided to end it all by throwing themselves in front of a train, but the injuries of the man in the tunnel were all the more horrific because of the way they'd been inflicted. This was no sudden death: the wounds had been inflicted one at a time, methodically, over a period of time. He shuddered.

The door to his office opened and his secretary showed in Tommy Reid and Nick Wright. Reid's cheeks were red and the superintendent could smell his minty breath from across his desk as the two men sat down. 'Well?' said Newton. 'What's the state of play?'

'White male, mid to late forties, multiple stab wounds and mutilations,' said Reid. 'That's all we know.'

'No identification on the body?' asked Newton.

'No, nothing,' said Reid. 'No clothes, no wallet, no jewellery.'

Newton slid one of the ten-by-twelves across the desk to Reid. 'Is that what I think it is in his mouth?' he asked disdainfully.

Reid nodded.

'A warning?'

'Maybe.'

'And the playing card?'

Reid shrugged.

Newton nodded thoughtfully. 'It's a messy one,' he said.

'I think it's a serial killer,' said Wright. It was the first time he'd spoken since entering the office.

Newton settled back in his chair and tapped his fingertips together as he studied Wright. Wright shifted uncomfortably under the superintendent's gaze. 'Why do you say that, Nick?'

Wright pointed at the glossy photographs. 'It's too . . .' he struggled to find the right word '. . . formal.' He frowned and ran a hand through his fringe.

'Formal?' said Newton. He raised his eyebrows archly.

'Organised,' said Wright hurriedly. 'It's too organised to be a gangland or a drugs killing. The way the body was nailed to the wall, it was as if someone was creating an image.' Wright's voice tailed off as he struggled to express himself.

'But I've not heard of any similar killings,' said the superintendent. 'And that would be a prerequisite for a serial killer, wouldn't it?'

The sarcasm didn't appear to register with Wright. 'It could be the start,' he said.

'It could,' said Newton, unconvinced. 'But at present we have a single killing. I think the time to start speculating about a mass murderer would be if and when there's a second victim. Until then I suggest you treat it as a straightforward murder investigation.' Newton tapped his fingertips on the desktop like a concert pianist warming up. 'I've been considering letting the Met continue with the case,' he mused.

Wright looked across at his partner for support. 'We've already started the preliminary work.'

'Nevertheless, the Met is geared up for murder investigations, and with the best will in the world—'

'We cracked the Everton case last spring.'

'The guy was caught with the knife in his hand,' said Newton patiently.

'It was still murder.'

'Manslaughter,' corrected the superintendent.

'Murder, manslaughter, what's the difference? This is a BTP case, sir,' said Wright. We can handle it.'

'Whatever happens, it's going to be a joint investigation,' said Newton.

'I understand that, sir, but it should be a BTP case first and foremost, with you as governor.'

'Nice of you to be so keen to increase my workload, Nick.' Newton kept his eyes on Wright as he gathered up the photographs. He stacked them neatly, then handed the pile to Wright. 'Okay. Have it your way. Tell Ronnie I want to see him,' Newton said eventually. 'He'll be liaison officer. Use the conference room in the basement as the incident room. I'll draw up a rota of officers to be assigned to the case. I'll arrange for temporary transfers and authorise the necessary overtime.' He took a deep breath as if reconsidering his decision. 'Ronnie can talk to the Met and have their officers sent over here, and I'll have half a dozen uniforms assigned. Oh, and the press have been on asking for details. I've arranged a press conference for four o'clock. The two of you can handle it. Ronnie's going to be too busy getting the incident room sorted out. Just give them the basics, and put out an appeal for witnesses. Don't mention the playing card. Keep that in reserve.'

'Our ace in the hole?' said Reid, deadpan.

Newton looked at him icily. 'And no mention of a serial killer.'

Reid and Wright stood up. 'Thank you, sir,' said Wright.

Newton acknowledged Wright's gratitude with a slight nod. 'It's not open ended, Nick. If it looks like you're not making any progress, the case goes to the Met.'

'Hey, Gerry, take a look at this!' Clive Edmunds gestured with a lit cigarette at the wall-mounted television above the office coffee machine. 'Those railway wankers are on Sky news.'

Gerry Hunter stopped pecking at his computer keyboard and looked up. 'Turn the sound up, will you?' he asked.

Edmunds looked around for the remote control and increased the volume. Tommy Reid was reading a prepared statement while Nick Wright sat next to him, toying with a ballpoint pen. Behind them was a blown-up map of the area where the body had been found. Hunter couldn't help smiling at Reid's appearance: the man's hair was damp as if he'd splashed water on it in an attempt to make it lie flat. Stray strands of hair were already coming adrift at the sides. He'd fastened the top button of his shirt but his collar was a size too small and clearly pinching his neck. Reid finished reading the statement and asked the assembled reporters if they had any questions.

'Do you have any motive for the killing?' asked a redhead holding a small tape recorder.

'Not as yet,' said Reid.

'And no suspect?'

Reid's jaw tightened. 'We're appealing for anyone who was in the vicinity of the tunnel to come forward,' he said. 'Even if they don't think they saw anything of significance, we'd still like to talk to them.'

'In fact, you don't even know who the victim is, do you?' pressed the redhead. Reid pretended not to hear her.

A middle-aged man in a crumpled blue suit raised an arm. Hunter recognised him as a crime reporter on one of the tabloids. 'When are you going to call in the Met?' he said.

Edmunds nudged Hunter in the ribs. 'The guys are running a sweepstake on that very question,' he chuckled.

'This is a British Transport Police investigation,' said Wright.

'We will be liaising with the Metropolitan Police,' said Reid. 'Officers from the Met will be assigned to the case.'

'Any other questions?' asked Wright, looking around the room.

'Do you think the killer could strike again?' asked a local radio reporter.

'It's a possibility,' said Wright.

Reid stiffened and put a hand on Wright's arm. Wright shrugged him off.

'A serial killer?'

Before Wright could answer, Reid stood up. 'I'm afraid that's all we have time for, gentlemen.' He added as an afterthought, 'And ladies.'

Wright looked up at his partner as if preparing to argue, but Reid gave a small shake of his head. The news broadcast cut away to a studio presenter.

Edmunds muted the sound and flicked ash into a waste-paper bin. 'They haven't a clue,' he said.

'It's a tough case, Clive.'

Edmunds snorted dismissively. 'Those two couldn't crack a fucking egg.'

'Maybe.' Hunter put his hand in his pocket and pulled out a crumpled ball of paper which he tossed to Edmunds. 'That wasn't funny,' he said.

Edmunds held his cigarette between his lips and flattened the sheet of paper. It was the list he'd given Wright earlier. 'Made me laugh,' he said.

'Yeah, well, go easy on him, will you? He's pissed off enough at me as it is.'

Edmunds folded the sheet into an aeroplane and threw it towards a wastepaper bin. 'Well, you are sleeping with his wife, Gerry.' The plane missed the bin by several feet and ploughed into a grey carpet tile. He took the cigarette between his forefinger and thumb and blew a smoke ring. 'When all's said and done.'

'Ex-wife,' said Hunter. 'Just leave him alone, huh?'

Edmunds held Hunter's look for several seconds, then realised that his partner was serious. 'Okay,' he said. 'They can have all the rope they need.'

'We were set up,' hissed Wright as he stormed down the corridor. 'It was that bastard Hunter. I'm sure of it.'

'Calm down, Nick.' Reid caught up with his partner and walked beside him. 'It wasn't too bad.'

Wright waved his hand in the air dismissively. 'You heard that shit from the *Mirror*.' He contorted his face and mimicked the crime reporter. '"When are you going to call in the Met?"'

Reid held up his hands in mock surrender. 'Hey, I'm on your side.' He went over to the coffee maker and filled two polystyrene cups. He took them back to the desk and poured in large measures of vodka, then passed one over to Wright.

Wright glared at his partner for several seconds, then

relaxed. It wasn't Reid he was mad at. He raised his cup and banged it against Reid's. 'Cheers,' he said, and drank gratefully. 'Are you working tomorrow?'

'What else is there to do on a Saturday? What about you?'

'Oh yeah, I'll be in. I need the overtime.' Wright flicked through his desk diary then groaned. 'Hell, I forgot, tomorrow's my day with Sean.'

'No sweat. Where are you going to take him?'

Wright closed his diary. 'I don't know. Trocadero, maybe. He likes video games. Where did you used to take Craig and Julie?'

'The old favourites. British Museum. Science Museum. The zoo. Football.'

'Been there, done that.' He reached over and took the prepared statement from Reid. He'd spent an hour working on it before the press conference but he still hadn't been happy with it. Wright was as aware as the journalists that the investigation had stalled before it had even started.

'All right, lads?' said a deep, Glaswegian voice.

Reid and Wright looked up. It was Detective Chief Inspector Ronnie Dundas, the fifty-year-old Glaswegian Newton had appointed as liaison officer on the investigation.

Wright put down his cup guiltily. 'How's the incident room going, sir?' he asked.

'Computers are in, HOLMES is up and running and there's a PNC terminal on line. We'll have two NCIS terminals connected by this afternoon.'

The Home Office Large Major Enquiry System would be used to collate all the evidence and interviews produced during the investigation, and the Police National Computer and National Criminal Intelligence Service would provide online databases and criminal intelligence.

'Who's office manager?' asked Reid.

'Are you putting yourself forward, Tommy?' Dundas perched on the edge of Reid's desk. His hair and moustache were unnaturally black, and he was rumoured to be dyeing both.

Reid flashed the chief inspector a sarcastic smile. 'You know me, Ronnie. I'm much more a foot-in-the-door man.'

'Arse on a bar stool, more like,' said Dundas. The banter was good natured: the two men had worked together for more than a decade. 'Anyway, Phil Evans has already been assigned.'

'He's well suited,' agreed Reid.

'What about the Met?' asked Wright. 'Have they said who they're sending over yet?'

Dundas shook his head. 'Only numbers. A DCI, two DIs, three DSs and six DCs. Same as us.'

'So when do we move downstairs?' asked Wright.

'Give it a couple of hours. They're still moving desks and getting the phones connected.'

'Time for a pint, then,' said Reid.

Dundas grinned. 'You read my mind,' he said.

The two senior officers looked expectantly at Wright, who sighed mournfully. 'Okay, I suppose so.'

There was a timid knock on the door and Dean Burrow looked up from the papers he was reading. Kristine Ross popped her head around as if she was trying to keep her body concealed from him. 'I'm the last one here, Senator,' she said. 'Is there anything you need?'

Burrow took off his reading glasses. 'Any sign of Jody Meacher?' he asked.

'He said he'd be here by seven, Senator.'

Burrow looked at his watch. It was half past seven. 'Okay, Kristine. You can call it a night.'

She flashed him a nervous smile and closed the door. Burrow toyed with his spectacles. Kristine was obviously still upset at the photograph. He wondered how she'd feel if she knew the real significance of the mutilated corpse. Then she'd really have something to worry about.

He was still daydreaming when there was a second knock on his door, louder and more confident than the first. The door opened wide and Jody Meacher strode in. He was a big man, at least twenty stone, with a waistline that was still expanding. He was balding with a greying beard and cheeks pockmarked with old acne scars. Meacher was one of the smartest men Burrow had ever met, and was a shrewd political operator. In his younger years he'd had his own ambitions of office, but his looks had been an insurmountable barrier and he'd settled for being one of the best spin doctors in the business instead. He'd helped two men get into the Oval Office already, and if everything went to plan, Burrow would be the third.

Meacher glided across the plush blue carpet. He moved majestically, with surprising grace for a man of his size. Burrow went around his desk to meet him and they shook hands firmly.

'Thanks for coming so quickly, Jody,' said Burrow. He

went over to his drinks cabinet and poured two measures of Jack Daniels, each with a single cube of ice. He handed a glass to Meacher and they toasted each other silently. Burrow waved Meacher over to two green leather couches placed at right angles to each other at the far end of the room. While Meacher eased his vast bulk down on to one of the couches, Burrow walked over to his desk and picked up the UPS package and the manila envelope.

'Something's cropped up,' said Burrow, going over to sit on the second couch. He put the package and the envelope on a low oak coffee table.

Meacher watched him with unblinking eyes and the same coldness with which an entomologist might study a beetle. Meacher rarely smiled, and on the few occasions that he did, the expression never looked sincere. To strangers he appeared aloof, hostile even, but Burrow knew that the man's facial expressions often belied his true feelings. It wasn't that he wore a mask, it was as if he simply didn't care how he looked, that his intellect was his only concern.

'I received something in the mail today,' Burrow continued. He opened the flap of the envelope and slid out the Polaroid photograph. He handed it to Meacher.

Meacher's expression didn't change. He studied the photograph for a full five seconds, then looked at Burrow expectantly. 'Everything,' he said softly. 'Tell me everything.'

Burrow spoke for ten minutes while Meacher listened, his hands in his lap as if meditating. When he had finished, Burrow drained his glass and went over to the drinks cabinet to refill it. Meacher's glass remained untouched on the coffee table.

'Remember what I said to you when I first agreed to join your team?' Meacher asked.

'Yes. I remember.'

'So why did you withhold this from me?'

Burrow sat down and adjusted the creases of his trousers. 'Jody, this all happened a long time ago. A lifetime ago.'

Meacher held out the Polaroid photograph so that it was just inches from the senator's face. 'And this? When did this happen?'

Burrow felt his face redden. 'I don't know.' He took another mouthful of Jack Daniels.

Meacher tossed the photograph on to the coffee table. 'You know what this means?'

'You don't have to spell it out for me, Jody.'

'Everything we've worked for, everything we've done, it'll all be for nothing if this gets out.'

'I know, Jody. I know.'

Meacher sat in silence, staring into the middle distance. Burrow crouched forward, his elbows on his knees. Burrow could practically hear Meacher's mind working.

'Who else has seen the photograph?' Meacher asked eventually.

'My secretary. Kristine Ross.'

'Would you miss her?'

Burrow flinched at the question. 'Is there no other way?'

Meacher's pale blue eyes bored into Burrow's. 'Senator, you know as well as I do the state of the Vice President's health. He's going to have to step down within the next few months, and you are the frontrunner to take his place.' He nodded at the Polaroid. 'What do you think will happen if what you've told me becomes public knowledge?'

Burrow drew a finger across his throat. The end of his career. The end of everything.

'So don't ask me if there's any other way out of this. There's only one way. My way.'

Burrow held Meacher's gaze for several seconds, then he nodded slowly. 'Whatever it takes, Jody,' he said, and drained his glass.

Tommy Reid grunted and fumbled in his pockets for his keys. Nick Wright beat him to it and slotted his Yale into the lock. He pushed open the door and allowed Reid in first. The two men walked down the narrow hall to the sitting room. Reid stopped dead. The room was a mess, with empty fast-food cartons on the floor, stacks of newspapers and magazines on a coffee table and a pile of dirty laundry in the corner by the television.

'Shit! We've been burgled,' said Reid. 'Call the cops.'

Wright pushed him in the small of the back. 'You always say that,' he said. 'If it annoys you so much, get a cleaning lady.'

'Who said it annoys me?' He staggered over to the window and pulled the curtains shut with a flourish. Dust drifted down around him. 'Is it snowing?' he asked.

'You're pissed,' said Wright, dropping down on to a sofa that had once been beige but had long ago turned into a dirty brown.

Reid exhaled and looked around the room. There were two overstuffed leather armchairs next to the sofa, both scuffed and worn from years of abuse, facing a portable television on a black plastic stand. 'What's on the box?' he asked.

Wright ran his hands through his hair. 'Who cares?' he said. The two men had spent several hours in a local Indian restaurant, challenging each other to increasingly hot curries and cooling themselves down with half pints of lager. All Wright wanted to do was sleep.

'Do you want a nightcap?' Reid asked. Wright shook his head. 'Okay, I'll get myself a beer and head off to bed. See you tomorrow.'

Wright gave Reid a small wave. He heaved himself up off the sofa and went over to the pine shelving unit which had been amateurishly screwed into the wall opposite the window. On the middle shelf, surrounded by well-creased paperbacks, was a mini stereo system. Below it were several dozen CDs, mostly jazz. Wright ran his finger along the cases and pulled out a Billie Holiday recording. From the kitchen he heard a dull thud as a can of beer hit the floor followed by a muffled curse. Wright slotted in the CD and pressed the 'play' button.

'Goodnight, John Boy,' shouted Reid as he ambled down the hall to the bedroom.

'Goodnight, Grandpa,' Wright replied unenthusiastically. He was starting to think that Superintendent Newton was right, that he had indeed been living with Reid for too long. Even the jokes were becoming stale. He pulled the cushions off the sofa and unfolded the bed where he'd slept for the past five months. It was small and uncomfortable, but cheaper than paying for a place of his own.

He went to the bathroom, cleaned and flossed his teeth, then took his quilt and pillow from the airing cupboard. As he returned to the sitting room, Billie Holiday was singing 'Lover Come Back To Me'. Wright threw the bedding on to the sofa and sat down to remove his shoes. He looked around the cramped room and a wave of hopelessness washed over him. His wife, his son, his house, his car; he'd lost everything. He'd been working for more than ten years and all he had to show for it were the two suitcases of clothes he'd taken from the house and the ageing Ford Fiesta he'd driven away in.

Wright went back over to the shelving unit and picked up a harmonica. He sat down on the edge of the sofabed and played along with the recording, the mournful notes echoing down the hallway.

The elevator wasn't working, and by the look of the rusting gate, it hadn't been used for several years. Jody Meacher took the stairs one at a time, resting for breath every couple of dozen steps. When he reached the third floor he took off his overcoat and draped it over one shoulder. By the time he was on the fifth floor, he had to mop his forehead with a large white linen handkerchief. The man he was looking for lived on the ninth floor, but Meacher doubted that he was ever fazed by the long climb. Len Kruse was a fitness fanatic and probably raced up all nine floors at the double.

Meacher transferred his black leather briefcase to his left hand, pulled out his gold pocket watch and flipped it open. It was five o'clock in the morning. Meacher had driven from Washington to New York. He hated driving but he didn't want to use an official car and there was a good chance he'd be recognised if he travelled by train or plane. The fewer people who knew he was in New York, the better. He leaned against the whitewashed wall and exhaled deeply. At his feet was a discarded used condom, glistening wetly like a trout that had just been pulled from a stream. Meacher grimaced and carried on climbing. He smelled stale urine and put his handkerchief over his mouth as he walked by a yellow stain on the wall.

There were no numbers to indicate the floors, but Meacher had been keeping count during his ascent. He pushed open a door and stepped into a corridor. The smell wasn't much better than in the stairwell. The corridor had a low ceiling with dim lights every fifty feet that did little to illuminate the drab walls and black-painted doors, every one of which appeared to have a minimum of three locks, and strips of metal along the jambs to prevent them being forced. Meacher walked slowly down the corridor, his heart still racing from the exertion of the climb.

He found Kruse's apartment at the end of the corridor, on the left. He stuffed his handkerchief into his trouser pocket and knocked gently on the door. Meacher waited. The paint was peeling off the ageing wood and a small glass lens stared blankly back at him. There were three locks in the door: a Yale and two high security locks. Meacher knocked again.

'It's open,' said a voice.

Meacher pushed the door. It squeaked open.

Kruse was sitting on a wooden chair in the corner of the room, his back ramrod straight and his hands resting on his knees. He was naked except for a pair of khaki boxer shorts, and his eyes were closed. It had been a little under three years since Meacher had seen Kruse but he didn't appear to have changed. His upper body was trim but muscular, his thighs thick and powerful. His hair was close cropped, light brown and flecked with grey at the temples, and there were lines around his eyes and mouth that made him look older than his twenty-eight years.

'Hello, Len,' said Meacher.

The room was little more than a cell, three paces wide and four paces long with a single bed that had been stripped of its bedding, a cheap wooden wardrobe and a door which Meacher presumed led to a bathroom. A bare lightbulb hung down from the middle of the ceiling. There was no curtain at the window, though a thin wire had been strung across the top of the frame as if one had once been there.

'Hello, Jody.' Kruse slowly opened his eyes. 'Long time, no see.' His face crinkled into a smile but there was little warmth in it, and the expression vanished just as suddenly as it had appeared.

Meacher walked into the room and closed the door behind him. There was no carpet, just bare floorboards, but they had been polished to a shine. Kruse was a fanatic when it came to cleanliness, and Meacher knew that if he ran his fingers along any surface they'd come away spotless. Kruse remained seated and watched Meacher with dispassionate eyes as he waited for him to speak.

Meacher smoothed his beard with his right hand. 'How've you been, Len?'

The corners of Kruse's lips turned down a fraction. 'Same old, same old.'

Meacher lifted the briefcase. 'Are you available for a short-term contract?'

The smile appeared again. 'Who do you want me to kill this time, Jody?' Kruse asked. His chest shuddered as he laughed, a dry, rasping chuckle that sounded more like a death rattle.

'Dad!' Sean's voice jolted Wright out of his reverie. He turned and grinned at his seven-year-old son. The boy ran forward for a hug and Wright scooped him up off the floor. 'Hiya, Dad,' said Sean, throwing his arms around Wright's neck.

'Whoa, you're choking me,' said Wright, but he didn't try to break free. Over his son's shoulder he saw Janie, her face a polite mask. She looked pointedly at her wristwatch.

Wright set his son down. He stepped forward, prepared to kiss Janie on the cheek, but her eyes hardened, leaving him in no doubt that the gesture wouldn't be appreciated. Wright's stomach lurched at the thought that she couldn't even bear to touch him any more. 'Do you want a coffee or something?' he asked.

Janie shook her head and looked at her watch again. 'I'll pick him up here at six.'

'That's okay, I can drop him off at home.'

'No,' she snapped. Her lips tightened as if she was holding something back, then she forced a smile. 'Here's fine.' She knelt down beside Sean. 'Give Mummy a kiss,' she said. Sean kissed her dutifully on the cheek. 'Be good,' she said.

Wright watched her go, her heels clicking on the tiled floor of the burger bar. He ruffled his son's hair. 'What do you want to eat?'

'Mummy gave me breakfast already,' said his son.

'Yeah? What did you have?'

'Muesli.'

'Rabbit food,' said Wright scathingly. 'Wouldn't you like a cheeseburger?'

'Mummy says red meat is bad for you.'

'Burgers aren't red. They're brown.' Sean giggled and Wright's spirits lifted. He might have lost his wife, but his son was still very much his son. Even if he was having muesli for breakfast. Flecks of rain peppered the window. 'So, where do you want to go?' Wright asked.

'Anywhere.'

'What about the Trocadero? We could hit the video games.'

'Mummy says I shouldn't play video games,' said Sean.

'She said what?'

Sean wiped his nose with the back of his hand. 'She says they encourage violence.'

Wright snorted softly. He knew that he shouldn't contradict his ex-wife, but sometimes she talked absolute nonsense. What did she hope to achieve by feeding the boy muesli and keeping him away from video games? She'd be putting him in a dress next. 'Okay,' he said. 'What do you want to do?'

Sean drummed his fingers on the table, his brow furrowed. 'We could go to the zoo,' he said eventually.

'You want to go to the zoo?' said Wright, surprised.

'Fine. I guess.'

'Okay, it's the zoo, then.'

They went out to the car park. Wright opened the door to the Fiesta for Sean and waited until he'd fastened his seatbelt before getting in himself. It took several turns of the key before the engine burst into life. Wright drove to Regent's Park, doing his best to keep the conversation going. His son seemed happy enough, but it was clear from the number of questions that Wright had to ask how little they knew about each other.

'Here we are,' said Wright, stopping in the zoo car park. As they walked towards the entrance, spots of rain began to fall. Sean pulled up the hood of his blue anorak. 'You're not cold?' asked Wright.

'I'm okay,' said Sean.

Wright looked up at the clouds gathering overhead. They were grey rather than black and the rain didn't seem to be getting worse, but Wright wondered if he should suggest going somewhere else. The problem was, he couldn't think of a single place to take a seven-year-old boy on a wet Saturday morning.

He paid for them to get in and they walked together towards the large cats enclosures, which was always Sean's favourite part of the zoo. They passed several other father-and-son couples. The zoo was a popular place for divorced fathers to go with their children.

'Can you see them?' Wright asked.

Sean shook his head. 'Lions don't like the rain,' he said.

Drops of rain began to pitter-patter on the hood of Sean's anorak and water trickled down the back of Wright's neck. 'I'm sorry,' said Wright. He put his hand on his son's shoulder.

Sean looked up at him. 'What for?'

'The rain.'

Sean smiled up at him. 'It's not your fault.'

In the distance there was a flash of light followed a few seconds later by a roll of thunder. Wright and Sean hurried back to the car as the skies opened.

Sean looked out of the window as Wright drove towards Tavistock Place. 'Where are we going?' he asked.

'It's a secret,' said Wright.

It was only when Wright pulled up in front of the Gothic-style brick building in Tavistock Place that Sean realised what their destination was.

'It's your office,' he said, his eyes wide.

'Smart lad,' said Wright. 'You should be a detective.' The black metal gate rattled up and Wright drove through to the courtyard. There were fewer than a dozen cars parked there and Wright pulled up next to Tommy Reid's Honda Civic.

They found the man himself in the CID office, slouched in his chair with a naked foot propped up on his desk, clipping his toenails. He seemed totally unfazed by the appearance of Wright and his son and continued to drop pieces of clipped nail into a wastepaper bin. 'I thought you were playing video games,' he said.

'Nah, they encourage violent tendencies,' said Wright.

Reid raised his eyebrows in surprise. 'Do they now?' he said. 'I must remember that.'

'Then Sean here said he wanted to see animals. So I thought . . .' He gestured around the office.

'What better place?' Reid finished for him with a wry smile. He put down his clippers and pulled on his sock. 'How are you doing, Sean? My name's Tommy.'

Sean said hello but he was more interested in a large whiteboard which Reid had placed in front of the window on an easel. On it Reid had stuck a photograph of the body in the tunnel. 'What's that?' asked Sean, pointing at the photograph. 'It's a body, isn't it?' he said, stepping forward for a closer look.

Too late, Wright realised what Sean was looking at, and dragged him away. 'What the hell's that doing up here?' he yelled at Tommy. 'It's meant to be in the incident room. That photo's enough to give the boy nightmares.'

'They've only just finished connecting the phones and computers downstairs.' Reid went over to the coffee machine. 'I'm still checking lists of missing persons on the Police National Computer.'

'Any joy?' asked Wright.

'Do you have any idea of how many middle-aged men go missing every year?'

'A lot?'

'Yeah. A lot. Mind you, I thought of doing a runner when my wife set her solicitor on me. You were probably the same, right?' He froze as he realised that Sean was listening. He looked across at Wright, who shook his head admonishingly. 'Do you want a coffee?' asked Reid.

'Sure,' said Wright coldly.

Reid made a gun of his hand and pointed it at Sean. 'Coke?'

'Yes, please,' said the boy. Sean looked up at his father, his face suddenly serious. 'You're going to find the man who did it, aren't you?'

Wright nodded. 'Sure I am.'

Jody Meacher pulled the door closed and walked down the dimly lit corridor. He took his pocket watch out and opened it. With luck he'd be back in Washington for lunch.

A door opened to his right and Meacher flinched, but a single eye glared at him for a second and then the door slammed shut again. Meacher put his watch away and pushed open the door that led to the stairs. This time the smell didn't seem as bad.

He switched the briefcase to his right hand. The briefcase had been mainly for show, a badge of office. The briefing he'd given Kruse had been entirely verbal: no papers, no photographs, not even a copy of the Polaroid that had been sent to the senator. Kruse had listened in silence as Meacher explained what had to be done. There had been no questions, a credit to the thoroughness of Meacher's briefing and the sharp intelligence of the man who had been nicknamed 'Missile' during his brief time in Special Forces. Kruse hadn't even asked how much he'd be paid this time.

Meacher wasn't concerned by the man's apparent lack of enthusiasm. Or by his curious living arrangements. Meacher knew that between missions Kruse simply shut himself down, like a piece of machinery that was surplus to requirements.

Meacher knew that in his resting phase, Kruse was almost robotic; but primed and briefed, given an objective, he became a human juggernaut. His personality underwent a transformation, too, like an actor assuming a role. Kruse would produce whatever characteristics were necessary to get the job done, almost on demand.

Meacher walked slowly down the stairs, taking care not to touch the walls. He had come across Kruse five years earlier, shortly after he'd left the army. Kruse had served with distinction in Desert Storm and had stayed behind in Saudi Arabia as part of a special anti-terrorist unit protecting the Saudi royal family, but one of his best friends had been killed by a suicide bomber. Kruse's retaliatory attack had killed three Iranian terrorists, but bad timing had led to two innocent bystanders being injured, one of them a Saudi prince. The Americans pulled Kruse out before the Saudis discovered that he was involved.

On his arrival back in the States Kruse was given a battery of psychological tests, the result of which was a recommendation that he be removed from Special Forces. He'd quit the military a week later, and according to an FBI report that had passed across Meacher's desk, he'd tried to begin work as a contract killer. He approached a New York Mafia family but they were suspicious of the non-Italian and sent three of their own men to kill him. They were found two days later in a dumpster, shot with their own guns. That was when Meacher approached Kruse, offering him a chance for occasional work on condition that he worked solely for him. The arrangement had worked perfectly so far.

Kruse didn't know the reason for the missions he was given, and as far as Meacher knew, Kruse was unaware that Meacher worked for a US senator. The man simply didn't care. All he cared about was being given the chance to use the skills he had. Killing skills.

Wright dropped Sean back at McDonald's to meet Janie, then after spending a lonely and depressing evening in an Indian restaurant he drove back to Tavistock Place, parked his car in the BTP courtyard and walked up to the CID office, showing his warrant card to the security guard at the entrance. The guard was reading a first edition of the *News of the World*, his feet on the desk. He nodded a greeting at Wright and then went back to his paper.

Wright went up to the first floor, but the CID office was deserted and the whiteboard had gone, so he took the stairs down to the incident room in the basement. He took off his coat and dropped it on the back of a chair, then went over to the whiteboard and stared at the photograph of the mutilated corpse for several minutes, rocking backwards and forwards on his heels. Wright picked up a black marker pen and drew an ace of spades next to the photograph on the whiteboard, carefully shading it in. He stood back and admired his handiwork. The playing card was the key to solving the murder, he was sure of that.

He tapped the pen on the palm of his hand as he nodded slowly. He smiled tightly, then stepped forward and began writing on the board in large capital letters. WHO? he wrote. WHEN? HOW? WHY? He circled the last word. Then he circled it again. And again.

Superintendent Newton pushed open the door to the incident room. It was seven o'clock in the morning and he didn't expect to see anyone in before him, but to his surprise Nick Wright was sprawled in a chair, his head slumped down on his chest. He was wearing a pale green cotton shirt rolled up to the elbows and khaki Chinos, and scuffed, dirty Nike training shoes. Newton frowned and his pale lips tightened into a straight line. It was most definitely not the standard of clothing he expected to see his plainclothes operatives wearing. Newton walked over to Wright and stood looking down at him. Wright continued to snore quietly. A thin dribble of saliva had run down his chin and plopped on to his shirt. Newton clasped his briefcase to his chest and coughed. Wright shifted his legs. On Wright's desk was an opened can of Coke and a plastic-wrapped sandwich. The superintendent realised that Wright must have spent the night in the office. He coughed again, louder this time. When Wright still didn't react, Newton gently kicked his leg.

Wright opened his eyes sleepily. 'Huh?' he said, trying to focus. 'What?'

'What are you playing at, Nick?' asked Newton.

Wright sprang to his feet. He ran a hand through his unkempt hair and grinned shamefacedly. 'Sir? Sorry. I was, er . . .' He swallowed and realised there was saliva on his chin. His hand flew up to cover his embarrassment and he wiped away the mess.

'Have you been here all night?' Newton asked.

Wright wiped his hand on his trousers. 'I must have fallen asleep,' he said. He picked up his can of Coke and drank, swilling the cola around his mouth before swallowing. 'Sorry,' he said. 'My mouth felt like something died in it.'

'When I said that you should move out of Tommy's place, I didn't mean to suggest that you should take up residence here,' said Newton dryly.

'Oh no, I wasn't—' began Wright, but he stopped short as he realised that the superintendent was joking. 'I'll go home and change,' he said.

Newton looked at Wright through narrowed eyes. 'Are you okay, Nick?' he asked.

'Yeah, really. I fell asleep, that's all.'

Newton nodded at the whiteboard covered with Wright's doodles. 'The tunnel case?'

Wright put down his can of Coke. 'I was going through the PNC, checking missing persons.'

Newton waved for Wright to sit down. Wright dropped down into his chair and Newton perched on the edge of his desk, his briefcase still in his arms. 'How far have you got?' he asked.

'Based on what little we've got, the PNC computer's generated some two hundred-odd possibilities,' said Wright.

'That seems a lot,' said Newton.

'That's the number of men aged between forty-two and fifty-eight who've been reported missing and who haven't been accounted for yet,' said Wright.

'Nationwide?' asked Newton.

'Except Northern Ireland,' said Wright, picking up a print-out of names and addresses. 'Trouble is, it's not an exhaustive list. A lot of men that age go walkabout and nobody misses them. Single men, contractors, tramps.'

'And you can't be more precise about the age?'

'Pathologist reckons fifty, give or take five years. We widened the age range a bit, just to be on the safe side.'

'And you're telling me that two hundred men in their forties and fifties have gone missing?'

Wright handed the print-out to the superintendent, who ran his eyes over it as Wright talked. 'They've been reported missing within the last three months, but a lot will have turned up, it's just that the police weren't told. People are quick to call up if someone goes missing, but not so quick to phone to say that the guy's turned up again. I've been going through the list, checking to see who's still not been accounted for and requesting photographs where possible. The problem is, sir, the face is in a real mess and I don't think we can rely on getting a match from a photograph. I want to narrow it down before we start bringing in people to identify the body.'

'Agreed,' said Newton. 'The last thing we want is a stream of people filing past the corpse wondering if it's their nearest and dearest. What about identifying marks on the body?' He smiled thinly. 'And I don't mean the fact that his dick was cut off.'

'The post mortem mentions some scars on his back but doesn't go into detail. We weren't in on the post mortem because the pathologist called in the Met instead. I'm going to talk to her to see if there's anything else that might give a clue as to who he is.'

'What about a search of the crime area?'

'We had a fingertip search of the tunnel and a general sweep outside, but there wasn't anything. It was well planned, his clothes had been taken away, there were several knives used. Anyone who went to that amount of trouble isn't likely to have left anything lying about outside.'

Newton exhaled deeply. 'And no witnesses?'

Wright shook his head. 'There are no houses or gardens overlooking the area, and anyone using the road can't see down into the culvert. There was some dog shit around so we've got a man there interviewing any dog walkers. We're going to start a house-to-house once we've got the rotas worked out.'

Newton stood up and went over to the whiteboard. He looked at the words Wright had written, and at the ace of spades he'd drawn. 'Who, when, how, why?' Newton read. 'Well, answer those questions, Nick, and the mystery is solved.' He turned around. 'I saw you on TV.'

'Ah.' Wright looked embarrassed.

'At least you didn't allow yourself to be drawn on that serial killer question.' Newton sighed despondently. 'I suppose I should be grateful for small mercies. Go home and change, Nick. You've got a busy day ahead of you.'

Kristine Ross rolled over and hugged her pillow, luxuriating in the warmth of her bed. She opened one eye and looked at the clock radio on her bedside table. It was just after two a.m. She closed her eye and tried to get back to sleep. Her alarm was set for six a.m. so that she could be in the office by seven thirty. She listened to her own breathing, then jerked involuntarily as she heard a soft scraping sound from the far side of her bedroom, as if the door had opened and brushed against the carpet. She opened both eyes. The door was closed. She sighed and tried to slip back into sleep.

Sleep wouldn't come. She tossed and turned and rolled on to her side. Working for Senator Burrow was demanding, both physically and mentally, and normally she was so tired that she dropped off as soon as her head touched the pillow. The skin on her back tingled as if she was sleeping in a draught. She pulled up the quilt and drew her knees up against her stomach, curling up into a fetal ball. It was no use. She was wide awake. She opened her eyes. Immediately she stiffened. There was a dark shadow in the corner of the room in a place where she'd never seen a shadow before. She frowned, wondering what it was, cursing herself for being so stupid, but then the shadow moved and she gasped.

'I've got a gun,' she said. 'If you don't leave now I'll shoot.'

There was a soft chuckle from the shadow. 'You didn't have a gun when I checked this morning, Kristine. I hardly think you bought one on the way back from the office.'

He knew her name, but Kristine was sure that she didn't know who the man was. She sat up, holding the quilt up to cover herself. Suddenly she realised what the man had said. He'd been in her apartment before. She began to panic and her hands shook uncontrollably. 'Take what you want,' she said.

'I intend to,' said the man. He walked over to the light switch and flicked it on.

Kristine blinked and tried to focus on the man. He was wearing a grey suit and a white shirt and a conservative tie in muted reds and greens. He looked more like a stockbroker than a burglar or a rapist, but then she'd seen enough police documentaries to know that burglars, rapists and even serial killers didn't always conform to type. His light brown hair was greying prematurely and it was cut short in military style. He was trim and fit but not over muscular, and he was, Kristine realised, the type of man she often went out with.

'Just don't hurt me. Please.' She felt weak and vulnerable and hated herself for it.

'I'll try not to,' he said.

Kristine was seized by fear. 'Oh God. Please, take what you want and go!'

The man pursed his lips and pressed his index finger to them. He was wearing gloves, Kristine realised. Tight-fitting black leather gloves. 'Try to keep your voice down, Kristine. I know how stressful this is for you, but if you raise your voice I'm going to have to use more force than I want to. Do you understand?' He raised his eyebrows and nodded and Kristine found herself nodding along with him. 'I want you to get dressed,' he said. 'There's a blue cotton dress in your wardrobe, the one with the white flowers. Put that on. Are you wearing underwear?'

'What?'

'Are you wearing underwear?'

'No,' she said, her voice trembling.

'Put a bra and panties on. White.'

She slid out from underneath the quilt and scampered across the thick-pile carpet to the chest of drawers where she kept her underwear. He watched her, but there was nothing salacious about the way he looked at her. She turned her back on him while she pulled up her panties and put on her bra.

'Do you work out?' the man asked.

'What?'

'Do you work out? Exercise? You've got a great body.'

'Thank you.' The words came out instinctively and she mentally cursed herself for thanking the intruder. She went over to the mirror-fronted wardrobes and pulled open the doors. The blue dress was on a hanger. She took it out and put it on.

'Let's go to the kitchen,' said the man.

Kristine was confused. 'What?'

'The kitchen. Now come on, Kristine, you're not being a very good host, are you?'

He was so close that she could feel his breath on her face. Kristine stared down at the man's jacket. She had seen enough Secret Service agents around Senator Burrow to know that no matter how well a weapon was concealed, there was always a telltale bulge.

The man smiled. It was an easy smile, showing perfect teeth. 'I don't need one,' he said, as if reading her mind.

'What?'

'You keep saying that, Kristine, and frankly I don't think it's especially polite. Didn't your mother teach you to say, "I beg your pardon" or "Excuse me"?'

Kristine shook her head, now totally confused and unable to speak.

'Let's try, shall we?' said the man. 'You can say, "I beg your pardon?" can't you?'

Kristine felt suddenly light headed and for a moment she feared she was going to pass out. She fought to steady herself. 'What do you want?' she asked. This wasn't a robbery. Did he want to kidnap her? That didn't make any sense: she wasn't married and her parents didn't have money.

'I think you need a drink,' he said. 'There's wine in the kitchen.' He held the door open for her. 'After you.'

He followed her along the hall to the kitchen. 'You know where most accidents happen?' he asked as she switched on the overhead fluorescent lights.

Kristine shrugged. 'The roads?' she guessed.

The man pointed a gloved finger at her. 'That's what everyone thinks. But it's the home. Home sweet home. More people are hurt at home than anywhere else. Homes are dangerous places.'

'Red or white?' she asked. She was feeling braver. He'd

made no move to hurt her and seemed to be going out of his way to put her at ease.

'You choose,' he said. Kristine pulled a bottle of Chianti from the rack by the door and picked up a silver-plated corkscrew, a housewarming present from her mother. She removed the cork and reached for two glasses. 'Just the one glass,' he said.

'You don't want any?' she said. It was important to keep him talking, she knew. She'd seen an Oprah Winfrey show once about how to deal with attackers, and a policeman had said that it was important to establish a rapport with the criminal.

'I don't drink,' he said.

Kristine half filled the glass, and raised it. 'Cheers,' she said. 'Do you have a name?' She stared at his face, trying to imprint it on her memory. It was important to remember details that couldn't be changed, the detective had said. Not clothing, or jewellery, which is what most witnesses fixated on. Things like the dimple in the centre of his chin. The light brown hair that was starting to grey. The pale hazel eyes.

'Len,' he said. 'Short for Leonard. Let's go into the lounge. Bring the bottle with you.'

He held the door open for her and she smiled at him as she walked by. 'Thanks, Len,' she said. Use his name if you knew it, the policeman had said. Make the process as personal as possible.

He followed her into the lounge and closed the door, then switched on a table lamp. 'Have some more wine, Kristine.'

She turned to face him. 'I don't want any more. I've had enough.'

'Do it for me anyway,' he said pleasantly.

Kristine shook her head. 'Please, really, I've had enough.'

The man's smile widened but all the warmth vanished. It was a cold, harsh smile, the smile of an attacking shark. Kristine shivered. 'I'm asking you nicely, Kristine, and I expect you to do as I ask. If you don't, I'm going to rape you, then I'm going to fuck you up the arse and then I'm going to shove a carving knife so far up your cunt that you'll get a nosebleed.' The warmth seeped back into his smile. 'So drink up. Please.'

Kristine drained her glass and refilled it with shaking hands. She forced herself to drink but she almost gagged and wine spurted from her mouth. 'I'm sorry,' she said.

The man ignored her apology. 'Keep drinking,' he said. He perched on the back of her sofa with his arms folded and watched as she forced down the wine.

Kristine began to giggle. Her stomach felt as if it were glowing and she could feel the alcohol coursing through her system. The most she usually drank was a couple of glasses of wine and that was while she was eating. She poured the last of the wine into the glass and put the empty bottle on to the coffee table.

'Very good, Kristine,' said the man. 'What about some music?' He nodded at the stereo. 'Something mellow.'

Kristine walked unsteadily over to the Panasonic stereo system and looked through the rack of CDs. Her mind was in a whirl as she frantically searched for a way out of her predicament. The wine was making her dizzy and she knew that she wouldn't be able to run. Besides, even if she was sober she doubted that the man would have any problem catching and restraining her. There was a telephone in the bathroom – if she could convince him that she had to go to the toilet then perhaps she could call the police. She chose a Lloyd Cole CD and slotted it into the player.

'I need to use the bathroom, Len,' she said. She brushed a stray lock of blonde hair from her face and tried to make herself look as appealing as possible. Make them think you were co-operating, the policeman had said. Then choose your moment.

'Later,' he said. 'There's still some wine in your glass.'

He walked over to the sliding window that led to the balcony. He flipped the lock and slid the window open. Kristine frowned, wondering what he was doing. She picked up her wine glass. Despite the threat he'd made earlier, he clearly wasn't going to rape her; he'd had every opportunity to do that in the bedroom. And if he was planning to rob her, why make her drink the wine? Maybe he thought the wine would knock her out so that he could make a clean getaway. But that didn't make sense either because all he had to do was tie her up.

'Beautiful view, isn't it, Kristine?' said the man. He had his back to her as he stared out at the lights of the nation's capital. 'Come and look.'

Kristine was totally confused. He was treating her more like a girlfriend than a hostage. She walked slowly across the room, both hands cupped carefully around the wine glass as if it was a sacred chalice.

The man moved to the side and gestured with his left arm for her to go out on to the balcony. It was a big balcony with room enough for a white-painted cast-iron table and three chairs, and was one of the main reasons she'd chosen the apartment. 'It's a beautiful home you have,' he said. 'Are you buying or renting?'

'Buying,' she said.

'You're a very lucky girl, Kristine,' said the man.

Kristine opened her mouth to reply, but before she could speak she felt a thump in the small of the back and she stumbled forward. Her arms flailed as she tried to regain her balance, but she was pushed again, this time harder, and she pitched across the waist-high rail, falling towards the car parking area eight floors below. She tried to scream but her throat was full of wine and vomit and all she could manage was a terrified gurgle before she slammed into the tarmac.

Nick Wright handed a cup of coffee to Tommy Reid, who looked at his wristwatch theatrically. 'Wet leaves on the line?' Reid said.

Wright sipped his coffee and sat down. 'I didn't leave until seven o'clock this morning,' he said. 'I got back to the flat just after you'd left.'

Reid snorted. 'I assumed you'd pulled a bird,' he said. He pointed at the polythene-wrapped sandwich on Wright's desk. 'I suppose that's still fresh, then?'

Wright shook his head in disgust. He tossed the sandwich to his partner.

Reid caught it one handed. 'Hey, I could have just eaten it before you got here.'

'That would've been theft,' said Wright. He took another sip of coffee. 'And I would've pressed charges.'

Reid unwrapped the sandwich and took a large bite out of it. 'You came back here last night?'

'Yeah.'

Reid gestured at the whiteboard. 'That's your artwork, then?'

Wright nodded. 'I was brainstorming.'

He picked up the list of missing middle-aged men. 'I've managed to eliminate a dozen names so far,' he said. 'I want to eliminate a few more before we start bringing people in to look at the body,' said Wright. 'We know our man's fingerprints aren't on file with New Scotland Yard's Fingerprint Bureau, so I want to check if any of those missing have had their prints taken. Any that have, we can eliminate.'

Reid nodded. 'Makes sense.'

'I've arranged for a DNA sample to be sent to the DNA database at Priory House in Birmingham but they're struggling with a backlog and it'll be at least five days before they get back to me. And I'm going to see the pathologist. See if there's anything else she can tell me about the body. Stuff that might help us identify him. Or at least rule out some of the names on that list.'

'Busy, busy, busy,' said Reid. He handed the list of names back to Wright and picked up the second sandwich.

'What about you?' asked Wright. 'Any thoughts?'

'Ronnie's asked me to canvas the area again for witnesses and check with the uniforms, the ones checking dog-walkers. But according to Ronnie, the Met boys'll be in later today and they'll probably take over that end of it. He says we'll stick with the crime scene and the forensic, the Met will handle the trace and any witnesses.'

'That's bollocks,' said Wright. 'We've already started trawling missing persons. Hell, between us we've already discounted twenty per cent of the names.'

'Don't argue with me, mate, speak to Ronnie.'

'Speak to Ronnie about what?' boomed the chief inspector from the doorway.

Wright twisted around in his seat. Dundas was carrying a pale blue file and a carton of milk. He had recently acquired an ulcer, and a pint of milk a day was his one concession to his doctor's plea for a change in lifestyle.

'I think we should handle the identification of the body,' Wright said.

'What, you've started so you want to finish?'

'Exactly.'

Dundas pretended to consider what Wright had said. He drank from the carton, leaving a smear of milk across his upper lip. 'Remind me again how you got on with your inspector's exam, Nick?' he said eventually.

Wright scowled but didn't reply. There was no need to. Dundas knew exactly how badly Wright had done.

'Oh, I remember,' said Dundas, waving around his carton of milk. 'Not an inspiring performance, was it?'

'And your point is?' sighed Wright.

'That when you're a chief inspector, you can call the shots. Until then . . .'

'Okay, okay, I get the drift,' said Wright. 'Do you have any objections to my going to see the pathologist? See if I can get any more physical characteristics?'

'Now you're sulking,' said Dundas. He gestured at Reid. 'What do you think, Inspector Reid?' he said, stressing Reid's title. 'Should we allow Sergeant Wright to go to speak to the nice pathologist?'

Wright shook his head in disgust.

Dundas and Reid exchanged grins. 'Might keep him out of trouble,' said Reid.

'Thanks, partner,' said Wright.

'What about you, Tommy? Any thoughts?'

'Thought I'd have a go at following up the playing card. The forensic boys haven't got any prints off it, but it must have come from somewhere.'

Dundas nodded approvingly. He looked around the incident room. There were half a dozen detectives sitting at desks and three female uniformed officers working on the computers. 'Lads and lassies, could I have your attention for a few moments, please,' he boomed. All heads turned to look at Dundas as he took another drink from the carton. 'Just to let you know that the Met team will be arriving later this afternoon. Twelve officers in all, the brightest and the best, no doubt.' He grinned and there were several guffaws from around the room. 'Most will be coming from the Battersea station and you'll probably recognise a few familiar faces. I see you've spread yourselves out but it might make more sense to stake a claim to one side of the incident room and let them have their desks together. They're a sensitive bunch and they feel happier in a pack. Phil, make sure they have enough phones and terminals, will you? I don't want them complaining that they're getting the short end of the stick.'

Phil Evans flashed Dundas a thumbs-up.

'Now, you know as well as I do how this is going to work. It's a joint investigation, with the BTP and the Met working hand in hand, brothers-in-arms in the fight against the forces of darkness. That's the PR shit. In reality we'll tell them fuck all and they'll treat us like mushrooms. I know I'm pissing in the wind, but please try to remember that we're supposed to be co-operating. Try to share something with them, otherwise we'll have two investigations going and that's not going to help anyone. Any questions?'

'Who's on the Met team?' asked Wright.

Dundas opened his file and held out a sheet of paper on which was a typed list of names. Wright scanned the list. His heart fell. The third name on the list was Detective Inspector Gerry Hunter. The sixth name was Detective Sergeant Clive Edmunds. He handed the list back to Dundas who gave it to Phil Evans. Dundas smiled at Wright. 'Any problems?' he asked.

'No, sir,' said Wright.

'Glad to hear it,' said Dundas. He left the incident room, humming to himself.

'Hunter's on the case?' asked Reid.

'Yeah.'

'That should produce a little creative tension, wouldn't you say?'

Wright drank the rest of his coffee and stood up. 'Maybe.'

On the way out, Wright checked his mailbox by the door. There was a single envelope, blindingly white, with his name and the address of the office typed on the front. He ripped it open on the way to the elevator. It was from the Child Support Agency, asking for details of any savings accounts he had. It was the third letter from the agency that he'd received that month. He treated it exactly the same way as he'd treated the previous two. He screwed it into a tight ball and tossed it into a wastepaper basket.

A middle-aged man wearing a bloodstained dark green glossy apron over light green scrubs squinted at

Wright's warrant card and told him that Dr Anna Littman was in the middle of a post mortem but that he could go in if he wanted. He nodded at a pair of green-painted swing doors with metal protective strips at waist height. Wright shook his head and said that he didn't mind waiting. The man pulled off bloody rubber gloves and dropped them into a bin, then stripped off his gown and put it in a black bag before going over to a stainless-steel sink and carefully washing his hands. 'Don't see many of you chaps here,' he said. 'What happened? Somebody fell under a train?'

'Murder,' said Wright. 'I'm Nick Wright.'

The man nodded. 'Robbie Ballantine.' He wiped his hands on a towel. 'Oh, of course, the body in the tunnel. Gruesome business that.'

'You saw it?'

'I helped Anna with the post mortem, actually. Is there a problem?'

'No, not really. I just wanted more information, that's all.'

'The report seemed comprehensive to me.'

'It's not that. I'm more interested in seeing if there was anything about the body that might help me identify the man.'

'You still don't know who he is?'

Wright shook his head. 'Can you think of anything? The scars on his back, for instance.'

Ballantine raised his eyebrows. 'Ah yes. The scars. They're in the report, aren't they?'

'The report refers to them as old scars, but doesn't say how they got there.'

'No real need to,' said Ballantine. 'They were very old

wounds. At least twenty years, I'd say. No connection at all with the crime.'

'Knife wounds?'

'Oh no,' said Ballantine. 'They were too jagged for that. Fragmentation scars, I'd say.'

'From a grenade? A war wound?'

'Could be.' He looked up at the ceiling and waggled his head from side to side as he thought about it. 'An explosion of some sort, certainly. It could have been a gas cylinder exploding, something like that.' He looked at Wright again. 'I actually hadn't given it much thought. Why are you so interested?'

'Because if it was a grenade I'd be looking for someone with a military background. If it was a bomb, then he could have been caught up in a terrorist incident.'

The swing doors behind Wright banged open and Anna Littman burst into the room, her gloved hands held out in front of her. Her hair was covered with a green plastic cap and she was wearing scrubs and a bloodstained green apron. 'Nick Wright,' she said. 'Rank unknown. To what do I owe the pleasure?'

Wright was surprised that she'd remembered his name. Surprised and flattered. She turned her back on him as she stripped off her protective clothing.

'It's sergeant,' said Wright. 'And I need your help.'

'Take two aspirins and call me tomorrow.' She took off her cap and her greying blonde hair spilled out. She looked over her shoulder at him and winked mischievously. 'That's a doctor joke,' she said.

'I just came to tell you that your car's been towed away,' he said.

'I only . . .' she began, but she stopped when Wright's face broke into a grin.

'That's a policeman joke,' he said.

Her green eyes flashed, then she smiled. It was an open, honest smile, thought Wright. He decided that he liked Dr Anna Littman. She seemed a lot less prickly than when they'd met in the tunnel. She went over to the sink and washed her hands.

'He was asking about the tunnel corpse,' said Ballantine, putting on a fresh apron.

'Was he now?' said Dr Littman. She pulled her hair back into a ponytail and fastened it with a small black band. 'You got my report?'

'Eventually,' he said.

'Oh yes, I'm sorry about that. I didn't know where to send it, so I figured that Gerry could hand it on to you.'

'The report was fine,' he said, putting his hands in his pockets. 'I just wanted to pick your brains.'

Ballantine pulled on rubber gloves. 'Duty calls,' he said to Wright, and used his shoulder to push his way through the swing doors.

'So, Sergeant Nick, pick away.' Dr Littman leaned back against the sink and watched him with amused eyes.

'I'm having trouble identifying the body,' said Wright. 'The face was messed up so badly it's impossible to get a match from photographs. Hundreds of men go missing every year, and other than the scars on his back there don't seem to be any identifying features. Robbie there was saying he thought they might be shrapnel scars. An old war wound. Or an accident. Something like that could help me identify him.'

'I see. Do you want a coffee?'

The change of subject took Wright by surprise and for a moment he was flustered. 'Coffee? Sure. Yeah, that'd be great.'

'Come through to my office.'

Wright followed her down a corridor. Even in the shapeless scrubs it was clear she had a good figure. Wright wondered how old she was. Late thirties, certainly. Maybe early forties. At least six or seven years older than he was. She opened a door and he followed her into a small office with a single window overlooking a car park. There were several feminine touches: a fern in a pot, a watercolour of a young girl playing with a puppy, and several framed photographs on the desk. One of the pictures was of a good-looking man wearing gold-rimmed spectacles with two young boys in his lap. Dr Littman poured two cups from a coffee-maker on top of a filing cabinet. 'No milk, but I've got Coffeemate,' she said.

'Coffeemate's fine,' said Wright.

'Sit,' she said. 'Sugar?'

'No, thanks,' said Wright, sitting in a leather armchair. On the wall to his right was a poster of a rock group, half a dozen beefy men with long hair and leather waistcoats holding their musical instruments in phallic poses. Wright wondered if Anna Littman had a thing about rock musicians. The poster certainly seemed out of place in the office.

She stirred white powder into the coffees, gave him his cup and then sat in the high-backed swivel chair behind the desk. 'I'm not sure how much of a help the scars on his back will be,' she said. 'They were very old, hardly noticeable. A wife would probably know about them, but they wouldn't be common knowledge.'

'Pity,' said Wright. 'Was there anything else that you

saw, maybe something that wasn't in the report but which I could use to narrow down the possibilities?'

Dr Littman looked at Wright over the top of her cup. Small frown lines appeared across her forehead. She put down her cup. 'He was circumcised,' she said. 'That should help. I think you'd probably be able to eliminate two thirds of the possibilities on the basis of circumcision alone.'

She warmed her hands on the steaming cup of coffee and chewed on the side of her lip, deep in thought, staring into the middle distance as she tried to recall the body.

'Contact lenses,' she said. 'He had contact lenses. The disposable type, the ones you wear for a day and throw away.' Suddenly her eyes widened. 'Oh God, I clean forgot. I think he played bass guitar.'

Wright burst out laughing. 'Come on, Anna. What on earth makes you say that?'

She looked at him seriously. 'I was checking his hands for defence wounds. They were soft, as if he wasn't used to manual work, but the skin on the fingertips of both hands was hard.'

Wright shook his head, still chuckling.

Her eyes flashed and she flicked her hair to the side like a horse swishing its mane. 'Do you want my help or not, Sergeant Nick?'

Wright did his best to stop laughing. 'I'm sorry,' he said, 'but that's a feat of deduction that Sherlock Holmes would be proud of.'

Dr Littman pointed at the poster. 'See the guy third from the left. With the bass guitar?'

Wright looked at the musician. A tall, good-looking man in black leather with shoulder-length jet-black hair and a white guitar thrusting up from his groin. 'Yes . . .' he said, not sure what she was getting at. Dr Littman turned the framed photograph of the man with two children around so that he could see it more clearly. He did a double-take. 'My God,' he said. 'You married a rock and roll star.'

'He used to dye his hair,' she said. She smiled at the photograph. 'And he has to wear glasses these days.' She looked up at Wright. 'He still plays. And I'd know a bass guitarist's hands anywhere.'

'Okay, I'm convinced, but why are you so sure he played bass and not lead guitar?'

Dr Littman sat back in her chair, smiling broadly. 'Lead guitarists use plectrums, so the skin isn't so hard on the fingertips of their right hands. And Spanish guitarists have long nails on their right hands so that they can pluck the strings.' She gave an exaggerated shrug. 'What can I say? I've been married a long time. My husband could probably tell you half a dozen causes of hypertension.' Wright was suddenly very envious of Dr Littman's husband. Her love and affection for him was written all over her face. Wright doubted that Janie had ever felt the same way about him. 'So, have I been of any help?' the pathologist asked.

Wright grinned. 'Of course you have,' he replied. 'I'm looking for a short-sighted, circumcised bass player. How hard can that be?'

When Wright got back to the office, Tommy Reid was devouring a carton of Kentucky Fried Chicken. 'Wanna piece?' asked Reid, offering a leg.

Wright shook his head. He sat down and studied a note that had been left on his desk. His ex-wife had called. Three times. Wright held up the note.

'Yeah, she's not a happy bunny,' said Reid. He wiped his greasy lips with a paper napkin.

'Did she say what it was this time?'

Reid picked up a handful of French fries. 'Nope.' He slotted the fries into his mouth and chewed contentedly. 'How did it go with the lady doctor?'

'I think I can narrow the list down quite a bit. Our man played bass guitar.'

'Yeah? What colour?'

'I'm serious. Playing the guitar affects the fingers, apparently.'

Reid pulled a face. 'You learn something every day,' he said.

'What about the card?' asked Wright.

Reid reached for his notebook and flicked through it. 'I had no problem identifying it. I took it to a magic shop in Kensington and the guy there knew what it was straight away. It's a Bicycle brand, one of the most common brands, unfortunately. Manufactured in Ohio by the United States Playing Card Company. They make millions of the things.'

'Any chance of telling where our card was bought?'

'If we had the box they came in, maybe. But not from the card itself. Game shops, department stores, magic shops, newsagents, they all sell playing cards. And a hell of a lot of them sell the Bicycle brand.'

Wright heaved himself out of his chair and went over to the whiteboard. He massaged his temples with his knuckles as he stared at the photograph of the mutilated corpse. 'I wonder what it's like to die like that?' he mused. 'To have your skin peeled off, bit by bit.'

'Hey, I'm eating here,' complained Reid. Wright turned and was about to apologise, but his partner was already biting into his chicken leg.

There were two detectives, big men in cheap suits with the careworn faces of cops who had been on the job long enough to have seen it all. They were polite enough, and the senior of the two, an inspector called O'Brien, had shaken the senator by the hand after they'd shown him their identification. The questions were routine, O'Brien had said, and he didn't expect to take up too much of Burrow's time. They'd rejected his offer of coffee and O'Brien's partner had taken out a pen and notebook after they'd seated themselves in front of the senator's desk.

'How long had Kristine Ross been working for you, Senator?' asked O'Brien.

'Just under two years.'

'As your secretary?'

'As one of three secretaries. Four, if you include my office manager, Sally Forster.'

'Did she seem depressed?'

Burrow leaned forward. 'I thought it was an accident? She tripped, I was told.'

O'Brien made a patting motion with his hand and shook his head emphatically. 'These are standard questions, Senator. Whenever we get an accidental death, we have to rule out any other possibilities. I wouldn't be doing my job if I did otherwise.'

Burrow sat back again. 'I understand, Officer, but Kristine was a delightful, high-spirited, wonderful girl, and I wouldn't want it to get around that she might have killed herself. No, she was most definitely not depressed.'

'To the best of your knowledge, did she have a drinking problem?'

'A drinking problem? Absolutely not. Why, was drink involved?'

'She'd drunk a bottle of wine before she fell.'

Burrows shrugged. 'That surprises me,' he said.

'Was she under a lot of stress here?'

'No more so than the rest of my staff. We all work long and hard here, Inspector O'Brien, but it goes with the turf. Kristine knew what was involved before she joined. She didn't appear to me to have any trouble coping, but Sally would know better than me. You should speak to her.'

'We have, Senator, and she agrees with you.'

Burrow held his hands out, palms upward. 'There you are, then.' He stole a glance at O'Brien's partner. The detective was scribbling in his notebook. He finished writing and looked up. Burrow flashed him a confident smile.

O'Brien stood up and held out his hand. Burrow shook it again and looked the detective in the eye. The senator knew how important eye contact was: it demonstrated sincerity and openness, qualities that Burrow was a master at projecting.

'Terrible business,' said Burrow.

'Accidents happen,' said the detective. His partner put away his notebook and nodded a farewell to the senator. 'Did you know that more accidents happen in the home than on the roads?' O'Brien asked.

'Is that so?' said the senator. 'I had no idea.'

He walked the two detectives to the door and showed them out. Sally Forster was waiting to escort them out of the main office. Burrow closed the door and sighed deeply. His heart had been pounding throughout the interview, even though he knew that Jody Meacher would have left nothing to chance. There wouldn't be anything to connect Burrow to the murder, and it was a murder, he was sure of that. Meacher hadn't said what he was going to do, or when it would happen, but Burrow knew that Meacher was behind Kristine Ross's death. More than that, Burrow didn't want to know. All that mattered was that Meacher was taking care of things, just as he'd promised.

Nick Wright spent the afternoon methodically working through his list of missing persons. The list had been generated by the Police National Computer after details of the corpse had been fed in: height, weight, eye colour, age, and distinguishing features. The wide age bracket was the main reason that the list was so long, but he hadn't wanted to narrow it any further. Each missing man had his own page giving physical details, the name and telephone number of the investigating officer and a PNC code that identified the police station involved in the enquiry. What the PNC didn't supply was a photograph, or details of next of kin; for that Wright had to contact the officer handling the enquiry. It was slow, methodical work. Often the officer involved wasn't available, so Wright had either to leave a message or find someone else who could pull the file for him. If there was a photograph available, Wright arranged to have it sent to Tavistock Place, either through the Photophone system that the Force Intelligence Bureau had on the third floor, or by faxing it to one of the two fax machines in the incident room. Sometimes he was able to eliminate a possibility solely on the basis of a photograph, but the mutilation of the face and the poor quality of the photographs meant that more often than not Wright would have to telephone the next of kin for further details.

At first he'd felt a little embarrassed asking relatives if the man who'd gone missing was circumcised, and several times he'd been accused of being a pervert and had had the phone banged down on him. Despite his embarrassment, he'd already ruled out more than twenty names. Wright was about to dial another number when the phone rang. He picked up the receiver and his heart fell as soon as he heard his ex-wife's voice.

'What the hell are you playing at, Nick?' she hissed. Janie rarely shouted. If anything, the angrier she got, the quieter she became.

Wright was stunned. He had no idea what he'd done to upset her. 'What's wrong?' he said.

'What did I say to you about telling Sean war stories?' she said. 'He had nightmares all last night and I had to take him to school with bags under his eyes. What the hell did you think you were doing?'

'He wanted to—'

'Just how long do you think the judge is going to allow you to see our son if he finds out the sort of photographs you've been showing him? Crime scene pictures, for God's sake. You showed him a photograph of a dismembered corpse.'

'Okay, I'm sorry.'

'Sorry doesn't cut it. I'm supposed to be able to trust you with Sean. I specifically told you not to talk about that case.'

'Janie, it was raining, the zoo was a washout, I couldn't think what else to do with him. It was a mistake. I'm sorry. What do you want me to do, open a vein?'

'An artery would be nice,' she said. 'Don't do it again, Nick.'

The line went dead. Wright banged the receiver back on its cradle. He put his head in his hands and closed his eyes. 'Shit,' he whispered. He stood up and went over to the coffee machine and poured himself a cup. He sipped it but the hot, bitter liquid couldn't shift the bad taste in his mouth. Wright went over to Reid's desk and pulled open the bottom drawer. The bottle of vodka was wrapped in a Kentucky Fried Chicken bag. Wright took it out and poured a slug into his coffee, then drank half of it in one gulp. He added more vodka, then put the bottle away and closed the drawer. Reid was out trying to interview dog-walkers and wasn't planning to put in an appearance that afternoon. More than likely he'd be in a pub somewhere. Wright raised his polystyrene cup in a silent salute to his absent partner.

Wright sat down at his own desk and ran his finger down the list of missing persons. He'd already discounted most of the names on the first sheet. As he flicked over to the second sheet, his mobile telephone rang. The noise startled him and coffee slopped over his hand. He cursed, put the cup down and licked his hand as he picked up the phone and held it to his ear. He had a sinking feeling that it was his ex-wife, but the voice on the other end of the line was cultured and soft-spoken, the sort of voice that might belong to the wife of a Conservative Member of Parliament. 'Sergeant Wright?' she said.

'Speaking,' said Wright.

'You left a message for me to call you,' she said. 'My name's May Eckhardt.'

Wright ran his eyes down the sheet. No Eckhardt. 'Do you by any chance have a relative missing, Mrs Eckhardt? A man?'

'My husband,' she said hesitantly. 'Have you found him?'

Wright found the name on the fourth sheet. Max Eckhardt. A forty-eight-year-old American living in Maida Vale. May Eckhardt didn't sound at all American, her accent was pure Home Counties. 'I just wanted to ask you a few questions about your husband, Mrs Eckhardt.'

'Have you found him?' she repeated, a harder edge to her voice this time.

'Mrs Eckhardt, at this stage all I'm trying to do is to eliminate names from a list of missing persons. A body was found in a railway tunnel and I'm trying to identify it. Could you tell me, was your husband circumcised?'

'Excuse me?'

'Your husband. Was he circumcised?'

She hesitated for several seconds. 'Oh, I see. Yes. Yes, he was.' She had obviously realised why he had asked the question, for which Wright was immediately grateful.

'Did he wear contact lenses?'

'Yes. Yes, he did.'

'And were there scars on his back? Old scars, small ones.'

'Oh my God,' she whispered.

'Mrs Eckhardt, did he have scars on his back?'

'Yes, he did. It's him, isn't it?'

'I really couldn't say, Mrs Eckhardt, but I would like you to come in and take a look at the body we have.'

'You think it's him, don't you?'

'It's a possibility,' Wright admitted.

'What about his wallet? He had a driving licence, his press card, his credit cards.'

'There were no personal effects on the body, Mrs Eckhardt.'

'But you said he was found in a tunnel. He was hit by a train, wasn't he?'

'No, he wasn't hit by a train. Look, Mrs Eckhardt, I really don't want to say any more until you've had the chance to identify the body.'

'When?'

'As soon as you can,' said Wright. He gave her the address of the mortuary and arranged to meet her there within the hour. Wright put his mobile phone into his jacket pocket. He drank the rest of his coffee, but the bad taste was still in his mouth. He hoped that the body wouldn't be that of May Eckhardt's husband, but he had a feeling that his search was over.

Wright arrived at the mortuary in St Thomas's Hospital fifteen minutes before he was due to meet Mrs Eckhardt. He wanted to check with Dr Littman that the corpse was in a fit state to be viewed. The last time Wright had seen it the face was cut to ribbons and smeared with blood. Dr Littman wasn't there but Robbie Ballantine was, washing up after yet another post mortem.

'What state's the tunnel body in after the post mortem?' Wright asked him. 'I've got a possible relative coming to identify him.'

'The face was pretty cut up,' said Ballantine. 'We've put it back together as best we can, but it's still a mess.'

'Recognisable?'

'I should think so. How close a relative?'

'Wife.'

'Poor cow,' said Ballantine sympathetically.

'If it's her,' said Wright. He looked across at the large clock on the wall over the sink. 'I'd better go along to reception. Can you get it ready?'

'Sure,' said Ballantine. 'Does she know about the injuries?'

'Not yet.'

'Because the body isn't . . . complete. If you see what I mean. His dick's in a specimen jar, to put it bluntly,' Ballantine said. 'So if she's any thoughts about checking up on other parts of his anatomy to confirm that it's him, I'd think twice before you let her pull the sheet back.'

Wright walked through to reception. There were two uncomfortable-looking orange plastic chairs to the left of the main entrance with a metal coffee table on which lay a few well-thumbed magazines. A bored receptionist was pecking away at a computer keyboard and she looked up as Wright walked up to the counter.

'I'm waiting for a Mrs Eckhardt,' he said. 'She's here to view a body. Can you point her in my direction when she gets here?'

The receptionist nodded but didn't say anything.

Wright went over to a window which overlooked the car park. Dark clouds rolled slowly overhead, threatening rain. A black VW Golf cabriolet nosed into the car park, driven by an Oriental girl. The top was down and as she parked she cast a nervous look at the sky. 'Yeah, it looks like rain,' Wright said out loud. 'Better safe than sorry.' He smiled to himself as she put the top up.

Wright picked up the magazines, wondering what sort of reading matter was thought suitable for a mortuary. Most of them were old copies of *Hello!*

He looked up as the Oriental girl walked in. She was a little under five feet six, with shoulder-length glossy black hair. As she approached Wright he realised that she was older than he'd first thought, certainly in her late twenties, maybe older. The fringe and her small frame gave her the appearance of a schoolgirl from a distance, but she walked with authority and he saw the swell of firm breasts under her open fawn Burberry raincoat. She had an expectant look on her face and Wright figured that she worked in the mortuary. He was about to point to the receptionist when she spoke.

'Sergeant Wright?'

Wright's mouth fell open in surprise. The cultured upper-middle-class voice was totally at odds with the petite Oriental. 'Yes?' he said, momentarily confused.

'May Eckhardt.' She held out her hand. 'We spoke on the phone.'

She seemed to be deliberately trying to put him at ease and he realised she must have sensed his confusion. 'I'm sorry,' he said, trying to regain his composure. 'Of course, Mrs Eckhardt, I'm sorry, my mind was elsewhere.' He immediately regretted the words. It was possibly the worst day of May Eckhardt's life and he'd told her he was thinking about something else. 'I'm sorry,' he repeated. He shook her hand. It felt tiny within his own, but it was strong and firm and he felt her nails press against his flesh. The sensation was decidedly sexual and he felt a slight tingle down his back. She withdrew her hand quickly and seemed flustered herself as if she'd sensed what he was thinking. 'Thank you for coming,' he added, and felt another surge of embarrassment. It wasn't as if he'd invited her to a party.

Wright took her down the corridor to the viewing room in silence. He didn't trust himself to speak without making a fool of himself again. The viewing room was little more than a cubicle, about six feet wide and ten feet long, painted a putrid yellow. The only furniture was a narrow table on which stood a white oval vase containing a bunch of faded silk flowers. Set into one of the walls was a white-framed window, and on the other side was one of the post mortem rooms. Robbie Ballantine was waiting on the other side of the glass. Wright nodded that they were ready and Ballantine pushed a trolley over.

The body was covered with a sheet the same colour as Ballantine's scrubs. He slowly pulled back the sheet until the face was revealed. It was considerably less bloody than when Wright had last seen it, but the cuts were clearly visible in the pale dead flesh.

Wright looked across at May Eckhardt. She was staring at the body, her face devoid of expression. 'Is it your husband?' he asked.

She didn't reply and Wright wondered whether or not she'd heard him. He was going to ask her again when she gave a small shake of her head. 'I'm not sure,' she said, her voice a hoarse whisper.

Ballantine looked at Wright expectantly. Wright shrugged. 'Take your time,' he told her.

She wrapped her arms around herself as if she was feeling the cold. 'It's just . . .'

She didn't finish, but Wright knew what she was trying to say. People never looked the same after death. 'There's no rush, Mrs Eckhardt.'

She turned to face him. 'Can I get closer?'

Wright wanted to dissuade her, but he knew that her request made sense. 'Okay,' he said. 'Come this way.' He took her along the corridor to the post mortem room. Ballantine had realised what was happening and was holding the door open for them. He flashed Wright a warning look as he went by, a silent reminder not to allow her to pull back the sheet. Wright nodded.

May seemed not to notice the non-verbal communication between the two men, and walked hesitatingly over to the trolley. She stared down at the body for a few seconds, then looked up at Wright. Her lower lip was quivering. She tried to speak, but words wouldn't come and she just nodded. Wright reached for her arm, wanting to guide her away from the trolley, but she took a step back, leaving him grabbing at empty air. She turned, bent down and kissed her husband on the forehead. Her hair swung across the corpse's face, then she straightened up and walked quickly out of the room.

Wright gave a small sigh of relief. He had feared that she might break down and he wasn't sure how he would have dealt with that. Her high heels click-clacked along the tiled floor and Wright had to jog after her as she hurried along the corridor. She rushed through the door to reception and it slammed in Wright's face. He pushed it open and called after her. She stopped in the centre of the reception area, facing away from him. The receptionist was engrossed in her computer.

Wright walked up behind her. 'I'm sorry, Mrs Eckhardt,' he said, 'but I have to ask you, for the record. Is that your husband in there?'

She spun around, her eyes filled with tears and contempt. 'What do you think?' she spat.

Wright held up his hands as if trying to ward off her rage. 'Please, Mrs Eckhardt, I have to ask. I can see you're upset . . .'

'Upset!' she hissed. 'Upset? That's my husband in there and you can see that I'm upset?'

Wright ran a hand through his hair, wondering what he could possibly say that would calm her down. 'I'll be asked at the inquest, Mrs Eckhardt. I'll be asked if you positively identified the body as being that of your husband, and it won't be enough for me to say that you reacted as if it were. I have to hear you say the words. I'm sorry.' He kept his head close to hers and his voice down to a hushed whisper.

She took a deep breath, and gradually regained her composure. 'No,' she said. 'I'm the one that's sorry. You're right, of course. Yes, that is my husband. Max Eckhardt.'

The strength seemed to fade from her legs and Wright reached for her as her eyes closed and she fell forwards. He grabbed her around the waist. She was as light as a child and he swept her up and carried her over to the chairs, where he sat her down and loosened her coat.

Wright looked over his shoulder; the receptionist was continuing to type obliviously. 'Excuse me, do you think you could get me a glass of water?' Wright asked her.

The receptionist gasped when she saw May slumped in the chair. 'Oh my goodness,' she said. 'That's the third one this week.'

'A glass of water,' said Wright. 'If it's not too much trouble.'

He fanned May's face with a copy of *Hello!* until the receptionist returned with a plastic cup of tepid water. By then May had opened her eyes again and she sipped gratefully at the water. 'What happened?' she asked.

'You fainted,' said the receptionist. 'You're the third one this week.'

Wright glared at her and she shrugged carelessly and went back to her desk behind the counter. He took the cup off May. The rim was smeared with pink lipstick.

'What happened to Max?' she asked.

Wright shook his head. 'I'm afraid he was murdered, Mrs Eckhardt.'

'Murdered?' What little colour remained in her face visibly drained away and Wright put a hand on her shoulder, afraid that she was about to faint again.

She shook him away. 'I'm all right,' she insisted, but she took the cup off him and drank again.

'Is there someone I can call for you? A friend? A relative?'

She shook her head. 'I don't have any friends in London,' she said. 'We've only been here a few weeks. And I don't have any relatives.'

'What about on your husband's side of the family?'

'He left home when he was a teenager.' She snorted softly. 'Not that he ever called it home. He hasn't spoken to his parents for thirty years, doesn't even know if they're alive.' She bit down on her lower lip. 'Didn't,' she corrected herself. 'He didn't even know if they're alive.' She looked at Wright with large, tear-filled eyes. 'When do you start thinking about them in the past tense?' she asked.

Wright took one of her small hands in his own. This time she didn't seem to resent the physical contact. 'It takes a long time,' he said. 'Sometimes you never get to think of them in the past.'

She shuddered and slowly withdrew her hand, a faraway look in her eyes. Wright gave her back the cup of water and she sipped it. 'What am I going to do?' she asked.

Wright didn't know what to say.

'I have to go home,' she whispered. 'I have to take the car in for its service. I have a lot of things to do.' The words came out singly, each separated by a distinct pause.

'Are you going to be all right?' he asked, the words sounding woefully inadequate.

She looked up at him as if she'd forgotten that he was there. 'I'm sorry?' she said, frowning. 'What did you say?'

'Will you be all right?'

She stood up and adjusted the belt of her raincoat. 'I'll be fine,' she said, her voice robotic.

'I'll need to talk to you again,' he said. 'There are questions I have to ask you.'

She turned away. 'Of course,' she said.

'I'll telephone you tomorrow,' he said.

She pushed open the door. 'Do that,' she said. The door swung closed behind her.

Wright went over to the window and watched as she went over to her car. He half expected her to break down in tears, but she opened the door, climbed in, and a few seconds later she drove away. She didn't look in his direction.

Ballantine walked into the reception area. 'Did she identify him?'

'Yeah. It's her husband. Max Eckhardt.'

'Okay, I'll do the paperwork. Do you want to stay and watch a post mortem? I've got a victim of parakeet poisoning.'

Wright frowned. 'Don't you mean paraquat?'

'Nah, someone shoved a parrot down his throat.' Ballantine chuckled and slapped Wright on the back. 'Just trying to lighten the moment, Nick.' He walked away, still chuckling.

Wright drove back to the office. Reid was squinting at his VDU and cross-checking a list of names against a computer printout.

'The victim is Max Eckhardt,' said Wright. 'Definitely.'

'Thank God for that,' said Reid. He sat back and massaged his right shoulder. 'I think I'm getting RSI,' he complained. 'You want to contact the press office?' He shook his hands, then clicked his knuckles.

'I think I'll wait until I've interviewed his wife.'

'Widow,' corrected Reid. 'Speaking of ex-wives, your solicitor rang.' He handed Wright a piece of a Burger King wrapper on which he'd scrawled a telephone number.

'Did he say what he wanted?'

Reid shook his head.

'Great,' sighed Wright. He was sure of one thing: it wouldn't be good news. 'Where's Ronnie?'

Reid gestured upwards with his thumb. 'With the governor.'

'I'd better tell him I've identified the body.' The door to the incident room was pushed open. 'Speak of the devil,' said Wright as Ronnie Dundas stepped into the incident room, closely followed by Superintendent Newton.

Wright got to his feet. 'Sir, we know who the victim is. Max Eckhardt. Number sixty-three on the PNC list.'

'Great,' said Dundas. The chief inspector turned to the superintendent. 'At least we can show the Met boys something, Governor,' he said.

Newton nodded, his mouth a tight line. 'Where are they going to sit?' he asked.

Dundas pointed at a group of desks that had been pushed together to the right of the door. 'We've given them their own HOLMES computer and I've asked Phil to assign two uniformed WPCs to input their statements and reports. I don't think they'll have any reason to moan.'

Newton pursed his lips as he looked around the incident room. He looked at his wristwatch. 'They're due in at three,' he said. 'Bring their chief inspector up to see me when they get here.' He turned and left the incident room.

Dundas went over to his desk and picked up a carton of milk. 'Okay, tell me about Eckhardt,' he said.

Wright logged on to the PNC terminal and called up Eckhardt's details. 'Forty-eight years old, American, married and lives in Maida Vale.'

Dundas cursed as his fingers slipped and the carton fell to the ground. Milk splattered over his shoes as he retrieved it. 'Why the hell do they make these damn things so difficult to open?' he asked. He took a long drink and wiped his moustache with the back of his hand. 'Missing since when?'

'A week ago. His wife reported it on Tuesday.'

'Did she say why he was in Battersea?'

'I haven't interviewed her yet,' said Wright. 'She was

pretty shaken up. I thought it best if she went home. I'll go along and see her later.'

'Okay,' said Dundas. 'Get a picture circulated. The Met boys'll be handling the house-to-house in Battersea. They'll be glad of the overtime.'

'Couldn't we handle that?' asked Wright. If there was going to be an early break on the case, it would probably come from a witness who'd seen the killer in the vicinity.

'It's a joint investigation, Nick.'

'Yeah, yeah, yeah.'

'I'm serious.' Dundas held his arm up in the air. 'That goes for everyone!' he shouted. 'I know we're not the best of buddies with the council cops, but the key word here is co-operation. Everything goes into HOLMES. Everything. No holding back tidbits for yourself. And at morning prayers we share ideas, not hurl insults. Is everyone clear on that?'

There were assorted mumblings from the detectives in the room.

'Good!' Dundas shouted. 'Just make sure we solve the case before the bastards!'

Roy Casper's office was little more than a broom cupboard, with half a window that looked down on a street of shops, most of which had 'For Sale' or 'To Let' signs in their windows. The office had once been twice the size but a plasterboard wall had been fitted, splitting it down the middle. There were no pictures or framed certificates hanging on the wall and Nick Wright wondered if the solicitor had been warned that it wouldn't take the weight. The few qualifications that Casper had hung on the wall by the door. Wright had never looked at them; for all he knew they could have been primary-school swimming certificates.

The office furniture wasn't dissimilar to that in Wright's own office: a cheap teak-effect desk, three shoulder-height metal filing cabinets, and swivel chairs covered in grey fabric. The solicitor had a computer on his desk but it was probably a decade older than the one Wright used. Casper hadn't even switched it on.

Casper was smoking a cigarette that he'd rolled himself and scattering ash over the file he was reading. Wright waited impatiently, knowing that he could only have been summoned to the poky little office to hear bad news.

'Here it is, sorry,' said Casper, pulling out a letter. Casper was only a few years away from retirement and Wright had the feeling he was coasting. Everything about the man suggested he'd given up taking care of his appearance. In a perfect world Wright would have had a more high-powered solicitor, but Casper was all he could afford.

Casper squinted at the letter, clicking his teeth as he read, and Wright had to fight the urge to grab the letter from him. Casper looked up at him. 'She wants to cut back on your visitation rights . . .'

Wright jumped to his feet so quickly that his chair flew backwards and banged into the wall. 'She what?' He grabbed for the letter, almost tearing it out of Casper's hand. His whole body shook as he read it.

'Calm down, Nick,' said the solicitor.

'Once a month!' Wright spat. 'She wants me to see him

once a month! For God's sake, he's going to forget who I am. She can't do this.'

Casper began rolling another cigarette. 'She can try,' he said. 'Read on.'

Wright read through to the end. Janie was claiming that Sean was having nightmares after the unauthorised visit to his office. 'This is bullshit,' said Wright.

Casper used a red plastic lighter to light his cigarette and he blew smoke over the file. 'Did you take Sean to your office?'

'Yes. I'd taken him to the zoo, it started raining, I figured he might like to see where I worked, that's all.'

'But your ex-wife specifically told you not to?'

Wright shook his head vigorously. 'No, that's not what happened at all. Look, whose side are you on?'

'You're paying my bill,' said Casper. 'Though I should mention that I'm still waiting for your last account to be settled.' He took a long pull on his roll-up. 'Your ex-wife alleges that your last visit has had a detrimental effect on your son's mental wellbeing. Accordingly, she wants to decrease your exposure to him.'

'Can she do that?'

'It'll have to go before a judge. But if she gets a medical report on her side, I wouldn't be surprised if the judge decided in her favour.'

Wright tossed the letter back on to the solicitor's untidy desk. 'Terrific,' he said bitterly.

Casper put the letter back in the file. 'How do you want me to proceed?' he asked.

Wright put his hands either side of his head and massaged his temples. 'What are my options?'

'I can say that we'd like our own psychologist to examine

your son. They'll have to agree to that, and by the time he's been examined, he'll probably be over the nightmares.' Casper put up his hands as Wright scowled at him. 'That's my recommendation, anyway.'

'I've a better idea,' said Wright. Casper raised his eyebrows expectantly. 'I could kill her.' Wright bared his teeth in a semblance of a smile. 'I'm only joking, Roy,' he said. 'Honest.'

May Eckhardt's address was an apartment in a four-storey mansion block in Maida Vale. Her black VW was parked in the road and Nick Wright pulled in behind it. The exterior of the mansion block was orange brick and white-painted pebbledash with a slate roof that looked brand new. There was a narrow well-tended strip of garden in front of the block and a black and white cat with pale green eyes watched him from the safety of a small chestnut tree as Wright walked towards the front door. There were eight bells and a brass speakerphone to the right of the door. Most of the bells had brass nameplates, but the one under the Eckhardt bell was written on cardboard. Wright pushed the bell. There was no answer and he pressed it a second time. There was still no reply, but the door lock buzzed and when he pushed the front door it swung open. He looked around and saw a closed-circuit television camera tucked away at the top of the entrance alcove. She'd obviously seen him on that. He smiled up at the lens, and immediately regretted it. He wasn't there on a social call.

There were two apartments on each floor. Wright walked up to the second floor where May Eckhardt already had the door open for him. She was wearing a baggy white sweatshirt with Exeter University on the front, the sleeves pulled up to her elbows, and blue Levi jeans. Her hair was tied back in a ponytail and she had dark patches under her eyes.

'Sergeant Wright,' she said flatly. 'I thought you said you'd telephone.'

'I'm sorry, but I was passing and . . .'

She turned away and walked down the hall, her bare feet slapping on the polished pine floorboards. Wright closed the door. When he turned around the hall was empty. There was a stripped pine door to the left and Wright peered around it into a big room with a bay window overlooking the street. May was sitting on a beige sofa, her knees drawn up against her chest. Apart from the sofa there were two armchairs in matching fabric and a Chinese-patterned rug on the floor. A big screen TV sat in one corner and a JVC stereo with waist-high speakers in another. An alcove opposite the door had been lined with shelves on which were stacked hundreds of records. Frank Sinatra was playing on the stereo.

'I thought I'd try, on the off chance . . .'

'It's all right,' she said. There was a bottle of white wine on the floor by the sofa and a half-filled glass.

'How are you?' he asked, sitting down in one of the armchairs.

Her eyes narrowed. 'How do you think I am?' she asked.

'I'm sorry, stupid question.' He looked around the room. A black bass guitar hung on the wall behind the sofa where May was sitting.

'Is that your husband's?' asked Wright.

May twisted around and stared at the guitar for several seconds as if it was the first time she'd seen it. 'Yes,' she said.

'He was a musician?'

She turned around again. 'No, it was a hobby. He was a photographer.'

Wright took out his notebook and a pen. 'Who did he work for?'

'Agence France Press. It's a news agency. He was moved to the London bureau three months ago.' She leaned forward and picked up the wine glass. 'We've only just moved into the flat. Half our things are still in storage.'

'When did he go missing?'

'Last Monday. He'd been sent to Brighton for the Conservative Party conference. The office wanted him to stay in Brighton rather than coming back to London each night.' She sipped her wine. 'He was supposed to be back on Monday but didn't show. That's not unusual so I didn't worry. But on Tuesday the office called me asking where Max was. He'd left Brighton on Monday. I thought perhaps he'd had an accident, and started calling around the hospitals. Then I called the police.' She finished her wine with several gulps and refilled her glass before holding out the bottle. 'Would you . . .?' she said.

Wright shook his head. 'I wouldn't mind a drink of water, though,' he said.

She began to get up but Wright beat her to it. 'Tap water will do just fine,' he said.

May settled back and looked at him over the top of her glass. 'The kitchen's first on the right,' she said.

Wright went along the hallway. The kitchen was all stainless steel and shiny white worktops and it reminded

Wright of the post mortem room, stark and functional. He picked up a glass off the draining board and ran the cold tap. There was a pine knife block to the left of the sink in which were embedded five knives, all with black handles. There was a space for a sixth knife. Wright put down the glass and pulled out one of the knives. It seemed to be a pretty good match to the one that had been impaled in Eckhardt's body. He took out a second knife. It was a bread knife with a serrated edge. Wright wondered which knife was missing from the kitchen block. He pushed the two knives back into the block and filled his glass from the tap. As he did, he looked down into a plastic washing-up bowl. Lying next to a toast-crumb-coated plate was the missing knife. Wright took it out of the bowl and slotted it into the block. It was a perfect match. Wright felt an inexplicable sensation of relief wash over him.

He went back into the sitting room with his glass of water. May didn't appear to have moved at all. Wright sat down and sipped his water. 'Was he driving back from Brighton?' he asked.

'No. He was taking the train.'

'So why did you think he might have been involved in an accident?'

She frowned as if she didn't understand the question. 'I don't know. I suppose I thought he might have had a heart attack or something. You know what flashes through your mind when someone goes missing. You always assume the worst.' She began to shiver and she gripped the glass so hard that Wright feared it would shatter. 'Who would do that to him?' she whispered. 'Why would anyone want to kill my husband like that?'

'Did he have any enemies?' asked Wright.

'Good God, no. Oh no. You don't think that someone who knew Max would . . . ?' Her voice tailed off.

'Is it possible that he was working on a story that brought him into contact with dangerous people?'

'Like the Conservative Party?' She smiled thinly. 'What is it they call it? Gallows humour? Isn't that what police are famous for?'

'Sometimes it makes it easier to deal with the sort of things we come across,' said Wright.

'Well, Max is . . . I mean, Max was . . . a senior photographer with the agency. They wouldn't have him doorstepping gangsters or drug dealers. Most of the time he covered wars. Crazy, huh? I never worried about him when he was here. It was always when he was abroad that I was scared. And we haven't been here long enough to have made enemies. You could talk to the office, though. His boss is Steve Reynolds.'

'Where were you before you moved to London?'

'The States. New York.'

'He was an American?'

She nodded.

'And you? If you don't mind me asking, where are you from?'

'Sale. Just outside Manchester.' She smiled tightly. 'Sorry to disappoint you if you thought I was from somewhere more exotic.'

'Oh, it's not that,' he said quickly. 'I know lots of Asians are born here these days—'

'Oriental,' she interrupted.

'I'm sorry?'

'I'm Oriental,' she said. 'Asians are Indians or Pakistanis.' She shook her head. 'It doesn't matter.' Her eyes glazed over and it was obvious her mind was elsewhere. They sat without speaking for several minutes. Frank Sinatra began to sing 'New York, New York'. One of life's little coincidences, thought Wright.

'He must have died in such pain,' May said eventually. 'I wonder if . . . ?' Tears welled up in her eyes.

Wright uncrossed and crossed his legs, embarrassed by the strength of her emotion. He looked down at his notebook and to his surprise saw that he'd been doodling, boxes within boxes.

'Why would anyone torture him like that? Why would anyone cut him so many times?'

'I don't know,' said Wright lamely. He knew that she wasn't fully aware of the extent of her husband's injuries and he didn't want to make her any more upset than she already was. 'It could have been a random killing. Someone who just wanted to kill, and your husband was in the wrong place at the wrong time.'

'Poor Max,' she said. 'Poor, poor Max.'

Wright and Reid had to wait in the reception area of Agence France Press for almost twenty minutes before a balding man in his late thirties ambled out. His jacket collar was up at the back as if he'd pulled it on in a hurry and one of his shoelaces was undone. 'Hiya. Steve Reynolds,' he said, holding out his hand. He had an American accent.

'Tommy Reid,' said Reid, shaking his hand. 'This is Nick Wright. Thanks for seeing us.'

Reynolds opened a glass door for them and they walked together down a white-walled corridor and through another set of glass doors into a large open-plan office full of shirtsleeved young men and women sitting at desks in front of VDUs.

Reynolds's office was to the left with a glass wall overlooking the main working area. 'Can I get you coffee or something?' he asked. Both detectives nodded and Reynolds asked a young blonde secretary for three coffees. Reid and Wright sat down opposite Reynolds's desk. Wright took out his notebook as Reynolds closed the door and sat down on the other side of his desk. 'So how can I help you guys?' Reynolds asked.

'We're looking for a reason why anyone would want to kill Max Eckhardt,' said Reid.

Reynolds grimaced as if he had a bad taste in his mouth. 'It's a mystery to all of us here,' he said. 'Max was the nicest guy you could imagine.'

'How long have you known him?'

'Personally, three months. That's when he moved here from our New York bureau.'

'He was a photographer?' asked Reid. The two detectives had agreed beforehand that Reid would lead the questioning and Wright would take notes. It was their usual way of operating, mainly because Reid's handwriting was so bad that he often had trouble reading back his notes.

'That's right. He's been with the company for more than fifteen years.' He reached across his desk and picked up a green file which he handed to Reid. 'This is Max's personnel file. I thought it might speed things up a little.'

Reid gave the file to Wright. 'The job he was on just before he died. The Conservative Party conference. Was that typical of the sort of work he did?'

'Good Lord, no,' said Reynolds. 'In fact, he fought like hell not to go.'

'Labour supporter, was he?'

Reynolds grinned and shook his head. 'War photographer. Max always wanted to be where the bullets were. Panama. Grenada. Kuwait. Northern Ireland. Bosnia. Never happy unless he was wearing a flak jacket.'

'That's why he requested a transfer from New York? To be closer to the hot spots?'

'Partly,' said Reynolds. 'He reckoned that Europe and the new Russia were going to be the major areas of conflict over the next decade. He tried to get a transfer to our Paris office, but there are no openings there.'

Wright looked up from the file. 'So it wasn't because of his wife?'

'His wife?'

'May Eckhardt. She's British. I thought maybe she wanted to come home.'

The blonde secretary reappeared with three plastic cups of coffee. Reynolds gestured at the file. 'There's a memo in there from Max requesting the London posting. He doesn't mention May. I don't think she had a problem travelling with him. She's a computer programmer, she can work pretty much anywhere. I don't think she especially wanted to come back to the UK.'

'You said he covered Northern Ireland. Is it possible he crossed one of the terrorist organisations?' Reid asked.

Reynolds leaned forward, his shoulders hunched over

the desk. 'Not really,' he said. 'Max was a photographer, not a reporter.'

'He could have photographed something he shouldn't have.'

Reynolds shook his head. 'Unlikely,' he said. 'He's been on soft jobs for the last month. Besides, terrorists would have just shot him or put a bomb in his car. They don't go in for torture.'

Reid nodded. 'You said he didn't want the Brighton job. Why did you send him?'

'We had a couple of guys off sick. And you can't cover wars all the time. It's not good for the soul.'

'And how was Max's soul?' asked Reid.

'That's a searching question,' said Reynolds, picking up a pen and twirling it around his thumb. 'Very philosophical.'

'For a policeman, you mean?'

'For anyone,' said Reynolds. 'Max was a driven man, you know? As if he was aiming for something, something that was always beyond his reach.'

'Or running away from somebody?'

The pen flew off Reynolds's thumb and landed on the floor. He bent down and retrieved it. 'Max was one of the most centred people I know. He wasn't a man on the run, he wasn't living in fear, he was just a bloody good photographer. He worked hard, harder than almost anyone I know, and I don't know anyone who didn't like or respect him. Most journalists, reporters and photographers are driven by something. They have to be. Long hours, low pay, no respect from the public, they have to have their own reasons for doing the job.'

'Tell me about it,' said Wright bitterly.

Reynolds grinned. 'I suppose there are a lot of similarities between our jobs,' he said. 'The search for the truth. The accumulation of facts.'

'The fiddling of expense sheets,' added Reid.

The three men laughed. 'Seriously,' said Reynolds, 'you'd be wasting your time looking for someone who wanted to kill Max.' He pointed at the file in Wright's hands. 'Look at his yearly evaluations. Every boss he's ever had has given him glowing references professionally and personally.'

'Could we look through his desk?' asked Reid.

'Sure,' said Reynolds. He stood up and took the two detectives out into the open-plan office. Several heads turned to look at them. They walked to the far end of the office where two white-shirted men bent over a light box studying a strip of negatives. Reynolds introduced the two men to Reid and Wright. The taller of the two was Martin Staines, the bureau's picture editor, the other man was his assistant, Sam Greene.

'They're investigating Max's murder,' Reynolds explained.

Staines nodded at the desk nearest the window. 'We weren't sure what to do with his stuff.'

'No one's touched it?' asked Reid, sitting down at the desk and pulling open the drawers.

'Nobody wanted to,' said Staines.

'Was it bad?' asked Reynolds. 'The papers didn't give too many details.'

'Yeah,' said Wright. 'It was bad.'

'You might want to look at his locker,' said Greene. He nodded at a line of light blue metal lockers. 'Max's is third from the left.'

Wright went over to the lockers. There was a combination padlock on Max's locker. 'Six two five,' said Greene. Wright raised an eyebrow. 'He left his address book in it one night and phoned me to get a number he wanted,' explained Greene.

Wright took the lock off and opened the locker door. Inside was a yellow waterproof jacket hanging from a hook and a pair of green Wellington boots. There was an extendable metal pole at the back of the locker. Wright took it out and examined it.

'It's for supporting a long lens,' said Staines. 'Max had some pretty heavy equipment.'

Wright replaced the pole. He checked through the pockets of the waterproof jacket but there was nothing there. 'What about the rest of his equipment?' asked Wright. 'His cameras and stuff?'

Staines and Greene exchanged looks. Staines shrugged. 'Photographers are responsible for their own gear,' he said. 'He took everything he needed with him to Brighton.'

Reid walked over to join Wright. 'Is that his wife?' he asked Wright, tapping a photograph that had been taped to the inside of the locker door.

Wright hadn't noticed the black and white photograph. It was May Eckhardt, smiling nervously at the camera as if she'd been caught unawares, one hand up to her face, the fingertips close to her lips. It was a good photograph; it had captured the softness of her skin, and the fact that it was in black and white emphasised the blackness of her hair against her pale skin. 'Yes. That's her.'

'I didn't realise she was Asian.'

'She's not,' said Wright quickly. 'She's Oriental.'

'What?'

'It doesn't matter.' Wright closed the locker door and

turned to look at Reynolds. 'Did you speak to Eckhardt after he'd finished in Brighton?'

'I spoke to him,' said Staines. 'He called to say he was leaving Brighton on the afternoon train.'

'Didn't he drive?' asked Reid.

'He did as a rule but he went down with one of our reporters, Pete Thewlis. They used Pete's car and were planning to come back together, but Pete was sent on to another job. Max was a bit pissed off, but it's not as if he was in the Outer Hebrides. We told him we'd pay for him to come back first class on the train.'

'And that was the last you heard of him?' asked Reid.

'That's right,' said Staines. 'That was on the Monday, and he was due in the office that afternoon. When he didn't show we assumed he'd missed the train, either by accident or design.'

'I don't follow you,' said Reid.

'Like I said, he was a bit annoyed at having to take the train. We thought maybe he'd gone AWOL as a sort of silent protest. When he didn't turn up for work on Tuesday, we called his home. That's when we realised he'd gone missing.

'To be honest, we weren't that worried,' said Greene. 'It wasn't unusual for Max to go chasing after his own stories. He always checked in eventually.'

'What about this Pete Thewlis, can I talk to him?'

'He's in Islington on that explosives seizure,' said Reynolds. 'He wont be back until late. I can give you his mobile number, though.'

'Would Thewlis have taken Eckhardt's camera equipment with him?' asked Reid.

'Definitely not,' said Staines. 'Photographers are very

possessive about their gear. They don't even like sharing lenses and stuff. Besides, Thewlis didn't know how long he'd be away.'

'So he'd have taken it with him on the train?' asked Wright.

'Sure,' agreed Staines.

'How much gear would he have had?' asked Wright.

Greene bent down and picked up a large canvas holdall. It was heavy and he used both hands to lift it on to the desk next to the light box. 'This is about par for the course,' he said. 'Three or four camera bodies, half a dozen lenses, a tripod, film. Max had a bag like this, and two leather cases containing his really long lenses.'

Wright put his notebook away and looked at Reid. His partner nodded. 'Okay, well, thanks for your time,' said Reid. He handed BTP business cards to the three men. 'If you should think of anything else, give me or Nick a call.'

Outside the AFP offices, Reid said, 'Can you call that guy Pete Thewlis? Check when he last saw Eckhardt?'

'Sure,' said Wright. 'What about checking the station to see if Eckhardt caught the train from Brighton? We've got to find out how he ended up at Battersea.'

'Yeah, okay. We'll go down this afternoon. We should do a sweep of the train, too. We'll need a few more bodies. Half a dozen, maybe. Can you clear it with Ronnie? We'll do the train that he was supposed to catch, and the ones either side. Oh yeah, and make sure someone goes to Edbury Bridge and views the Victoria surveillance tapes. They're supposed to hold them for twenty-eight days before wiping them, but put in a call today just to make sure.'

'I'll arrange it.'

Reid looked up and down the street.

'I hope you're not looking for a pub, Tommy,' said Wright.

'Last thing on my mind,' said Reid.

'They're not open yet.'

'I know a place. Just around the corner. Come on, hair of the dog.'

Wright shook his head emphatically. 'I'll see you back at the office.'

'Ah, come on, Nick,' Reid whined. 'You've got the car, how am I going to get back?'

'Well, duh, Tommy. What's wrong with the Tube?'

'You know I hate public transport,' scowled Reid, but Wright was already walking away.

Wright collected his Fiesta from the underground car park and headed back to Tavistock Place.

Wright got caught in heavy traffic and it took him the best part of an hour to get back to the office. Superintendent Newton was in the incident room, studying a whiteboard on which the various assignments had been written up. Ronnie Dundas was hovering at the superintendent's shoulder and he winked at Wright.

'Morning, Nick,' said Newton.

'Morning, sir.'

'Tommy not with you?'

'We were at Eckhardt's office. Tommy's checking his personal effects.'

Newton looked at Wright with slightly narrowed eyes, his

lips pressed so tight together that they had practically disappeared. Wright instinctively knew that the superintendent didn't believe him. Dundas grinned and made a cut-throat motion with his hand.

Wright ignored the chief inspector's antics and took out his notebook. 'We know what train he was supposed to be on. We'll do a sweep of the stations, and we'll put men on the trains interviewing passengers. I'll get the video surveillance tapes from Victoria and have them checked. If he got on the train at Brighton it could be he was forced off at Battersea.'

'The train doesn't stop there, does it?'

'No, but it goes close by and sometimes the trains are held up if Victoria's busy.'

Newton nodded his agreement. 'Any sign of a motive?' he asked.

'I'm afraid not, sir.'

Newton turned to Dundas. 'Any progress on the knife?'

'It's a common kitchen knife,' said Dundas. 'We've identified fifteen different suppliers in London alone, including three chain stores. The Met boys'll continue looking, but I don't see it providing us with a lead.'

'When Eckhardt went missing he had a bagful of camera equipment with him,' said Wright. 'I'm going to arrange a sweep of secondhand shops to see if I can turn it up.' For the first time Wright realised that the superintendent was holding a sheet of paper. It was a fax.

'Well, maybe the cavalry will help,' said Newton dryly.

'Cavalry?'

Newton held out the fax. 'An FBI agent, on secondment from FBI headquarters in Washington.'

Wright took the fax and scanned it quickly. It was a brief

memo from an assistant director of the Federal Bureau of Investigation, notifying the BTP that a Special Agent James Bamber was being sent to assist in the investigation and to act as liaison with the FBI.

'Is this normal?' asked Wright. 'Do the FBI usually send people over on murder enquiries?'

'Eckhardt was an American citizen,' said Newton.

'Yes, but even so. Do we send cops over to investigate deaths overseas?'

Newton took back the fax. 'It's not unknown,' he said. 'To be honest, we should just be grateful for the additional manpower.' He gestured with his thumb at the list of assignments. 'We can't keep this many detectives assigned to the case indefinitely.' The superintendent went back to his office.

'You missed my briefing this morning,' said Dundas.

'Yeah, sorry. We went straight to AFP to talk to Eckhardt's boss.'

'Just so you know, the Met team is handling the house-to-house, the knife, and they'll look into Eckhardt's background. We'll concentrate on the forensics, the playing card, and anything else that turns up in the tunnel. We'll be sharing information on a daily basis at morning prayers, and we'll all have access to the HOLMES database. I've recommended that the two teams eat together in the canteen to talk informally but I won't be holding my breath. If you think there's anything that they should know about urgently, tell me and I'll brief my opposite number, Chief Inspector Colin Duggan, aka the Welsh Wizard. He's a twenty-year-man with a lot of murder enquiry experience and if your paths cross I'd recommend treating him with kid gloves. Okay?'

'Okay,' said Wright unenthusiastically.

'I gather there's a bit of friction between you and Gerry Hunter,' said Dundas.

'A bit.'

'Well, I know you're man enough not to let it interfere with the job,' said Dundas. 'There really shouldn't be any reason for the two of you to talk, you'll be following separate lines of enquiry.'

'It won't be a problem,' said Wright.

'Glad to hear it,' said Dundas. He took another swig from his milk carton and went over to one of the HOLMES terminals.

Two BTP DCs were sitting at neighbouring tables, their faces close up against VDUs. They were both in their late twenties, but other than their jobs, that was all they had in common. Dave Hubbard was tall and bulky and played rugby in his spare time. Julian Lloyd was anorexically thin and was one of the best amateur squash players in the South of England. They'd been assigned to checking on sexual offenders with a record of attacking men. It had been Reid's idea, but hadn't provided any tangible leads so far.

'Hey, guys, can one of you call Victoria, see if you can get the surveillance tapes for last Monday,' Wright shouted. 'Eckhardt was supposed to catch an afternoon train from Brighton. We might get lucky.'

Lloyd waved, his eyes still on his screen. 'I'll do it.'

There were more than a dozen surveillance cameras around Victoria, and with a four-hour window, that would mean around fifty hours of tape to view. Tapes were rarely easy viewing, either, especially when you were trying to identify one face among thousands. With his holdall and two leather cases, hopefully Eckhardt would be relatively easy to spot, but even with half a dozen officers it would still take the best part of a day to go through the tapes. And all that would prove was whether or not Eckhardt had arrived at Victoria.

'Get back here by noon,' said Wright. 'We're going down to Brighton to do a sweep through the station and then we'll be coming back on the train. Dave, we'll need you. Tommy's coming, and we'll need another four bodies. See who you can round up.'

'Will do,' said Hubbard.

Wright sat down and flicked through his notebook. He found the number of Pete Thewlis's mobile and dialled it. Thewlis answered, his voice a Liverpudlian drawl. Wright told the journalist who he was and asked him when he'd last seen Max Eckhardt. Thewlis said they'd had breakfast together in their Brighton hotel and that Thewlis had left first, driving to York. Wright made a note of the hotel and thanked the journalist for his help.

He was about to call the hotel to find out exactly when Eckhardt had checked out when Reid walked into the office and flopped down into his chair. He pulled open his top drawer, took out a pack of mints and popped two into his mouth. 'So, what's new?' he asked.

'The Yanks are coming,' said Wright, putting down his phone.

'What?'

'The FBI are sending an agent over. To help. I guess they think we Brits aren't up to solving the case.'

Reid put his mints back into the drawer. 'Yeah, well, they can join the queue, can't they?'

'Line,' said Wright. 'Americans call it a line.'

'Yeah? Well, we're really going to have problems if I tell

him I want to smoke a fag, right?' He opened his bottom drawer and looked into it. 'Fancy a coffee?' he asked.

The occupant of seat 17A was practically the perfect passenger. If Gwen could have her way, only men like him would be allowed to fly. He'd smiled politely when he'd boarded, had no carry-on luggage with him, and hadn't asked for a thing to eat or drink. There had been no salacious looks, no clumsy attempts to chat her up, just a small shake of the head when she'd offered him his dinner tray. Gwen wondered what he did for a living. His clothes gave nothing away: a nondescript grey suit, white shirt and a neatly knotted tie. He looked like the typical business-class passenger. What wasn't typical was his lack of a briefcase or laptop computer. Most businessmen had come to regard the cabin as an extension of their office, and those who didn't work caught up on their sleep. Passenger 17A didn't work or sleep, nor did he bother to use his inseat entertainment. He kept his seat up and simply stared ahead of him, his hands together in his lap, almost as if he was meditating. He wasn't in a trance, though, because whenever Gwen spoke to him he answered immediately.

'What do you think about the quiet one, Tony?'

Tony Kelner was working business class with her, and was a good judge of passengers. He was gay and had the inbuilt radar which allowed him to spot other gays without a word being spoken. He pouted as he looked over her shoulder. 'Definitely my type, darling,' he said. 'But he's definitely hetero. Cruel lips.' He mimed a shiver. 'Oooh, I think I'd better go and lie down.'

'Not until you've helped get the breakfasts ready,' laughed Gwen. 'What's his story?' It was a game she and Tony often played, making up fictitious backgrounds for their passengers.

Tony folded his arms and put his head on one side. He pressed a finger against his lips as he studied the passenger. 'He works out,' he said. 'Look at those thighs. What is he, twenty-seven, twenty-eight?'

'His hair is starting to go grey,' said Gwen.

'Prematurely, darling,' said Tony. 'Nothing a little Grecian Two Thousand wouldn't hide.'

'Is that what you use?'

'Bitch!' hissed Tony playfully. He ran a hand through his own unnaturally blond and coiffured hair. 'A little peroxide, that's all I allow near my locks.' He put his forefinger to the side of his face as he glanced at the profile of the passenger. 'He's a professional footballer,' he said eventually. 'Played for a first division club, but was plagued by injury—'

'Didn't have a limp,' interrupted Gwen.

'Is this my story or yours?' asked Tony. 'Knee problems, or Achilles tendon. Nothing serious, but enough to keep him from giving his best, so he decided to quit playing before he was over the hill. He's just joined a second division club, as assistant manager.'

'Oh, did I mention that he was American?' said Gwen.

'They play soccer in the States,' said Tony. 'All right, Miss Know-it-all, what do you think?'

'Mafia hitman,' she said. 'Look at his eyes. Cold, cold eyes. That man could pull the trigger and not care. The Mafia send him all over the world to get rid of people who are causing them problems. He gets well paid for what he does, but he doesn't do it for the money.'

Tony raised his eyebrows. 'Interesting,' he said. 'I wonder if I could persuade him to indulge in a little S and M.'

Gwen giggled and Tony gave her a playful push. The man in 17A turned his head slowly and looked at them across the cabin. His eyelids were half closed and his face was devoid of any emotion, but Gwen and Tony both stopped laughing immediately. Tony shivered, and this time Gwen knew he wasn't faking it. He turned away and began to busy himself with one of the trollies. The passenger held Gwen's look for several seconds, but to the stewardess it felt like an eternity. She was transfixed by his pale hazel eyes, unable to tear herself away. The man smiled, but his lips didn't part. It was a humourless smile and it sent a chill down Gwen's spine. Eventually he looked away. Only then did she realise that she'd been holding her breath all the time he'd been staring at her, and she exhaled like a deflating balloon.

Tommy Reid put down a cup of coffee in front of Nick Wright. 'Morning prayers in five minutes,' he said.

Wright sipped his coffee. 'Yeah, I know,' he said. The two detectives went downstairs to the incident room. Most of the BTP detectives were already there, sitting on tables or standing around, drinking coffee or chewing on bacon sandwiches brought from the canteen. Only half of the Met contingent had turned up, but Hunter and Edmunds were there, huddled over a HOLMES terminal. Several of the detectives fidgeted with pens or pencils – Newton was a vehement anti-smoker and had banned smoking in the room. The detectives would have to wait until after the briefing before lighting up.

The superintendent walked in, a clipboard under one arm, followed by Ronnie Dundas and the Met's senior officer on the investigation team, Chief Inspector Colin Duggan, a balding Welshman in a dark blue suit. The assembled detectives stopped talking and waited while Newton studied his notes. 'Day eight, gentlemen. One week and a day. I have so far approved four hundred and eighty hours of overtime and I appear to have precious little to show for it. I know you're all keen to have that central heating installed or upgrade your car or pay for that foreign holiday next year, but the powers that be are going to want to see some sort of return on their investment. And frankly, so am I.' His upper lip barely moved throughout his speech, though his eyes fixed on each of the detectives in turn. Most of them averted their eyes under his stony gaze; they were all well aware of how slowly the investigation was proceeding.

'So, let's recap. We know that Max Eckhardt left his hotel intending to walk to the station, but none of the station staff remembers seeing him. Nick, have we spoken to every member of staff?'

'Everyone who was working on the Monday. And if he did buy a ticket, he didn't use a credit card.'

'We've interviewed passengers on the train that he should have caught,' said Reid. 'And the trains either side. We'll do another sweep next Monday, just in case there are passengers who only travel then. It's a long shot, but it's worth a try.'

'Agreed,' said Newton. 'Julian, any joy on the surveillance tapes?'

'Afraid not,' said Lloyd. 'We've been through all of them, but there's no man with a holdall and two leather cases. We're trying to decide whether we go through them again to see if he's lost the gear, but that's going to take days. We'd have to look at the face of every white male, and the quality's not that good.'

'I think we should,' said Wright. 'It's the only way we have of finding out if he arrived back in London.'

The detectives looked at Newton, waiting for him to reach his decision. His lips tightened to the point where they almost disappeared, then he relaxed. 'Okay. But organise it so it's done between other enquiries. No overtime. What about forensics?'

'Nothing,' said Reid. 'At least nothing that we can definitely say belonged to the killer. If we had a suspect, it's possible we might be able to link him to the crime scene.' He grinned. 'But then if we had a suspect, we could just beat a confession out of him anyway.' He held up his hands. 'Joke.'

The superintendent glared icily at Reid. 'As always, we're grateful for you trying to lighten the moment, Tommy. But I'd rather you left the song and dance act until we'd at least got some of the way towards solving this case.' Newton looked around the room as if daring any of the others to crack a joke. 'Gerry, anything new on the knife?'

'Nothing,' said Hunter. 'When we eventually get a suspect, maybe we'll be able to link them to the knife, but it's not going to point the way. I'm more concerned at the moment about finding Eckhardt's camera equipment. I've distributed serial numbers and descriptions. That equipment's worth over two thousand pounds, it must be somewhere.'

Newton nodded. 'Good,' he said. 'I want that equipment found, and found soon.' He looked around the assembled detectives before tapping his clipboard. 'Right, two more things. First, we're going to hold another press conference tomorrow. We'll announce that we've identified the victim, then release his picture and appeal for witnesses again. I'm also going to release details of the missing camera equipment. This time I'll conduct the press conference, along with a press officer. That's tomorrow at three. Second, Max Eckhardt's funeral is this afternoon. Tommy and Nick, I want you two to attend.'

'It's a bit sudden, isn't it, sir?' asked Wright.

'Not really. It's been more than a week, and the cause of death isn't going to be disputed,' said the superintendent. 'The pathologist says they don't need anything else, so they contacted the widow. She called in a firm of undertakers and they had a slot today. I gather there weren't any other relatives to inform, and it suits us to have the funeral before the press conference so that we don't have a pack of photographers pestering the mourners.' He looked around the room. 'Any other thoughts?'

None of the detectives spoke. The first few morning briefings had produced a stream of ideas and theories, but the initial flush of enthusiasm had faded and most of the detectives were now resigned to the fact that the case, if it was ever going to be solved, would be solved by routine investigation rather than a flash of deductive reasoning. That, or a lucky break.

The superintendent didn't appear to be surprised or disappointed by the lack of response. 'Okay, let's get on with it,' he said, heading for the door. 'Oh, by the way. For those that don't know already, an FBI agent has been seconded to the investigation. James Bamber's his name. He has no jurisdictional powers in this country. That means he has no powers of arrest, no right to acquire a warrant or to question suspects. That said, he's to be offered every assistance.'

The superintendent left the room, and half a dozen of the detectives immediately went upstairs to light up. Hunter and Edmunds took their coats off the rack by the door and headed out.

'Shit,' said Reid.

'What?' said Wright.

'I'm not wearing my black suit.' He grinned, expecting to get a smile out of Wright, but Wright wasn't amused.

'Newton's right, you know. Sometimes you're not funny.'

There was a single red rose on the polished pine coffin, and it vibrated as the wooden casket slid along the metal rollers and through two green velvet curtains. Recorded organ music oozed out of black plastic speakers mounted on shelves close to the ceiling. The vicar closed his leather-bound Bible as if impatient to get on with his next function, be it a wedding, a christening or a funeral. Wright wondered if the young vicar, who was still in his twenties, showed a similar lack of enthusiasm for weddings as he'd shown for the funeral service. It had taken a little more than ten minutes and he'd hardly looked up from the Bible, as if embarrassed by the handful of mourners who'd gathered to say farewell to Max Eckhardt. There were eight in all, including Reid and Wright, who stood together in the pew furthest from the vicar and his lectern, their hands clasped across their groins like footballers in a defensive wall.

May Eckhardt stood alone in the front pew, wearing black leather gloves and a lightweight black coat that reached almost to her ankles. Her hair was loose and she kept her head down throughout the service so that it fell across her face, shielding her features like a curtain. The rest of the mourners were Eckhardt's co-workers: Steve Reynolds, Martin Staines and Sam Greene were there, along with two young women who looked like secretaries.

'Not much of a turnout,' whispered Reid.

'She said he didn't have many relatives,' said Wright.

'None by the look of it. No friends of the family, either. Just colleagues.' The curtain slid over the rear of the coffin and the organ music stopped abruptly. The vicar looked at his watch.

Wright wondered how many mourners there would be at his funeral if he were to die tomorrow. His mother was in a nursing home in the West Country and he only visited her two or three times a year. He had a brother in Australia, but they hadn't spoken for more than five years. He looked across at Reid. His partner would be there, Wright was certain of that, probably wearing the same brown raincoat and carrying the same tweed hat. And Reid would probably twist a few arms to get some of his colleagues to attend. Superintendent Newton would be there, but out of duty rather than friendship. Would Janie attend? Probably, with Sean at her side. Wright could picture her in black, a comforting hand on their son's shoulder, telling him not to worry because Sean had another daddy who loved him just as much as his real daddy did. Wright shivered.

May Eckhardt was walking down the centre aisle, the vicar at her side. The top of her head barely reached the vicar's shoulder and he had to stoop to talk to her as they walked. She saw Wright and gave him the smallest of smiles. For a brief moment their eyes locked and Wright felt something tug at his stomach. Wright smiled back at her but she looked down as if the contact had frightened her.

The mourners filed out of their pews and followed May and the vicar out of the church. The vicar stood at the doorway with May and together they thanked each person for attending. Wright and Reid were the last to leave. Wright nodded at the vicar, but had no interest in talking to him. The service had been perfunctory and the man appeared to have been operating on auto-pilot throughout. Wright felt that May had deserved better.

'Thanks for coming, Sergeant Wright,' said May, and she held out a slim gloved hand.

He shook it. Her hand felt like a child's in his. 'How are you?' he asked.

She withdrew her hand. 'I don't know,' she said. 'How are people usually? After . . .' She faltered and put her hand to her head.

'I'm sorry,' said Wright quickly. 'Stupid question, really.' The news agency staff stood together on the pavement as if unsure what to do next. 'Is there a reception?' Wright asked.

May shook her head. 'No, I just wanted a service. In fact, I didn't really want that. Max wasn't one for religion. He always said that the Apaches had the best idea: lay the body on a rock and let the birds eat it.' She forced a tight smile. 'I didn't think Westminster Council would look too kindly on that. Besides, Steve Reynolds called me and said some of the people in the office wanted to say goodbye . . .' Her voice faltered again. She brushed away a tear.

Wright wanted to step forward and comfort her. She tensed as if she'd read his thoughts. 'What are your plans now?' he asked.

'I'm going to go back home. Then I . . . I don't know. I've been taking it one day at a time. His clothes are still on the chair in the bedroom . . .' She mumbled incoherently, then shook her head as if clearing her thoughts. 'I'll be fine, Sergeant Wright.'

'Nick. Call me Nick.'

She looked at him for several seconds until he began to feel that he was lost in her soft brown eyes, as if she was pulling his soul towards hers. He blinked and the spell was broken.

'Nick,' she said. 'Thank you for coming.' She thanked the vicar and then walked away.

The church was only half a mile from her flat so Wright assumed that she was going to walk, but then he noticed her VW Golf parked at the roadside. He watched as she unlocked the door and climbed in. She put on her seatbelt and started the engine. At the last moment she turned and looked at him. She flashed him a quick smile and gave him a half wave, then drove away.

Reid finished talking to the vicar and came up behind Wright. 'Okay?' he asked.

'Yeah. I guess.'

Wright turned and looked up at the outside of the church.

It was a modern building, all brick, the windows shielded from vandals by wire mesh screens. It looked more like a fortress than a place of worship, bordered by roads on three sides. A poster on a noticeboard by the door advertised the services of the Samaritans and next to it was a handwritten notice asking for donations of clothing to send to a church project in Africa. The young vicar disappeared inside and closed the door.

'He didn't even know her,' said Wright. 'There was nothing personal in the service.'

'That's the way it goes these days. People don't go to church, but they want weddings and funerals. I asked the vicar and he said he'd never seen the Eckhardts, didn't even know where they lived other than that they were local.'

'What happens to the coffin?' asked Wright. There was no graveyard attached to the church.

'It gets taken to the crematorium,' said Reid. 'Then she takes delivery of the ashes.'

'I wonder what she'll do with them?'

'Bury them maybe. There's a place at the crematorium. Or maybe he wanted them scattered somewhere.'

'Yeah? What would you want doing with your ashes?'

Reid rubbed his hands together. 'I'm going to have them thrown into my ex-wife's face,' he said. 'By a nineteen-year-old blonde with big tits.'

'You old romantic, you,' laughed Wright. They watched the AFP staff hail two taxis and climb into them. 'Not much to show for a life, is it?' asked Wright. 'Half a dozen mourners, a handful of ashes, then nothing.' He shivered, though it wasn't a cold day.

They walked together to Reid's Honda Civic. 'Can you do me a favour?' asked Wright.

'Depends on what you want,' said Reid, cautiously.

'I want to go and look at the tunnel,' said Wright.

Reid looked puzzled. 'What's the story?'

'No story. I just want to get a feel for what happened.' It was clear from Reid's face that he didn't understand. 'I thought it might help me get inside the killer's head.'

Reid looked even more confused but didn't say anything.

Wright felt that he had to justify his request, but words failed him. 'I can't explain it,' he said. 'I just feel that I have to go and have a look.'

Reid raised his eyebrows. 'Okay, if that's what you want, we'll go.'

'Alone,' said Wright. 'I want to go alone. Can I borrow the car?'

Reid rubbed the back of his neck. For a moment it looked as if he was about to argue, but then he handed the car keys to Wright. 'I'll get a cab,' he said.

'Thanks, Tommy. I'll see you in the office in a couple of hours.'

'Just be careful,' said Reid. 'With the car.' He walked away, but after a few steps he hesitated, then turned and shouted to Wright that there was a flashlight in the boot.

Wright got into the car and drove south to Battersea. He pulled up at the side of the road that ran parallel to the disused rail line. He retrieved the flashlight from the boot, and stood for a while staring down the overgrown embankment. A cold wind blew from his left, tugging at his hair and whispering through the grass and nettles that hadn't been trampled down by the investigation team. The sky above was pale blue and clear, but there was a chill in the air. Wright shivered inside his raincoat. He went down the embankment, his hands out at his sides for balance, skidding the last few steps and coming to a halt next to the rusting rails.

The cutting sheltered Wright from the wind, and there was a stillness around him as if time had stopped. Wright headed towards the mouth of the tunnel. As it came into view, he saw that a wooden framework had been constructed across the opening. Yellow tape with the words 'Crime Scene – Do Not Enter' had been threaded through the wire and the message was repeated on a large metal sign. Wright cursed himself for not realising that the tunnel would have been sealed off. He walked up to the wire and peered through it into the blackness of the tunnel. He heard a noise, a scuffling sound, and turned his head to the side, trying to focus on whatever it was, but the noise wasn't repeated. He remembered the rats and what they'd done to the body of Max Eckhardt.

Wright stood back and examined the barrier. It had been well put together and bolted into the stone of the bridge. He walked across the mouth of the tunnel, stepping over the tracks and running his left hand over the mesh so that it rattled and shook. He realised a doorway had been constructed in the barrier, a wooden frame with a double thickness of mesh, three hinges on one side, a bolt with a padlock through it on the other. Wright stared at the padlock. It was hanging open. He reached for it and unhooked it from the bolt. It didn't appear to have been forced. He put it in his coat pocket, then slid open the bolt. The door creaked on its hinges and Wright opened it just enough so that he could slide through the gap. His coat snagged on a piece of wire and he felt it rip. He reached behind his back and pulled himself free, then slipped inside.

The darkness was almost an impenetrable wall, a finite boundary that he hesitated to cross. He switched on the flashlight and a yellow oval of light appeared on the ground, illuminating one of the rails. He held the flashlight out in front of him but the darkness seemed to swallow up the beam. Wright felt his heart pound and he realised he was breathing faster than normal. He took slow deep breaths and tried to quell the feeling of unease that was growing stronger by the second. He closed his eyes. His fingers tensed around the body of the flashlight until it was the only thing he could feel.

He flashed back in his mind to another time when he'd faced darkness, to a time when he'd been eleven years old. It wasn't the mouth of a tunnel he faced then, it was an open door, a door that led down to the basement. The eleven-year-old Nick Wright took a step forward, then another, until he was standing on the threshold. The darkness was absolute as if the basement had been filled with tar, a darkness so thick and black that the eleven-year-old Nick was sure he would drown in it. More than twenty years later, the adult Nick struggled to remember where the light switch was, or even if there was one, but he could vividly recall the terror he felt as he dipped his right foot into the darkness and felt for the first step. He was alone in the house, of that he was certain. Alone except for what lurked in the basement, waiting for him. He put his weight on his right foot and probed with his left, both hands gripping the wooden rails as if they were a lifeline to the light behind him. He took a second step, and a third, and then the blackness swallowed him up.

Wright opened his eyes. His face was drenched in sweat and he rubbed his forehead with his sleeve. He pointed the flashlight at the floor and stepped in-between the rails. There was a damp, slightly bitter, smell to the air, a mix of stale urine and rotting vegetation, and Wright tried to block out the stench by breathing through his mouth. He stood with his feet together on an ancient wooden sleeper, like a high-diver preparing to jump. He took a step forward, concentrating on the rust-covered rails highlighted by the yellow beam of the flashlight. The light flickered. The batteries were old, Wright realised. He shook the flashlight and the beam grew stronger for a few seconds but then faded back to its original yellow glow.

Wright began walking, stepping from sleeper to sleeper. He wondered how long the batteries would last, and how he would react if the torch died while he was in the bowels of the tunnel. And he wondered why he was deliberately testing himself, pushing himself into a situation that was almost more than he could bear. It wasn't just that he hated tunnels. He hated all dark places. Dark places and confined spaces. He was thirty-two years old and he was scared of the dark, but today was the day that he was going to prove to himself that his fears were groundless.

Wright swung the beam from side to side. The walls of the tunnel were stained black, streaked with green moss and dotted with silvery cobwebs that glistened with moisture. Wright shivered. Last time he'd been in the tunnel he hadn't noticed how cold it was.

Suddenly he stopped. He'd heard something ahead of him. It wasn't the same sort of sound he'd heard outside the tunnel; this was a gravelly crunch, the sort of noise a foot might make if it slipped off a sleeper. A human foot. He crouched down and listened. All he could hear was the sound of his own breathing. He held his breath. There was nothing. He stared ahead but couldn't see anything outside the beam of his flashlight. He put his hand over the end of the flashlight so that the light glowed redly through the flesh. The darkness seemed to wrap itself tighter around Wright and he took his hand away. He crouched lower, instinctively trying to make himself a smaller target even though he didn't know what he was protecting himself from.

He listened, but the sound wasn't repeated. Something brushed against his cheek and he spun around, sweeping the flashlight beam around his head like a claymore, but he was alone. A large moth fluttered up to the roof of the tunnel where it dislodged flecks of soot that fell around him like black snow. Wright's panic gradually subsided and he stood up again. He looked over his shoulder. He'd only walked fifty feet or so into the tunnel. Through the opening he could see the lush green embankment and a strip of sky. Fifty feet. He could run that far in seconds, yet it felt a lifetime away. Part of him wanted to run back into the open, to get the hell out of the tunnel, but he knew that he had to fight his phobia; he had to break its hold on him before it gripped him even tighter.

Wright turned back. Someone was standing in front of him. Wright yelped in fright and dropped the flashlight. It crashed on to the rail and the light went out. Wright put his hands up to protect himself.

'Whoa, take it easy,' said the man. He had an American accent.

Wright tried to regain his composure. 'Who are you?' he asked, attempting to sound authoritative but all too well aware just how much his voice was shaking. The man was an inch or so shorter than Wright but his shoulders were wider and he stood confidently between the rails, his hands swinging freely at his sides. 'Who are you?' repeated Wright, with slightly more confidence this time.

'I was here first,' said the man. 'Maybe I should be asking you who you are.'

Wright wanted to pick up his flashlight but he was too close to the man to risk bending down. 'You're trespassing on Railtrack property,' he said. He could only make out the man's silhouette. He looked down at his hands, trying to see if he was carrying a weapon. There was something in his right hand, but Wright couldn't make out what it was.

'I might say the same about you,' said the man.

'I'm a policeman,' said Wright.

Bright white light suddenly blinded Wright and he turned his head. The light went off. Wright blinked, trying to recover his night vision. He took a step back as he realised how defenceless he was.

'You don't look like a policeman,' said the man. He sounded amused, and although Wright couldn't make out his features, he knew he was grinning.

'Look, I'm a policeman and you're trespassing. I want you out of here. Now.' He shouted the last word and it echoed down the tunnel.

The man stood where he was. When he spoke, his voice was a hushed whisper. 'Suppose I said no. What would you do then? Do you think you could make me?' He chuckled. 'I don't think so.'

Wright took another step backwards, then swiftly bent down and retrieved the flashlight. He flicked the on-off switch but it had no effect. The bulb must have broken. He tapped the flashlight against the palm of his left hand. It wasn't much of a weapon but it was all he had.

'Bet you wish they let you carry guns, huh?' said the

man. 'Never understood that. Ninety-nine per cent of people will do as they're told if you ask them the right way, but what do you do when someone just says no? You have to use necessary force, right? But how do you decide what's necessary? And what if the guy you're up against isn't intimidated by force?'

Realisation dawned and Wright sighed with relief. 'You're the FBI agent?'

'Jim Bamber at your service,' said the man.

'Why the hell didn't you say so?' asked Wright angrily.

'Hey, you weren't exactly quick to identify yourself,' said Bamber. 'Anyone can say they're a cop.'

'Yeah? Well, anyone can say they're an FBI agent.'

Bamber took his wallet out of his jacket pocket and switched on his flashlight. Wright squinted at the credentials, FBI in large blue letters and a small photograph of an unsmiling man in his late twenties with a strong jaw and a prominent dimple. 'Of course, you probably wouldn't be able to tell if it's real or not,' said Bamber. 'Same as if you showed me yours. How would I know, right?' The flashlight went off.

'Do you think you could leave that on?' asked Wright.

'Sure,' said Bamber. He did as Wright asked, keeping the beam low, illuminating the rails.

'I'm Nick Wright,' said Wright, realising that he still hadn't identified himself. 'Our superintendent warned us you'd be coming.'

'Warned?'

'Maybe warned's the wrong word. He said the FBI was sending someone over to work on the case.'

'And here I am,' said Bamber. He held out his hand, shining the beam of his flashlight on to it, and

Wright shook it. 'How come you're here, Nick?' asked Bamber.

'I just wanted another look at the crime scene,' said Wright. 'I had some crazy idea about getting a feel for the killer.'

'Not such a crazy idea,' said Bamber. 'That's what I was doing. The superintendent let me view the video and the stills, but that can't tell you everything. The smell, the sounds, the atmosphere, it's all part of it. You can feel what the victim felt, right up to the moment he was killed.' He looked around the tunnel. 'Not a good place to die, huh?'

'Is there a good place?' asked Wright.

'A five-star hotel room, in a king-size bed with busty blonde twins and a bottle of champagne,' suggested Bamber. He started walking deeper into the tunnel and Wright hurried after him. Bamber ran the flashlight beam along the bottom of the tunnel wall. A large brown rat scuttled along the floor, trying to escape from the light. 'They must have made a mess of the body,' said Bamber.

'Yeah. It was down here for a couple of days before it was found. Most of the lower parts of the legs had been eaten away.'

'According to the autopsy report, the body was already well mutilated.'

'Post mortem,' said Wright. 'We call them post mortems here.'

Bamber played the beam along the wall, back and forth. He picked out the rusty brown smears where the body had been and headed towards them. 'Must have taken some time,' Bamber continued. 'Do you reckon it was because they wanted information from him?'

'We're not sure,' said Wright. 'You said "they", do you reckon there was more than one?'

'How else would they get him in here?' said Bamber. He nodded at the entrance to the tunnel, a squashed oval of light in the distance.

'He could have been carried in, unconscious.'

'Maybe,' said Bamber. He stepped closer to the wall and played the beam down the bloodstains. There were scrape marks where the forensic people had taken away samples. 'It was all the same blood group?' asked Bamber.

Wright nodded. 'Have you ever come across anything like it in the States?'

'Not personally,' said the FBI agent, 'but I've only worked on a dozen or so homicides. I'm running a check through our Behavioral Science Services Unit. They'll spot any patterns that match similar deaths. Have you considered a Satanic connection? Ritual sacrifice?'

'We spoke to a few experts, and they said that Satanic symbols would have been used, candles and the like. Eckhardt was also the wrong sort of victim. Sacrifice would normally involve children or young women.'

'Drugs?'

'He certainly wasn't a user, and he didn't appear to be the sort who'd have drug connections.'

'He was a news agency photographer, right? Could he have been photographing the wrong people?'

'Nothing controversial,' said Wright. 'At least, not in the UK.'

'We're looking at his New York background, but I've already got a negative from the DEA and he doesn't have a criminal record, other than a few speeding tickets. He's just a regular citizen.'

'That's what we figured,' said Wright. 'An innocent bystander. Wrong place, wrong time.'

Bamber straightened up. 'I want to switch the flashlight off. Are you okay with that?'

Wright felt his chest tighten and his breath caught in his throat. He forced himself to relax. 'Sure,' he said.

The light winked off. Wright immediately felt as if he was falling. He gasped and put out his hands, but there was nothing to hold on to. He twisted around and fixed his eyes on the entrance to the tunnel, focusing all his attention on the patch of light, but that only made his disorientation worse. Time seemed to crawl by, and with each passing second the darkness seemed to become more and more stifling, a creeping cloud that threatened to suffocate the life out of him. The flashlight came back on and Bamber walked over to stand next to Wright again.

'Gives you a feel for what it must have been like,' said the FBI agent. He looked across at Wright. 'Are you scared of the dark, Nick?'

'Why do you ask?' asked Wright, defensively.

'Because it's as cold as a witch's tit in here, and you're sweating.'

Wright wiped his hand across his forehead. It came away wet. 'I'm a bit claustrophobic, that's all.'

Bamber chuckled. 'Yeah? That's funny, isn't it? You being a transit cop and all.'

'It's transport, not transit,' said Wright. 'And I joined for the trains, not the tunnels.'

'I didn't think of that,' said the FBI agent. He stopped laughing. 'Hey, you really are uncomfortable, aren't you?' He handed Wright the flashlight. 'Come on, let's get out of here.'

The two men walked back along the track and out into

the sunshine. Wright took the padlock from his pocket and relocked the gate.

'How did you get here?' Wright asked. 'I didn't see a car.'

'It's about half a mile away. I picked up a rental at the airport.'

They walked away from the tunnel. 'How long are you going to be in town, Jim?' asked Wright.

'As long as it takes. We don't take kindly to our citizens being murdered overseas.'

They climbed up the embankment. Bamber went first. He moved quickly and gracefully, with swift, sure steps that took him up the slope at twice Wright's speed, and whereas Wright was panting when he reached the top, Bamber wasn't affected at all. Bamber looked as if he worked out regularly; he wasn't over muscled, but he was lean and hard without a spare ounce of fat on his frame.

'Do you want to follow me back?' said Wright, figuring that Bamber would have difficulty finding his way across South London to the office.

'I thought I'd go and talk to Eckhardt's widow,' said Bamber.

Wright stiffened. 'Now's not a good time,' he said. 'The funeral was today.'

Bamber stood looking down at the tracks below. He wasn't wearing a coat and the wind was tugging at the lightweight material of his suit but he didn't appear to feel the cold. 'That's the best time,' he said. 'She'll be off balance.'

'She's not a suspect,' said Wright quickly. Too quickly, he realised.

Bamber turned to look at him. He didn't say anything

for several seconds, then he slowly smiled. 'Pretty, is she?'

'Don't be stupid,' Wright said brusquely. He could feel himself start to blush and he looked away.

'Stupid? I just meant that maybe she had a lover, maybe she wanted her husband out of the way.' He craned his neck forward, his head twisted to the side like a hawk eyeing up potential prey. 'What did you think I meant, Nick?'

'She's not a suspect,' Wright repeated. Bamber continued to look at him, smiling. 'It's not what you think,' said Wright.

'Yeah? What do I think?'

'You think I fancy her.'

'And do you?'

Bamber was still smiling. It was a good-natured, open smile, and Wright felt that the FBI agent wasn't being malicious. Wright grinned despite his embarrassment. 'Maybe,' he said. He shook his head. 'I don't know, it's weird. I keep thinking about her, you know? At night, when I'm driving, when I'm shaving. Pretty sick, huh? Her husband's only just been cremated and I want to get inside her pants.'

'Actually, it's understandable. She's vulnerable, she's hurting, it brings out the protective instinct in you. You want to take care of her. It's happened to me before, Nick.'

Wright rubbed his nose. 'Yeah. Maybe.'

'Okay, I'll follow you back to the office. I'll go get my car.' He walked away as Wright climbed into Reid's Honda. As he waited for Bamber to return, Wright thought over what he'd said about May Eckhardt. He wondered whether it had been a good idea to open up to the FBI agent, to a man he'd only just met. Bamber had been sympathetic, though, in a way that Reid would never have been. If Wright had told

Reid how he felt about May Eckhardt, his partner would have reacted with guffaws and sarcasm. Wright massaged the back of his neck, kneading his fingers into the base of his skull in a vain attempt to ease the tension that was building there.

Louise Malone had been a chambermaid for almost eight years but she had never come across a guest as strange as the man in room 527. According to the register he was an American, James Bamber, but he'd never spoken to her so she hadn't heard his accent. On the few occasions she'd seen him, he'd merely smiled and nodded. Hadn't said a word. That in itself was unusual because he was a good-looking guy in his late twenties, exactly the sort of man who'd normally make a pass at her. With her shoulder-length blonde hair, green eyes and curvy figure obvious even under her housecoat, Louise received more than her fair share of passes and she wasn't used to polite indifference. It was a shame that he wasn't interested, because she was between boyfriends and he had a firm, hard body and hazel eyes that made her go a little weak at the knees.

It was the state of his room that Louise found so unusual. She had come across all sorts during her years cleaning rooms, from an Arab who insisted on defecating in the wardrobe, to a family of wealthy Hong Kong Chinese who took the lightbulbs with them when they checked out, but she'd never encountered a guest who cleaned his own room. Louise prided herself on her standards, but she had to admit that his bathroom positively sparkled. He'd even cleaned the shower curtain and managed to dislodge the limescale that had discoloured the toilet overflow. There was never any rubbish in the litter bins, not even a scrap of paper, and his bed was always made, no matter what time of day she checked the room. If she hadn't seen him entering and leaving the room, she'd have been convinced that no one was staying there. She'd been so intrigued by the mysterious Mr Bamber that she'd gone through the drawers and the wardrobe looking for any clues as to what he did for a living, but there were no personal effects to be found, just a few items of laundered clothing, still in protective wrappers. Still, there was nothing wrong with being neat and tidy. Maybe he was gay. That at least would explain why he hadn't made a pass at her.

Two desks had been lined up in front of three large floor-mounted boards. On the centre board were the words 'British Transport Police' and underneath it was the force's logo. On the left-hand board was a photograph of Max Eckhardt, one of several that Nick Wright had borrowed from the widow, blown up to poster size. Underneath were photographs of camera equipment similar to that owned by Eckhardt. On the board on the right was a large photograph of the tunnel entrance and below it a map of the area. More than two dozen reporters and photographers were already in the room when Duggan and Dundas followed Superintendent Newton to their places.

A pretty brunette from the press office was handing out press releases and photographs of the victim. She flashed the superintendent a nervous smile and thrust the remaining press releases at a television reporter before chasing after the officers. She caught up with Newton as he sat down. 'Sorry, sir, could you just hang on a few minutes? Sky TV want to go live and they're having problems in the studio.'

Newton sighed heavily. 'Do we have to?'

'It's good coverage, sir. And they'll reuse it in their hourly bulletins.'

Newton looked at his wristwatch and sighed again. 'Okay, but we haven't got all day.'

The press officer held up her hands for silence and explained to the assembled journalists that the press conference wouldn't be starting for several minutes. There were grumbles from the newspaper reporters. 'Bloody Sky,' shouted one. The press officer suggested that the photographers use the opportunity to take pictures. Newton blinked under a barrage of photographic flashes.

Nick Wright stood at the side of the room next to Tommy Reid, looking at the reporters. They were a mixed bag: earnest young men in sharp suits, middle-aged women with tired skin, grey-haired men in sheepskin jackets. Most had notebooks and pens though several were also holding small tape recorders. A tall blonde wearing a black mini skirt was reading the press release and underlining parts of it. She crossed her long legs. Wright looked across at Reid. His partner was openly staring at the girl's thighs.

'Try to keep your mind on the job, Tommy,' whispered Wright.

A bearded man with a plastic clipboard made a thumbs-up gesture at the press officer. She took her place next to the superintendent and nodded at him. Newton stood up, took his glasses out of his top pocket, and read through the press release. It consisted of barely a dozen paragraphs, identifying the victim as Max Eckhardt, a brief biography, and an appeal for anyone who had been in the vicinity of the tunnels at the approximate time of the murder to call the incident room. They were also appealing for any motorists who had driven along the road that ran parallel to the disused line to come forward, in the hope that they had seen any parked vehicles. Eckhardt's missing camera equipment was listed on a separate sheet. The superintendent asked if there were any questions and there was a flurry of raised hands. They all started to shout at once, so the press officer stood up and pointed at one of the older journalists. Wright recognised him as a crime reporter from one of the heavier Sunday papers.

'Is it possible for us to speak to the man's widow?' he asked. 'It might add weight to the appeal if we could have a quote from her?'

'I'm afraid not,' said Newton. 'She's made it clear that she doesn't want to speak to the press. It's a very difficult time for her.'

'Can we at least have an address for her?'

'No, I'm afraid we can't release that information,' said the superintendent.

Two of the tabloid reporters exchanged hushed whispers. Wright knew that the Eckhardts were ex-directory, but most newspapers had contacts within British Telecom who'd be prepared to disclose the information for the price of a couple of bottles of Scotch. He made a mental note to warn her.

The blonde in the black mini skirt raised a languid hand. 'Are you any closer to discovering a motive?' she asked.

She had a strong Geordie accent which was at odds with her elegant appearance.

'We are pursuing several lines of enquiry,' said Newton.

The blonde uncrossed her legs and tapped her lips with a gold ballpoint pen. 'Have there been any similar murders in the past?' she asked.

'Similar in what way?'

She recrossed her legs. Wright looked across at Newton but the superintendent was staring fixedly at her face. Wright admired the man's self-control.

'The way the body was mutilated. I understand the man's penis was cut off.' Several of the male reporters laughed but the blonde wasn't distracted. She appeared to have the same degree of self-control as the superintendent. 'And then stuffed in his mouth.'

The guffaws intensified and the superintendent waited for the noise to die down before speaking. 'We haven't released details of the man's injuries,' he said.

'Yes, I know that. But we do have our own sources. Perhaps I should rephrase the question. In your experience, have there been any murders in the past where the victim's genitalia have been removed and placed in the victim's mouth?'

Wright and Reid exchanged looks. The blonde had good contacts, either within the police or the pathologist's department. Reid grinned wolfishly and Wright immediately knew what had passed through his mind. Her long legs and short skirts probably opened a lot of doors.

'No, we don't know of any murders which have involved injuries such as you described,' said Newton.

'But you can confirm that Max Eckhardt was mutilated in the way I've described?'

'I'll repeat what I said earlier. We haven't released details of the man's injuries.'

'Because?'

'Because we might need the information to identify the person responsible.'

One of the television reporters, a thirty-something man in a dark blue double-breasted suit, raised his arm and the press officer pointed at him. 'Have you had many hoax confessions?' he asked.

'Fifteen,' answered Newton. Duggan leaned across and whispered into his ear. 'Correction,' said Newton. 'As of today there have been seventeen.'

'Do you have an opinion on people like that who waste your time and resources?'

'Not one that you can print,' said Newton.

A man in a sheepskin jacket stood up. Wright recognised him as the reporter from the *Daily Mirror* who'd been at the last press conference and who had goaded him about the Met being called in. The press officer pointed at him. 'Ted Vincent,' she said to the superintendent out of the corner of her mouth. *'Daily Mirror.'*

'Other than the seventeen hoaxes, how many suspects do you have at present?' said Vincent.

It was a rhetorical question, Wright knew, serving no purpose other than to embarrass the superintendent. 'We are pursuing several lines of enquiry,' Newton said eventually.

'Yes, you said that,' said Vincent. 'But do you have any actual suspects?'

'No,' said Newton coldly. 'That's why we are making this appeal for witnesses. We want anyone who was in the area to come forward—'

'You're asking the public to solve the case for you,' cut in the reporter, punctuating his words with short jabs of his pen. 'This is the second appeal for witnesses in as many weeks. Isn't it time that this case was turned over to more experienced investigators? Such as the Met?'

'Mr Vincent, the Met are already assisting the BTP with this investigation. Officers from both forces are working together. We have more than two dozen officers on the case and are prepared to increase our manpower resources if necessary.'

Vincent shrugged and muttered something as he sat down. The questions continued for more than half an hour and Newton fielded them deftly. None of the reporters was as hostile as Ted Vincent had been, and the *Mirror* reporter made no move to ask any further questions.

When the press conference was over the press officer ushered the superintendent to the back of the room where the television crews wanted to record individual interviews.

Wright and Reid slipped into the corridor. Reid made a drinking motion with his hand and wiggled his eyebrows. 'Yeah, okay,' said Wright wearily.

They walked past the pub nearest their office, figuring that the press pack would be sure to pile in to compare notes before heading back to their papers. The one they chose was already filling up with office workers, and two waitresses in black and white uniforms rushed around with trays of food, everything with chips.

'Solids?' asked Reid disdainfully as they stood at the bar.

Wright shook his head. 'Just a Coke.'

'Bloody hell, Nick. You're over eighteen, you know. Have something stronger.' He waved a ten-pound note and a red-haired waitress in a white blouse gestured with her chin to let him know that he'd attracted her attention. 'Vodka and tonic, love. Make it a double.' He looked meaningfully at Wright.

'Okay, okay. Lager shandy.'

'Pint of lager shandy,' Reid relayed to the waitress, who was already putting his vodka and tonic on the bar in front of him. Reid sipped his drink and smacked his lips. 'How do you think it went?' he asked.

Wright grimaced. 'Better than the one we did, that's for sure.'

'Smooth, isn't he?'

'He's a politician. And he's been on courses for television, press conferences, the works.'

The waitress brought Wright's shandy over and Reid paid her. The two men turned their backs to the bar and leaned on it. The door opened and in walked Ted Vincent, his hands thrust into the pockets of his sheepskin jacket. The journalist grinned when he saw the two detectives.

'Men after my own heart,' said Vincent.

'Ideally with a stake through it,' said Wright.

Vincent laughed good naturedly. 'Can I buy you two gentlemen a drink?' he asked, edging between them and pulling out his wallet.

'That'd be fraternising with the enemy,' said Reid. He pretended to consider the offer for several seconds. 'Mine's a vodka and tonic. A double.'

'Funny guy,' said Vincent. 'Good to see you can keep your sense of humour in the face of adversity.'

'And what adversity would that be?' asked Wright.

'Come on, you know as well as I do that you're getting nowhere on this case.'

'It's early days,' said Wright.

Vincent ordered Reid's vodka and a beer for himself. He raised an eyebrow at Wright but Wright shook his head. 'It's been almost two weeks. What leads have you got?'

'You were at the press conference,' said Wright.

'You've got fuck all,' said Vincent. 'You've got fuck all and you know it.' Reid and Wright looked at each other, then together they turned their backs on the reporter. He wasn't fazed in the least by their show of indifference. He patted them both on the shoulders. 'Look, we're on the same side here, lads. We shouldn't be arguing.'

'How do you figure that?' asked Reid. His vodka and tonic arrived and he downed it in one swift gulp.

Vincent waved at the waitress, pointing at the empty glass and at his own. She brought fresh drinks. 'You want to solve the case. And I want to write about it. It's no bloody story if it stays unsolved. You can see that, right? You guys should learn how to handle the press.' He tapped a cigarette out of a pack of Rothmans and slipped it between his lips.

'A ten-foot barge pole springs to mind,' said Wright. His glass was only half-empty but he pushed it away. 'I've got to go.'

Wright's Fiesta was parked ten minutes' walk from the pub. He sat in the car for several minutes, wondering what he should do. Other than Reid's flat, he had nowhere to go, and he was in no mood to sit down in front of Reid's portable television with a takeaway meal in his lap and a can of supermarket lager on the arm of his chair. He decided to go to see May Eckhardt.

The early afternoon traffic was heavy but flowing smoothly and he reached Maida Vale in twenty minutes. A Suzuki Jeep was pulling out of a pay and display parking place close to the Eckhardts' mansion block and Wright eased his Fiesta into the gap.

As he walked towards the block he realised that he was too late. Half a dozen photographers were clustered on the pavement, five men and a girl, all with cameras and lenses hanging around their necks. They all wore thick jackets and one of the men was pouring steaming coffee from a Thermos flask into plastic cups. Wright put his hands into the pockets of his coat and slouched past. They didn't even look at him.

He walked up to the block and pushed the button for the Eckhardt flat. There was no reply so he pressed it again. And again. When she still didn't reply, Wright kept his thumb on the buzzer for a full minute. When it became clear that she was either out or ignoring the bell, Wright took his mobile phone and tapped out her number. She answered on the fifth ring. 'Yes?' she said.

'Mrs Eckhardt? This is Nick Wright.'

'Nick Wright?'

Wright felt an involuntary twinge of regret that she didn't recognise his name. 'Sergeant Wright,' he said. 'British Transport Police. I'm at the entrance to your block, can you buzz me in?'

'Are you the one who's been ringing my bell?'

'I'm afraid so.'

'There've been so many journalists trying to get in, I didn't . . .' Her words dried up. 'Okay, I'll let you in,' she said. The line went dead and a couple of seconds later the lock buzzed and Wright pushed the door open. He went upstairs. This time she didn't have the door open for him and he had to knock. She had a security chain on the door and it only opened a few inches. Wright caught a quick glimpse of May's face before the door closed again. He heard the rattle of the chain being taken off and then the door opened wide.

May Eckhardt was wearing a white towelling robe that was much too big for her. For a brief moment Wright thought that she'd just got out of the shower but her hair was dry, and then he noticed that she had jeans on under the robe. Her eyes were red and puffy and she turned her face away from Wright as she closed the door.

'Are you okay?' he asked, and immediately wished he'd bitten off his tongue instead. Of course she wasn't okay. Her husband had been brutally murdered and a pack of press photographers were camped on her doorstep.

She walked by him into the sitting room and curled up on the sofa again. There was a box of tissues on the coffee table. 'What do you want?' she asked.

Wright shrugged apologetically. 'I actually came to warn you that the press would be after you. It seems I was too late.'

'Yes, you were,' she said coldly. May leaned forward and picked up half a dozen sheets of paper. She held them out to Wright and he went over to her and took them. Their fingers touched and Wright felt a small shock, like static electricity. May didn't react and Wright wondered if he'd imagined it. He looked at the pieces of paper. They'd been torn from different notebooks and were offers of money in exchange for an exclusive interview. A woman reporter from the *News of the World* had written three times, each time raising her offer. The amount she finally offered was more than Wright earned in a year. 'They were ringing my bell and stuffing these into my letterbox for hours,' she said.

Wright nodded at the telephone. 'Have they phoned yet?'

May shook her head. 'No, we're ex-directory.'

'That won't stop them,' said Wright. 'Can I sit down?' he asked. She nodded and Wright dropped into one of the armchairs.

May brought up her knees against her chest and wrapped her arms around her legs. 'What am I going to do?'

'Is there somewhere you can go?'

'I told you before, I don't have any relatives here.'

'You said you were from Manchester. Can you go back there?'

She threw back her head and gave a short laugh that sounded almost like a cry of pain.

'Friends?'

She shook her head. 'We haven't really been here long enough to make any,' she said. She rubbed her cheek against the towelling robe. Wright realised it was her husband's robe and that she was inhaling his scent.

'I'm sorry,' said Wright lamely. He always seemed to be lost for words in her presence. She looked so small and helpless that he felt an overwhelming urge to protect her, yet he knew there was nothing he could do. The press had a right to pursue her, and they weren't breaking any law by posting messages through her letterbox or waiting on the pavement outside. 'They'll get bored eventually,' he said. 'It's a story today, but that's because there was a press conference.'

'A press conference? Why?'

'We were releasing your husband's name. And appealing for witnesses.'

She held her legs tighter and rested her head on her knees. 'So you're no closer to discovering who killed Max?'

Wright looked away. 'No, I'm afraid not.' There was a

photograph of the Eckhardts on one of the shelves in the alcove, both of them smiling at the camera. Wright didn't remember seeing it last time he was in the flat. 'By the way, an American might get in touch with you. An FBI agent.'

May's eyebrows knotted together and her forehead creased into a frown that made her look suddenly much older. 'FBI?' she said.

'Yeah, his name's James Bamber. The FBI have sent him over to help with the investigation.'

Her frown became even more severe. 'Why? Don't they think you can find Max's killer?'

'It's not that, he's just here to help co-ordinate with the Americans, Max being an American and all. He said he might want to talk to you.' Wright looked around the room, not wanting eye contact with her. Something strange happened to his stomach each time he looked into her soft brown eyes. 'Do you have food?' he asked. She looked puzzled. 'So that you don't have to go out to the shops,' he added. 'The photographers outside are waiting for a picture. If you stay inside, they'll go away eventually.'

'I've enough food,' she said. 'I don't have much of an appetite, anyway. How long? How long do you think they'll stay there?'

'A couple of days, then they'll be chasing after another story.'

'That's all Max's death is? A story?'

Wright sat forward. 'No, of course not,' he said earnestly. 'I meant that's how the media regards it. It's much more than that to me. And to my colleagues.' A tear rolled down her cheek. 'I will find his killer, May. I promise you.'

She rubbed her cheek against the robe. 'Thank you,' she whispered.

There were half a dozen empty glasses lined up on the bar and Tommy Reid tapped them one at a time, trying in vain to play a recognisable tune.

Vincent patted him on the back. 'My round,' he said. In fact, they'd all been Vincent's rounds. Alcohol loosened tongues, and loose tongues produced page leads. He winked at the waitress and she produced fresh drinks without being asked. 'Your partner's a bit touchy, isn't he?'

'Nick? He's okay.'

'Oh, sure,' said Vincent hurriedly, not wanting to offend the detective. 'But it's like he's got something to prove.'

'He's young.'

Vincent finished off his cigarette and stubbed it out in a plastic ashtray. 'Dog in a manger,' he said.

'Bollocks,' said Reid. 'He's co-operating with the Met team, and with the guy the FBI sent over.'

Vincent's heart began to race, but he kept his face expressionless. It was the first time anyone had mentioned an FBI involvement and he sensed a good story. He decided to use a softly-softly approach. Reid was drunk but he was clearly used to consuming large amounts of alcohol and Vincent didn't want to scare him off. 'He hasn't been on a murder case like this before, has he?'

'I don't think any of us has ever seen anything like it before,' said Reid. 'It's a one-off.' He gulped down his vodka and tonic and looked at his wristwatch.

'Not in the States, even? There's all sorts of weird stuff goes on there.'

'The FBI guy says no.'

'So why's he come over, then?' Vincent pulled a ten-pound note from his pocket and waved it at the barmaid.

'Because Eckhardt's an American.'

'They do that? They send over an FBI agent when an American dies?'

Reid shrugged. 'I guess so. I'd better be going.'

Their drinks arrived. 'You might as well have one for the road,' said Vincent, picking up his pint. 'So what's his name, this guy?'

'Bamber,' said a voice behind him. 'Jim Bamber.'

Vincent turned around. The speaker was a man in his late twenties, slightly shorter than Vincent with light brown close-cropped hair that was greying at the temples. Bamber's hand was outstretched. Vincent transferred his glass to his left hand and they shook. The American had a firm grip but Vincent had the feeling that he wasn't using all his strength. 'Ted Vincent.'

'Careful what you say, Jim,' said Reid. 'He's a journalist.'

'Yeah? Which paper, Ted?'

'The *Mirror*. Can I buy you a drink?'

'Sure. Scotch. On the rocks. How's it going, Tommy?'

Reid shrugged as Vincent ordered Bamber's drink. 'Did you see the press conference on TV?' asked Reid.

'Sure did.'

'So you know how it's going.'

Vincent handed Bamber his whisky and they clinked glasses. 'Cheers,' said Vincent. 'I was asking Tommy if it was normal practice to send an FBI agent over to investigate the death of an American national.'

'Depends on the circumstances,' said Bamber.

Vincent could already see the headline: 'Train Cops Call In FBI.' He sipped his beer, taking his time. 'And are you taking an active part in the investigation?'

'I'm asking a few questions, sure. This isn't an interview, is it, Ted? I wouldn't want to say anything on the record.'

'Sure, sure,' said Vincent dismissively. He pulled his pack of Rothmans from the pocket of his sheepskin jacket and offered a cigarette to Bamber. The FBI agent declined and Vincent lit one for himself. 'What's your perspective on this, Jim?' Vincent asked. 'How do you think the investigation's being handled?'

'It's a tough case,' said Bamber.

'Would they do it different in the States?'

'Like I said, it's a tough case. We just have to wait for a break.'

'Yeah? Well, without a witness and without some sort of forensic evidence, it all comes down to motive, that's what I reckon.'

Bamber sniffed his whisky but didn't drink it. 'You might be right, Ted.'

'So which office do you work out of?'

'Washington.'

'FBI headquarters?'

Bamber nodded but didn't reply.

'I've got to tell you, Jim, what I'd really like to do is have an interview for my paper. An exclusive.'

'I don't think so,' said Bamber quietly.

'It might help bring people forward. Any publicity is good publicity and all that.'

'I don't think so,' Bamber repeated. His voice was barely audible, little more than a soft whisper, but there was a hard edge to it.

Vincent sensed the man's reluctance and tried to put him at his ease by smiling broadly and squeezing him on the shoulder. Bamber didn't react to the physical contact. He stared unsmilingly at Vincent and the journalist took his hand away. 'How about another Scotch?'

The FBI agent smiled, but without warmth. 'I'm okay,' he said.

Vincent ordered another pint for himself and a vodka and tonic for Reid. 'So, how long will you be over on this side of the pond?' asked Vincent.

'Depends,' said Bamber.

'The Bureau's happy to leave it open ended? Some murder investigations take months.'

'And some are never solved,' said Reid. He ran his fingers along the top of his empty glasses. The waitress returned with fresh drinks and reached out to take the empty ones, but Reid waved her away. 'I need an A flat,' he explained.

'I mean, can you imagine the BTP sending one of their men to investigate a death in another country?' said Vincent. 'Wouldn't happen.'

'Nah, you're dead wrong there,' said Reid, banging the flat of his hand down on the bar. 'British cops have been sent to the Falklands, to Kenya, lots of places.'

'Yeah? But you're talking about real police, not the BTP.'

Reid looked sideways at the journalist. 'Hey, you don't hear me saying that the *Mirror*'s not a real newspaper, do you? You don't hear me saying that it's a comic with a reading age in single figures.'

'And I'm grateful for that, Tommy. You're all heart.'

Bamber put his drink on the bar. 'Do you two always fight like this?'

'This?' said Reid. 'This is just the warm-up.' He chuckled and rested his arms on the bar.

'It's a symbiotic relationship,' Vincent said to Bamber. 'We publicise their successes, we help with appeals for information, and in return they give us stories to help us sell papers. Which brings me back to you, Jim. I'd really like to do a story on you and your involvement in the tunnel murder.'

'I don't think so,' said Bamber.

'Come on, Jim. I don't actually need your co-operation, you know. Freedom of Information Act and all that. I can call Washington and get the scoop from them. They'll have a press office, right?'

'I'd rather you didn't, Ted,' said Bamber.

'So talk to me. Give me an interview. That way you'll be able to put your own slant on it.'

'No,' said Bamber. He took a step forward so that his face was only inches away from the journalist's. His pale hazel eyes stared at Vincent so intensely that the journalist flinched.

Vincent was a good two inches taller than the FBI agent and several pounds heavier, but he still felt intimidated by the man. 'I'm just trying to do my job, Jim,' said Vincent. He heard his voice wavering and laughed to cover his embarrassment. It was a hollow laugh and Bamber continued to stare at him. Vincent took a drag at his cigarette. His hand was shaking and he dropped it to his side, not wanting Bamber to see the effect his stare was having on him. Reid watched them in the mirrored gantry.

'Okay, I guess I'd better be going,' said Vincent, taking a step back.

'Yeah, see you,' said Reid unenthusiastically.

Vincent waved to Reid's reflection, still backing away.

'Nice meeting you, Ted,' said Bamber. He smiled and the hardness faded from his eyes. He seemed suddenly friendlier, and when he stuck out his hand Vincent shook it. Bamber put his left hand on top of Vincent's as they shook. 'It's been a rough day,' said the FBI agent. 'I didn't mean to offend you.'

Vincent felt suddenly relieved, as if a snarling dog had begun wagging its tail. He smiled gratefully at the FBI agent. 'No offence taken, Jim.'

Len Kruse pressed the doorbell. It buzzed and a few seconds later the hall light went on. The door opened and Ted Vincent peered out. 'Jim?' he said.

Kruse grinned good naturedly. 'Hiya, Ted. I wanted to apologise for giving you a hard time earlier.'

The journalist ran a hand through his unruly hair. He was still wearing his suit but he'd removed his tie. 'No problem.' He frowned. 'How did you know where I lived?'

'Tommy Reid told me.'

'Tommy knows my address?'

'I guess so. Look, I had a long talk with Tommy, and he convinced me that we've more to gain by co-operating.'

'Co-operating?'

'On your article. I thought maybe we could do the interview tonight.'

Vincent looked at his watch. From upstairs a woman called. 'Who is it, Ted?'

'It's okay, it's for me,' he shouted. He shrugged apologetically at Kruse. 'My wife,' he explained. 'Can we do this tomorrow?'

Kruse gave him a pained look. 'No can do. I'm heading up to Manchester tomorrow morning.'

'What's in Manchester?'

'A lead on the tunnel killing.' Kruse shivered. 'Can I come in?'

The journalist opened the door. Kruse walked into the hall. He looked up the stairs. There was no sign of Vincent's wife. On the wall alongside the stairs hung dozens of framed newspaper articles and photographs of Vincent in several trouble spots. In one Vincent was standing in front of three blazing oil wells. 'Kuwait?' Kruse said, nodding at the photograph.

'Yeah, I was there during Desert Storm.'

'Must have been hell,' said Kruse.

'It was rough,' agreed Vincent.

Kruse nodded. He could have told Vincent a few stories about how rough it had really got in Kuwait. As a journalist covering the war, Vincent would have been fed the Allied line: smart missiles, clean kills, the antichrist as the enemy. It wasn't as clear cut as that, Kruse knew, but he wasn't there to enlighten Vincent. 'It must have been,' he said.

Vincent closed the door. Upstairs, the landing light clicked off. Kruse wondered if the wife had been listening. 'Through there,' said Vincent, pointing towards a door. Kruse pushed it open. It was a sitting room, large and airy with white walls, pine furniture and lots of potted plants, with wooden blinds on the windows. More framed articles and photographs hung on the walls. Modesty clearly wasn't one of Vincent's qualities. There was a wedding photograph on top of a big-screen television, Vincent in his twenties about to kiss a frightened blonde. He looked more like a vampire about to go for the throat than a just-married groom preparing to kiss his bride.

'Pretty girl,' said Kruse. There were no photographs of any children and no toys in the room. 'No kids?'

'Not yet,' said Vincent. 'Still trying. Fancy a drink?'

'No, thanks,' said Kruse. 'But don't let me stop you.'

Vincent nodded at a mug of coffee on a pine table next to a crystal ashtray in which a half-smoked cigarette smouldered among a dozen or so butts. 'I was having coffee. Do you want one?'

Kruse waved his hand dismissively. 'Never touch it,' he said.

'Can I tape our conversation?' asked Vincent. 'My shorthand's a bit rusty.'

'Sure.'

Vincent went over to a rack of shelves filled with paperback books. There was a small tape recorder on one of the shelves. Kruse pulled a pair of black leather gloves from his suit pocket. He slipped them on and walked quickly behind the journalist. He clamped his right hand over Vincent's mouth and gripped the man's throat with his left, applying pressure to the carotid arteries with his fingers and thumb. Vincent tried to turn but Kruse pushed him forward, taking care not to bang his head against the shelves. Vincent clawed at Kruse's gloves but his strength was already draining away as the brain began to feel the effects of the curtailed blood supply. Kruse was more than capable of crushing the man's windpipe with his left hand but he didn't want to do major damage. A post mortem wouldn't show up tissue damage, but broken cartilage or bones wouldn't be missed. It was a delicate balance, but it wasn't the first time that Kruse had choked a man to death, and he knew exactly how much pressure to apply. Too much and there'd be small haemorrhages under the skin and pinpricks of blood in the whites of the eyes.

Vincent's chest began to heave. He let go of Kruse's gloves and started to flail around with his arms. Kruse pulled him away from the bookshelves until they were standing in the centre of the room. Kruse shuffled to his right so that Vincent wouldn't hit the coffee table when he fell. He felt the journalist's legs begin to buckle, and watched in the mirror over the mantelpiece as Vincent's eyes fluttered and eventually closed. Kruse let him slide slowly to the ground, maintaining the pressure on the man's arteries all the way down.

Kruse lay down next to Vincent, his hands still around the man's neck. If he kept the grip on long enough Vincent would die from suffocation, but that wasn't what Kruse wanted. There had to be smoke in the lungs, and corpses didn't inhale. He stayed curled against Vincent like an attentive lover until he was satisfied that the journalist was unconscious, then he took his gloved hands away and stood up.

He listened intently, but the only sounds he could hear were the clicking of the water heater in the kitchen and the rustle of leaves outside. He walked on tiptoe to the foot of the stairs, then crept up them, keeping close to the wall so that the stairs wouldn't creak. Four doors led off the landing, but only one was ajar. Kruse peeked in. Vincent's wife was lying in bed, reading a paperback by the light of a table lamp. He pushed open the door and walked quickly across the plush pile carpet.

'Who was it?' she asked, still reading.

Kruse said nothing. He moved around the side of the bed. The curtains were drawn. The woman lowered the book. Her eyes widened in terror and she opened her mouth to scream, but before she could make a sound Kruse sat down on the bed and put his left hand across her mouth and nostrils. She dropped the book and clawed at his face but he grabbed both of her wrists with his right hand and forced her arms down. She struggled but she was no match for him. He straddled her on the bed, taking care not to bruise her flesh. The fire would probably obliterate all traces of tissue damage, but Kruse took a professional pride in his ability to kill without leaving marks. He pinned the woman's hands to her stomach, gripping with his thighs so that he could use his right hand on her neck. He found the carotids with his thumb and fingers, pushing in between the muscle to block off the blood supply. The woman kicked and bucked but Kruse was too heavy and strong. The brain held only enough oxygen for between ten and fifteen seconds, and she was soon unconscious. Kruse waited a further minute, to be absolutely sure, before climbing off the bed.

He put the woman's book on the bedside table, then went downstairs. He picked up Vincent and slung him effortlessly over his shoulder. Vincent was breathing heavily. Kruse knew from previous experience that the man would be unconscious for at least fifteen minutes. He carried him upstairs and lay him down on the bed before stripping off all the journalist's clothes. There was a raffia laundry basket under the window and Kruse dropped Vincent's shirt, underwear and socks into it. He took a wooden hanger from the wardrobe and hung up Vincent's suit. Kruse put the shoes Vincent had been wearing at the bottom of the wardrobe next to three other pairs. He closed the wardrobe door and looked around the room. The tie was downstairs, on the back of the sofa, but Kruse decided to leave it where it was. He quickly checked through the drawers of the dressing table and a cupboard, but there were no pyjamas. Vincent obviously slept in the nude, as did his wife.

Satisfied that everything was as it should be, Kruse rolled Vincent under the quilt, lying him on his back. He went downstairs and stood in the centre of the sitting room, checking that nothing was out of place. He went through to the kitchen and locked the back door. In the sink there was a pile of dirty dishes but Kruse figured that Vincent was the type who'd have left them until the morning.

He switched off the kitchen light and went back into the sitting room. The cigarette was still burning in the ashtray. Kruse picked up the ashtray and a box of matches that were lying on the coffee table and took them upstairs.

He knelt down by Vincent's side of the bed, then pulled the man's arm from underneath the quilt and slid the lit cigarette between the first and second fingers. After a final look around the bedroom to check that everything was as it should be, he took one of the matches out of the box and lit it. He held it against the quilt cover. It went out almost immediately. He lit a second match. This time the cotton quilt cover began to burn.

The fire spread quickly across the quilt. Kruse knew that the room with its wooden furniture, woollen carpet and cotton curtains would be an inferno within minutes. He switched off the light and went downstairs. He pulled the front door shut behind him and walked quickly down the street, his footsteps echoing in the night air.

Clive Edmunds stopped off at a video rental store in Camden High Street on his way home. He left his car on a double yellow line with his hazard warning lights flashing while he went inside. The girl behind the counter smiled, recognising him as a regular customer. 'Anything new come in?' he asked, heading for the new releases section.

'Not since you were last here,' she said. 'Well, there's another of them talking dog whatsits, but they're not really your thing, are they?'

'Bloody right,' said Edmunds, running his eyes along the video cases. He was an avid movie watcher and there was nothing on the shelves that he hadn't already seen or dismissed as not worth viewing. He pulled a face and went over to the action section. He fancied a good action movie, something with blood and guts. An early Schwarzenegger maybe, or a late Jean-Claude Van Damme. His eyes stopped at *Apocalypse Now*. It was the widescreen version, released after the film had won two Oscars in 1979, for Best Cinematography and Best Sound. It deserved more, Edmunds reckoned, but it was ahead of its time, before America was prepared to come to terms with Vietnam.

Edmunds turned the case over. On the back were two stills taken from the film, one of Marlon Brando, one of Martin Sheen. Edmunds scratched his bald spot. There was something at the back of his mind, something niggling him, that kept the video in his hands even though he'd seen it three times already, once on the big screen and twice on video. He tapped the video case against his forehead as he struggled to work out what it was about the movie that was troubling him, but the more he tried to concentrate, the more elusive the feeling became. It was like a mild case of *déjà vu*, but it wouldn't go away. He took the case over to the counter and handed it to the girl. 'I'll have this,' he said.

Len Kruse was in the middle of his third set of sit-ups when the telephone rang. He unlinked his fingers from behind his neck and reached over for the phone. 'Yes?' he said.

'Jim? It's Clive.'

Kruse got to his feet. 'Yes, Clive, what's up?' Kruse was bathed in sweat but there was no sign of strain in his voice. He stared at his reflection in the mirror on the front of the wardrobe. His face was a blank mask.

'What do you know about the Vietnam War?' asked Edmunds.

Kruse's face remained impassive. 'I know it's one we lost, Clive. What exactly do you have in mind?'

'Can you come around to my place now? There's something I want you to see.'

Kruse picked up a pen from the bedside table. 'Give me your address, Clive. I'll be right over.'

Nick Wright parked his car opposite May Eckhardt's flat and switched off the engine. He sat back in his seat, his hands gripping the steering wheel. He wasn't quite sure what he was doing. It was almost midnight. He should have been at home. Wright snorted. He didn't have a home any more, he thought ruefully. All he had was a sofabed in Tommy Reid's tiny flat. He looked across at the mansion block where May's apartment was. The lights were off and the curtains were open. The moon was reflected in the sitting-room window, glaring down at him like a single baleful eye. Wright wiped his hands on his face and then up through his hair. He'd actually been on his way home. Maida Vale was well out of his way, but he'd been struck by a sudden urge to see May Eckhardt.

May Eckhardt had been very much on his mind over the previous few days. He'd telephoned several times but there'd been no answer. There was something vulnerable about her, something that made Wright want to take care of her, to protect her from the world that had killed her husband. She was so different from his ex-wife.

Wright had never felt that Janie needing looking after, even when she was ill. Wright had once read in a magazine that couples were always referred to in order of dominance. He wasn't sure if it was true or not so he'd asked several of his friends and they'd all agreed that it was Janie and Nick. It had come as something of a shock because Wright had always felt that their marriage was a partnership of equals.

But the more he'd thought about it, the more he'd realised that when it came to making decisions, usually Janie got her way. She'd chosen the house, she'd had the final word on what car they bought, and it had been her decision to come off the pill when she did. They always talked through their problems, but it was always Wright who gave way. Because he loved her and she knew it.

He'd read in another magazine that the most successful marriages were where the husband loved the wife more than the wife loved the husband. Wright was living proof that the theory was flawed.

He wondered what May Eckhardt's marriage had been like. Had it been Max and May, or May and Max? He closed his eyes and rested his head on the back of the seat, trying to recall her face. Wright shivered. The car interior had cooled quickly with the engine off and he rubbed his arms, trying to keep warm. An old man wearing a raincoat and a flat cap walked by with a Yorkshire terrier on a bright red lead. He turned to look at Wright as he walked by. Wright smiled and gave him a small wave.

Wright looked up at the window again. The room was still in darkness. He checked the parked cars but there was no sign of her VW. Wright rubbed his chin. She didn't strike him as the sort who'd stay out late. He climbed out of his Fiesta and stretched, then locked the door and walked down the path towards the entrance to the mansion block. A light came on, presumably motion-activated because no one opened the front door. He ran his finger down the bell buttons, then frowned. The piece of cardboard with Eckhardt written on it had gone. He stared at the blank space under the bell, his forehead creased into a puzzled frown.

'Can I help you?' said a voice behind him.

Wright jumped as if he'd been poked in the ribs. He whirled around to see the man in the flat cap standing behind him, his dog cradled in his arms. The man was in his seventies and there was an aggressive tilt to his chin as if he suspected Wright of being up to no good. The dog yapped twice and the man put a hand on its muzzle to silence it.

'I'm a policeman,' said Wright, recovering his composure.

'Really,' said the man. 'Well, I'm with the Neighbourhood Watch and I've never seen you around here before.' The terrier struggled to escape the man's grip on its muzzle. 'Hush, Katie,' the man whispered.

'I suppose that's your guard dog,' said Wright good naturedly, but the joke fell flat.

The man tilted his chin higher. He was a small man, barely reaching Wright's shoulder, but he wasn't intimidated by Wright's relative youth or height. Wright had the feeling that he was a former boxer, and that if push came to shove he'd be prepared to take a swing at Wright, despite his age. Assuming he put the dog down first.

'I'd like to see your identification,' said the man.

'Sure,' said Wright. He reached into his inside pocket, took out his wallet, and opened it to show his warrant card and badge.

The man released his grip on his dog's muzzle and took the wallet. He stared at the warrant card as if committing it to memory. 'This says you're with the British Transport Police,' he said.

'That's right.'

The man compared the photograph on the card with

Wright's face, then handed it back. The dog growled softly. 'So you're not a real policeman, then?' he said.

Wright smiled tightly but said nothing.

'And who is it you're here to see, Sergeant Wright?'

'May Eckhardt,' said Wright. 'Flat four.'

The man smiled smugly. 'She's gone,' he said. 'Good thing too, the photographers were a bloody nuisance. Night and day, standing on the pavement, talking and laughing. Called the police but they said there was nothing they could do, they weren't trespassing.'

'Gone?'

'Moved out.'

'Do you know when?'

'Why? Is she a suspect now?'

'No, she's not a suspect, Mr . . .?'

'Jenkins,' said the man. 'I live in the flat below the Eckhardts.' He fished a key out of his raincoat pocket and Wright stepped aside so that he could unlock the door. 'Two days ago, that was when she left.'

'There's no "for sale" sign up,' said Wright.

'They rented,' said Jenkins.

'From who?'

'The landlord's a Mr Sadiq, I believe. Never met the man, though. He owns several flats in the area.' He pushed open the door and put down his terrier. It ran along the hallway and up a flight of stairs, its stub of a tail wagging furiously.

'I don't suppose you've got a telephone number for him, have you?' asked Wright.

The man shook his head, then pointed to a noticeboard on the wall. Several letters were pinned to it. 'The managing agents should be able to tell you. That's their address.'

Jenkins turned to follow the dog, but Wright asked him

if he could spare a few minutes. Jenkins looked at his wristwatch, then nodded.

'What sort of couple were they?' Wright asked.

Jenkins narrowed his eyes suspiciously. 'What do you mean?'

'I meant when they lived above you. Were they quiet? Did they argue?'

'Never heard a peep,' said Jenkins, taking off his hat and unbuttoning his raincoat. 'Hardly saw them. I was a bit worried when they first moved in, her being Chinese and all. I was a bit worried about the smell, you know?'

'The smell?'

'Cooking. Chinese food. The smell lingers, doesn't it? It was never a problem, though. Delightful girl. Spoke perfect English.'

'What about her husband?'

'Oh, he's American. Terrible English.'

'I meant what was he like?'

'A photographer. That's all I know. He liked jazz. I had to complain about the noise one Sunday, but generally they were perfect neighbours.' He looked at his watch again. 'Anyway, if there's nothing else, Sergeant Wright, I have to give my wife her medicine.'

Wright thanked him. Jenkins waited while he copied down the name and telephone number of the managing agent, then closed the door behind him.

Dean Burrow smiled at the office receptionist and wished her a good morning. He pushed through the glass door that led to his outer office and almost bumped into a black UPS deliveryman on his way out. Burrow held the door open for him and the deliveryman nodded his thanks.

'Good morning, Sally,' he said to his office manager. Sally Forster had been on his staff for more than fifteen years and was one of his most devoted staffers.

She looked up from the stack of mail on her desk and put a hand up to push her spectacles higher up her nose. 'Good morning, Senator,' she said brightly. A cigarette smouldered in a small brass ashtray. Sally smoked sixty cigarettes a day and the non-smoking members of staff had twice tried to declare the senator's office a no-smoking zone. They'd failed both times: Sally was as adept at office politics as she was at running the senator's diary.

'You work too hard, Sally,' said the senator. It was a common refrain. She generally put in a sixteen-hour day, and appeared to have no life outside the office.

She made a dismissive waving motion with her ringless left hand. 'Bullshit,' she said. 'If you want something doing . . .'

'And there's no one does it better than you,' said the senator. 'But you make me look bad by always getting in before me.'

She grinned slyly. 'I could give you an early morning alarm call, Senator.' She picked up her cigarette and inhaled.

Burrow chuckled. Sally was the only member of his staff who could get away with such teasing.

Burrow spotted a UPS document package on her desk and he twisted his neck to get a better look. It was from Bangkok. He reached for it but Sally beat him to it. 'It's not been scanned, Senator.'

'Who's it from?'

Sally read the waybill affixed to the package. 'Eric Horvitz. Bangkok, Thailand.'

Burrow felt a chill run down his spine. 'That's okay, I know Mr Horvitz,' he said.

She held the package out. 'You're sure that's his signature?'

Burrow didn't even look at the scrawl. 'Yes, don't worry, I've been expecting this.'

Sally let go of the package and Burrow took it. 'Coffee?' she asked.

Burrow shook his head. 'No, thanks. Maybe later.'

'There's a list of calls on your desk. And the *Washington Post* wants an interview. You've got a twenty-minute slot at three.'

'Three's fine. Who are they sending?'

'Jane Owen. With a photographer.'

Burrow nodded. 'Okay, go ahead and confirm. Better have Kimberly in to do my hair at two thirty.'

'Already booked,' said Sally.

Burrow acknowledged her mindreading ability with a slight nod and went through to his own office. He ripped open the package as he walked around his desk. There was only one thing inside – a Polaroid photograph.

Burrow stopped dead. For a second or two he felt faint and he reached out with his free hand to grip the desk. He stared at the image, his pulse pounding in his ears. It was almost identical to the previous Polaroid he'd received. A man, his flesh turned ghostly white, spreadeagled against a wall, shiny red blood smeared over his mouth and chest. Burrow narrowed his eyes as he looked at the face of the corpse. It had been more than a quarter of a century since he had last seen Eric Horvitz, but Burrow was reasonably sure that it was Horvitz in the photograph.

The senator dialled Jody Meacher's number and put the picture on to his blotter as the telephone rang. Meacher's answering machine cut in and Burrow left a brief message.

There was a discreet tap on his door as he replaced the receiver, and Sally popped her head in. 'Ready to go over your diary?' she asked.

Burrow opened the top right-hand drawer of his desk and tossed the photograph into it. 'Sure,' he said, closing the drawer and flashing his 'everything's all right with the world' smile. 'And I'll have that coffee now, too.'

There was an ambulance in the road outside Edmunds's house but the blue light wasn't flashing and the driver stood by the rear doors smoking a cigarette. Two police cars were parked on the opposite side of the road, both empty. Gerry Hunter climbed out of his car and locked the door. A group of housewives huddled together on the pavement, staring over the hedge at the front door. An old woman in a faded housecoat and slippers saw him coming and Hunter heard her say 'CID'. They all turned to watch him walk towards the gate.

'Isn't there something on television you could be watching?' shouted Hunter bitterly. One of the women had the decency to blush, but the rest were unfazed by his outburst. 'Go on, piss off!' he said.

One old woman tut-tutted and Hunter had a sudden urge to push her over the hedge, or better still to drag her into the house so that she could see for herself what was inside. Maybe if she came face to face with a few corpses she wouldn't be so keen to gawp. Hunter glared at her so aggressively that she took a step backwards.

He pushed his way through the onlookers and walked briskly down the path to the front door. It was ajar and he pushed it open with his foot. A uniformed constable was there, picking his nose. 'Get those people out of here!' Hunter barked. 'This is a crime scene, not a circus.' The constable opened his mouth but before he could speak Hunter cut him short with a warning finger. 'Just do it,' he said. 'Where's the body?'

'Upstairs, sir,' said the constable.

'Doctor?'

'She's there already, sir.' The constable edged past Hunter and out of the front door. Hunter closed it.

A second uniform came out of the sitting room, this one a sergeant. Hunter recognised him. 'Hiya, Mick,' said Hunter.

'Gerry. Have you been upstairs?'

'Not yet. What's the story?'

'Choked on his own vomit by the look of it.'

'Jesus.' Hunter walked through to the sitting room and looked around. He'd spent many an hour in that room, drinking and watching Sky Sport with his partner, their feet propped up on the coffee table. It was a comfortable room, a man's room, with cigarette burns on most of the furniture, and irregular-shaped stains on the brown carpet. Edmunds had never been married and his house was a female-free sanctuary for his friends and colleagues.

'Nothing suspicious?'

Mick shook his head. 'Made himself a snack and drank the best part of a bottle of whisky.'

Hunter rubbed his jaw. Edmunds was a heavy drinker, though he tended to drink in company rather than on his own. 'No visitors?'

'Doesn't look like it. Just the one glass.'

Hunter sighed. He wasn't sure if he'd have been happier if there had been suspicious circumstances. Dead was dead, when all was said and done. 'Okay, cheers, Mick. I'll go up and see the doc.'

Hunter went slowly upstairs, holding on to the banister as if afraid that he'd lose his balance. A third uniformed officer was in the bedroom, standing at the window and staring down at the street. He turned as Hunter walked into the bedroom. It was Sandy Peters, an old friend of Hunter's. They'd joined the force at the same time, and despite the fact that Peters had remained a constable while Hunter had risen relatively quickly through the ranks, they were still firm friends.

'Hiya, Gerry,' said Peters.

'Sandy. Thanks for the call.'

Dr Anna Littman was bending over the bed, examining the body. She nodded a greeting to Hunter.

Peters walked over to Hunter. 'Yeah, they said it was your day off, but I thought . . .' He shrugged, not sure what to say.

'I'm glad you did,' said Hunter.

'I'm sorry,' said Peters. 'He was a good guy.'

'Yeah. I know. Who found the body?'

'Me. His car was giving him trouble and I was going to pick him up from the garage. He didn't turn up so I came here. The curtains were drawn and I thought maybe he'd overslept. Tried his mobile, no answer.'

'How did you get in?'

'Broke a back window. I'll have it fixed.' He fiddled with his tunic. 'I'd better go downstairs, check that everything's sorted.'

Hunter nodded. He patted Peters on the arm as he went by.

Dr Littman stood up and draped the quilt over Edmunds's body. 'I'm sorry, Gerry.'

'Yeah,' said Hunter.

'You'd worked together for quite a while?'

'Three years. Give or take.' Hunter walked over to the window. Outside, the young constable was shepherding the neighbours away. 'What do they expect to see?' asked Hunter. The doctor didn't answer. 'What happened, Anna?'

'Choked on his own vomit. You'd be surprised how often it happens, Gerry. A lot of drunks . . .' She walked up behind him and put a hand on his shoulder. 'I'm sorry. I didn't mean that Clive was . . . you know what I mean.' She squeezed his shoulder gently. 'Are you okay?'

'It's such a stupid way to die,' said Hunter quietly. 'If he'd been on duty, if he'd been shot . . .'

'Then you'd have a murder to investigate. You'd be ablc to do something.'

Hunter sighed. 'Yeah, I guess that's it.'

'It's your day off, isn't it? Go home.'

'Yeah, and drink something sweet. A nice hot cup of tea. I know the routine.' He closed his eyes and massaged the bridge of his nose. 'I'm sorry, Anna. I didn't mean to snap.'

'I could give you something . . .'

Hunter shook his head. 'I'll be okay. I'll have to go and see his mother. She'll have to be told. Jesus, what do I tell her? He choked on cheese on toast?'

'Just say he died suddenly in his sleep. There's no need to go into details.'

'They always want details,' said Hunter.

The doctor took her hand away from Hunter's shoulder. 'Do you want a copy of the post mortem report?'

'Not unless there's anything unusual.'

'There won't be, Gerry. I'm sorry.' She went back to the bed and picked up her medical bag. 'Come on,' she said. 'Come downstairs with me.'

Hunter continued to stare out of the window. 'Just give me a few minutes,' he said.

He waited until she'd left the room before going over to the bed. He stared down at the bump in the quilt and reached out his hand, but then changed his mind. He didn't want to see his partner's corpse, he wanted to remember him as he had been. 'You stupid, stupid, bastard,' he whispered. Tears filled his eyes and he wiped them away with his sleeve.

Tommy Reid unscrewed the cap off his bottle of vodka and poured slugs into two polystyrene cups of coffee. He handed one to Nick Wright. 'Congratulations, partner,' he said.

They bashed their cups together and toasted each other.

'Never thought we'd get the bastard,' said Wright.

'All things come to him who waits,' said Reid, drinking his coffee and smacking his lips.

The mugger who had escaped from Wright during the undercover operation had finally been caught and was safely under lock and key in a custody suite at Edbury Bridge, the BTP's area headquarters. He'd almost killed an old man on the Victoria Line with his stun gun but had been overpowered by a group of rugby players on their way home from a training game. They'd almost broken one of the mugger's legs and blacked both eyes before handing him over to the British Transport Police. Reid and Wright had been over to identify him as the mugger they'd pursued through Paddington. It was definitely him – he was wearing the same motorcycle jacket. They'd left him screaming obscenities and threatening to sue the rugby players for assault.

Wright would have preferred to have caught the man himself, but he was happy to settle for second best. He sipped his spiked coffee and swung his feet up on to the desk.

'Hey, Nick, did you get the box?' called Dave Hubbard.

'Box? What box?'

Hubbard pointed over at the far corner of the CID office. 'Came first thing this morning.'

Wright pushed himself up out of his chair and went over to the large cardboard box and knelt down beside it.

'Not ticking, is it?' shouted Reid.

It had been delivered by a courier firm and Wright studied the documentation stuck to the top of the box. 'It's from my ex-wife,' he said.

'Bloody hell, it probably is a bomb!' shouted Reid. He

and Hubbard giggled like a couple of schoolboys and Wright scowled across at them.

He pulled open the box. Inside were pieces of model railway track and more than a dozen small parcels swathed in bubble-wrap. He picked one of them up and carefully unwrapped it. It was a green and black model steam engine.

'You bitch, Janie,' said Wright under his breath. Stuck into the side of the box was an envelope. Wright opened it, read it, and ripped it in half.

Reid walked over and looked down into the box. 'A train set?'

'Brilliant deduction,' said Wright sourly.

Reid knelt down and picked up the model locomotive. 'Beautiful,' he said.

'My dad's,' said Wright. 'It was in the loft. Janie's had a clear-out.'

'Must be worth a bit?'

'Probably.' He stood up and went over to his desk. He picked up the phone and banged out Janie's number. She answered after half a dozen rings. 'Janie, what the hell are you playing at?'

'I don't know what you mean.'

'The train set.'

'Good. It arrived, did it?'

'That's for Sean. You know I gave it to him.'

'Sean doesn't want it. He's too old to play with trains.'

'He's seven.'

'Exactly. Anyway, he doesn't want it. It was just cluttering up the attic.'

'That's what attics are for, to be cluttered up.'

'I'm having it converted,' she said. 'Into a sewing room.'

'Hell's bells, Janie. I wanted Sean to have it.'

'He doesn't want it.'

'Can I speak to him?'

'He's at school.'

'I'll call later.'

'If you like.' She hung up.

'Bitch!' shouted Wright. He slammed the phone down.

'Ex-wives, huh,' sympathised Reid. 'What can you do with them?' He leaned forward conspiratorially. 'I've got an idea.'

'What?'

'Why don't you kill mine, and I'll kill yours. Like in *Strangers On A Train*. The Hitchcock movie.'

Wright shook his head in disgust. As far as he was concerned, his ex-wife's vindictiveness was no laughing matter.

Phil Evans walked over, grim faced. 'Hey, did you guys hear about Clive Edmunds?'

'Yeah? What did he do?' asked Reid. 'Break the habit of a lifetime and buy a round?'

'He's dead, Tommy.'

Reid's face fell. 'Shit. What happened?'

'Choked on his vomit. Died in his sleep.'

'Bloody hell.' Reid looked across at Wright. 'Better make sure I kip on my stomach from now on.'

Evans glared at Reid. 'Gerry Hunter's been on the phone. The funeral's next Friday. The Super thinks we should be represented.'

'Is Newton going?' asked Wright.

'Nah. Budget meeting with Railtrack. Can either of you two make it?'

Reid and Wright shook their heads.

'Great, that makes a grand total of zero so far. At this rate I'm going to have to go myself.'

'Well, it's his own fault for being such an unlikeable bastard,' said Reid.

'Come on, Tommy, he's dead,' said Evans.

'I'll go,' said Wright.

'You sure?' asked Evans.

'Yeah. He was a cop, he deserves to have someone there from the office.'

'Cheers, Nick. I'll get the details for you.' He went over to ask Hubbard and Lloyd.

'I can't make you out,' said Reid. 'You hated him. He was forever taking the piss out of you.'

Wright shrugged. 'Professional courtesy.'

'You're a soft bastard.'

'Yeah, maybe you're right.'

Reid sipped his coffee. He groaned. 'Okay, you can stop looking at me like that.'

Wright raised an eyebrow. 'Like what?'

'Like a puppy that wants to go for a walk. Okay, I'll come with you. Just don't expect me to throw myself on the coffin.'

'You're a soft bastard, too,' said Wright, grinning.

Reid leaned forward. 'Maybe. But if you tell anyone, I'll kill you.'

Gerald Manville rolled over on to his back and stared up at the ceiling fan which was doing its best to keep the air circulating in the windowless room. He raised his arm and looked at his wristwatch. He'd booked the room for two hours and he still had fifteen minutes left. He dropped his arm and groaned. It was his fifth day in Pattaya and he was exhausted. Sun, sea, sand and sex – Thailand was the perfect holiday destination, especially for a man with needs like Manville's. Three times a year he flew over to the Land of Smiles, to enjoy the sort of sex he could only dream of back in Plymouth. He had hit the bars within hours of getting off the plane from Heathrow, and since then the days and nights had blurred into one long session of sex and drink, with the occasional visit to a restaurant for food.

He turned on to his side and ran his finger down the silky smooth back of the figure next to him. Thai skin was so unbelievably soft, like silk. Manville kissed the boy between the shoulderblades, revelling in the salty taste of the thirteen-year-old skin. He felt himself grow hard again but he hadn't the inclination to start something he didn't have time to finish. They'd soon be knocking on his door to let him know that his time was up.

He patted the boy on the hip and went over to the shower. He rinsed himself clean and wrapped a threadbare white towel around his waist. When he went back into the bedroom, the boy was already dressed in a T-shirt and shorts and was sitting on the edge of the bed. Manville picked up his jeans and pulled out his wallet. He gave the boy a five-hundred-baht note. The boy smiled and put his hands together in a 'wai' of thanks, bowing as if he was saying his prayers, then he scampered over to the door and rushed out.

Manville smiled to himself as he dressed. He loved

Thailand. He loved the food, he loved the climate, and he loved the boys. He had another six years before he could retire from his job on a halfway decent pension, then he'd be on the first plane out with a one-way ticket. He'd have more than enough money to rent a small house with a garden, close to the beach, to run a car and to buy himself all the companionship he needed. Six more years. It seemed like a lifetime.

He checked himself in the bathroom mirror, then left the room. The door opened out on to a small concrete area across which a thick purple curtain had been drawn. Many of the customers at the short-time hotel arrived in cars, and the curtain hid their vehicles from prying eyes. Manville had walked from the nearby bar so he put his hands in his pockets and strolled out into the sunshine. Two chambermaids in blue uniforms giggled as they hurried by with a cart piled high with sheets and towels.

Manville decided he'd have a drink on the beach before heading back to his own hotel. He walked along the narrow street that led to the beach road, shading his eyes from the bright afternoon sun with the flat of his hand. Two Thai boys sitting on a low wall smiled up at him hopefully. Manville had already been with one of the boys, but he didn't recognise the other. Neither was much older than fourteen. Manville arranged to meet them both later that night and gave them each a one-hundred-baht note to seal the deal. Both boys gave him a formal 'wai' and he was almost tempted to go back to the short-time hotel with them there and then.

He crossed the road and walked down on to the beach, where Manville bought a copy of the *Bangkok Post* from a newspaper vendor. Spread out across the vendor's table were a number of Thai newspapers, and several had photographs of a corpse splashed across them. The Thai newspapers were even worse than their British counterparts when it came to running blood and gore. Manville bent over the table to get a better look.

The largest of the photographs was of a light-skinned bearded man, his mouth a bloody mass and his eyes staring lifelessly at the camera lens. It looked as if the man was lying on his back, but as he looked more closely Manville realised that he was actually spreadeagled against a wall and that the picture had been twisted around for reasons of space. There was something familiar about the corpse. Not the face, but the injuries and the position of the body.

Manville frowned and gathered up copies of all the papers that carried the photograph, paid the vendor and went across the sand to a row of deckchairs. He sat down under a faded red and yellow striped umbrella and spread the Thai newspapers over the sand. An old Thai woman with skin like an old leather briefcase came over and asked him what he wanted to drink. Manville asked for a Singha beer, his eyes fixed on the newspapers. He flicked through one. There were more photographs on the inside pages. In one of them, a playing card was impaled on the victim's chest. Manville lifted the paper up and stared at the card. He couldn't make out what it was.

'Hello, Jack,' said a voice.

Manville looked up. It was Poonsak, an eighteen-year-old Thai boy whom Manville had known for several years. Poonsak knew him as Jack, as did most of the underage boys whom Manville took back to the short-time hotel. Poonsak had grown too old for most of the sex-tourists who visited Pattaya, and now made a living procuring younger boys.

'Hello, Poonsak. Come here, will you?' Poonsak squatted down next to Manville's deckchair. 'Translate this for me, please.' Manville tapped the headline and story around the picture of the brutalised corpse.

Poonsak put his head on one side as he read through the story. 'It say farang was killed. Someone cut him, very bad.' He looked up but saw from Manville's face that he expected more. He looked down at the paper again and tugged at his lower lip as he read. 'His name is Eric Horvitz. He's an American. He had a place for children with no parents.'

'An orphanage?'

'Yes. An orphanage. He was found in the *haung tai din*. The basement. The basement of the orphanage. He was tortured, with knives. Somebody cut off his dick and put it in his mouth.' Poonsak pulled a face. He peered at the photograph as if to confirm that that was indeed what had been done to the man, and grimaced.

'What does it say about the playing card?'

Poonsak read through the article. 'An ace of spades. It was stuck on a knife that had been stuck into his chest. Police say they think it was maybe a drugs killing.'

'Why do they say that?'

Poonsak read more, then shook his head. 'It not say, Jack.'

'When did it happen?'

'The body was found yesterday. They not know when he was killed.'

Manville flicked through the *Bangkok Post*. The English-language newspaper was generally less salacious than its Thai rivals. It seldom printed gory photographs and tended to hold back on the details of murders and rapes. He found the murder story on page three, with no photograph. There were only a dozen paragraphs giving details of the victim and his orphanage. The playing card was mentioned right at the end of the story, but no significance was attributed to it.

'Did you know him?' asked Poonsak.

The old lady brought Manville's beer to him on a battered tray. He took it and smiled his thanks. The woman gave him an ice-cold wet towel and he wiped his face and neck before handing it back to her with another smile.

'No,' said Manville. 'No, I didn't know him.'

Poonsak stood up, brushing sand from the knees of his jeans. 'Do you want me to get you a friend tonight? I know a new boy, only just arrived in Pattaya. Almost a virgin.'

Manville chuckled. According to Poonsak, virtually every boy he supplied was as pure as the driven snow. 'No, thank you, Poonsak. I'm fixed up tonight.'

Poonsak smiled. Manville patted him on the back of the leg. He really was a delightful boy. Pity he'd grown so quickly. Poonsak's smile widened and Manville realised he'd misunderstood the gesture. Manville shook his head and took away his hand. The teenager shrugged and wandered away towards a group of Scandinavian tourists who were paddling in the surf.

Manville gathered up the newspapers. He knew now why the photographs had seemed familiar. There'd been a similar murder back in England a month or so previously. A circular had passed across Manville's desk from a British Transport Police detective describing a torture-killing in South London and requesting details of any similar murders. Manville had drawn a blank and had replied on behalf of the Devon and Cornwall Constabulary. There had been several vicious drugs-related killings in Plymouth but the injuries didn't match those of the London murder, and no playing cards were involved.

Manville began tearing out the articles. He'd put them in the post when he got back to the UK. That'd be the best and safest way of passing on the information. He didn't want to have to explain why an unmarried chief inspector was holidaying alone in Thailand.

Dean Burrow walked across the grass, his hands thrust deep into the pockets of his cashmere overcoat. Over to his right two Secret Service agents stood by a nondescript saloon parked behind his limousine. A third agent walked some distance behind him. Washington at night wasn't the safest of cities, but Burrow had wanted some fresh air and the Memorial was as good a place as any to meet Jody Meacher. Sirens wailed in the distance, three police cars by the sound of it. Burrow shivered. It was a full moon but he only saw glimpses of it as thick grey clouds scudded across the night sky. He stepped on to the cobbled path that led down to the Memorial and walked by the metal lecterns containing the books listing all those who had died during the Vietnam War. Not long after the slabs of black marble had been erected, Burrow had spent hours poring over the books, checking that the names of the friends he'd lost during the war were included, then he'd gone to the Memorial and satisfied himself that their names were carved there and that they'd been spelled correctly. There had been no omissions, no mistakes.

The black marble glistened in what little moonlight managed to filter through the clouds. It was the simplicity of the Memorial that made it so effective. Just a list of names. Burrow wondered what the tourists made of it, the Europeans and the Asians and the Arabs who came to photograph it because it was on the list of things to see in Washington, a ten-minute stop on a tour of the nation's capital. To them it could be nothing more than a list of names, but to Burrow and to the rest of the nation's veterans, it was something far more poignant, far more meaningful. It represented legs blown off by landmines, heads splattered by snipers' bullets, chests crushed by exploding mortars. Countless images of dismemberment and death flashed through Burrow's mind as he walked past the marble slabs and their silent roll call.

A lone figure stood midway down the Memorial. There was no mistaking Jody Meacher's massive profile, swathed in a dark overcoat the size of a small tent. Meacher continued to stare at the Memorial as Burrow approached. 'What a waste,' he said.

'The war, or the Memorial?' asked Burrow.

'The deaths,' said Meacher.

'What would you have done, Jody? Negotiated?'

Meacher shook his head. 'Who knows, Senator? Twenty-twenty hindsight is a wondrous thing. What's past is past. It's the future we have to be concerned about.'

He held out his hand, his eyes still on the Memorial. Burrow reached inside his coat and took out the Polaroid photograph with a gloved hand and gave it to Meacher. Meacher studied it for several seconds, then pocketed it. Burrow opened his mouth to protest but Meacher shook his head.

'Leave it with me, Senator.' His hand reappeared from his pocket and he stroked his greying beard thoughtfully. 'Eric Horvitz, you said?'

'That was the name on the UPS package. And it's him in the photograph. Whoever it is, they're not going to stop, Jody. They're going to keep—'

'It's going to stop, Senator,' interrupted Meacher. 'Don't worry.'

The Secret Service agent who was following the senator had stopped some fifty feet away, though his head still swivelled from side to side and periodically he mumbled into his hidden microphone.

Burrow arched his back and rubbed his knuckles into the base of his spine. 'I should get more exercise,' he complained.

'We all should,' agreed Meacher. 'But we don't always do what's good for us.'

Burrow began to walk along the path, and Meacher fell into step beside him.

'The Vice President will be stepping down within weeks, Senator.'

Burrow's eyebrows shot up and he stopped walking. 'You know that for sure?'

'From the horse's mouth. Well, the horse's doctor's mouth. The cancer is growing faster than they'd thought and the Vice President wants to spend more time with his family.'

'Jesus,' said Burrow, shaking his head sadly.

'Don't feel too sorry for the man, Senator. At least he knows it's coming; at least he's got time to put his affairs in order and say goodbye properly. Most of us don't get the chance.'

Burrow began walking again. 'I was at Kristine Ross's funeral today,' he said.

'It had to be done, Senator. There's too much at stake.'

'I know, I know.' They walked in silence for a while, their breath feathering in the night air. 'How many so far?' Burrow asked eventually.

'Four. Including your secretary.'

'Who were the other three?'

Meacher hesitated as if reluctant to answer the question, then shrugged almost imperceptibly. 'A journalist and his wife. And a policeman.'

Burrow put a hand up to his forehead. 'A policeman? Oh God.'

'Policeman, secretary, dental hygienist, their career path doesn't make any difference, Senator. All that matters is that this doesn't get out. The policeman was getting close.'

'How were they killed?'

'Need to know, Senator. And you don't need to know.'

'That may be, Jody. But I want to know.'

'It's not in your best interest.'

'Damn you,' hissed Burrow. 'I deserve to know. He's doing it for me.'

The two men stopped walking again. Meacher stared at Burrow for several seconds, then nodded. 'It was an accident,' he said. 'I mean it was made to look like an accident. No one will ever know different.'

'And it was the same guy who killed Kristine?' Meacher nodded. 'Who is he, this man?'

Meacher turned away from the senator and began walking towards the Secret Service agent. The agent mumbled into his hidden microphone and headed back along the path. 'That really *is* need to know,' said Meacher.

'At least tell me something about him.'

'He was in Special Forces. His specialty was to make his assassinations look like accidents. Falls, car crashes, food poisoning. Now he works for me and a few other individuals who have need of his particular skills.'

The senator looked incredulous. 'The army has people like that?'

'Hopefully you'll never know half of what goes on in the military,' said Meacher. 'There are black departments in the Pentagon that answer to no one. Not even the President.'

'So how does this guy end up working for you?'

'A friend of his was killed in Saudi Arabia. Iranian suicide bomber, remember? Killed a dozen Marines.'

'I remember.'

'This guy found one of the men who'd planned the operation and tortured him until he gave up the names of the other two men in his cell. Then he doctored their car, fixed it so it'd crash when it hit sixty miles an hour. Worked perfectly, but when the car spun out of control it crashed into a Mercedes being driven by a member of the Saudi royal family. A prince. The prince ended up in hospital with a broken back. The military pulled their man out and sent him back to the States.

'How much have you told him?'

'The bare minimum to ensure that he gets the job done, Senator.'

They left the memorial behind and walked by the lecterns. The Secret Service agent was now off to their left. 'And what is his job, Jody?'

'His instructions are to take care of anyone who discovers your secret. It's open ended.'

'So he'll go to Bangkok?'

'Once we're sure that the London situation is under control, yes.'

They walked by the bronze sculpture of three war-weary American soldiers. 'What if whoever it is comes after me, Jody?'

'You're a US senator. You're well protected.'

'So why am I being sent these pictures?'

'To scare you.'

'It's working.' They walked together back to the road. 'Can I give you a lift, Jody?' asked Burrow, nodding at his limousine.

'No, thank you, Senator. I'm going to walk for a while.'

'Are you sure? Washington's a dangerous place at night.'

Meacher smiled thinly. 'Not just at night time, Senator.' The two men shook hands, then Meacher walked away as gracefully as a galleon under full sail.

Nick Wright lay on the folded-out sofabed, staring up at the ceiling. It had been one hell of a day. In between handling his regular caseload, his efforts to track down May Eckhardt had come to nothing. Neither the managing agents nor the owner of the Maida Vale flat had had a forwarding address for her. He'd contacted British Telecom but an extensive search hadn't produced a new telephone number for a May Eckhardt anywhere within the United Kingdom. He'd spent the best part of two hours trying to obtain a

National Insurance number or tax reference for her, but without success. He wasn't sure what else he could do.

He sat up and ran his hands through his unkempt hair. The cardboard box containing his late father's train set was by the side of the sofa. Wright had tried to speak to Sean on the phone more than a dozen times but Janie had insisted that he wasn't at home. First he was at school, then at piano practice, then at a friend's house. After nine o'clock in the evening all he got was the engaged tone. Janie had left the phone off the hook.

Clive Edmunds's funeral had taken place late in the afternoon, and it had been a depressing affair, hardly better attended than the funeral of Max Eckhardt. Wright and Reid had represented the British Transport Police, and there had been a dozen Met officers, including Gerry Hunter. There had been no relatives, and no grieving widow.

Wright swung his legs off the sofabed and went over to the stereo. He put a Muddy Waters CD on and turned the volume down so as not to disturb Reid in the adjoining bedroom. His harmonica was on the shelf above the CDs and he stood by the fireplace, playing softly. He figured that if he was feeling depressed, he might as well play the blues.

Len Kruse was midway through his second set of press-ups when the telephone rang. He locked his elbows. Naked except for his khaki boxer shorts, his body was bathed in sweat, though his breathing was steady, his chest barely moving. He supported his weight with his right arm and reached over with his left to pick up the telephone from the bedside table. 'Yes?' he said.

'Are you alone?' It was Jody Meacher.

'Yes.' Kruse lowered himself so that his chest was only inches from the carpet. His arm muscles bulged but there was no sign of strain on his face.

'There's been another event,' said Meacher. 'In Bangkok.'

Kruse pushed himself up until his arm was rigid. 'Can you send me details?'

'You'll have them tomorrow. Have things stabilised in London?'

'Everything's under control. I'll book my ticket.'

'It might be a good idea to get a visa for Vietnam while you're in London. Just in case.'

'Agreed.' Kruse replaced the receiver and continued his press-ups, increasing the pace until the muscles in his arm began to burn. The pain didn't bother Kruse. In fact, he welcomed it.

Gerry Hunter parked his car as close as he could get to Clive Edmunds's house. None of the houses in the street had garages, and it was early evening so he had to walk almost a hundred yards to the front door. Hunter had been surprised on two fronts when the solicitor had telephoned: surprised that Clive had actually made a will, and even more surprised that he'd made Hunter joint executor of it.

For a man whose life appeared to be in a constant state of disorganisation, Clive had organised his death down to the last detail. He'd even paid for a burial plot in a graveyard in North London and listed the hymns that he wanted to be played at his funeral. He had a hefty mortgage on his house, but even so, his assets, including two life insurance policies, came to more than a hundred and fifty thousand pounds, the bulk of which he'd left to his three nieces in Australia. The will stipulated that Hunter take anything from the house that he wanted and arrange to have the rest sold or given to Oxfam.

Hunter had put off going there for as long as he could, but the solicitor had called to say that a buyer had been found for the house so Clive's belongings had to be cleared out. He slotted the key into the lock and pushed open the door. The air was stale and Hunter grimaced. He closed the door behind him and stood in silence for several minutes. The red light on the answering machine was blinking and Hunter realised that he'd forgotten to have the telephone disconnected. He pushed the 'play' button. It was a girl from a local video rental store, asking Clive to return a video. *Apocalypse Now*.

Hunter went through into the sitting room and knelt down in front of Clive's video recorder. He rifled through the cassettes stacked on top of the recorder but most of them were tapes that Clive had recorded himself. There was no sign of *Apocalypse Now*. He pressed the 'eject' button on the video recorder but no tape emerged from the slot. Hunter drummed his fingers on the top of the machine and looked around the room. He stood up. His fingertips were smeared with dust and he wiped them on the back of the sofa. He checked the sideboard, the bookcase, and the cupboard on which

Edmunds kept framed photographs of his parents and his brother's family. There was no videotape.

He went back into the hall and replayed the message. The girl didn't say which shop she worked for, but a quick flick through the *Yellow Pages* turned up four within half a mile. The third one that Hunter called had Clive down as a member and the man who answered the phone confirmed that he hadn't returned the video.

'There's a big fine,' said the man gruffly. 'And it's growing by two quid a day.'

'When did he take it out?' Hunter asked.

'Ten days ago.'

Hunter counted backwards in his head. 'Thursday?'

'Yeah. Thursday.'

Thursday was the day Clive died. 'Are you sure?'

'Of course I'm sure, it's all on computer. Now when am I going to get it back?'

'I'll see if I can find it for you,' said Hunter.

'Why can't Mr Edmunds tell you where it is?'

'Because Mr Edmunds is dead,' said Hunter, and slammed down the receiver.

He took Clive's keyring out of his pocket. His car keys were on it. Hunter tossed them in the air and caught them. Maybe Clive had left the cassette in his car. He went outside and found the car but there was no sign of the video cassette. Hunter went back to the house and sat down on the sofa with his feet on the coffee table, deep in thought. Assuming Clive had come straight home with the video, and assuming he'd watched it before going to bed, then the cassette should still be in the house. And if it wasn't, then somebody else must have taken it. But there were no signs of a break-in, and any self-respecting burglar would have taken the television and video recorder. Hunter couldn't imagine why anyone would want to steal a rental copy of *Apocalypse Now* and nothing else.

Wright put two cups of coffee down in front of his partner and blew on his fingers. 'That coffee's getting hotter and hotter,' he said. He picked up his own cup again and carried it over to his desk. A large white envelope was propped up on his computer terminal.

'I got your mail for you,' said Reid.

'You're all heart,' said Wright. He sat down, sipped his coffee, and picked up the envelope.

Reid looked across at the envelope in Wright's hands. 'What is it, a birthday card? It's not your birthday, is it?'

'No,' said Wright, ripping it open.

Wright pulled out the contents of the envelope. It was a collection of newspaper cuttings. He spread them out. Most of them were in a strange language, the letters totally different to the English alphabet with hardly any spaces between words. 'What the hell's this?' he muttered.

Reid stood up and peered over at the pieces of newspaper. 'What is it, Indian? Arabic?'

'No idea,' said Wright. Several of the cuttings had grainy photographs on them. Photographs of a corpse. Wright looked carefully at the pictures. 'My God,' he said. 'Look at this, Tommy.'

Reid hauled himself out of his chair and stood behind Wright. He looked down over his shoulder.

Wright pointed at one of the photographs. 'It's a playing card,' said Wright.

'Is it an ace of spades?' asked Reid.

Wright held the cutting closer to his face. 'I can't tell.' He handed it to his partner. 'What do you think?'

As Reid scrutinised the picture, Wright picked up the only cutting that was in English. It had been cut out to include the name of the newspaper and the date. The *Bangkok Post*. Twelve days ago.

'Thailand,' said Wright. 'They're Thai newspapers.' He picked up the envelope. The postmark was Plymouth.

'I can't see what card it is,' said Reid. He picked up another of the cuttings.

Wright scanned the *Bangkok Post* article. 'It's the same,' he said.

'What's the same?'

'A man in his forties, tortured and killed. His dick cut off and shoved in his mouth.' He reached the last paragraph. 'And impaled in his chest . . . an ace of spades.'

Reid stepped back theatrically. 'Coincidence? I think not!' he boomed.

Wright glared at his partner. 'Come on, Tommy. This is important.'

Reid went back to his desk. 'It's Thailand, Nick. It's the other side of the world. What do you think's going on? A serial killer who's collecting frequent-flyer miles?'

Wright waved the cutting in the air. 'It's the same man. He's killed twice. And he's going to kill again.'

'You don't know that.'

Wright stood up. 'There are times when you really piss me off,' he said coldly. Reid shrugged and sipped his coffee. Wright wanted to say more but he could see that he'd be wasting his time. He stormed off, the cutting clutched in his right hand.

Newton's secretary looked up from her typing as Wright walked up to the door to the superintendent's office. 'Yes, Nick, is there something I can do for you?' she asked.

Wright stopped dead. 'I have to see him, Nancy.'

'He's in a meeting,' she said.

'When will he be free?'

She looked at him over the top of her gold-framed glasses. 'I don't know,' she said. 'Would you like me to call you when he is?'

Wright looked at the cutting, then at the closed door. 'I'll wait,' he said.

'Nick, I don't know how long he's going to be.'

'I'll wait,' he repeated.

There were three hard-backed chairs against the wall facing Nancy's desk. Wright sat on the middle one. Nancy continued to watch him for several seconds, then she pushed her glasses higher up her nose with her forefinger and resumed her typing. Wright reread the cutting as he waited. The victim was an American, Eric Horvitz. He ran an orphanage in Bangkok and he'd been discovered in the basement. There weren't many details of what had been done to the body, but what there were tallied with the corpse that had been found in the tunnel near Battersea.

The door to Newton's office opened and two men wearing suits and carrying briefcases walked out. Wright stood up but the door closed firmly. He looked across at Nancy expectantly, who gave an impatient wave of her hand.

'Go on, go on,' she said.

'Thanks, Nancy,' said Wright. He knocked on the door and opened it without waiting for a reply.

The superintendent was dipping a biscuit into his cup of tea and he looked up guiltily. As he did so, half of the biscuit broke off. Newton stared distastefully at the cup. 'Yes, Nick?'

'Sir, I've had a lead on the tunnel murder.' He gave the cutting to Newton.

The superintendent took a pair of reading glasses from his shirt pocket and put them on. He read the cutting, grimaced, and gave it back to Wright. 'So?'

'So I was right. It's a serial killer.'

'No, Nick. It's two similar murders, five thousand miles apart.'

'Both with an ace of spades left on the corpse? Come on, sir. It's the same killer. It has to be. Sir, this is a break. I want to follow it up.'

'Nick, the simple fact is, we just don't have the resources to pursue this lead. We answer to different masters here, masters who are ultimately responsible to shareholders. It's all about money, Nick. I'm sorry, but that's the way it is.'

'So profits come before justice?'

'That's not what I'm saying,' said Newton. 'I'm saying that I have to operate within a strict budget. I can't afford to send you halfway around the world to follow up a lead that might prove to be nothing.'

Wright reached over and took the cutting back. 'Let me go over there, sir. I just know the murders are related, and I know I can crack the case. Just one week, and I promise I'll get a result. It'll reflect well on the BTP, you know.'

Newton hesitated for a few seconds, then leaned forward. 'Okay, you can go, but the Met boys will have to know about it, and I want you reporting back anything you find out immediately. You've got exactly one week.'

Wright punched his fist in the air. 'Thanks, sir.'

'Just be careful, Nick. And for God's sake, don't get into trouble out there. Thailand can be a dangerous place.'

There was something about the Oval Office that inspired respect, even when its occupant was less than presidential. Some of the most important decisions facing mankind had been taken in the office: wars had been started and ended, economies had been ruined or revived, men had seized the opportunity for greatness or lied their way into infamy. Dean Burrow could sense the history in the room, so strongly that he could virtually smell it, even above the oversweet aftershave of the man who stepped towards him, arm outstretched.

'Dean, good to see you,' said the President, smiling easily. The word on the cocktail circuit was that the presidential smile had cost somewhere in the region of thirty thousand dollars and that there was now so much metal in his mouth that the Secret Service had had to reduce the sensitivity of the metal detectors at the entrances to the White House. They shook hands. The President's grip was firm, his hand dry. 'How's Patricia?'

'She's fine, Mr President. Thank you.'

'And Bill? I gather he's top of his class at Yale.'

'We're both very proud of him.'

'You should bring him in for lunch some time. I'd like to meet him.'

'He'd be honoured, Mr President.'

The President patted Burrow on the shoulder and guided him to a chair. 'You're looking good, Dean. Real good.' The President gestured to his own ample waistline. 'That's the big drawback in this job: there's never enough time for exercise.' He sat down in a chair facing Burrow and crossed his legs. 'Your health is the most important thing, Dean. Nothing else matters. Money, power, none of it means anything if you haven't got your health.'

Burrow nodded. The meeting had been called at short notice, and there could be only one reason for it.

'Glenn's condition is deteriorating, Dean. He wants to throw in the towel now and spend more time with Elaine. She lost her father, you know.'

'Yes, Mr President.'

'Hell of a business, prostate cancer. Not an easy way to die.' The President shivered. 'I've asked him to hang on in there for two more weeks, until the China trade talks are out of the way. Glenn's always gone down well in Beijing, being fluent in Mandarin and all. He's agreed. God bless him for that.'

The President brought his sky-blue eyes to bear on Burrow. The effect was almost hypnotic and while the contact lasted it felt as if Burrow was the centre of the President's universe, that nothing else mattered to him other than the man sitting opposite him. It was something all the best leaders seemed to be able to do at will, a skill that Burrow himself was working to acquire.

'Forty-eight's a good age to be Vice President, Dean. Can you handle it?'

'Absolutely,' said Burrow. He felt a surge of elation which he fought to keep under control. He'd known he was front-runner, but he'd been counting chickens right up until the moment the President said the words. He wanted to leap up out of his chair and punch the air, but he confined himself to a tight, almost regretful, smile. When all was said and done, it was still a case of dead man's shoes.

'The timing's perfect from your point of view,' the President continued. 'Economy's on the up and up, the Middle East is as quiet as it's ever going to get, no dark clouds on the horizons, none that I'm aware of anyway. Two years' time, you could have this job.'

Burrow said nothing. He wanted the job more than he'd ever wanted anything in his life, but burning ambition was something best kept hidden, especially when the only obstacle to your desire was sitting just a few feet away.

'Two weeks today I'm going to be in Washington – I plan to announce it then. Clear your schedule for the day, and the day after. You're going to have the world's media on your tail. I'd appreciate it if you'd hold off from telling Patricia. You know how the girls love to talk.' He stood up and extended his hand again. The second handshake was as firm and dry as the first. Burrow could feel that his own palms were damp with sweat.

'Congratulations, Dean.' He put a reassuring hand on Burrow's shoulder. 'It's going to be good to have you on the team.'

'I won't let you down, Mr President.'

The President chuckled. 'I'm relieved to hear that.' He let go of Burrow's shoulder, but continued to shake his hand for a few seconds more. 'It goes without saying that I've had you checked out, Dean. And it also goes without saying that you passed with flying colours. First-class war record, which is more than I can say for myself, huh? Never been caught taking drugs, and other than a handful of parking tickets you're clean as a whistle.' He fixed his eyes on Burrow again. 'There was that business with your secretary, of course, but you handled that well.'

Burrow felt his chest go suddenly cold and he caught his breath. He forced himself to keep smiling. 'Secretary?' he said. Did he know? Did the President know about Kristine Ross? And if he did, why in God's name wasn't he being taken away in chains instead of being given the second most powerful job in America? The President was known as a vindictive man, but why on earth would he dangle the prize and then snatch it away?

'Mary-Louise Wilson,' said the President. 'She's been as good as gold since the . . . operation. She seems to have settled nicely in Cleveland.'

Burrow suppressed a sigh. The abortion. 'Yes, Jody Meacher paid her off.'

'And you haven't seen her since? She hasn't approached you?'

'She got what she wanted. There are no records, no written proof. In a worst-case scenario it would be her word against mine, and I doubt that the media would use it without some sort of corroboration. I can assure you there is no evidence that would back up her story – Meacher took care of that. Besides, it was a long time ago.'

The President nodded. 'And you can give me your cast-iron guarantee that no other skeletons are going to emerge from some long-forgotten closet?'

'Absolutely, Mr President.' Burrow returned the President's gaze and flashed him a confident smile, despite the images that flitted through his mind, whirling and twisting like bats at dusk. Bodies crucified, with bloody mouths and playing cards impaled on their chests.

'Because if there are, we should clear them out now.'

Burrow shook his head. 'I am as pure as the driven snow, Mr President.'

Gerry Hunter tossed his jacket on to the back of his sofa and knelt down in front of his video recorder. He slotted in the tape. He'd had to visit three video rental stores before finding one that had a copy of *Apocalypse Now*. The store manager was a bearded man in his late twenties who had refused to allow Hunter to take away the tape until Hunter had filled out an application form and provided him with two pieces of identification. Hunter had shown him his warrant card and told him that he needed to borrow the tape as part of a murder investigation, but the manager had been adamant: no membership, no tape.

Hunter pressed the 'play' button and sat down on the sofa. The telephone rang and he cursed. He leaned over and picked up the phone.

It was Janie Wright. 'Hiya, honey,' she said. 'What are you doing?'

'I'm watching a video,' said Hunter, his eyes on the screen.

'Come and watch it with me,' she said.

'It's work related,' he said.

'That doesn't matter,' she said. 'Come on, Gerry. I haven't seen you for two days.' Hunter looked at his watch. 'I'll cook,' she said. 'Pasta.'

'It's late, Janie.'

'Please,' she whined. 'Please, please, please.' He could picture her pouting and swinging her shoulders from side to side, playing the little girl lost like she always did when she wanted to get her own way. It might have been attractive when she was in her teens, but Hunter was starting to find it irritating in a woman in her early thirties.

Hunter knew that it was pointless to argue with Janie when she was in one of her demanding moods. Besides, she was right, he hadn't seen her for two days, he'd been so tied up with work. 'Okay, I'll be there in twenty minutes,' he said.

'I'll open a bottle of wine,' she said.

Hunter retrieved the video cassette, grabbed his jacket, and drove to Janie's house.

He parked behind her car and walked up the driveway. She opened the door before he reached it. She was wearing a pink silk dressing gown and full make-up and she'd obviously just brushed her hair. Wright thought she looked gorgeous, and he knew immediately that she'd lied about the pasta. She was dressed for the bedroom, not the kitchen. Hunter kissed her on the cheek and caught her favourite scent. Her arms slid around his neck and she kissed him on the mouth, pressing her body hard against his. Hunter could taste wine as her tongue slid against his teeth.

'Thank you for coming,' she said when she eventually broke away.

He held up the video cassette. 'I have to watch this,' he said.

'Right now?'

'Right now. It won't take long.'

She took it off him and examined it. '*Apocalypse Now*?

That's at least two hours long, isn't it?' She held it behind her back. 'Bed first.'

'Video first,' Hunter insisted.

Janie could see that she wasn't going to get her way, so she gave him the video and flounced off to the sitting room. Hunter followed her and loaded the video into the recorder. He dropped down next to Janie on the overstuffed sofa opposite the television. A half empty bottle of wine and two glasses were on the coffee table next to Janie. The screen flickered into life and Hunter picked up the remote control and fast-forwarded through the piracy warning and trailers for other movies.

Janie picked up her glass and sipped her wine. She put her glass down and slid across Hunter, straddling him. Her dressing gown rode up her thighs as she put her hands on either side of his face and pressed her lips against his. Hunter tried to protest but as he opened his mouth wine spilled between his lips and he had to swallow. Janie thrust her tongue deeper into his mouth and ground her backside against his groin. Wine dribbled from between their lips and ran down Hunter's chin. Janie took her hands away from his face and wriggled out of her robe. She was naked underneath.

Hunter put his hands on her shoulders and pushed her away. She was panting and there was an almost manic gleam in her eyes. 'Janie,' he protested.

'Do as you're told,' she said. She seized his wrists and placed his hands on her full breasts. The nipples were hard and he couldn't stop himself caressing them. She smiled, sensing that she'd won, and slipped her hands down to his groin, rubbing and probing and making him hard.

'Where's Sean?' he asked.

'Sean's in bed, asleep.' She raised herself up and undid his belt. Her right hand found him and Hunter gasped. Janie pressed her mouth against his again and as she kissed him she slid him inside her.

The British Airways flight to Bangkok was full and Nick Wright was lucky to get a window seat. He was seated next to two Australian backpackers who seemed to be intent on drinking as much free beer and wine as they could. They were pleasant enough but there was no chance of Wright getting any sleep. Two hours into the flight he decided that he might as well join them in their binge, and together they downed the best part of a case of lager by the time they landed in Thailand.

It took more than an hour for Wright to clear immigration. The queues were long and the brown-uniformed immigration officials seemed in no hurry to process the arrivals. His suitcase was waiting for him on the carousel, so he collected it, handed in his Customs form and headed through the 'Nothing To Declare' exit.

Several Thai men in blue blazers and black slacks tried to shepherd him towards counters offering hotel and limousine services but the Australians had already warned him that they were overpriced. They'd told him to walk on to the public taxi counter and given him the names and addresses of several reasonably priced hotels to go along with those he'd already picked from the *Lonely Planet* guide to Thailand.

At the public taxi counter a young girl in a white blouse

tried to persuade him to accept a non-metered taxi, but the backpackers had told Wright to refuse and to insist on a taxi with a meter. Reluctantly, the girl handed him a chit stamped with 'Taxi Meter'. On it she'd written his destination, one of the hotels that the backpackers had recommended. It was off Sukhumvit Road, a mile or so from the orphanage where Eric Horvitz had worked.

A driver materialised at Wright's shoulder, a bulky Thai in his forties wearing a blue T-shirt and beige slacks. He took the chit, picked up Wright's suitcase and led Wright across the crowded terminal building. Wright stopped to change the sterling he'd brought with him into Thai baht then they walked outside.

He was hit by a wall of humidity that took his breath away. Beads of sweat gathered on his face and he wiped his forehead with his sleeve. He slipped off the blazer he was wearing.

The driver grinned at his discomfort as he held open the door of the white Toyota. 'First time in Bangkok?' he asked.

'First time in Asia,' said Wright. In fact, it was his first time outside Europe. Janie loved France and Italy, and apart from a couple of weeks in Spain, they'd spent most of their holidays there.

The driver put the suitcase in the boot, climbed into the front seat and drove off. Wright leaned forward and pointed at the meter. 'Meter,' he said.

The driver shook his head. 'Not working.'

The backpackers had told Wright that it was common practice to claim that the meter was out of order so that the drivers could negotiate a higher fare. Wright jabbed his finger at the meter. 'Use the meter,' he said.

The driver shrugged and pressed a button on the front of the meter. Red numbers glowed. 'You want massage?' said the driver.

'No,' said Wright.

'You want girl?'

'No.'

'Boy?'

Wright laughed and the driver laughed along with him.

The traffic was heavy and they soon slowed to a crawl. Cars and trucks seemed to stretch towards the horizon. In the distance tower blocks glinted in the early morning sun. The light was dazzlingly bright, a stark contrast to the grey drizzle he'd left behind in England. Wright settled back and dozed, his head resting against the window.

It took them almost two hours to get to the hotel, which as far as he could judge was only ten miles from the airport. Wright had become so used to the taxi stopping and starting that he didn't realise they'd arrived until the driver twisted around in his seat and pointed, saying, 'We here.'

Wright stretched and rubbed his eyes. They were in a narrow street in front of a five-storey building that had once been white but that was now a grubby grey. Streaks of rust ran down from leaking pipes and the windows were covered with a film of dust. Wright pulled out his wallet, paid the driver and carried his suitcase into reception.

A security guard in a blue uniform was fast asleep on a grey sofa, his peaked cap over his face, and the young girl at the reception desk had her head on her arms and was snoring softly. Overhead a wooden-bladed fan turned slowly and in the corner of the reception area a small television showed a Thai news programme, the sound muted. The girl opened her eyes and looked up at him sleepily. She smiled, reached under the desk for a check-in form and slid it across to him. She smiled again and put her head back on her arms.

Wright filled in the form, and just as he finished the girl opened her eyes and handed him a key. She was snoring once more as he picked up his suitcase and headed for the stairs.

His room was on the third floor, clean but basic with a double bed, two cane chairs and a small circular table, a mirrored built-in wardrobe, a television and a small refrigerator. Wright heaved his suitcase on top of the wardrobe and sat down on the bed.

Bangkok was six hours ahead of London, but despite not sleeping on the plane he didn't feel tired. There was a telephone by the bed and a *Yellow Pages*. He flicked through it but it was all in Thai. He took his notebook out of his blazer pocket and read through the notes he'd made on the Eric Horvitz murder. He'd managed to find a translation agency in the West End that had translated the Thai cuttings, and one of them had contained a quote from a policeman who was involved in the investigation. Wright reckoned he would be as good a place to start as any, but first he needed a contact number.

He showered and changed into a pair of brown slacks and a white shirt, then took his notebook down to reception, woke up the receptionist and showed her the policeman's name in his notebook. She frowned, not understanding. Wright pointed at the inspector's name and mimed using a telephone. The girl squinted at his writing, then smiled and shook her head. 'Not speak English,' she said.

'Directory enquiries?' asked Wright, pointing at her telephone, but it was clear from the look on her face that she didn't understand. The girl's smile widened, as if the smile would solve his problem. He banged his notebook against his leg as he considered his options. The orphanage where Horvitz had worked seemed the best bet.

He went outside and looked up and down the narrow street but there was no sign of a taxi. He headed for the main road and within seconds he was bathed in sweat. The Bangkok air assailed his nostrils, a stifling brew of exhaust fumes, sewage and fried food. He stepped across an open drain and as he looked down something moved in the grey sludge, something with a tail and hard, beady eyes.

A large Mercedes went by, the wing mirror narrowly missing Wright's arm. He walked by an open-fronted shop selling tinned food and canned drinks. He bought a can of iced coffee and sipped it as he walked.

The traffic on the main road was locked solid. Wright looked at his wristwatch. Nine thirty. Obviously still rush hour. In the distance a traffic light turned from red to green and the traffic began to crawl forward. A green taxi with white Thai writing on the side had its red 'For Hire' light on in its windscreen, so Wright flagged it down and opened the rear door.

'Sukhumvit Soi Two,' he read, hoping that he was pronouncing it correctly.

The young driver smiled and shook his head. Wright tried again. This time the driver made a waving motion with his hand. Wright showed him the notebook but the driver refused to look at it. Horns blared out behind them, illogical because the traffic was barely moving.

'Look, I want to go here. This is Sukhumvit Road, right? I want to go to Sukhumvit Soi Two. It can't be far away.'

The driver turned away and sat motionless with his hands on the wheel. Wright sat back and silently cursed. What chance did he have of solving the case if he couldn't even tell a taxi driver where he wanted to go? He got out of the taxi and walked back along the side street.

When he got back to his hotel the sleeping girl had been replaced by a young man in a black suit and a starched white shirt whose collar was about three sizes too big for him. He smiled at Wright and held out a key for him. 'Good morning, Mr Wright,' he said, flashing a grin of perfect white teeth.

'How did you know my name?' asked Wright.

'My colleague told me that you had checked in, and she described you as a good-looking man wearing brown trousers.'

Wright shook his head in amazement. Faultless English and flattery combined, it was almost too good to be true. 'What's your name?' he asked.

'Somchai,' said the teenager. 'At your service.' He bowed slightly, still holding out the key.

'Somchai, you're just what I need,' said Wright, showing him the notebook. 'I want to go to this address. Can you help?'

Somchai put the key back in its cubbyhole and studied the page. 'An orphanage?' he said.

'That's right.'

'Sukhumvit Soi Two. The main road is called Sukhumvit. The soi is the street off the main road. We are in soi twenty-six.'

'So how do I tell the taxi driver?'

'You say Sukhumvit Soi Song. And to get back here you say Sukhumvit Soi Yee Sip Hok.' He picked up a pen and a sheet of hotel notepaper and wrote on it in Thai. 'This will be better,' he said. 'Show the driver this, and when you want to come back, show him the printed address.'

'You're a lifesaver, Somchai,' said Wright, pocketing the piece of paper. He went through the notebook and found the name of the police inspector. He showed it to Somchai. 'I want to speak to this man. He's a police inspector. Can you get a telephone number for him?'

'Do you know which police station he is based at?'

'I'm afraid not.'

Somchai copied down the name. 'I will see what I can do,' he said. He smiled expectantly at Wright. Wright smiled back. Somchai's smile widened so that it seemed to encompass the whole of his jaw. Realisation dawned and Wright took out his wallet and gave the teenager a hundred-baht note.

This time Wright had no problem persuading a taxi driver to take him to the orphanage. It was only a mile or so away from the hotel but the journey took almost an hour. If it hadn't been for the searing heat and humidity, Wright could have walked it in less than half the time. Even the Thais seemed affected by the heat. A line of schoolchildren stood in the shadow cast by a telegraph pole; female office workers in pastel-coloured suits shielded their faces with their handbags as they walked along Sukhumvit Road; a crew of workers resurfacing a section of the road wore wide-brimmed straw hats and had swathed their faces with cloth to protect themselves from the sun.

The road was a mix of old and new: gleaming shopping malls with boutiques and ATMs, and small open-fronted shops where bare-chested old men worked on ancient Singer sewing machines. There were roadside stalls selling T-shirts and cheap watches, and others offering noodle soup and fried fish balls on sticks from the shade of spreading umbrellas.

The orphanage was in a quiet side street, barely wide enough for two vehicles to pass at the same time. Wright heard the sound of laughing children as he climbed out of the taxi and paid the driver.

The orphanage was surrounded by a high wall into which was set a pair of huge wrought-iron gates encrusted with dirt. A security guard in a pale blue uniform with a gleaming gold badge on the breast pocket opened the gate for Wright.

'Who's in charge?' asked Wright.

The guard smiled and worked a toothpick between his front teeth. Wright repeated his question but it was clear that the man didn't understand.

Wright looked around helplessly. The orphanage was a large concrete two-storey building, painted a pale pink colour with a red tiled roof. The laughter he'd heard came from one of the rooms on the ground floor. The windows were wide open and inside he could see children sitting at desks while a Thai nun in a white habit stood in front of a blackboard. The gardens around the building were well tended with neatly trimmed bushes and a large expanse of grass where the children could play. In the far corner of the garden, close to the wall, were a slide and a set of swings. It wasn't at all how Wright had pictured a Thai orphanage: he'd expected a drab, dreary place where hollow-cheeked malnourished children held up empty bowls and begged for more.

Wright nodded at the guard and headed along a flagstoned path that led to the main entrance. Two stone lions stood guard at the front door, each coming up almost to Wright's shoulder. He walked past them and into the building.

There was no airconditioning but large fans whirled overhead in the wood-panelled hallway and it was much cooler than outside. A highly polished rosewood table stood to the left, with a large visitors' book next to a vase of pink and white orchids.

'Can I help you?' asked a voice behind him.

Wright jumped. 'Jesus!' he exclaimed. He whirled around to find himself face to face with an amused European nun, a woman in her forties with striking green eyes and a sprinkling of freckles around her nose.

'Hardly,' she said. 'Though we do like to feel that we have his blessing in our work.' Her accent was Irish, a soft, feminine brogue that suggested she enjoyed teasing men.

Wright felt his cheeks flush with embarrassment. 'I'm sorry, Sister,' he said. 'You caught me by surprise.'

The nun clasped her hands together. She was wearing a white habit and stray locks of red hair peeped out from the cowl as if reluctant to stay hidden. 'And what brings you to our establishment, Mr . . .?'

'Wright. Nick Wright. Are you in charge?'

'For my sins,' she said. 'Sister Marie is my name. Taking care of children, my game. And you, Mr Wright?'

'I'm a policeman,' said Wright. He took out his warrant card and showed it to her.

She studied both sides, then handed it back to him, suddenly serious. 'It's about Eric, I suppose?'

Wright nodded. 'Is there somewhere we can talk?'

'My officc,' she said. 'This way.' She swept down the hall, past an ornate crucifix and a small font, and down a second tiled hallway to a wooden door. She was a tall woman, the spreading cowl emphasising her height, and she had to duck slightly as she walked through the doorway. The habit concealed her figure and Wright couldn't help but wonder what Sister Marie's body looked like. He shook his head, disgusted with himself. She was a nun, for God's sake. A bride of Christ.

Sister Marie stood to the side and ushered him to a straight-backed wooden chair next to the window. She closed the door and glided over to her desk. 'Can I offer you a drink?' she said.

'It's a bit early for me,' said Wright.

'I meant water,' she said archly. 'Or iced tea.'

Yet again Wright was flustered. He was so used to Tommy Reid offering him a hair of the dog that refusals had become second nature. 'I'm sorry,' he said. 'Iced tea would be fine. Thank you.'

Sister Marie pressed a small button on the side of her desk and a moment later the door opened and a Thai nun opened the door. Sister Marie spoke to her in Thai and the nun nodded and closed the door. 'So tell me, Inspector Wright. Why is a transport policeman from England investigating Eric Horvitz's murder?'

A good question, thought Wright. And one that he wasn't sure how to answer. 'There was a similar murder some weeks ago. In London. I thought there might be a connection. The victim was also an American. His name was Max Eckhardt. I don't suppose you know if Mr Horvitz knew him, do you?'

'I don't think so,' said Sister Marie. 'It's certainly not a name I'm familiar with.' She opened one of the desk drawers and took out a Filofax. She flicked through it, then shook her head. 'No, there's no Eckhardt here. This is Eric's. Was Eric's, I mean.'

There was a timid knock on the door and the Thai nun carried in a tray containing a jug of iced tea and two glasses which she placed on the desk. Sister Marie murmured her thanks, and waited until the nun had left before picking up the jug. 'I suppose I'd better be mother,' she said.

Wright grinned. He couldn't help wondering why a sexy, self-assured woman like Sister Marie had turned her back on the outside world and offered her body and soul to Christ. He went over to the desk and took the filled glass from her. 'Cheers,' he said.

She raised her own glass. '*Slainte*,' she said, toasting him.

When he'd sat down again, Wright asked her what Eric Horvitz had been doing in Thailand.

'His job, you mean? He didn't actually have one. He ran the orphanage, took care of any repairs that needed doing.'

'And who paid his salary? Who did he work for?'

'Oh, didn't you know? This is his orphanage. He bought the building, he paid the running costs, sponsored the older children to go to university.'

'That must cost a fortune.'

'He never talked about money. But whenever we needed it, it was there. The Lord will provide, he used to say, but I know it was his own money.'

She went suddenly quiet and Wright could sense that she was uneasy talking about Horvitz, as if she was betraying his secrets.

'Do you know of anyone who might have wanted to kill him?' he asked. 'Anyone who would have profited from his death?'

'He left everything to the orphanage,' said Sister Marie. 'We haven't got the money yet, of course, things take time in Thailand. But his lawyer said we were the only beneficiary in his will.'

'And enemies?'

She smiled and shook her head. 'Eric had no enemies,' she said. 'He wasn't the sort to make enemies. He was quiet, even tempered, he was at peace with himself.'

'He was a religious man?'

'Oh no. He didn't believe in God, and I was never able to convince him otherwise.' She looked across at another chair, a leather armchair almost within reach of her desk, and Wright knew that that was where Horvitz used to sit whenever he visited Sister Marie in her office. He knew also that it would remain Horvitz's chair for a long time to come and that was why she'd shown him to the one by the window.

'How did you meet him?' asked Wright.

'I like to think that it was God who sent him to us, despite his lack of belief,' she said, fingering her glass of iced tea. Wright sipped his. It was sweet and sickly, but he was grateful for the ice. Like the rest of the building, Sister Marie's office had no airconditioning. 'Our order had an orphanage in Vietnam, in Saigon,' she continued. 'Or Ho Chi Minh City as they insist on calling it these days. Eric came with a group of Americans to look around. They were part of a goodwill tour arranged by some war veterans association. The idea was for the vets to come to terms with the war by meeting the people they'd once fought against. We were part of their itinerary. The orphanage had looked after hundreds of Amerasians who had been abandoned by their mothers.'

'When was this?'

'Seven years ago.' She frowned. 'No. Eight.'

'Sister Marie, Max Eckhardt wasn't on the tour, was he?'

She frowned and put a hand up to her cowl. 'No, I'm pretty sure he wasn't,' she said eventually. 'Actually, I can't be sure, because I wasn't told all their names. There was a guy called Lehman, Dan Lehman, and a man with an artificial hand called Larry.' She smiled as if recalling a fond memory. 'The reason I remember their names is because although they came as part of the goodwill tour they returned a few months later and gave the orphanage a lot of money.' She paused and sipped her tea.

'How much, if you don't mind my asking?'

She held his look for several seconds. 'A lot,' she said. 'Enough to solve all our financial problems. Dan and Larry stayed in Vietnam for a few months then returned to the United States. Eric stayed.'

'Do you know how I can contact them?' asked Wright.

She shook her head. 'I'm afraid not. We occasionally get Christmas cards from Dan, but he seems to move around a lot. Believe me, none of them would want to hurt Eric. You never saw such close friends.'

A bell began to ring and seconds later came the sound of children laughing and running down a corridor. It was a happy place and Wright felt that the atmosphere had a lot to do with the fact that Sister Marie was in charge.

'What happened to the orphanage in Vietnam?' he asked.

'Oh, it's still there, and our Order still runs it, but the Vietnamese made it harder and harder for foreigners like myself and Eric to stay there. It became increasingly difficult for us to get visas and the authorities made it clear they'd rather have the orphanage in Vietnamese hands. It's still a Communist country, you know, and the petty bureaucracy has to be seen to be believed. At first we paid off the right people, but after a while even that wasn't enough and we had to leave.'

Wright smiled at Sister Marie's admission of bribery, but he guessed that in her mind the end justified the means. Even so, he couldn't help but wonder what other transgressions there had been in the nun's life. He wanted to ask her if she'd always been a nun, or if prior to taking holy orders she'd had a normal life, of pubs and dances and boyfriends. Wright could imagine a lot of broken hearts when Sister Marie turned her back on the outside world and chose a life of chastity and prayer.

'Eric offered to set up a new orphanage here in Bangkok.' She waved her hand, indicating the room they were in. 'He paid for everything. The building. The staff. Medical care.'

'And no ulterior motive?' Wright regretted the words as soon as they'd left his mouth.

She stiffened and her eyes narrowed. 'What do you mean?' she said.

Wright smiled awkwardly. 'I'm sorry,' he said, 'but I think like a policeman. I'm not used to dealing with philanthropists. Everybody I meet has a dirty secret, an axe to grind . . .' He tailed off as he realised he was rambling.

'Not Eric Horvitz. He was truly a good man.'

'I'm sorry. I didn't mean to imply otherwise.'

She smiled and inclined her head, accepting his apology.

'You said his two friends went back to the States. What about here in Bangkok, does he have many friends here?'

'Some,' she said. 'He chose his friends carefully. He played jazz with a group at a bar in Lang Suan.'

'Lang Suan?'

'It's an area near the embassies. Upmarket nightclubs, expensive restaurants. Eric played at a club called Cowboy Nights. He sang and played percussion.'

'Drums?'

'No, not drums. The tambourine, and those things you shake.'

'Maracas?'

'That's right, maracas. He had a good singing voice.' She smiled at the memory.

'You went to a jazz club to hear him?' asked Wright, surprised.

Sister Marie raised an eyebrow. 'I'm not a prisoner here, Sergeant Wright. They do allow me out from time to time.'

'Could you give me the address?' he asked.

She reached for a sheet of paper and wrote on it. When she handed it to him he realised it was in Thai. 'You read and write Thai?' he said.

'And Vietnamese. I was always good at languages. I studied French and German at university.'

'Don't you miss it?' asked Wright. 'The real world?'

There was more laughter outside and running footsteps. Sister Marie smiled as if she had a secret only she knew. 'This is the real world,' she said softly. 'I'm not hiding under these robes. I chose them.'

Wright emptied his glass. She didn't offer to refill it. A sudden thought struck him. 'Oh, I've been trying to get hold of the policeman in charge of the investigation. I don't suppose you know who he is, do you?'

'Of course,' she said. There was a Rolodex on her desk and she flicked through it and pulled out a business card. 'He hasn't been in touch for a while,' she said. 'I think they haven't made any progress and he's too embarrassed to tell me. It's a question of face, you see.'

She handed him the card and Wright studied it. There was an ornate crest and writing in Thai. He turned the card over. The man's name, title, address and telephone number were reprinted in English. Police Colonel Vasan Srihanam, the officer quoted in the newspaper. He slipped it into his wallet, put his empty glass on the tray and thanked her.

'I'll show you out,' she said.

'He was found in the basement, wasn't he?' asked Wright.

Sister Marie shivered but quickly regained her composure. Wright wondered if she had been the one who'd found the body. 'Yes,' she said quietly.

'Can I take a look?' he asked.

The nun shook her head. 'It's been locked and sealed by the police,' she said. 'Colonel Vasan said the seals mustn't be broken.'

Wright felt a sudden surge of relief. He hadn't relished the prospect of going down into the basement.

'Maybe you could ask him for permission,' said Sister Marie.

She walked him out of the orphanage and to the gate. A dozen children, boys and girls, were playing on the swings and the slide, laughing and giggling. She was absolutely right, Wright realised, this was the real world, children were all that mattered. He wondered how long it had been since he had heard Sean laugh. Far too long.

Sister Marie interrupted his thoughts. 'You were asking about Eric's motives for helping us,' she said. Her face was turned towards the children and he couldn't see her expression. Wright said nothing, sensing that there was something she wanted to tell him. 'He had his own demons to deal with, that much I can tell you. He was at peace here, with the children, but I think that perhaps you're right, he was atoning for something, something in his past. He never spoke about the war, but I think that was where his demons lay. Whatever he did back then, he's more than made up for it since.' She turned to face him and the sun glinted off her white cowl so brightly that Wright had to avert his eyes. 'He was a saintly man,' said the nun. 'Maybe not a saint, but a saintly man.'

She left him at the gate and Wright watched her walk back to the building. Two children, a boy and a girl, both wearing white shirts and red ties, ran over to Sister Marie. They stood either side and she took a hand each and they walked together, a huge white mother hen and her clucking chicks. Wright felt an urge to see his son again, a longing so strong that it made him gasp.

Gerry Hunter lay back on the sofa, the remote control in his right hand. Janie had gone upstairs to bed soon after they'd finished making love, taking with her the bottle of wine. It wasn't the first time that she'd taken the initiative so aggressively, but it had still caught him by surprise. He wondered if it had had anything to do with the fact that he'd been so keen to work on the Eckhardt case. Janie demanded constant attention and Hunter felt that she was as jealous of his police work as she would be if he looked at another woman. It was almost as if she wanted to prove to herself that he loved her more than his job, and once she'd proved it she was happy to go to bed alone.

Hunter watched the television and tried to push Janie out of his mind. He wouldn't need much encouragement to follow her upstairs and slip under the quilt with her. Janie had one of the sexiest bodies he'd ever seen, taut and soft, the skin flawless, her breasts soft but firm and showing no signs of her having had a child. And Hunter knew from experience that she was at her sexiest when she'd had a couple of drinks. Alcohol seemed to wipe away what few sexual inhibitions she had and it was all he could do to keep up with her. He sat up and forced himself to concentrate on the movie. He had all night to join her in bed.

He leaned forward with his elbows on his knees and his hands supporting his chin. Hunter wasn't a fan of war movies, in fact he didn't enjoy watching any films containing violence. He'd spent too much time clearing up the aftermath of violence to take any pleasure in watching it on the big screen, and he preferred comedies or historical dramas as entertainment.

His attention was caught by a scene early in the movie, at the start of Lieutenant Willard's journey down the river in search of Colonel Kurtz. He watched Robert Duvall striding through a Vietnamese village in the aftermath of an American attack. He was wearing a black cavalry officer's hat and a silk scarf wrapped around his neck as he strutted arrogantly past a line of corpses. A soldier ran up and handed Duvall a pack of playing cards. Duvall ripped the pack open and began throwing a playing card on to each body. Martin Sheen, as Willard, had picked up one of the cards and was staring at it. 'Death card,' said Sheen. 'Lets Charlie know who did this.'

Hunter sat bolt upright, his eyes wide. He scrambled closer to the television so that his face was inches from the screen. There wasn't an ace of spades and he couldn't make out what brand the cards were, but Hunter knew that if Edmunds had watched the movie he'd have seen the connection with the Eckhardt case. Hunter retrieved the remote control from the sofa and replayed the scene. Had Edmunds seen the movie on the night he died? Hunter wondered. And if he had, what had happened to the video cassette?

Hunter stood up and paced around the sitting room, all thoughts of Janie forgotten.

When Nick Wright arrived back at his hotel, Somchai had gone and his replacement, an elderly man in a stained T-shirt, was asleep with his head in his arms. Wright collected his key from behind the counter, then went upstairs and showered. He lay down on his bed, swathed in two thin towels.

When he opened his eyes again it was dark outside. He stared at his wristwatch. It said four o'clock. He frowned. Four o'clock in the morning? Impossible. Then he remembered that he hadn't reset his watch to local time. Bangkok was six hours ahead of London, so it must be ten o'clock at night. He'd slept for the best part of eight hours.

He sat up and swung his legs off the bed. It was sweltering in the room and his mouth was dry. He went into the bathroom and drank from the tap, then splashed water over his face.

He dried his face and looked at himself in the bathroom mirror. There was a small yellow sticker in the corner of the mirror warning guests not to drink the water from the tap. There was still a bad taste in his mouth and he took his washbag out of his suitcase and cleaned his teeth. His hair had dried in a mess, unkempt and spiky, and he dampened it and recombed it.

Wright's original plan had been to call on the police colonel, but that would have to wait until tomorrow. He changed into a fresh shirt and a pair of black Levis and left the hotel.

The first taxi driver that Wright stopped had no trouble reading the note that Sister Marie had given him. Wright flopped down in the back seat. The traffic was much lighter than it had been during the day, though the roads were still far from quiet. There were motorcycles everywhere, buzzing around the cars and trucks. Some were clearly being used as taxis, the riders wearing brightly coloured vests with numbers on; others were workhorses, piled high with cartons or bags.

The pavements were as busy as the roads. Small restaurants had been set up, with plastic chairs and folding metal tables, and old women ladied out noodles and roast duck and steaming vegetables. Lines of stalls sold T-shirts and cheap dresses and wristwatches, and vendors called out to the tourists who walked by. Small children ran around the stalls, laughing and playing, and skinny dogs with curly tails lay at the roadside, panting in the evening heat. At one of the makeshift restaurants two Thai businessmen in suits were eating noodle soup, their portable phones standing to attention on the table in front of them, while next to them two labourers in threadbare T-shirts and shorts argued over something they were reading in a Thai newspaper. It was like no other city Wright had ever seen, a jarring mixture of old and new, East and West.

They drove past a park where the trees had been bedecked with hundreds of tiny white lights. In the distance, Wright could hear a band playing, a tune he vaguely recognised but accompanied by Thai words.

'You want massage?' said the driver, his guttural voice lancing through Wright's thoughts.

'What?' replied Wright irritably.

'Massage,' repeated the driver, twisting around in his seat even though they were speeding down a main road. He handed a creased glossy brochure to Wright. 'Many pretty girls. We go now?'

Wright studied the brochure. It featured a massage parlour and the main photograph consisted of more than a hundred smiling Thai girls dressed in white togas, each with a numbered blue badge pinned to her left breast, presumably to aid in identification.

'Okay?' asked the driver, nodding vigorously. The taxi narrowly missed smashing into the back of a bus packed with strap-hanging passengers, but at the last second the driver looked back at the road and swerved across into the next lane. 'Okay?' he repeated.

'Not okay,' said Wright, giving him back the brochure. It seemed that every time he got into a taxi he was offered sex. He'd never complain about London cabbies and their banal chatter again.

'You not like Thai girls?' asked the driver as he powered through a red light.

A huge elephant stood on the pavement, a bare-chested man sitting astride its neck. A second man was selling small bunches of bananas to passers-by who took it in turns to feed the animal.

'I don't like paying for sex,' said Wright.

'Huh?'

'Sex. I don't want to pay for sex. Not give money for sex.' Wright realised that he was behaving like the typical Englishman abroad: if the natives don't speak English, talk loudly and slowly in the hope that they'll get it in the end. Surprisingly, it actually worked, and the driver began to laugh.

'Everybody pay,' he said. 'Nobody get free sex.' He slapped his leathery hands on the steering wheel and rocked backwards and forwards.

The driver was still chuckling when the taxi came to a halt outside a three-storey building which had been lined with wooden planks to make it look like a building from the Wild West. A group of young Thai men in leather jackets lounged around on motorcycles smoking cigarettes and drinking Thai whisky from a bottle. A lazy saxophone solo leaked out from the double doors which opened inwards saloon-style. To complete the Western motif there was a hitching post on either side of the doors, and a gold-embossed wooden sign across the middle of the building read 'Cowboy Nights'.

Wright paid the driver and climbed out of the car. The Thai motorcyclists stared at him but without hostility. The guy with the bottle raised it in salute and when Wright smiled they all smiled back.

He pushed open the doors half expecting to see men in cowboy hats and boots, but the people inside were conservatively dressed: Thai thirty-somethings in fashionable outfits, Westerners in suits, a group of teenage girls in short skirts and pullovers sipping Cokes through straws. The club was on two floors, with a wooden spiral staircase leading up to a second level from where balconies looked down on a dancefloor and a small raised stage where the band was performing.

Around the edge of the dancefloor a dozen large leather sofas were grouped around wooden coffee tables, and winged leather armchairs that would have been more at home in a London gentlemen's club filled the corners of the room. Framed oil paintings were hung around the walls, between brass light fittings with green shades. There were two bars, one on the far side of the dancefloor, where a group of Westerners sat on barstools holding bottles of beer and tapping their feet to the music, and a longer bar to the right where two waistcoated waiters juggled cocktail shakers. The nightclub was full, all the sofas and chairs occupied, and a sea of faces, mainly Thai, looked down from the balcony.

A young Thai waitress with her hair pinned up smiled at Wright and held up one finger. He nodded and she led him to an empty bar stool. Wright sat down and ordered a lager from one of the bartenders. A Heineken arrived and Wright followed the example of the Westerners and drank from the bottle.

He swivelled around so that he could watch the band perform. They were all Thais and Wright doubted that any of them was older than twenty-five. They were professional and played tightly, but they lacked emotion. It was as if they'd learned to play by listening to records, and though they could hit the right notes and keep the rhythm going, there was next to no improvisation. They didn't look at each other; each was concentrating intently on his own instrument, like session musicians who'd been brought together for a single gig.

Another waitress appeared in front of Wright, holding a

menu. She waited with her hands clasped behind her back while Wright read through it. It was in English and contained a selection of Western and Thai food. Wright realised the last thing he'd eaten was the tray of food he'd been given on the plane, and he'd left most of that untouched. He didn't want to dive into the unknown and order Thai food so he plumped for a club sandwich. The waitress frowned when he told her what he wanted, so he pointed at the menu. She nodded enthusiastically. Wright smiled. He felt that he was starting to get the hang of Bangkok.

The group finished the song to scattered applause, as if the audience realised that they'd been short-changed artistically. Wright wondered why there were so many people in the club, because what he'd heard so far couldn't in any way be described as a crowd-puller. The lead guitarist said something in Thai and the musicians began packing away their instruments. Wright looked at his watch. It was only eleven o'clock so presumably there'd be more acts to follow. He drained his bottle and ordered another. The man on the bar stool to his left accidentally knocked Wright's arm and he apologised, his accent vaguely French.

'No sweat,' said Wright. He introduced himself and the two men shook hands.

'Alain Civel,' said the man. 'From Montreal. Are you on holiday?'

'Sort of,' said Wright.

'You like jazz?'

'Love it.'

Civel was drinking a bottle of the local beer, Singha, and he waved it at the stage. 'That was *merde*. Crap.'

'It wasn't great,' admitted Wright.

'Now the next group, they really are something. Not

kids like that lot. You can't play jazz unless you've lived.'

'Unless you've suffered?'

'Life. Suffering. One and the same, Nick.' He pronounced it Neek.

'Can't argue with that,' said Wright, and the two men clinked bottles.

Wright's sandwich arrived. It was a massive triple-decker, filled with chicken, cheese and a fried egg, cut into four triangles, each of which was impaled on a miniature plastic sword, and served with a pile of French fries. Wright's stomach growled. He saw Civel looking covetously at the sandwich and Wright offered him a piece.

The two men chewed as a middle-aged Westerner and two Thais carried instrument cases on to the stage and opened them. The Westerner was in his late forties, the two Thais maybe a decade older. The bigger of the two Thais, a beefy man with a weightlifter's shoulders, was carrying a double bass, which he unpacked and began to tune. Two waiters put a dust cover over the drums that the previous band had used and pulled a cover off a second kit in the middle of the stage. It was considerably bigger than the first, a professional set-up that must have cost several thousand dollars. On the bass drum was the name of the band: The Jazz Club.

The Westerner had combed-back greying hair, a drinker's eyes, watery blue and flecked with red veins, and pale white skin as if he avoided going out in the sun. He opened his case and took out a saxophone.

'That's Doc Marshall,' said Civel. 'You've never heard anyone play a horn like Doc.'

A young waiter handed Doc a bottle of Singha beer, and

Doc drank it as he surveyed the crowd, nodding at familiar faces. The younger of the two Thai musicians, square jawed with an Elvis quiff and sideburns, opened a guitar case and took out a red and black guitar which he leaned against a stand at the side of the stage, then he went over to a pair of chest-high congas and stood behind them.

A Westerner in a wheelchair rolled across the dancefloor towards the stage. A big man with a round face, he had grown what hair he had left and tied it back in a ponytail. Behind him stood a hefty black man with a wide chest and powerful legs, and a stick-thin Latino who had also tied his glossy black locks into a ponytail. The two men lifted the crippled man and his wheelchair on to the stage and the Latino handed him the guitar.

'Dennis O'Leary,' said Civel, nodding at the man in the wheelchair. 'They say he played with Clapton once.'

'He's a regular here?'

'The whole band is. Been playing together longer than I can remember, and I've been coming to Bangkok for ten years, on and off.'

Wright leaned towards Civel, and lowered his voice. 'I don't suppose you ever saw a guy called Eric Horvitz play with them, did you?'

'The guy that was murdered? Damn right.' He drained his bottle and Wright bought him another. 'Great singer, voice that could rip your heart out.' He jabbed Wright's shoulder with a forefinger. 'Now Horvitz was a guy who'd suffered. You could hear it in his voice when he sang. Like a knife through your soul, man.'

On the stage, O'Leary began strumming on his guitar, his head tilted to the side as he listened to the chords. The big black man went to stand behind a keyboard and began to do what looked like martial art moves, presumably his own style of warm-up exercises. His hands moved through the air in a slow-motion dance, curving and flexing, first relaxed then tense, and even from across the bar the strength in his upper body was obvious.

'Bernie Hammack,' said Civel.

'And the drummer?' said Wright. The Latino had sat behind the drum kit and was adjusting a wing nut on top of one of the high hats.

'Sergio Ramirez.' Two fresh bottles of beer arrived and the two men clinked them together. 'The girls love him.' He nodded over at the group of Coke-sipping teenagers. 'His fan club.'

Ramirez was a good-looking guy with skin the colour of burnished oak, eyes of a brown so dark that they appeared black, and high cheekbones that a catwalk model would kill for. A silver crucifix glittered at his throat and he wore a tight polo shirt that showed off his chest.

The customers in the bar gradually fell silent and all faces turned towards the stage. The lights dimmed and the six members of the band were picked out in individual beams of soft yellow light. Ramirez started first, tapping a simple four-four beat on the high hat, his eyes half closed, nodding as he played. He brought in the bass drum with an off beat, and at the same time he was joined by the Thai on the double bass, laying down a solid rhythm with a simple bass riff.

O'Leary began to play along with them, picking out the notes with the ease that came from thousands of hours of practice, then Hammack joined in on his keyboard. Doc stood with his back to the audience, watching the band play. He nodded at the Thai percussionist, who started to drum the palms of his hands on the congas, a lilting counterpoint to Ramirez's hypnotic beat. Doc listened to them play for several minutes, then he put the mouthpiece of his saxophone to his lips and turned and began to play.

Wright sat transfixed as he listened. The jazz the men played was on a whole different level to the Thai group. A whole different planet. It was like listening to a single entity, a single creature that could sing with different voices, each individual but connected, voices that took it in turns to lead and follow, to increase the pace and to slow it down. At first it seemed to Wright that the band members were deciding among themselves who should improvise, but he gradually realised that it was Doc who was running the show, communicating with the rest of the band with looks and signals so subtle that it was no wonder Wright had missed them. A sideways look at Hammack, and the black man would go off on his own, his huge hands moving confidently across the keyboard, his finger span so big that he barely had to stretch. Wright watched Hammack's face as he played: the man's eyes were open but he seemed to be staring off into space. He was chewing gum, and the faster he played, the harder he chewed.

Doc took the lead back from Hammack with no more than a nod of the head and a deep breath, then he took the tune into a short solo accompanied only by the Thai percussionist and the bass player before slowing the pace and moving into a Roland Kirke number that Wright hadn't heard for years. The transition was so smooth that Wright sat back in amazement.

'*C'est superbe, huh?*' said Civel, and Wright instantly resented the man's intrusion into his enjoyment of the music. Wright didn't take his eyes off the stage, just nodded to show that he'd heard.

Doc cued O'Leary with a quick glance. The guitarist had been watching for the gesture out of the corner of his eye and again the transition was seamless. The lights slowly dimmed until O'Leary was the only one picked out on the stage. He played for a full ten minutes, the rest of the band accompanying him so unobtrusively it was as if he was playing alone. It was the best live guitar playing that Wright had ever heard, and he'd seen all the greats.

When he finished playing the silence lasted several seconds as if the audience didn't want to believe it was over, then there was a sporadic clapping followed almost immediately by tumultuous applause. Wright clapped enthusiastically.

Civel nudged his arm. 'What did I tell you?' he said.

'Brilliant,' said Wright. 'Bloody brilliant.'

The spotlights came back on. Doc leaned forward to his microphone and thanked the audience, then introduced the band members one by one. They acknowledged the applause with a nod or a half wave, then at a nod from Doc they moved effortlessly into a Van Morrison number, 'Days Like This', with the saxophone taking the part of Morrison's voice. They played for almost an hour, everything from traditional jazz and blues to Lennon–McCartney, but with their own distinctive feel, nothing was predictable. Occasionally Hammack would sing, but usually they stuck to instrumentals, and Wright wondered how the band had sounded when Horvitz had sung along with them. He sang like a man who'd suffered, the Canadian had said. One thing was for sure, he'd suffered before he died.

Wright was jerked out of his reverie by ecstatic applause and he realised that the band had finished their set. He joined in, and when several of the Westerners in the audience began cheering, Wright cheered along with them.

'Thanks,' said Doc, unscrewing the reed from his saxophone and leaning towards his mike. 'And don't forget, tomorrow night's jam night, so come prepared to show us what you can do.'

The lights went down and conversation started up. The group of Coke-sipping girls clustered around the drummer, laughing and vying among themselves for his attention.

'They never do an encore,' said Civel. 'They play what they play, then they stop.'

'Best way,' said Wright. 'Leave the audience wanting.' He drained his lager and Civel ordered two more bottles.

Hammack and Ramirez helped lift O'Leary and his chair off the stage and went over to two green leather sofas placed at right angles to each other close to the bottom of the spiral staircase that led up to the balcony. Hammack and Ramirez sat down and O'Leary parked his wheelchair in the gap. A few seconds later they were joined by Doc. The two Thai members of the band headed for the doors, the big musician carrying his double bass as if it were no heavier than a briefcase.

When Wright's lager arrived he said goodbye to the Canadian, and went over to the table where the band were sitting and drinking beers. The four men looked up at him as he approached. 'Mind if I join you?' he asked.

Ramirez, Hammack and O'Leary looked across at Doc. Doc in turn squinted up at Wright. 'We know you?' he asked.

'My name's Nick Wright. I'm a policeman. From England.'

'Jolly old England, what?' said Doc in a passable imitation of an upper-class English accent. 'Hello, hello, hello, what's all this, then?' He laughed and his three companions laughed along with him. 'Do you have any identification, Mr Wright?'

Doc asked, his face suddenly serious and the English accent forgotten.

Wright showed him his warrant card.

'British Transport Police?' said Doc. 'Someone stolen a train, Sergeant?'

'It's more serious than that,' said Wright. He indicated an empty space on the sofa next to Doc. 'Okay if I sit down?'

Doc stood up. He was an inch or so taller than Wright, but thinner. 'If it's serious, maybe we should have a little privacy,' he said. He spoke in Thai to a waitress and she nodded at a door close to the bottom of the spiral staircase. Doc thanked her. 'There's a private room we can use over there,' he said, handing the warrant card back to Wright. Wright followed Doc as he weaved through the armchairs and sofas.

The far wall of the nightclub was filled with framed photographs of the bands that played there, and Wright saw several featuring The Jazz Club as he walked by. Doc was always centre stage, the focus of the group.

The thickly carpeted room that Doc led Wright into was gloomy and lined with books that appeared to have been bought by the yard. There were several leather armchairs and, incongruously, a pinball machine up against one wall.

Doc sat down in the armchair furthest from the door and lit a Marlboro with a Zippo lighter as Ramirez, Hammack and O'Leary made their way into the room. Hammack waited until O'Leary's wheelchair had crossed the threshold, then he closed the door and stood with his back to it. Again, the three musicians waited for Doc to speak.

Doc blew smoke through tightly pursed lips and studied the detective for several seconds. 'So what brings you to

Bangkok, Sergeant Wright?' He put his Zippo on the table next to him.

'I'm investigating a murder,' said Wright.

'Eric's?' said Doc.

'Maybe.' He squinted at the lighter. It was an old steel model, worn and scratched from years of use. Engraved on it was a cartoon rat, not a friendly rodent like Mickey Mouse but a shifty-looking creature with narrow eyes and a malicious grin. In one hand it held a flashlight, in the other a gun.

Doc said nothing, his watery eyes boring into Wright's.

'What do you mean, maybe?' asked O'Leary, but he was deterred from saying anything else by a quick sidelong glance from Doc, a look that could have frozen antifreeze.

'I'm investigating a similar murder that took place in London several weeks ago.'

'Similar in what way?' asked Doc.

'An American. Tortured and killed.' He paused. 'With an ace of spades impaled in his chest on a knife.'

Wright heard a slight gasp from behind him, but he had no way of knowing if it was O'Leary or Hammack. Wright kept his eyes on Doc. The man showed no reaction at all: his hands were rock steady, he didn't even swallow.

'According to the newspaper reports I've read, that's how Eric Horvitz died. I'm working on the theory that the murders are connected.'

Doc nodded slowly. 'And this American, the one who was murdered in London. What was his name?'

'Max Eckhardt.'

Doc's face was as unyielding as a granite cliff. He stared at Wright and took another long draw on his cigarette.

'Doesn't ring a bell,' he said. He flicked ash into a large crystal ashtray.

'Max Eckhardt,' repeated Wright. He spelled out the surname.

Doc shrugged. 'It's an unusual name, I'm sure I'd remember it.'

Wright turned around to look at O'Leary, who was staring at Doc with wide eyes. 'What about you, Mr O'Leary? Does the name Eckhardt ring any bells with you?'

O'Leary shook his head, but he kept looking at Doc, like a loyal Labrador waiting for instructions from its master.

'Are you sure?' pressed Wright.

O'Leary looked up at him. 'I'm sure,' he said, but Wright could sense the tension in his voice.

'And you, Mr Hammack?'

Hammack stood impassively, his massive arms folded across his chest. 'Not a name I'm familiar with,' he said. He grinned, but there was no humour in the expression. A gold tooth glinted in the left-hand side of his mouth.

Wright looked sharply across at Ramirez. 'Want to make it unanimous, Mr Ramirez?' he said.

Ramirez flashed Wright a movie-star smile but said nothing.

'Three wise monkeys,' said Wright. 'Hear no evil, see no evil, speak no evil.'

'There are four of us,' said Doc. 'Actually.'

'And you never met Max Eckhardt?'

'You won't get a different answer by asking the same question over and over again,' said Doc, stabbing out the butt of his cigarette.

'What makes you think it's the same killer?' asked O'Leary, a nervous tremor in his voice.

Wright turned to face him. O'Leary was clearly the weak link in the group. 'There are too many similarities for it to be a coincidence,' he said. 'The way the body was tortured, the playing card, the fact that the victim's penis was placed in his mouth, the fact that the body was found underground . . .'

'Underground?' repeated O'Leary. 'What do you mean, underground?'

'Horvitz was found in the basement of his orphanage. Eckhardt was tortured and murdered in a disused railway tunnel in South London.'

'A tunnel?' repeated O'Leary. His head swivelled around to look at Doc, who silenced him with a small wave of his hand.

'But you've no motive, no explanation of why someone would want to kill two men that way?'

'No,' admitted Wright. 'We've no motive.'

'And no suspect?'

'I was hoping that by finding a link between the two victims, I'd be able to come up with a motive and a suspect. It seems I was wrong.'

'It was worth a try, though,' said Doc, lighting up another Marlboro. 'I'm sorry we couldn't be of more help, but Eric's murder is a mystery to us, and we've never heard of Eckhardt.' He blew a thin plume of smoke up at the ceiling. 'Is there anything else we can help you with?'

'Yeah, just one thing,' said Wright. 'How come this place is called Cowboy Nights?'

Doc grinned. 'Used to be a country and western place, line dancing, banjos, the works. The Thai guy who owned it lost a bundle and sold out to the present owners. They liked the name, thought it had class, so they did up the interior and left the outside as it is. Typical Thailand.' He took another long pull on his cigarette, his watery blue eyes fixed on Wright's face. 'Okay?' he said.

Wright nodded and headed for the door. Of all the questions he'd asked of the four men, it was probably the only one that he felt had been answered truthfully. 'Thanks for your time,' he said, wiping his sweating hands on his slacks. 'And for the music.'

Hammack stepped to the side and opened the door for him, then closed it behind him.

Wright stood for a while, looking at the framed photographs that lined the wall at the bottom of the spiral staircase. He wondered what the men would say when they were alone. And he wondered why they'd lied to him. The proof that the four Americans knew Max Eckhardt was hanging on the wall among the scores of other photographs. One of the pictures was an old one of The Jazz Club, by the look of it taken more than a decade earlier. Eric Horvitz wasn't in the photograph, but Max Eckhardt was, standing next to Doc and cradling a bass guitar.

'Max is dead,' said Ramirez quietly. 'How could it have happened and we not know about it?'

'We're not his next of kin, Sergio,' said Doc. 'Why would anyone tell us?'

'We're family,' said Ramirez bitterly. 'We should have been at the funeral. We pay our respects to the dead, when it's family.'

'Doc, did you know what had happened to Max?' asked Hammack, who had remained standing with his back to the door.

Doc flicked ash into the ashtray. 'No, Bernie, I did not. Do you think if I had known, I'd have kept it from you?'

'First Max. Then Eric. Who's next, Doc?' O'Leary's voice rose in pitch and there was a look of panic in his eyes.

'We don't know that anyone's going to be next,' said Doc.

O'Leary gestured with his chin at the door. 'The Brit knows,' he said.

'He knows nothing,' said Doc calmly. 'Hell, Dennis, what do any of us know?'

'He's not dead,' said O'Leary. 'He didn't die down there and now he's coming back for us.'

'That's crazy talk,' said Doc.

'What, that's a professional opinion, is it, Doc?'

Doc looked at O'Leary through a cloud of cigarette smoke. 'Maybe it is, Dennis.'

Ramirez laughed sourly. 'Maybe I could prescribe him a little something, hey, Doc?'

Doc went to stand with his back to the pinball machine. 'Time for a sitrep,' he said. 'Eric was murdered in his basement, by a person or persons unknown. In a manner with which we are all familiar. We've just been told that Max has also been murdered under similar circumstances. Whoever killed them knows what we know, but there are no such things as ghosts, gentlemen. He died down there, he's dead and buried, so we have to look elsewhere for our killer.'

'The card, Doc?' said Ramirez. 'What about the card?'

'The card is being used for exactly the same reason that

we used to use it. The fear factor. Somebody's trying to scare us.'

'They're fucking well succeeding,' said O'Leary.

'Someone knows what we did,' said Hammack quietly. 'Someone knows what we did and is paying us back.'

'Maybe,' said Doc. 'So we've got to find out who it is, not worry about ghosts from the past. The dead don't walk, the dead don't talk. The dead don't do anything. That's what dead means.'

'Maybe he's not dead,' said Hammack.

Doc's upper lip curled back in a sneer. 'Your memory playing tricks on you, Bernie?' he said.

Hammack shrugged. 'They were tough motherfuckers, Doc. We've seen them walk when they should be crawling, crawl when they should be dead.'

'After what we did?' asked Doc. 'Time for a reality check, gentlemen. Is there anyone here who seriously thinks that he's not dead?' He looked from man to man, and could see indecision in all their faces. He shook his head in disgust. 'I don't believe this,' he said.

'Who else could it be?' asked O'Leary. 'Who else knows what we did? Max? Eric? They're dead. The four of us? Well, I sure as hell know I didn't do it, and I'd trust you guys with my life.'

'There's Rabbit,' said Ramirez.

'Rabbit's in the States, hasn't been out here in more than twenty years. And he's too high profile these days. Are you suggesting that Rabbit flew to London to murder Max, then got on a plane to Bangkok and did Eric?'

Ramirez shrugged. 'I'm just listing the possibilities, Doc,' he said.

'Well, if you're doing that, what about Jumbo?'

'Jumbo?' repeated O'Leary.

'Yeah, maybe Jumbo wasn't dead. Okay, maybe we had his blood all over us, okay so his neck was hacked to bits, and I know I helped put the corpse on the helicopter myself, but maybe an angel came down and blessed him and gave him another chance, maybe the dead can walk again . . .'

'Jumbo's dead,' said Hammack flatly.

Doc clenched his left hand in frustration and banged it against the side of the pinball machine. 'I know he's fucking dead!' he hissed. 'That's what I'm trying to tell you. They're both dead, we all know they're both dead.' He turned his back to them and stared at the book-lined walls as if hoping to draw inspiration from the volumes.

'Doc, who else could it be?' asked O'Leary, hesitantly.

Doc turned around. 'I'm going to ask you one at a time. Do you think he's alive or not? Dennis?'

'I think he might be, yes,' said O'Leary, averting his eyes.

'Jesus H. Christ. Sergio?'

'I don't know,' said the Latino. 'I really don't know. Like Dennis said, who else could it be? There were only seven of us came out alive, and two have been murdered. That leaves five, and four of us are here. Rabbit's got no motive, and if he had, why would he wait so long? He's always known where we were.'

Doc blew cigarette smoke in Ramirez's direction and shook his head sorrowfully. He looked across at Hammack. 'Bernie?'

'Maybe,' said Hammack. 'Maybe he is, maybe he isn't. I wouldn't like to place a bet one way or the other.'

Doc dropped his cigarette on to the floor and ground it into the carpet with his heel. The emotion seemed to drain from his face and he visibly relaxed. 'Fine,' he said. 'We have a might be, a don't know, and a maybe. And as my vote is a definite no, that means we have nothing approaching a consensus.' He sat down and folded his arms. 'So what do we do now?' he asked them. 'I'm open to suggestions.'

'We could talk to the cops,' said O'Leary.

'And tell them what we did?' said Doc.

O'Leary shrugged. 'It was a long time ago, in a war situation.'

'And if someone is trying to kill us all, you think the Thais will protect us?'

O'Leary pulled a face. 'I guess not.'

'We could go back,' said Hammack.

'And do what?' said Doc.

'See if the body's there.'

'And if it's not? Then what?'

'Then at least we'd know,' said Hammack.

Doc leaned forward and scratched his neck. 'And if there's no body, Bernie? If it's not there?'

'Then at least we'd know,' said Hammack. 'Either way, we'd know.'

Doc said nothing. He stared at Hammack and the two men locked eyes as if both were unwilling to be the first to look away.

'Okay,' said Doc eventually. 'We'll vote on it. You first, Bernie.'

'I'm not exactly losing sleep over it, but the card business makes me think it's connected with what happened back then. Yeah, Doc, I wanna go back for a look-see.'

Doc nodded. 'Sergio?'

The Latino shrugged. 'Waste of time,' he said. 'It doesn't matter who did it, what matters is if they try again.

And there ain't nobody gonna get close to me to cut me up.'

'So you vote no?'

Ramirez nodded. Doc looked at O'Leary. 'Dennis?'

O'Leary slapped the wheels of his chair. 'What's the point of me voting? I'm not going back, am I?'

'Dennis,' said Doc quietly. O'Leary looked up. 'We're a team, Dennis,' said Doc quietly. 'You get to vote.'

O'Leary smiled tightly. 'Then I vote yes. I want to know if he's dead or not.'

Doc sat back in his chair. 'Two votes for yes, one for no,' he said. 'You're out of your minds.' He looked at Hammack and at O'Leary. 'Out of your fucking minds.' He turned to Sergio, and the Latino wrinkled his nose and shrugged. 'Okay, I vote yes,' said Doc. 'Is that okay with you, Sergio? No one's going to force you.'

Sergio laughed harshly. 'Think I'd let you two go back down there alone?' he said. 'You wouldn't last five minutes. Besides, have you taken a look in the mirror lately? You're both about twenty pounds heavier than you were back then.'

Doc stood up and went over to O'Leary. 'Okay, we go. We'll need visas, but I've got a guy who can get them for us pronto.' He held out his right hand, palm down. O'Leary reached out hesitantly and put his hand on top of Doc's. Hammack walked over and put his massive black hand down on top, and Ramirez did the same.

Doc nodded. 'Not worth a rat's ass,' he said. One by one the men repeated the phrase. 'You are a bunch of crazy bastards,' said Doc.

'Yeah,' agreed Hammack. 'But you love us really.'

When Nick Wright arrived back at the hotel, the elderly man in the stained T-shirt was still fast asleep, slumped across the reception desk. He'd been joined in his slumber by the security guard who had reoccupied his spot on the sofa and was snoring softly, his peaked cap pushed down over his face. Half a dozen keys were lined up on the counter and Wright took his.

Wright went up to his room and sat down on the bed, wondering how he was going to deal with Doc and his band. Why were they lying about not knowing Max Eckhardt? Did they know who the killer was? If they did, why hadn't they told the police? And if they didn't, what were they hiding? None of it made any sense. He stood up and paced around the room, then stood for a while staring out through the window.

His room was at the back of the hotel and overlooked a sprawl of tin shacks with corrugated iron roofs scattered around a construction site where foundations were being laid. Concrete columns intertwined with steel mesh sprouted from the ground like stunted trees and a group of mangy dogs sat staring at a cement mixer as if they expected it to provide food at any moment. Wright ran his finger down the window, then slowly traced out the word 'Why?' on the glass.

He went over to the wardrobe and took his harmonica out of his suitcase, then stood at the window again. He began to play, a slow mournful tune that he'd heard once but never discovered the name of, his brow furrowed as he concentrated. Down below, one of the dogs pricked up its ears and stared up at his window.

Gerry Hunter lifted down the cardboard box and went through the contents. Several notebooks, a small tape recorder, a pencil sharpener with 'World's Best Uncle' on it, stationery and pens, and a couple of science fiction paperbacks. No video. Hunter hefted the box back on to the metal shelf. He'd cleared out Edmunds's desk the day after he'd died, but he hadn't known what to do with his stuff and had left it in the evidence room for safekeeping. Hunter stood with his hands on his hips, wondering if there was anywhere else Edmunds could have left the *Apocalypse Now* video. He'd searched his flat and his car and he'd asked all his colleagues and friends but none of them had been given a video by Edmunds.

Hunter went back to the incident room and sat down at his desk. The ace of spades playing card was in a clear plastic evidence bag, propped up against Hunter's computer keyboard. Hunter stared at it. It was crusted with dried blood and there was a jagged hole in the centre of the card where the knife had been. Hunter picked up the evidence bag and looked more closely at the card within. In the middle of the black ace was the ghostly figure of a woman, and the hole went through her chest. Was there any significance about the ace of spades? Hunter wondered. He knew that there was a death card in the Tarot pack, but he didn't know if the ace of spades was connected to death or murder. There hadn't been an ace of spades in the *Apocalypse Now* video; Duvall had been throwing down cards at random. He turned the card over. There was more blood on the back than the front, but there seemed to be nothing unusual about the card itself. It obviously meant something to someone, however. Had Edmunds solved the mystery? Hunter wondered. Had he uncovered the significance of the card before he died?

Hunter dropped the evidence bag on to his desktop and sat back in his chair, staring up at the polystyrene tiles above his head. A card had been left on mutilated bodies in South London and Bangkok. Playing cards had been left on bodies in the Vietnam War. What was the connection? He wondered if Wright's investigation in Bangkok had turned anything up yet.

He leaned forward and tapped out the commands on the HOLMES computer keyboard that called up the background notes on Max Eckhardt. He had been forty-eight years old. Old enough to have served in the Vietnam War. There was no mention of military service in the notes, but as it would have been a quarter of a century earlier, Hunter wasn't surprised. He called up the post mortem file and scanned it. There had been old scars in the man's back. Shrapnel wounds, perhaps. A war wound? Hunter took his notebook out of his jacket. He was a compulsive note-taker, had been ever since he'd been a twenty-year-old constable on foot patrol. There were two lines of enquiry that he wanted to follow: he had to find out if Max Eckhardt had served in the Vietnam War, and he had to nail down the significance of the ace of spades.

Somchai was back on duty when Nick Wright went down to reception. 'Good morning, Mr Nick,' the Thai said, smiling broadly. 'I have good news for you.'

'Good news?' said Wright. He was wearing a blue linen jacket, white shirt, light brown slacks and his BTP tie.

Somchai produced a sheet of hotel notepaper with a flourish. 'I have found the policeman you wanted. Colonel Vasan.' He handed the paper to Wright. In capital letters he'd written Vasan's name, a telephone number and an address, and he'd noted down the address in Thai. Wright didn't have the heart to tell him that he already had the man's business card in his wallet. He smiled and thanked the Thai teenager and gave him a five-hundred-baht note.

'Can you do me another favour? Can you call and fix up an appointment for me?' He looked at his wristwatch. It was ten a.m. 'Say in about an hour?'

'It will take you more than an hour, Mr Nick,' said Somchai. 'Traffic very bad today. Maybe an hour and a half.'

'Okay. Can you arrange it?'

'I can try,' said Somchai. He picked up the telephone and dialled Colonel Vasan's number. He spoke for a minute or two then was put on hold. After a few minutes he spoke to someone else and was then put on hold again. Somchai smiled apologetically.

Wright went over and sat on one of the sofas by the side of the entrance. He picked up a copy of the *Bangkok*

Post and tried to read an incomprehensible article on Thai politics. There had just been an election but with no outright winner all the participants were manoeuvring to put together a workable coalition. Wright found the story difficult to read: the English was unwieldy and the names of the people involved were so impossibly long and unpronounceable that he couldn't remember them from one paragraph to the next. From time to time he glanced over at Somchai who was waiting patiently with the phone held against his ear.

Wright read through the news section and then the sport section, which contained a surprisingly large number of stories on British football. He read the business section, then flicked through the classified advertisements. He looked at his wristwatch. Half an hour had passed and Somchai was still on the phone. Wright sighed and put his feet up on a small table. He closed his eyes.

He was woken up by someone shaking his shoulder. It was Somchai. Wright rubbed his eyes and took his feet off the table. 'What?' he said, momentarily confused. He looked at his watch again. He'd been asleep for half an hour.

'Colonel Vasan is very busy,' said the receptionist, 'but his secretary said if you come and wait, maybe he can see you.'

'So is that an appointment or not?'

Somchai's cyebrows knotted together. 'I don't understand.'

'If I go, will he definitely see me? I don't want to waste my time.'

'Maybe,' said Somchai, smiling ingratiatingly.

Wright hauled himself up off the sofa. His mind felt woolly and he was having difficulty concentrating. It was probably jetlag, he figured, coupled with the humidity and the alcohol he'd drunk the previous night. He thanked Somchai and went out in search of a taxi.

It was a swelteringly hot day and his shirt was soon drenched with sweat. He walked down the soi to Sukhumvit and stood at the roadside, trying to breathe through his nose because the air was thick with traffic fumes. A coach crawled by, the windows wide open and most of its passengers dozing in the heat. Black smoke belched from its exhaust and Wright stepped back. Emission controls were clearly not a priority in the city.

A motorcyclist in a wraparound helmet and wearing a bright green vest over a T-shirt stopped in front of Wright. 'Where you go?' he asked.

Wright shook his head. He peered down the traffic-packed road. The only taxis he could see were already occupied.

'Where you go?' the motorcyclist repeated. He was barely in his twenties with skin burned almost black from the sun. He wore ragged jeans and had rubber flipflop sandals on his feet.

Wright showed him the police colonel's business card.

'Forty baht,' said the motorcyclist. About one pound sterling.

Wright took another long look around. There wasn't an empty taxi in sight and the traffic was barely moving. 'Okay,' he sighed and climbed on the small motorcycle. The driver twisted around and handed Wright an old pudding-basin-type black helmet with a frayed strap. Wright inspected the interior for lice, found none, and put it on. It wasn't a bad fit. Before he could fasten the strap the motorcyclist pulled away from the kerb and began weaving through the traffic. Wright held on to the metal bar at the rear of the seat.

They made surprisingly quick progress. The cars and trucks all left plenty of space between their vehicles, giving the motorcyclists room to get by. On the few occasions they reached a blockage, the car drivers would do their best to create a gap so that the bikes could get through, acts of generosity that were acknowledged with nods of helmeted heads.

They reached a set of traffic lights where more than fifty motorcycles had already gathered, engines revving. Wright tried holding his tie over his mouth but it provided little in the way of protection from the fumes. The air was deadly, and he could understand why most of the traffic policemen he'd seen wore white cotton masks over their mouths and noses.

The lights turned green and Wright almost fell off the pillion as his rider sped away. All the girl passengers he saw were riding side-saddle, one leg on the foot rest, the other suspended in mid air, their handbags on their laps. Many appeared to be office workers or housewives in pastel-coloured suits. There were many child passengers, too, some so small that they sat astride the petrol tanks, their tiny hands gripping the handlebars as their fathers drove. On one 250cc Yamaha he saw a husband and wife and three children between them, packed like sardines on to the seat.

There seemed to be construction sites everywhere Wright looked, and the skyline was peppered with cranes atop half-built office blocks and apartments.

A Mercedes pulled out of a side street and the bike swerved to avoid a collision, but it all happened so quickly that Wright didn't even have time to be scared. They turned off Sukhumvit and roared down a four-lane road, but within half a mile hit another traffic jam and began weaving in and out of unmoving cars. At one point the driver took the bike up on to the pavement and drove slowly, nodding apologies to those pedestrians he inconvenienced.

Several times they were forced to stop at traffic lights and had to wait an inordinate length of time. The lights appeared to be operated almost on a random basis by brown-uniformed policemen who sat in glass-sided cubicles. At one intersection they were held up for a full ten minutes and when Wright looked over his shoulder he could see a queue of cars almost half a mile long.

They left the main road and sped through a network of narrow side streets. Behind walls topped with broken glass stood houses with red-tiled roofs, wide balconies, shielded by spreading palm trees. The air was fresher, though occasionally Wright was hit by the stench of an open sewer or the odour of overripe fruit or animal faeces. The small streets had no pavements and the driver kept having to swerve to avoid pedestrians. There were clusters of shops with apartments above them, high-class shops selling Italian furniture and Thai antiques, and others offering haircuts or same-day laundry.

Many of the side streets were one-way, being too narrow for cars to pass, and they had to zigzag left and right with little or no indication of who had the right of way. They cut through the car park of a large hotel where a security guard in a grey uniform and white gloves pushed a mobile barrier out of the way so they could get by, then joined another main road. Wright had lost all sense of where he was; the city seemed to be one huge sprawl with no obvious centre.

They eventually came to a halt close to a white three-storey building with a huge car park in front. Above the main entrance porch was a huge gold and red insignia and large Thai letters which ran almost the full length of the building. Brown-uniformed policemen manned the barrier restricting entrance to the car park. Wright dismounted and paid the motorcycle rider, then strode up to the barrier. The policemen smiled at him but didn't ask what he wanted so Wright walked by and headed for the main entrance. He pushed open a glass door and went inside.

A dozen or so Thais sat on several rows of wooden benches, and two men in denims lay on one of the benches, snoring softly. An elderly woman was peeling an orange and handing pieces of the fruit to a little girl in pigtails. The benches faced a wooden counter behind which stood half a dozen uniformed men and women. Two of them, young men with red braid on the left shoulders of their tunics and strips of bright-coloured medals on their breast pockets, were talking to visitors and taking notes but the rest didn't seem to be doing anything. Wright couldn't see a queuing system in operation so he walked up to the counter. A girl who was barely out of her teens smiled at him.

'Do you speak English?' he asked.

She smiled and shook her head.

'Does anyone here speak English?' asked Wright, pointing at the uniforms behind the counter.

Her smile widened. She shook her head again.

Wright and the girl stood smiling at each other. He wondered if it was a test of wills, if she was seeing how long he could wait with an inane grin on his face. If it was a test, Wright failed. He took out Colonel Vasan's business card and handed it to the girl.

'I want to speak to him,' he said.

She read the card and then looked at Wright with renewed respect, speaking to him in rapid Thai.

Wright shook his head. 'I don't understand,' he said. He was starting to feel helpless. The language was so unfamiliar, the sounds so strange, that he couldn't even begin to guess what she was talking about.

A female officer and a middle-aged man came over and took it in turns to read the card. The man spoke to Wright in Thai.

'I'm sorry,' said Wright. 'I don't speak Thai.'

'Name you?' said the man.

'Ah, yes,' said Wright. He took out his wallet and gave the officer one of his British Transport Police business cards. It was studied with equal solemnity.

'Sit, please,' said the man, indicating the benches.

Wright went and sat down. The officers talked among themselves, then the young girl picked up a phone. Wright sighed. That hadn't been too difficult.

Half an hour later he was still waiting. He went back up to the desk and in pidgin English tried to ask how long it would be before Colonel Vasan could see him. He was faced with more smiles and nods towards the benches. He went and sat down again.

Forty-five minutes later a matronly woman in a pale blue dress came up behind him. 'Mr Nick?' she said.

Wright stood up. 'Yes,' he said. 'Nick Wright. I'm here to see Colonel Vasan.'

'He is very busy today,' she said, handing him his business card. 'Can you come back tomorrow?'

'I don't mind waiting,' he said.

The woman hesitated, then smiled. She turned and went through one of four doors in the wall opposite the counter. Wright sat down. Behind him the two men continued to snore quietly. Wright wondered if like him they were also waiting to see someone, of if they had just come in to take advantage of the airconditioning.

It was a full hour before the woman returned. 'Colonel Vasan will see you now,' she said.

Wright followed her through the door, along a corridor, up a flight of stairs and along another corridor, lined on both sides with dark wooden doors bearing the names of police officers. The woman took Wright into an office which contained a desk and a dozen filing cabinets. On the desk was a photograph of two smiling children and next to it a gold Buddha statue around which had been draped a garland of purple and white flowers. She knocked on a door and disappeared.

When the woman reappeared a few minutes later she nodded at a chair by the door. 'Please wait here,' she said, smiling. 'He is busy again.'

Wright began to feel that he was getting the runaround, but he smiled and sat down as asked. He could only imagine what sort of reception a Thai detective would get if he turned up at BTP headquarters unable to speak a word of English, so he was prepared to be patient. He sat with his hands on his knees and resisted the temptation to keep looking at his watch.

The woman busied herself with paperwork, occasionally pecking at a large electric typewriter that shuddered so much that her desk vibrated every time she pressed a key. After fifteen minutes she stood up, opened the door to the colonel's office and told Wright that the colonel was ready to see him. There had been no phone call, no signal from the colonel, and Wright knew for sure that he'd been deliberately kept waiting in the outer office.

Colonel Vasan was a short, stocky man with jet black

hair that glistened as if it had been oiled and steel-framed spectacles that sat high up on a prominent nose. He wore a chocolate-brown uniform with gold insignia on the shoulders and a thick chunk of ribbon medals on his breast pocket. His left cheek was pitted and scarred as if it had been scraped against a rough surface a long time ago. He had a square face with a wide jaw that he thrust forward as he studied Wright. He had Wright's business card on his desk and he looked down at it and then back at Wright's face.

'Thank you for seeing me, Colonel Vasan,' said Wright, holding out his hand.

The colonel looked at the hand, then at Wright's card, then back to Wright's face. He spoke in Thai. Wright was about to say that he couldn't speak Thai when the secretary spoke behind him.

'Colonel Vasan prefers to conduct interviews in his own language,' she explained. 'I will translate for him. He asks that you sit down.'

Wright sat on one of two wooden chairs facing Vasan's desk. The secretary sat next to him, her hands clasped in her lap.

'I am Sergeant Nick Wright. I am a detective with the British Transport Police in London investigating a murder that took place several weeks ago.'

Wright waited for the secretary to translate. The colonel stood up as the secretary spoke and strode over to a window that overlooked the car park. Wright noticed a large holstered handgun on Vasan's right hip, and a radio transceiver hooked to his belt. His trousers were tucked into black boots that had been polished to a lustrous shine. He looked more like a soldier than a policeman.

'I understand from press reports that there has been a

similar murder in Bangkok. A man called Eric Horvitz. I was hoping that you might tell me what progress had been made on the case.'

When the secretary finished translating, the colonel turned. He spoke in Thai and the secretary turned to Wright.

'Colonel Vasan asks that you tell him about the case you are investigating,' she said.

Wright took an envelope out of his jacket pocket and handed it to Vasan. Inside was a printout of the pathologist's report, a description of the crime scene, photographs of the crime scene and the body, Max Eckhardt's biography and several newspaper cuttings. Vasan studied them. Wright wondered if he was able to read English or if he was only pretending to.

'The victim was a forty-eight-year-old American photographer, married but with no children. He'd only recently arrived in London. He had no enemies as far as we can see. Some camera equipment and his wallet were taken, but we don't think robbery was the motive. The wounds were inflicted over a long period and amount to torture.'

The colonel nodded, even though the secretary hadn't started translating. When she did begin talking, Vasan seemed more interested in the newspaper cuttings than in what she was saying. Wright reckoned the Thai policeman's English was more than adequate for a conversation, but that he preferred to use the woman as a buffer. Vasan waited until she'd finished before speaking to her in Thai.

'Colonel Vasan asks why there is no mention of the playing card in the newspaper articles you have given him,' she said.

Wright explained that investigating officers often withheld

information in the hope that it would help identify the culprit at a later date. The secretary translated and the colonel nodded. He sat down again behind his desk and spread the photographs out, studying them in silence for several minutes.

'What I'd like is to have a look at the evidence you collected from your crime scene, and perhaps to speak to your officers,' said Wright. 'It has to be the same killer.'

The secretary didn't start translating until the colonel looked up from the pictures. He replied in Thai.

'Colonel Vasan asks what is it that you want to know,' she said.

Vasan gathered up the photographs and handed them to Wright, but kept hold of the printouts and newspaper cuttings.

'The playing card,' said Wright. 'I'd like a look at it.'

Again, Vasan reacted before his secretary translated. He said something to her and nodded at a bank of filing cabinets. She went over to them and pulled out a drawer. She had a pair of spectacles hanging on a chain around her neck and she put them on, then riffled through the grey cardboard files. She took one out and gave it to Wright.

It consisted mainly of written reports, all in Thai, none of which made any sense at all to Wright. Most appeared to be handwritten. There was a hand-drawn diagram which he realised must be the basement where the body was discovered. 'Are there any photographs of the crime scene?' he asked.

Colonel Vasan shook his head before the secretary had time to translate.

'No, there are not,' she said.

At the back of the file was a plastic bag containing a

blood-stained ace of spades. The black ace filled most of the card and in the centre of it, where it had been punctured by a knife, was the ghostly figure of a woman. It was the same brand that had been found in the Battersea tunnel.

'It's the same,' he said. 'The card we found in London was the same as this.' He held it up.

The secretary translated.

'Would it be possible for me to have translations of these reports?' asked Wright, indicating the file.

The secretary spoke to Vasan, who shrugged and replied.

'It is possible, but it will take time,' said the secretary. 'If you tell us where you are staying, we will have them delivered to you.'

Wright nodded. 'Thank you.'

'There will be a charge for the service, however,' she said.

Wright was surprised but tried not to show it. 'Fine,' he said.

She spoke to Vasan and the colonel smiled.

'And I'd appreciate a look at the rest of the files on the case,' said Wright.

The secretary frowned. 'There is only the one file,' she said.

Wright was stunned. 'That's all there is?' he said. 'For a murder invcstigation? Are there no computer files? Witness reports?'

She translated and listened as the Colonel replied. 'That is the only file,' she said, 'but Colonel Vasan will answer any questions you might have.'

'Does he have a suspect? Any motive, a reason why anyone would want to kill Eric Horvitz?'

Through his translator, the Thai policeman said that enquiries were continuing, but so far they had no theories, that Eric Horvitz had been well liked, had no financial problems, and so far as the Thai police were concerned, no enemies.

'And what about the card? Do you have any idea of the significance of the ace of spades?'

The secretary translated and the colonel shook his head. Assuming that Vasan wasn't keeping anything back, the Thai police had made as little progress as Wright and his colleagues had on their case.

The colonel spoke to his secretary. 'Colonel Vasan asks if you know of any other connection between the two dead men,' she said.

A good question, thought Wright. He'd gone to the police station with the intention of sharing the information he had, and of telling Vasan that Eckhardt and Horvitz had both played with The Jazz Club in Bangkok, but now he was having second thoughts. Vasan seemed more concerned with playing power games than with solving the case. Wright shook his head. 'Not yet,' he said.

When he left the office, Wright didn't offer to shake hands.

Gerry Hunter got AFP's number from directory enquiries and called up Steve Reynolds. 'I'm calling about Max Eckhardt,' explained Hunter. 'Do you by any chance know if he served in Vietnam?'

'I've already been through this with another officer,' said Reynolds tetchily.

Hunter tensed. 'Who?'

'Edwards. A sergeant, I think.'

'Clive Edmunds?'

'That's it.'

'When was this?' asked Hunter.

'A while back, I think. He called late one evening just as I was on my way out of the office. Insisted I pulled Max's personnel file.'

Hunter gripped the ballpoint pen in his right hand so tightly that his fingers started to turn white. 'Can you remember what you told my colleague?' he asked.

'I know I was able to tell him that Max had been in Vietnam. Look, give me a second, I'll get the file.'

Reynolds was only away from the phone for a few seconds, but it felt like an eternity to Hunter. 'Yeah, here we are. He did a tour of duty in 'sixty-seven and 'sixty-eight.'

'Does it give any details of what he did?'

'No, it's an old CV, from the 'seventies, and back then people tended to gloss over what they did during the war. There was a lot of anti-war feeling in the States, right up until the Reagan years, I guess.'

'What about you, did you go?'

'Hell, no,' said Reynolds. 'I missed it by five years. Why are you so interested in what Max did during the war?'

'It's just a line we're following up,' said Hunter. 'Do you have any idea how I could find out more about his war record?'

'I can tell you the same as I told Edmunds,' said Reynolds. 'You should try the Pentagon. The Defense Department. I'm sure they'd have him on file. Edmunds said he would speak to your FBI agent about it. And there's May, of course.'

'May?'

'Max's wife. She'd probably know.'

'Oh, right, sure.' Hunter thanked Reynolds and hung up.

He sat staring at the wall, his mind in turmoil. Clive had been on to something, but what? He'd tied Eckhardt to the Vietnam War, a war where playing cards were used as death cards. Had Clive taken it any further before he died? Hunter picked up the evidence bag containing the ace of spades. There was nothing in the HOLMES file about Eckhardt's war service, and while Clive was notoriously lax at filling out his reports, Hunter figured that he must have been working on the Vietnam link just before he died. What else had he found out?

Wright pushed open the swing doors and walked into Cowboy Nights. He'd changed into a white cotton shirt and black Levi jeans. The crowd was pretty much the same as the previous night, and he recognised several faces.

The Canadian, Alain Civel, was standing at the bar and he waved at Wright. 'Ah, Neek,' he called, 'back for more?'

Wright joined him and ordered a lager. A waitress put a bowl of roasted peanuts down in front of him and he took a handful. 'What time are The Jazz Club on?' he asked.

'Ten minutes or so. You know it's jam night?'

'Yeah. Are you going to play?'

Civel grimaced. 'Not me, man. They're way out of my league.'

The Thai band finished their set to lukewarm applause. Wright carried his bottle over to the spiral staircase and examined the framed photographs hanging on the wall. The one featuring Max Eckhardt had gone. Wright methodically looked at all the photographs on the wall in case they'd been rearranged, but there was no mistake.

Wright turned around. Doc was standing on the stage, holding his saxophone. He was staring at Wright. Wright raised his bottle in salute and grinned. Doc flashed Wright a tight smile, then turned away.

Wright went back to Civel. 'You've been coming here for ten years, you said?'

'Oui,' said Civel. 'I work in Saudi, but every chance I get I fly over. Beer and women on tap, what more could a man want?'

The question was rhetorical, Wright assumed. 'Ever come across a guy called Eckhardt? Max Eckhardt. Played bass guitar.'

Civel shook his head. 'Don't think so. Why?'

'I saw his picture on the wall, playing with the band.' He nodded at the stage, where Hammack and Ramirez were lifting O'Leary's wheelchair. They spent a few minutes tuning their instruments while the audience waited expectantly.

The band went straight into 'Dimples', a John Lee Hooker song, with O'Leary stabbing at his guitar, rocking his head violently in time with the beat, and Doc's saxophone taking the place of the vocals. Then they eased into two more John Lee Hooker blues tunes, 'Walkin' The Boogie' and 'I See When You're Weak', both giving Doc ample scope to show his flair and originality. Civel jabbed Wright in the ribs and Wright nodded appreciatively.

Hardly had the applause broken out than the band launched into a Muddy Waters classic, 'Got My Mojo Working'. Hammack sang as he played on the keyboard, chewing his gum between verses.

For half an hour the band jammed, and once again it was Doc who was firmly in control, allocating solos with nods and glances. They ended to tumultuous applause, and Doc introduced the members of the band. Then he announced that it was jam night, and that members of the audience were welcome to take part.

The first volunteer was a middle-aged Westerner in a Coca-Cola T-shirt and cut-off jeans. He played drums and Ramirez went over to stand with his fan club while the band ran through two Phil Collins numbers, 'In The Air Tonight' and 'Another Day In Paradise'. The drummer tried to be too clever and several times lost the beat after attempting complicated fills. He left the stage to supportive applause, but there was a self-satisfied look on Ramirez's face as he took his place behind the drum kit.

Next up was a stocky Japanese man in a shiny black suit, who sang 'My Way' in a near-perfect imitation of Sinatra, down to the phrasing and gestures of the great man. It owed more to karaoke than jamming, but The Jazz Club gave him musical and moral support, and joined in the applause when he finished the number. He beamed as he went back to a group of Japanese businessmen clustered around the bar and several of them slapped him on the back.

'Any more volunteers?' asked Doc.

'Here we go,' Wright said to the Canadian. 'Wish me luck.' He walked towards the stage, taking his harmonica from the back pocket of his jeans. Doc raised a querulous eyebrow. 'Okay?' said Wright, holding up the harmonica.

Doc gave him an exaggerated bow and made a sweeping gesture with his arm. 'Feel free,' he said.

Wright stepped up on to the stage. A spotlight moved across and settled around him. O'Leary was staring open mouthed. Wright was obviously the last person he'd expected to see on stage. Ramirez grinned and said something to Hammack and the keyboard player chuckled. '"Before You Accuse Me",' Wright said to Doc. 'You know it?'

'One of my favourites.'

'Guess we don't need to rehearse, then,' said Wright, raising his harmonica to his lips.

Doc looked at him with an expression that came close to amazement, then he shrugged and nodded curtly at Ramirez. The drummer came in quickly as if trying to catch Wright off guard, four taps of his sticks to get the beat and then straight into it. He was joined almost immediately by O'Leary.

Wright took the chorus, his harmonica taking the place of the vocals, and Doc stood at the side of the stage, listening and tapping his right foot. Wright closed his eyes and concentrated on hitting the notes right.

As he finished the chorus, Hammack joined in, but it was Doc who took the solo, turning his back on Wright and putting everything into it.

Doc turned sideways on and flashed a look at Wright, letting him know that the chorus was his again, but Wright didn't lift his harmonica. Instead he sang, with his eyes closed because he didn't want to see Doc's reaction or be distracted by it.

There was a whooping cheer from the far side of the bar

and Wright opened his eyes. It was the Canadian, pumping his fist into the air.

The bass player joined in as Doc took the next verse. Doc threw in a few improvisations as if trying to show Wright what he was capable of. Wright remained stony faced, his eyes fixed on the saxophone as he tried to get a feel for Doc's rhythm. Doc finished the verse and nodded at Wright. Wright raised the harmonica to his lips and played, this time keeping his eyes on Doc's face. Doc smiled and folded his arms around his saxophone. When Wright finished the chorus, Doc nodded again.

Wright stepped closer to his microphone, arching his neck up as he sang. Doc turned to O'Leary as the verse ended and nodded, then gave Hammack a sideways glance. They all hit the chorus together, and Wright joined in with his harmonica. They finished with a flourish and the audience erupted. Wright felt the appreciation wash over him. Ramirez was grinning and Hammack gave Wright an enthusiastic thumbs-up.

Doc walked over to Wright. 'A singing policeman,' he said. 'Where the hell did you learn to sing?'

'I was in a band at university,' said Wright. 'Pubs and stuff.'

'You're good,' said Doc.

'Nah,' said Wright.

'You wanna do another?'

'Sure.'

'You know "It's Rainin' In My Life"?' Doc asked.

'Yeah. Mine too.' Wright grinned. 'Yeah, I know it.'

Doc turned around and primed the rest of the band, then went immediately into it. Wright played harmonica, singing only when he came to the chorus, but when they moved seamlessly into 'Honky Tonk' Wright started to sing again.

Without a break they went into a medley of Howlin' Wolf songs. Wright felt as if Doc was testing him, seeing if he was able to spot the cues. Several times Doc threw solos at him, allowing Wright to jam on the harmonica, then quickly coming in on his sax, taking the lead back and switching tunes, then throwing it back to Wright. Wright enjoyed the challenge, and after half an hour was confident enough to be able to relax and enjoy himself. When Doc eventually brought the set to a halt, the nightclub burst into applause.

Wright went back to the bar where Civel hugged him and clapped him on the back. 'Bloody brilliant, man. *Fantastique*.'

Wright picked up his bottle and drank the last of his lager. Civel ordered him another.

'You can sing, man,' said Civel. 'You can really sing.'

'Thanks.'

The members of The Jazz Club were making their way over to their regular seats. Wright clinked bottles with Civel, then went over to join them.

Doc was whispering something to O'Leary, but he moved back as Wright approached. 'Pull up a chair, Nick,' said Doc.

'Nice harp-playing,' said Ramirez.

'It's just a hobby,' said Wright, sitting down on the sofa next to Hammack.

'You could do it professionally,' said O'Leary, pouring the contents of his bottle of Singha into a glass.

'You could, too,' said Wright. 'Why don't you?'

O'Leary shrugged. 'Not much call for wheelchair-bound

musicians,' he said bitterly. 'These days it's all pretty boys and dance routines.'

'Bullshit,' said Wright. 'You're a musician, a good one. You could play with any band in the UK or the States. Civel said you played with Clapton.'

'He was out here on tour and he dropped by one night, that's all.'

'You held your own, Dennis,' said Doc. He stabbed his cigarette at Wright. 'Clapton offered Dennis a gig in the States, but he turned him down.'

'It wasn't a definite offer, Doc,' said O'Leary.

'Damn was, Dennis, and you know it. You just didn't want to leave your wife alone.'

Ramirez's fan club clustered around him, four young Thai girls in short skirts and tank tops. They were flirting outrageously, vying for his attention, flicking their long hair and batting their eyelashes like crazy. Ramirez talked to them in Thai and they giggled.

'I went to see the cop who's investigating Eric Horvitz's death,' Wright said to Doc. 'He didn't seem to be making much progress.'

'And you're surprised at that?' asked Doc. 'Eric was a farang.'

'A farang?'

'It's what they call foreigners. Investigating the murder of a farang isn't exactly a money-making opportunity, so we're pretty low on their list of priorities.'

'What's money got to do with it?' asked Wright, confused.

Doc sighed as if he'd been asked by a child to explain why the sky was blue. 'People here don't join the cops out of a sense of public service,' he said.

'What, like they do in the States?' interrupted Hammack, his voice loaded with sarcasm. He spat the gum he'd been chewing into an ashtray.

Doc ignored him. 'They join for one reason – to make money. The traffic cops take bribes from motorists, the guys back in the station take a percentage, everyone gets a cut. The higher up the ladder they can climb, the more they get. You want to open a bar in Bangkok, you have to pay the cops. You want to start a business, you talk to the cops. You get arrested, you pay off the cops.'

'Are you saying they don't investigate murders here?'

'No, that's not what I'm saying. Most murders are domestics: a wife stabs her unfaithful husband, husband has one drink too many and hits his wife too hard, kids arguing with parents over money, and they get put away, though they usually serve less than ten years. No, what I'm saying is that if the crime doesn't solve itself, they're not going to put in any effort, not unless there's going to be a pay-off.'

'And where would the pay-off be in solving a murder?'

Doc looked across at Hammack and winked. 'The innocent abroad, isn't he?' He waved his bottle of Singha at Wright. 'Did you tie your white horse up outside, Nick? Checked your suit of armour at the door? You're not in bloody old England now. You can get someone killed in Bangkok for less than a hundred US dollars. Hitman on a motorbike, bullet in the back of the head.' He mimed pulling a trigger. 'Pop!' He took a swig from his bottle. 'Happens every day. Now, do the cops investigate? Yes, if the victim's rich or well connected, because if the victim's a somebody, then the guy who paid for the hit is probably a somebody, too. And being a somebody in this country means only one thing: money. So sure, they'll try to solve the murder then, because if they can come up with a suspect who's got money, they can take a bribe to let him off.'

'That happens?'

'Sure it happens. The hitman will probably go to prison for a few years, but the guy who paid him will take care of his family and give him a bonus. It's typical Thailand, everyone comes out of it making a profit.'

'Except the victim?'

'Yeah. Except the victim.'

'So you reckon this Vasan isn't going to solve Eric's murder?'

'Eric didn't have any rich enemies; hell, he didn't have any enemies at all. He wasn't the boss of a big company, the orphanage was a non-profit-making body.'

'He had money, though.'

'Who told you that?' asked Doc, leaning forward. He pulled a cigarette out of its pack, lit it with his Zippo, and put the red and white pack and the lighter on the low table in front of him.

'One of the nuns. She said Eric paid for everything.'

'He did, but through a trust fund he'd set up. No one could have made a profit from Eric's death.'

Wright put down his bottle of lager. 'Where did Eric get his money from?'

Doc shrugged. 'He never said. He turned up in Bangkok five years ago. Before that he was in Saigon. Before that he was in the States, living rough on the Canadian border.'

'Living rough?'

'I guess he went a little crazy after he got back home. Went off to live by himself in the woods.'

'Back home?'

Doc went suddenly still as if he'd just realised that he'd said too much. Hammack, Ramirez and O'Leary sat looking at him. Ramirez waved the girls away. They pouted and went over to stand by the bar. Wright waited, knowing it was a turning point in the conversation: Doc could either shut up, change the subject, or continue. It was a moment Wright recognised from countless interviews with suspects and witnesses and he knew there was no way he could influence the way Doc would jump. All he could do was wait.

Doc blew smoke out through his nostrils as he stared at Wright. 'Back to the world,' he said eventually. 'From Vietnam. He was a Vietnam vet, and he had a rough war. Post traumatic stress syndrome they call it now. Crazy, they called it back then. Eric went crazy, but no more than thousands of others. Did you know that fifty-eight thousand Americans died in the war? But many more than that went on to commit suicide after they got back. You don't see their names on the wall.'

'The wall?'

'The Vietnam War Memorial in Washington. All the names of the dead are on that wall, they say, but that's shit because they forget about the ones that took their own lives. Tens of thousands of suicides, probably more than a hundred thousand if you count all the car wrecks and drug overdoses. Where are their names, Sergeant Wright? Who remembers them?'

'What about your war, Doc?' asked Wright quietly. 'What was your war like?'

Doc looked at him, his eyes bloodshot and watery. He looked suddenly tired. 'You don't want to know about my war,' he said.

'I can't imagine what it must have been like, to have been sent thousands of miles away from your home to fight a war in a country you knew nothing about. I can barely walk through Bangkok without getting covered in sweat, it must have been hell to have been sent into the jungle carrying a gun. Being shot at.'

'Ever been in a war zone?' asked Doc.

Wright shook his head.

'So you'd never understand, even if I spent a hundred years trying to describe it.'

'And Eckhardt? What was his war like?'

Doc's eyes hardened. Wright could feel the barriers building up. 'How would I know?' asked Doc.

'I just thought that maybe he was a Vietnam War vet, too. That seems to be the common thread, right? You, Eric. And Bernie, Sergio and Dennis, you're all about the same age, all American, I just assumed . . .'

'You assume a lot,' said Doc coldly.

'What about you, Dennis?' Wright asked O'Leary.

O'Leary flinched as if he'd been struck. 'What?'

'Your tour of duty in Vietnam. Is that where you were injured?'

O'Leary looked at Doc. Doc gave a small shake of his head, the sort of gesture he used to such good effect when they were playing. O'Leary looked away and said nothing.

'Maybe it's time you left,' said Doc.

'Why did you take the photograph down?' Wright asked.

'What photograph?' asked Doc.

'You know what photograph. Did you think I hadn't seen it? Did you think that if you took it down I'd convince myself that I'd imagined it?'

Doc said nothing.

'What's going on?' Wright pressed. 'Why the secrecy? They were friends of yours and they were murdered. Don't you want to know who the killer is?'

'We know,' said O'Leary bitterly.

Doc flashed him a withering look and O'Leary put up his hands as if warding off an attack.

'Why don't we tell him?' asked O'Leary.

'This isn't the time or the place,' said Doc.

'You name it,' said Wright.

Doc glared at the detective. 'You're an outsider here, Sergeant Wright, and you've overstayed your welcome.'

'There are still some questions . . .'

'You're not in England now,' said Doc. 'We don't have to tell you anything.'

'I just thought . . .'

'You just thought that if you came along and jammed with us then we'd open up to you like shucked oysters.' Doc stood up. He looked across at Hammack. Hammack stood up, too, his massive arms swinging at his side. 'You can leave under your own steam, or I can provide an alternative. It's up to you,' said Doc.

Wright could see that it was pointless arguing. 'Okay, I can take a hint,' he said. 'Do you mind if I have a cigarette?' Before Doc could say anything, he leaned over and picked up the pack of Marlboro and the lighter.

'Didn't realise you smoked,' said Doc.

Wright took out a cigarette and lit it. He looked at the Zippo. The rat engraved on the side grinned up at him. Wright flipped the lighter over. A Latin phrase was inscribed on the back: *Non Gratum Anus Rodentum*.

Doc took the lighter and the pack from Wright. He nodded at the door.

Wright smiled thinly and held up his hands in mock surrender. 'I can tell when I'm not wanted,' he said. On his way to the swing doors he stubbed out the unsmoked cigarette.

The three flaming torches soared high in the air and the juggler looked up optimistically, his top hat perched precariously on the back of his head. He caught them one by one to scattered applause while a young girl with braided blonde hair walked around with a Harrods bag collecting change from the spectators. As he continued to whirl the torches around his head, the juggler flicked off his top hat and caught it deftly with his right foot.

Gerry Hunter walked behind the crowd and headed for a row of small speciality stores at the far end of Covent Garden. The shop he was looking for was in the middle. Game For A Laugh, it was called, and the window display consisted of board games and books, including more than a dozen different chess sets. Hunter pushed open the door and a bell ding-donged at the back of the store. A balding, overweight man in rolled-up shirtsleeves was sitting behind the counter reading a chess book. He looked up and nodded at Hunter, then went back to his book.

Hunter was the only customer. There were glass-display cases containing more chess sets and stacks of board games, some like Monopoly and Cluedo that Hunter remembered from his childhood, but many that he'd never seen before. Hunter went over to the glass counter. On a shelf below it he saw what he was looking for: dozens of packs of playing cards.

'Help you?' said the man, putting down his book.

Hunter showed him his warrant card. 'I'm interested in a playing card,' he said, taking the plastic bag containing the ace of spades from his coat pocket.

The man took it. 'Is that blood?' he asked.

Hunter nodded. 'Do you know who made the card?'

'Sure do,' said the man. 'The United States Playing Card Company. Biggest card company in the world.' He turned the card over. 'What made the hole?' he asked. 'A bullet?'

Hunter ignored the question. 'Is there anything special about the card?'

The man's lower lip jutted forward and he frowned, as if thinking was an effort. 'Not that I can think of,' he said. He scratched his bald head, and flakes of skin drifted down on to the counter. 'They've got several brands. This one they call Bicycle.'

'Any idea why?'

The man shrugged. 'Just a name, I think.' He showed the front of the card to Hunter. 'See the woman here? The white figure? That's only on the Bicycle brand.'

Hunter took the card off him. 'Do you know much about the cards?'

'I'm more of a chess buff,' said the man, indicating the display case full of chess pieces and boards. 'If I had my way that's all I'd sell, but there's not the call for them that there was. It's computers or fantasy games. Even playing cards don't sell like they used to. What is it you want to know?'

'That's the thing,' said Hunter. 'I'm not really sure.'

The man nodded at the card in Hunter's hand. 'It's a clue, right?'

Hunter smiled thinly. 'Yeah, it's a clue. A big clue. But I haven't the faintest idea what it means. Do you know of anyone who is a real card expert? Somebody who might be able to tell me something about the history of playing cards, stuff like that.'

'Try the card company,' said the man. 'Their head office is in Cincinnati, Ohio.' He scratched his peeling scalp again.

Hunter thanked him and headed back to his office. He wasn't sure what the time difference was between Cincinnati and London, but he figured it must be about six hours. He had time for a quick bite in the canteen before he called the company.

Wright managed to find a taxi driver who spoke reasonable English and he explained that he wanted to sit and watch the bar for a while. 'Five hundred baht for one hour,' said the driver.

'Whatever,' said Wright. He settled back in his seat. The driver tuned his radio to a Thai pop station and adjusted the airconditioning. After an hour, there was still no sign of the members of The Jazz Club leaving Cowboy Nights.

The driver turned around and held out his hand. 'One more hour, five hundred baht,' he said. Wright handed over another purple banknote.

Three elephants walked slowly down the road, trunks and

tails swinging in unison. Each had a man sitting astride its neck, and ahead of them walked a man carrying a string bag full of coconuts.

Thirty minutes later a grey minivan pulled up in front of the bar, driven by a middle-aged Thai man in a pale blue safari suit. The man went into the bar and a few minutes later the swing doors opened and he reappeared, followed by Doc, who was pushing O'Leary's wheelchair. They all headed over to the minivan. The driver climbed back into the cab and opened a side door. A lifting mechanism swung out and down and Doc pushed O'Leary's wheelchair on to it. The wheelchair slowly lifted into the air and back into the van. Doc climbed in with O'Leary and the two men were deep in conversation as the van pulled away from the kerb.

Wright pointed after the van. The driver nodded and followed.

O'Leary lived half an hour's drive from Cowboy Nights, in a row of modern townhouses in a quiet side street. Wright told the driver to keep his distance and they stopped at the end of the street, behind a black pick-up truck. The van parked and the safari-suited driver helped Doc unload O'Leary and his wheelchair. Doc pushed O'Leary up a ramp to the front door and into the house.

Wright's driver turned around and looked expectantly at Wright. The detective handed over another purple banknote.

Doc left the house fifteen minutes later. He climbed into the front of the minivan and it drove off down the road.

Wright waited a few minutes, then went over to the front door and knocked on it. A Thai woman answered it, barefoot in T-shirt and jeans. Wright told her who he was and said that he wanted to speak to Dennis. She stepped to the side to let him in.

Dennis O'Leary was sitting in his wheelchair at the far end of the room, a bottle of whisky on the table next to him. An Eric Clapton CD was playing on an expensive stereo system under one of the windows. Wright recognised the album. *Journeyman*.

'What do you want?' O'Leary asked.

'Just a chat,' said Wright. The girl who'd opened the door padded up an open wooden staircase and disappeared into a bedroom. 'Your wife?' asked Wright.

O'Leary shook his head. 'No. Not my wife.' He drank from a tumbler. 'Doc says we shouldn't talk to you.'

'Do you do everything Doc says?' asked Wright.

O'Leary put his head on one side as he considered the question. 'Pretty much,' he said.

The room was large, with dark wooden floorboards and rosewood furniture and several large Buddha statues, most of which looked very old. Thai embroideries hung on the walls. At one end of the room there were two guitars on stands, like sentries on duty. There was no airconditioning but two metal fans whirred overhead and the windows had been left open so that a gentle night breeze blew across Wright's back. Two doors led off the main room and both had been widened to accommodate O'Leary's chair. Across one of the doorways was a metal pole which Wright guessed O'Leary used for arm exercises, and in the far corner of the room was a set of dumb-bells and weights.

'Nice place,' said Wright.

O'Leary shrugged but said nothing. His face was flushed. He'd untied his ponytail and his long hair hung around his shoulders like some sort of Viking warrior. A crippled warrior, thought Wright. Maybe that was why he was drinking so heavily.

Wright gestured at the bottle of whisky. 'May I?' he said.

'I thought you were a lager drinker,' said O'Leary.

'I'll take what I can get,' said Wright.

O'Leary waved at the bottle. 'Help yourself,' he said.

Wright took a glass from a cabinet. There were several photographs in brass frames on a shelf below the glasses. Pictures of O'Leary with a pretty Thai woman and two children, a boy and a girl. In none of the photographs was O'Leary in a wheelchair.

'Yeah,' said O'Leary from behind him. 'That's my wife.'

'She's lovely,' said Wright. 'Great kids, too. How old are they there? Four and six?'

'The girl was five then, the boy seven. They're sixteen and eighteen now.'

'They don't live with you?'

O'Leary sneered and took another long pull at his whisky. 'No profit in it any more,' he said, and slapped the wheelchair. 'Half a man.'

Wright sat down on a wooden chair that had elephants stencilled into the back of it. 'I'm sorry about before, when I was asking if it happened during the war.'

'That's okay,' said O'Leary. 'In a way it would have been better if it had happened then. At least then I'd have got disability payments. Two tours of duty without a scratch and I have to fall off a fucking motorcycle.'

'It's not going to get better?' asked Wright.

O'Leary shook his head. 'I'm in this chair for life,' he said. 'My wife came to see me in hospital, spoke to the doctors, and I haven't seen her or the kids since. She sold my business, the house, the car, took the money and went upcountry. That was seven years ago.'

'That's rough,' said Wright.

'It's Thai style,' said O'Leary. 'No matter how much you think they love you, no matter how much you give them, they always want more. She knew I'd never walk again so she figured she'd better look for another man before she got any older.'

'And the kids?'

'She probably told them I'd died.' He drank and swirled his whisky around the glass as he stared into it. 'Might have been better if I had. Bastards.'

Wright wasn't sure who O'Leary was cursing. He went over and refilled the man's glass, then poured more whisky into his own.

'Thais,' said O'Leary, as if sensing Wright's confusion. 'Give them your finger and they'll take your hand. Give them your hand and they'll want your arm. Give them your arm . . .' He scowled. 'Been to the bars yet?'

Wright shook his head. He sat down again.

'Pat Pong, Nana Plaza, Soi Cowboy. The red light areas. You'll meet beautiful girls there, stunners, and they'll be all over you. They'll smile and they'll bat their gorgeous brown eyes at you and they'll fondle your dick and they'll take you for everything they can.'

'Yeah, but you're talking about hookers,' said Wright.

'Ha! They're all fucking hookers,' said O'Leary. 'Every last one of them. Any girl you see driving an expensive car in Bangkok has either fucked someone rich or is the daughter of someone who's been fucked by someone rich. It's all about money, and when my wife thought her gravy train had come off the rails, she ran like the fucking wind.'

'What about this?' said Wright, indicating the room. 'This is a nice place.'

'It's Doc's,' said O'Leary. 'He lets me live here. If it wasn't for Doc, I'd be on the fucking street.'

'It's a better place than where I'm living,' said Wright. He told O'Leary about his own domestic situation, about his divorce and the arguments over access to his son.

O'Leary nodded sympathetically. 'Yeah, it's the kids I miss most,' he said. 'Not knowing what they look like, what they're doing. Not knowing if they even know that I'm alive. Don't let her keep your son away from you, Nick. Do what you have to do. Fight and don't stop fighting, okay?'

Wright raised his glass in salute. 'Here's to that,' he said, and the two men toasted each other. Wright could feel the warmth of the spirit spreading comfortingly across his stomach and he stretched out his feet.

'Tell me about Doc,' said Wright.

'Like what?'

'You met him in Vietnam, right?'

'Yup.'

'And you've all stayed together for twenty-five years? I don't think I've any friends from twenty-five years ago. There must be something special between you all to keep you together.'

O'Leary flicked his hair away from his shoulders with a quick movement of his head. 'Do you know much about Vietnam, Nick?'

Wright shook his head. 'Not much.'

O'Leary helped himself to more whisky. The bottle was almost empty when he put it back on the table. 'Doc wasn't being facetious about it taking a hundred years to describe what it was like,' he continued. 'If you weren't there, you'd never understand. There's a bond formed with the people you fought with, a bond that's stronger than marriage, than family, than loyalty to your country.'

Wright cradled his glass with both hands. O'Leary stared at the floor, almost as if he was talking to himself.

'The VC had a network of tunnels right across the country, built when the French occupied Vietnam, and then expanded when we went in to help the South. By the time the war was almost over, they had hundreds of miles of tunnels, stretching from Saigon to the Cambodian border. They started off as a way of getting from village to village without being seen, but by the time we were there they had huge underground installations: training rooms, armament factories, bomb shelters, hospitals, dormitories. Thousands of VCs and civilians lived underground, coming out to fight at night, then disappearing as soon as they came under fire.'

A cockroach scuttled across the floor in front of O'Leary's wheelchair, a big insect several inches long, but O'Leary didn't appear to notice it.

'We all went down the tunnels, Doc, Bernie, Sergio and I. Max and Eric, too. Bernie, Sergio and Max were with the Twenty-eighth Infantry, First Engineer Battalion. Eric was with Special Forces, but he was attached to the Tunnel Rats for six months. I was supposed to be mapping the tunnel network. Doc was a medic. You asked what sort of war we had? It was a shitty, dirty, nasty war, Nick. A war fought underground, in the dark, with guns and knives because there wasn't room to use anything bigger, in a battleground totally of the enemy's making, booby-trapped, full of poisonous snakes and spiders and God knows what else.' He shivered and rubbed the bridge of his nose as if trying to stave off a sneeze.

'Five of us stayed in South-East Asia after our tour of duty: Doc, Bernie, Sergio, Max and I. Max went over to the States in the 'eighties, then we met up with Eric five years ago.'

'Why were you so reluctant to tell me that yesterday?' asked Wright.

O'Leary looked across at him, his jaw set tight. 'Why should we tell you anything? What happened back then is nothing to do with you.'

Wright didn't say anything for several seconds. O'Leary looked away and took a mouthful of whisky. He gulped it down.

'What did happen?' Wright asked eventually.

O'Leary didn't answer, nor did he look at Wright. The only indication that he'd heard the question was a slight shrug of his shoulders.

'Is it connected to the way Horvitz and Eckhardt died?' asked Wright.

O'Leary continued to avoid Wright's gaze.

Wright decided to try a different approach. 'Tell me about Doc's lighter,' he said. 'The Zippo.'

'What about it?'

'There's a rat on one side, a rat with a torch and a gun. And a Latin motto on the other.' He screwed up his face as he tried to recall the words he'd read. '*Non Gratum Anus Rodentum*. Rodentum is rat, I guess.'

O'Leary smiled. 'Not worth a rat's ass,' he said. 'More of a credo than a motto.'

'That's how you felt?' asked Wright.

'We lost a lot of friends down the tunnels,' said O'Leary.

'Were you volunteers?'

'The Tunnel Rats? Sure. There's no way they could force you down there.'

'So why do it?'

O'Leary pressed his glass against his cheek. 'That's the question,' he said quietly. 'If you could answer that, you'd know a hell of a lot about human nature.'

'Self-destructive, was that it? Some urge to punish yourself?'

O'Leary shook his head. 'We didn't go down there to get killed, or to punish ourselves. We fought to stay alive, we took every precaution we could.'

'But you didn't have to go down in the first place.'

O'Leary flashed Wright a lopsided grin. 'Doesn't make sense, does it?'

'What about Doc's motivation? Why did he join the Tunnel Rats?'

'He was already a veteran of the tunnels when I met him. I think he wanted to make sure we didn't get hurt. He likes to take care of people, does Doc. He likes to lead, he likes responsibility.'

'And Ramirez?'

'Ramirez? I think he just wanted to prove that nothing scares him.'

'Prove to who? To you? Or to himself?'

'Another good question.'

'Hammack?'

O'Leary swatted a mosquito that had settled on his left leg. 'Bernie wanted to be special. There weren't many blacks down in the tunnels.'

'What about Horvitz?'

'Eric was Special Forces. I think of any of us he was the one most reluctant to go. I don't think he had anything to prove. But he was a good soldier and he obeyed orders.'

'And Max?'

'I didn't really know Max, we only went on the one mission together.'

There it was, out in the open. Wright said nothing, allowing the pause to get longer and longer. O'Leary drained his whisky. He poured the rest of the bottle into his glass. A motorcycle roared by outside and Wright caught a whiff of exhaust fumes through the open windows.

'I can't tell you any more,' said O'Leary softly.

'You have to,' said Wright. 'You owe it to Eric and Max.'

O'Leary shook his head. 'We can't ever tell. Any of us.'

'But it was twenty-five years ago, Dennis. A quarter of a century.'

'I know,' said O'Leary bitterly. 'You think I don't know exactly how long it's been?'

'Two men have died, and it's connected with whatever happened in Vietnam. You said you knew who it was. Who, Dennis? Who's killing the Tunnel Rats?'

O'Leary drained his glass and looked mournfully at the empty bottle. 'A ghost,' he whispered.

'A ghost?'

O'Leary looked up, and there was no disguising the fear in his eyes. 'He isn't dead,' he said, his voice a dry rattle. 'He isn't dead and he's coming back for revenge.'

O'Leary slumped back in his chair and his eyes closed. Wright sat and watched him. After a minute or so O'Leary began to snore, and his head fell forward on to his chest.

He'd drunk almost three quarters of the bottle of whisky, plus several beers at Cowboy Nights.

Wright stood up. One of the two doors led through to a kitchen, beyond which was a patio with a barbecue pit. A brown and white dog looked up at Wright and then settled back to sleep. The other door led to a large bedroom containing a king-sized bed swathed in mosquito nets. The furniture appeared to have been designed with O'Leary's disability in mind: there was a dressing table built so that there was room for the wheelchair, and the wardrobes were all low so that O'Leary could remove his clothes while sitting. Wright went back into the main room and pushed O'Leary into the bedroom. He was a big man and it took all Wright's strength to lift him out of the chair and roll him on to the bed. He loosened O'Leary's shirt, then switched off the light and left.

International directory enquiries had no problem coming up with a number for the United States Playing Card Company. Hunter got through to a fast-talking girl in the public relations department whose enthusiasm came bursting out of the telephone with all the force of a tornado. She was even more excited when Hunter told her that he was a policeman investigating a murder, though considerably less pleased to discover that one of her company's products was involved. Hunter explained that he wanted to speak to someone about the playing cards in general, and in particular any role they played in the Vietnam War.

'I can't think of anyone in the company, not off hand,' she said, 'but we do have a museum devoted to playing cards. They've got more than a hundred thousand different decks. Why don't you call them?'

Hunter took down the number of the museum and thanked her. This time a man answered, and he spoke in slow, measured sentences as if he was considering each word before he allowed it to pass his lips. His name was Walter Matthau. 'Not the actor,' he said. 'But we do share the same birthday. My friends call me Wally.'

Hunter explained why he was calling and asked Wally if the Bicycle brand had played any special role in the Vietnam War.

'Sure did,' said Wally.

When Wally didn't elaborate, Hunter had to prompt him. 'Could you tell me exactly what that role was?' he asked.

'The ace of spades,' said Wally. 'It was the death card.'

Hunter felt a surge of excitement. 'Death card?' he repeated.

'They were left as calling cards by the Twenty-fifth Infantry Division. And by Special Forces in Operation Phoenix.'

Hunter was so shocked that for several seconds he couldn't speak. He hadn't expected to strike gold so quickly. 'What do you mean, calling cards?'

Wally sniffed before continuing, and Hunter suspected that the man had just wiped his nose. 'It was back in 'sixty-six, I think. The company got a letter from two lieutenants in the Twenty-fifth Infantry Division. Seems they'd been leaving the cards behind whenever they attacked the Viet Cong. They reckoned the VC were scared of the cards, you see? Part of their folklore, the ace of spades, it represents death. And the soldiers preferred the Bicycle brand because of the woman. The woman in white. The VC thought it was a ghost. You know what I'm talking about, Inspector Hunter?'

'Yes, I've seen the card. It was always the ace of spades? I was watching *Apocalypse Now* and in the movie they used all sorts of cards.'

'Yeah, I remember that scene. Robert Duvall, right? I don't know what that was about. I heard of one long-range reconnaissance patrol that used one-eyed jacks, but generally it was our ace of spades. It was started by the infantry but Special Forces started using it as well once they realised how effective it was. They were so popular that they wanted us to send them a thousand aces of spades.'

'A thousand?'

'That's right.'

'And the company was happy to help? Despite what they were being used for?'

'Our company has a long and proud history of supporting the military,' said Wally. 'We ended up sending several million aces of spades, in special packs. Didn't charge them a cent. We designed a special pack. "Secret Weapon, Bicycle Ace of Spades", it said. Don't know if they were all used. Is this of any use to you, Inspector Hunter?'

'A great help, Wally. Believe me. You said something about an Operation Phoenix. What was that about?'

'It was a plan to destroy the VC by getting rid of as many members as possible. They used bribery, military attacks, and there were rumours of assassinations. The South targeted some ten thousand VCs who were reckoned to be crucial to the organisation, from local politicians up to full generals. Thousands of them died.'

'Thousands of assassinations?'

'Depends who you believe,' said Wally. 'The official

line was that most were killed in military engagements. Jane Fonda and her lily-livered liberals would probably accuse our boys of personally torturing and butchering every last man.'

Hunter made copious notes in his notebook, grateful for the man's slow delivery. 'And who was involved in this operation?'

'Now, I'm no expert on the Vietnam War, Inspector Hunter. Playing cards are my specialty. You'd better talk to someone who knows what they're talking about. I wouldn't want to steer you wrong.'

Hunter clicked his ballpoint pen shut. 'Wally, I can't thank you enough,' he said.

Dennis O'Leary awoke, struggling to breathe. He tried to twist his head to the side but something was clamped across his chin, pressing him down on to the bed.

'Don't struggle, and don't make a noise, Dennis,' hissed a man's voice.

O'Leary tried to turn to face the man but he couldn't move his head.

'I mean it, Dennis,' said the man. 'I don't want to have to kill your maid or anyone else who's in the house, but I will if they wake up. Do you understand?'

O'Leary nodded.

'Now, I'm going to take my hand away, and I don't want you to make a sound until I've finished speaking, do you understand, Dennis?'

O'Leary nodded again. He didn't recognise the voice, but the accent was American.

'I've got a knife, Dennis, a very sharp knife, and I know how to use it. If I even think you're going to shout for help I'll slit your throat. Understand?'

O'Leary closed his eyes and nodded. The hand went from his mouth and he felt the man move around the bed and sit down on the edge of it. O'Leary opened his eyes. The man was in his late twenties with a military haircut and a prominent dimple in his chin.

'What do you want?' O'Leary whispered.

The man held a finger to his lips and held up a knife. It had a long, thin blade and was curved slightly at the point. 'I want you to tell me everything you told Nick Wright,' said the man. 'And then I want you to tell me everything that you didn't tell him.'

Gerry Hunter dialled the number of Jim Bamber's hotel. The female receptionist who answered had an East European accent and spoke English that was slightly too correct, as if she'd learned from a textbook published in the 'fifties. Hunter asked to speak to Bamber.

'I am terribly sorry, but the gentleman is no longer resident at our establishment,' she said.

'Are you sure?' asked Hunter. The FBI agent hadn't said that he was planning to change hotels. It was unprofessional of him not to have informed the Met.

'I am certain. The gentleman checked out on Tuesday last.'

'Did he leave a forwarding number? Somewhere I can reach him?'

'I am afraid that he did not.'

Hunter thanked the girl and replaced the receiver. He called over to a WPC who was inputting data into her HOLMES computer and asked her if she had an up-to-date number for Bamber. She shook her head. Hunter had hoped that Bamber would be able to suggest the name of someone who could brief him on the Vietnam War and in particular Operation Phoenix. He also wanted to ask him if Clive had voiced any suspicions about there being a Vietnam connection to Eckhardt's murder. Reynolds had said that Clive was going to ask Bamber to help him get information on Eckhardt's war service record from the Defense Department. Now he'd have to wait until the FBI agent got in touch.

He decided to call his local library. There was a lady there, Miss Blackstone, who often helped him with enquiries. He'd never actually met her, but he pictured Miss Blackstone as a fifty-something matronly figure, several stones overweight with ornate spectacles and purple-tinted hair. She worked in the reference section, and always seemed pleased to hear from him; he felt that she probably enjoyed telling her friends how she helped Scotland Yard crack their most difficult cases.

'Why, Gerald, it's so nice to hear from you,' she said when he got through to her. She insisted on calling him Gerald, even though no one else, not even his parents, used the full version of his name. Hunter explained what he wanted. 'Operation Phoenix,' she whispered as if she was frightened of being overheard. 'What's the case, Gerald?'

'It's confidential at the moment, Miss Blackstone. I'll be

able to tell you more once I've got a suspect, but at the moment I'm just looking for background information.'

'We do have an extensive military history section,' she said. 'Let me see what I've got on the Vietnam War.'

'Could you do me a favour, Miss Blackstone? Could you fax me over anything you find?' He knew from past experience that the librarian would do such a thorough job that it could take her several hours. Miss Blackstone said she'd be delighted to and Hunter gave her the fax number before hanging up.

Hunter sat back in his chair. He was worried about Bamber checking out of his hotel without telling him. Everything else about the man had been extremely professional; it was out of character for him not to have been in touch. He obtained the American Embassy's telephone number from directory enquiries and asked to be put through to the FBI's office. He got through to one of the Bureau's representatives who introduced himself as Ed Harris, a legal attaché. Hunter explained who he was and that he was trying to track down Jim Bamber.

'Never heard of him,' said Harris.

'Are you sure?'

'Sure I'm sure. There are only five of us here in London. What office does he work out of?'

'Washington,' said Hunter.

'And he's here in what capacity?' asked Harris.

'Shouldn't you know? He's one of your agents.'

'Not necessarily,' said Harris. 'The London office is part of the FBI's legal attaché programme. We're here to liaise with the local police forces and security services. We exchange information, we don't investigate crimes.'

'But this guy Bamber, he said he'd been seconded here from Washington. He said—'

'Don't get me wrong, Inspector Hunter, I'm not saying it's not possible, I'm just saying that he's not working out of the London office. He could be reporting direct to Washington or to the Bureau's intelligence division. What exactly is he doing here?'

'He's helping us with a murder enquiry. An American by the name of Max Eckhardt. But he's checked out of his hotel and I don't know where he is.'

'Well, I can assure you he hasn't made contact with us,' said Harris. 'But I'll speak to headquarters, he shouldn't be too hard to track down. Give me your number and I'll get back to you.'

Hunter did as Harris asked and thanked him. He replaced the receiver. His stomach growled and he decided to pop over to the canteen for a quick meal. He had a hunch that it was going to be a long night.

Nick Wright was in a cold, dark place. His hands were shaking and his legs were trembling. He was afraid. 'Dad?' His voice echoed around the darkness, but there was no reply. 'Dad?' he called again. There was a ringing sound off in the distance, muffled as if it was coming through water. He opened his eyes. It was a telephone.

He groaned, rolled on to his stomach, and reached for the phone by his bed. He put it to his ear and heard a dialling tone. The ringing continued. He dropped the receiver back on its cradle.

The ringing was coming from Wright's suitcase. He pulled it down from the top of the wardrobe and opened it. It was his mobile ringing. 'Yeah?' he said, putting it to his ear.

'Nick?' It was Tommy Reid.

'Hey, Tommy.'

'Wasn't sure if your mobile would work,' said Reid.

'It's a GSM, same as yours,' said Wright. 'Should work anywhere in the world.'

'Satellites,' said Reid. 'Bloody marvellous, aren't they? How's it going, mate?' He was slurring his words. Wright looked at his wristwatch. It was just after midnight back in London. 'You alone, or have you got some lovely Asian babe with you?'

'I'm alone, Tommy. Alone and asleep. What do you want?'

'Just wanted to see how you were getting on.'

'Great. Eckhardt and Horvitz served together in Vietnam,' said Wright. 'In a unit called the Tunnel Rats. Something happened twenty-five years ago, something they want to keep secret.'

'Yeah? What was that?'

Wright closed his eyes. 'Tommy, if they want to keep it a secret, why the fuck would they tell me?'

'Because of your smooth tongue? Because they like you? Because you're a sodding policeman?'

'Yeah, well, I was talking to one of them tonight, a guy called O'Leary, but he'd only open up so much.'

'What about the Thai police? Are they any help?'

'Don't seem interested. But I did have a look at their file on Horvitz's murder, and guess what: the card on the chest is exactly the same.' Wright heard the chink of glass against glass. Reid was obviously pouring himself another drink.

There was a knock at the door. Wright went over to answer it, but realised he was naked and hurried to the bathroom for a towel.

'Hold on a minute, Tommy,' said Wright. He pulled open the door.

Jim Bamber was standing there, an easy grin on his face. The grin disappeared when he saw that Wright was on the phone.

'Fuck me,' said Wright.

'But you're so far away, darling,' said Reid, giggling.

'Not you, you soft bastard. Jim. Jim Bamber. He's here.' Wright opened the door for the FBI agent. Bamber was wearing his usual grey suit and white shirt and he looked fresh and relaxed as if he'd just showered. Wright gestured at the phone. 'Tommy,' he mouthed.

Bamber nodded and went to stand by the window.

'What's he doing there?' asked Reid.

'Tommy wants to know what you're doing in Bangkok,' said Wright, closing the door.

'The second murder,' said Bamber.

'Same as me,' said Wright into the phone. 'The second killing.' Bamber was standing looking out of the window, his arms folded. 'Look, tell Hunter what I've told you, will you? I'll talk to you tomorrow, okay?'

'Ah,' moaned Reid. 'Can't you read me a night-night story?'

'Goodnight, Tommy,' said Wright.

'Goodnight, John Boy.'

Wright cut the connection and put the telephone on the dressing table. 'Sorry about that, Jim. Tommy likes to talk when he's pissed.'

'Pissed?' Bamber turned around, frowning. 'What's he pissed at?'

'Pissed. Drunk.'

Bamber smiled. 'Oh, right. I get it. Two nations divided by a single language.'

'Something like that. When did you get to Bangkok?'

'Three days ago. I didn't realise you'd come to Thailand. Who told you about the murder in Bangkok?'

'Anonymous tip-off,' said Wright. 'Someone sent in some newspaper cuttings.'

'So Superintendent Newton sent you to Bangkok?'

'He's as keen as I am that the BTP solve this case.'

'Seems a little unusual, that's all. An American murdered in Bangkok. Not really your jurisdiction.'

'The two cases are obviously connected,' said Wright. 'It's got to be the same killer.'

'No doubt about it', said Bamber. 'That's what I told my bosses. So what progress have you made?'

'O'Leary's one of four Americans who play together at a club called Cowboy Nights.'

'Near Lang Suan. I know.'

'Yeah, there's Dennis O'Leary, a guy called Doc Marshall who's sort of the group leader, Bernie Hammack and Sergio Ramirez. And the victims both played with the band. Not together, Eckhardt left before Horvitz arrived, but they all knew each other in Vietnam, twenty-five years ago. They were all Tunnel Rats, fighting the Viet Cong underground.'

Bamber raised an eyebrow, clearly impressed. 'You've found out a lot in a short time,' he said.

'I was lucky,' said Wright. 'I saw a photograph of Eckhardt with the band in Cowboy Nights, and I managed to get O'Leary to talk to me a little. We've both had woman troubles. And he'd been drinking. What about you? What have you found out?'

Bamber adjusted the cuffs of his jacket. 'I'd pinned down the Tunnel Rats connection. Our Washington office checked up on the service records of both men and discovered they'd served together for a time towards the end of the war. I haven't approached the four surviving members in case one of them is the killer.'

'What?' said Wright, stunned.

Bamber frowned. 'Hadn't you considered that? It seemed obvious to me. Either Marshall, Hammack or Ramirez could be behind the murders. O'Leary we can rule out because of the chair, but the others are definite suspects. Immigration is doing a check for me to see if any of them were out of the country at the time Eckhardt was killed.'

Wright sat down on the edge of the bed. 'But whatever it was that happened twenty-five years ago, they've all kept the secret. Why start killing now?'

'I don't know, Nick. But I did find out something else. They're all going back to Vietnam. Back down the tunnels. All except O'Leary, of course.'

'Why?'

'I'm not sure. All I know is that they've already applied for their visas and have booked tickets on Wednesday's Thai flight to Saigon.'

'How the hell did you find that out?'

'We've had them under surveillance,' said Bamber.

Wright rubbed his eyes. 'This is crazy, Jim. If one of them is the killer, why would he want to go back down the tunnels?'

'Maybe he wants to finish the job.'

'So why would the other two go? Why put themselves in harm's way?'

Bamber opened the minibar. 'Okay if I have a soda?' he asked. Wright nodded. Bamber took out a can of Sprite and popped the tab. He sipped it. 'Nick, you're asking questions that I don't have the answers to. But I know for sure that the solution lies down in the tunnels. We have to go, Nick. It's the only way we're going to solve this case.'

Wright's jaw dropped. 'You have got to be joking!' he exclaimed.

Bamber drank from his can. 'It's the only way,' he said.

Wright shook his head emphatically. 'O'Leary said there were hundreds of miles of tunnels, all the way from Saigon to Cambodia. How are you going to find out where they're going?'

Bamber grinned, crushed his empty can and tossed it into a wastepaper bin. 'I'm getting a map sent over. The Defense Department mapped a big chunk of the tunnel network, and the mission that Horvitz, Eckhardt and the rest went on was recorded. I'm getting the file pulled from the Pentagon, and it and the map are being sent over to our office here.'

'And you're going down the tunnels?'

'Not just me. We. It's going to take two, Nick. I need you down there with me.'

Wright swallowed. His mouth had gone completely dry. 'I'm not sure if I'm up to it,' he said.

Bamber looked at him levelly. 'You want to solve this, don't you? That's presumably why you came.'

'Yes, but . . .'

'There are no buts. The answer lies down in the tunnels. That's where they're going and that's where we have to go. Okay?'

'Okay,' said Wright, reluctantly.

Bamber walked over to stand in front of Wright. The detective looked up at him. For a wild moment he thought that the FBI agent was going to strike him. The feeling was so strong that he had to force himself not to flinch. 'I mean it, Nick. I need you on this. I need you to be one hundred per cent committed.'

'I am,' said Wright, more sure this time.

'Good man. I'll arrange the tickets. I've already got my visa for Vietnam, I can pull a few strings to get yours done quickly. I'll need your passport.'

Wright got his passport from his dressing table and handed it to Bamber.

'One more thing,' said the FBI agent. 'Keep a low profile for the rest of the time you're in Bangkok. Don't go back to Cowboy Nights, don't speak with The Jazz Club, or the police. And don't mention me to anybody. I don't want anyone to know that the FBI's involved.'

Wright nodded. 'I understand.'

'Be ready to leave on Wednesday.'

Wright nodded again. His stomach began to churn.

Bamber went over to the door. He made a gun with the fingers of his hand and pointed it at Wright. He made a clicking noise, then let himself out.

Gerry Hunter sat down at his desk and drank from a can of 7-Up.

'Anything good in the canteen?' asked Steve Denning, a middle-aged DS with a thickening waistline and a tendency to snack on Mars bars during periods of stress.

'If there was, I missed it,' said Hunter, massaging his stomach.

'What did you have?'

'Sausage and chips, but I'm regretting it. Anyone call for me?'

Denning shook his head but pointed at a wire basket on the desk next to Hunter's. 'Fax came for you, though.'

Hunter reached over and retrieved the stack of pages. There were almost two dozen in all. Miss Blackstone had done him proud. There were photocopies of articles from several encyclopedias and selected pages from military history books and biographies.

He read through the pages and from time to time he made notes in the margins and underlined words and phrases that he thought might be significant. Hunter himself hadn't even been ten years old when South Vietnam fell, and for him the conflict was as distant an event as the First and Second World Wars. Many of the references to people and events meant nothing to him.

Gradually Hunter began to build up a picture of Operation Phoenix and its significance. It came towards the end of the war, when it was clear to most commentators that the

United States wasn't capable of winning by conventional means. The army thought that a change of tactics might produce results, and in 1968 Operation Phoenix was born. The aim was to identify and target specific members of the Viet Cong infrastructure: its fighters, its political cadres and its rank and file members. It was initially set up as a means of pooling intelligence information, which up until then had rarely been shared. The Americans didn't trust the South Vietnamese, and vice versa, and both sides guarded their intelligence jealously. Operation Phoenix set up official guidelines on how information was to be shared, and once targets had been identified they were arrested and interrogated. Some eighty Operation Phoenix offices were set up around South Vietnam, collating information with the aid of computers.

If proven to be Viet Cong sympathisers, targets would be either imprisoned or persuaded to change sides. It was, Hunter realised, the same technique that the British had used against the Provisional IRA in the 'seventies. In Northern Ireland the technique had paid dividends, with a number of notable successes, but in Vietnam, Operation Phoenix was regarded as a failure. There were allegations of torture and assassination, and time and time again Operation Phoenix was described as a front for government-sponsored assassination. Included among the photocopies were articles from American newspapers alleging that Operation Phoenix was primarily an assassination plot and that the CIA was targeting individual members of the Viet Cong and murdering them. All such allegations were denied by Defense Department spokesmen. The official view was that any deaths were the result of military action, not assassination.

According to some of the articles Miss Blackstone had photocopied from encyclopedias, Operation Phoenix wasn't regarded as a success because of all the negative publicity it generated, but it did come close to achieving its objectives. In 1968, almost 16,000 Viet Cong cadres and fighters were either captured, killed or switched sides. In 1970 the number was 21,000, and US intelligence experts estimated that over the four years that Operation Phoenix was underway, the Viet Cong infrastructure was reduced by a total of almost 75,000 men.

Nowhere in the information Miss Blackstone had sent was there any mention of the ace of spades death card. Wally Matthau had said that Special Forces had used the card, but there was no mention of Special Forces involvement in Operation Phoenix.

By the end of June 1972 all American advisers had been pulled out of South Vietnam, and a few months later the Saigon government ended Operation Phoenix.

Hunter sat back in his chair and stared up at the ceiling. What did he have so far? He had a dead middle-aged American, tortured and killed in London with a card impaled in his chest which had been used as a death card in the Vietnam War, and another in Bangkok which Wright was following up. Eckhardt had served in the Vietnam War. Had he come into contact with the soldiers using the death cards? Had Max Eckhardt himself been involved in Special Forces operations in Vietnam? Jim Bamber would probably be able to find out, but until Hunter could get in touch with the FBI agent he'd have to pursue his own line of enquiry, and the dead man's widow seemed the best bet. He picked up his coat.

'I'm going to see Eckhardt's widow,' he told Denning.

'You want company?' asked the detective sergeant.

'Nah. If Jim Bamber calls for me, tell him he can get me on my mobile.'

Denning gave him a thumbs-up without taking his eyes off his computer screen.

Hunter drove to the Eckhardts' flat in Maida Vale and parked in front of it. He walked down the path and peered at the doorbells. None bore the name Eckhardt. He took his notebook out of his raincoat pocket and checked the address. It was the right building. One of the bells didn't have a name attached to it and he pressed it hopefully. There was no response and he didn't bother pressing it again. Hunter heard a noise behind him and he turned to see a postman walking down the path pushing a mail cart. He showed the postman his warrant card and asked about May Eckhardt.

'Haven't had anything for them in a few days,' said the postman. 'I think they've moved.'

'Did they leave a forwarding address?'

The postman shook his head and began slotting letters through the communal letterbox. 'You could try asking old man Jenkins, Flat Two. He's the local busybody.'

The postman pushed his trolley back down the path and Hunter pressed the bell for Flat 2.

'Who is it?' asked a disembodied voice.

'Police,' said Hunter.

'Your name, please,' said the voice.

'Gerry Hunter. Inspector Gerry Hunter.'

'Hold your warrant card up to the camera behind you, please,' said the voice.

Hunter did as asked, suppressing a smile.

'Thank you,' said the voice. The door lock buzzed. 'You can come up.'

Hunter pushed open the door and went upstairs. He knocked on the door to Flat 2 and it was opened by a man in his seventies.

'Are you Mr Jenkins?'

'Yes,' said the old man, scrutinising Hunter through narrowed eyes. A security chain prevented the door from being opened more than a few inches. A dog yapped from somewhere behind him. 'Hush, Katie,' said Jenkins. 'It's only the police.' The dog continued to bark.

'Can I have a word with you about one of your neighbours?' said Hunter.

Jenkins undid the security chain and opened the door for Hunter. The flat stank of vomit and disinfectant and the detective wrinkled his nose at the smell.

'First on your right,' said Jenkins. 'It's about the Eckhardts, I assume,' he said as he followed Hunter into the sitting room. It was akin to stepping into a time warp. The wallpaper, carpets and furniture all seemed to be relics of the 1950s, clean but shabby. A gas fire surrounded by a green-tiled fireplace hissed like a deflating balloon and in the corner a six-foot-tall grandfather clock ticked off the passing seconds. 'Sit down, please,' said Jenkins, indicating a green velvet sofa that had worn bare in places.

Hunter sat down. Jenkins was wearing a blue dressing gown and tartan slippers, one of which had a hole in the toe through which poked a gnarled, yellowed toenail.

'I spoke to a Sergeant Wright some time ago,' said Jenkins. 'Of course, he wasn't a real policeman. Transport Police, he was.'

'That's right,' said Hunter.

'He was a rum sort,' said Jenkins. 'I couldn't understand why a transport policeman was involved in a murder investigation.' He drew out the word 'murder' as if reluctant to finish saying it.

'The body was found in a railway tunnel,' explained Hunter.

'Oh, I know that,' said Jenkins. 'But murder requires real police work, doesn't it?' Again he drew out the word 'murder' as if relishing the sound.

A bell tinkled and Jenkins flinched as if he'd been slapped. 'My wife,' he explained. 'She needs her medicine.'

Hunter felt suddenly sorry for the old man, living out his final years with a yappy dog and an invalid wife. It had been more than six months since Hunter had seen his own father, the detective realised. Six months was way too long. He sat and listened to the hissing gas fire and the ticking clock until Jenkins returned carrying a Yorkshire terrier. He perched on the edge of an armchair at the side of the fire, his back ramrod straight.

'So do you happen to know where Mrs Eckhardt is?' asked Hunter.

'Haven't seen her for a few weeks. Her car's not outside so I presume she's moved. Is she a suspect?'

'We just want to ask her a few questions,' said Hunter. 'Did she leave a forwarding address?'

'Not with me. As I told Sergeant Wright, the landlord or the managing agent might know. The agent's name and address is on the noticeboard by the front door.'

'What about her furniture? Did a removal van call?'

'Didn't see one, but I think they rented the flat furnished.'

'And you've no idea where she might have gone?'

Jenkins stroked the Yorkshire terrier behind the ears. 'Maybe she went home to China,' he said absentmindedly.

'China?' said Hunter. 'What makes you say that?'

'She was Chinese. Didn't you know? Spoke perfect English, but she was Chinese.'

'Are you sure she was from China?' asked Hunter.

'Well, she was Oriental, no mistaking that, but she wasn't Japanese, I'm damn sure.' The old man shuddered. 'I spent two years in a Japanese POW camp so I know what bloody Japs are like.' The old man shrugged. He looked suddenly older and there was a faraway look in his eyes as if his mind was elsewhere.

Hunter stood up. He thanked Jenkins for his help and shook his hand. His grip was surprisingly strong for a man of his years, and the memory of it and the smell of sickness stayed with Hunter for the rest of the day.

Kruse settled back in the taxi and closed his eyes. His meeting with Nick Wright had taken a completely unexpected turn and he had a lot of thinking to do. He'd gone to Wright's hotel room intent on killing the British detective, but the phone call had put paid to that. Kruse couldn't risk being associated with Wright's death, whether or not it looked like an accident. Tommy Reid might have an alcohol problem, but he wasn't stupid. The idea of taking Wright with him to Vietnam had come out of the blue, but Kruse was used to thinking on his feet and he knew it made perfect sense. Down in the tunnels anything could happen, and there'd be no witnesses. Getting a visa for Wright at short notice wouldn't be difficult: anything could be obtained in Bangkok for a price, and Jody Meacher had made it clear that money was no object.

Kruse went over the conversation he'd had with Wright, looking for any slips he might have made. He hadn't liked having to lie about getting information from the Pentagon, because that could be checked, but it was the only way he could think of explaining how he knew about the service records of the members of The Jazz Club. And he needed an explanation for the map that he'd taken from O'Leary's house. Suggesting that one of the surviving members of The Jazz Club might be the killer had been a flash of brilliance. It would keep Wright off balance, trusting no one.

The question of who the killer was still troubled Kruse. His thirty-minute conversation with O'Leary had provided no clues. Kruse knew exactly what had happened down the tunnels a quarter of a century ago, and he understood why the men needed to go back, but he didn't believe in ghosts and he didn't believe that dead men waited twenty-five years before coming back for revenge. The killer was real, flesh and blood, and Kruse knew that when the men went down the tunnels, the killer would be going too. Kruse smiled to himself. The witnesses would be there, the killer would be there, and the detective investigating the case would be there. And once Kruse had finished his work, all would be dead and buried deep below the earth. It was perfect, so perfect that the anticipation was almost painful.

The loud knocking on Wright's door woke him from a dreamless sleep, the taste of vomit still at the back of his mouth. 'Yeah, who is it?' he called. There was no reply and the banging continued. Wright wrapped a towel around his waist and opened the door.

Two policemen in dark brown uniforms stood there. The taller of the two was wearing Ray-Ban sunglasses. He spoke to Wright in Thai.

Wright frowned. 'You'll have to speak English,' he said.

A third figure moved into view behind the two policemen. Somchai. He looked worried. 'They want you to go with them, Mr Nick,' he said.

'Why?' queried Wright.

'They won't say.'

'Tell them to wait while I get dressed,' he said. He moved to close the door but the smaller policeman stuck out his arm and held it open.

As he dressed, Wright looked at his watch. It was ten o'clock in the morning. He'd only slept for two hours after Bamber had left and he was exhausted. He ran a hand over his jaw and wondered if he should shave, but the policeman in sunglasses made an impatient clicking sound and motioned with his hand for Wright to hurry up, so Wright threw on his jacket and followed them down the corridor.

A white police car and a uniformed driver were waiting outside the hotel. Wright got into the back with the smaller of the men; the one with sunglasses climbed into the front. A garland of purple and white flowers and a small gold Buddha in a transparent plastic case hung from the driver's mirror. Wright knew it was pointless to ask any questions so he stared silently out of the window as they drove through the crowded streets.

It wasn't until the car turned into the small side street that Wright realised they were heading for O'Leary's house. Three other police cars and a Jeep were parked haphazardly outside the building, red lights flashing on their roofs, and two brown-uniformed police motorcyclists in knee-high boots and white helmets were talking to a small group of onlookers, obviously telling them to keep back.

The car stopped behind the Jeep and the cop next to Wright pointed at the front door. Wright got out of the car, a sick feeling in the pit of his stomach. He'd liked Dennis O'Leary, and this amount of police activity could only be bad news.

Colonel Vasan was in the main room, standing by O'Leary's desk and watching two uniformed officers rummage through the drawers. They weren't wearing gloves, Wright noticed. Vasan looked across at Wright, then turned his head away, deliberately ignoring him. Wright waited by the door, not wanting to walk across the room without being asked.

After several minutes Vasan walked over, his gleaming black boots squeaking on the wooden floor. He stared at Wright through the lenses of his steel-framed spectacles, but said nothing. He was, Wright realised, trying to intimidate him with silence.

Wright smiled. 'Is there a problem, Colonel Vasan?' he said.

The colonel said nothing. He nodded at a uniformed officer who was standing by the kitchen door. The officer opened the door and ushered out the maid who'd admitted Wright the previous night. She'd been crying.

The colonel spoke to her in Thai. She looked at Wright and nodded tearfully. He said something else to her and she hurried back into the kitchen and closed the door.

The colonel scratched his pitted cheek and studied Wright with hard eyes. 'Why were you here last night?' he said.

'I wanted to talk to Mr O'Leary.'

'About what?' Any pretence that Vasan wasn't able to speak English had disappeared.

'About the murder of Eric Horvitz. They played together in a band. Horvitz was a singer, O'Leary—'

'Played guitar. Yes. I know the connection between the two men.'

'Was there an ace of spades?' asked Wright.

Deep furrows appeared on Vasan's forehead.

'On the body. Was there an ace of spades?'

'How did you know he had been killed?' asked Vasan. 'I didn't say he had been killed.'

Wright sighed patiently. 'The maid's in tears, your men are all over the place and there's no sign of a robbery.'

Vasan glowered at Wright. 'You are quite wrong,' he said. 'There has been no murder.'

A sudden thought struck Wright and he caught his breath. 'He didn't kill himself, did he?'

Vasan shook his head. He turned his back on Wright and walked towards the door to O'Leary's bedroom. Wright followed him. Vasan pushed upon the door. A uniformed officer was going through O'Leary's wardrobes, patting down the pockets of his clothes. Another policeman stood guard at the open door to the bathroom. Vasan motioned for Wright to take a look.

O'Leary was sprawled on the floor next to the toilet, his head up against the wall, his neck at an awkward angle. The belt to his trousers was undone and his flies open. The wheelchair was on its side, next to the bath. The man had soiled himself in death and Wright put his hand over his mouth, trying to block out the smell of urine and faeces.

'Mr O'Leary had been drinking?' said Vasan.

'Yes. Almost a full bottle of whisky.'

'He was trying to use the toilet. He must have overbalanced.'

'It certainly looks that way,' said Wright.

'Bathrooms can be dangerous places, even for those who aren't in wheelchairs.'

Wright tried to remember where he'd left O'Leary's wheelchair when he put the man to bed. Had it been within reach? Had O'Leary woken up, levered himself into the chair and rolled himself into the bathroom? It was possible, he decided. An ugly, unnecessary accident. Guilt washed over Wright. He'd allowed O'Leary to get drunk in the hope that he'd talk. Encouraged him, even. He was partly to blame for the man's drunken state, and that meant he was partly responsible for his death.

'Is there something on your mind?' asked Vasan, looking at Wright over the top of his spectacles.

'It seems such a waste,' said Wright, backing out of the bathroom.

The colonel stroked his chin. 'Did you obtain anything useful from him? During your talk?'

'No,' said Wright. He went through the bedroom. The policeman who had been going through the wardrobes was slipping something into his own pocket. Wright flashed a look at the colonel, but Vasan appeared not to have noticed what the man was doing.

'According to the maid, you were with him for almost an hour.'

'Thirty minutes, at most.'

They went through to the main room. More uniformed policemen arrived, all with holstered guns and radios on their belts. They were walking around and examining O'Leary's possessions as if they were at a jumble sale.

'And you learned nothing of interest?'

Wright was determined not to tell Vasan anything. Nothing he'd seen so far had suggested that the colonel was anything other than incompetent. Even if O'Leary's death was an accident, there was no excuse for allowing so many men to be trampling around the house. 'He confirmed that Horvitz had no enemies, and he couldn't think of any reason why anyone would want to torture and kill him. The rest of the time we talked about music.'

'Music?'

Wright nodded at the two guitars. 'He played guitar. He was good, he played with Eric Clapton once.'

'Eric Clapton? Who is Eric Clapton?'

'A famous guitarist. It doesn't matter.'

Vasan nodded. His hand rested on the butt of his gun as if reassuring himself that it was still in its holster. 'So you talked about music, then you went back to your hotel?'

Wright shrugged. 'That's about it.'

Vasan stared at Wright, who held the colonel's gaze. 'I would prefer that you inform me in advance of any future interviews you wish to conduct,' Vasan said eventually. 'I would like one of my investigating officers to be present.'

'I have no problem with that.'

A uniformed policeman picked up one of O'Leary's guitars and strummed it. Vasan looked across at the man, but there was no trace of annoyance on his face.

'In my opinion you would do best to visit our temples,' said the colonel. 'Maybe go and see the pretty girls we have in Pat Pong, then go home.'

Wright ignored the suggestion. 'Is it okay if I leave now?' he asked.

'My men will drive you back to your hotel,' said Vasan. He turned his back on Wright and went through to O'Leary's bedroom, his shiny black boots squeaking like hungry rats.

Tim Marshall was updating the medical records of the patient he'd just seen when the intercom on his desk buzzed. 'Yes, Ma-lee?' he said, storing the file.

'There are two men to see you, Dr Marshall. They don't have an appointment but they say they are friends. Mr Hammack and Mr Ramirez. I have asked them to wait in reception.' Ma-lee had only been with the surgery for three weeks and was already proving herself an asset. She was university educated and spoke good English, and wasn't in the least intimidated by farangs.

'Thank you, Ma-lee, you can show them in.'

A few seconds later the door to his consulting room opened and Bernie Hammack and Sergio Ramirez came in, both men visibly shaken. 'It's Dennis,' said Hammack as he closed the door. 'He's dead.'

'What!' said Doc. 'What happened?'

'An accident, according to the cops,' said Ramirez. 'We went around to pick up the map and the police were all over the house.'

'Seems he was drunk and he fell out of his chair trying to use the toilet. Broke his neck.'

Doc sat back in his chair and ran his hands through his thinning hair. 'Shit. Poor Dennis.' He narrowed his eyes. 'There's no doubt about this? About it being an accident?'

'They seem sure,' said Hammack.

'Just a lousy coincidence?'

Ramirez sat down on a low sofa by the window. 'I don't think it is a coincidence, Doc. Max, Eric, now Dennis. What are the odds, huh?'

'Pretty extreme, I'd say,' said Doc. 'But if it's the same killer, why make it look like an accident? He tortured Max and Eric, ripped their bodies apart and left a calling card. Why go to all the trouble of making Dennis's death look like an accident?'

'None of this makes any sense,' said Hammack. 'Question is, what do we do now?'

'Did you get the map?'

'They wouldn't let us into the house. Besides, I wouldn't know where to look.'

There was a small red birthmark on the back of Doc's neck and he scratched it, deep in thought. Ramirez and Hammack sat in silence, waiting.

'We don't need the map,' Doc said eventually. 'We can find our way back.'

'We're still going?' asked Ramirez.

'We took a vote,' said Doc.

'I think we should make a stand here, in Bangkok,' said Ramirez. 'On our turf. If it is him, if he has come back, I'd rather face him out in the open.'

'We took a vote,' Doc repeated, a harder edge to his voice. 'We go back.'

Ramirez's jaw tightened and for a moment it looked as if he was going to argue, but then he relaxed and nodded. Doc looked at Hammack. The black man nodded, too.

'I'm pretty sure I can remember the layout. What about you, Bernie?'

'Ain't never gonna forget,' said Hammack. He grinned and his gold tooth glinted at the side of his mouth.

'Sergio?'

The Latino sighed. He nodded slowly. 'I might have trouble finding the entrance, but once I'm down there, I'll know my way around.' He smiled ruefully. 'A map would have been nice, though.'

'Like Bernie said, we don't even know where Dennis kept it.' Doc stood up. 'I'm getting the visas tonight. We fly out tomorrow at eleven. We'll pick up the equipment we'll need in Saigon.'

'What about weapons?' asked Ramirez.

'We won't need them,' said Doc. He stood up. 'The only thing we're going to find down there is a skeleton.'

'I meant for the snakes and stuff. The VC might have moved out, but the wildlife's going to be well entrenched by now. Scorpions, rats. The works.'

Doc nodded. He took off his white coat and hung it on the back of the door. 'There's no way we can get guns through the airport, and I wouldn't know where to go about buying them in Vietnam. We can get knives in Saigon, that's about it.'

'I'd feel happier with a gun, Doc.'

'I hear you, Sergio, but I don't see how it's going to be possible.'

'And if he's not down there, Doc,' said Hammack. 'What then?'

'Let's cross one bridge at a time, gentlemen. One bridge at a time.'

Nick Wright spread the typewritten sheets over the bed. There were more than twenty in all. They had been delivered by a young uniformed policeman who had demanded five thousand baht before handing them over. Wright hadn't had enough cash in his wallet and he'd had to go to an ATM to withdraw Thai money. The officer turned out to be a motorcycle policeman and he'd offered Wright a lift. It had been almost surreal, driving through the traffic along Sukhumvit Road, riding pillion behind a traffic cop. The policeman had even turned on his flashing red light, forcing traffic to pull to the side to allow them to pass. After he'd withdrawn the money, the cop had driven him back to the hotel, and laboriously written out a receipt before taking the money and handing Wright the manila envelope containing the translated reports. He'd even saluted Wright.

Wright was surprised at the thoroughness of the reports. There was a summary of the post mortem, and the injuries were identical to those of Max Eckhardt's. The body had been discovered by a nun just after breakfast, and there was a statement from her and from the rest of the nuns in the orphanage including Sister Marie. Neighbours had also been interviewed, but to no avail. No one had seen or heard anything unusual. There was a breakdown of Horvitz's financial situation and photocopies of bank statements from Thai Farmers Bank and Bangkok Bank. Horvitz had had almost a quarter of a million dollars on deposit. There had been no major withdrawals before or after Horvitz's death. Extortion or robbery had been ruled out as a motive. Doc had been interviewed, but not the other members of The Jazz Club. Doc had told Vasan as little as he'd told Wright on their first meeting. Wright could find nothing in the report about the playing card, other than in the description of the crime scene. Vasan had obviously decided that it wasn't a clue worth following up.

He went over to the minibar and took out a can of lager and a can of Sprite and mixed himself a shandy. Wright stood looking out of his window as he drank. A group of bare-chested children were running around a corrugated-iron shack, laughing and giggling. Wright wondered what Sean was doing. He looked at his watch. It was just after two o'clock in the afternoon. Back in London, Sean was probably getting ready for school.

He sat down on the bed and began to read through the translated reports again, hoping to find something that he'd missed on his first reading. If he could come up with a clue as to who the killer was, maybe he wouldn't have to go down the tunnels.

He toyed with the idea of phoning Hunter, but remembered

that he'd already asked Tommy to update him on what he'd found out so far.

There was a knock on the door and Wright went over and opened it. Jim Bamber stood there, a black holdall in one hand.

'How's it going, Nick?'

'Fine,' said Wright. He closed the door and handed the typewritten sheets to the FBI agent. 'Colonel Vasan sent over a translation of his file on the Horvitz killing, but there's nothing of any use.'

'Did you really expect there to be?' asked Bamber. He unzipped the holdall and handed Wright his passport and a folder containing an airline ticket.

Wright opened his passport and flicked through it. The Vietnam visa filled an entire page, blue writing with a large red seal.

'The guys are flying out tomorrow morning on Thai Airways. We're booked on the flight after them. It's Vietnam Airlines, I'm afraid, but there's no way we can travel on the same flight.'

Wright picked up his glass of shandy. 'Jim, I'm having second thoughts about going down the tunnels.'

'We've no choice,' said Bamber. 'The answer to the murders is down there. We have to go.'

Wright began to pace up and down in front of the window. 'Look, you know I'm claustrophobic. You know the state I was in when you switched off your torch in the tunnel. Think how bad I'm going to be underground.'

Bamber grinned. 'I think I've solved that,' he said. He reached into the holdall and pulled out what looked like a bulky pair of binoculars. He handed them to Wright. There were two lenses and an adjusting knob, and a black rubber facepiece with webbing straps to hold it in place. 'It's a nightsight.'

'Yeah, I know.' Wright had used something similar on night-time anti-vandal surveillance operations. 'But they won't work underground.'

'What do you mean?'

'They work by gathering what light's available and amplifying it. Starlight, whatever. But underground there's a total absence of light. Nothing to amplify.'

Bamber shook his head. 'That would be true for the passive systems, but these operate on infra-red. They'll work. Took me ages to find. I've got two sets, plus a stack of batteries. Has the bathroom got a window? Try them in there.'

Wright went into the bathroom, switched on the light and closed the door. He put the goggles on and adjusted the straps, then switched the unit on. It took ten seconds or so to warm up, whining in a high-pitched tone that was almost out of his hearing range, then the eyepieces flickered and he had a white-flecked green view of the bathroom. He switched off the light and moved his head from side to side. They were heavy and the view was initially a little disorientating, but they worked.

'Yeah, they work,' he shouted.

'Should hope so,' said Bamber.

Wright opened the bathroom door. 'How long do the batteries last?'

'The guy said six hours. That probably means four.'

Wright took off the headset. 'How long are we going to have to be underground?' he asked.

'Twelve hours or so, max.'

Wright's mouth opened in surprise. He wondered if he'd misheard. 'Twelve hours?'

'Twelve hours, maximum. But probably less.'

'Twelve fucking hours!'

Bamber held out his hand. 'I'll look after them until we get there,' he said.

Wright gave the headset to the FBI agent. 'Jim, I can't stay underground for twelve hours.'

'That's what it's going to take,' said Bamber. 'The main tunnel complex is about two miles from the entrance they used. It's a communications tunnel, but it's the only way to the complex. The only way that's been mapped, anyway. Down in the tunnels you can make about half a mile an hour. And that's assuming we don't make a wrong turn along the way. So it's going to take about three hours just to get there.' He put the headset into the holdall.

Wright pressed his glass against his cheek. 'Twelve hours,' he said.

'Twelve minutes, twelve hours, twelve days. It takes as long as it takes, Nick. Do you want to crack this case or not?'

'You know I do.'

'So we go down the tunnels. We find out what's so important that Marshall, Hammack and Ramirez feel they have to go back after twenty-five years.'

Wright nodded. 'Yeah. You're right.'

'I know I'm right. You'll be just fine. And I'll be with you every step of the way. It'll be a walk in the park, Nick.'

Wright drained his glass. Despite Bamber's confidence, he was gripped by an overpowering feeling of dread. He smiled weakly. 'If you say so, Jim.'

Gerry Hunter was putting on his coat ready to go home when Steve Denning shouted across to him that he had a call.

'Who is it?' called Hunter.

'FBI,' said Denning. 'Guy called Harris.'

Denning transferred the call to Hunter's extension. 'Hiya, Ed. Thanks for calling back,' he said.

'Yeah, sorry I didn't get back sooner,' said Harris. 'It took longer than I thought. Can I just confirm the spelling of this guy's name. B-A-M-B-E-R, right? First name James?'

'That's it,' said Hunter.

'In that case, we have a problem,' said Harris. 'There's only one agent of that name in the FBI, and he's a twenty-year veteran working out of our San Francisco office. I spoke to him an hour ago.'

'So the James Bamber who's been part of our murder enquiry team is an impostor?'

'Looks that way, Gerry. You saw his ID, right?'

'Not personally, but I'm sure it must have been looked at somewhere along the line. This doesn't make any sense. Why the hell would anyone want to sit in on a murder enquiry that's going nowhere?'

'Maybe he wants it to stay that way,' said the FBI agent. 'Look, we'd like to speak to this guy, whatever his motives. If nothing else, it's a federal offence to pass yourself off as an FBI agent. Have you got an address?'

'He checked out of his hotel last week. I haven't a clue where he is now.'

'What about fingerprints? Have you got anything he touched? A cup, a typewriter?'

Hunter looked around the incident room. Bamber had only visited the room twice and he couldn't recall him touching anything, and the hotel room would already have been cleaned. 'I don't think so,' said Hunter. 'If I think of anything, I'll let you know.'

Hunter replaced the receiver and slipped off his coat. He slumped down into his chair and ran his hands through his hair. There were so many strands to the investigation that his mind couldn't cope with them all. He picked up a pen and a sheet of paper. He wrote the name JAMES BAMBER at the top. Underneath he wrote MAX ECKHARDT. Then MAY ECKHARDT. Then ERIC HORVITZ. Underneath that he wrote the name of his dead partner. He stared at the five names and chewed the inside of his lip. James Bamber, an American claiming to be with the FBI. Max Eckhardt, an American brutally murdered. An American who had served in the Vietnam War. A playing card impaled on his chest that had been used as a death card by American Special Forces. May Eckhardt, an Oriental girl married to the victim, vanished. Clive Edmunds, dead after renting a Vietnam War movie. No sign of the video cassette. The cassette disappears, so does Jim Bamber. Hunter drew an arrow connecting Bamber to Edmunds. Was the timing coincidental? He remembered Eckhardt's boss Reynolds saying that Edmunds was going to check with Bamber for details of Eckhardt's Vietnam record, and he shuddered involuntarily. He drew another arrow between Bamber and May Eckhardt. Were their disappearances connected in some way? He drew a third arrow linking Bamber to Max Eckhardt, and a fourth between Bamber and Horvitz. Was Bamber the killer? Was his desire to be part of the murder enquiry some perverse voyeurism? He underlined Bamber's name several times. Hunter had a growing sense of dread, a fear that perhaps his partner's death wasn't a tragic accident.

He drew a circle around May Eckhardt's name. Where had she gone? Had she too been killed? He wondered if it would be worth getting a search warrant and giving the flat a going over, but decided against it. If she had moved out, the landlord would have checked the premises. Besides, Jenkins had said that her car was missing, so presumably she'd driven away.

'You okay, Gerry?' asked a Welsh voice.

Hunter looked up to see Colin Duggan scratching his fleshy neck.

'That guy Bamber, apparently he wasn't with the FBI. I've just been on to their London bureau and they've never heard of him.'

'Fuck me,' said Duggan. 'Who the hell is he?'

'No idea. But he had to have some reason for hanging around.'

'Jesus, they say that murderers always return to the scene of the crime, but this is the first time I've heard of one joining the investigating team. Put a couple of guys on it, will you? Unless you fancy taking it on?'

'I want to chase up May Eckhardt. She's gone AWOL, too.'

Duggan ran his hand over his bald patch. 'What a fucking mess,' he said. 'This Bamber, it was the BTP that brought him in initially, right? Nothing to do with us?'

Hunter nodded. 'Newton introduced him,' he said. 'I've

got a memo somewhere saying that we should offer him every assistance.'

Duggan winked at Hunter. 'Not our fault, then, huh? If the shit hits the fan we're in the clear. Dig out the memo and send it to me, will you?'

As Duggan left the room, Hunter went over to a HOLMES terminal and logged on. He pulled up the interviews that Nick Wright had done with May Eckhardt and read through them. There was nothing untoward and the BTP detective had done a professional enough job. There were no details of her family, but according to the background, she'd studied at Exeter University. Hunter looked at his watch. It was too late to call the registrar's office, he'd have to do it first thing in the morning.

Doc handed the three passports and tickets to the girl behind the check-in desk. 'Three seats together,' he said.

She smiled and began tapping away at her computer console.

Doc turned around to look at Ramirez and Hammack. 'Okay, guys?'

The two men nodded. 'I could do with a beer,' said Hammack.

'We've plenty of time before we board. We can get a drink airside.'

'Any bags to check in, sir?' asked the Thai Airways girl.

'Just hand baggage,' said Doc. 'We won't be staying for long.'

From their vantage point up on the second floor, Wright and Kruse looked down on the three Americans as they walked away from the check-in desk towards immigration. 'They're travelling light,' said Wright.

'They're not planning to stay long,' said Kruse. 'Straight up to the tunnel complex, then down.'

The men walked through the barrier to the immigration area and passed out of sight. 'Are you sure we won't lose them in Vietnam?' asked Wright.

'We know where they're going. The map I've got is incredibly detailed. We can find the entrance, and once we're in the tunnels we know where they're going.'

'They're going to have a hell of a start on us.'

'Not really,' said Kruse. 'We'll get to Saigon about three hours after them, and they don't seem to be taking much in the way of equipment with them. They're going to be picking up their supplies in Saigon, say an hour. Maybe two.' He kicked the metal suitcase at his feet. 'We've got all the stuff we need right here. I reckon we'll reach the tunnel entrance an hour or two after they get there. They'll only be half a mile or so ahead of us, and that's not too big a margin. Sound will travel down there, so we won't want to get too close.'

Wright rubbed his chin thoughtfully. 'What are we going to find down there, Jim?'

'The answer,' said Kruse. He leaned on the rail that ran around the balcony. He already knew what the Americans hoped to find when they reached their destination, deep underground. A body. O'Leary had told him everything before he died: where the map was; where the body was buried; what had happened twenty-five years earlier and why the Tunnel Rats were so convinced that their past had come back to haunt them.

Kruse didn't believe in ghosts. He didn't care who was responsible for the murders, but he needed to know the identity of the killer and he needed to make sure that everyone who knew the secret of the tunnels was silenced for ever. He looked across at Wright and smiled. Kruse's speciality was making deaths look accidental, but down in the tunnels that wouldn't be necessary. 'What say we get breakfast, Nick? We can't check in for a couple of hours yet.'

The Thai Airways 737 turned off the main runway and headed for the terminal. 'Never thought I'd be back,' said Hammack. 'Once I was on the Freedom Bird, I swore that was it.'

'I don't think any of us ever expected to return, Bernie,' said Doc, peering out of the window. The plane taxied past curved concrete shelters that had protected US warplanes from VC mortar attacks during the last years of the wars. Most stood empty and were overgrown with weeds but a few contained small cargo planes. At the peak of the war, Saigon airport was the busiest in the world, with huge transporters ferrying in the hundreds of thousands of troops and all the armaments and equipment needed to keep them in combat, and bombers queuing up to drop their loads on whatever targets the top brass had earmarked for devastation that day. The airport was still busy, but now it was civilian airliners that were rolling up and down the taxiways.

The plane stopped and three buses pulled up next to it. The passengers poured off the plane and were ferried to the terminal, where they handed in yellow health forms that said they had no contagious diseases, and then joined the queues for immigration. Most of the passengers were Japanese and Chinese businessmen, though there were a few Westerners, mainly backpackers.

'Just like Bangkok, huh?' said Ramirez, nodding at the queues.

'I guess we make it just as hard for foreigners arriving at JFK,' said Doc.

They waited for more than an hour before handing their passports and visa forms to a stony-faced immigration officer in a green military-looking uniform, then passed through Customs where another green-uniformed official gave their holdalls a cursory inspection after passing them through an X-ray machine.

The three men walked out of the terminal into blinding sunshine, and stood in silence, looking out over the acres of tarmac, filled with gleaming taxis and chauffeur-driven luxury cars. Drivers in blue trousers and white shirts waited expectantly. Beyond them were large billboards advertising Japanese computers and American cigarettes. All were struck by the same thought: they'd left a war zone, and returned to an economic boom town.

Two Vietnamese girls walked by wearing the traditional *ao dai* costume – long blouses slit up the side over flowing, baggy pants. They were carrying cans of Coke and sipping their sodas through straws. From the open window of one of the taxis came the thumping beat of an Aerosmith song.

'Remind me again who won, Doc,' said Hammack. 'It was the Communists, right?' He ripped open a pack of chewing gum and slotted a piece into his mouth.

A young Vietnamese man came over. 'Taxi?' he asked.

'We want to go to the Rex Hotel,' said Doc. 'How much?'

'All taxis have meters, sir,' said the man. He motioned with his arm to the queue of taxis where a driver had already opened his boot for them.

'Beats Bangkok,' said Ramirez. 'You always end up bargaining with the cabs at the airport.'

They loaded their holdalls into the boot and climbed into the back of the Toyota taxi. The airconditioning was on and the interior was spotless.

It was a half-hour drive to the hotel. The bulk of the traffic on the roads was of the two-wheeled variety, bicycles and motorcycles. Unlike Bangkok, the traffic flowed freely and the air didn't shimmer with exhaust fumes. Construction seemed to be going on all around them and the skyline was littered with cranes and the skeletons of half-completed tower blocks. The three Americans stared out of the windows. The last time they had seen Saigon it had been a military town, packed with Jeeps and trucks and US military personnel. Now the only uniforms were worn by the policemen standing in the middle of the crossroads directing traffic. They drove by a sidewalk café where waiters in white shirts and black trousers served coffee to a group of businessmen, then by a line of shops filled with lacquerware and rosewood furniture. The car slowed as they eased through a group of young women pedalling old bicycles, all wearing pastel-coloured *ao dais* and what appeared to be long evening gloves, presumably to protect their hands and arms against the fierce Vietnamese sun.

It was a city in transition. One block would consist of a gleaming office tower with smartly dressed secretaries carrying briefcases, the next a boarded-up tenement block with peeling paint and rusting balconies, obviously awaiting demolition. Alongside modern stores with expensive display cases stood open-fronted shops selling secondhand motors covered in grime and oil, and advertising hoardings promoted everything from vitamins and baby powder to cigarettes and cognac.

'It's not what I expected,' said Hammack.

'What did you expect?' asked Doc.

'I dunno. Everyone in Mao tunics, maybe. The NVA on the streets. Tanks. Communist slogans. Martial music broadcast through loudspeakers. This is just like Bangkok.'

'It's capitalism, but under Communist control,' said Doc. 'They're trying to bring in Western products but without Western politics. Same as China.'

'And foreigners can go anywhere? No restrictions?'

'Pretty much,' said Doc. 'They're trying to encourage tourists. And that's what we are, tourists.'

The taxi turned down a tree-lined avenue. Ahead of them a sandy-coloured building sported a huge crown. 'The Rex Hotel,' said Doc. 'It was where the military used to brief the press corps. I thought it was appropriate. We can have a final briefing here before we head upcountry.'

It was a long time since May Eckhardt had worn an *ao dai*. The silk was soft against her skin and it rippled in the warm wind that blew down Nguyen Hue Boulevard from the Saigon River behind her. In front of her stood the red-roofed white and yellow building that was the Hôtel de Ville, home of the Ho Chi Minh City People's Committee. The Vietnamese flag, a yellow star on a red background, fluttered above it. To her left was the Rex Hotel. She stood astride her Yamaha scooter, her sandalled feet flat on the ground. No one gave her a second look in her pale blue *ao dai* and conical hat, she was just one of many. A small beggar boy, nine years old at most, held up a handful of packs of chewing gum. She shook her head. *'Toi khong muon . . .'* she said, but he pouted and pushed the gum at her.

She relented. She didn't want the chewing gum but she could remember when she was nine years old and alone on the streets of Saigon. She gave him one US dollar and took a pack. He grinned, showing a mouthful of yellowing teeth, then skipped away to bother an overweight German couple who were loudly bargaining to buy an opium pipe from a roadside trader.

May stared up at the Rex Hotel. She'd followed the three Americans from the airport, keeping close behind them on her scooter, until she was sure of their destination. She was disappointed that the one called Rabbit wasn't with them. She'd hoped that by sending him photographs of what she'd done, he would have contacted the others and travelled to

Vietnam with them. She'd been wrong. Still, there was a certain irony in leaving him until last, because he was the one she hated most. She kicked the scooter into life and drove away from the kerb. She weaved between the packs of cyclists making their way towards the Hôtel de Ville, and turned left on to Le Loi Boulevard, then into the narrow side street where she'd rented a small house. In front of the house was an Isuzu pick-up truck, the red paintwork starting to rust. She parked the scooter behind the Isuzu and went inside to change. The Americans wouldn't stay in the hotel for long, she knew. And where they were going, her *ao dai* would be useless as camouflage.

The woman in the registrar's office wouldn't take Gerry Hunter's word that he was a detective inspector and insisted on taking down his warrant card number and calling him back. When he picked up the receiver again she apologised profusely but explained that a year ago a jilted boyfriend had obtained confidential information from the university by falsely claiming to be a police officer. Hunter told her that he was trying to track down a former student who had studied computing at the university. 'Her name's May Eckhardt but she's married and I'm afraid I don't know her maiden name,' he said.

'Do you know when she was here?' asked the woman.

'About fifteen years ago, but could you check five years either side?' said Hunter. Wright had shown her date of birth as September 1965, but there was nothing in his report to say when she'd gone to university. 'I think her parents were from Sale in Cheshire. She's Oriental. Chinese, maybe.' He gave the woman May Eckhardt's date of birth, and she promised to check with the Department of Computer Science and get back to him as soon as possible.

Nick Wright scratched his ear with his pen. 'So many bloody forms to fill in,' he complained. 'Customs, immigration, health.'

'You've got to remember it's still a Communist country, Nick,' said Jim Bamber. 'The bureaucracy controls everything.'

Wright finished copying down his passport details on to the immigration form and put away his pen.

A stewardess with bright pink lipstick smiled and asked Wright if he wanted another drink. He shook his head. They were about halfway through the eighty-minute flight from Bangkok.

'Tell me about the tunnels,' Wright asked.

'What do you want to know?'

'O'Leary said they had all sorts of stuff underground. Factories, hospitals, training areas. How come the Americans didn't just blow them up?'

'They tried,' said the FBI agent. 'Cu Chi, to the north-west of Saigon, is riddled with tunnels. They reckon the network there is more than a hundred and fifty miles long, spread over something like three hundred square miles of an area they called the Iron Triangle. The Americans knew the tunnels were there, and they sent in tens of thousands of troops, but they uncovered only a tiny fraction of the network. They bulldozed the jungle, they sprayed the area with defoliants, practically killed every tree and blade of grass, but still they couldn't find the tunnels. Bomber pilots returning to Saigon were told to dump their unused bombs and fuel on the area, and then they started carpet-bombing with B-52s. Couldn't move the VC, though. They just dug in, deeper and deeper. The only way to get them out was to send in American soldiers.'

'The Tunnel Rats?'

'That's right. Hand-to-hand combat, deep underground.'

'Maybe I'm being obtuse, but why didn't they just pump the tunnels full of gas?'

'They tried, but the tunnels were built with water traps so that the gas could only go so far. Like a sink trap. Then they tried using dogs, but so many were killed by booby traps that they had to stop. They tried filling the tunnels with explosives and setting them off, but there are so many kinks and bends that the damage was always limited.'

'What I can't work out is why they're going back. What can be down there that's so important?'

'If we knew that, Nick, we wouldn't have to go down ourselves.'

Wright shivered. 'What about the reports you were getting from the Defense Department?'

'My people are having trouble tracking them down. They hope to have them by the time we get back to Bangkok.'

'But you've got the map, right?'

'Sure.'

'Can I see it?'

Bamber looked around. The plane was full. 'I'd rather wait until we've got a bit more privacy,' said Bamber.

'I guess so,' said Wright. 'But we're going to Cu Chi, right?'

'About thirty miles further north,' said Bamber. 'Cu Chi has been turned into a tourist area, believe it or not. They've widened some of the tunnels, even installed electric lighting. The tunnels that our guys are heading for haven't been opened up, and have probably been deserted for the last twenty-five years.'

A thin sheen of sweat had formed on Wright's face. A male steward offered him a cold towel with a smile and Wright accepted it gratefully. 'What sort of state are they going to be in?' he asked. 'Won't they have collapsed?'

'Shouldn't have,' said Bamber. 'The earth is mainly soil and clay, but it doesn't soak up water so most of the time it's as hard and dry as brick. It's softer during the rainy season, which is when the VC did most of the digging, but at this time of the year it's rock hard. It's perfect for tunnelling: it doesn't turn to mud, yet it doesn't crumble. The water table is about fifty feet below the surface, so they don't flood. The network we're going to is more than ten miles from the Iron Triangle, so it should have escaped the bulk of the B-52 bombing. Even so, the tunnels were so well built that even a bomb from a B-52 would only affect the upper levels.'

'I don't understand this business about levels,' said Wright.

'I'll be able to show you better on the map,' said the FBI agent. 'But basically the upper levels were communication tunnels, linking villages, firing posts and all the trapdoor entrances. They were usually about ten to fifteen feet down.

There are trapdoors leading down from the communication levels to the second level, about thirty feet below the surface. That's where they had sleeping chambers, air-raid shelters, training rooms and hospitals. Even further down, forty or fifty feet, were the command headquarters and storage areas.'

'Sounds like a whole city underground.'

'It was, Nick. At one point there were supposed to be something like twelve thousand VCs based in the various tunnel networks.'

A stewardess interrupted their conversation, asking them to put up their tray tables and to make sure that their seatbelts were fastened as they were preparing to land. Wright wiped his face with the cold towel. He was still sweating. He stared out of the window at the rice fields below and wondered what it would be like to be deep below the surface, crawling through the earth like a tunnelling animal. He shivered.

Sergio Ramirez and Bernie Hammack were already sitting around a wrought-iron table with cups of coffee in front of them when Doc walked on to the terrace. They had ordered a cup for him and it sat with its aluminium coffee dripper on top of it. He lifted the dripper off and poured milk into the inky-black brew.

'Rooms okay?' asked Doc. He sipped his coffee. It was bitter and strong.

'Hard to believe it's Saigon,' said Hammack. 'It's as good as anything in Bangkok.'

'And they speak better English,' said Ramirez.

A group of Japanese businessmen were sitting at a neighbouring table, peering at a blueprint. Two Chinese entrepreneurs in polo shirts and Chinos slurped noodles and argued over a balance sheet. Doc could almost smell the money being made. The terrace bar was tacky in the extreme, with garishly painted statues of animals, including two grey elephants and a white horse, standing amid tubs of ornately clipped bushes, and around the perimeter of the roof faded flags fluttered gently in the wind. At the far end of the terrace was a statue of a crouching Oriental archer, drawing back his bow. A Japanese girl posed next to it while her boyfriend snapped away with a small camera.

'I've booked the rooms for three days,' said Doc. 'I expect to be back here tomorrow, so if everything goes smoothly we can have a couple of days R and R.'

'If,' said Hammack. 'That's a big if, Doc.'

'We go down, we check it's still there, and we come back.'

'And if he's not there?' said Hammack. 'If he's not dead?'

'Then I'll eat my fucking hat, Bernie.'

'That's not what we should be worrying about,' said Ramirez. 'If he's not dead, if he is the killer, then it's going to be easy enough to protect ourselves. But if it's not him, then we have a big, big problem. Who killed Eric, Max and Dennis?'

'Dennis was an accident,' said Doc.

'Maybe,' said Hammack. 'But the point is, someone knows what we did. And someone wants to make us pay.'

'Whatever, we take this one step at a time. And step one is to get ourselves equipped. There's a market not far away where we can get everything we need.' He took a sheet of paper from the pocket of his denim shirt and dropped it on the table in front of Ramirez and Hammack. 'I've drawn up a list of what I think we'll need. Can you see anything I've missed?'

Ramirez ran his finger down the list. 'A double-action Smith & Wesson .44 magnum would be nice,' he said.

Doc smiled thinly. 'Much as I'd like to oblige, short of stealing one, we're not going to get a gun.'

'String,' said Hammack. 'You forgot the string. And rope.'

Doc took a pen out of his pocket and added string and rope to the list.

'How are we getting up to the tunnels?' asked Ramirez.

'Bikes,' said Doc. He smiled when he saw the look of disbelief on Ramirez's face. 'Motorbikes,' he clarified. 'Foreigners can't hire cars without a local driver, but we can rent motorbikes. I asked reception and there's a place around the corner that can help us.'

The three Americans went down together in the lift and walked through the marble-floored foyer where a group of Taiwanese tourists were checking in. There was a line of white Toyota taxis outside the hotel and they climbed into the first one. Doc told the driver where they wanted to go and he smiled and flicked on the meter. It was, thought Doc, a pleasant change from Bangkok where more often than not getting into a taxi meant several minutes of bargaining, depending on how heavy the traffic was and whether the driver wanted to go in a particular direction.

'You tourists?' asked the driver. He was in his fifties with greying, spiky hair and skin that was as leathery and weatherbeaten as an old saddle.

'Sort of,' said Doc.

The driver looked at them in his rearview mirror as he negotiated a way through several dozen bicycling schoolchildren.

'You here during war?' he asked.

The Americans looked at each other. Doc shrugged. 'Yeah,' he said.

'American GIs, Number One!' he cackled.

They passed two cyclos, hybrids of bicycles and rickshaws, with two thin Vietnamese teenagers pedalling hard up an incline, ferrying two obese tourists in T-shirts and shorts who were filming each other with video cameras. A beautiful young girl in a pale green *ao dai* and black evening gloves drove by on a Honda moped. She smiled at Ramirez and he beamed back.

'You were a soldier?' asked Hammack.

'Damn right,' said the driver, cackling again.

'What, with ARVN?' The Army of the Republic of South Vietnam. The soldiers who were supposed to be fighting alongside the Americans, but who more often than not proved to be a liability rather than an asset.

The driver laughed louder. 'No, me VC!' he said, thumping his chest.

'You've got to be joking,' said Ramirez.

'VC. Damn right!' He twisted around in his seat. 'We won, huh?'

'Yes, you did,' said Doc. He looked across at his two companions. Hammack and Ramirez sat stony faced, their arms folded across their chests.

The driver dropped them in front of a bustling market with stalls bedecked with clothes and shoes, vendors selling food, and tables strewn with cheap plastic toys. The three

Americans threaded their way through to the rear of the indoor market where most of the clothing was in camouflage fabric and the plastic toys and electrical equipment gave way to war surplus equipment. There were lines of old gas masks, combat boots, webbing belts, canteens, flashlights; enough cquipment to outfit an army. Hammack and Ramirez stood with surprised looks on their faces.

'How did you find out about this place?' asked Hammack.

'It's in the guide book, believe it or not,' said Doc. 'Dan Sinh Market. Most of it is reproduction, tourists love it.'

Ramirez was looking at a rack of field stretchers and a medical kit with a red cross on it. 'This looks genuine,' he said.

'Some of it is, but a lot of it is made here.'

Ramirez tossed him the medical kit and Doc opened it. Inside were bandages, dressings, sutures and hypodermics. The quality looked as good as anything he had back in his surgery in Bangkok. He wondered whether buying it would be taken as a bad omen by his two companions, but he decided that it would be essential, to deal with the cuts and bruises they'd get just negotiating the tunnels. He bought it, along with several tubes of antiseptic ointment and mosquito repellent from a neighbouring stall.

The three Americans chose the clothing they'd wear, all opting for T-shirts and jeans, knowing how hot it would get underground. They selected small nylon rucksacks, checking them for fit, and plastic canteens because they'd sweat like crazy and dehydration would be one of their biggest problems.

Ramirez found a stall selling knives and they argued for a while over which would be the best type to buy.

Ramirez wanted a killing weapon, but Doc's view was that they'd be most useful for probing for booby traps and hidden trapdoors. Eventually they agreed to differ: Ramirez selected a large hunting knife, Doc chose a bayonet-type knife and Hammack a smaller weapon in a plastic scabbard. A neighbouring stall sold compasses, including several aviation models that appeared to have been stripped from planes. They chose the most rugged and easy-to-read models they could find.

Doc took out a pen and crossed off the items they'd purchased. 'Flashlights,' he said.

They bought flashlights and spare batteries, three green canvas kitbags with 'USMC' stamped on them, and the rest of the equipment that was on the list. The last thing that Doc bought was a small folding shovel. Hammack and Ramirez looked away as Doc put it in one of the kitbags with the rest of his purchases.

It took Nick Wright and Jim Bamber more than an hour to pass through immigration, and it was another hour before their bags rolled out on to the carousel. They carried their bags over to Customs where two green-uniformed young women with waist-length hair helped load them through an X-ray machine.

'This doesn't make sense,' said Wright. 'Shouldn't they be X-raying luggage before it goes on the plane?'

'It's not about safety, it's about contraband,' said Bamber.

'There's a lot of duty imposed on stuff brought into the country, computers and the like.'

One of the girls pointed at Bamber's case as it rolled out of the X-ray machine. 'I bet I know what this is about,' he sighed. He popped the locks and opened the case. She went through his clothes and pulled out the two sets of infra-red goggles. Bamber smiled easily. 'Binoculars,' he said, miming putting a pair to his eyes and looking through them. 'For night-time. For watching birds at night-time.'

She held out her hand for the Customs form he was holding. Wright's suitcase emerged from the X-ray machine and a middle-aged man with a squint motioned for Wright to open it. He riffled through the contents and took out Wright's portable telephone and charging unit.

'You have receipt?' the girl asked Bamber. The FBI agent shook his head. She pointed at the form. 'You have to put down how much they cost.'

Her colleague held Wright's form a few inches away from his face. 'Fill in form properly,' he said.

Wright borrowed Bamber's pen, detailed the phone and charging unit on the back of the form. They handed over their forms and were told they could go. They walked out into the arrivals area.

'Are we going to hire a car?' asked Wright.

'No can do,' said Bamber. 'Guide book says you can't drive here. Cops'll stop any foreigner they see at the wheel. We have to take a taxi.'

They went outside and Wright was hit by a wave of heat and humidity that made him gasp. 'Jeez! It's hotter even than Bangkok, and Bangkok was sweltering,' said Wright. He put down his suitcase and holdall and surveyed the line of gleaming white Toyotas. 'One of them?' he asked.

Bamber rubbed his chin thoughtfully. 'Might be a bit suspicious climbing into a cab here and heading straight out into the country,' he said. 'I reckon we should go to Saigon and switch cars there.'

'Whatever,' said Wright. Bamber seemed to know what he was doing so Wright was happy to let him take charge. Wright was having trouble concentrating – all he could think about was the tunnels.

Hammack kicked his motorcycle into life and blipped the throttle. 'Sounds sweet,' he said.

Hammack was sitting astride a Yamaha trail bike, his kitbag tied to the back. Doc and Ramirez were on fairly new Honda trail bikes, the wheels of which were crusted with mud. All three Americans were wearing jeans and white cotton shirts with the sleeves buttoned at the wrist to provide protection from the sun, and they had rented gloves and full-face helmets with tinted visors from the man who'd supplied the bikes.

Ramirez gave Doc a thumbs-up. 'Rock and roll,' he said.

'Remember, the roads can be dangerous, so we take it slow and watch out for potholes,' said Doc. 'I don't want to have to do any needlework on the way up, okay?'

Hammack and Ramirez nodded.

Doc flicked his visor down and led the way out of the shop, bumping carefully off the pavement and on to the road. Hammack and Ramirez followed. The three motorcyclists headed north, nudging their way through the battalions of cyclists and moped riders.

A red Isuzu turned out of a side street and headed after them.

'Okay, stop here,' said Bamber, tapping the taxi driver on the shoulder. At the roadside was a line of shabby cars, and a group of Vietnamese men stood in the shade of a tree, watching a flickering television fixed to the inside wall of one of the shops that lined the road.

Bamber paid the driver with a handful of Vietnamese currency as Wright climbed out. The two men put their suitcases and holdalls on the pavement and watched their taxi drive away.

'Now what?' asked Wright.

'I'm pretty sure these guys are for hire,' said Bamber.

'They don't have taxi signs,' said Wright.

Two of the men who'd been watching television walked over. 'You want car?' the taller of the two asked.

Bamber winked at Wright. 'Told you.' He nodded at the car at the head of the queue, a Mercedes with rusty wings that must have been at least twenty years old. 'How much for one day?'

The two men spoke to each other in Vietnamese. The shorter one shook his head. 'Where you want to go?'

'North,' said Bamber. 'Past Ben Suc, up by the Thi Tinh River.'

The two men pulled faces and shrugged. 'One hundred and twenty dollars for one day,' said the shorter one.

'Eighty,' said Bamber.

'One hundred,' said the man.

Bamber nodded. 'Okay.' He grinned at Wright. 'What the hell, the Bureau's picking up the check, right?'

Wright picked up his suitcase. The man already had the boot open and he helped Wright heave it in. 'My name Chinh,' he said.

'I'm Nick. He's Jim.'

'Nick. Jim.' The driver said their names several times as if trying to commit them to memory as he loaded Bamber's metal suitcase on top of Wright's. Bamber and Wright got into the back of the car with their holdalls. The driver went into one of the roadside shops and emerged with a carrier bag containing two plastic bottles of mineral water. He handed them to Wright and started the car. Clouds of black smoke billowed from the exhaust and the engine coughed, backfired, then roared. 'Diesel,' said the driver. 'Okay soon. Where we go?'

'Head for Ben Suc, then I'll show you.'

A policeman blew a whistle and held up a white gloved hand to stop the traffic. Chinh braked hard, throwing the Americans forward. 'You want to go down the tunnels?' said Chinh. 'Better you go to Cu Chi. Many tourists go there. Lots of fun.'

'We don't want to go to the Cu Chi tunnels,' said Bamber, as hundreds of bicycles rolled by. 'We want to go further north. And we want you to wait for us.'

'How long?'

'Ten hours. Maybe longer.'

Chinh clicked his tongue. 'Where you go?' he asked.

'That's not your problem,' said Bamber. 'You drop us, you wait for us, you drive us back to Saigon.'

The policeman blew his whistle again and Chinh put the taxi in gear and edged forward.

'Okay,' said Chinh. 'You the boss.'

May Eckhardt drove through a small village where women were using hoes to spread rice along the roadside so that it would dry in the baking hot sun. Several of the women looked up as she went by – it was still unusual to see a woman behind the wheel in Vietnam. May accelerated as she reached the outskirts of the village, veering over to the wrong side of the road to give a wide berth to a cart being pulled by two massive water buffaloes, their spreading horns at least six feet wide. The cart was piled high with sacks of rice, grains of which dribbled from the sides of the cart. Rice splattered against the Isuzu like rain, then she was past the cart and powering down the dusty road. Rice paddies stretched on either side almost to the horizon, lush and green, and young men stood knee deep in the canals that ran around the rice fields, fishing with nets that thcy threw like lassos.

In the far distance she could just make out the three motorcyclists and she slowed down. There was no need to get too close. She knew exactly where they were going. Her hands were light on the steering wheel, caressing rather than gripping, and she hummed softly to herself.

Jim Bamber unzipped his holdall and took out a green plastic map case. He unfolded it and held it up so that Wright could see it. It was hand drawn in black ink, the paper yellowing at the edges.

'This is a Defense Department map?' asked Wright. 'They let you have the original?'

'Yeah, I was surprised, but I guess they've got copies,' said Bamber.

The map was in five parts, each a sheet about two feet square. The top sheet showed features of the landscape – hills, a river, several small villages – and there were several crosses marked on it. In the top right-hand corner of the map was a compass showing north.

'This area was called the Long Nguyen Secret Zone,' said Bamber. 'It covered both sides of the Thi Tinh River. The Iron Triangle was about fifteen miles south, here.' He pointed at the map.

'And the crosses?'

'Tunnel entrances,' said Bamber.

'I thought there was only one way in?' said Wright.

Chinh pounded on his horn. From the moment he'd left the outskirts of Saigon he'd insisted on using the horn every time he came up behind a cyclist, letting them know that he was about to overtake. The constant noise irritated Wright, but despite several times asking him to stop doing it, Chinh persisted.

'There are entrances all over the area,' said the FBI agent, 'but they're not all connected. That was one of the reasons the army found it so difficult to close them down.'

He flipped over the first sheet, which also had a compass in the top right corner. Written across the top in capital letters was 'FIRST LEVEL'. The map had black crosses that coincided with the crosses on the first sheet.

'This is where the entrances lead to,' said Bamber. 'See what I mean? They're not all connected.'

The various entrances were linked by a network of tunnels. Some of the tunnels simply ran from one entrance to another, apparently connecting firing points, while others ran to larger rooms. Scattered across the map were four red crosses. Wright tapped one of them.

'What do they represent?' he asked.

'Hatches that lead down to the second level,' said Bamber.

He flipped the sheet over. Underneath was a map marked 'SECOND LEVEL', with matching red crosses on it. The second level contained much larger rooms and fewer tunnels. Wright peered at the notes that had been made alongside several of the squares that denoted the different rooms.

'A cinema?' he said in amazement.

'Yeah, they used to show propaganda movies underground. And they had dance troupes that used to tour around giving performances, poetry readings, the works.'

'And this,' said Wright, pointing at the map. 'This is a well?'

'That's right. They could draw their own water without leaving the tunnels. They had water, food stores, supplies of fuel. They could live down there for months.' He turned the sheet. 'This is the third level. They only discovered one way down, so much of the third level is unexplored.' He pointed at a blue cross. 'And this is the only way down to the fourth level.'

'The fourth level? I thought you said there were only three.'

Chinh slammed on the brakes and swerved into the middle of the road. Wright and Bamber were thrown apart and the map tore. Chinh pounded his horn. A flock of more than a hundred white ducks with bright orange bills scattered across the road. Two young Vietnamese boys with long canes jogged after the birds, shouting and waving. Bamber inspected the damaged map. It was only a small rip.

Chinh swung the car back on to the right side of the road. He twisted around in his seat and smiled apologetically. 'Roads bad up country,' he said.

'Sure are,' agreed Bamber. Ahead of them loomed a truck piled high with boxes of fruit. Bamber pointed at the truck and raised his eyebrows. Chinh turned around and narrowly avoided crashing into it. Two women riding bicycles piled high with firewood watched open mouthed as the car flashed by, missing them by inches.

Wright reached over and turned to the last page of the map. There were only two chambers drawn; a large one linked by a short length of tunnel to a second, smaller, room. The only writing on the sheet was the words 'FOURTH LEVEL'.

'That's obviously where they're going,' said Bamber. 'It must have been important to be so far underground.'

'How far below ground is this?' asked Wright, tapping the page.

'Fifty-five feet, I guess.'

Wright sat back and closed his eyes. He rubbed his temples with the palms of his hands. He could feel the pressure building behind his eyes, the prelude to a major headache. 'O'Leary mentioned booby traps,' he said.

Bamber folded up the sheets and slotted them back into the map case. 'Don't worry,' he said. 'I'll be ahead of you. If there are any problems, I'll come across them first.'

Problems sounded innocuous; problems sounded like small obstacles that could easily be overcome. O'Leary hadn't said problems, he'd said booby traps. 'What sort of problems?' asked Wright.

'Punji sticks in pits.'

Wright opened his eyes. 'What?'

Bamber smiled easily. 'Nick, we'll be following Doc and the rest. They've been down there already, they'll have exposed any traps.'

'You can't be sure of that.'

'They're almost fifty years old. You think they'd be putting their lives at risk if they didn't think they could handle it?'

'Maybe,' said Wright, unconvinced. 'Is there anything else I should worry about?'

Bamber put a hand on Wright's shoulder. 'It's going to work out just fine,' he said reassuringly.

Wright looked out of the window. They drove through a small village, on the outskirts of which was a school, little more than a long single-storey building and a dusty playground surrounded by a waist-high metal fence. Groups of young children in bluc and white uniforms lined up in front of an open doorway while a teacher carried out a head count. It reminded Wright of the orphanage in Bangkok, and the basement where Eric Horvitz had died. He wondered what it must have been like, dying in a cold dark place, tortured and killed, begging for mercy and receiving none. He shuddered.

Doc pulled in at the side of the road and took a map out of the holdall strapped to his petrol tank. Hammack and Ramirez stopped their bikes either side of him. Doc flipped up his visor and studied the markings on the map. He checked his milometer and ran his finger along the thin line that represented the road they were on. He looked across the rice fields to a lone hill, a bump in the landscape that was much the same shape as the conical hats that the peasants wore.

'Much further?' asked Ramirez, using his sleeve to wipe away the red dust which had coated his visor.

'About an hour,' said Doc. 'Then we leave the road. There's a track that leads to the river. According to the map it's three miles from this road. Once we reach the river, we should be able to find the entrance.'

'You think we'll be able to find it, after twenty-five years?'

'We'll find the rock formation. That won't have changed,' said Doc. 'And then all we've got to do is to find the rock that we put over the hatch. It's not going to be a problem, Sergio.'

Hammack rubbed his arms. 'My arms are going numb,' he complained. 'Makes you miss the old Hueys, doesn't it?'

'You'll be telling us next that you miss the war,' said Doc.

Hammack shook his helmeted head. 'No fucking way,' he said.

Doc put the map away. 'Okay?' His two companions nodded. Doc put the bike in gear and roared off.

While Gerry Hunter waited for the woman in the registrar's office to call him back, he went over to make himself a coffee. He picked up the wrong mug by mistake, then realised with a jolt that it was Clive's. He stared at the chipped white mug with its map of Australia on one side and a grinning kangaroo on the other, wondering what to do with it. It was too personal to throw away, but he didn't want anyone else to use it. He took it back to his desk. He still expected Clive to walk into the incident room at any moment, cursing the London traffic or the weather or the canteen food or whatever it was that was annoying him that day.

Hunter picked up his telephone and dialled Anna Littman's number. Even as the phone rang out, Hunter wasn't exactly sure what he was going to say to her, and when she answered the words tumbled out in a rush.

'Anna, look, this is Gerry. I know this is crazy and I know you'll say that I'm clutching at straws and that I'm making something out of nothing, but is it in any way possible that Clive's death wasn't an accident?'

For several seconds she didn't speak. 'Gerry, you know what I'm going to say,' she said, her voice a concerned whisper.

'I know, I know. I want to feel that I'm doing something, I want to have someone to blame, I can't accept that sometimes shit just happens. I know the drill. I get it all the time, Anna, people who've lost their nearest and dearest and who aren't prepared to accept that it was an accident. They're convinced that it was an arsonist and not a faulty electrical heater or that someone tampered with the brakes and it wasn't just carelessness that sent the car off the road. I know, Anna, I'm not stupid.'

'No one said you're stupid, Gerry, but you've just lost a close, personal friend. More than that, a partner, someone who trusted you and relied on you. It's only natural that you're going to feel guilty.'

'I know all about survivor guilt, too, Anna.'

'So what do you want me to tell you? That Clive's death wasn't an accident?'

'Is it possible?'

'God, Gerry, how long have you been in the job? Anything's possible, you know that. But just think what that would mean. Someone would have had to have got into Clive's flat and forced him to drink the best part of a bottle of whisky, then forced him to throw up and choked him to death. Does that sound at all likely to you?'

Hunter put his hand up to his forehead. 'No, of course it's not likely. But is it possible?'

Dr Littman sighed. 'Yes, Gerry. It's possible. It's also possible that I'm really a visitor from another planet and that you're going to win the lottery this weekend. Anything's possible. But do I think that there's any likelihood that Clive was murdered? No, Gerry. I don't. You're going to have to let it go. Grief is all well and good, it's part of the—'

'— healing process, I know. I know. That's not what this is about.'

'What is it about, Gerry?'

Hunter considered her question. He wanted to tell her about Bamber, a man pretending to be an FBI agent. He wanted to tell her about the missing video cassette, about the ace of spades being a death card, but he knew that it wouldn't make any sense to her. It barely made any sense to him. 'I don't know, Anna. It's been a bad week.'

'Do you want to come around and talk about it? I serve an excellent coffee.'

Hunter ran his finger down the kangaroo on Clive's mug. 'Thanks, Anna, but I'll be okay.'

'My door's always open,' she said. 'Hell of a draught, but what can you do?'

Hunter laughed. When he replaced the receiver the phone rang almost immediately. It was the woman in the registrar's office, apologising for the delay in getting back to him.

'May Hampshire graduated in 1986, with first-class Honours,' said the woman.

'Hampshire?' queried Hunter. He'd been expecting an Oriental name.

'She was the only May in Computer Science, and I checked from 1980 right up to last year, just to be sure,' said the woman. 'The date of birth matches so there's no doubt that it's the girl you're looking for. Oh, you're worried about the name? I wondered about that because you said she was Chinese. Her photograph was on file and she's definitely Oriental. Very pretty girl.'

'Do you have her address?'

'I do. It's in Sale, just like you said. Her parents are Peter and Emily Hampshire.' The woman gave Hunter the full address and a telephone number. Hunter thanked her and cut the connection.

He sat staring at Clive's mug, thinking over what Anna Littman had said, wondering if she was right when she suggested he was suffering from survivor's guilt. He shook his head. No, there was a nagging doubt that wouldn't go away, no matter how dispassionately he thought about his partner's death. The missing video couldn't be explained, not unless someone else had been at Clive's flat. Then there was the Vietnam War connection: the movie, Eckhardt's war service, and the ace of spades death card. All were somehow linked, he was sure of that. He needed to talk to May Eckhardt, to find out what she knew of her husband's wartime experiences.

He dialled the number the woman had given him. Emily Hampshire answered the phone, her voice apprehensive as if she didn't get many calls and those that she did get rarely brought good news. Hunter identified himself.

'Mrs Hampshire, I'm actually calling about your daughter . . .'

'May? What's . . . ?'

'Mrs Hampshire, please don't worry. I just need to ask you a few questions, there's nothing for you to be alarmed about, really.' Hunter looked at his watch and came to a sudden decision. He could drive up to Sale in four hours or so, assuming the motorway was clear. 'Mrs Hampshire, will you and your husband be at home this afternoon?'

'Yes, I suppose so,' she said hesitantly.

'I'd like to pop along for a chat,' said Hunter. 'Nothing to worry about, I can assure you. Let's say three o'clock, shall we?'

The handlebars of Doc's motorcycle kicked from side to side and he fought to keep the machine moving in a straight line. Ramirez and Hammack followed in single file. The track was wide enough for a car, but it was uneven and dotted with potholes. They passed a small village, a cluster of houses with corrugated-iron roofs and television aerials on poles more than twenty feet long. A group of small children rushed out to watch the motorcycles drive by. They giggled and waved and Ramirez waved back. In the middle of the village was a large hut, open at the sides. Inside more than a dozen men sat in deckchairs watching an old black and white television set. None of them noticed the Americans ride by.

Beyond the village were acres of rice paddies. Half a dozen farmers in conical hats were burning rice stalks and the grey smoke blew over the track in billowing clouds. The three Americans drove through the smoke. The smell brought back memories for Doc, memories of helicopters hovering above a village, the rattle of AK-47s and the dull crump of mortars exploding in the paddies. Huts were on fire, the thatched roofs crackling and hissing like the burning rice stalks, and from inside the huts came screams and cries for help. Doc shook his head, trying to clear the thoughts from his head. It was no time for flashbacks.

They followed the track to the river, and then headed north. The rice paddies gave way to undergrowth, and then secondary jungle, areas which had been defoliated during the war but which had been reclaimed by trees, shrubs and ground-hugging plants. Doc took a look at his milometer and slowed his bike, looking around for landmarks. Twenty-five years ago the area had been as barren as a lunar landscape.

He saw what he was looking for over to his right, a jagged spar of rock amid the trees, leaning to the side like a massive javelin that had stuck point first in the ground. Next to it was a smaller rock formation, shaped like the comb of a rooster.

Doc stopped and put his feet on the ground. Ramirez and Hammack pulled up either side of him. All three were coated in red dust. Doc flipped up his visor and pointed at the rocks.

Hammack nodded. 'That's it,' he said. 'You did it, Doc. You got us here.'

Ramirez looked around. 'I never thought anything would grow here again, what with all the Agent Orange and shit they dumped and all.'

'Yeah, must have worked its way right through the food chain by now,' said Hammack.

Doc climbed off his bike. 'We won't be here long enough for it to affect us,' he said. 'Tomorrow lunchtime we'll be back in Saigon drinking beer and laughing at this.' He pushed his bike off the track and into the undergrowth.

'Yeah, I sure hope so,' said Hammack. He dismounted and pushed his bike after Doc. Ramirez followed.

All three men were bathed in sweat by the time they reached the sandstone rock formations. They parked their bikes and took off their helmets and gloves. Ramirez wiped his forehead with his sleeve, smearing red dust across his skin.

Doc went over to an anvil-shaped rock that came up to his waist. 'This is it,' he said. Hammack and Ramirez walked over to stand by him. They stood in silence, staring at the rock.

'I can't believe we came back,' said Ramirez.

'Believe it,' said Doc. 'We're here.'

All three men put their shoulders against the rock and pushed. It slid slowly to the side.

'That's enough,' said Doc. He knelt down and began scraping away the red soil with his hands until he found the trapdoor. Ramirez helped him and together they lifted up the wood and bamboo hatch, revealing the hole underneath.

'We know one thing for sure,' said Doc. 'No one came out this way after us. They wouldn't have been able to budge the rock.'

'That doesn't mean anything,' said Ramirez. 'There could be lots of other ways out that we didn't know about.'

'Always looking on the bright side, aren't you, Sergio?' said Doc sarcastically. 'Okay, let's get our gear on.'

They went back to their bikes and untied their kitbags. After stripping off their dusty clothes they changed into T-shirts and jeans and slung their rucksacks on. Doc and Hammack pulled on soft caps made of camouflage material, and Ramirez tied a scarf of green and brown around his head. They put their clothes into the kitbags, along with their helmets and gloves and the keys to the motorcycles.

'Okay?' asked Doc.

The two men nodded. 'Let's do it,' said Ramirez.

'We'll leave the kitbags down in the tunnel,' said Doc.

They carried the bags to the tunnel entrance. All three men were breathing heavily and sweating. Hammack's T-shirt was already soaked. They dropped their bags and stood around the hole, looking down. Doc patted Ramirez on the shoulder. 'Do you wanna lead the way, Sergio?' he said.

'Happy to,' said Ramirez.

He switched on his flashlight and sat down on the ground, swinging his legs into the square of darkness. He took several deep breaths and then crossed himself. He slid down through the hatchway, then dropped into a crouch and shuffled to the side. Doc and Hammack passed the kitbags down. Ramirez stacked them at the far side of the tunnel and then moved away from the hatch.

Hammack eased himself into the hole, his shoulders scraping against the wooden frame. He grunted, then he was through, bending his legs and crawling forward. Doc followed. He switched on his flashlight and then pulled the cover across the entrance.

'Stop here, Chinh,' said Bamber, pointing at a roadside shack. Chinh jammed on his brakes and they shuddered to a halt in a cloud of dust.

Wright opened his eyes. 'Are we there?' he asked.

'Not yet,' said the FBI agent. He opened the door and got out. 'I figured we should get some water.'

Bamber went over to the shack where an old woman in a wide-brimmed hat was hacking away at a coconut with a machete. Wright climbed out of the taxi and joined him. In the back of the shack was a refrigerator full of cans of soft drinks and bottles of water. An old man was sprawled on a sun-lounger, his head turned to a wall.

He was skeletally thin, his ribs clearly outlined through his mahogany skin.

Bamber pointed at the water and held up four fingers. The old woman gave him four bottles. 'Do you want a Coke or something?' Bamber asked Wright.

Wright shook his head. An ancient bus rattled down the road towards Saigon, scattering a group of scrawny chickens that had been pecking at spilled rice grains. He rubbed the back of his neck, trying to loosen the knotted muscles there. The sun was dipping towards the horizon. 'How long until it gets dark?' he asked.

'A couple of hours,' said Bamber. 'Don't worry, we'll be there well before the sun goes down. And once we're underground, it won't matter whether it's night or day.' He handed two of the bottles to Wright. 'You okay?'

Wright smiled tightly. 'Getting a bit of a headache, that's all.'

'It'll all be over in a few hours,' said Bamber, patting him on the back and guiding him towards the taxi where Chinh was gunning the engine impatiently.

May Eckhardt climbed out of the Isuzu and stretched lazily. The heat of the afternoon sun had been almost unbearable, even with the pick-up's airconditioning full on, but now it was early evening and there was a soft breeze from the north. She was wearing a faded sweatshirt and blue jeans, which she stripped off and tossed into the back of the pick-up truck. She kicked off her sandals and took off her bra and pants and stood naked, enjoying the feel of warm wind on her skin. She had a sudden urge to run across the sand, to go jumping over the rocks and skipping around the trees as she had done as a child. She smiled to herself. She wasn't a child any more and she had an adult's work to do.

She took the blue and green holdall off the passenger seat and took out a pair of black pyjamas, the sort that peasants still wore when they were tending their fields. She shrugged them on, then tied a black and white checked scarf around her neck. The sandals she put on were old and worn, but comfortable, the soles cut from truck tyres, the strip that ran between her toes made from an old inner tube. She took a leather belt and fastened it around her waist, then attached two metal water canteens, one either side. Also in the bag was a long hunting knife in an oiled leather scabbard, and she clipped that to the back of the belt. Everything else she needed was down in the tunnels already. The only food she was taking was a ball of rice wrapped in a silk handkerchief and placed in a small cloth bag that she tied to the front of the belt. She didn't need food to sustain her. Hate would be more than enough.

May used a rubber band to tie back her hair in a ponytail, locked the doors of the Isuzu and slid the key into the exhaust pipe. From the back of the pick-up she took a long flashlight. She walked confidently through the undergrowth, skirting a bomb crater half filled with green stagnant water.

The three motorbikes were in the shade of the jagged rock. One by one she pushed them to the water-filled crater and rolled them in. When she'd finished she stood at the edge watching the oily bubbles gradually subside until the surface was still once more. She wiped her hands on her trousers and walked over to the anvil-shaped rock.

The hatch covering the tunnel entrance had been pulled back into place but there had been no one to replace its covering of dirt. She pulled it open, and put her head to the opening, listening. There was only silence. She dropped down into the tunnel. Three kitbags lay to one side. Closing her eyes, she breathed in, sniffing like a tracker dog. She smelled sweat, cigarette smoke and beer, and the minty odour of toothpaste.

She pulled the hatch over her head, blocking out the light. It was a perfect fit and the darkness was absolute. May sat for a while, her back pressed against the hard, dry clay, breathing in the smell of the tunnels. The entrails of Mother Earth held no fear for her. They would protect her, as they had done in the past. She twisted around and began to move down the tunnel in a half crouch, still in total darkness because she wanted to use the batteries of her flashlight as little as possible. Besides, there were no traps in the early part of the tunnel. All the dangers lay ahead.

Ramirez played the beam of his torch along the floor of the tunnel. It ran for some fifty feet before it bent to the right. The roof was arched and the tunnel was slightly wider at the base than at the top. It was about three feet tall, so Ramirez could crawl on his hands and knees without banging his head. The Viet Cong, being smaller and slighter, were able to run along in a low crouch, giving them the advantage of speed. Ramirez knew, though, that speed wasn't what counted when exploring the underground labyrinth. Care and caution were the watchwords. The tunnels were a death trap for the unwary.

'How's it going, Sergio?' asked Hammack. The black man was about ten feet behind Ramirez.

'No problem,' said Ramirez. 'Makes all the difference knowing that a VC isn't just around the corner with a loaded AK-47, doesn't it?' Ramirez looked over his shoulder. Sweat was pouring off Hammack's face and he wiped his forehead with his massive forearm. 'Don't forget to drink,' said Ramirez. 'It's easy to get dehydrated down here.'

Hammack grinned and his gold tooth glinted. 'You wanna teach me to suck eggs while you're at it?' he said.

Ramirez smiled. 'Bet you're regretting all that fried chicken now, huh? You must be what, twenty pounds heavier than last time we were down here?'

'At least,' said Hammack. 'You want me to go point, thin man?'

'Hell no,' said Ramirez. 'This is the fun part.'

He turned away from Hammack and began to crawl forward, his flashlight in his left hand, his knife in his right.

'There,' said Bamber, pointing at the jagged rock formation to their right. He grabbed Chinh by the shoulder and told him to stop. He checked the map, looked at the milometer, then rechecked the map. 'Yup, this is it,' he said.

He pointed to the side of the road. 'Can you pull off here?' he asked Chinh.

The driver frowned. 'No road,' he said.

'I know there's no road, but the undergrowth isn't too thick, you can drive through it.'

Chinh pulled a face. He shook his head.

Bamber took a handful of Vietnamese banknotes out of his pocket and thrust them at the driver. 'If it's your paintwork you're worried about . . .'

Whether or not Chinh understood what Bamber had said, he grabbed the money and put the car in gear. He edged the Mercedes off the road and through the vegetation.

'I just want us away from the road,' said Bamber. 'Just in case someone goes by and wonders why Chinh's waiting.'

'Sure,' said Wright. He peered out of the window at the darkening sky. 'We made it just in time.'

'It's perfect,' said Bamber. 'We'll be out again at dawn. And the car's less likely to be spotted at night.'

The Mercedes slowed to a crawl. It had to skirt a bomb crater and then circle around a clump of tall trees covered with vines. Bamber looked over his shoulder. He couldn't see the track they'd left. 'Okay, Chinh, this'll do fine,' he said. Chinh brought the car to a halt.

Bamber opened the door and climbed out. Wright followed him. 'Is it far?' Wright asked.

'Over by the rocks,' said Bamber. 'According to the map, it's by a rock shaped like an anvil.'

He popped open the boot and clicked the combination locks on his suitcase. 'Mickey Mouse or Snoopy?' he asked.

'What?'

'The mouse or the dog? Which do you prefer?' He held up

two knapsacks, the sort children used to carry their books to school. One had a grinning Mickey Mouse on it, the other featured Snoopy lying on his kennel.

'Either,' said Wright.

Bamber tossed him the Mickey Mouse bag. 'You'll need this to carry your stuff,' he said. He handed him one of the infra-red goggle sets, spare batteries, a flashlight, and a large plastic bag.

'What's the plastic bag for?'

'You'll find out,' said Bamber, packing his stuff into the Snoopy knapsack. He took his jacket off and threw it into the boot. 'I suggest you strip down to the basics,' he said.

Wright removed his jacket. He was wearing dark brown Chinos and a fake Lacoste polo shirt that he'd bought for a couple of pounds on Sukhumvit Road. He loosened the straps on the knapsack as far as they'd go and put it on his back. It was a snug fit, but not uncomfortable. He took it off again and filled it with the equipment that Bamber had given him, then put in the two bottles of water.

'Ready?' asked Bamber.

'As I'll ever be,' said Wright.

Chinh got out of the car as Bamber slammed the boot shut. 'Where we go now?'

'You don't go anywhere,' said Bamber. 'You stay here, with the car.' He looked at his wristwatch. 'We'll be back here in twelve hours.'

Chinh looked at the two men, totally confused. 'You go walking at night?' he said.

'Don't worry about what we're doing,' said Bamber. 'Just make sure you're here when we get back.' He took a one-hundred-dollar bill from his pocket, tore it in two and gave one half to Chinh. 'You get the rest tomorrow,' he said.

Chinh nodded enthusiastically. 'No problem,' he said.

Bamber put the map case under one arm. 'Okay, Nick, let's go.' He walked towards the rocks and Wright followed. A bird squawked off to their left, then fell silent. The colour was draining from the trees and bushes, turning them from bright green to a muted grey. Something settled on Bamber's neck and he felt a sharp stabbing pain. He ignored it. He studied the map, and took a bearing with a small compass. 'This way,' he said, pushing through a cluster of broad-leaved bushes. Hundreds of small flies swarmed around them and a large purple dragonfly buzzed over their heads.

They walked through a clearing, then around a clump of tall palm trees. The ground dipped and then they stood in front of the rock formation, weathered from centuries of wind and rain. Bamber looked around. He pointed at the anvil-shaped rock. The wood and bamboo hatchway was clearly visible in the dirt. Bamber went over and pulled it up. He peered inside.

Wright came up behind him. 'That's it?' he said.

'That's it,' said Bamber. 'That's the way in. Doc and the rest are already down there.'

Wright crouched down. 'It looks so small,' he said.

'More than enough room,' said Bamber. He folded the map case. 'Why don't you go down first, just to get a feel for it. I'm going to make sure that Chinh understands he has to wait.'

'Okay,' said Wright.

Bamber walked through the undergrowth, making almost no sound. Crickets clicked all around him, like Geiger counters gone crazy. The sun slipped down below the horizon, leaving behind only a red smear in the sky. Dark clouds scudded overhead and beyond them stars began to become visible, winking into existence one at a time.

Chinh was standing at the back of the car, the boot open. He was fiddling with the catches to the metal suitcase. Bamber crept up behind him. In a smooth, fluid movement he grabbed Chinh's head and twisted it savagely, snapping his neck like a dry twig.

The tunnel dipped down ahead of him and Sergio Ramirez felt his centre of gravity move forward so that more of his weight was on his hands. Grains of dirt sprinkled down from the roof and pitter-pattered on his scarfed head. Behind him he could hear Hammack grunting with exertion. They'd been underground for almost an hour and by Ramirez's reckoning they'd covered about half a mile. The muscles in his shoulders were aching and he'd scuffed his palms in several places. The floor of the tunnel was rock hard, and it was like crawling along a road.

Ramirez stopped and played his flashlight beam along the length of the tunnel. Something moved and Ramirez stiffened.

'What?' asked Hammack, behind him.

'Centipede,' said Ramirez. It was more than six inches long, dark green in colour with countless legs, and it was moving purposefully towards the Americans, its antennae twitching. Ramirez had once been bitten by a similar insect and his arm had swollen up like a football for more than a week.

The centipede seemed oblivious to the flashlight. Ramirez pressed himself against the side of the tunnel and raised his knife.

'Kill it, man,' hissed Hammack.

'Well, Jeez, Bernie, why didn't I think of that?'

'What's the hold-up?' called Doc, from the rear.

'Centipede,' said Hammack.

'Just kill it and let's get moving,' said Doc.

'Yeah, well, if I had a gun, I'd just shoot it, but seeing as I've only got a knife I'm gonna have to wait until it gets close, okay?' said Ramirez. 'Now will you guys just pipe down and let me take care of business?'

Doc and Hammack fell silent, but Ramirez could still hear them breathing. The centipede stopped and its antennae twitched as if probing for vibrations in the air. 'Come on, lovely,' whispered Ramirez. He held the knife in his fist, point downwards. 'Come to Papa.'

The centipede's legs began to ripple again and the insect moved forward. It headed towards the wall and ran along it. Ramirez jabbed the knife at the middle of the insect and impaled it. The centipede reared up and tried to snap at his hand. Ramirez twisted the knife and it made a crunching sound. Still the centipede refused to die. Ramirez scraped it along the tunnel wall but it continued to thrash about. He held it down with the knife and squashed its head with the end of his flashlight, gently so that he wouldn't break the bulb. Green, milky fluid squirted from the insect's body and splashed along Ramirez's hand. Eventually it went still and Ramirez pulled his knife out. He flicked the dead insect out of the way. 'Okay,' he said. 'Let's go.'

Nick Wright sat with his legs down the hatchway, staring into the darkness. Around him insects clicked and whirred and he heard something slithering on the rocks behind him. There'd be snakes, he was sure of that. Snakes and spiders and God knows what else. He shuddered. His mouth had gone dry and he wanted to drink some of the water in his knapsack but knew that he should save it for later. He held the flashlight in both hands. It was made from black rubber and was long enough to hold three batteries. How long would three batteries last? he wondered. Six hours? Twelve?

A figure materialised in the gloom. It was Bamber. 'Okay?' Wright asked.

'Yeah, he knows what he's got to do,' said the FBI agent. He crouched down next to Wright and illuminated the map with his flashlight. 'The first part's a piece of cake,' he said. 'The tunnel runs pretty much north all the way. There'll be kinks and bends but nothing to worry us.'

Wright nodded. He switched on his own flashlight. Bamber's face shone a deathly white in the beam.

'I'll go first,' continued Bamber. 'Stay fairly close. You'll probably find that you don't need to have your flashlight on.'

'What about the goggles?'

'Let's see how you get on with the flashlight first,' said Bamber. 'You'll find the goggles uncomfortable if you wear them for more than an hour or so.' He gestured at the hole. 'Do you wanna go down?'

Wright swallowed. His throat felt as if it had shrunk to half its normal size. 'Okay,' he said. He edged forward and slid his legs into the hole, taking his weight on his arms. For a second his feet swung freely and then his toes scraped on the floor and he dropped down. He scraped his cheek against the side of the tunnel as he wriggled through.

Wright twisted his neck up so that he could see the square of light above his head. Bamber was looking down on him, smiling. Wright flashed him a thumbs-up and tried to grin. He ducked down and examined the tunnel. To the north, it ran off into the distance, then curved to the left. Wright could just about shuffle forwards in a crouch, his knees up against his chest, but it was painful and he knew he wouldn't be able to keep it up for long. He squatted back down. There wasn't enough room to walk bent double, and his only option was to crawl.

'Okay, Nick?' called Bamber.

'Yeah,' replied Wright. He moved back, making room for Bamber to come down. He bumped against something soft. It was a green kitbag, with 'USMC' stencilled on it in white letters. 'There's some stuff down here. It looks like they left it.'

Bamber's feet dropped through the hole. The FBI agent's toes scraped against the side, kicking down a small avalanche of dirt, then he lowered himself down and squatted, facing Wright. The beam of Bamber's flashlight was shining up under his chin and it gave him a ghostly appearance, his eyes transformed into black pits in a stark white face. He reached up to grab hold of the cover.

'Leave it,' said Wright, quickly. Too quickly, he realised. He could hear the panic in his own voice.

'Nick, we're going to be almost two miles away from here,' said Bamber. 'Open or closed, it's not going to make any difference.'

'Humour me,' said Wright.

More grains of soil tumbled down from the hatchway. Wright shone his flashlight along the sides of the tunnel. He patted the tunnel wall with the flat of his hand. The earth was hard, like concrete, reddish in colour.

'It's solid,' said Bamber. 'It's been like this for twenty-five years, it's not going to collapse now.'

Wright rested the back of his head against the clay. 'I know,' he said. He took deep breaths. The air was hot and sticky and it felt as if he had to drag in each lungful. He looked up at the hole and the stars behind. They were maybe four feet underground. Just about the depth a coffin would be. He tried to block the image out of his mind but it kept returning: a black coffin, lowered into the ground, a group of mourners standing on artificial grass as a robed priest muttered Latin, then a handful of wet earth thrown down, thudding against the polished walnut. Wright standing next to his mother, holding her hand and listening to her cry, squeezing her fingers to let her know that he was there, but getting no reaction from her.

'Nick?'

Wright snapped back to reality. 'What?'

'Time to go.'

Wright nodded.

Bamber shuffled around and crawled forward on his hands and knees. The beam of his flashlight danced crazily, throwing eerie shadows against the tunnel walls. Wright tried to clear his throat but almost choked, and he began coughing, the noise echoing around the confined space. Bamber was almost fifteen feet away and the light from his flashlight was already fading. Wright crawled after him, his eyes fixed on the soles of Bamber's training shoes.

Ramirez emerged into the chamber and stood up, arching his spine and exhaling deeply. He was drenched and his hair and skin glistened. The chamber was almost twenty paces long and ten wide and about twice the height of a man. Hammack crawled out behind him. He too was soaked to the skin. He stood up and surveyed the room with Ramirez. There were reed mats on the floor, and on the far end of the chamber a sheet that had once been white was pinned to the wall. At the opposite end an old projector sat on a wooden table, covered in cobwebs and dust.

'Wonder what the last feature was?' said Ramirez.

'Probably *A Thousand And One Ways To Kill The White Devil*,' said Doc as he crawled into the chamber. He ran his hand over his face, wiping away the moisture that clung to his skin, then took off his rucksack and shook it. It too was dripping wet. He took a swig from one of his canteens, spat, then drank deeply. He wiped his mouth and offered his canteen to Ramirez.

There was a flurry of movement above their heads and dozens of small black shapes whizzed by, spinning and curving through the air. All three men ducked instinctively.

'What the . . .' said Hammack.

'Bats,' said Doc. 'They're harmless.'

The bats flew around the chamber, their sonic radar allowing them to whiz by the men so closely that they could feel the draught from their wings, then almost as one they flew off down a side tunnel to the left of the makeshift movie screen.

Ramirez handed the canteen back to Doc. Doc had taken a Marlboro pack and his Zippo lighter from a small plastic bag and he lit up.

Ramirez shook his head. 'Can't see why a doctor smokes,' he said.

Doc exhaled and grinned at Ramirez. 'This from a man who snorts heroin?'

'Recreational use, Doc,' said Ramirez.

Hammack was walking around the perimeter of the chamber. Three tunnels led off the room: the one they'd come through, the one the bats had flown down, and another, midway along the wall. In the far corner, to the right of the screen, was a jagged hole in the floor. Hammack went over to it. The hole was about three feet deep and at the bottom were sharpened bamboo spears, pointing up. 'Damn near lost my foot to that thing,' said Hammack.

'Yeah, well, you should know they always put punji traps in the corners,' said Ramirez. 'That's where you hide when you're scared of the dark.'

Hammack sneered. 'Hell, I weren't ever scared of the dark,' he said.

'That's right,' said Ramirez. 'When you closed your eyes and your mouth you were damn near invisible.'

Hammack laughed throatily. He popped a fresh piece of chewing gum into his mouth and went over to the tunnel the bats had flown into. He knelt down and looked inside.

There were fragments of metal embedded in the red clay. Hammack pulled one out and held it in the palm of his hand. Doc peered over Hammack's shoulder.

'Max was lucky,' said Hammack, probing the metal with his finger. 'Got down just in time. Another second and it would have killed him.'

'Shouldn't have gone in without probing for tripwires first,' said Ramirez. 'It was an obvious place.'

'Easy enough to say after the event, Sergio,' said Doc.

'Come on, Doc. He was panicking, he wanted to get out and he took the wrong tunnel. If you hadn't heard the click, if you hadn't shouted . . .'

'Yeah, well, I did and he got away with a backful of shrapnel,' said Doc, crushing his cigarette with his heel. 'Come on, let's go.' He slipped his rucksack on. 'Bernie, are you okay going point for a while?'

'Sure,' said Hammack.

'I can do it,' said Ramirez defensively.

Doc shook his head. 'You've been in front for two hours, Sergio. You need a rest. You take the rear.'

Ramirez looked for a moment as if he was going to argue, but Doc's eyes hardened and Ramirez nodded. Hammack went over to the hole in the middle of the wall. He pointed his flashlight into the darkness, ran the beam over the walls and ceiling, and crawled in. Doc and Ramirez followed.

Nick Wright had no idea how deep he was. The tunnel had been sloping downwards for some time, a gradual incline but a definite one. He wondered how much earth was above his head. If there was a collapse, he'd never be able to claw his way to the surface, of that he was sure. The tunnel sides seemed to be pressing in on him, and the roof seemed to be lower than it had been in the first section. Occasionally his back would bang against it and there'd be a small shower of red dirt. The tunnel had zigzagged left and right until he'd lost all sense of direction, though Bamber had insisted that they were still heading north. Wright wondered what they'd do if the way ahead proved to be blocked. The tunnel was so narrow that he doubted he'd be able to turn around, they'd have to shuffle backwards for upwards of three hundred metres to a small chamber which had apparently been a resting place for VC on their way to the main tunnel complex. The thought brought on feelings of panic and Wright tried to think of relaxing images: trees, fields, beaches. He closed his eyes and tried to imagine he was out in the open, that above his head was clear blue sky and not unyielding clay.

It was bad enough fighting the claustrophobia. Wright couldn't imagine what it must have been like for the Tunnel Rats, knowing that the enemy was waiting for them somewhere underground, an enemy with guns and knives, hiding in the darkness.

His hands and knees were sore and his back and neck ached, and the rough surface kept scuffing and scratching his skin. Gritty dust constantly worked its way into the cuts and abrasions on his hands, stinging and burning.

He opened his eyes. Bamber was ten feet or so in front of him, crawling with slow, regular movements. Wright tried to follow the FBI agent's rhythm, right arm and right leg moving together, then left arm and left leg. It produced a rolling motion that would have been soothing if it wasn't for the friction on his palms and knees.

His shoulders banged against the concrete-hard walls. He'd never be able to dig his way out if anything went wrong. He pictured himself clawing at the impenetrable clay, his fingers bleeding, his nails breaking, screaming for help with no one able to hear him. Wright's chest began to pound. He was underground, he was surrounded by the earth, he was buried deep below the ground and if the roof were to collapse he'd die with his mouth full of soil and clay with no one to help him. He shook his head. Nothing was going to go wrong, he told himself. The tunnels had been there for decades, there was no reason for them to start collapsing now. He took deep breaths, willing the panic to subside.

His hand squashed against something soft and mushy and he jerked it back. He shone his flashlight on to his palm. There were pieces of dead insect on it. Something long and thin with dozens of legs. Wright flinched. His head banged against the roof of the tunnel and he yelped. He frantically wiped his hand on the wall, trying to get the mess off his skin. There was another, longer, piece of centipede on the floor, its legs sticking lifelessly up into the air.

'What's wrong?' asked Bamber. He'd stopped and was looking over his shoulder.

'I put my hand on a centipede,' said Wright. He rubbed his hand on his shirt.

'Did it bite you?'

'I think it was dead already.'

'You okay?'

'I've been better.'

Bamber nodded. 'We're almost at the main complex,' he said. 'Then we go down to the second level.'

Wright nodded. He took deep breaths, fighting to stay calm, knowing that if he did panic there was nowhere to go. He couldn't turn around, and the FBI agent blocked the way forward. He had never felt so trapped and helpless in his life.

Doc leaned back against the wall of the chamber and sighed. 'I'm too old for this,' he said.

'We're all too old for this,' agreed Hammack. He unwrapped a stick of gum and put it in his mouth. He offered the pack to Doc and Ramirez but both men shook their heads.

Doc flipped his Zippo open and lit a cigarette. He looked around. The chamber they were in was conical, like a concrete teepee, with two tunnel entrances. It was big enough to hold four people and Doc knew it had been constructed as an air-raid shelter for Viet Cong cadres. The conical structure was virtually indestructible, even by a direct hit from a 750-pound bomb dropped by a B-52. The shape of the structure amplified sound from above ground so that the cadres would be able to hear the planes long before they arrived over the tunnel complex.

Ramirez drank from his canteen and wiped his mouth with the back of his hand. 'We must be fucking crazy,' he said.

Doc looked at his wristwatch. They'd been underground for four hours. 'If we're crazy now, think how crazy we were twenty-five years ago,' he said.

Hammack nodded. 'We were young. We thought we'd live for ever. I did, anyway. I was fucking invincible. I was the man.'

Doc blew a smoke ring up at the apex of the chamber.

'Secondary smoking kills, Doc,' said Ramirez, grinning.

The three men laughed, but it was an uneasy, disjointed sound and it echoed eerily around the chamber.

'Do you ever think about what happened, last time we were here?' asked Hammack when the last echo had faded.

'About Jumbo?'

'About Jumbo. About what we did.'

Doc rolled his shoulders and twisted his neck from side to side. 'I try not to,' he said.

'I think about it every day,' said Hammack. 'Especially at night.'

Ramirez nodded. 'Yeah. The nights are the worst. Sometimes I wake up and for a moment I forget where I am. It's like I'm back down in the tunnels, in the dark. Then I'll hear a noise and I'm up in a crouch, hands out.' He flashed a humourless smile. 'Scares the shit out of the girls.'

'That's not what I meant,' said Hammack. He interlinked his fingers and cracked his knuckles. 'I get flashbacks and stuff, but anyone who was in 'Nam gets them. I'm talking about guilt.'

Doc and Ramirez exchanged looks, then stared at Hammack. Hammack raised his hands.

'I'm just saying, that's all. I think what we did was wrong.'

Doc stubbed his cigarette out on the floor. 'We were fighting a war, Bernie. They killed Jumbo, slit his throat like they were killing a pig.'

'Yeah, but—'

'There are no buts, it was kill or be killed.'

Hammack shook his head. 'Not at the end it wasn't, Doc. It was murder.'

Doc's eyes hardened. Before he could speak there was a scrabbling noise from one of the tunnels and all the men jumped. A large grey rat rushed out of the hole next to Ramirez, leaped across his outstretched legs, and disappeared through the other hole.

Hammack put his hand on his chest and let out a long sigh. 'I almost had a seizure,' he said. 'That'd be one for the books, wouldn't it? Killed by a rat.'

May Eckhardt sat in the darkness, listening to the laughter echoing down the tunnels. She sat cross-legged, her unlit flashlight in her lap. The darkness was total, but her other senses were telling her everything she needed to know. She could hear the men, even though they were more than five hundred feet away. She could smell the cigarette that Doc had smoked and the spearmint gum that Hammack was chewing. On her right cheek she could feel a light breeze, fresh air blowing in through a small ventilation tunnel only a few inches in diameter. She placed the flat of her hand on the floor, feeling the vibrations made by the men as they started to move again.

She knew exactly where they were going, and the route they would take. May had all the time in the world. She knew her way around parts of the tunnel complex that the

Americans didn't even know existed. She took her knife out of its scabbard and used her black and white checked scarf to polish it, smiling to herself as she worked.

Bamber stopped and opened his map case. Wright crawled up behind him. 'What?' he said.

'You'll need to get the plastic bag out,' said the FBI agent.

Wright knelt back, ducking his head so that it wouldn't scrape along the tunnel roof. 'What are you talking about?'

The tunnel had widened a little, giving Bamber enough room to twist around so that he was facing Wright. He kept his flashlight down so as not to dazzle him. 'You remember I told you about the water trap? The U-bend, to stop gas going all the way through the complex.'

Wright realised what Bamber was getting at. He shook his head fiercely. 'No,' he said. 'No way.'

'It's no big deal,' said Bamber. 'Eight feet at most.' He put the map on the ground and pointed at a length of tunnel. 'We go through the water, then we go down to the second level.'

Wright continued to shake his head.

'Nick, we've no choice. It's the only way forward. Doc and the rest have already gone this way.'

Wright felt suddenly light headed. He was hyperventilating. He held his breath for a while, then exhaled. He shone his flashlight over Bamber's shoulder. An oval pool of water glistened. Beyond it was nothing but red clay. 'Eight feet?' he said.

'Maximum. You hold your breath and you crawl down, then up. You don't even have to swim.'

'What about the flashlights?'

'What do you mean?'

'Are they waterproof?'

'They're rubber coated, but I wouldn't want to risk exposing them under water.'

'Jim, you don't know how tough it is for me to be down here in the first place. It's all I can do to stop myself from screaming. There's no way I can go underwater in pitch darkness.'

'You can, and you will.'

'I can't be in the dark. I'll freak out.'

'Because of your claustrophobia?'

Wright nodded.

'Hell, Nick, you're already underground. What is it with you and dark places?'

Wright put his hands over his face. 'It's a long story,' he said.

'Give me the short version. We don't have too much time.'

Wright sighed. 'When I was a kid, my father built me a train set, a huge one, scenery, stations, points, the works. He built it and I helped him. It got so big we had to put it in the basement. When I was ten, he and my mum got divorced. To this day I don't know why. I don't remember any rows, it's not as if he used to hit her or anything. But my mum moved out, and I went to live with her. We didn't live far away so I used to go around to my dad's house all the time. I had a key so I could I let myself in.'

Wright went quiet as the memories flooded back. Bamber waited patiently for him to finish.

'I went around one Saturday afternoon. I rang the doorbell but there was no answer. Sometimes he went away, he was a salesman, selling life insurance and stuff, and he often went on sales trips. I let myself in. The light in the basement wasn't working, but there were lights on the train set, for the stations and the houses, and I knew the switch, for that was in the far corner, so I went down in the dark. I got halfway down the stairs and the door closed. I kept on going, figuring I could find the switch in the dark.'

Wright fell silent again as he relived the experience in his mind. Walking slowly through the dark, his hands stretched out in front of him. He shook his head.

'I bumped into something, something hanging from the ceiling. He'd hanged himself. At first I didn't know what it was, then I felt his shoes. They were wet and there was a funny smell. He'd pissed himself. People who hang themselves always do.'

'I know,' said Bamber quietly.

'I turned and ran, slap bang into the table. Knocked myself out. I woke up a couple of hours later, didn't know where I was or what had happened. It was pitch black. I don't know how long it took me to find my way back up the stairs and to open the door, but it seemed like for ever. It still does.' Wright smiled ruefully at Bamber. 'That's the abridged version,' he said. 'But the upshot is, I always leave a light on when I sleep, because if I wake up in the middle of the night and it's dark, I panic.'

Bamber looked at him for several seconds. 'I don't know what to say. You want to go back? You want to quit?'

'No, I don't want to quit,' said Wright quickly. The words

came out without thinking, but he realised that he meant what he said. Just then nothing meant more to him than finding out who had killed Max Eckhardt and Eric Horvitz. He wasn't going to quit, not after he'd come this far. He shrugged off the knapsack and took out the plastic bag. He put the knapsack into the bag, then put his flashlight inside, still switched on, before twisting the neck of the bag to form a seal.

Bamber followed Wright's example. The lights were dimmer, but they still illuminated the tunnel around them. 'I'll go first,' Bamber said. 'Give me thirty seconds, then follow me through. If you can, I'd recommend you keep your eyes closed, there's no telling what shit's in there.'

He turned around, took a deep breath, and plunged head first into the water. His legs kicked, then they disappeared, leaving only ripples in the surface. Water spilled on to the floor of the tunnel, and then ran back into the pool. Wright stared at the water. It was inky black, like oil. He wondered if there were snakes in the water, or worse. They were bound to find their way into the tunnels; what would he do if he got bitten? He imagined himself writhing in agony, already entombed in the earth, dying alone, in the dark. He twisted the plastic bag so that the beam of the flashlight ran along the length of the tunnel behind him. It was clear. How fast could snakes move? he wondered. Would they attack him from behind, or did they only bite if threatened? Wright didn't know, and he didn't want to find out.

He looked back at the pool. Its surface was still once more, a black mirror through which he had to pass. He had no way of knowing if Bamber had got through safely. He could be trapped under the surface, the last breath escaping from his body. Wright shuffled up to the edge of the pool.

His reflection stared back at him. 'Eight feet,' he whispered to himself. 'It's only eight feet.'

He swallowed, then took deep breaths. He said a silent prayer, then dipped the bag into the pool. He took a final breath of air and ducked his head under the surface. He pushed himself forward, his hands and knees scrabbling on the tunnel floor. The water pushed him up and his head banged on the roof and he arched his back and pushed again with his toes. He felt as if he was hardly making any progress. The back of his head scraped the clay again. His natural buoyancy and the air in the plastic bag were pushing him up against the roof. His eyes began to sting and he clamped them shut.

His feet floated up and he kicked them but he was being pushed against the tunnel roof so strongly that he couldn't move forward. Wright's lungs began to burn and he knew he was only seconds away from drowning. He tried to claw his way along the tunnel floor but he couldn't get a grip. His head slammed into the roof again.

He opened his eyes but the water was so dirty that he could only see a few inches in front of his face. He tried kicking again, but his feet had nothing to push against and his heels flailed uselessly against the roof. His chest began to heave and he clamped his jaws shut tight. He hadn't even reached the halfway mark; the roof was still curving down. Wright twisted around so that his face was turned towards the roof. He scrabbled with his hands and feet, the plastic bag banging into the side of his head, but finally he managed to get a grip on the slippery clay and he pulled himself down. The tunnel began to curve up again and his buoyancy pulled him around the bend and he popped up to the surface, crying and gasping for air.

A hand gripped him by the collar and pulled him out of the water. 'What the hell kept you?' asked Bamber. Wright rolled on to his hands and knees and retched. The FBI agent slapped him on the back. 'I'd just about given up on you,' said Bamber.

Wright coughed and spat. 'You and me both,' he gasped. He flicked his wet hair out of his eyes. 'Are you telling me that the VC did that every time they used the tunnel?'

'Sure did. Probably with a bit more finesse than you, though.' He fastened the straps of his knapsack, then took Wright's out of its plastic bag.

Wright put his knapsack on and wiped his face with his hands, then picked up his flashlight. Bamber was already crawling down the tunnel and Wright followed him. The air seemed staler, and it was an effort to breathe. The tunnel bent sharply to the left and for a few seconds Bamber was out of sight. Wright had a sudden feeling of panic and he crawled faster.

Bamber had stopped around the corner and Wright almost bumped into him. The FBI agent was pulling at a hatch in the floor. He tossed the wooden cover to the side and peered down.

'This is where we go down?' asked Wright.

'That's right,' said Bamber. He opened the map case and studied the hand-drawn plan of the second level. 'We've got several chambers to get through, but the tunnels linking them are quite short,' he said.

Wright nodded. 'How does air get down to the lower levels?' he asked.

'Ventilation tunnels,' said Bamber. 'There are a few marked on the map. They're small tunnels that lead up to the surface, usually facing into the wind so that air blows into them.' He slipped the map case underneath his shirt. 'Okay, let's do it,' he said. He lowered his legs through the hatchway and dropped down. Wright took a couple of deep breaths to steady his nerves and then followed him.

Peter and Emily Hampshire's house was a neat mock-Tudor semi-detached in a tree-lined avenue off the main road that cut through Sale, much the same sort of house that Gerry Hunter had lived in as a child. A small patch of grass was surrounded by carefully pruned roses and next to the front door was a wooden sign on which had been painted 'The Hampshires' in white flowery script. Hunter pressed the doorbell and a tune he didn't recognise chimed for a full ten seconds.

The front door opened and a woman in her sixties frowned out at him. Hunter smiled and showed her his warrant card. 'Mrs Hampshire? I'm Detective Inspector Gerry Hunter, I spoke to you this morning.'

The woman peered past him as if fearing he'd parked a squad car with flashing lights in her driveway, but she visibly relaxed when she saw his blue Vauxhall Cavalier. Hunter figured he was probably the first policeman to have called at her house. She opened the door wider and ushered him inside. She was a large woman, only a few inches shorter than Hunter and considerably broader, and he had to squeeze past her in the narrow hallway.

'My husband's in the sitting room,' she said. 'Just to your right.'

The sitting room was feminine and fussy: lace trimmings on the sofa and armchairs, glass display cases filled with pottery figures and glass animals, brass knicknacks on the mantelpiece, ornately framed pictures on the walls. Among the clutter Hunter almost overlooked Mr Hampshire, a small man with bird-like features, perched on the edge of the sofa as if he feared being engulfed by the overstuffed cushions. Hunter shook hands gingerly, his own hand dwarfing the older man's.

'How about a nice cup of tea?' asked Mrs Hampshire. 'I've got the kettle on.' She had a barrel-like figure, the excess weight blurring her breasts, waist and hips into one smooth, featureless body mass. Her face, however, wasn't fat at all and she had strong cheekbones and thin lips. It was a forceful face and Hunter reckoned she had probably been quite attractive when she was younger. She was at least twice the weight of her husband and Hunter couldn't stop himself picturing the couple in bed together. He wondered what positions they favoured, because if she went on top there was a good chance the poor man would be crushed to death.

'Tea would be lovely,' he said, smiling.

He sat down as she left the room and smiled at Mr Hampshire who was wearing a blue blazer with a regimental crest on the pocket and grey slacks.

'How were the roads?' Mr Hampshire asked, peering at the detective over the top of tortoiseshell-framed reading glasses.

'Fine,' said Hunter. He got the feeling that Mrs Hampshire had told her husband not to discuss the reason for his visit while she was out of the room.

'The traffic just gets worse and worse, doesn't it?'

Mr Hampshire pushed his glasses up his nose with his finger. 'Do you collect stamps, by any chance?'

'Afraid not,' said Hunter.

'Ah,' said Mr Hampshire. He looked at the lace curtains around the bay window and raised his eyebrows. The two men sat in silence as a grandfather clock ticked off the seconds.

Hammack used the point of his knife to pry open the hatch. 'I'll take over from here, Bernie,' said Doc.

'I don't mind going first,' said Hammack, putting his knife away.

'No,' said Doc, sharply.

'There's nothing down there, Doc,' said Hammack. Doc stared at Hammack, his jaw set tight. 'Okay,' said Hammack. 'Have it your way.' He crawled over the hatchway and turned around.

Doc shuffled over to the hole, his face impassive. He sat back on his heels and looked down into the dark. Twenty-five years earlier, he'd sat in the same position. Hammack had been there, and Ramirez. Horvitz had been at the rear, with Eckhardt, and Burrow had been just behind Doc, waiting to hear Doc's decision. O'Leary had been marking the hatchway on his map. And Jumbo had been there, looking over Doc's shoulder, saying that it was his turn, that he should go down first.

Doc had thought long and hard, back then. They'd mapped the first and second levels, but this had been the first time they'd found a way down to the third level, so it had meant going into the unknown. Ramirez would usually have been Doc's choice but the Latino had taken the lead for three hours and the strain was starting to tell on him. Horvitz had volunteered but he'd almost fallen into a punji trap earlier in the day and his nerves were still on edge. Hammack was just about the least experienced of the Tunnel Rats, and Burrow, well, Burrow was with Psyops, psychological operations, he wasn't a tunnel specialist. Jumbo had been the obvious choice, and he was so damn keen.

Jumbo had drawn his knife and checked his flashlight, then slowly eased himself through the hatch. He'd reached the bottom, then looked up and grinned at Doc. Doc had wanted to warn him, to tell him not to let down his guard, but before he could open his mouth there had been a flash of steel around Jumbo's neck and a look of terror in his eyes, then the knife had disappeared and the blood had flowed in a scarlet curtain down his chest.

Doc had plunged headfirst through the hatchway and grabbed Jumbo under the arms. Jumbo was gurgling, his legs thudding against the tunnel floor, his eyes wide and imploring as if begging Doc to help him. Burrow had pulled Doc's legs and together they'd dragged Jumbo back up to the second level. Doc had done his best, but the cut was too deep. It had taken Jumbo more than a minute to die, sixty seconds during which Doc had had his hands clamped around Jumbo's throat in a vain attempt to stem the flow of blood, whispering words of encouragement even though he had known it was hopeless.

'Doc?' said Ramirez.

Doc shook his head. 'Okay,' he said. 'I'm going down.'

Ramirez put his hand on Doc's shoulder. 'It was Jumbo's decision,' he said.

'No, Sergio. It was my call. He wanted to go but it was my call.'

Doc's knife was in its scabbard, hanging on his belt. He reached for it but then hesitated. Hammack was right, there was nothing down there. The VC had long gone, taking their place above ground as victors of the war against the Americans. He nodded curtly at Ramirez and Hammack, and lowered himself through the hatchway. The vertical tunnel was three feet deep, so Doc had to bend his knees and duck his head to look around the third level. He turned his body through three hundred and sixty degrees, his heart racing, images of Jumbo flashing through his mind. The tunnel was clear, north and south. He looked up and gave Ramirez a thumbs-up.

Doc crawled a short way down the tunnel so that Ramirez and Hammack could join him. As they dropped down into the tunnel, something bit Doc on the back of his neck and he slapped it with the flat of his hand. It was an ant, half an inch long. He felt another sharp pain, just below his ear, then another, on his ankle. He shone his flashlight along the tunnel wall. There were hundreds of ants scurrying around. He'd been so intent on checking that the tunnel was clear that he hadn't seen the insects. He jerked his hand back as an ant bit him on the thumb. 'Watch it, guys, ants!' he said, as he took off his rucksack.

Ramirez and Hammack scuttled backwards. Hammack began slapping his legs and cursing.

Doc pulled a can of insecticide out of his rucksack and sprayed the sides of the tunnel. The ants shrivelled into black balls and dropped to the floor. The bitter smell made Doc gag and he put his hand over his mouth and nose. Dead ants fell from the tunnel roof and rolled off his cap. Live ants were still biting at his neck and he slapped himself.

'Throw me the spray, Doc!' shouted Hammack, and Doc tossed him the can. Hammack pushed it down the front of his pants and sprayed himself, wriggling his legs so that the insecticide could work its way down. 'The little bastards are biting my nuts!'

Ramirez was laughing at the black man's discomfort, but then he too began to slap himself. 'Fuck, they're everywhere,' he shouted.

Hammack sprayed the inside of his shirt, then the ground on which he was sitting. He passed the can to Ramirez.

More ants ran along the tunnel walls, hundreds and hundreds of them. Doc pulled another can of insecticide out of his rucksack. He took off his cap and used it to cover his mouth as he sprayed the walls and floor. He felt ants wriggling along his back, biting his flesh, but he ignored the discomfort as he crawled down the tunnel, spraying everywhere. Hammack and Ramirez crawled after him.

After fifty feet or so the walls were clear and the floor of the tunnel behind them was littered with dead insects. The three Americans sat down and disposed of the remaining ants on their bodies, with slaps and sprays of insecticide. Doc pulled up the legs of his trousers and inspected his legs. There were dozens of small red bumps where he'd been bitten and they were already starting to itch. Hammack asked Ramirez to clear his back and Ramirez pushed his shirt up and killed them one by one.

May Eckhardt finished attaching the thin metal wire to the bamboo cage and backed away. When she was a safe distance she turned around. In the distance she could hear the Americans talking. When they'd come across the ants she'd heard them from five hundred feet away as she lay in a sleeping chamber in the second level. The sleeping chamber was a safe place to hide: there were four exits and entrances, two of which were booby-trapped. They were careless, the Americans, because they weren't afraid. They thought that there was nothing down the tunnels that could harm them. She smiled to herself. They were so wrong.

She bent double, her spine parallel to the floor of the tunnel. With her head down and her knees slightly bent she could run, moving at a speed that would be beyond the Americans. She ran silently towards the hatchway that led down to the third level. Soon they would realise that the tunnels were now more dangerous than they had ever been.

Wright and Bamber emerged from the tunnel into the chamber. 'My God,' said Wright. 'It's huge.'

Bamber dropped his knapsack on the floor and stretched. 'It's where they used to show movies, hold lectures, stuff like that.' He took a deep breath. 'The air's fresher, too, did you notice?' He pointed at two large holes close to the ceiling. 'It's coming from there.' He held his palms up. 'You can feel the breeze. VC airconditioning, huh?'

Wright took off his knapsack and put it on the floor. He stripped off his shirt and screwed it up to wring out the water, then used it to wipe his face and hands. 'How far underground are we here?' he asked.

'This is still on level two, so about thirty feet, I guess.'

Wright looked around the chamber. 'How the hell did they dig this out?'

'With their hands. Small shovels, maybe. Like I said, during the rainy season the clay is softer.'

'But all the earth must have been carried back along that tunnel. It must have taken for ever.'

'I guess they figured they had for ever,' said Bamber. 'The VC philosophy was that they didn't have to win the war, they just had to make sure they didn't lose.' He knelt down and picked up a squashed cigarette butt. He sniffed it, then dropped it back on to the floor.

Wright went over to the white sheet pinned to the wall. To the right was a hole in the floor. He looked down at the sharpened bamboo stakes that lined the bottom. 'Bloody hell,' he said.

Bamber joined him. 'The VC used to smear them with shit so that any wounds would get infected.' He unfolded his map, looked at it, then nodded at the tunnel that led from the middle of one of the chamber walls. 'This way,' he said. He put his knapsack on and crouched down, using his flashlight to illuminate the tunnel.

Wright looked around the chamber. It was a relief to be in a place where he could stand up and where the walls didn't feel as if they were closing in on him. It was just about bearable. He got down on his hands and knees and crawled across the reed mats to the hole. It was smaller than the tunnel they'd arrived in, so narrow that his shoulders brushed either side as he crawled into it.

The tunnel walls weren't as dry as they had been in the upper level, and the air smelt damp and fetid. The knees of Wright's trousers were frayed and torn and he winced with each movement of his legs. His hands were grazed and bleeding, too, but he gritted his teeth and continued to crawl. He'd come this far, and he was damned if he'd give up now just because of a few cuts and scratches.

The tunnel was thankfully short and opened up into another conical chamber, this one with three exits. Wright looked up at the apex and flinched. The top of the chamber was filled with a mass of white feathery cobwebs, and several dozen large spiders stared down at him. Each spider was about the size of Wright's hand with long, hairy legs.

'Jim,' said Wright. He pointed with his flashlight.

Bamber looked at the spiders and shrugged. 'They won't bite,' he said, unfolding the map.

One of the spiders stepped off the web and moved down the side of the chamber, its beady eyes fixed on Wright. Two black jaws clicked back and forth.

'Come on, Jim, let's get out of here,' said Wright through gritted teeth.

'We have to choose the right exit,' said the FBI agent. 'The wrong one could be rigged with a booby trap.'

The spider stopped. Another, slightly larger, moved off the web and walked slowly down the chamber wall. It raised its two front legs and seemed to be sensing the air with them.

'Jim . . .'

'Hang on,' said Bamber.

The larger spider ran down the chamber towards Wright. Half a dozen more left the web and began moving down the wall in a black, spindly mass.

Wright lashed out with his flashlight and squashed the big spider against the wall. It fell on to Wright's leg and he jerked it out of the way. The spider rolled on to the floor, its legs scrabbling in the air. Wright stamped on it, keeping his head down so that he wouldn't brush against the web.

The rest of the spiders kept coming and Wright hit them with his flashlight. He squashed one, then another, but still they came down the wall towards him.

'Okay, this way,' said Bamber, crawling into the right-hand tunnel.

A spider dropped from the web and landed on Wright's head. He gasped and used his flashlight to knock it from his hair. He knelt down and smashed it with his flashlight. The glass shattered and the bulb went out. He was alone in the dark. For a moment he panicked, forgetting which way Bamber had gone. He groped with his hands, trembling at the thought of touching one of the spiders, then found empty space and knew it was the exit. He ducked down and crawled into it, immediately seeing the yellow glow from Bamber's flashlight. He crawled after the FBI agent, breathing furiously. He glanced over his shoulder, but it was pitch dark behind him and he had no way of knowing if the spiders were pursuing him.

He practically stumbled into the back of Bamber. 'Hey, easy,' said the FBI agent.

'The spiders . . .' gasped Wright.

'They won't bite,' said Bamber. 'And if they did, it

wouldn't be fatal. There isn't a single spider in the world with a fatal bite, unless you're very old or very young.'

'How do you know that?'

'Read it somewhere,' said Bamber. '*National Geographic*, maybe.' He emerged into another chamber and Wright hurried after him.

'My flashlight,' said Wright. 'It's broken.'

Bamber turned around and shone his flashlight on Wright's.

'It's the bulb,' said Wright. 'Have you got a spare?'

'Sorry, no.'

Wright threw his useless flashlight to the ground. 'Shit,' he said. 'I'm going to use the goggles.'

'I'd save them if I were you,' said Bamber. 'You'll need them on the way back.' He illuminated the map. 'We're almost there, Nick. Stick close to me, you'll be all right.'

Bamber shone his flashlight around the chamber. It was huge, twice the size of the one where the VC had showed movies. The walls were covered in a dark green silky fabric. Wright reached out and stroked it. It was soft to the touch.

'Parachute silk,' said Bamber. 'Watch where you put your feet. According to the map they didn't check all the floor area. There could be traps.'

They walked together to the centre of the chamber. 'What is this place?' asked Wright.

'The map says it's an ammunition chamber,' said Bamber. He played his flashlight on the ceiling. It was reinforced with sheets of corrugated iron and thick steel beams that had turned brown with rust. Long-disused oil lamps hung from the beams.

Wright shivered. He was still soaking wet from the water

trap. He stood close to Bamber, not wanting to get too far from the flashlight in the FBI agent's hand. The disc of light travelled along the roof and down one of the walls. It picked out a row of machines, vertical lathes and grinding equipment, covered with dust and cobwebs. Behind the lathes was a stack of wooden boxes. Bamber went over to them and pried off one of the lids.

'Ammunition,' said Bamber, peering into the box. 'For AK-47s by the look of it.' He replaced the lid.

He ran the flashlight along the bottom of one of the walls and picked out a tunnel. 'We go along there for about six hundred feet, through two more chambers, then we should find the way down to the fourth level.'

Wright nodded. His feelings of claustrophobia had lessened, mainly because of the sheer size of the chamber he was in. He wasn't sure how he was going to cope with the fourth level, but if he was ever to get to the bottom of the mystery of the Tunnel Rats, he had no choice but to go deeper.

Mrs Hampshire returned with a tray filled with tea things. She poured weak tea into three delicate cups, handed a cup and saucer to Hunter, then sat down on the overstuffed sofa next to her husband, almost bouncing him into the air. 'Well now, it's about May, is it?' she asked.

Gerry Hunter nodded and pulled out his notebook. 'When was the last time you saw her?' he asked.

'Nineteen eighty-six,' said Mrs Hampshire.

Hunter frowned. 'Nineteen eighty-six?' he repeated. 'That was when she graduated, wasn't it? You haven't seen her since?'

'That's right,' said Mrs Hampshire. 'She didn't even tell us that she was graduating. We weren't invited to the ceremony.'

Mrs Hampshire heaved herself up off the sofa and waddled over to a sideboard that was bedecked with bowls and vases. She bent down, opened a cupboard and took out a framed photograph. She handed it to Hunter without looking at it. It was a family group, an Oriental girl in her teens with a much younger Mr and Mrs Hampshire either side. The girl had a tight, nervous smile as if she didn't like being photographed. Mrs Hampshire was beaming proudly at the camera and Mr Hampshire was looking across at them, adoration in his eyes.

'When was this taken?' Hunter asked.

'About nineteen seventy-seven, I think.'

'She's a lovely girl,' said Hunter. 'Did something happen?' he asked. 'Is there a reason you haven't kept in touch?'

'You'd have to ask her that,' said Mrs Hampshire, her voice loaded with bitterness. 'We gave her everything: we gave her a home, an education, a good start in life, and how did she thank us? We don't even get Christmas cards from her. It was a mistake, right from the beginning. I said so, but Peter insisted, said that it was a chance for us to have a family. A real family.' She glared across at her husband and he winced from the intensity of the look. 'He can't have children, you see. We've seen specialists.'

Peter Hampshire stared silently out of the window, his hurt and embarrassment making Hunter's stomach churn. Resentment and suppressed anger hung in the air like a storm about to break. Hunter could picture Peter Hampshire taking an axe to his wife one day, then sitting in court and pleading guilty with a satisfied smile on his face. 'So she's adopted?' said Hunter.

'She came to us when she was ten years old,' said Mrs Hampshire.

'From?'

'From Vietnam.'

Hunter stiffened at the mention of Vietnam. 'She was Vietnamese?'

'Didn't you know? She was an orphan. The *Daily Mail* helped rescue her, along with almost a hundred others. Flew them out just before the end of the war. In nineteen seventy-five. She was quite a celebrity for a while; her picture was always in the local paper.'

Hunter picked up his cup and sipped his tea, giving himself time to gather his thoughts. Mrs Hampshire put two heaped teaspoons of sugar into her tea and stirred it slowly.

'A journalist from the *Mail* rang us a few years ago. They were doing an article about what had happened to the orphans, twenty years on. I had to tell the girl that I didn't know where May was. I was so embarrassed, I can tell you.'

Hunter was finding it harder and harder to smile at Mrs Hampshire. He sipped his tea again. Mr Hampshire was still staring at the window. Hunter wondered if he, too, was considering running away and never coming back.

'You never said why you were looking for May,' said Mrs Hampshire. She offered him a plate of custard cream biscuits but Hunter shook his head.

'There's no easy way to say this,' said Hunter. 'I'm afraid her husband was murdered several weeks ago.'

'She was married?' said Mrs Hampshire. She looked sharply across at her husband as if accusing him of keeping secrets from her. 'She didn't even tell us she'd married.' She looked back at Hunter. 'Does she have any children? Do I have grandchildren?'

'Not that I know of,' he said. 'The thing is, Mrs Hampshire, I need to talk to May and I was hoping you might have some idea where she'd be.'

Mrs Hampshire shrugged her large shoulders. 'Now you know different,' she said. She took Hunter's empty cup and put it on the tray with the rest of the tea things. 'She got what she wanted from us and then she made a life of her own. You know what I feel like, Mr Hunter? I feel like I had a cuckoo in my nest. I fed her, nurtured her as if she was my own daughter, but all the time she was just using me, waiting for the opportunity to take wing.' She stood up and dusted her flower-print dress with her hands. 'She was the biggest mistake of my life,' she said, her voice trembling.

She picked up the tray and left the room. Hunter could tell that she was close to tears.

The three Americans stood in the antechamber, breathing heavily. Doc stood at the threshold, Ramirez and Hammack at either shoulder. They played their flashlights around the main chamber, their beams reflecting off the shiny silk lining that covered the walls. Ramirez took off his headscarf and used it to wipe his face.

The room was about thirty feet square and just over ten

feet high. At the far end was a wooden desk which had once been painted brown but which was now rotting and peppered with white fungus. An oil lamp stood on one end of the desk.

'I remember it being bigger,' said Hammack, his voice a hoarse whisper.

'This is definitely it,' said Doc. He aimed the beam of his flashlight at the far corner of the room.

'I know,' said Hammack. 'I know this is it.'

'Come on, let's get on with it,' said Ramirez. 'The air's bad down here.'

Doc stepped into the main chamber. He walked slowly across the reed mats. There were rusty-coloured patches all over the floor. Old bloodstains. Doc tried to avoid stepping on them, like a child jumping over the cracks between paving stones. There was a rhyme that went with avoiding the cracks, something that Doc had sung as a child, but he couldn't remember the words. Something about breaking a grandmother's back. Hammack and Ramirez followed him into the chamber.

Doc jumped at the sound of water splashing and whirled around, his hand groping for the knife in his belt. Ramirez was holding his water canteen above his head and dousing himself. He grinned sheepishly at Doc.

Doc turned his back on Ramirez and pulled the reed mats away from the corner. He threw them to the side, then took off his rucksack. Ramirez and Hammack stood just inside the entrance as if trying to put as much distance as possible between themselves and what was buried in the chamber. Doc took the folding shovel from his rucksack and straightened it out. He took a deep breath, then began to hack away at the earth, the blows echoing around the chamber like the crunching of a giant's footsteps.

Wright's arms and legs were shaking uncontrollably and he closed his eyes and imagined he was outside, above ground, forcing out the images of being buried alive and replacing them with pictures of Sean: Sean at the zoo, Sean playing football, Sean falling asleep in front of the television. He opened his eyes. The walls and floor of the tunnels were damp and in places pieces of wet clay had fallen from the roof. The tunnel they were in had dipped down and he figured they must be close to the water table. He wondered what would happen if it began to rain, whether the water would rise. He dismissed the idea. The Viet Cong would never have constructed the tunnels so that they'd flood every rainy season.

Bamber was crawling purposefully forward and Wright had to struggle to keep up. The back of Bamber's shirt was caked with wet mud from where the FBI agent had scraped against the tunnel roof. The tunnel forked and Bamber headed down the left-hand section.

'Where does the other one go?' asked Wright, peering into the darkness. The air smelled fresher in the right-hand tunnel.

'The map doesn't say,' said Bamber. 'We'd better keep clear of any areas that aren't mapped.'

'How much further?'

'Fifteen minutes.'

'Feels like the tunnel's getting narrower.'

Bamber chuckled. 'Optical illusion,' he said.

A piece of wet clay fell on to Wright's hair and rolled down his neck. He shivered. Every breath was an effort, as if the fetid air had to be pulled into his lungs. He wondered what it would be like to be buried alive, to have the soil force its way into his mouth and nose, to have the dirt pressed against his face, his eyes, to feel nothing but earth around him. How long would it take to die? he wondered. More than seconds, surely. Minutes, at least. It would depend on how much air was trapped with him. He wondered how he'd face death, whether he'd just lie down and accept it, or if he'd die screaming and futilely trying to claw his way out.

He closed his eyes and concentrated on his movements, keeping his crawl at a steady rhythm. There were tons and tons of earth above his head, but Wright tried not to think about it. A tunnel was a tunnel, he told himself, it didn't matter how deep it was. He tried to convince himself that the tunnel he was in was just below the surface, that if anything went wrong he could just force his way up through a few inches of topsoil and be able to breathe clean, fresh air. He knew it was a lie, but it helped to calm his nerves. He realised that he was panting and he struggled to slow down his breathing.

'Nick!'

Wright opened his eyes. Bamber had stopped a few feet ahead of him. 'What?'

'Don't move.' Bamber's voice was icily cold.

Wright stopped in his tracks.

'There's a snake here.'

'Can you kill it?' asked Wright.

'It's about four feet long,' said the FBI agent, 'and all

I've got is my flashlight. There's a knife in my knapsack, but I don't want to risk reaching for it.'

'What's it doing?'

'It's coiled up in the middle of the tunnel. I think it's asleep. Get my knife out, will you?'

Wright swallowed.

'I'm going to switch the flashlight off in case the light disturbs it.'

'No!' said Wright hurriedly.

The tunnel was plunged into darkness. Wright became suddenly disorientated and his head swam. He felt as if he was falling and he put both hands flat on the tunnel floor, wanting to feel something solid on his skin. He inched forward.

'Come on, Nick. Hurry up. I can hear it moving.'

'Switch the flashlight on,' said Wright.

'Not yet,' said Bamber.

'I thought snakes couldn't see well, anyway. I thought they used their tongues to sense air movements.'

'If you were in front, I'd probably take the risk, but as I'm here, I think I'll stick with the flashlight off. Now get a move on, will you?'

Wright bumped into Bamber's feet. He felt his way up the FBI agent's back and ran his hands over the knapsack. Wright undid the flap and groped inside. It was like a party game he'd played as a child, touching objects under a cloth and trying to recognise them from their shape. He could feel the infra-red goggles, and hard metal cylinders that he assumed were batteries, and the two bottles of water. His fingers touched something plastic, long and thin, with a metal edge. He held it in his palm. It was a Swiss Army knife, he realised. Every Boy Scout's best friend. He pulled it out.

He fumbled with the knife, trying to pry out a blade with his thumbnail. 'Turn the light on, Jim,' he said.

'Have you got the knife?'

'Yeah, but I can't open it, I can't see what I'm doing.'

The light flickered on. Wright looked at the knife in his hand. He'd been trying to pull out a nail file.

'Nick. It's moving.'

The knife slipped from Wright's fingers and he cursed.

'Now what?' hissed Bamber.

'I've dropped it.' The knife was covered with red mud, and so were Wright's hands. He picked up the knife but couldn't get a grip on the blade. 'Where's the snake?' he whispered.

Bamber didn't reply.

'Jim? The snake. Where is it?'

The FBI agent had stiffened. As Wright looked up, he saw why. Two glass-hard eyes were staring at him from a diamond-shaped head. The snake had pushed itself between Bamber's legs and was heading purposefully down the tunnel towards Wright. A shiny black forked tongue flicked out as the snake slid forward.

'Can you see it?' whispered Bamber.

The snake stared at Wright, inches away from his face. The tongue flicked out again. Wright was on his knees, the unopened knife in his hands. His centre of gravity was so far forward that he couldn't shuffle back.

The snake began to move its head from side to side, its eyes still fixed on Wright. He managed to get his thumbnail into the groove on the side of the main blade and he eased it out. The snake stopped moving.

'Nick?' said Bamber.

Wright said nothing. He didn't know if snakes could hear

but he didn't want to risk doing anything that might cause it to bite. He held the knife in his right hand.

The snake started moving again, its red and black striped body slithering silently across the muddy tunnel floor.

Bamber bent his head down and peered back between his legs. The snake's tail brushed against his thigh.

Wright raised the knife slowly. The snake stopped moving forward and lifted its head off the ground. The tongue flicked out and the snake opened its mouth revealing two white fangs. Wright held his breath. He'd only have one chance.

Bamber's left knee cracked, and the snake turned its head towards the sound. Wright brought the knife down, driving the point into the snake's head. It crunched through the bone and then bit into the floor of the tunnel. The snake thrashed around, its tail flailing like a whip. Bamber grabbed the tail with both hands. The knife jerked in Wright's hand and he gripped it tighter, pressing the blade into the ground as hard as he could so that the snake couldn't move its head. With his left hand he pressed down on the snake's body. He could feel the animal's immense strength; even in its death throes he couldn't keep the body still.

The snake's mouth kept opening and closing and its eyes glared at Wright, silently cursing him. Bamber dropped down on the snake, using his bodyweight to keep it from thrashing about.

Wright twisted the knife around, shuddering at the crunching sound it made, but knowing that he'd hasten the snake's death by mashing up its brain. Dark red blood oozed out around the blade and the animal's movements became slower and slower, though it was a full two minutes before the snake was completely still.

Wright pulled out the knife and wiped the blade on his trousers. He refolded the knife and handed it to Bamber.

'Let's go,' said Wright.

The snake's lifeless eyes continued to stare accusingly at Wright as he crawled over it.

'Would you like to see some more pictures of her?' asked Mr Hampshire, his voice a conspiratorial whisper as if the offer was somehow subversive. His wife was in the kitchen, washing the teacups.

'I'd love to,' said Hunter.

Mr Hampshire walked over to the sideboard and knelt down beside it. He pulled out a large green photo album and handed it to Hunter. 'I put this together,' he said. 'Emily keeps saying that I should throw it away, but . . .' He left the sentence unfinished as if he feared retribution for defying his wife. Mr Hampshire leaned forward. 'She loves May, there's nothing she'd like more than for her to walk through that door. You'll never get her to admit it, though. Never in a million years.'

Hunter opened the album. The first page contained a newspaper article about the plight of Vietnamese refugees in Saigon at the end of the Vietnam War. Hunter read it quickly. Just before the North Vietnamese overran Saigon, hundreds of orphan babies and children were stranded and there were fears for their survival. The American government had organised an airlift to America, and as the defences around the city began to crumble, the *Daily*

Mail had joined in the appeal for something to be done about the children. Hunter turned the page. There was a second newspaper cutting, this one detailing a horrific crash in which 189 orphans were killed when a United States Air Force cargo plane crashed on take-off at Saigon airport.

Mr Hampshire sat down on the arm of Hunter's chair. 'She was on that flight,' he said, pointing at the newspaper cutting. 'One of eighty-nine who survived. God, what that little girl went through. To have lived through a war, then be told you were being flown to safety and to see so many die in the crash. Can you imagine what that must have been like, at ten years old?'

Hunter shook his head. 'What about her parents?' he asked. 'What happened to them?'

'We've no idea,' said Mr Hampshire. 'All their records were destroyed when the plane crashed. We don't even know her family name. She didn't speak a word for the first year she was in this country. Post traumatic stress syndrome, the doctors said. Love and affection was what she needed, they said. And we gave her that, Mr Hunter, don't doubt that for one moment. She had more love than any child could ask for. Don't let my wife make you think otherwise. She wasn't always like this. She had so much love to give, to me and to May. She really wanted children of her own.'

'I understand,' said Hunter, and he meant it. He felt a sudden wave of compassion for Emily Hampshire and her bird-like husband.

'It really was a miracle,' said Mr Hampshire. 'It was a miracle that she survived the crash, and it was a miracle that they found a place for her on the *Daily Mail* flight. Turn the page.'

Hunter did as he was asked. There was another cutting, which like the rest had yellowed with age around the edges. It was from the *Daily Mail*, detailing how the editor, David English, had decided that leader articles and calls for action weren't enough, that something had to be done. The newspaper was chartering its own plane, and sending in a team of doctors and nurses to help evacuate as many children as they could.

The next article detailed the mercy flight, how the *Daily Mail*'s Operation Mercy airlift plucked ninety-nine children from the beleaguered city in a Boeing 707 just days before the North Vietnamese stormed into Saigon.

'The Americans got about a thousand children out,' said Mr Hampshire. 'The *Daily Mail* rescued ninety-nine. Most of them were malnourished, and three died within hours of arriving in Britain. Fair broke our hearts, it did, the suffering and everything. We applied to adopt one of them and they gave us May.'

Hunter turned the page. There was only one photograph, black and white, the sort that might have been used in a passport. A young girl stared vacantly at the camera, the face so lifeless that it could have been that of a corpse. On the page opposite was a letter from an adoption agency saying that the Hampshires' application had been approved.

'You should have seen her,' said Mr Hampshire. 'They weren't sure how old she was because all her paperwork was destroyed in the Galaxy crash. She looked like a six-year-old, so thin that her ribs were showing through and her legs were covered with bites and scars. The doctors reckoned she was ten and they gave her a birth date, just made it up because she'd need it for school and passports and so on. We always celebrated it as her birthday, but we knew that it wasn't real.'

Hunter looked at the photograph and wondered what horrors the little girl had seen, an orphan trapped in a war zone. 'She came here? To this house?'

Mr Hampshire nodded. 'We moved in the day after we married and we've been here ever since. I can show you May's bedroom if you want. It's just the same as when she left to go to university.' He leaned forward so that his face was only inches away from Hunter's. 'Emily still hopes . . . you know?'

Hunter smiled thinly. He knew.

'Her husband? What was he like?'

'An American,' said Hunter, his eyes still on the small black and white photograph. 'He was a photographer. They'd only been married for a couple of years.'

'Murdered, you said?'

'I'm afraid so.'

Mr Hampshire took off his spectacles and began polishing them with a white handkerchief. 'How is she?' he asked quietly.

'I really don't know,' admitted Hunter. 'I haven't actually met her. She was interviewed by a colleague.'

'She must be devastated,' said Mr Hampshire softly. 'She must need us.' He looked up and Hunter saw that his eyes were brimming with tears. 'Why hasn't she been in touch with us, Mr Hunter?'

'I don't know,' said Hunter. He averted his eyes, embarrassed by the raw emotion etched on the man's face. 'I'm sorry,' he added.

Doc stopped digging and shouldered his shovel. 'Is it there?' asked Hammack from behind him.

'Come and look for yourself,' said Doc.

Hammack walked slowly across the chamber, the beam of his flashlight dancing crazily across the parachute-silk-lined walls. Ramirez stayed where he was, retying his camouflage scarf around his head.

Doc was looking down into an oblong hole just over five feet long and a couple of feet wide. He'd piled the earth up next to the wall. The surface had been hard and he'd had to chip his way through, but several inches underneath the red clay was damp and pliable. A skull leered up at them, the bone glistening in the damp earth. A worm wriggled from an eye socket and burrowed into the soil. Doc knelt down and used his shovel to scrape away the earth from the skeleton's chest.

'It's definitely him?' asked Hammack.

Doc sighed with exasperation. 'For God's sake, Bernie, how many corpses do you think there are buried down here?'

Hammack flinched as if he'd been slapped across the face.

'I'm sorry,' said Doc.

'No sweat,' said Hammack. 'It was a stupid question.' He rubbed his jaw. 'At least now we know,' he said.

'What do we know?' asked Doc. 'We know he's not the killer, that's all.' He reached down and picked up a piece of card. He wiped it on his trousers. It was a playing card. An ace of spades. He gave it to Hammack who stared at it and then passed it to Ramirez.

Doc straightened up and wiped his hands on his trousers. 'We've wasted our time.'

'What do we do now?' asked Ramirez, throwing the playing card on to the skeleton.

'Bury it again and go home,' said Doc. He picked up the shovel.

'Wait!' said Hammack. 'Max's dogtags. He had Max's dogtags. We should take them with us.'

Doc nodded and knelt down and grabbed the right arm of the skeleton. It made a sucking sound as he pulled it out of the damp earth. The hand was clenched into a fist. Doc used the end of his shovel to pry open the bones, one by one. He looked up at Hammack, deep frown lines furrowed across his brow. He showed him the hand. It was empty.

Hunter turned over the page. There were half a dozen colour photographs, three per page, of the ten-year-old May playing in the back garden. May on a red swing. May with a doting Emily Hampshire. May throwing a ball to Peter Hampshire. May sitting on the grass reading a picture book. In none of the photographs was the little girl smiling.

'That was during the first few months,' said Mr Hampshire. 'She was like a little robot. She did as she was told, she played when we asked her to play, ate when we gave her food, slept when we put her to bed. But she never smiled, never looked at us, never showed any emotion at all.'

'Perhaps she didn't speak English,' said Hunter.

'No, she understood. And she was a very quick learner. Very bright.'

Hunter remembered that May had graduated with first-class Honours. He told Mr Hampshire, who smiled proudly. 'I was the one who got her interested in computers,' he said. 'I was cataloguing my stamp collection and putting it all on disc. She used to sit and watch me.'

Hunter turned the page. More photographs. A slightly older May. Occasional smiles. May riding a pony. May holding a bow and arrow.

'She won prizes for archery,' said Mr Hampshire. 'We used to have her trophies in here, but Emily . . .' He looked away, the sentence unfinished. The bow she was holding was almost as tall as she was. In another picture she was taking aim at a distant target, the bow at full stretch.

Hunter looked closely at the photograph. There was something around her neck. A necklace with two oblong objects hanging from it. Hunter frowned. He flicked back several pages and looked at another photograph, May in her school uniform, a brown leather satchel on her back. There was something in her right hand. It looked like the same necklace. He looked across at another of the pictures. May balancing on a bicycle. She was holding something in that picture, too. Hunter flicked back to the previous page. Whatever it was, the girl was holding it in all the photographs.

'What is that?' he asked, pointing at the picture of May throwing a ball. 'In her right hand? She's wearing it in some of the later pictures.'

Mr Hampshire finished polishing his spectacles and put them back on. 'They're dogtags,' he said. 'It was the funniest thing. She had them in her right hand when they flew her out of Saigon, and she never once let go of them. All the time she was in the orphanage in Vietnam, all the time she was on the plane, when she was in hospital in the UK, she wouldn't let go of them. The doctors tried but she screamed and screamed until they decided it was better to let her have them. She had the end of the chain wrapped around her wrist and her fingers were clenched as if she was scared that she'd lose them. For the first year she was with us, she never unclasped that hand, even when she was asleep. Eventually she wore them around her neck, and as far as I know she never once took them off. When she was older, we asked her who they belonged to, but she never told us. Emily and I thought that maybe they belonged to an American soldier who'd saved her life, that maybe he'd died and she kept them as a reminder.'

Hunter put his face closer to the photograph. 'Do you have a magnifying glass?' Hunter asked.

'Of course,' said Mr Hampshire. He scurried over to the sideboard and returned with a magnifying glass like an eager-to-please puppy carrying his master's slippers. 'I use them for my stamps.'

Hunter focused the glass on the dogtags. He could just about make out the letters and numbers. The soldier's date of birth. His religion. His blood group. His name. Hunter froze. He felt as if a block of ice was being drawn slowly up his spine. The name on the dogtags was Eckhardt, M.

The three Americans stared at the bony fingers of the skeleton's hand. 'They're not there,' said Hammack.

'Maybe the other hand,' said Ramirez. 'Maybe he was left handed.'

Doc prised open the fingers of the skeleton's left hand. It too was empty. He stood up, wiping his hands on his trousers, and took a step back from the open grave.

For several seconds the only sound in the chamber was that of their breathing, then Doc spoke. 'Someone else was here,' he said quietly. 'Someone saw what we did.'

He backed away from the skeleton, his hands twitching. He kept on moving until his shoulders were up against the wall.

'Impossible,' said Ramirez. 'There's only the one way in, through the antechamber, and Eric was standing there. If anyone had been watching, Eric would have seen them.'

Doc turned around and grabbed a piece of the parachute silk that lined the chamber. He ripped it down, revealing the damp clay wall behind it. Dozens of tiny centipedes scuttled away from the flashlight beams.

'What are you doing?' asked Hammack.

Doc ignored him. He reached for another piece of green silk and pulled it away from the wall. At the base of the wall was an arched hole, cut into the clay, just big enough for a man to hide in if he crouched down.

'Shit,' said Ramirez.

'So now we know,' said Doc quietly.

Wright opened his mouth wide and took deep breaths. He squatted back on his knees, his face inches from the damp tunnel floor. The air seemed thick, almost like liquid, and each lungful was an effort.

Ahead of him, Bamber was finding the going equally tough. He was panting and moving one limb at a time. The tunnel had narrowed considerably and Wright couldn't see beyond Bamber's feet and backside. Wright was in almost complete darkness and several times he'd come close to telling the FBI agent that he wanted to put on the infra-red goggles. The only thing that stopped him was the realisation that even with the goggles on he wouldn't be able to see any further forward.

Wright couldn't imagine how the Viet Cong had managed to live underground for years at a time. Even allowing for the fact that they'd have been able to go up for fresh air at night, they'd still have had to cope with the dirt and the bad air, the snakes and insects, and the constant pressure of knowing that at any moment they could be buried alive.

Sweat poured off Wright and his clothes were dripping wet. 'Jim!' he called. 'I've got to have a drink.'

Bamber stopped. 'Okay.'

Wright struggled to remove his knapsack. He had to lean forward and wriggle his shoulders to get the straps off, then push himself against the tunnel wall to drag the bag between his legs.

He took out one of the plastic bottles. The water was

hot but he gulped it down. 'How much further?' he asked Bamber.

'Five minutes, at this rate,' said Bamber.

'Do you want some water?'

'Yeah,' said Bamber. He reached back for the bottle and Wright passed it to him. There were only a couple of mouthfuls in the bottle and Bamber emptied it. He tossed it to the side.

Wright had no idea in which direction they were heading, or how deep they were. Bamber had the compass, and Wright had only glanced briefly at the map.

'Ready to move on?' asked Bamber. His flashlight flickered and he slapped it against his palm. The beam intensified.

'Yeah,' said Wright.

'Not long now, Nick,' said Bamber confidently. 'It'll soon be over.'

Doc, Ramirez and Hammack crouched together under the hatch. Doc wiped his hands on his trousers.

'Who could it be, Doc?' asked Hammack. 'Who could have been there?'

'Let's talk about it when we're up top, Bernie,' said Doc. 'There's nothing we can do down here.'

Hammack nodded. He played his flashlight around the hatchway. 'Yeah, you're right,' he said. 'We can talk it through over a few beers at the Rex. Maybe it won't seem so bad then.'

'Don't count on it,' said Ramirez. He took a drink from his canteen but it only contained one mouthful. He shook his second canteen but that too was empty. 'You got any water?'

Hammack shook his head. Doc handed one of his canteens to Ramirez. 'That's the last of mine,' he said.

'Save it,' said Ramirez.

'Take it,' said Doc. 'Three hours and we'll be back on the surface.' He looked up at the hatch. 'I'll go first.'

Ramirez drained the canteen and handed it back to Doc. 'It's my turn, Doc,' he said.

Doc was about to argue but Ramirez had already got to his feet. Ramirez checked his flashlight and took his knife out of its scabbard. He winked at Doc, then eased himself up through the hatch. 'Last one out's a sissy,' said Ramirez, his voice muffled by the sides of the tunnel.

Doc clipped the empty canteen to his webbing belt. 'Okay, you go next, Bernie,' he said. 'I'll bring up the rear.'

Hammack nodded grimly. He was obviously still troubled by what they'd found in the chamber, but Doc was determined not to discuss it while they were down in the tunnels. Doc put a hand on Hammack's shoulder, just as Ramirez's legs began to kick and judder.

'Stop messing about, Sergio!' Doc shouted.

One of Ramirez's feet smacked into Hammack's head.

'Cut it out, you wop bastard!' shouted Hammack. 'It's not funny!'

Suddenly Ramirez's legs stopped kicking. Doc shone his flashlight up at the hatch. Blood was dripping down between Ramirez's waist and the hatchway. Red spots peppered the lens of Doc's flashlight, turning the beam pink and casting a macabre glow around the tunnel.

Hammack shuffled away from the feet, his eyes wide. Blood plopped down on the tunnel floor.

'Oh Christ,' gasped Hammack. 'What the fuck's happening?'

'Bernie, help me get him down,' said Doc. He grabbed Ramirez's feet and pulled while Hammack took hold of the man's knees. 'Harder,' said Doc. 'Pull harder.'

The two men tugged on Ramirez's legs but they couldn't shift him.

'Something's holding him,' said Hammack.

Rivulets of blood trickled down from the hatchway and smeared Hammack's face. Hammack let go of Ramirez's knees and wiped his face with the bottom of his shirt.

Doc put his hand up between Ramirez's legs and felt for a pulse in the man's groin. He couldn't find one.

'I didn't hear anything, did you?' asked Hammack. 'No gunshot, no explosion, nothing. He didn't make a sound.'

Doc shrugged but said nothing.

'It wasn't a booby trap, was it?' said Hammack, his voice a hoarse whisper. 'If it was a booby trap we'd have seen it coming in. Somebody killed him, Doc. Somebody up there killed Sergio, just like they killed Jumbo.'

'I know,' said Doc, staring up at the blocked hatchway. He shook his head. 'I should have gone first,' he said quietly.

'The killer's down here with us, Doc,' said Hammack, holding his flashlight in front of him as if it were a knife. 'What are we going to do?'

Doc sat back on his heels and stared at the lower half of the lifeless body. 'We're going to have to find another way out,' he said as his flashlight began to flicker. He opened his rucksack, took out three spare batteries, and slotted them in.

'What about Sergio?'

'We can't pull him down. If we can get up to the third level and double back, we'll be able to pull him up.'

Doc got on to his hands and knees and began to crawl back to the main chamber.

'Doc?'

Doc turned to look at Hammack.

'What if there isn't another way up?'

Gerry Hunter could sense Emily Hampshire staring at him through the net curtains so he didn't look around. He drove away from the Hampshires' house, fumbling for the mobile phone in his inside pocket. He'd stored the BTP incident room number on autodial and it was already ringing as he turned the corner and pulled in at the side of the road. Tommy Reid answered.

'Tommy, it's Gerry. Have you heard from Nick yet?' I need to talk to him. About May Eckhardt.' Hunter explained about May Eckhardt's adopted parents, and what he'd seen in the photographs. It was obvious from Reid's silence that the BTP detective hadn't grasped the significance of the discovery.

'A ten-year-old girl is rescued from Vietnam clutching the dog-tags of an American soldier she marries almost twenty years later,' said Hunter. 'Two years after they marry, he's murdered. This isn't a love story, Tommy. It's revenge. I don't know why, but she killed him, I'm sure of it. And now she's bolted.'

'Jesus Christ.'

'Do you know if Nick's uncovered anything about Horvitz over there?'

'Oh Jesus,' said Reid. 'I was supposed to pass the details on to you. Apparently Eckhardt and Horvitz served together in Vietnam in an outfit called the Tunnel Rats. Something happened out there that they're desperate to keep a secret. Jim Bamber's out there with him.'

'Bamber's there? Shit, I need to talk to Nick,' said Hunter. 'Do you know what hotel he's staying at? This is important.'

'You can try his mobile. I got him a few days ago. It's a GSM so it works out there, assuming it's switched on.'

Reid gave Hunter the number and he keyed it in, read it back to Reid, then cut the connection. He pressed the 'send' button and waited impatiently for it to ring, hoping that the BTP detective hadn't got himself into trouble.

Bamber stopped crawling. Wright thought he was about to consult his map again so he waited, concentrating on the FBI agent's back and breathing slowly so as not to hyperventilate in the damp, sour air. Wright had to keep fighting off images of collapsing tunnels: the walls were damp and each time he rubbed against them small avalanches of red dirt spilled on to the floor. Bamber made no move to open his map case.

'What's wrong?' Wright asked.

'We've got a problem,' said Bamber.

'What?'

Bamber rolled to the side and pressed himself against the wall of the tunnel, allowing Wright to see ahead. The beam of Bamber's flashlight illuminated the head and chest of Sergio Ramirez, his eyes closed, his mouth open in a silent scream. A bamboo spear was impaled through his stomach and blood seeped through his mud-stained T-shirt. One end of the spear had been thrust into the tunnel wall, locking the body into position. He had a flashlight in one hand and a knife lay on the floor in front of him.

'Was it a booby trap?' asked Wright.

'No. Somebody did that to him,' said Bamber. He crawled forward and took something that was poking out from Ramirez's T-shirt. He handed it to Wright. It was a playing card, smeared with blood. An ace of spades.

Wright stared at it. 'Oh Christ,' he whispered. 'The killer's down here with us.'

Bamber bared his teeth. 'Of course he is, Nick. What did you expect?'

Wright stared at the FBI agent in horror. 'You knew?'

'What did you think all this was about?' He pulled the playing card from Wright's hand. 'Why do you think he left the cards on the bodies? So that they'd know that he knew their secret. He wanted them to come back here, he wanted them down the tunnels so that he could kill them.'

'Why?' asked Wright. 'Why does he want them dead?'

Bamber threw the card on the ground. 'Come on,' he said, 'we have to get him out of there. It's the only way down.'

'Down? We're going down?'

'We have to follow this through to the end. Doc and Hammack are down there, and the killer will be after them.'

Wright pointed at Ramirez. 'Jim, whoever killed Ramirez is still up here, in the third level.' He felt a presence behind him and jerked around, but there was nobody there.

'You're jumping at shadows,' said Bamber. 'And you're wrong, Nick. My map only shows one way down to the fourth level, but there are bound to be others.' He crawled forward and grabbed Ramirez by the shoulders. He pulled but the bamboo spear was wedged into the damp clay, preventing him from moving the body. He twisted the stick savagely to the side, ripping open the wound in Ramirez's stomach. Greasy grey intestines spilled out.

'Oh Jesus,' whispered Wright, turning his head away.

'He's dead, Nick.'

'I know he's dead,' said Wright. 'That doesn't make it any more pleasant.' Intestinal gas bubbled out of the wound, making Wright gag.

'You're going to have to help me,' said Bamber. 'I can't move him myself.' He yanked at the spear and it snapped.

Wright crawled over to Bamber. Together they heaved Ramirez's body out of the hatchway. Wright prised the flashlight out of the dead man's hand. He reached for the knife but Bamber beat him to it.

'I'll go first,' said Bamber, nodding at the hatch. There was a gleam in his eyes that was almost manic in its intensity. He looked as if he relished the opportunity of meeting the killer face to face.

'Okay,' said Wright. He gripped the flashlight tightly and looked away as Bamber crawled over the body, his knee digging into the stomach wound with a sickening squelching sound.

Bamber put his head down the hatch and slithered down,

opening his legs wide and pressing them against the tunnel walls for leverage. The hairs on the back of Wright's neck stood on end and he whirled around, his flashlight held high like a club. There was nobody there. He forced himself to relax.

Bamber pulled himself back into the tunnel 'It's clear,' he said. 'Wait till I call you.' He slid his feet through the hatchway and dropped down.

Wright edged towards Ramirez. Slippery grey tubes slid snake-like out of the gaping belly wound and pooled in a steaming mass on the damp clay floor. Wright kept as close to the tunnel wall as possible but he couldn't avoid contact with the entrails. He'd seen more than his fair share of bodies and had sat in on several post mortems, but seeing was one thing, physical contact with a corpse was another. He closed his eyes and crawled over it, wrinkling his nose at the smell.

'Okay, Nick,' Bamber called from below.

Wright squatted over the hatch and lowered himself down.

Doc and Hammack ripped the sheets of parachute silk from the walls of the chamber, gathered them up in their arms and dumped them on the floor. 'Come on, there has to be another way out,' muttered Doc.

Hammack tossed a rolled-up piece of silk into the middle of the chamber. 'What if there isn't?' he said.

'This was the command centre,' said Doc. 'They'd have been crazy not to have had an escape route.' He pulled a large sheet away from the wall, revealing damp clay underneath. Three of the walls were now bare. Other than the hiding place, the walls were perfectly flat.

Hammack wiped his forehead with his arm. Suddenly he looked up. 'Did you hear that?' he asked.

Doc stopped peeling away a piece of silk. 'What?'

Hammack held up his hand. 'Listen,' he said.

The two men stood in silence. 'I don't hear anything,' said Doc eventually.

'I thought . . .' Hammack shook his head. 'I don't know. Maybe I imagined it.' He bent down and picked at a section of parachute silk, then slowly pulled at it. It came away with a sound like tearing paper.

Doc cleared the rest of the wall, then stood back with a look of dismay on his face. The wall was flat and featureless. He frowned. 'Impossible,' he said. 'No one would build a command centre with just one way in.' He looked around the chamber. The pile of parachute silk in the centre of the room almost came up to his waist. 'The floor,' he said.

'Give it up, Doc,' said Hammack, squatting down, his back against the wall.

Doc began ripping up the mats that covered the floor. There was damp, hard clay underneath. He tossed two of the mats to the side, then bent down and picked up another. A trapdoor lay underneath, the sides flush with the floor. Doc grinned triumphantly. 'I knew it,' he hissed.

He used his knife to prise the hatch open. Hammack

scrambled to his feet and joined Doc. The two men shone the beams of their flashlight into the darkness.

'Wonder where it leads to?' said Hammack.

'There's only one way to find out,' said Doc, dropping down through the hatch.

May played the rope between her fingers until she felt the bucket hit the surface of the water, some twenty feet below where she lay on the floor of the tunnel. She allowed the bucket to sink, then slowly pulled it back up. She sniffed the water cautiously, and then sipped it from the plastic bucket. It tasted fresh and clean but she drank sparingly. The Americans had sprayed tons of Agent Orange on the ground above and it still seeped through the soil into the water. May had been to local hospitals and seen the damage the chemical was still doing to newborn babies more than a quarter of a century later.

She put the bucket on the floor and pressed her ear against the tunnel wall so that she could hear the two Americans moving along the tunnel from the command centre. She smiled to herself. They thought they had found a way out, but they were wrong.

Suddenly May tensed. Her forehead creased into a worried frown. She shuffled over to the other side of the tunnel and put her ear against the clay. There was someone else in the network. She listened intently. Two people. Two men. Moving into the command centre. She could hear the dull murmur of their voices, but couldn't make out what they were saying.

Wright ran his flashlight beam along the floor and up the walls. 'What the hell were they doing?' he asked.

'Looking for a way out, is my guess,' said Bamber. He nodded at the open hatchway in the floor. 'And they found it.'

Wright went over to the fungus-covered desk. He stopped short as he saw the open grave and the skull leering up at him. 'Jim. Come here,' said Wright quietly.

The FBI agent joined Wright and shone his flashlight on the skeleton. Something glinted in the beam.

'What's that?' asked Wright.

'An old playing card,' said Bamber.

Wright knelt down and picked it up. He showed it to Bamber. 'The ace of spades,' he said.

Bamber took the card from Wright and examined it. 'Bicycle brand,' he said. 'Same as in London.'

'And Bangkok,' said Wright. 'Except this one is twenty-five years old. This is what it's all been about,' he said, straightening up. 'They killed this guy. Killed him and buried him here.' He frowned. 'But why? And who killed Eckhardt and Horvitz?'

Bamber went over to the hatch and looked down into the tunnel below. 'Why don't we catch them up and ask them?' he said.

Wright walked around the perimeter of the chamber, examining the walls. He stopped when he got to the alcove cut into the clay. He bent down and examined it, running his fingers along its smooth sides. He wondered what it was. A storage area maybe. He looked at the silk that had once covered the walls. The hole would have been concealed. Perhaps it was a hiding place. But for who?

'Come on,' said Bamber, swinging his legs through the hatch. 'They can't be far away.'

The tunnel was only a few inches wider than Doc's shoulders and he had to haul himself along with his arms, dragging his legs behind him. Behind him, Hammack grunted with each movement.

'Bernie, are you okay?' whispered Doc.

Hammack laughed harshly. 'Let's just say that I know what a fucking sperm feels like,' he said.

The tunnel sloped upwards. Doc put the end of the flashlight between his teeth so that he could grip with both of his hands. He had to stretch his arms out, get as much leverage as he could with his palms and forearms, then pull himself up. The best he could manage was six inches at a time. Every muscle in his body ached and he had to strain to breathe. They'd taken off their rucksacks and tied them to their waists with lengths of string so that they could drag them along behind.

'Doc, have you any idea where this tunnel leads to?' asked Hammack.

Doc stopped where he was and took the flashlight out of his mouth. 'The third level, I guess,' he said. 'We're heading west, so with any luck we'll link up with a passage that we recognise.'

'And if we don't?'

'Then we keep heading north and up.'

Doc put the flashlight back in his mouth. He stretched his arms out and splayed his fingers on the tunnel floor. He gripped with his fingertips, but as he did he felt a sliver of something hard and smooth running perpendicular to the tunnel. He froze.

'What's up?' asked Bernie from behind him.

Doc moved his head, directing the beam of the flashlight at his hands. His neck burned with the effort of keeping his head up. All he could see was the back of his hands and the muddy floor of the tunnel. He moved his left hand slightly. He could just about make out a thin piece of bamboo set into the tunnel floor. He eased his head down and allowed the flashlight to rest on the ground.

'Can you back up, Bernie?'

'Oh shit,' said Hammack. Doc heard him scrabble backwards, breathing heavily.

'Don't be too long about it, Bernie. I'm not sure how long I can keep my hands still.'

'What is it?'

'I can't see. I think I've tripped it already, whatever it is.'

Doc put his forehead on the tunnel floor. His fingers felt as if they were on fire and the muscles in his arms were aching.

Hammack stopped. 'I'm not leaving you,' he said.

'There's no point in both of us getting it,' said Doc.

'I'm staying.'

'Do as you're fucking told, Bernie.'

Doc heard a rustling sound from behind him, then a grunt.

'What are you doing?'

'I'm getting the rope out of my rucksack.'

'We don't have time for this,' said Doc. 'I can't hold my hands steady for much longer.'

Doc felt rope being looped around his ankles, then tied tightly. 'It's about thirty feet back to the hatch,' said Hammack. 'That's about how much rope I've got.'

'Bernie, it's going to take you at least five minutes to get back. The tunnel's too tight.'

'I'll make it. Just hang on.'

'I can't.'

'You can. If I can get to the hatch, I can pull you back. If I can get you away fast enough . . .'

'It won't work, Bernie.'

'It's worth a try.'

Doc heard Hammack back slowly down the tunnel. Doc's fingers were in agony. Sweat was pouring off his hands and he felt them begin to slide off the bamboo. 'I can't hold it,' said Doc, his voice a hoarse whisper. His arms began to tremble and he gritted his teeth, willing the shaking to cease. For a moment he managed to get the trembling under control but then his fingers slipped and the piece of bamboo flicked upwards. He heard a click, then another, and soil cascaded down from the roof.

His first thought was that it was a cave-in and that he'd be buried alive, but then among the soil and mud he saw shiny black creatures with claws and stinging tails. Scorpions, he realised. Deadly scorpions.

'No way,' said Wright. 'There's no way I'm going in there.'

Bamber shone his flashlight down the narrow tunnel, and lowered himself through the hatch. 'It won't be far,' he said.

'You don't know that.'

'It's an escape route, a way to get out if there was a problem with the main entrance.'

'So maybe it's never been used,' said Wright. 'Maybe it's blocked.' He was lying on the floor of the chamber, looking down through the hatch.

'That's the way they went,' said Bamber. 'We have to follow them.'

Wright shook his head. 'It's too narrow.'

'Hammack went that way. Neither of us is bigger than him. If he can squeeze through, so can we.'

Wright shook his head again. He backed away from the hatch. 'I'll go the other way, the way we came in.'

Bamber stood up and poked his head and shoulders up through the hatch. He had his flashlight in his left hand and Ramirez's knife in his right. For several seconds he locked eyes with Wright. 'I don't think that's a good idea, Nick,' he said quietly.

The skin on the back of Wright's neck began to tingle. He got to his feet. Bamber continued to stare at him, and Wright took a step backwards. Bamber put his elbows on either side of the hatch. He pushed himself up, his eyes fixed on Wright. Wright shivered. It reminded him of the dead stare that the snake had given him.

'What's wrong?' Wright asked.

Bamber was halfway out when he cocked his head on one side. He looked at Wright quizzically. 'Did you hear that?' he asked.

Wright's voice caught in his throat. He coughed and shook his head.

Bamber popped back down the hatch. A few seconds later he reappeared. 'They're coming back,' he whispered. He pulled himself up and moved on tiptoe to the side of the chamber. He waved Wright back. Wright flattened himself against the wall. Bamber motioned for Wright to switch off his flashlight. Wright did as he was told. Bamber's flashlight went out a second later.

Wright could hear the FBI agent's shallow breathing from across the chamber, and even though the darkness was absolute he could sense Bamber staring at him. Wright shivered and held the flashlight close to his chest. Wright didn't know what had come over Bamber, but he knew one thing for sure: when the FBI agent had emerged from the hatch with the knife in his hand, there had been murder in his eyes.

His train of thought was interrupted by a scraping noise from the hatch. Wright held his breath. He heard whispering, then the sound of something being dragged across the ground. There was a muffled curse, then more scraping. The hatchway was suddenly filled with a warm glow, then a flashlight beam carved through the darkness of the chamber. Wright ducked as the beam sliced above his head.

Hammack grunted and heaved himself through the hatch, then lay sprawled on the floor, gasping for breath. He rolled on to his back, his chest heaving.

Thirty seconds later Doc's head popped through the hatch. He was also exhausted and it took him several attempts before he managed to claw his way into the chamber. 'Thanks, Bernie,' he groaned. 'If you hadn't pulled me back . . .'

'Forget it,' said Hammack. 'It don't even make us close to even.'

Wright switched his flashlight on. Doc and Hammack jerked as if they'd been stung. Hammack jumped to his feet and pulled a knife from his belt.

'Easy,' said Wright. 'It's me, Nick Wright.'

Doc sat up. His face and hat were smeared with red mud. As Wright walked closer to Doc he realised that there was also blood on his face, from dozens of small scratches that crisscrossed his flesh.

'What the hell are you doing here?' asked Doc.

Hammack lowered his knife. He was staring at Wright in amazement.

Bamber's flashlight came on and Doc and Hammack whirled around to face him.

'What happened down there?' asked Wright.

'There was a booby trap,' said Doc, breathing heavily. 'A cage full of scorpions rigged to open when a bamboo trigger was touched.' He took off his cap and used it to wipe his forehead. 'If Bernie hadn't yanked me away, I'd be dead for sure.'

'Scorpions?' said Wright. 'They can't have been there for long, can they? Days, at most.'

'That's right,' said Doc. 'It was set up by someone who knew we were coming. Someone who knew we'd be using the tunnel.'

Doc sat down with his back to the wall. He shook one

of his water canteens, but it was empty. Wright took his remaining bottle of water from his knapsack and gave it to him. Doc drank gratefully.

'What are you doing here?' Doc asked. He poured water into a cupped hand then splashed it on to his face, wincing as it got into the cuts and scratches.

'Following you,' said Wright.

'You must be mad. Stark raving mad.' Doc handed the bottle to Hammack.

Wright grinned ruefully. 'Yeah, you might be right,' he said. He sat down next to him. 'What's it all about, Doc?' he asked. He gestured at the open grave at the far end of the chamber. 'Who was he?'

Doc shook his head. 'Still asking questions, Detective?'

'Fuck you, Doc!' Wright hissed. 'I'm down here with you, I've earned the right to ask.'

'You've earned nothing,' said Doc.

'We're in this together now,' said Wright. 'Whoever killed Horvitz and Eckhardt killed Ramirez, too. That means he's down here with us.'

'You think I don't know that?'

Hammack gave the bottle of water back to Wright, who put it into his knapsack.

'Think about it for a moment, will you?' said Wright. 'He wants to kill you and Bernie and he's damn well going to want to make sure that there are no witnesses. Jim, am I right?'

Bamber nodded slowly. 'Makes sense to me,' he said.

'And who the fuck are you?' asked Doc.

'He's with the FBI,' said Wright.

Doc stared at Bamber in disbelief. 'The FBI?' he said.

'What happened, Doc?' said Wright quietly. 'What happened all those years ago?'

Doc shook his head and looked away. He put his head in his hands.

'Tell him, Doc,' said Hammack. 'If you don't, I will.'

Doc stared at the open grave.

'Doc,' prompted Hammack.

Doc took a deep breath and held it for several seconds, then he sighed and began to speak, hesitantly at first. 'There were eight of us,' he said. 'To start with, anyway. It was my mission, I was the ranking officer. Not that rank meant anything in the Tunnel Rats. Experience was the only thing that mattered. Experience and luck.'

He rested the back of his head against the damp clay wall. 'Bernie, Sergio, Eric, Max and Dennis, you know about. There were two others, a Tunnel Rat we called Jumbo and an intelligence guy called Rabbit. We were down here for three days. Three fucking days.'

Hammack squatted down against the wall facing Doc. He put his massive forearms on his knees and interlinked his fingers.

'We were tracking a VC major, a guy called Vin,' continued Doc. 'Dennis had been mapping the network for months, and he added to his maps as we went deeper and deeper. We used string and compasses, measuring it inch by inch, all the time getting closer and closer to Vin.'

'As part of Operation Phoenix?' asked Bamber.

Doc shook his head. 'We were on some Phoenix operations, but this was something else. Half a dozen bombs had gone off in Saigon, big ones. More than twenty of our boys had been killed, fifty civilians. Vin was behind the bombs and we knew there were more on the way. Cinemas, bars, shops, the VC didn't care who they killed. You know about bombs, don't you, Sergeant

Wright? You're from London, you've seen what terrorists can do.'

Wright nodded. He took off his Mickey Mouse knapsack and placed it on the floor next to him.

'Rabbit was an interrogation expert,' Doc continued. 'Our mission was to get Vin and find out where the next bombs were going to be planted. We knew he had a command centre down in the fourth level, but we'd never been further than the second level before. Three days, can you imagine being down here for three days?'

Wright shuddered, and shook his head.

'We ate cold rations, drank the minimum of fluid, just enough to keep going. We were living on our nerves. They had snakes, you know? Snakes tethered with wires. The VC knew how to pull the wires back so that they could get by, but we shot the snakes, shot them with silenced guns. The VC had trip wires connected to grenades, others that caused cave-ins. Pits with stakes smeared with shit. With shit, Sergeant Wright, so that any wounds would get infected. They were sick bastards. Sick, sick bastards. They weren't soldiers, they were terrorists.' He ran his hands through his hair.

Hammack had rested his forehead on his arms and was breathing heavily.

'On the third day we found the way down to the fourth level. Jumbo went down first and they cut his throat. He died in my arms, begging me to help him. There was so much blood.' He put a hand up to the bridge of his nose. 'So much fucking blood. You wouldn't believe there was so much blood in a man.' He shook his head, then put his cap back on.

'We killed half a dozen VC to get here. Took us three

hours to find Vin.' He gestured at the room. 'We caught up with him in here. Jumbo's blood was still wet. It was dripping off me, like sweat.' He took a deep breath as if gathering his strength for what was to come. 'Vin was a tough motherfucker. Wouldn't talk. Wouldn't say a fucking word. Just stood there with a secret fucking smile on his face like he thought there was nothing we could do to stop him. Rabbit threatened him, offered him bribes to change sides. He tried everything he could to get him to talk. Nothing worked. Then Rabbit hit him. Just a slap, across the face. Wasn't even that hard.'

Doc leaned forward and took off his rucksack. He reached inside and took out a plastic bag containing a pack of Marlboro and his Zippo lighter. He lit a cigarette and blew smoke up to the ceiling.

'Vin just glared back at him, smiling the way they do. Smiling like he didn't give a fuck. So Rabbit hit him again. Harder. Vin's lip started to bleed but he just kept on smiling.'

He took another long pull on his cigarette. 'Max was close to Jumbo, really close. Jumbo had saved Max's life more times than either of them could remember. He started urging Rabbit to hit him harder. And Rabbit did. Punched him in the gut, in the face, in the balls. Vin didn't even flinch. He was like a fucking rock. Like there was nothing Rabbit could do to get to him. He just kept staring at the wall.'

He flicked ash on to the floor, then stared at the alcove that had been carved into the wall of the chamber. His eyes widened. 'He wasn't staring at the wall,' he whispered. 'He was staring at the hiding place. Making sure that whoever was there stayed put.' He closed his eyes and banged the back of his head against the wall. 'I should have guessed,' he whispered. 'That's why he didn't cry out.'

'What do you mean?' asked Wright.

'No matter what we did to him, he didn't say a word. He didn't scream, he didn't cry out, he didn't even beg us to stop. Now I know why.'

Wright looked across at the alcove, then at the pile of parachute silk that had previously lined the walls. 'Someone else was down here?'

Doc nodded. 'Someone was down here and they saw what we did to Vin. And afterwards, after we'd buried the body and gone, whoever it was crawled out and took Max's dogtags.'

'Dogtags?' repeated Wright.

Doc stubbed the butt of his cigarette on the ground. 'When we eventually got out, Max discovered that his dogtags were missing. He remembered that Vin had grabbed them.' He gestured at the open grave. 'They're not there now.'

'So whoever was hiding there knew who Eckhardt was. Are you saying they spent twenty-five years tracking you all down?'

'That's the way it's starting to look,' said Doc.

'That's a hell of a long time to wait for revenge,' said Wright.

'You don't know the Vietnamese,' said Doc. 'They dug most of these tunnels by hand, knowing that it would take years before they were finished. Time doesn't mean the same to them, it's the passing of seasons, that's all. Part of the cycle.'

'What exactly did you do to Vin?' asked Bamber.

Doc looked across at the open grave. He shook his head.

'You butchered him,' said Wright. 'You cut him up. You cut him up and you cut off his dick.'

Doc winced under Wright's verbal attack. 'We lost it,' said Doc. 'We'd been through hell, we'd seen Jumbo die in front of us, and we knew that the bastard was in the process of planting more bombs in Saigon, bombs that would kill our boys. We had to get him to talk.'

Hammack laughed harshly, a guttural roar that made Wright jump. 'Bullshit,' said Hammack. 'It wasn't about getting him to talk. It was murder. Cold-blooded murder.'

'Cold it wasn't,' said Doc, his voice barely a whisper. 'We were angry, we wanted revenge, we wanted to hurt him the way he'd hurt our friends.'

'And you were all involved?' asked Wright. 'You all had a hand in it?'

Doc nodded and lit another cigarette.

'Rabbit and Max started it,' said Hammack. 'Max telling Rabbit to kick the shit out of him. Then Ramirez pulled out his knife and slashed him across the face. Something happened when we saw the blood. It was like we were with Jumbo again, watching him die.' He put his forehead down on his folded arms again.

'After a while we stopped asking questions,' said Doc. 'We just kept cutting him. Cutting and cutting. The little bastard didn't cry out once. That just made us madder. If he'd just said something, if he'd begged us to stop, maybe we'd have realised what we were doing. Maybe we'd have stopped.'

He closed his eyes and banged the back of his head against the wall again. The cigarette smouldered between his fingers.

'It took him hours to die. Fucking hours.'

'Who cut his dick off?'

'Rabbit. He'd lost it by then. He wanted to do more to the body, but Bernie and Eric pulled him off.'

'And the card?'

'That was Rabbit, too. Psyops used to leave them as calling cards.'

He opened his eyes and looked at Wright. 'I'm not trying to pass the buck, we were all to blame. Every one of us.'

'You tried to stop them, Doc,' said Hammack. 'You told them they were going too far.'

'We were a team, Bernie.'

'All for one and one for all?' said Wright. 'Like musketeers?'

Doc gave him a withering look. 'You wouldn't understand,' he said.

'Maybe not. But I understand murder.'

'It was a war,' said Doc.

Wright pushed himself up against the wall, then went over to the grave and looked down at the skeleton.

Doc got to his feet. 'We have to get out of here,' he said.

'How?' asked Hammack. He nodded at the hatch in the floor. 'Scorpions down there.' He gestured at the antechamber with his thumb. 'The killer's up there.'

'Maybe not,' said Wright. 'We got down all right.'

'Once we'd moved Ramircz's body,' said Bamber.

'So what are you saying?' asked Doc, dropping his cigarette on the floor and grinding it into the clay with his heel. 'We go back the same way? Maybe it's a trap, maybe the killer let you down so that he could kill us on the way back up.'

Wright stared at the grinning skull. He'd seen bodies before, but never a skeleton. It made him realise what lay ahead. No matter how he lived his life, no matter what he did, he would end up the same way, bones in the ground. He shuddered and turned away. He nodded at Bamber. 'What about the map, Jim? Does it show any other way out?'

'Map?' said Doc, wiping his hands on his trousers. 'What map?'

'We've got a Defense Department map of the tunnel complex,' said Wright. 'Jim got it from the Pentagon.'

Doc frowned. He looked at Hammack, then back to Wright. 'Impossible,' he said. 'We never gave the map to headquarters. Why would we want anyone else coming down here and seeing what we'd done?' He stared at the map case in Bamber's hand.

Wright reached for the case, but Bamber moved it out of his reach.

'What's going on, Jim?' Wright asked.

Bamber said nothing. He tossed the map case to Doc. Doc opened it and flicked through the maps. He looked across at Wright, his eyes narrowing. 'These belong to Dennis,' he said coldly.

Wright turned to look at Bamber, confusion written all over his face. 'Tell him, Jim.'

The FBI agent ignored him. He was staring at Doc, the knife in his hand twitching from side to side.

Gerry Hunter had tried Wright's number more than a dozen times as he drove back to London. It was ringing, but Wright wasn't answering and each time a recorded voice cut in asking if he wanted to leave a message. He had begun to hate the prim, prissy female voice and would cheerfully have strangled the woman if she'd been in the car with him. After trying for more than an hour, he called up the company that had supplied Wright's mobile and asked to speak to somebody on the technical side. A man with a slight stutter explained that the recorded message meant that the phone was responding to the signal sent out over the satellite network. It wasn't a case of the phone being switched off. If the signal had reached the phone and it had been switched off, Hunter would hear a different message.

'I think it's in Bangkok, would that make a difference?' asked Hunter.

'Shouldn't,' said the man. 'We cover most of South-East Asia. Parts of Thailand might be out of our range, but certainly Bangkok is well covered. The person you're calling just isn't answering the phone.'

Hunter thanked the man, though he'd been no more help than the prerecorded message. He punched in Wright's number again and hit the 'send' button.

'Jim, what the hell's going on?' Wright's voice echoed around the chamber.

'I'll tell you what's going on,' said Doc. He pulled his knife from his belt and held it out in front of him. He threw the map at Wright's feet. 'That map belongs to Dennis. I want to hear how he got it.' He took a step towards Bamber.

Bamber stood his ground, his own knife held low, the point aimed at Doc's stomach. He was smiling.

Hammack got to his feet, a puzzled frown on his face. He slid his own knife from its sheath and stood holding it as if unsure what to do next.

'Sergio and Bernie went to get it the day after he was killed,' said Doc. 'If he's got the map, he must have seen Dennis. What I want to know is if Dennis was alive when he went around to the house. And if he was, I want to know how he managed to persuade him to part with it.'

Bamber continued to smile at Doc. He took a step forward, keeping the knife low.

'Come on, Jim, stop this,' said Wright. Bamber ignored him. 'Just tell him how you got the map.'

'Yeah, Jim,' said Hammack. 'Tell us how you got the map.'

'I don't have to tell you anything,' said Bamber. He waved his knife and it glinted in the beam of his flashlight. 'It's been a long time since you used a knife, hasn't it? You're not really sure how to hold it, are you?'

Doc threw Hammack a quick glance and Hammack moved to the side, widening the gap between them.

Bamber moved into the middle of the chamber, closer to the pile of parachute silk. 'You're an old man now, Doc. Your reflexes aren't what they were. Eyesight's going. Muscle tone's deteriorating.' He moved his knife in a slow circle.

Doc looked at Wright and made a small gesture with his chin, telling him to move behind Bamber so that the three men were equally spaced around him. Wright wasn't sure what was going on, but this time there was no mistaking the murderous intent in Bamber's eyes.

'I guess you're feeling pretty happy about the odds right

now,' said Bamber. 'Three against one. I guess you're thinking that three of you can take me. But you're wrong, Doc. Dead wrong. Nick here's a pussycat. You're an old man, and the nigger, well, I've never met a nigger yet that I couldn't fight one handed.'

'Fuck you,' said Hammack. He stepped forward, his knife raised.

'Bernie, no!' hissed Wright. 'He's just trying to rile you.'

'Man's succeeded,' said Hammack, but he lowered his knife.

'Always like to see a nigger kept in his place,' said Bamber.

Hammack roared and lashed out at Bamber. Bamber moved quickly, stepping to the side and drawing his knife across Hammack's chest in a fluid motion. Hammack yelled, but Wright couldn't tell if it was from anger or pain. The black man stabbed at Bamber but Bamber was too quick for him and he spun around like a matador goading a bull before slashing out again, this time to Hammack's upper arm. Blood spurted in a crimson stream and Hammack's knife dropped from his nerveless fingers. Blood was flowing down Hammack's T-shirt in a jagged red curtain and he sank to his knees, a look of despair on his face. Bamber raised his knife once more.

Wright could see that Bamber was going to slash Hammack's throat. He yelled 'No!' and threw his flashlight as hard as he could. It smashed into Bamber's arm and the light winked out. Hammack pitched forward and fell on to the pile of parachute silk, one hand clutching the wound on his chest. Doc dashed forward but Bamber struck out with his knife, hacking at Doc's stomach. Doc moved back.

Bamber bent down and picked up Hammack's flashlight, switched it off and tucked it into his belt. He backed up, his bloodstained knife moving in a lazy figure of eight, alternating between Doc and Wright.

'We can take him, Doc,' said Wright.

'Sure you can, Nick,' said Bamber. 'You can't even handle your own wife, how do you think you're going to be able to stop me?'

Wright didn't reply. He held his arms out to the side, fingers splayed, looking for an opportunity to grab the knife.

'I mean, how much of a man can you be, letting another guy screw your wife in your own bed? You've taken being pussy-whipped to a whole new level.'

Wright felt a surge of anger, but he fought to stay calm. He looked at Doc. Doc made a small gesture with his chin and the two men moved further apart so that Bamber had to turn his head to keep them both in vision.

'Screwed him with your boy in the next room, hey? Do you think he heard them? Rutting like pigs? What if she screamed out his name? How do you think little Sean would feel? His mother screwing another man? And you letting her?'

Hammack groaned. Blood trickled from between his fingers, staining the parachute silk.

Wright's pulse pounded in his ears and he took a step forward.

'Nick . . .' said Doc.

Wright smiled tightly. 'I know, Doc, don't worry.' He glared at Bamber. 'It's not going to work,' he said. 'Sticks and stones.'

A look of uncertainty flashed across Bamber's face, but he quickly regained his composure. 'Remember what it was like when you found your father, Nick? Remember what it was like when you were locked in with his body, in the dark? How alone you felt? How vulnerable?' He grinned evilly. 'Time for a flashback,' he whispered. He switched off the flashlight and the chamber was instantly plunged into darkness.

Wright stepped back, then dropped into a crouch. He heard Bamber move, but couldn't tell in which direction. He had visions of Bamber slashing his knife from side to side like a scythe and his stomach tensed. He took another step back and his foot caught on the pile of parachute silks, sending him tumbling backwards. He gasped as he hit the ground, and immediately rolled over, knowing that Bamber would be able to pinpoint the sound. He kept on rolling, then realised that if he wasn't careful he'd end up in the shallow grave with the skeleton. He stopped moving and listened intently.

'Nick?' hissed Doc. 'You okay?'

'Don't talk,' snapped Wright. He got up but kept low, and took several steps back, skirting the parachute silk. Wright heard a footfall to his right, and he froze. Hammack moaned and the silk rustled as he shifted his position.

Wright's brain, starved of visual stimulation, began to manufacture its own images. He saw whirling circles and multicoloured grids, strange shapes that disappeared when he tried to focus on them but reappeared as soon as he looked away. It was as if he was floating in a universe of computer-generated shapes, and he swayed on his feet as his sense of balance began to desert him. He blinked several times and shook his head, but then felt as if he was falling, so he dropped down into a crouch and put his hands on the floor.

Wright heard more footsteps, fainter this time, then a

scraping sound. He waited several seconds, but heard nothing else. 'Doc?' he said hesitantly.

'Yeah, I think he's gone.'

'Where's your flashlight?' Wright asked.

'In the tunnel. I dropped it when the scorpions fell on me.' Hammack groaned in pain again. 'Bernie, are you okay?' asked Doc.

Hammack muttered something unintelligible.

'Bernie?'

'I'm bleeding bad, Doc.'

'Hang on, we'll get to you.'

'Your Zippo, Doc,' said Wright. 'Where is it?'

'On the floor, where I was sitting.'

'Let's see if we can find it.'

Wright tried to picture the chamber, but he couldn't even recall which direction he was facing. He got down on his hands and knees and groped around. His hand touched the pile of parachute silk torn from the walls. He moved to his left, feeling with his fingertips.

His hands brushed against a mat, then the damp floor. He crept forward. There was a scraping noise from the opposite side of the chamber. Wright knew it was Doc, but he couldn't stop himself thinking of snakes and scorpions and spiders. He crawled slowly, patting the ground with his right hand.

Hammack moaned again. 'Doc . . .' he gasped.

'We're coming, Bernie,' said Doc.

The ground in front of Wright disappeared and he pitched forward, his head slamming into the wooden sides of the trapdoor. He cursed.

'What's wrong?' asked Doc.

'Damn near fell in the hatch,' said Wright, pushing

himself up. He touched his head. His hand came away wet with blood.

'You okay?'

'Yeah.'

Doc had been sitting about six feet from the hatch, so at least Wright now had his bearings. He crawled away from the trapdoor, brushing the ground with his fingertips. He touched something soft and picked it up. It was the Marlboro pack. He put it down and patted the area around his knees. His left hand fell on something metallic. The lighter. He picked it up, pulled open the top and flicked the wheel. There was a shower of sparks and a flickering yellow light.

Wright held up the Zippo. Doc was on his hands and knees, close to the chamber wall. He got to his feet, picked up his rucksack, and ran over to Hammack.

Hammack was lying on his back, his hands clutched to his chest, his eyes closed tight. Doc took his medical kit out and slapped a dressing on Hammack's chest. 'Nick, hold this for me. Keep the pressure on,' he said.

Wright held the burning Zippo in his left hand and clamped the dressing to Hammack's wound with his right. Doc pulled a second dressing out and wrapped it around Hammack's bleeding arm.

'How bad is it?' Hammack asked through gritted teeth.

'Not too bad,' said Doc. He shook four white tablets out of a plastic bottle and held them up to Hammack's mouth. 'Swallow these,' he said. 'They'll help with the pain.'

Hammack opened his mouth and swallowed the tablets one by one.

The Zippo got hotter and hotter until Wright couldn't hold it any longer. He cursed as it fell from his fingers, plunging the chamber into darkness once more. 'Sorry,' he said. He grabbed for the Zippo but it was still too hot to touch. He tossed it from hand to hand and blew on it, then flicked it into life again. Doc handed him another dressing.

'Wrap this around it,' said Doc. 'It'll act as insulation.'

Wright held the Zippo up in the air and watched as Doc applied sticking plaster to the wound on Hammack's arm.

Doc nodded at Wright, who took his hand away. Doc tossed aside the soiled dressing, inspected the wound, then smeared antiseptic ointment across the bloody flesh. He placed a fresh dressing over it and applied strips of sticking plaster to keep it in place.

'Is he going to be okay?' Wright asked.

'Yeah, Doc, will I be able to play the piano again?'

Doc grinned at Wright. 'I think that answers your question, Nick,' he said. 'If he can make jokes, he can walk out of here.' He helped Hammack to sit up.

'Where'd the crazy guy go?' asked Hammack.

Doc gestured at the antechamber. 'Back up to the third level. Who is he, Nick?'

'He's an FBI agent, investigating the two murders.'

'Like hell,' said Doc. 'He's the killer, I'm sure of it.'

'Couldn't be,' said Wright. 'He didn't kill Ramirez. And I know for a fact that he was in the UK when Horvitz was murdered.'

Doc put an arm around Hammack to support him. Hammack was weak, but he could stand.

'He killed Dennis, though. And he would've killed the three of us, given a chance.'

'So that means what? Two killers?'

Doc shrugged. 'I can't think of any other explanation.'

Despite the dressing around the Zippo, Wright could feel the lighter getting uncomfortably hot. 'What are we going to do about a light?' he said. 'This isn't going to last much longer.'

'What about your flashlight?'

'The bulb went when I threw it at Bamber.'

Doc pointed at his rucksack. 'I've got spares in there. See if they'll fit.'

Wright picked up the broken flashlight and went over to the rucksack. He put the burning Zippo on the ground and in its flickering light found and fitted one of the bulbs. To his immense relief, it worked. He flipped the Zippo shut and pocketed the lighter.

'Have you got any weapons?' Wright asked Doc.

'Knives. I've got one, so does Bernie.'

'I don't think I'm gonna be winning any knife fights,' said Hammack.'

Wright went over and retrieved Hammack's knife. He stuck it into his belt, then crouched down next to his knapsack. He pulled out the goggles.

'What the hell are those?' asked Doc.

'Infra-red goggles.'

'They work?'

'I bloody well hope so. We're not going to get anywhere with one flashlight between three of us.'

May sat with her ear pressed against the clay wall, listening intently. She'd heard angry voices, then there had been silence, then a man had left the command centre and moved up to the third level. She knew where he was, about three hundred feet west of her position. The three other men were still in the command centre, talking in hushed voices, so she couldn't make out what they were saying.

The chamber she was in had once functioned as a dormitory area for families. There were still sleeping mats on the floor and in one corner stood two large earthenware pots that had once stored water for drinking and washing. So far as May was concerned, the main advantage of the chamber was that it had four exits. From where she was she could easily reach the second level, and get quickly to most parts of the tunnel complex.

She went over to one of the pots. It came up almost to her waist and she leaned into it and pulled out a case. She sat cross-legged on the floor as she opened it. Inside was a crossbow and six bolts. She assembled the weapon with practised ease, then slotted the bolts into a plastic clip that attached to the bottom of the crossbow. May hoped she wouldn't have to use the weapon. She wanted to get close enough to use her knife, to look into their eyes as they died.

'He could be up there,' whispered Doc, looking up at the hatch. Ramirez's blood was still wet on the wooden sides of the hatchway.

'I'll go,' said Wright, fastening the straps on his goggles.

'No!' said Doc sharply. 'I'm leading.'

Wright shook his head. 'You're going to have to take care of Bernie,' he said. He tapped the goggles. 'Besides, I've got these. It's better I go first.'

'You know which way to go?'

'I think so. If I have a problem, I'll shout back to you. Bernie, are you okay?'

Hammack forced a smile. 'I'll make it,' he said.

'Keep your distance,' said Wright. 'There's no telling what's up there now. Don't get too close in case . . .' He left the sentencc hanging.

Doc squeezed Wright's shoulder. 'Good luck.'

Wright had a last look around the tunnel, took Hammack's knife from his belt, then edged slowly through the hatch, turning his head from side to side, ready to duck back at the first sign of a threat. Except for Ramirez's corpse, the tunnel above was clear. He pushed himself up, using his elbows for leverage.

He backed away from the hatch, then helped Hammack through. The big man was clearly in pain but fighting not to show it. He was weak, too, and Wright realised there was no way Hammack would have been able to get up without his and Doc's help.

Doc crawled over to Ramirez and felt for a pulse in the man's neck.

'He's dead, Doc,' said Wright quietly, but Doc threw him a warning look. Wright nodded, acknowledging that the two men had a friendship going back more than a quarter of a century and that Doc had the right to check for himself.

Doc made the sign of a cross over Ramirez, and closed his eyes for a few seconds as if in prayer.

Wright looked down the tunnel, wondering where Bamber

was, and what he was doing. He could think of no reason why the FBI agent had acted in the way that he had. Whatever Bamber's motives, his actions suggested that Doc had been right, that Bamber had taken the map from O'Leary. If he'd taken the map, he'd probably killed O'Leary, too. But why? And why had Bamber been so determined to come down the tunnels?

Kruse took the infra-red goggles out of his Snoopy knapsack and slipped them on, adjusting the straps so that they stayed firmly in place. He switched them on. Within seconds they'd warmed up and he turned off his flashlight. He put the flashlight back in the knapsack and eased it over his shoulders.

He was looking forward to the hunt, relishing the opportunity to use his killing skills. For too long he'd been limited by the environment in which he'd operated, where every killing had to be made to look like an accident. Deep underground, there were no restrictions. No limits.

He caressed the knife he'd taken from Ramirez. It was a good weapon, a killing knife, razor sharp with a slightly curved end so that it would slip easily between the ribs. It had sliced cleanly through the black man's chest and arm, and only Wright's thrown flashlight had prevented Kruse from cutting Hammack's throat. Kruse smiled at how easily he'd made Hammack lose his temper. Kruse wasn't a racist, but he'd known instinctively that racial abuse was Hammack's weak spot, in the same way that he'd known that he could get to Wright through the policeman's feelings for his ex-wife. Kruse was as expert at finding weak spots as he was at killing.

Kruse had never intended to kill the three men in the chamber. He'd wanted to weaken them, to injure them if possible, but he wanted them alive. He needed them as bait.

Kruse crawled towards the hatch that led up to the second level. He'd wait there for his victims, assuming that the other killer didn't get to them first. He smiled at the thought of a slogan he'd once seen printed on a T-shirt: 'Yeah, though I walk through the valley of the shadow of death, I fear no evil. Because I am the meanest son of a bitch in the valley.' Kruse's smile widened. Of one thing he was sure: he was the meanest son of a bitch down the tunnels.

Wright waited under the hatch that led up to the second level, sitting to one side so that he wasn't exposed from above. The hatch was closed, but he had no way of knowing if Bamber had already gone through or not. He looked back along the tunnel to where Hammack was dragging himself along. The tunnel was narrow, so Wright couldn't see Doc, who was bringing up the rear, but he could hear his whispers of encouragement.

There was nothing either man could do physically to help Hammack, as there wasn't enough room to pull or push him. Hammack grunted with each movement, and he was able to use only his left arm as he crawled. Doc had used Ramirez's headscarf as a sling to support Hammack's injured arm and Hammack kept it close to his chest in an attempt to maintain pressure on the dressings there.

It took Hammack almost twenty minutes to crawl the hundred feet to where Wright was sitting. He grinned ruefully at Wright. 'Sorry 'bout this,' he said.

'Hey, there's no rush,' said Wright. 'I'm tired, too. This pace is fine.'

Hammack lay down on his side and groaned. 'I could sleep for a month,' he said.

'We can rest here for a while,' said Doc.

'How 'bout you call room service and order us all a beer?' said Hammack. He chuckled, but the chuckle swiftly turned into a series of coughs that wracked his chest.

Wright took off his goggles and blinked as his eyes became accustomed to the pale yellow light from Doc's flashlight. 'Have you got spare batteries for that?' asked Wright.

'Three more,' said Doc. 'I figured I'd wait until these fail completely before I put them in.'

Hammack's chest began to rise and fall slowly and he snored quietly.

'Do you think he's going to be okay?' asked Wright.

'He's lost a lot of blood,' said Doc, 'but he's not in shock, not yet, anyway. He's tough. He'll make it.'

'I think it might be better if you went ahead of him,' said Wright. 'Let him bring up the rear.'

'We're not leaving him,' said Doc.

'That's not what I meant,' said Wright.

'What did you mean?'

'If anything did happen, you'd be trapped behind him. If you were in the middle, you could still move.'

'If he dies, you mean?'

Wright sighed. 'Look, don't be so defensive, Doc. I just mean that in the event of there being a problem, there'd be no point in you being stuck behind him. Besides, you've got the flashlight, you should be in front of him, not behind. He can't use the flashlight, not with his injured arm.'

'The man's right, Doc,' said Hammack, his eyes still closed.

'I thought you were asleep,' said Doc, patting him on the leg.

'Too much noise to sleep,' said Hammack. 'Time we started moving, huh? We haven't got all day.'

Kruse crouched down in the conical chamber, his knife in his hand. He switched off his infra-red goggles to get rid of the distracting high-pitched humming noise they made, then took them off and laid them on the floor. There were three exits leading from the chamber, and Kruse knew that his quarry would be coming down the tunnel he was facing. They were making slow and noisy progress, which was just what Kruse wanted. If he could hear them coming, so could the killer. All Kruse had to do was to watch and wait, and when the killer eventually struck, Kruse would be there to take care of the business. He smiled in the darkness.

He stiffened as he heard a scraping sound behind him. He pulled on the goggles and switched them on. They hummed and after a few seconds they flickered into life. He headed towards the source of the sound, his knife poised.

May moved slowly down the tunnel, the crossbow out in front of her. A group of red ants marched purposefully in single file across the floor of the tunnel, out of one tiny hole and into another. She took care not to trample on them as she crossed over their ranks. She squatted down and took a drink from her canteen. A sudden noise made her look back the way she'd come. She grabbed for the crossbow. A bolt was already in place, and she slid her finger over the trigger.

She heard another noise, then the rustle of clothing. She sniffed softly, moving her head back as she inhaled. She could smell a man's sweat.

The tunnel she was in stretched for a hundred and fifty feet behind her. She couldn't risk turning around to get away because she'd have to expose her back. She crouched down. Ahead of her was a thirty-foot length of tunnel, just big enough for her to kneel up in. It met a T-junction, with larger tunnels running east–west. To the east was a conical air-raid chamber; to the west was a hospital chamber. May had set a booby trap at the entrance to the hospital: a cage containing scorpions, similar to the one she'd placed in the escape tunnel leading from the command centre. Whoever it was would probably continue straight ahead; there was no reason to take the smaller tunnel, the one she was in. She switched off her flashlight, put it on the ground, and waited.

She heard the man move slowly forward, then stop. May

frowned in the darkness. She held the crossbow with both hands. There was no glow at the end of the tunnel, no light to show that he was approaching. Could he be moving in the dark? She dismissed the thought immediately. It was impossible. Even she wouldn't move through an unexplored section in total darkness: there were too many dangers for the unwary. Although she knew where all the traps were, there were still the snakes and insects to contend with.

Another sound came from the man's direction – a high-pitched whine, like a mosquito. She put her head on one side, focusing her attention on the sound. There was another rustling noise, like a sleeve brushing against the tunnel wall. He was moving again. Still there was no light.

May took her left hand off the crossbow and picked up her flashlight. The crossbow wavered as she pointed the flashlight down the tunnel and switched it on.

She stifled a scream. Crouched at the T-junction was a monster, a huge insect-like creature with glassy eyes and a bulbous head, looking straight at her. It was holding a knife in its hand. May backed away in horror. She didn't believe in ghosts or demons – all the horrors she'd witnessed in her life were the actions of men – but this, this was something that could only have crawled out of hell. It had the body of a man and the head of a giant locust, and whatever it was, it could see in the dark. The creature moved towards her, its mouth parting to reveal human teeth. Its blank eyes stared at her, and she could see her own reflection in its stare. She saw the look of horror on her own face, the scarf around her neck, and the crossbow shaking in her hand. The crossbow. She'd forgotten about the crossbow. She put the flashlight on the ground, its beam highlighting the monstrous creature, and aimed her crossbow with both hands.

As she sighted along the bolt, she realised it wasn't a monster she was facing, but a man, a man wearing a mask. No, not a mask, something else, something that helped him to see in the dark. She aimed at the man's chest and pulled the trigger. The man was already moving and the bolt hit him in the shoulder. He fell back against the tunnel wall. May fumbled for another bolt.

Hammack groaned and lay down on the tunnel floor. 'Doc, I'm beat,' he gasped.

'It's not much further, Bernie,' said Doc.

'Don't kid a kidder,' whispered Hammack. 'We're not even up to the second level yet. I'm bleeding again. And I need water.'

Doc reached over his back and undid the top of his rucksack. He pulled out his medical kit and passed it back to Hammack. 'Take a dressing out and slap it on the wound,' he said. 'And if the pain gets worse, chew on another tablet.'

Hammack reached for the kit with his good arm.

'I'll go ahead and bring the Brit back,' said Doc.

'Then what?'

'He's got water in his backpack. Enough for you, anyway. He had Dennis's map, maybe he can remember where the well was and we can find water.'

'That's a big maybe, Doc.'

'I'm going to have to leave you in the dark. You okay with that?'

Hammack nodded. He rolled over on to his back, opened the medical kit and took out a dressing. Doc waited until he'd put it over his wound before crawling away.

Hammack rested his head on the floor and sucked in the warm air. Every breath sent stabbing pains through his chest wound. He put his hand up and placed it on the dressings, using pressure to stem the flow of blood. He shivered. He could feel his body temperature dropping, despite the heat of the tunnel. 'Hurry back, Doc,' he whispered.

Kruse gritted his teeth and pulled out the bolt. He probed the wound with his fingers. It was painful but there didn't appear to be too much damage. He flexed his fingers. The bolt seemed to have missed the nerves and the blood flow was far from life threatening. He'd been lucky, if lucky meant reflexes honed almost to perfection by years of training. A woman had been the last thing he'd expected to see down the tunnels, especially a woman dressed in the black pyjamas uniform of a Viet Cong guerrilla. That was what had slowed him down, kept him rooted to the spot while she'd aimed her crossbow. She must have been surprised too, because her aim had been off.

He dropped the bolt on the floor and began crawling again. He had to put as much distance between himself and the woman as he could. She had the advantage of range, so in the long tunnels she'd have the upper hand. To be sure of defeating her he'd have to lie in ambush, wait for her to show herself, using the darkness as a cloak. One of the chambers would be the best bet. He could wait in the dark and the beam of her flashlight would announce her presence. Then he could move in close, with the knife.

Kruse didn't care who the woman was. All he cared about was that he now knew who he was up against. The fact that it was a woman made it a little more interesting, but he gave no thought as to who she was or why she wanted to kill the Tunnel Rats. Jody Meacher could deal with the questions; all Kruse cared about was his mission – to kill everyone who knew the secret that had lain buried in the fourth level for so long.

He moved quickly along the tunnel, through a small resting chamber, not even bothering to consult the map. He ducked into a side tunnel, scampering along on all fours, his knapsack rubbing against the tunnel roof. He stopped suddenly as he heard voices ahead. It was Doc and Hammack, talking in hushed voices.

Kruse crawled forward cautiously. The tunnel he was in merged with another. Doc and Hammack were around the corner. Kruse crept along to the point where the two tunnels intersected, and leaned against the clay wall. He could see along the full length of the tunnel ahead of him, but didn't want to risk looking around to see where the two men were. In the distance he had a back view of Nick Wright about two hundred feet from the intersection. Kruse tightened his grip on his knife. It wouldn't take him long to catch up, then he could plunge his knife into Wright's back without him ever knowing what had happened. He was about to crawl after Wright when he heard someone moving along the tunnel. Kruse backed up, his knife out in front of him. It was Doc.

Kruse moved further back down the tunnel to where

it zigzagged so that Doc wouldn't be able to see him. He waited until he was sure that Doc had passed the intersection before crawling back into the tunnel. He looked after Doc, only thirty feet away and clearly trying to catch up with Wright. Kruse turned to look at Hammack. The black man was lying on his side, his eyes closed. Kruse decided to go after Doc.

Kruse moved quickly and easily gained on Doc. He raised his knife and slashed at Doc's legs. Doc yelped and Kruse stabbed him in the thigh, using the knife as leverage to pull himself up on Doc's legs. Kruse felt like a cheetah bringing down a running antelope; once it had its claws embedded into the animal's flanks, it was all over.

Doc screamed in pain. Kruse saw Wright twist around in the tunnel, and grinned. He grabbed Doc's hair and pulled back the man's head, waited until he was sure that Wright could see what he was doing, then slashed at Doc's throat so savagely that he almost severed the neck. Blood spurted over the sides of the tunnel and Doc's body went into convulsions.

'You're next!' Kruse shouted at Wright. He crawled over Doc's body but Doc's rucksack blocked his way. There wasn't enough room to get by. Kruse pounded the rucksack, trying to flatten it down. It was no good. Kruse clawed at the straps and yanked the bloodstained rucksack off Doc's back. He passed it through his legs then clambered over Doc's body. Wright had already disappeared around a bend in the tunnel. Kruse sped after him, the smell of blood so strong in his nostrils that it made him giddy.

Hammack heard a soft scraping sound and opened his eyes. He had no way of knowing how long he'd been lying in the tunnel as he'd been drifting in and out of consciousness. A flashlight beam illuminated the ceiling and he twisted his head back to see who was coming.

'Doc? That you?'

There was no reply but he could still hear whoever it was crawling towards him. Hammack swallowed.

'Doc?' His voice echoed around the tunnel.

The light wavered, then got stronger. Hammack forced his head back but all he could see was red clay. Something fluttered across his face and he flinched. He spluttered and brushed whatever it was away with his hand, but it wasn't an insect, it was a piece of card. Hammack groped for it and held it in front of his face. It was a playing card and he was looking at the back of it. He knew what it was before he'd even turned it around. An ace of spades. He gave a groan of resignation and closed his eyes.

When he opened them again a face was looking down at him, the face of a woman. A Vietnamese woman. Around her neck was a black and white checked scarf, the sort that the VC used to wear. Hammack wondered if he was having a flashback, if the medication Doc had given him was producing hallucinations. He tried to speak, but his throat was too dry. Even though her face was the wrong way up, Hammack could see that she was pretty, with a small mouth, high cheekbones, and soft, brown eyes. He smiled up at her. She didn't smile back. Something flashed at the periphery of his vision. It was only as it sliced through his throat that he realised it was a knife.

Wright crawled out of the tunnel and emerged into a large chamber. He looked around at the lathes and metal-turning machinery and the stacks of boxes. He was in the ammunition chamber. He turned and listened. He could hear Bamber in the tunnel, coming after him. Wright looked around for somewhere to hide. The boxes were the best bet. They gave him a sudden idea. He climbed up on a stack and took down one of the old oil lamps that hung from the overhead metal beams. He shook it. There was still oil inside.

His heart raced as he unscrewed the oil filler cap. He yanked open the box that Bamber had prised off last time they'd passed through the chamber and splashed oil over the cartridges. He trickled oil over the rest of the boxes, then dropped the lamp on to the floor and went back to the tunnel. He bent down and peered inside. Bamber was only twenty feet away, and roared as he saw Wright.

Wright ducked out of thc way, then ran to the centre of the chamber and pulled Doc's Zippo out of his pocket. He flicked it, but it stubbornly refused to light. 'Come on,' he hissed, and flicked the metal wheel with his thumb again. There were sparks, but still no light.

Wright shook the Zippo and tried again. This time it burst

into life. He tossed it on to the pile of ammunition boxes and they immediately caught light with a whooshing noise.

Wright ran to the exit. He turned in time to see Bamber stagger out of his tunnel. He ran across the chamber, towards Wright, his knife high in the air. Wright stared in horror, knowing that he was no match for Bamber in a knife fight. Or any sort of fight, for that matter.

The top ammunition box exploded in a series of ear-splitting bangs. Wright ducked instinctively. Dozens of cartridges detonated and bullets thwacked into the parachute silk that lined the chamber.

A pool of flame spread across the floor and the reed mats ignited easily. Plumes of choking black smoke billowed up between Wright and Bamber, and Wright stepped back. There was another explosion as a second crate caught fire.

Wright bent down and scurried into the exit tunnel. He crawled frantically. A few seconds later there was a third, even bigger explosion, that sent a wave of burning hot air down the tunnel. He crawled faster, coughing and spluttering. After fifty feet or so he turned and looked behind him. There was no sign of Bamber.

He lay on his back, gasping for air, but started crawling again as soon as he'd caught his breath. He wasn't sure how much life there was left in the batteries of his goggles.

He crawled along to the conical chamber which had contained the spiders and rushed through it, just in case they bore any grudges from his last visit. He kept his head down and didn't look up as he passed through, not stopping for a rest until he'd reached the cinema. He sat on the floor by the white sheet screen with his back to the parachute-silk-lined wall, fighting off the feelings of nausea that washed over him.

His throat was painfully dry and his nose and lips were coated with thick dust. He took off his goggles and rubbed his face. The rubber seal irritated his skin, but it was still a small price to pay for being able to see.

He put the goggles back on and crawled out of the cinema chamber. All he had to do now was to find the hatch up the first level, and get through the water in the U-bend. Wright laughed harshly. After everything he'd been though, he figured that this time it'd be a breeze.

May wrapped her scarf around the lower part of her face and narrowed her eyes against the stinging dust. She had no idea what had caused the explosion in the ammunition chamber, but she could see the after-effects for herself. The tunnel leading to it had collapsed, and the chamber itself had almost certainly caved in. The chambers had been built to withstand bombs falling outside, not explosions from within. She backed away, then twisted around. There were a number of different ways up to the first level and from there she knew of several ventilation tunnels that she could use to get to the surface.

Wright knelt down beside the water. He slipped off his goggles, dipped a hand into the water and splashed it over his face, taking care not to get any of it in his mouth. He put the goggles back on and rummaged through his knapsack. The plastic bag wasn't there. He searched again but it had definitely gone. He must have lost it when he'd taken the water bottles out. He cursed. He wasn't sure how the goggles would stand up to being immersed in water. They were rubber coated, but that didn't mean they were waterproof.

He took off the goggles and put them in the knapsack, trying not to think about the dark. He tucked his knife in the back of his belt, all the time keeping his eyes firmly closed, clinging to the illusion that he wasn't in total darkness, that it was something he'd chosen, that at any time he could open his eyes.

He slipped his arms through the straps of the knapsack, and felt for the water. He took two deep breaths, then threw himself headfirst into the pool. He kicked, then immediately turned around so that he could use his hands and feet to propel himself through the U-bend. His fingers dug into the wet clay and he pulled himself down.

The air trapped in his knapsack pushed him up against the tunnel roof and he banged his head, but he kicked with his feet, surged around the bend and popped up to the surface, barely out of breath. He grinned to himself as he climbed out of the water. It had been easy compared with his chaotic first attempt.

He crawled away from the water and knelt on the tunnel floor, flicking his wet hair from his eyes. He shrugged off his knapsack and felt for the goggles. He fitted them, then said a silent prayer as he switched them on. They clicked and hissed, and after a tense five-second delay they flickered into life. Wright sighed with relief and leaned back against the tunnel wall. He was going to make it. All he had to do now was to get up to the first level and then find the trapdoor.

He reached for his knapsack, and as he did, Bamber shot out of the water, his mouth wide open. His shirt was scorched and torn and there were burn marks on his hands and arms. In his left hand he held his flashlight and infra-red goggles wrapped in a plastic bag; in his right hand a wicked hunting knife. Water cascaded from Bamber's body as he surged forward, his knife raised in the air.

Wright screamed, holding his knapsack up for protection. The knife slashed into it, slicing through Mickey Mouse's smiling face. Bamber slashed again and again as he pulled himself out of the water, roaring with each blow. Wright scuttled backwards and kicked out with his feet. He caught Bamber under the chin and the FBI agent fell back.

Wright threw his knapsack at Bamber and it struck him a glancing blow on his cheek. Bamber slashed down with the knife and Wright felt a burning pain in his left calf. He kicked out again and struck Bamber in the chest. Wright groped behind him, trying to find his own knife. It wasn't there. It must have fallen out while he was under water.

Bamber grunted and drew back his knife. It glistened with blood. Wright grunted and drew both his legs up to his chest. Bamber shuffled towards Wright, waving the knife from side to side. Wright lashed out with both feet, catching Bamber in the stomach.

Bamber fell backwards, his head slamming into the roof of the tunnel. Wright scraped his right foot along the tunnel roof, kicking red clay into Bamber's face, then kept up the attack, shuffling forwards on his backside and kicking, forcing Bamber back down the tunnel towards the water.

As Bamber wiped the soil from his eyes, Wright lashed out at the bag in his hand. It fell to the ground and Wright stamped on it, smashing the flashlight with his heel. He kicked it again and heard the lenses of the goggles smash. At last he had the advantage. Bamber couldn't see.

Wright picked up the bag full of broken metal and glass and slammed the end against Bamber's head, again and again, whipping it back and forth.

Bamber tried to stab him with the knife but Wright easily evaded the blows. Bamber cocked his head on one side, listening intently. Wright held his breath so as not to give away his position, but he realised that Bamber was listening for the buzzing of his infra-red goggles.

Wright pulled the flashlight out of the bag and stabbed the end of it into Bamber's face, grinding the broken glass into his cheek. Bamber cried in pain and Wright brought the flashlight down on his nose with a satisfying crack. Bamber put his hands up to his broken nose and fell back into the water. He disappeared under the surface, head first. Wright crouched over the water, the flashlight raised like a club, waiting for Bamber to reappear, but after half a minute the ripples had subsided and the surface was as flat as a mirror. Wright counted a full two minutes in his head before lowering the broken flashlight. He turned and began to crawl along the tunnel, looking over his shoulder every few seconds, just in case. He'd hit Bamber hard, but he was reasonably sure that he hadn't him hit hard enough to kill him.

May undid the trip wire. It was connected to a small bamboo cage containing two venomous snakes that she'd bought from a dealer in Saigon. She crept by the cage, which she'd set into the tunnel wall, then retied the trip wire. The three Americans who'd come down the tunnel were all dead. She'd killed Ramirez and Hammack herself, though the man in the strange headset had beaten her to Doc Marshall. Still, she'd managed to place an ace of spades on Marshall's corpse. That had given her no small satisfaction. There were two men still in the tunnels: the man in the goggles and the other man, whom she hadn't yet seen. Neither concerned her. She'd completed her work in the tunnels and was now intent on getting back to the surface and out of Vietnam.

The tunnel she was in was relatively tall and the roof arched, so that she was able to run along it providing she kept her upper body thrust forward and her knees slightly bent. She cradled the crossbow in her hands as she ran, a bolt in place even though she didn't anticipate meeting anyone. The two men were the other side of the collapse, and one had probably died in the explosion.

She reached the end of the tunnel and paused for breath in a resting chamber large enough to hold six men. A slight breeze came from a small hole close to the roof of the chamber. May turned her head towards it and let it play over her face.

As a child she'd crawled through ventilation tunnels, despite her father's warning that it was dangerous, that they weren't built to such a high standard as the chambers and the communication tunnels. She had grown since then, but she knew that she would still be able to crawl up through the ventilation tunnel, all the way to the surface. It would be a tight fit, and she would come out almost half a mile from her pick-up truck, but it was still the quickest route out. She drank the last of her water, then stood up and pushed her crossbow into the hole. She used both hands to get a grip on the hard clay, and heaved herself up.

The green flickering image faded and the buzzing of the infra-red goggles became suddenly fainter. Wright had a sick feeling in the pit of his stomach. The infra-red image had been getting steadily worse over the past few minutes, but he'd tried to convince himself that he was imagining it. Now there was no doubt. He couldn't see more than ten feet ahead of him and his field of vision was fading fast. He crawled faster, wanting to take advantage of what little life remained in the equipment, but he'd barely managed twenty feet before they failed completely. Despair washed over him and he beat his hands on the ground.

He ripped off the goggles and threw them down. He cursed himself, he cursed the tunnels, and he cursed Jim Bamber. He started to hyperventilate and fought to steady his breathing.

'It's okay,' he whispered to himself. 'It's one straight tunnel. A walk in the park.' He started to crawl forward, groping ahead with his fingers, staring ahead with unseeing eyes. 'A walk in the park,' he repeated, though he could hear the uncertainty in his voice.

Gerry Hunter opened the front door. 'Hey!' he called.

'Hiya, honey!' Janie shouted from the kitchen. 'We're in here.'

She was standing by the dishwashing machine. Sean was helping her to load it.

'Hiya, Sean,' said Hunter, dropping his briefcase next to the kitchen table. 'How was school?'

'Okay,' said Sean. He closed the door of the machine and rushed out of the kitchen. Hunter watched him go.

Janie kissed him on the cheek. 'He'll get used to you,' she said, and slipped her arms around his neck. 'I'm pleased to see you.' She kissed him on the lips. 'But you're late.'

'Yeah, Nick's in trouble.'

Janie held up her hands. 'I don't want to hear any more,' she snapped.

'But—'

'No, Gerry. He's out of my house, he's out of my life, I don't want to talk about him.'

'You're over-reacting, Janie.'

'You didn't have to live with the man, Gerry. With his moods, his nightmares, his fixation with work. You didn't get woken up in the middle of the night to find him downstairs playing his bloody mouth organ.' She stamped her foot. 'Damn him, damn him for never leaving me alone.' She turned on her heel and stormed out of the kitchen.

Hunter groaned and took off his coat. He was finding it harder and harder to deal with Janie's mood swings. When he first met her he'd thought that the break-up of her marriage had been Nick Wright's fault, but the longer he spent with her the more he realised that Janie was far from the catch she first appeared. She was moody, spoiled and selfish, and while the sex was terrific, she was impossible to live with. In fact, Hunter had made it a point not to live with her. She'd given him a key, and he often stayed until the early hours, but he was never there in the morning. He always left before first light, partly because he didn't think it fair on Sean, but partly because he didn't want to make a commitment to Janie which he might have to break.

He switched on the kettle, then took his mobile phone out of his briefcase. He tapped out Wright's number. To his surprise, after half a dozen rings, it was answered by a laconic male voice.

'Nick?'

'What?'

'Nick? It's Gerry.'

'Gerry who?'

It wasn't Wright, Hunter realised. He checked the number with the man. He was one digit out. He apologised for bothering the man, and redialled, taking care to press the correct buttons. It rang out for a while, then he got the recording again, asking him to leave a message.

Wright probed forward with his fingers, testing the dirt ahead for trip wires. He had no idea what he'd do if he did touch something. What could he possibly do in the dark? He would have no way of knowing what sort of trap it was. Bamber had mentioned snakes, and Doc had said there had been a scorpion trap down in the escape tunnel. What would he do if he touched a snake or a stinging insect? He could feel blood trickling from the wound on his calf each time he moved his left leg but he blanked the pain from his mind, focusing all his attention on the tunnel ahead of him.

He had no sense of time passing, no way of knowing if it was day or night outside. He couldn't see his watch, so for a while he'd tried to mark the passing of time by counting. He'd given up after reaching three thousand. Three thousand seconds was fifty minutes, almost an hour, but he couldn't tell how far he'd crawled during the time he'd been counting. At least his infra-red goggles had held out until he reached the upper level. He would never have been able to get up from the second level without being able to see the trapdoor.

A sudden thought gripped his heart. What if the trapdoor had been replaced? What if Chinh had found the entrance and had put the hatch back? Maybe Wright had already crawled under the trapdoor and was now heading away from it, crawling to oblivion, to a waterless, lightless, lonely death. He shook his head. No, the kitbags were in the tunnel. To miss the hatch he'd have to pass the kitbags the Americans had left. All he had to do was to crawl until he reached the kitbags. Unless Chinh had taken them, figuring he was better off stealing what they contained than waiting for Bamber's half of the hundred-dollar bill. He pushed the thought out of his mind and began counting again, ticking off the seconds as he crawled.

May squeezed through the last section of the ventilation tunnel. She could feel the breeze on her face, stronger than before, and hear the sound of birdsong and running water. She pushed the crossbow ahead of herself, then pulled with her arms and wriggled with her legs.

She burst through a veil of spindly white tree roots and hauled herself out into the sunlight. The tunnel opened into the wet clay of a riverbank and some six feet below muddy water rippled past. She slid down towards the river, but grabbed on to a rock and swung her legs to the side until she managed to get a grip on the slippery clay. She dragged herself up and lay on her back on the bank, gulping in lungfuls of clean, fresh air.

Wright had counted to two thousand when he saw the patch of light ahead of him. He stopped and stared at the sunbeam that lanced through the dusty air of the tunnel. It looked solid, almost as if it could be sliced with a knife. He started crawling, oblivious to the pain in his leg, all thoughts of booby traps forgotten, his eyes fixed on the small square of light, staring at it as if he feared it would disappear at any moment.

He roared with triumph as he got closer, an animal-like bellow that swelled to fill the tunnel. He'd made it. He'd survived.

He dragged himself up through the opening, and rolled over and over in the sand like a puppy. He stared up at the brilliant blue sky and the white feathery clouds that moved slowly across it, revelling in the fact that he was alive, then rolled on to his front and sat up on his knees, his eyes half closed against the blinding sun. He shaded his eyes with his hand and squinted around, trying to recall where the Mercedes was. If he could find the car, then Chinh, the driver, would help him.

He tried to get to his feet but he had no strength left and fell back on to his hands and knees. He kept his head down and began to crawl, his left leg dragging in the sand. After several minutes he realised he was in the shadow of a rock formation. He clawed himself up the sandstone rock, then twisted around and sat with his back to it, breathing heavily.

He rolled up his trouser leg and examined the wound on his calf. His ripped jeans were stained with blood, but the cut itself wasn't too deep. Wright could see grains of dirt among the cut tissue and he realised there was a good chance of the wound becoming infected if he didn't clean it soon. He didn't have any antiseptic or water, so he put his head close to the cut and spat at it several times, then smeared the saliva around it. He tried to spit again but his mouth was too dry.

'Chinh!' he shouted, but his voice wasn't much more than a hoarse whisper.

The elation that he'd felt as he climbed out into the open began to fade, and Wright's mind started to wander. A series of disjointed images flashed through his mind. Eckhardt's mutilated body in the Battersea tunnel. The blood streaming from Hammack's chest wound. Bamber, the crazed look in his eyes and the knife in his hand. His father, hanging from the beam, his shoes stinking of urine.

Wright's head slumped forward and the jolt woke him up. He slapped his face several times, but barely felt the blows. His whole body seemed to have gone numb. He had to find Chinh. He pushed himself up, using the rock for leverage, and scanned the surrounding vegetation. There were no features that he recognised. He staggered out of the shadow and back into the searing sunlight, shading his eyes with his hands. Once he'd walked some distance from the rocks, he turned to look at them, trying to recall what they'd looked like when he and Bamber had first approached the hatch. He stood staring at the rock formation for almost a minute, then figured that they'd come in from an angle to his left. He looked down to see if there were any footprints, but the wind had obliterated all tracks.

A large black and yellow bird flew overhead and settled in the branches of a spreading tree. Wright staggered towards a gap in the vegetation, wincing each time he put his weight on his left leg. He had to stop after a dozen steps to rest. He wiped his forehead with his hand and it came away sopping wet. Sweat was pouring off him. He put his hands on his hips and took deep breaths, then started walking again.

He heard a noise behind him and whirled around. Bamber was crawling out of the hatch, his knife in his right hand.

'Wright!' he yelled.

Wright felt as if he'd been punched in the solar plexus. Any remaining strength he had seemed to drain away from him and his arms hung uselessly at his sides. He was exhausted. He couldn't run. He couldn't hide. He couldn't fight back. He stood and watched as Bamber hauled himself out of the tunnel.

'It's over, Wright!' shouted Bamber. He walked slowly towards Wright, the knife raised in the air. The steel glinted in the harsh sunlight. The yellow and black bird cawed and took flight.

Wright's heart began to race and he felt a surge of adrenalin. He turned and staggered into the jungle, pushing branches and vines away with his hands, barely managing a fast walk, his left leg dragging, a dead weight. It was like walking through treacle, as if the ground was sucking at his feet, slowing him down so that every step required a superhuman effort. Wright looked over his shoulder. Bamber was gaining. He too was exhausted, but he didn't have an injured leg and he had a knife.

Wright turned and forced himself to jog, though every step was agonising. He could hear Bamber breathing and snorting behind him, and the sound of his feet slapping into the dirt. Wright stumbled over a fallen branch and pitched forward. He fell on to his hands and knees, his chest heaving, tears of frustration and rage stinging his eyes. He pushed himself up. In the distance he could see the Mercedes, its windscreen a mass of reflected sunlight. He got to his feet and staggered towards the car, his arms outstretched as if reaching for it.

His legs became heavier and heavier with each step, but behind him Bamber maintained his pace, breathing like a bull at stud. Wright risked another look over his shoulder. Bamber was only six paces behind him, the knife held high. He was grinning maniacally, his eyes wide and staring, his face smeared with blood and mud like hastily applied warpaint.

Wright fell again. He hit the ground hard and rolled over on to his back, his hands up in front of his chest in an attempt to defend himself against the attack he knew would come. Bamber slowed and stood over Wright, a look of total triumph on his face.

Bamber opened his mouth to speak, but before he could say anything, there was a swooshing sound and something thwacked into his neck, just below his right ear. The look of triumph turned to one of disbelief. His hand clawed up at the object in his neck, but as he touched it his legs folded under him and he fell to his knees. Blood streamed from his neck, and Wright watched in horror as Bamber's mouth worked soundlessly. It was a crossbow bolt, Wright realised. Someone had shot Bamber with a crossbow bolt.

Wright scuttled away on his back like a startled crab, but he couldn't take his eyes off Bamber's face. Bamber reached out a hand as if begging Wright to help him, but then he fell face down into the sand.

Wright rolled on to his front and crawled, head down, towards the car. He had to find Chinh. Blood was pouring from the wound in his leg, but he ignored the pain.

He crawled into a clearing and towards the Mercedes. 'Chinh!' he shouted hoarsely. There was no sign of the driver.

As he got closer to the car, Wright heard a muffled ringing sound. It was his mobile telephone. 'The phone!' he muttered. He could use it to call for help. He struggled to the rear of the car and pulled himself up, grunting with the effort.

He pulled open the boot, then stepped back in horror. Chinh was there, his eyes staring lifelessly up at the sky, dried blood over his chin. The telephone continued to ring. It was inside his suitcase, at the bottom of the boot. Wright grabbed the body by the arms and heaved it out. It dropped on to the dirt with a dull thud. Wright pulled Bamber's metal suitcase out of the boot and placed it next to the body, then opened his own suitcase.

The mobile was under a pair of Levis. He put it to his ear. It was the last person in the world he expected to hear from. Gerry Hunter.

'Nick!' said Hunter. 'Thank God.'

'What the hell do you want, Hunter?' asked Wright.

'The killer,' said Hunter. 'I know who the killer is.'

Wright smiled grimly. He slammed down the boot door. 'Yeah, well, you're about three hours too late,' he said, looking down at Chinh's corpse.

'Nick, shut up and listen, will you?' interrupted Hunter. 'It was Eckhardt's wife. May. She's the killer.'

Wright stiffened. He heard a footfall behind him and turned around, slowly. May Eckhardt was looking at him, a puzzled frown on her face. She was wearing black pyjamas and sandals, and around her neck was a black and white checked scarf. She had her hair tied back and her face was streaked with dirt. In her right hand she carried a loaded crossbow; in her left, the knife that Bamber had been holding.

Gerry Hunter paced up and down the hallway, his mobile phone pressed against his ear. 'Nick? Are you there?' The phone buzzed and clicked. 'Nick?'

'Yes, I'm here.'

'Did you hear what I said? May Eckhardt killed her husband.'

'Are you sure?'

'Positive. She was flown out of Vietnam when she was a kid, holding a set of dogtags. The dogtags belonged to Max Eckhardt.'

There was a longer silence. Then the line went dead.

'Nick? Nick, can you hear me?' There was no reply.

The phone dropped from Wright's hand. 'Why, May?' he asked.

May slung the crossbow on her back and transferred the knife to her right hand.

'He was going to kill you,' she said flatly.

'Not Bamber!' he shouted. 'Your husband. And the rest of them.'

'They killed my father,' she said. 'They tortured him and they cut him to pieces. They deserved to die.'

Wright staggered back against the boot of the Mercedes. 'You were down there? You saw them? You saw what they did?'

'I saw everything,' she said, her voice a dull monotone.

'But you couldn't have been more than . . .'

'I was eight years old,' she said. 'I'd been living down the tunnels with my father for almost a year. My mother had been killed in the fields.' There was a faraway look in her eyes as she relived the memory in her mind. 'I saw her die, too. She was planting rice with a group of women from her village, and a helicopter flew overhead. We were always told to wave at the American helicopters, so that they'd know that we weren't VC.' She put a hand against the black pyjama top. 'The peasants wore tunics like this, but so did the Viet Cong.' She shrugged. 'My mother refused to wave. She stood glaring up at the helicopter, glaring at it as if she wanted it to fall out of the sky. I was at the side of the field, fishing in a canal. The helicopter circled around her, then there were gunshots, lots of gunshots, from the big gun they had inside. There was a black man firing and laughing, and lots of splashes around my mother, like tiny fish jumping, then she fell back and the water became red. The helicopter flew away. They didn't even land to see what they'd done.'

Wright leaned back against the Mercedes and slowly slid to the ground, his legs out in front of him.

'They burned our village a week later, and my father took me down into the tunnels.' She stared at Wright. He expected to see tears, but her eyes were dry. 'You don't want to hear this,' she said.

Wright looked from her face to the knife in her hand, and back to her face. 'I do,' he said.

She swallowed. 'It wasn't so bad down in the tunnels. There were lots of children there. We played games, we had lessons, we helped catch snakes and scorpions for the booby traps. We even helped dig the tunnels. We were small so we could get into difficult places.'

'Weren't you scared?'

She shook her head. 'Never,' she said. 'The tunnels were our homes. We were safe there.'

'Until the Americans came.'

'That's right,' she said. 'Until the Americans came.' The faraway look returned to her eyes and she stared off into the middle distance. Wright wondered if she intended to use the knife in her hand, if she was intent on removing all witnesses to what she'd done. The one thing that gave him hope was that she'd killed Bamber to save his life.

'My father heard them coming, but we didn't have time to use the escape tunnel. He hid me in the wall and told me not to come out, no matter what happened, no matter what I heard. I said I wanted to stay with him but he made me promise. Then he went back to his desk, just as they burst into the chamber. They were like madmen, Nick. Like animals. I could see through a tiny gap in the parachute silk. I saw everything.'

'They said they interrogated your father. That they started out by asking questions.'

She laughed harshly. 'A lie,' she said. 'They had a bloodlust. They just wanted to hurt and to kill. I saw everything they did to him. Everything.'

For the first time she looked as if she was about to cry, but she shook her head, refusing to allow the tears to come. 'Afterwards, they buried him, as if they were finally ashamed of what they'd done. The one called Burrow threw a playing card on my father's body. The ace of spades. Then they left. I waited for hours in the dark, convinced that they would come back for me. Can you imagine what it's like, Nick, to be trapped in a pitch-black room with your dead father, too scared to move?'

She moved closer to Wright. The sun was behind her and Wright had to shade his eyes to look up at her. 'Actually, May, I can,' he said quietly. 'You probably won't believe me, but yes, I can appreciate what you went through.'

She continued to talk as if she hadn't heard what he'd said. 'Eventually I crawled out of my hiding place. I dug the earth away from my father with my bare hands. That's when I found the dogtags. Eckhardt, M. Max Eckhardt. I took the tags and reburied my father.'

'And you waited more than twenty years to find Eckhardt?'

She nodded. 'That's how long it took. And then I had

to get him to tell me who his friends were, who he'd served with in Vietnam.'

'And to do that, you had to marry him?'

'I did what I had to do to avenge my father.'

'How could you do that?'

'How could I do what? Seduce him? Sleep with him? Every time I opened my legs to the man, I thought of what he'd done to my father and what I would one day do to him. The hatred kept me going.'

'For more than two decades?'

She shrugged. 'How long it took didn't matter. All that mattered was that my father's death was avenged. Now it's almost done. Soon I'll be able to rest.'

She knelt down and Wright flinched. She smiled, and used the knife to tear a slit up the leg of his trousers. She put the knife on the ground, then reached behind her back. Her hand reappeared with a green plastic pack. It was Doc's medical kit. She took out a piece of cotton wool and a bottle of iodine and cleaned his wound, smiling again when he winced with pain.

As she placed a dressing on the wound, Wright cleared his throat. 'May Eckhardt, I am placing you under arrest for the murder of Max Eckhardt.' The words sounded oddly stilted and he stumbled over the word 'murder'.

May smiled and brushed a stray lock of muddy hair from her face. She picked up her knife and slid it into its scabbard.

'You are not obliged to say anything, but—'

She placed a hand on his chin and kissed him softly on the cheek. 'Goodbye, Nick,' she said. 'Take care.'

She turned and walked away without a backward look. Wright slumped down against the wheel of the

Mercedes and watched as the jungle swallowed her up.

His mobile phone began to ring again. He groped for it and put it to his ear. It was Tommy Reid. 'Hell's bells, Nick, where've you been?' asked his partner. 'I've been trying to get hold of you for hours. What have you been doing, fooling around with some gorgeous Asian babe?'

Wright's arm fell to the side and the mobile phone knocked against a small rock. He could still hear Reid talking, his voice buzzing like a trapped wasp. Wright threw back his head and began to laugh, louder and louder, until the laughter became an ugly, pain-filled scream that echoed around the jungle, quietening even the insects and birds.

Dean Burrow removed his reading glasses and surveyed the cheering crowd. There were more than five thousand people, and the sound of their clapping and shouting vibrated through his body like an earthquake tremor. He could understand why rock stars became addicted to performing; nothing came close to the sensation of being on the receiving end of the adulation of thousands of people. Placards praising his virtues and huge posters of his face were displayed at strategic intervals, placed to obtain maximum television coverage from the cameras that were scattered around the auditorium.

It had been the best speech Burrow had ever given; modest but farsighted, laying out his vision of a united, prosperous, caring America. Jody Meacher had done him proud. The only minor criticism that Burrow had raised was that the speech seemed more suited to a presidential campaign, but Meacher had just smiled at that. Both men knew that the Vice President's job was just a stepping stone.

Burrow put up a hand to acknowledge the cheers, then turned to look at his wife. She smiled on cue, the pride and admiration pouring out of her, a look as practised as any of Burrow's gestures. Flashes went off as the assembled photographers captured the image. That would be the one splashed across the morning editions of the world's newspapers. That or the picture of the President shaking his hand, congratulating him on becoming the second most powerful man in the world.

The cheering began to die down and Burrow put his glasses on. He had considered wearing contact lenses, but Meacher had disagreed, pointing out that the glasses gave Burrow a more serious air, adding maturity but not detracting from his looks. The time would come when Burrow would want to lose the glasses and some of the grey that was spreading through his hair, but that time was almost a decade away. Burrow had ceded to Meacher, knowing that when it came to image-making, Meacher was second to none.

Burrow looked across at the bank of television cameras that were transmitting the event around the world. It was all about image now. Getting elected was a matter of presentation, of media manipulation, of not making mistakes, and Jody Meacher would be there to guide him every step of the way. Burrow scanned the crowd as the cheering swelled again. Meacher's enthusiastic young team scattered through the audience would keep the applause going for a full two minutes before giving him the chance to continue his speech. Meacher wasn't in the auditorium, he was in an office upstairs watching the television coverage on a bank of monitors.

Burrow held up both hands as if trying to quieten the audience down. He knew it was futile; Meacher had stipulated the two minutes at rehearsal and there was nothing Burrow could do to change the programme. The gesture showed modesty, though, humility, even. Burrow smiled and gave a small shrug as if finally accepting that there was nothing he could do to stop the applause.

He waved at the audience. It was a good mixture: nobody too old, nobody too young, nobody too black, nobody too disabled. A camera-friendly melting pot that showed how all America was behind the new Vice President.

Suddenly Burrow stiffened. An unsmiling face glared at him with undisguised hatred, an Oriental woman with high cheekbones and shoulder-length hair. Her eyes bored into his as if she was staring into his soul. Burrow swallowed. The crowd around the woman cheered and waved, but she sat motionless, her lips set tight, her arms folded across her chest.

Burrow looked around to see if any of his Secret Service agents had noticed her. There were six of them, all in dark suits with radio earpieces and dark glasses, strategically placed around the stage. They were all scanning the audience but none appeared to be looking in the direction of the woman. There was nothing he could do to attract their attention, not with the world's cameras aimed at him.

He forced himself to smile and turned back to face the audience. The woman had gone. He couldn't even find the place in the crowd where she'd been. Burrow's smile widened and he raised both arms in a victory salute. The cheering welled around him. Maybe he'd imagined her. Besides, he had nothing to worry about. He was the Vice President of the United States of America and only one man in the country was better protected. He had nothing to fear from a sullen-faced Oriental woman. Nothing.

Pay Off

For Zita

PART ONE

Only a mother could have loved the bearded, brooding face of Get-Up McKinley. Only someone with vast amounts of maternal instinct to draw on, who'd changed his nappy and breastfed him through countless sleepless nights, could have seen him as anything other than a nasty piece of work, mean, moody and malevolent. But even McKinley's own mother would have been wary of this glowering man-mountain whose face matched the grainy picture in the newspaper cutting I'd folded and unfolded time and time again in a succession of East End pubs, until the newsprint was grimy and smeared and I'd had to repair its tattered edges with Sellotape.

I'd watched him over the top of my chipped glass, studied his reflection in the mirror behind the crowded gantry, and walked close by him to the toilet. I was sure it was him long before I heard the acne-ridden young barman call him by name.

McKinley was standing in the professional drinker's pose, his feet shoulder width apart, his knees locked, his left hand resting on the beer-stained bar while the right held his glass, elbow crooked and parallel to the ground, the whisky emptied down the throat with a flick of the wrist, an economy of movement that a conjuror would have envied.

How do you describe six feet four inches of grizzly bear in a green corduroy jacket? I guess that's a good start, but you'd also need to throw in a few simple adjectives like big and ugly, and try to get across the barely-suppressed aggression of the man. McKinley was angry, very angry, and I couldn't take my eyes off the hand on the bar which was clenching and unclenching like a rattlesnake about to strike.

I'd spent three long weeks sniffing at McKinley's trail, but I was in no position to speak to him, not yet. Give me an asbestos suit and a couple of SAS-trained bodyguards and maybe I'd have been brave enough to approach him. Maybe, but don't hold your breath. McKinley wasn't in a particularly receptive frame of mind just then.

The source of his displeasure was a couple of young drunks, neither good-hearted nor bad, just boisterous and rowdy, leather-jacketed, flush with drink and youth. The taller of the two had twice knocked McKinley's drinking arm, the second time hard enough to spill his drink. Not deliberate, you understand, but that wasn't the point, not as far as McKinley was concerned, anyway.

There's an elaborate procedure to be followed when you spill somebody's drink, and it depends on the sort of pub you're in. If it happens in one of the trendy Fulham wine bars you smile politely and say how awfully sorry you are, OK yah? And you joke and it's forgotten. In your average suburban pub you apologize and offer to buy another, an offer which is always refused, and it's relaxed and friendly. If it happens in an inner-city drinking den, the sort of men-only places you find in Glasgow, Birmingham, Liverpool and the East End of London, anywhere the unemployment rate is high and the black economy booming, then the politeness is exaggerated, the apologies ritualistic, just in case the drunk you're dealing with is a dangerous drunk.

'Are you all right?'

'Aye.'

'Are you sure?'

'Aye.'

'Can I get you another?'

'Aye.'

We were in Kelly's Bar in Leyton, and it's fair to say that it isn't my normal sort of London drinking establishment; no ice or lemon to go in my G and T, overflowing ashtrays, one underworked barman paid for by the YTS who was doing nothing to quieten the two rowdies as he gave a few half-washed pint mugs a casual wipe with a grubby cloth and placed a full bottle of lemonade on the bar, just out of McKinley's reach. No, my sort of place was about six miles or so due west, in the City or the West End, where they know the difference between a Wallbanger and a Sloe Comfortable Screw, where you need a collar and tie to get in and a full wallet to enjoy yourself, where noisy drunks don't bump into dangerous drunks and trouble is nipped in the bud.

Everyone called McKinley Get-Up because of an unfortunate incident that happened almost seven years ago, seven years which he'd spent in Wormwood Scrubs cooped up with prisoners who went to a lot of trouble to be nice to him.

At the age of twenty-nine he'd found his vocation as a bodyguard-cum-thug protecting a wholesale drugs dealer who arranged for heroin and cocaine to be brought in from Amsterdam, Ireland, or America, anywhere he could get it, and mixed it with talc or sugar or whatever white powder was floating about before selling it on to smaller dealers.

It was cash and carry and the seventy-five per cent profit margin was more than enough to pay McKinley a decent wage. His downfall came when the drugs dealer decided to branch out and put up the money for an armed robbery.

Three up and coming young villains had made him an offer he hadn't wanted to refuse. If he put up two thousand pounds for the shotguns, the getaway car and other expenses, he would be in for half of whatever they got from the superstore in Hackney they'd been casing for the best part of two weeks, and they reckoned the take could be as high as £65,000.

The three geniuses behind the plan were Alvin Miller, Dick Wallace and Charlie Leonard, three ne'er-do-wells whose combined IQ was less than the tube fare from Clapham Common to Clapham South.

They'd already done over a couple of filling stations and a post office with flick knives and hatchets, but the money had been frittered away. Now they reckoned they were ready for the Big Time, but for that they needed a stake. Ronnie Laing, McKinley's boss, was just the man to help three youngsters along the path to riches. For a price.

Laing slipped them the cash in used notes in a brown envelope and waited. Three days later Miller phoned to say that the job was off. Leonard had all but lost his leg slipping off a ladder while decorating his mum's front room. He was in hospital, in pain and no way was the job going ahead with just the two of them. A hundred and eighty pounds was left in the kitty and Ronnie was welcome to that and the three sawn-off shotguns.

No chance, said Laing. Get someone else or all three of you will have broken legs. Like who? asked Miller. Like McKinley, said Laing, and now I'm in for sixty per cent of the action.

Twenty-four hours later McKinley, Miller and Wallace were sitting in a four-year-old Rover with Miller's brother Tommy acting as driver, going over the plan for the last time.

All three would go in carrying holdalls, put a few things in wire baskets, use three separate check-outs and then pull out the shooters. Miller would fire his, they'd get the girls to empty their cash registers while Wallace got the manager to empty his safe in the office. Simple. They'd already gone through it three times for McKinley as he sat in the back seat, his shotgun dwarfed by the fingernail-bitten hands in his lap.

They moved. Miller went in first, Wallace second. McKinley counted to fifty and followed. All the blue-handled wire baskets had gone so he grabbed a trolley and pushed. One of the rear wheels was sticking and it squeaked sideways along the tiled floor as he wandered down past the cereals picking up packets of Cornflakes and Frosties. He threw in a tin of dog food – he'd always wanted a dog – and by the time he got to the check-out Miller and Wallace were waiting, fuming silently. McKinley frowned an apology and Miller nodded twice. All three threw off their woolly caps, pulled down their stocking masks and brought out the guns. Miller pointed his at the ceiling and pulled the trigger. The noise was deafening, bits of the plasterboard ceiling fell around him in a cloud, sticking to his stocking like pieces of tissue paper to a cut chin.

'Right, get down on the floor. Now!' he yelled, but nobody moved. One of the young girls sitting in front of a cash register started to cry quietly. The manager came out of his office, stopped and raised his hands above his head. Still nobody moved. The fire sprinklers came on, a shower of cold water washed the pieces of plasterboard from Miller's stocking mask and a trickle ran down the back of his neck. A couple of the girls held plastic bags over their heads and watched him anxiously.

'Down on the floor. Everybody down on the floor. Now,' he screamed and fired the gun again. This time everyone moved. 'Oh Jesus, no. Get up, McKinley! Get up!'

They were all caught five minutes later in the carpark by a passing plain clothes police car packed with armed Flying Squad detectives just about to go off duty.

McKinley didn't fare too badly in court. His gun hadn't been loaded; Miller and Wallace reckoned he'd have sawn the wrong end off his shotgun given the chance and there was no way they were going to let him loose with a loaded gun. That, coupled with a surprising lack of previous convictions, kept the sentence down and he was out in seven years with a criminal record and a nickname that stuck.

A bit thinner now than he looked in the newspaper photograph, taken as he had left the Old Bailey handcuffed between two beefy police officers, McKinley was scowling in much the same way.

Eventually his patience snapped and he turned to his right, banging his glass down hard on the bar.

'Why don't you two twats just piss off?' he thundered, but he didn't wait for an answer, just drew back his massive fist and smacked the shorter one in the mouth, sending him spinning and staggering across the bar, blood streaming from his splattered lips.

His friend took a step back and put his hand inside his leather jacket, bringing out what looked to be a butcher's knife wrapped in cardboard which he stripped off to reveal a polished steel blade. McKinley seemed not to notice and pulled back his fist again.

I thought the sound of the lemonade bottle in the barman's hand would have made much more noise when it connected with the back of McKinley's head, but it didn't smash or even crack, it just went 'thunk' and McKinley's legs folded up like a collapsing deck-chair and he slumped to the floor. The two lads decided that discretion was the better part of valour and made for the door.

'Are you going to bar him?' I asked the barman as together we helped the unconscious McKinley to an empty seat by the gents.

'Are you joking?' he replied. 'Would you try to stop him coming in? Besides, he was provoked. McKinley's OK so long as he's left alone.'

The sleeping giant began growling and I didn't want to be around when he woke up with a sore head, so I said I'd be back and walked out into the cold night air. One down, three to go.

Killers come in many forms. The old man going too fast in a car and mowing down a child on a zebra crossing. The thug with a knife who wants your wallet and doesn't care what he does to get it. The pensioner who can't stand to see his wife suffering from incurable arthritis any more and pushes a pillow against her face. The soldier firing his gun in the heat of battle.

The poisoner, the strangler, the axe murderer. There are men you can hire to kill, men who'll beat in a man's skull for a few hundred pounds. There are men whom you'll never meet, who will kill for a six-figure sum paid into a Swiss bank account, half in advance, half on completion. The world is full of killers, and so are the prisons.

Me, I could never take a life. My father took me when

I was twelve years old to his brother's grouse moor near Inverness and helped me to fire his favourite twelve bore, rubbing my shoulder better when it hurt, kidding me for missing, not knowing that I didn't want to hurt the birds or his feelings and pretending to be in pain was the only way to save both.

I guess he understood because the next time he tried was when I was fifteen, but I hadn't changed and this time I was old enough to tell him so, to tell him that blasting birds with shotguns wasn't my idea of fun and what was the point of raising birds just to shoot them out of the air and honest, father, I'd really rather not. It did hurt him, I know, but he didn't say anything and the guns went back to his study and he never took them out of the guncase other than to clean them from that day on.

He was of the old school, my father, huntin', shootin' and fishin', until a riding accident put paid to all but the fishing. Even that pleasure caused him pain, standing thigh high in fast flowing freezing water flicking flies at salmon, and his orthopaedic surgeon told him more than once that it was doing him no good. Humbug, my father told him, fishing and work are the only pleasures I've got left and I'm damned if you're going to take either away from me. He reckoned that the only good advice the surgeon ever gave him was to lie on the floor if the pain got too bad. It seemed to work and I'd often go into his study and find him lying on his back with his ebony stick by his side, reading one of his leather-bound books or going over a balance sheet, Bach playing on the stereo.

I'd sit by him and he would explain things like shareholders' funds, liabilities and provisions, loan capital; and by the time I was fourteen I could read a balance sheet and profit and loss account like a comic, understanding how a company operated just by looking at the figures. I was hooked faster than a careless salmon, which is exactly what he'd intended, because he had my career mapped out from the time I was born and there was no way on God's earth that I wasn't going to end up in my uncle's merchant bank.

He was a gentle man, and a gentleman, and other than where foxes, grouse and salmon were concerned he lacked the killer instinct. I was the same. I might not have inherited his passion for country pursuits but he had taught me to be honourable in business, never to cheat or lie, and to feel guilty if I broke any of his rules and now that was holding me back, and I had to find a killer because I knew I wouldn't be able to do the job myself.

Killers come in many forms but I wanted a professional, a mercenary. I'd arranged for a newsagent near my flat in Earl's Court to get me a copy of *Professional Soldier* magazine. It took him two weeks to get hold of it, and by the time he gave it to me it was a month out of date. It's one of the few places where mercenaries actually advertise their services between pages devoted to a thousand and one ways of killing silently and what's new in portable rocket launchers. You can buy everything you need to start or fight a war through the adverts in *Professional Soldier*, from jungle clothing and survival rations to the latest military hardware. You can also buy men. I picked out three possibilities and circled them in blue Biro.

SAS-trained small-arms expert requires work, distance no object. Experience in explosives, anti-tank combat and hand-to-hand. Box No. 156.

Have gun, will travel. Does anyone out there need a combat vet who wants a piece of the action? London based. Box No. 324

Ex-para needs work. Anything considered. Box No. 512

I wrote the same letter to all three, telling them that I had an interesting proposition to put to them, that I'd pay well and that they were to phone me at the flat if they were interested. I stuck the envelopes down, put on first-class stamps and walked down the two flights of stairs to the street and put them in the nearest post box. The first call came two weeks later from mercenary number one, the SAS expert.

'You the man with an interesting proposition?' asked a rough Liverpool accent. 'This is Box 156.'

'You've got the right number,' I said. 'Who are you?'

'First things first. What's the job, where is it and how much are you paying?'

'I'd rather meet you first, then we can go over the details.'

'When and where?'

'The American Bar at the Savoy Hotel, Wednesday lunchtime, say half past one. How will I recognize you?'

'You won't. I'll find you. Carry a copy of *The Times*.'

'I imagine most of the people in the Savoy would be reading *The Times*. Make it the *Mirror*. I'll be wearing a dark blue suit and a red tie and I'll be sitting at the bar.'

'I'll be there.'

* * *

Wednesday at one o'clock, I got out of a taxi on the Strand and walked past the Savoy Taylors Guild to the huge canopy that marks the entrance to the Savoy. Across the road stonecleaners were scouring the dirt off the National Westminster Bank, and a thin film of white dust settled on my shoes. Porters in the Savoy's green and yellow livery were loading calfskin suitcases into a blue Daimler, while a suntanned executive sorted through his wallet. All were covered in white flecks of dust.

The foyer was almost deserted, so at least my friend Box 156 wouldn't have any trouble recognizing me. I dropped the *Mirror* onto the bar and asked for a Tamdhu as I slipped onto the stool. Caricatures of Liza Minelli, Lauren Bacall, Ginger Rogers, Fred Astaire and Greta Garbo, all by Almud Bonhorst, glared down at me from the walls and I raised my glass to them. I was proud to be performing in front of Hollywood's finest.

I spotted him as soon as he walked into the bar. He was impossible to miss: close cropped hair, a camouflage combat jacket and scruffy jeans. The boots were cherry red. He walked with his feet splayed outward, hands thrust deep into the pockets of his jacket as his head jerked left and right like a startled rabbit. Somehow I'd managed to lumber myself with a twenty-four carat headbanger, and if the only thing identifying me had been a copy of *The Times* I could have got rid of it and played innocent, but I was labelled as clearly as a jar of Nescafé at Sainsburys. Not only was I the only man in the Savoy carrying a copy of the *Mirror* and wearing a blue suit and red tie, but I was also the only person in the bar. All that was missing was a large neon sign above my head flashing the word 'sucker'. Hell, hell, hell.

'You the man with the mission?' he asked from six feet away. No, son, I'm the Avon lady. The barman's eyebrows shot up like clay pigeons, his chin dropped and my stomach turned over. Hell, hell, hell, should I bluff or run?

'Could be,' I said. 'What can I get you?'

'Guinness, a pint. And a packet of crisps. Salt and vinegar.' The drink he got, the crisps were off. I took him over to a table by the baby grand piano where he could nibble at the stuffed olives and not be within earshot of the barman.

'So what are you up to?' he asked, a piece of olive stuck firmly in the gap between his front teeth. I leant back in the decidedly uncomfortable chair, crossed my legs and narrowed my eyes. Bluff or run? No question about it. I might as well enjoy myself.

'First things first,' I said. 'Have you been in action before?' He looked uncomfortable, shifting in his seat and rubbing his boots together.

'Not as such, no, but I spent four years with an SAS territorial regiment, trained with them in Wales, live firing, explosives, the works.'

'Parachuting?'

'Some.'

'Freefall?'

'No, but I made four static line jumps.'

'That'll be a problem, the job I'm setting up requires a HALO from twenty thousand feet with full kit, at night. And there could be enemy fire.'

'Jesus, what are you planning?'

'I'm not planning anything, the planning has already been done. I'm just handling the recruitment. Two hundred men, hand-picked, for the Sultan of a small but very rich country out in the Middle East. Or more accurately the brother of the Sultan who wants to take over. There's a lot of money at stake because the country is swimming in oil. Our team will be freefalling in from a couple of Hercules and splitting into three sections, taking out the palace, the oil fields and the communication systems.

'The whole mission should take less than twelve hours, and we'll be taking no prisoners, on either side. In fact that's one of the stipulations of the job. A suicide pill will be placed inside a fake tooth. The Sultan's brother can't afford to have anything go wrong with the attack, and if it does he wants to make sure there's nobody around to tell tales. And the sort of money he's paying he's entitled to expect that.'

By now the young 'SAS expert' was sweating and his cheeks were flushed. It was difficult to tell if it was the thought of having a dentist's drill in his mouth or swallowing poison or the Savoy's chair which was causing him the most distress. Hell, if he swallowed this story he'd swallow anything, the tooth, the poison, even the chair.

'We're going in with bazookas, mobile missile launchers, grenades, the works. It should be one hell of a war. And if, I mean when, we take over there's a good chance we'll be kept on as the new Sultan's bodyguard, unless the cunning old bastard tries some sort of double cross.

'He'll also be looking for help on the interrogation side afterwards. It seems the present Sultan has been tucking away hundreds of millions of dollars in bank accounts all around the world and our employer would obviously like to know where the money is. I hope you've got a strong stomach, it's liable to get a bit messy.'

I don't know what the guy was looking for, cheap thrills,

hard experience to beef up his part-time toy soldiering or what, but my Arabian tales had put the wind up him and no mistake. He'd stopped chewing on the stuffed olives and most of his pint was untouched.

'Well, I'm your man,' he said, and neither of us believed him for a moment. I took a few details from him, told him I'd be in touch and off he went into the wide blue yonder, a first-class prat and a second-class time-waster. I wanted a killer and I'd turned up a pussycat.

I never did hear from the *Have gun, will travel* vet. Maybe it was a joke, maybe he was lying bleeding to death on some far-off battlefield I couldn't pronounce in a month of Remembrance Sundays, or crouching in ambush high in the hills of Afghanistan, maybe I've just got an overactive imagination, who knows? I never found out, anyway.

The ex-para got in touch two days after the headbanger. Quiet, confident, no messing about. His name was Jim Iwanek, he'd left the Paras eighteen months ago and had been working as a bodyguard for a casino operator until recently. Where could we meet? I wasn't superstitious so the Savoy seemed as good a place as any. He agreed. 'I'm about five-eleven, short black curly hair and I'll have on a brown check sports jacket,' he said, like a policeman giving evidence from his notebook. 'I look forward to meeting you.'

He was bang on time and just as he'd described. OK, he missed out the brown cord trousers, the brown brogues, the crisp white shirt and the light brown tie, but who's counting?

I went over and introduced myself, bought him a double Teachers and took him to the table by the piano.

There was another thing he hadn't mentioned, his eyes. They were blue, a cold blue, difficult to read until maybe it was too late. Eyes that looked me over, measuring me up, calculating distances and angles, eyes that could just as easily work out twenty-four different ways of killing me bare-handed as they could spot a lie before it left my lips. You can tell a lot from a man's eyes: if he's lying, how he'll react to stress, sometimes even what he's thinking. Iwanek's eyes were as cold and hard as ice daggers and he hardly blinked as he crossed his legs, smoothed out the creases in his trousers and asked me what it was I was offering.

I took a sip of my whisky. He hadn't touched his. 'I'm thirty-two years old and I am what's called a corporate financier, a sort of merchant banker without a bank. I help arrange bank loans, company takeovers, share flotations, that sort of thing. Sometimes I act as a company doctor, find out where a firm is going wrong, why it's losing money, suggest a remedy. I make a lot of money doing what I do because I do it well, very well. I'm an expert and in the City I'm a survivor. More than that, I'm a winner. But I have a problem, a big problem, and it's one that I can't cope with own my own.'

Iwanek hadn't moved while I talked, but I knew I was being measured up, assessed, and labelled as either truthful or not to be trusted.

He leant back in his chair and steepled his fingers under his broad chin. His hands were smooth with long, delicate fingers and perfect, well-manicured nails. A stainless steel watch peeped out of his left sleeve as he gently tapped his two index fingers against his upper lip and looked into my soul.

'I've been wronged, badly wronged, and I'm out for revenge. Two men have done me a grave injustice, just how bad I can't tell you and maybe I never will but they deserve what's coming to them. You'll have to trust me on that score.

'One is a drugs dealer and property developer with very nasty criminal connections and a stack of dangerous friends. The other is one of his associates, a business man of sorts, a whizz kid who's acting as a front for the other guy's money.

'If these guys had crossed me in the City, if it had been business, then I could have coped on my own, I could have fought back. If they'd broken the law I could have gone to the police, or sued, but they were far too clever for that.'

'What did they do?' he asked.

'I can't tell you that. I just need your help, and I'm prepared to pay for it. And to pay well.'

'You want them killed,' he said, and it was a statement, not a question.

'I want them dead, or put away for a long time. And I don't want to be directly involved. I have a conscience, Jim, a set of values that was drilled into me from a very early age so no, I couldn't point a gun at either of them and pull the trigger.'

'You want someone else to do your dirty work.' Another statement.

'Yes, but not in the way you think. Sure, I could go into any of a dozen pubs in the East End, spend a little money and have their legs broken, maybe even killed. What would it cost me, a few hundred pounds? I could do that, but I couldn't live with myself afterwards. All my time working in the City I've been honest, I've never doublecrossed anybody or deliberately hurt them. My word is my bond might sound corny in this day and age but that's what my father taught me and those are the values that I've stuck to. I can't betray him or myself, and I won't even try.'

'It's not corny, but it puts you in a very difficult position. Maybe an impossible position. You want two men dead yet you're going around saying "thou shalt not kill" like some pious prophet. Either put up or shut up, you can't have it both ways. And if it's an assassin you want then you've got the wrong man. I've killed, but in battle and that's a whole different ball game. It's one thing to run down a Falklands hill firing at men trying to kill you, it's another to sneak up and shoot someone in the back of the neck. Soldiers have standards, too, and backshooting isn't one of them.' He started to get up, but I held out my hand and motioned him to sit down.

'You don't understand, just hear me out.' He settled back in the chair but there was a tenseness about him, an unease that was making both of us uncomfortable.

'One of the things I do best is to lay down strategies, to calculate how people will react in certain situations. To gauge the reactions of directors and shareholders, to anticipate the actions and reactions of others and to plan accordingly.

'I have a plan, a set of actions which, if I put them into effect, will give me the result I'm looking for. I think I can get my revenge without pulling the trigger or paying someone to do it for me.'

'A set up,' he said. 'You're going to set them up.' He was smiling now.

'Yes, and for that I'm going to need help, people with skills I don't have. It's the same in business. You need advice, you bring in a consultant, you pay him to provide the services and knowledge you don't have yourself. It works with computers, marketing, public relations, so why shouldn't it work for me? I need expertise which you have and I'm willing to pay for it.'

I leant forward and looked into the ice blue eyes. 'I'm not going to lie to you and say that I'm putting all my cards on the table. You're smart enough to know that I'll be keeping a couple of aces up my sleeve and probably a joker, too.

'I'm going to set these two creeps up to be knocked down, and I need your help. At some point I'm going to get involved with drugs dealers and I need someone who can handle a gun, someone who is obviously prepared to use it. I'm virtually certain that you won't have to fire it and I'm damn sure you won't have to kill anyone, but I have to have someone who looks the part. And of course it'll be useful to have someone who isn't afraid to shoot just in case anything goes wrong. Are you in?'

'I'm in,' he said.

'I don't know when I'll be going ahead but from start to finish the whole operation should take less than a month. I think I'll need you for two days, and I'm willing to pay you five thousand pounds. What I propose to do is to give you a retainer of a thousand, a show of good faith on my part. When I know I'm ready I'll give you a further thousand and the balance on completion. When I ring I'll need you right away, so if you're taking on anything else make sure you can leave at short notice, like immediately.' I took out a brown envelope from my inside jacket pocket and handed it to him. He didn't even bother to count the twenty pound notes inside. I passed him a card and asked him to write down a number where he could be contacted, any hour day or night.

'You're forgetting something,' he said. I raised my eyebrows. 'The gun,' he said.

'I assumed you could provide that.'

'You assumed right, but we have to decide what we're going to use and you're going to have to pay for it.'

'What do you suggest, something small?'

'No. You want to show we mean business so you want something impressive. If you're going to kill it doesn't matter what it looks like so long as it does the job. If you mean what you say about not wanting to kill then you want something threatening. That's why so many villains use sawn-off shotguns. OK, I know you can get them without individual licences and the shot can't be identified, but at the end of the day they're used because they look so bloody big and menacing.

'Look down the barrels of a sawn-off twelve bore and you're guaranteed to piss yourself. Yet when you actually fire one they do little serious damage unless you're right up close. The shot spreads out all over the place, painful and uncomfortable but usually they don't do too much damage beyond a range of twenty feet.'

'That sounds fine by me – can you get one?'

'Sure – but it'll cost you – another four hundred pounds.'

I handed him the cash from my wallet. 'Look after it until I call you.'

'I'll be ready – and waiting. And don't forget, the retainer only holds me for one month.' He stood up to go, holding out his hand. I shook it firmly.

'Jim, it's been a pleasure doing business with you.'

Two down, two to go.

Highway robbery they used to call it, when a guy dressed in black astride a huge sweaty horse pointed a blunderbuss at stagecoach drivers and yelled 'stand and deliver'. It was easy money in days of yore, no police, no street lights, no problem. The only thing that could go wrong was the coach driver plucking up enough courage to draw a weapon and fight back. It didn't happen much. Even Get-Up McKinley could have made a go of it way back then. Things have changed, though.

Nowadays there is a much more profitable form of highway robbery, stealing cars. McKinley wasn't bright enough to break into a car and get the engine started without a key – hell's bells, he'd taken his driving test eight times – but there are hundreds of men and women around who make a nice living stealing cars.

Best profits are made at the luxury end of the market, the same as selling them legally. To make a profit selling Ford Escorts you need a high turnover, with Jaguars and Rolls-Royces you only have to get rid of a few a week to live well. Car thieves know that, so it's only the joyriders and youngsters who steal anything worth less than £10,000. The professionals stick to the classier models.

It's easy money, too. Step one, take an advance order from South Africa, Hong Kong, Australia, anywhere where they drive on the left is best. It's not too vital, though. If some Saudi prince wants to jump the queue for a Rolls it will be his chauffeur who'll be driving, so he's not going to be too bothered about which side the steering wheel is on. Step two, select your car. In London that's no great problem: stand in the Strand with your eyes shut and throw a spanner – chances are that it will bounce off a Porsche or a Rolls or a BMW. Find the car you want and break in, then drive it to the sort of garage where nobody is going to ask any awkward questions. That's the difficult part over.

The next step is to open the bonnet and get the chassis, frame and vehicle identification numbers and stroll along to any main Post Office and fill in Form V62 – it'll set you back all of two pounds. You'll have to sign a declaration that the original registration document hasn't been passed on by the previous owner or been lost, destroyed, mutilated or accidentally defaced. OK, so strictly speaking you are telling a lie but then you did steal the car in the first place so that shouldn't keep you awake at night.

Two weeks later, three at the most, your new registration documents arrive from DVLC Swansea – isn't new technology wonderful? They handle more than a thousand of the V62 forms every week and they don't bother checking – they haven't the time or the resources.

You, sir, are now the proud owner of a luxury car complete with relevant documents. Drive it into a crate or container and deliver it to the nearest docks. Simple. It's big business – in Britain alone a car is stolen every six minutes and never recovered. Right now Scotland Yard's C10 Stolen Vehicle Investigation Branch is looking internationally for more than twelve hundred Mercedes, a thousand Jaguars, two hundred and fifty Porsches and a hundred Rolls-Royces. They've more chance of finding Lord Lucan than of turning them up.

The hardest part of the whole operation is actually getting inside the car, and for that you need a professional. I don't know how to do it, you probably don't, you need someone with experience, someone who can deal with central locking systems, and who won't panic when a policeman taps him on the shoulder and says, 'Having trouble getting into your car, sir? Can I be of help?'

The trouble is car thieves don't advertise, you only hear about the amateurs who get caught and appear in the magistrates' courts, and I wasn't after an amateur.

I'd rented a lock-up garage a couple of hundred yards from my flat, and the morning after I'd met Iwanek in the Savoy I picked up the keys off the lounge table and walked down the two flights of stairs and into the early sun. It was a short walk to the garage and I unlocked the up-and-over door and went inside, pulling it closed behind me.

I switched on the light and it gleamed off a brand new red Porsche 911, well, almost brand new, anyway. I'd bought it nine months ago as a present to myself after handling the flotation of a local radio station. The fee I earned for placing the shares on the Unlisted Securities Market was more than enough to pay for the Porsche, and what the hell, you only live once. That was before my mother died in a car accident, though; that had taken most of the pleasure out of driving.

In the corner was a second-hand blue and white Honda 70cc that I'd picked up for £120 through an advert in the London *Standard*, and a full set of mechanics' tools that had set me back five times that figure. I took off my pullover and jeans and slipped on a pair of brand new green overalls and got down to what I knew was going to be several days of hard work.

It took me a full day to get the head off the engine, and two hours to mangle the insides of the cylinders and give it the sort of treatment it wouldn't have had with twenty-five years of constant use – Mr Porsche would have cried his eyes out, and to be honest I felt pretty bad at ruining one of the best cars I'd ever driven.

A Porsche mechanic could have done the job a lot quicker but that would have been like asking a plastic surgeon to amputate a leg, and besides, no mechanic in his right mind would cripple a car without wondering why. It took me another day and a half to put the bits back together again; I only went back to the flat to eat and sleep and I eventually emerged from the garage with an aching back, my skin and hair dirty and oily and my hands covered in cuts and bruises, but the Porsche was well and truly knackered.

Back in the flat, after showering and throwing away the stained overalls, I rang up a Porsche dealer and asked for the price of a new engine. Ouch. I spent the next week driving around as many backstreet garages as I could find, tucked away in unfashionable mews, hidden under railway arches and behind blocks of rundown flats in areas which were in no danger of ever becoming gentrified.

Most of the mechanics just sucked their teeth and said they couldn't even begin to tackle a masterpiece of Teutonic engineering that was obviously on its last legs, several suggested I tried a Porsche dealer and a couple quoted a price which wasn't far off the official cost and told me it would take weeks, if not months, to get a new engine.

Eventually I struck gold. His name was Bert Cook and his lock-up garage in Camden wasn't much bigger than mine. He was bent over a yellow Jag which had seen better times when I drove up, and he waited until the

Porsche juddered to a halt before he came over, rubbing greasy hands on a piece of grey cloth hanging out of his overall pocket.

'Sounds rough,' he said, rubbing his pencil-thin moustache below a mottled, bulbous nose. 'Very rough. Cylinders are definitely on their way out, you're kicking out a lot of smoke.' He wiped his nose on the greasy cloth.

'Performance is right down, too,' I said. 'It used to kick you in the pants when you put your foot down, but now it's worse than a twelve-year-old Cortina. Haven't had it that long either.'

'Should still be under warranty, then?' he said, putting the cloth back in his pocket, grease smeared over his nose.

I tried to look sheepish, a guilty schoolboy caught with his pockets full of stolen apples. 'I'd rather get it done on the QT, actually.'

'Ah,' he sighed, and winked. 'I get your drift. Well, I might be able to help. Hang on while I make a call.'

He busied off to the back of his lock-up, keen to help now that he reckoned he knew the score. When somebody wants to pay good money to fix a car that's still under warranty that can mean only one thing. And if he thought my pride and joy was stolen, who was I to put him right?

He came back after five minutes, a grin on his oil-stained face. Bert just happened to have a friend who had a friend who could get me a complete Porsche engine for half the price the dealer had wanted, including fitting, no questions asked.

'Have to be a cash deal, though,' he said. 'You bring her in Saturday morning and she'll be back with you by Sunday night.' I tried to look relieved and grateful, shook Bert by the greasy hand and drove back to Earl's Court and parked my battered Porsche.

An hour later I was back in Camden, this time on the Honda in a massive black anorak, red crash helmet and yellow plastic trousers, a clipboard pinned to the handle-bars, just one of the hundreds of would-be cabbies doing the Knowledge in London.

It was four o'clock, Thursday afternoon, and if Bert wanted my Porsche in on Saturday morning the chances were that he'd be going off for the engine tonight or tomorrow. I felt lucky, and an hour after I arrived back at his garage he locked up and walked over to a battered red pick-up. I was about a hundred yards down the road so he didn't hear me start up the bike. He pulled out from the pavement, grey smoke belching from the exhaust, and I followed as he turned into Camden High Street and down past Euston Station and its throngs of home-going commuters.

There was no problem at all in keeping up with him, in the rush hour traffic the Honda was much faster than his truck and it was so distinctive I could hang well back.

He drove through Bloomsbury, and before long we were over the Thames and heading for Battersea. I felt luckier and fifteen minutes later he pulled up in front of another lock-up garage, much the same as his own except this one had the legend 'Kleen Karparts' above the brown-painted twin doors.

Bert wiped his nose again on the dirty cloth and sounded his horn three times. A door opened and he disappeared inside. Kleen Karparts was in the middle of a row of small businesses, a bathroom shop with suites for £199, a bookmakers, three or four shops with shutters down and 'For Sale' signs up and a couple which were open for business but with nothing in the windows to give a clue as to what they sold.

At the end of the road was a narrow passage which led to a muddy track behind the backyards of the shops. Karparts was fourth from the end and set into the wall there was a weatherbeaten door painted the same dirty brown as the front entrance. The door had warped badly and by pressing against it I could get a pretty clear view of what was going on inside.

A man wearing dark blue overalls and a welding visor was cutting away at what appeared to be a brand new Mercedes, and as I watched he pulled away the rear wing in a clatter of metal. At the front of the car a young lad, sixteen or seventeen at the most, was using a winch to take out the engine. There were two or three other cars in the back yard in various stages of being stripped, and one of them looked like a Porsche, but as there was virtually just a chassis left it was difficult to tell. Lying around were piles of electric wiring, headlamps, carbs, bumpers, enough parts to build yourself several complete cars if only you could work out how to put them back together again.

Another youth came into view, small and dark and wearing a black leather motorcycle jacket, laughing with Bert who was wiping his nose yet again. They walked up to the man in the welding visor who had now moved over to the driver's side. He noticed the two of them, switched off his cylinders and pulled away his visor revealing a crop of purple hair and three gold earrings in one ear.

'Dinah,' said Bert. 'How's it going?'

'Triffic,' replied Dinah as he pulled at his virgin ear. 'Should have these done by tonight and then I'll start cutting up the chassis for scrap. I can't strip them fast enough, we've done two Mercs this week and I've got a backlog of orders for Jags, BMWs, the lot. I might even have to go legit.'

'I bet,' said Bert. 'The Porsche ready?'

'It's inside. Can I do you for anything else, body panels, lights, windows?'

'No thanks, Dinah, just the engine, that's all I need for this job. I'll tell you what, though. I'm going to be needing a rear axle for a Merc 500 SL some time in the next couple of weeks, maybe a gearbox too. I'll give you a bell.'

'Consider it done, there's always a market for Merc parts. Not the easiest cars to get hold of, though, but I'm working on it.'

'Yes, well, you know what they say, Dinah, practice makes perfect, and when it comes to getting hold of cars there's no one getting more practice than you.'

'Nice of you to say so, Bert, but I'm still not going to give you a discount. Harry, give Bert a hand with the Porsche engine and for God's sake count the money first.' He reached up and pulled the visor down and turned back to the Mercedes, laughing as the two men walked back towards the garage.

I crept back down the passage and waited at the entrance to the road until the two men came into view, pushing a mobile winch which they used to load what seemed to be a brand new engine onto Bert's pick-up. He pulled himself into the driver's cab, started it with a shudder and drove off, smoke still pouring from the rusty exhaust.

There was a pub opposite Karparts, a run-down drinking man's den, the varnish on the windows cracking with age and the rough-cast stained where rainwater had flooded down from a blocked gutter. I stripped off my waterproof gear and pushed it into the carrier on the back of the bike and walked inside the gloomy bar.

The ex-boxer of a barman asked, 'What can I get you,

chief?' and I paid for a whisky and sat at a creaky circular table circa 1950 in the corner facing the door. Twenty minutes later Dinah came in, his overalls swapped for jeans and a grubby green sweater which clashed perfectly with his purple hair. With him were the two youngsters from Karparts, and Dinah brought out a wad of five-pound notes from his back pocket to pay for a round. At the back of the pub was a pool table and after a few minutes Dinah's companions walked over, pushed in two ten-pence pieces and started to play. I picked up my glass and went over to Dinah, sitting alone at the bar.

'How's it going, Dinah?' I asked.

He turned from his glass and looked me up and down. 'Do I know you?' he asked.

'Not yet, Dinah, but you will, you will. I need a car and I think you're just the chap to help me get it.'

He shook his head. 'Try a garage, mate – I deal in parts and spares.'

'Second-hand parts by the look of it, and most of them hot enough to cook sausages on.'

'What are you getting at? You the law?'

'Do I look like the police?'

'As a matter of fact you do. Sod off and leave me alone.'

'Look, Dinah, the fact that I'm here talking to you in the pub and not bursting into your yard with a search warrant should prove to you that I'm not a cop, but if you want I could give them a ring. I think they'd be fascinated to hear about the operation you're running over there. Pays well does it?'

'What operation? What do you think I am, a surgeon?'

'Of sorts, Dinah, of sorts. How did you get a name

like Dinah in the first place? Parents expecting a girl, were they?'

The change of subject took him by surprise and his mouth hung open in amazement. 'My name's Maurice, Maurice Dancer—'

'I don't believe it,' I said interrupting. 'Maurice Dancer? Somebody in your family must have had a sense of humour. Had a tough time at school did you?'

He shrugged. 'Yeah, I guess so. For a while, anyway, then Maurice was shortened to Mo and then I got the car bug and got stuck with the nickname Dyna-Mo and that got shortened to Dinah. What's it to you, anyway?'

'I just want a chat, Dinah, that's all. Let me get you another. What are you having?'

'Bitter, a pint.'

'OK.'

'And a double whisky.'

'Expensive tastes, Dinah, can you afford them?'

'If you're paying, I don't have to. Get us a meat pie as well, hey? I haven't eaten today.'

I bought Dinah his supper, and we went over to the corner table where I watched his two mates scuffing the pool table and spilling lager down the pockets as Dinah attacked his pie and drank his whisky in two swallows.

'What's your game?' he asked finally, brushing crumbs onto the floor and picking up his beer.

'As I said, Dinah, I need a car, and I think you're just the man to get it for me.'

'But I've already told you that selling cars isn't my game.'

'Dinah, I'm not stupid. I know exactly what your game is. And it's not Subbuteo.'

'What are you getting at?' he asked, and started tearing a soggy beermat into tiny pieces, flicking them into a dirty ashtray.

'Dinah, it's simple. You're a car thief, and I presume you're a good one. Your yard over the road is packed with parts you've taken from almost new cars, you steal them and strip anything of value. The chassis and any other identifiable bits you probably sell for scrap. Am I right?'

He said nothing, his eyes fixed on the table, fingers busy destroying the wet cardboard.

He obviously wasn't going to reply, so I continued. Maurice Dancer, this is your life. 'It's virtually the perfect crime. The only risk is when you actually take the car away, and the way you look you'd probably be able to claim it was a first offence and that all you were doing was taking it for a joyride, officer, and you're very sorry but it won't happen again, your honour, because you're the product of a broken home and an uncaring Government and you'll get nothing worse than a few months' probation.

'But underneath that ludicrous purple hair I reckon there's a brain a bit too smart to be caught red-handed. Am I right?'

He looked up and smiled, showing crooked teeth. 'Maybe. Maybe you are. But I still don't know what you want from me.'

'You asked me what your operation is, Dinah. Well, I think you're making a nice living selling bits of cars that would cost an arm and a leg if you bought them honestly. Luxury cars, the Rollers, the Mercs, the Porsches, cars where you're talking three figures for a spare wheel and four for an engine.

'You supply a need, Dinah, like all good entrepreneurs.

You sell parts, no questions asked, to cut-price mechanics. They get the spares they need, you get a roll of fivers in your back pocket. Everyone's happy, the only loser is the guy whose car you've knicked and he'll be able to claim on his insurance.

'The beauty of the scheme is that once you've taken the cars apart all the evidence is gone, it's virtually impossible to trace things like axles, body panels, windscreens and lights. And once you've changed the numbers, selling an engine is no problem. I like it, Dinah, I like it a lot. If a business like yours qualified for the Business Expansion Scheme, you'd have investors queuing up halfway round the block.'

'I haven't stolen a car from you, have I?' asked Dinah, realization breaking across his face like an early dawn.

'No, Dinah, you haven't.'

'Thank God for that. That's been a nightmare of mine for years, that one day somebody will tap me on the shoulder and ask for their motor back before plastering me all over the wall. There's some very dodgy people driving Rollers, you know?'

'You don't have to tell me, Dinah. Now listen. I want you to steal a car for me. Two cars to be precise, a Merc and a Rolls.'

'No sooner done than said. Any particular colour?'

'Not just a particular colour, I want two particular cars. And I don't want to keep them.' His eyes brightened. 'And I don't want you to strip them, either, so you can forget any thoughts you had on that score. I want to borrow them and return them so that no one is any the wiser.'

'You planning a robbery or something? If you are you can count me out. I'll steal cars, sure, but that's as far as I go.'

Villains are like that, each to their own. They specialize and are usually reluctant to operate in territory they're unfamiliar with. They might progress upwards through the criminal hierarchy, acquiring new skills, but at no point would a safeblower get involved with a fraudster, or vice versa. Dinah would no more consider taking part in a robbery, no matter how far removed he was, than a solicitor would think about extracting a tooth.

'No, Dinah, I'm not planning a robbery, but I'm not prepared to tell you why I need the motors. What I am prepared to do is to offer you a thousand a car, half in advance. Then, when I'm ready, I want you to break into the Rolls and wire it so that I can drive it. I'll use it for a couple of days and then I want it put back in perfect condition. The Merc's a different matter. All I want you to do there is to open the boot and relock it. That's all you have to do, Dinah, and I'll pay you two grand.'

'Mine's a pint, and you're on.'

I got Dinah his pint from the bar and stood it in front of him along with the half-inch thick brown envelope I'd been carrying in my inside pocket.

'One other thing, Dinah. This buys your silence as well. Don't let your two pals in on the act, no subcontracting. I'm paying for you. And I want a telephone number where I can reach you. The job will be at short notice, very short notice. It could be any time within the next three or four weeks. Just be ready.'

He wrote a telephone number on a scrap of paper and raised his glass. 'To a long and profitable partnership,' he said.

'No, Dinah, to a short and profitable one. Make no

mistake, this is a one-off job, there'll be no repeat fees. I'll be in touch.'

Back outside, I pulled on the waterproofs and crash helmet and drove back to Earl's Court where I dumped them with the bike behind a busy service station and walked to the flat. Three down, one to go.

I'd gone to a lot of trouble to find Dinah but it had been worth it, and now I had three in the bag and all I needed to complete the set was a woman. Not just any woman but one who would sleep with a man for money, and do a few other extra little tasks for me. Got it in one, I was after a prostitute, but the last thing I wanted was a woman who looked like a whore. That would have been a dead giveaway, like using a plastic maggot to catch a wily old pike. No, what I needed was something luscious, a tasty morsel that the old predator would fall for hook, line and sinker.

Bleached hair, heavily rouged cheeks and thick eyeliner were out, she'd have to be young, intelligent and enthusiastic, but a professional. The sort of girl you'd be happy to see marry your brother, if you had a brother and if he was the marrying kind. My brother, David, isn't. And he never will be.

So, step one, find your whore. That didn't appear to be a major problem, they're not hard to find in a big city. Or in a small town come to that. In Glasgow you'll find them around Blythswood Square, huddling on street corners waiting for a lift to the nearest multi-storey carpark where lusts are satisfied, almost, for as little as ten pounds.

Birmingham, Manchester, Bristol, they've all got their red light areas, and what the hell I was in London which has more whores per head of population than anywhere else in Britain. One of the growth industries, servicing the foreign tourists and visiting businessmen.

There was no way I was going to go kerb crawling around St Pancras or walking through Soho on the off chance that I'd bump into the perfect pro to complete my gang of four. The only thing I'd pick up that way was an infectious disease. Doctor, doctor, I think I've got Hermes. Don't you mean Herpes? No, I think I'm a carrier. I'd been lucky getting Iwanek so I was pretty impressed with the power of advertising. At a local newsagent, not the one who'd got me *Professional Soldier*, I picked up a couple of guides to what's on in London and also managed to find a contact magazine, 'Middle-aged executive with own house and understanding wife seeks young blonde with big breasts for friendship with a view to unnatural sex', you know the sort of thing.

The contact magazine was worse than useless and went straight in the bin. One of the London guides had a series of adverts for massage parlours and private masseurs that looked more promising, some of them offering a rub down in private apartments, discipline in your own home, a few were even in Arabic.

Five seemed hopeful, three in the West End, one in the City and another south of the Thames. I rang them all and the Kennington number was answered by a man so that was a definite non starter. The other four sounded like the same girl, a treacly deep voice, stroking the back of my neck and tickling me under the chin, all could fit me in, when did I want to come round, what was my name, they looked forward to seeing me.

Despite the personal nature of the adverts the three in the West End were all massage parlours, the only privacy was in the form of tiny cubicles and a production line of girls in bikinis and sweat, cold eyes and warm hands. I didn't bother revealing I was a reporter, I just left.

The girl in the City turned out to be five feet four,, long blonde hair and blue eyes and living on the tenth floor of one of the tower blocks in the Barbican complex. She was in her late thirties with a good figure that was starting to go and small lines around her eyes that crinkled as she smiled but threatened to become deep ravines within a few years. But she was bright and warm and fun despite being ten years older than I needed so I stayed for an hour and left her flat feeling a lot better than when I'd arrived. I'd paid her fifty pounds in advance, but as I went I gave her another ten pounds and I couldn't help smiling and nodding when she asked if she'd see me again. I was getting soft, but then I hadn't been too hard to start with. I decided to go up to Pitlochry to see David.

Shona picked me up at Edinburgh Airport and drove me the seventy miles to Shankland Hall in her Rover, or rather our Rover as it was leased to our company, Scottish Corporate Advisors. Shona and I had met at St Andrew's University, but while I cut my financial teeth in my uncle's merchant bank after getting a lower second-class degree, she pocketed a first with no trouble at all and went off to work for the stockbrokers Wood Mackenzie in Edinburgh in their research department, specializing in the retail sector, followed by a spell examining the inner workings of the gilt-edged market. When I decided to set up on my own she leapt at the chance of joining me. I was lucky to get her and now we were partners, equal partners.

As she settled back in the driving seat of the Rover she looked more like an aerobics instructor in one of the plusher dance studios, bright pink tracksuit, white tennis shoes and her long dark hair tied back in a pony tail with a pink ribbon. She looked about seventeen. But put her in a dark two-piece suit and she'd more than hold her own in any boardroom, big brown bedroom eyes or not. One very, very clever lady and she wasn't spoiled one iota by the fact that she knew it. I just wished she wouldn't keep teasing me about her superior degree, but that was a small price to pay.

She powered us past a removals lorry before turning and asking, 'How's the Big Smoke?'

'Big,' I said. 'And smokey. How's business?'

'How do you think? You've been away for almost a month and the cracks are starting to show.'

'You're a big girl, you can handle it.' She could, too, and the little girl lost act wasn't fooling anyone. She relished the opportunity of showing what she could do on her own.

'Do you want a rundown on what's happening?' she asked.

'No, Shona, not just now. Later.'

'Damn you, when are you coming back to work?'

I rested my hand on her knee but she jerked it away angrily. 'Soon,' I said. 'I only need a few more weeks, maybe a month.'

'It's been almost three months and that's time enough

for grieving. Getting back into harness would be the best thing for you.'

'Yes, doctor.'

'I mean it.'

'I know you do. I'll be back soon, I promise. How's David?'

'Missing you. Wants to know when he can live with you again. He keeps asking if you're dead, too. Don't leave him there too long – he panics. So do I.' Then she smiled to herself and pressed the accelerator hard to the floor. Little girl lost, indeed.

'They're looking after him all right?'

'Of course they are,' she replied with a toss of her pony tail. 'They're professionals, and the sort of money you're paying reflects that. The food's better than I'm getting. I'm thinking of taking a few of our clients there instead of to the North British. The service is probably better, too.'

She spent the rest of the drive filling me in on business, whether or not I wanted to hear. I had other things on my mind but I listened with half an ear, nodded when she asked if I agreed with the way she was handling things and offered her a few words of advice. She was doing fine.

We pulled into the gravelled drive which curved in front of the grey stone building that was Shankland Hall only two hours after I'd landed at Edinburgh. Originally built as the private residence of a wealthy tobacco baron who decided to devote his retirement to the pursuit of country pastimes, it had been sold to pay off death duties just after the Second World War and was now one of the best, and most expensive, private nursing homes north of the border. Tucked away in a sheltered valley to the east of Pitlochry it's a case of out of sight, out of mind for many of the residents, dumped there by uncaring relatives with money to spare. In David's case, though, it was a temporary home, he wouldn't be there long. I hoped.

He was waiting at the top of the stone steps leading to the large oak double doors, holding the arm of a nurse in a dazzlingly white starched uniform. He was jumping up and down with excitement and waving with his free hand. My daft brother.

As I got out of the car he left the nurse and ran down the steps to grab me around the neck, and he squeezed me so tight that I couldn't breathe. 'Missed you, missed you, missed you, missed you,' he whispered into my ear. 'Don't go, don't go, don't go.'

'It's all right,' I gasped, and reached behind my neck to unclasp his hands. I held them in front of me and looked into his brown eyes which were starting to fill with tears. 'It's all right, I'm here.'

A tear rolled down his plump cheek, dripped off his round chin and onto his blue linen trousers. David's my younger brother, my only brother, and he's nineteen years old. The only difference between David and you, me and the Duke of Edinburgh is that David was born with one extra chromosome in each of his cells, a tiny amount of genetic material that's enough to throw his whole body out of kilter and produce a baby that will never, ever, grow up to be 'normal'.

It happens in something like one out of every 660 births and they used to call them Mongols and now they call it Down's Syndrome but David is David and that's all there is to it. The doctors keep measuring his IQ and coming up with numbers between sixty and seventy which is bright for a Down's Syndrome adult but so low as to deny him a life on his own, not that he'd want one.

He is happy, most of the time, and fun and affectionate and occasionally flashes of intuition would come shining through like a lighthouse beam slicing through fog.

Then he'd spoil it by trying to eat his soup with a fork and laugh because he knew full well what he was doing – teasing me. He'd hug me and ask me to promise never to leave him and I'd say I wouldn't ever leave him for good and that he was safe with me. My daft brother.

'Go and say hello to Shona,' I said and pushed him away.

He rushed over to Shona and grabbed her from behind as she locked up the Rover, picked her off the ground and gave her a bear hug that made her gasp.

'Put me down, David,' she laughed. 'You're hurting.' But he wasn't, he knew his own strength and he knew by the way Shona was laughing that she was enjoying it. He giggled and put her down, seized her hand and then pulled her over to me and caught mine, linking the three of us together.

'All for one,' he shouted.

'And one for all,' we chorused. It was his favourite joke, but it was more than that, it bound us together and he knew that he could depend on us both.

Now he was laughing and giggling and squeezing my hand tight, swinging it back and forth. He'd been at Shankland Hall for about three months now, since the day after the funeral, and it wasn't doing him any good, I could see that.

His eyes flicked nervously from face to face, eager to please and anxious not to offend. Even Shona's visits weren't enough and she was getting to see him every couple of days, but he wouldn't be right until he was back in a house with me, knowing that I'd be home every night and there to read to him before he fell asleep.

'Come on, David,' I said. 'Let's go for a walk. Shona has to see the sister.'

'Man talk,' he giggled and released Shona's hand. As we walked down the drive and over the close-cropped lawn he kept turning back to look at her like a spaniel being taken away from his owner, but the tight grip on my hand showed that he was glad to be with me.

The lawns sloped down to a string of trees, an oak, a sprinkling of silver birch and a line of conifers marking the path of a stream that meandered across the estate.

David sat with his back against the oak, scratching like a cat while I lay on the ground beside him, picking tufts of grass and shredding them, staining my fingers bright green. It was a fresh, clean day, the sort of day for a picnic, a day for playing football or for just lying by a stream tickling trout. 'Shoes off,' I yelled and helped him pull off his big black boots and roll up his trouser legs. I followed suit and we were soon up to our knees in the cold, sparkling water.

David stomped and splashed and got us both so wet we were in line for a row from the sister when we got back. He soon tired me out and I dragged him over to a large, dry rock in the middle of the stream and we sat there with our feet dangling in the water.

He draped his arm across my shoulders and rested the top of his head against my neck, breathing deeply as if he were fast asleep. His legs were swinging gently, making slow whirlpools in the stream and he was humming quietly to himself, a tuneless tune with no structure, no pattern. I began talking, he loved to be talked to, following the rhythm of speech even when he couldn't always grasp the meaning. Empathy rather than understanding.

'I've run into a problem, David,' I said. 'I found Get-Up McKinley easily enough – I told you I would. It took me a couple of weeks to track him down and make friends with him but now he's on the payroll part-time. Sometimes he drives me about and sometimes I use him as a minder. It's his first steady job in a long time. Oh, and I found out why he's called Get-Up.'

I told him the story of how the unfortunate McKinley got lumbered with his nickname and he giggled, kicking water over me.

'I've found a good man with a gun, too. His name's Iwanek and he's one of the paratroopers who fought in the Falklands but now he's out of the army and he's been working as a bodyguard. I'm going to have to be very careful with him, he's very clever and very fit, if he decides to turn against me or to go it alone then I really will have problems.'

David looked worried and his grip tightened so I added quickly, 'Don't worry, I know what I'm doing, you know how carefully I've planned all this. Nothing can or will go wrong.' He relaxed again. 'Iwanek is providing his own gun and I'm going to give him a call when everything's set up.

'The car thief was easy, too. His name's Dinah, that's short for Dyna-Mo, and he's the strangest looking young man you could imagine. Remember those punks we saw when we went shopping in Princess Street before Christmas?' He nodded excitedly. 'Well, he wears clothes like them, a black leather jacket with shiny chains and scruffy jeans with holes and tears. And his hair is purple and spikey and he's got three gold earrings in one ear, like a pirate. But he's bright and there's nothing he doesn't know about cars and let's face it, who'd believe that a purple-haired punk was a top car thief?'

'Not me,' he laughed. 'He sounds fun.'

'Funny he is, but I'm not so sure about him being fun. He takes his work seriously and he's made a lot of money without ever getting caught. He's the least of our worries because we only have to use him twice and he has no way of knowing what he's getting involved in. And I know enough about him to make sure that he won't talk to anyone else about the deal.

'So I'm three-quarters of the way there, David, but I'm having trouble getting hold of a suitable girl.'

'Like Shona,' he said, suddenly serious and frowning slightly, forehead furrowed as he looked into my eyes, almost nose to nose, his hot breath on my lips. 'She's nice.'

'Shona's too nice, you daft brush. We want a woman of easy virtue, a high class lady of the night who'll charm her way into Ronnie Laing's pants and lead him astray. She's got to be pretty, witty and fun but hard enough to cope with a villain like Laing. And we've got to be able to trust her completely. She's a vital part of the plan, David, but I can't find her. The sort of girl we're after doesn't walk the streets and she doesn't have to advertise. What am I going to do?'

The question was rhetorical but David took it seriously, he shrugged and tilted his head from side to side like a budgie gazing at its reflection in a mirror. He was biting his lower lip with his uneven teeth, his face pained with concentration as he tried to help, feet now unmoving in the rushing water.

'Don't look so serious,' I chided, and ruffled his hair. 'I'll think of something. It's going to be all right. Trust me.'

Eventually he spoke, slowly and with a great deal of concentration. 'Tony like girls, you told me,' he said, eyes wide open, head tilted back, proud because maybe he'd found the solution.

Tony had come to stay with us three months ago, before I'd gone down south, and he'd delighted David with his stories of life in London and his visits to the Middle East and suddenly I realized what he was getting at. 'Sometimes you amaze me!' I yelled and dragged him to his feet and hugged him hard.

'Come on, back to the house, last one there's a cissy – and whatever you do don't blame me for your wet clothes.'

I scooped up our shoes and socks as he rushed off and I held back to let him win. We were both out of breath and panting when we reached Shona who was leaning against the Rover, smiling and waving. 'Having fun?' she shouted.

'Yes, yes, yes, yes,' chanted David. She helped him on with his shoes and socks and we went in for tea. Afterwards, as Shona and I drove away from Shankland Hall, I watched him waving goodbye from the top of the steps, still holding hands with the nurse, and even from the end of the drive I could see he was saying 'Don't go' over and over again.

'Sometimes he amazes me,' I said to no one in particular.

'Who?' she asked.

'David,' I said. 'My daft brother.'

She drove in silence, handling the car expertly in and out of the twisting bends back towards Edinburgh.

'I have to go back to London. Tonight,' I said and winced inwardly as her face fell.

'No, you don't,' she answered and flicked her pony tail in annoyance. 'I meant what I said about the cracks starting to show. I've got a couple of big headaches and I need your help.'

'Tell me,' I said, prepared to be convinced.

'The main one concerns Crest Electronics. I'm having trouble convincing them that they should go ahead with their employee share ownership scheme. They know they can afford it, they know the benefits it'll bring, and I've trotted out all the old arguments until I'm blue in the face. They've got one foot poised over the edge, they just have to be persuaded to take the plunge. I think you'd swing the balance. Will you stay?'

I couldn't help but smile. 'Yes, I'll stay. You knew I would.'

'I hoped.'

'One day,' I said. 'One day is all I can spare. Then I have to get back to London.' Tony could wait twenty-four hours.

'Agreed,' she said, and drove me to her Edinburgh flat where we spent the night, together but apart.

Shona and I had made the unspoken decision years ago not to get involved. Friends yes, lovers no. People who knew us as a pair found it hard to believe that it was possible for us to work so closely together and to perform as well as we did as a team without going to bed.

We'd never talked about it but it came to a head a couple of months after we'd set up Scottish Corporate Advisors, and were spending the night in a hotel in Aberdeen after helping an up-and-coming diving firm negotiate a six-figure loan from the Clydesdale Bank.

We'd booked separate rooms but we were so high on the adrenaline of a job well done that we spent most of the evening at Gerards, a top class restaurant, not just for the food and drink but for the sheer pleasure of each other's company, basking in the glow of mutual success. We were talking and laughing and touching as the waiters waited patiently to close up for the night, and then we reached the point where our eyes met and the air was thick and time stopped and we either had to take it further or kill it.

I can still remember the moment as we both silently came to the same conclusion, and we smiled and Shona shook her head slowly. What we had was too important, too special, too precious, to risk spoiling. It would follow a pattern that could end with us losing everything. I read it in a book once, one of Stephen King's I think, but I can't remember which one. 'First it was love,' he wrote, 'then it was like love, and then it was over.' Becoming lovers would have given it a beginning, a middle and an end, and I didn't want ever not to know Shona.

I guess what we had now was love without being lovers. And we had the business. We knew we were heading for the top, together but apart.

We were in the office bright and early going through the newspapers.

It's surprising just how much business you can pick up that way, from profiles of businessmen on the way up, recruitment advertisements pointing to a firm expanding and maybe in need of new capital, rumours of multinationals moving into Scotland to take advantage of Scottish Development Agency incentives and the twenty per cent unemployment rate, all were opportunities waiting to be grasped.

I ploughed through the *Glasgow Herald* while Shona read the *Scotsman*. Glasgow and Edinburgh are separated by a forty-minute train ride but they're poles apart, and nowhere is that more reflected than in their newspapers. Neither is a true national newspaper, they are far too parochial for that. There's hardly any overlap in circulation, which has led to both becoming complacent in their newsgathering, each maintaining only a token presence in the other's camp. There's no competition because a Glaswegian would no more think of buying the *Scotsman* than he would of giving up his seat to a lady on the bus. Equally, if you see a copy of the *Herald* in the capital then it was probably brought over by a passenger on the early morning train, and he was almost certainly riding in the first-class compartment. But any Scottish businessman worth his salt reads both.

My sortie down south had cut me off from much of the Scottish news, which always gets a poor showing in the English papers and London-based television. It's a different country, no doubt about it.

The people from Crest arrived at ten, there were three of them carrying identical black briefcases, middle-aged men starting to thicken around the waist after too many expense account lunches and too many hours at their desks.

Normally Shona and I tried to meet our clients on their home ground, it puts them at ease, but they'd wanted to get away from their factory for a few hours.

It was a doddle. Shona had been right; the three of them, the managing director, his deputy, and the financial director, all knew what they wanted, their minds were already made up. All they wanted was to be told what clever chaps they were and to have their egos massaged. By both of us.

I'm in two minds about employee share schemes. Its supporters will tell you that it gives the workforce an interest in their company as well as an incentive to keep the firm on a healthy profits curve. It's supposed to cut down absenteeism, reduce strikes, slash wastage and probably cure the common cold.

I suppose I'd better explain how it works. A company agrees to set aside a proportion of its profits, usually above a certain limit which it sets itself, and it converts the cash into shares which it then divides among the workforce according to salary, length of service and so on. Some of the country's biggest firms do it – ICI has one of the longest running and they reckon it's a great success. Me, I'm a cynic. I reckon most employees prefer a cash bonus to the shares and anyway it usually ends up getting pissed against a wall. And there's a lot to be said for working for one company and holding shares in a competitor – that way if your employer goes bust you don't lose your savings as well. Still, we were getting a very healthy fee from Crest for setting up their scheme, so who am I to knock it?

Crest Electronics is one of the Scottish new wave companies, non-union, full of earnest young men and women grateful to have a job and keen to work long and hard for the good of the firm. They'd have been right at home in Japan, in fact it was the land of the rising yen that had saved many of them from the dole queue. The Japanese had set up a few assembly plants in Scotland along with their American counterparts, and before long they'd created the so-called Silicon Glen, and anybody who was anybody, Motorola, IBM, National Semiconductor, had to be represented north of the border. Soon the big boys were investing millions in wafer fabrication facilities to churn out tailor-made silicon chips, and there was a golden opportunity for local entrepreneurs to get in on the act, supplying services and components.

But unlike Aberdeen, where the locals were quick to make a killing by ripping off the oil industry, the Scots were slow to exploit the sunrise industries, with one or two notable exceptions.

Crest is one of those exceptions, manufacturing things like circuit boards and electronic bits and bobs that I couldn't begin to understand. Profits had risen through the roof and they'd be going public before long, assuming the bubble didn't burst.

They wanted to share their good fortune with the work-force and Scottish Corporate Advisors was more than pleased to help.

There were a few minor creases to be ironed out, and they'd wanted to redo their profit forecasts in the light of a pick-up in advance orders, but they left after an hour and a half eager to tell the workers the good news at the next daily industrial liaison discussion circle, or maybe they'd interrupt the lunchtime aerobics class. Whatever, our five-figure fee would be in the post.

'You didn't really need me today,' I told Shona as she drove me to the airport.

'Don't you believe it,' she said. 'They aren't the only clients who are getting edgy because you're not around.

We're not a one-man band, we're a team. When we bill them it's on the basis that they're getting both of us, our combined experience and skills, not just mine. Your presence convinces them that they're getting their money's worth.' The voice hardened, it had an edge that I didn't like, I'd heard her use it on bolshy carpark attendants and unhelpful shop assistants. On a good day she could use it to slice cheese. 'Let's be honest, you're not pulling your weight. For the moment I can handle it, but not for much longer.'

Message received, Shona, loud and clear, don't rub it in. 'I'll be back soon, I promise. Three weeks maximum. Cross my heart.'

She nodded curtly and didn't say another word until she dropped me at the airport and kissed me on the cheek. 'Be careful,' was all she said before driving off. At least she didn't say 'Don't go.'

The first time I met Tony Walker was more of a head-on collision than a meeting. We were both after a small meat processing firm in Paisley, outside Glasgow. It did little more than take in carcases at one end and throw out plastic-packaged joints and chops at the other. It had been a family-run business for years but the directors were a far cry from the nineteenth-century founders.

They all drew very high salaries, ridiculously high in view of the dwindling sales and non-existent profits. They drove around in brand new BMWs, except for the old man of the firm who kept the chairman's title, salary and Rolls.

In its heyday Young's Meat Processing plc was a gold mine, and during the sixties it had gone public with investors desperate to buy shares. Things started to go wrong some fifteen years later, and by the time Tony and I were interested it was on the slippery slope to liquidation while the family swanned around in their flash cars and spent more time on the golf course than they did in the office.

The main factory was run-down and nothing short of demolition would put it right, and customers were vanishing as the big supermarket chains pushed north of the border. Young's once had a healthy stack of gilts and for a long time the interest from them had boosted profits, but they had gradually been sold to pay off borrowings and the firm was now sinking deeper and deeper into debt.

It did have one worthwhile asset, though, and it was more than enough to keep the vultures hovering. Young's had a Stock Exchange listing, and I was approached by an up-and-coming grocery chain which wanted to go public but which didn't want the expense or the trouble of going to the market on its own.

My brief was to arrange a mutually beneficial takeover, an agreed bid that would give my client the prestige of a public company – and access to City fund raising – and give the Young's family the chance of taking the money and running. Or more likely driving away in the BMWs. Easy enough, you'd think, and normally it would have been but in this case I'd reckoned without Tony Walker.

He'd spotted the potential of Young's as a shell company all the way from London and had managed to buy up about three per cent of the shares in the market for £72,000. He'd then persuaded one of the older directors to sell him his stake for cash and that took Tony's holding to twelve per cent, and then he started putting pressure on for a seat on the board.

Tony had started professional life as an accountant, but soon realized he could do a lot better by running companies himself instead of just looking after their books. He'd borrowed something like a quarter of a million pounds from his father, a retired farmer, and started buying strategic stakes in companies ripe for takeover.

It was a bit like betting on racehorses, but more often than not the favourite romped home and the winnings piled up. Then he came to the conclusion that he could do even better if he took part in the race himself, buying shares in companies and then negotiating for them to be taken over, more often than not from a position of authority within the firm. He usually made a double profit, a healthy management fee from the company and a boost to the value of his shareholding, which he would sell soon after the bid went through.

He was doing the same at Young's and had just got his seat on the board and had a West Midlands electronics company all ready to reverse into it when I came onto the scene. By then the share price was already on the way up, partly because the market was well aware of Walker's reputation and also because you can't do anything in this business without making ripples and the brokers knew there was a battle in the offing. My only chance was to put together an agreed bid, a package that all the directors would accept and recommend to the rest of the shareholders.

My tack was to appeal to their chauvinism and play on the Scottish roots of my client, 'Wouldn't it be a terrible shame to let this proud Scottish name be taken over by a crowd of heathen Sassenachs, remember Culloden', and so on. My pleas fell on deaf ears and glazed eyes while Tony was out wining and dining the sixty-eight-year-old matriarch of the Young's clan and playing golf with the rest of the board at a level well below his seven handicap.

I was fighting an uphill battle and the City watchers of the *Glasgow Herald* and *Scotsman* had just about given up on me when I decided to take Shona for a meal in one of Edinburgh's plusher restaurants.

We'd planned to overhaul our strategy in a bid to snatch victory from the jaws of this wide-mouthed London predator, but as it turned out we saw Tony Walker shoving smoked salmon and shrimps into his mouth in a secluded booth with the chairman who had hired me to spearhead his offer for Young's. Shona and I turned on the spot and drove back to our office in Charlotte Square without speaking.

Not until we had walked through the door did she say, 'Bastard, bastard, bastard' with a venom that was not completely out of character. She flung herself into her dark green leather chair and put her feet on her desk, knocking the blotter to one side. 'Bastard, bastard, bastard.'

There were any number of reasons why Tony could be having a quiet tête-à-tête with our client: a shared interest in good food was one, a chance meeting was another, but they were both about as likely as scoring a hole in one on the Old Course at St Andrews by teeing off at Bearsden Golf Club.

If it had been above board and Tony was offering to sell his stake or switch his allegiance then Shona and I would be involved, so what was going on was obviously not the sort of behaviour likely to win Brownie points from the Takeover Panel.

The reason why the two so-called adversaries were dining

together had flashed into our minds at the same moment – our bid was nothing more than a red herring to boost the share price so that Tony and the directors could make an even bigger profit on the deal when his electronics company eventually gained control, a profit which would no doubt be shared by our client.

Which was great news for everybody except the West Midlands firm, which would be paying over the odds, and Shona and me. A failed takeover bid wouldn't do much for our reputations – or our fees.

We spent the rest of that evening putting away the best part of a bottle of Tamdhu and planning what we'd do to Mr Tony Walker. He'd booked himself a suite on the fifth floor of the North British Hotel and the following day I went to see him.

To this day I'm not sure how it happened but I walked into his room fuming and ready to take a swing at him but within half an hour we were the best of friends. It just happened. It wasn't personal with Tony, it was always business, just business, and when it came to making money there wasn't a stroke he wouldn't pull. He admitted that quite openly, he didn't apologize, he just smiled and said I wasn't to take it personally and that if it would make me feel any better then OK, I could take a swing at him but wouldn't I really prefer that he bought me a good lunch?

To make myself feel better I ordered the most expensive items on the menu, but by the end of lunch we were laughing and joking and the prospect of Scottish Corporate Advisors losing a takeover battle didn't seem like the end of the world. He became a firm friend, I'd trust him with my life if not my money, David loved him, and after Shona he was the first person I rang when my father died. He was on the first

Shuttle up to Edinburgh, I cried on his shoulder and he helped organize the funeral and sat by me at the inquest.

As it turned out Scottish Corporate Advisors didn't win or lose the fight for Young's. The West Midlands company suddenly lost interest and I wasn't altogether surprised when our client decided to drop out, too. Tony got his fingers burnt to the tune of £30,000, though he managed to cut his losses by selling his shares at a much lower price to an Edinburgh life office which saw Young's as a possible recovery situation.

It was only much later that I discovered Shona had phoned down to Birmingham and dropped a few hints about what Tony was up to. She's a lot harder underneath than I am, and she bears grudges, but now even she'd warmed to Tony. There was still a vague wariness about her whenever he was near, though.

Eventually word got round and Tony found it harder and harder to play the takeover game, and some eighteen months ago he'd joined up with a friend from his old university and now worked as an armaments middleman, selling mainly to the Middle East and doing a fair amount of juggling with end-user certificates. It was far from being a clean business, Tony had to make up most of the rules as he went along, and that often meant shunting money into Swiss bank accounts and encouraging buyers with wine, women and cocaine. With Tony it was just business, nothing personal.

As soon as I arrived back in London I phoned Tony and offered to take him for a drink that evening in a wine bar down the road from his Mayfair office. He was already sitting at a brass and glass table nursing a white wine and soda when I arrived.

'Doctor's orders, sport,' he said after he'd jumped to his feet, and shook my hand and slapped my back and rattled my teeth. 'Told me to lay off the hard stuff, liver trouble and all that. Can't say I like this muck, though. And it's about twice the price of a half-decent whisky.'

'You can afford it, Tony, stop complaining,' I laughed. 'I've seen you collect enough receipts to know the sort of expenses you get. Just to make you feel bad I'll have a double Glenmorangie, and you can pay for it.'

He slouched over to the bar, tall and fair in a dark blue business suit and highly polished shoes. He'd grown a moustache since the funeral and it added about fifteen years to his long, thin face. A thick rectangle of black hair, it half covered a thin scar that ran from the left side of his lip up to the middle of his cheek. The few times I'd asked him about the scar he'd laughed it off with jokes about jealous husbands, scorned lovers and frustrated business partners and after a while I'd stopped asking. There was a lot I didn't know about Tony Walker but I loved him like a brother.

He brought the tumbler of malt back to the table and sat opposite me, careful to cross his legs so that the sole of his shoe faced away from me, a hangover from dealing with Arabs. He caught my look and smiled, reaching for the peanuts on the table with his left hand, just to show me that he wasn't fully converted to Middle East customs.

'How's the lovely Shona?' he asked.

'She's fine. Sends her best.' Not true, she didn't know I was going to see him.

'And David?'

'He's well. He's staying at a private nursing home for a few months just until I get myself straight. They look after him really well but he can't wait to get back with me.'

'And when will that be?'

'Soon. Soon, I hope.'

'I hear Shona is handling most of the business herself at the moment. And handling it well by all accounts. She's a capable girl, you should watch her. I should have paid more attention to her myself – I could have saved myself several thousand pounds.'

'Now, now Tony, down boy. And what big ears you have.'

'Word gets round, sport. You know how the grapevine works. Been down here long?'

'Just arrived off the Shuttle, the noo,' I said, lapsing into a music hall Scottish accent that made him smile.

'Flying visit, or business, or social?' he asked, and it felt suddenly as if I were being interviewed by a high-powered headhunter, feeling my way through traps set for the unwary. Tony raised his thick eyebrows and looked me straight in the eyes through long, dark lashes, but unlike Iwanek's penetrating gaze Tony's was warm and friendly and caring.

'Business, Tony, but it's got more in common with your line of business than mine. I'm in the middle of setting up an export deal with a West African country, dictatorship to be more accurate, and I'm due to entertain one of their Trade Ministers in London next week.'

'Entertain?'

'Exactly. And I'm afraid it's not the sort of business I'm au fait with.'

'What's his predilection? Boys, girls, camels? Drugs?'

'Girls, or at least a particular type. He likes them classy, very classy, the ultimate Sloanes. He likes them pretty, well-groomed and intelligent. This guy was educated at Sandhurst, he's not out of the jungle. She'll have to be talkative, witty, charming . . .'

'And screw like a rabbit?'

'Exactly.'

'Not quite your line of country, sport,' he said, sipping his drink and grimacing.

'We're branching out.'

'Are you sure you're being one hundred per cent honest with me?'

No, Tony, I'm lying through my teeth but if I told you the real reason I want the girl you'd try to stop me. 'Hell, Tony, if I could go into details I would, but I can't. Now will you help?'

'Of course I will. You knew that or you wouldn't have come to me. I just want to make sure that you aren't getting in above your head. Is there anything I can do to help? Some of these tin-pot states can be murderous.'

'Just give me a name, Tony. I know what I'm doing.'

He took one of his gold embossed business cards from his wallet and scribbled a number on the back. 'Her name is Carol Hammond-Chambers. You'll have to mention my name or you won't even get past her answering machine. Carol is very selective and very, very pricey. But by Christ she's worth it.'

'You haven't?'

'Of course I have. You wouldn't buy a car without test driving it first, would you? There you are, then. I've introduced some very important clients to her and it was vital that I knew what they were getting into – if you get my drift.'

'And how is she?'

'The best, the absolute best. Worth every pound. Sexy, but very bright with it. You can't go wrong with Carol. She lives with another girl, Sammy. She works for me from time to time as well. A nice pair.' Freudian slip? Probably not, knowing Tony.

'Why do they do it?' I asked.

He sipped his wine before answering. 'Different reasons,' he said. 'Carol has an expensive habit to fund and working for me means she gets well paid and moves in the sort of circles where the coke flows freely and is as pure as the driven snow. Best of both worlds.'

'I tried sniffing coke once but the bubbles got up my nose,' I said and Tony laughed.

'What about the other girl, this Sammy?' I asked.

'Sammy's more of a mystery. You'll understand what I mean if you meet her. She's very smart, very sociable. She enjoys the company of stimulating men, men with power, men I can introduce her to. She's more than able to handle the physical side, too, and I think she enjoys that as well. To be honest I've never been able to work her out. Sometimes she'll turn a job down simply because she doesn't like the man's politics or his sense of humour. Strange girl. And I know for a fact the money's not important, she comes from a wealthy family, father's a Surrey landowner and farmer. Look, sport, are you sure I can't help?'

'If you could you'd be the first person I'd come to, believe me. You've done more than enough giving me Carol's name.'

'Good. I mean it, if things get tough call me. And take

care. You can give me your number in London before you go, too. Now, have you heard what happened to Ferguson over at Kleinwort Benson?'

Then he was off, gossiping and joking like the Tony I knew, but he was worried about me now and perhaps it had been a mistake going to him.

The voice on the answering machine was smooth and soothing, the sort of voice that relaxed you but at the same time gave you a hint of pleasures to come, illicit pleasures, pleasures to make your toes curl.

It was the sort of voice that usually belongs to fifty-year-old telephonists with spots and halitosis who flirt outrageously with men they'll never meet, but in this case Tony had promised me it belonged to a body that would more than live up to my expectations. I left my name and number and said that Tony had suggested I give her a ring.

My phone rang ten minutes later, which meant she'd just got in, had been in the shower, or more likely that she'd been in all the time and had rung Tony first to check up on me. Whatever, her warm sultry voice seemed to float out of the receiver, wash down my neck and tickle my back and I could feel my toes pressing against the top of my shoes. It wasn't Carol, it was Sammy. Tony's first choice was all set to fly to Oman for an extended 'holiday with friends' but she was sure she'd be able to help. It was Sammy's voice on the answering machine. If ever I get knocked down by a bus and go into a coma, play me tapes of Sammy's voice. I'll either wake up or die happy.

I asked her if she'd like to go for a drink and she said why didn't I just go round because she had more than enough drink for two, and I couldn't help wondering what Tony had told her as my toes fought and slashed to cut their way out of my shoes.

An hour after the call I was at the door of her Kensington flat, one floor up in one of those white buildings that used to hold one very rich family but are now home to several very, very rich families. To the side of the building were parking spaces for three cars and standing next to each other were a Rolls, a Mercedes and a Jeep – Dinah would have loved it. McKinley waited outside in our rented Granada. I was still waiting for my Porsche to be repaired, and even when it was I doubted that I'd ever let him take the wheel.

The names above the entryphone at the main door had said S. Darvell and C. Hammond-Chambers but there was no label on the shining white door to the flat itself, just a brass knocker in the shape of a diving dolphin.

She opened the door and I saw a flash of red hair cascading down to sun-browned shoulders, a wide mouth with teeth every bit as white and sparkling as the front door, then my eyes drifted down to breasts thrusting to get out of a backless white dress which stuck to her waist and hips and ended above the most perfect calves I'd ever seen.

Sammy was a cracker, an absolute angel who'd turn heads and necks and even whole bodies in order to get a better look. My eyes returned to her face, eventually, and the slightly mocking smile told me that she was getting the sort of attention she was used to and which she expected.

'Come in,' she breathed and I walked into a room which

looked like a soap powder commercial. Everything – walls, carpet, settee, coffee table – everything was white, even the blue-eyed cat which lay on a sheepskin rug and purred and stretched and sounded every bit as sexy as its mistress was a dazzling white.

Another girl walked into the whiteness from a bedroom, toting a green fabric suitcase and a matching holdall. Carol? Couldn't have been anyone else. I thought of Tony's test drive and I grinned.

'You must be Carol,' I said, and held out my hand to a curly-haired brunette with big brown almond eyes, lips that formed a permanent pout and a figure that matched Sammy's inch for inch, though she was a hand shorter. The leather jacket was white and so was the blouse, but the skirt was black and slit to the thigh and the legs were brown and sleek and long.

'Must I?' she asked, dropping the suitcase with a dull thud and taking my hand. She glanced at Sammy and smiled. 'Yes, I suppose I must.'

The voice was pure Cockney, belying the name and the body, and I mentally cursed Tony and his twisted sense of humour. Ultimate Sloane, indeed.

'I love the flat,' I said, looking round and releasing the cool, scarlet-fingernailed hand. 'How on earth do you keep it clean?'

'Why should it ever get dirty?' asked Carol. 'Sit down, I'll get you a drink.'

'It's OK, I'll get it,' said Sammy. 'Anyway, I thought you had to go.'

'Shit, yes, what's the time? Oh no. Was there a cab outside?' she asked me, her eyes widening.

'No,' I said, but just then we heard a horn sound in the

street below and she picked up the case and headed for the door.

'I must dash,' she said. 'I'm sorry I can't stay, but I'm sure you'll get on with Sammy. Oh, and when you see Tony next, give him my love. Tell him I'll phone when I get back and he can check my tan.'

'I'll tell him,' I laughed, and then the door slammed and she was gone.

'Hectic,' I said to Sammy.

'Yes,' she nodded, shaking her head so that the waterfall of red hair swung back and forth. 'She got a call from a friend in Oman. Here today, gone tomorrow. That's the way it is with Carol. No ties, no commitments.'

'The flat?'

'The flat's mine. Carol helps out with the rent but she'd never take on a mortgage in a million years. In the sixties they'd have called her a free spirit.'

'And now?'

'Irresponsible, I suppose. No, that's not fair, Carol just has different priorities to me.'

She walked past me and something smelled sweet and expensive, the sort of perfume that back-street chemists make cheap copies of and sell out of cardboard boxes in shopping precincts.

Walking over to the four-seater sofa was like wading through an uncut lawn, the thick lush pile came halfway up my shoes. I dropped onto the soft white upholstery and slowly sank into it until my backside was a good six inches below my knees.

The cat purred and rolled over, eyes fixed on my shoelaces. It was probably grateful to see something, anything, that wasn't white. Hell, I'm surprised the poor thing hadn't gone snow blind living with Sammy and Carol. I felt so sorry for it that I let it play with them, dangling my foot over its eager paws.

As the cat and I got acquainted Sammy came back from the drinks cabinet, which stood next to a large picture window overlooking a verdant garden square where sparrows fought and squabbled and a thrush sang its heart out. That's what the residents pay rates of £1.68 in the pound for, I guess.

I didn't think I could stand without an overhead winch so I was grateful when she walked over and handed the glass down to me. I was even more grateful when I discovered it wasn't white wine or white rum or white anything. It was a malt, a good one, and it came with a splash of water which is just the way I like it and that meant she had a severe case of woman's intuition, she'd made a lucky guess or she'd had a long chat with Tony and I wondered what he had told her and if he'd asked her to go ferreting for him. Or maybe she had just smelled the whisky I'd drunk for Dutch courage before I left my flat.

Our fingers touched as I took the crystal tumbler and I got a slight shock of static electricity, a combination of the carpet, her dress and the thin film of sweat that I could feel all over my skin. The girl made me nervous, she was almost too beautiful, too well-groomed. It was difficult being in the same room as her, I was like a schoolboy on his first date and it was all I could do to stop biting my nails.

She floated down into the settee next to me and pulled her knees up onto the cushions so that one brushed against the outside of my leg. I didn't jump but my heart soared and I just melted as she looked at me and ran her finger up and down the stem of her glass. I came to as the cat began scratching its claws down my socks and I cleared my throat and started the semblance of a conversation.

'Have you known Tony for long?' I asked and wished I'd bitten my tongue instead.

'About three years, on and off,' she said. 'I work for him every couple of months, usually Arabs, and usually they want something a little different.' She raised her eyebrows, daring me to ask what was different, but I didn't rise to the bait, all I could think of was the warmth of her leg against mine.

'What is it you want me to do?' she asked. 'Tony said you had something special in mind but he wouldn't tell me what.'

'Tony was teasing you,' I said. 'I want you to do much the same as you do for him, only for a client of mine. Only he isn't a client of mine. I'm not explaining this very well, am I?' I was embarrassed, that's why, discussing sex with this beautiful girl that I fancied something rotten as if I were talking about a secretarial job.

'No, you're not. Let me get you another.' She uncurled and drifted up and off the settee, God knows how but I suppose the long suntanned legs had something to do with it. She returned with another whisky and I don't remember drinking that one either. She made me laugh, she told me stories about Tony that I would dredge up next time I saw him so long as my memory held out; she told me about her parents, her time at Oxford, we touched on everything but her profession though after a while it became clear that it was more of a hobby than a job. I told her about David and Shona and before long I told her everything.

I needed someone to talk to, and I knew that unless I gave her good reason she wouldn't help me and she was perfect for the job. It wasn't pillow talk, that would come later, this was just getting it all off my chest. Like a chat with an analyst, that's the way I looked at it. I was pissed, and when I'm pissed I talk too much.

If you've got a couple of thousand pounds to invest there are a number of things you can do. In fact a host of friendly advisors will beat a path to your door with a view to tucking away your nest egg in one of their many and varied schemes.

You can shove it into a building society or deposit account and forget about it, collecting the interest every few months. It's boring, to be honest, and you'll never make a fortune unless you start with half a fortune and wait ten years or so, but your capital is as safe as houses.

You can put the lot into Premium Bonds, and wait for Ernie to pick one of his electronic ping pong balls out of his electronic hat with your number on it. You've more chance of winning than you have of being struck by lightning but statistically you're better off putting your hard-earned loot in the care of Mr Bradford and Mr Bingley. If your luck's in you could cream off a fortune, but that could also be said of the football pools. I guess that's why so many people are glued to their TV sets on Saturday afternoons – dreaming of the big one, but if it doesn't come off, well, there's always next week, isn't there? It's a mug's game. You might as well toddle into a casino and plonk the lot on zero. Sometimes that comes up, too.

At the opposite end of the financial spectrum are the

out and out gambles, the City equivalent of betting on a 250–1 outsider running in the Grand National. There are get-rich-quick schemes like buying those large containers used to ship antiques over to America, disgraced diplomats to Nigeria and stolen cars to the Middle East. You rent them out to export companies and pocket a healthy profit, in theory, but more likely they'll just lie rusting in some disused dockyard and your money will evaporate faster than goodwill at a creditors' meeting. Not to be recommended.

Anyway, back to Mr Average looking for a home for his two grand. He's probably heard about the stock market, the mystical exchange where fortunes are won and lost, and if he is a little curious he's maybe read about penny shares, buying them at 9p each and selling a few months later when they're worth £6.15. Mr Average, being average, is more than a little greedy and reckons that the stock market is the place for his hard-earned cash.

He might be right, but he'll be playing in one of the biggest casinos in the world, with rumours and counter-rumours sending share prices soaring and crashing, a bad set of results blighting a firm's shares for months, a takeover bid sending them through the roof.

Putting all your eggs in one basket is a doubtful way of investing, but Mr Average's £2,000 would have to go on one share to make any sense at all, dealing costs and stamp duty see to that, and picking that one share makes it a gamble. Back to the racecourse.

There is an alternative: a unit trust or an investment trust. Different animals but with a similar aim, the spreading of risk. Get together a group of investors, pool their capital and put their money into several shares, gilts, maybe even property. Then spread the rewards. There'll obviously be a few misses, but the many hits will more than cover them.

The main difference between unit and investment trusts is that investment trusts come in the form of shares listed on the stock exchange. To buy unit trusts you go to the firm which manages them. Both sorts of trusts specialize, in sectors like electronics or natural resources, or in parts of the world like the Far East or America.

Edinburgh has always been a major centre of investment trusts, going back to the days when canny Scots realized there was many a mickle to be made out of America, but they were also canny enough to realize that there was safety in numbers. Shareholders made small fortunes out of their investments, but even bigger fortunes were made by the men who managed the funds. That's still the case.

Take a gold sovereign and place it over a small scale map of Edinburgh centred on Charlotte Square, and you're probably covering more millionaires per square foot than anywhere outside the City of London. Many of them are fund managers, men who make their money by looking after other people's.

These days most of the Ivory & Simes and Martin Curries have branched out into other lucrative areas like pension fund management, but my father had always stuck to what he knew best, looking after an investment trust that was his pride and joy. He'd managed Scottish Commercial Overseas Trust, SCOT as it was called, since he was a young man fresh out of St Andrews University with a first in economics.

My grandfather got him the job by pulling a few well-greased strings. My family's always been like that: doors are opened and more strings pulled than at a campanologists' convention to make sure the next generation gets a head start on their peers. Don't knock it until you've benefited from it.

Father took to it like a duck to water, long expense-account lunches, meeting old friends from school and university, drinks with the G and T brigade, and free publicity in the quality Scottish press. All he had to do was to keep up with the FT Index, and he had the experience of a flock of Scottish stockbrokers' analysts to draw on. OK, I'm making it sound easy, but running an investment trust is a darn sight more fun than breaking rocks for a living.

It's just a matter of running with the pack, switching into sectors as they become popular and ditching them when sentiment goes against them. Japan this year, America next, making sure you sell at a profit wherever possible but never being afraid to cut loose a dead loss.

The really good guys, the ones that earn £100,000 a year and more, set trends rather than follow them. They know, based on instinct or research, where to invest and where to sell, but everyone knows who to watch and the sheep follow the wolves and everyone makes a good living, my father included.

For the whole of his working life my father ran the SCOT investment trust with John Read, another St Andrews graduate. But when Read died of a massive stroke two years ago my old man was left in sole charge, and the mantle didn't fit too well on his shoulders.

He should have taken on more staff right away, beefed up the research side, maybe even taken on a few more non-executive directors, but at fifty-nine years old it was the first time he'd had his hands on the reins and he was reluctant to give them up.

By then SCOT was doing fairly well, with investments

worth a total of fifty-two million, though its performance lagged well behind the high-flyers. In fact SCOT had under-performed the investment trust sector average for the past five years but it had still done better than many. It was just after Read's death that Ronnie Laing, drugs dealer, and Alan Kyle, property developer and self-styled City tycoon, crawled out of the woodwork.

There's another big difference between unit trusts and investment trusts. A unit trust is an open fund, the more money that comes in the more units are created. If investors withdraw their money then the number of units is reduced.

An investment trust is different, it's a closed fund, set up with a limited number of shares. The only way to increase the share capital is to issue more shares, which sometimes happens. You buy them through a stockbroker and it's the City that sets the price. A share that's in vogue or is doing particularly well will have more money chasing it than a dullard, and its price will rise.

Now, the fact that investment trust shares are sold on the stock market leads to an interesting phenomenon called the discount. The price you pay for a share is more often than not less than the actual value of its investments.

Say a fund's investments are worth a hundred million and there are fifty million shares, then the net asset value, the value of each share, is two pounds. But you'll be able to buy the shares for quite a bit less, perhaps for as little as £1.50. In that case you'll be getting the share for three-quarters of its value and the discount would be one quarter, or twenty-five per cent. That's not an unusual figure.

That's fine and dandy, it means that shareholders are actually getting a boost to their investment, every

£1.50 they put in has two pounds working for them and producing dividends. But it wasn't too long before some wily investment trust managers realized that they could take over smaller trusts and take on ready-made portfolios at a bargain price. A hundred million pounds worth of investments might cost only seventy-five million on the stock exchange.

Well, it's not exactly as simple as that because once the City gets wind of what's happening the discount narrows pretty rapidly and the share price is soon the same as the net asset value. Timing is obviously crucial and the faster the takeover goes ahead the more money the predator makes. Tony dipped his toe into the investment trust pool and came out smiling once or twice.

It's a good deal for the predator, who gets investments on the cheap, and the shareholders are happy because they make a quick profit, though more often than not they're prepared to take shares in the predatory investment trust in place of cash. The only losers are the managers of the original trust who lose the goose that's been laying their golden eggs, but they can always go back to accountancy, or soliciting, or selling shoelaces on street corners, or whatever it was they used to do before climbing on the gravy train of fund management.

Once investment trusts started snapping each other up other interested parties began to take notice; private trusts and pension funds didn't need telling that they too could do a lot with cheap investments. They could keep the stocks and shares they liked and sell the rest through the market, a highly lucrative form of asset stripping, on a par with buying up cheap tenanted property, getting rid of the occupants and selling the freeholds. Nice work if you can get it.

PAY OFF

She'd sat patiently by me on the virgin white settee and her eyes never left my face other than the two times when she'd refilled my glass. She hadn't yawned, she hadn't spoken. Sometimes she pushed her hair behind her left ear but it wouldn't stay put, and occasionally she reached over and touched my shoulder gently and listened, head slightly on one side, which is why her hair kept falling across her eye. The cat had long since become bored with my shoelaces and lay on the back of the settee, eyes closed and paws opening and closing as it tortured dream mice. I'd stopped feeling her leg against mine and I wasn't looking at her any more, I was looking at the window but not through it, just looking into the middle distance as I talked in a quiet voice that I barely recognized as my own, getting it out of my system like a fever that has to be sweated out.

Of course other people recognized a good thing when they saw it, and that's how Laing and Kyle came on the scene. Laing was a drugs dealer with a cash flow that would make a Swiss banker blush with pleasure, Kyle was a downmarket version of Tony Walker.

For Kyle it wasn't just business, it was a pleasure to grind people's faces into their misfortune, particularly if it was a misfortune he'd brought about. Kyle was a short, stocky man with a hard face and a harder heart and a reputation for losing his temper, if he'd ever managed to find it in the first place.

He always dressed immaculately; his silk tie matched by a handkerchief, he wore sharp suits with a gold-buckled leather belt and his shoes never cost less than the average weekly wage.

He'd started his career as a property developer, doing up run-down buildings and selling them at an inflated profit, breaking rules and legs and trampling over anybody he could to get a leg up the ladder. Sometimes he'd trample on people just for the hell of it, just for practice, just because he liked it. He graduated to the City, set up a company offering financial services, took over an office cleaning firm, a pool table business, a couple of minor hotels that were barely disguised brothels. He was still breaking heads and working an eighty-hour week in his office near Bishopsgate.

He'd met Ronnie Laing one night in a gambling club in Mayfair, tall, willowy Ronnie Laing with his pale blond hair and deep set blue eyes covered by green-rimmed glasses, a blonde on each arm and a wide gold band on his wedding finger. Kyle liked him immediately, and liked him even more when Laing split the pair of blondes right down the middle, one each. The following morning they got to talking and that's how the partnership was born. That's what I heard, anyway, but that was afterwards when I was looking for information and paying for it and howling at the moon for revenge.

I don't know how or why they picked on SCOT, maybe it was the twenty-eight per cent discount, maybe it was its size, maybe it was the fact that my father was in sole charge and less able to protect his baby than one of the larger investment houses, but they chose SCOT and went for it with all the subtlety of a Chieftain tank.

They attacked in two waves, each buying quietly in the market, softly softly until they reached just below the five per cent mark at which point they would have a notifiable stake. Then they pounced, lumped the two stakes together, snapping up another ten per cent in the market on the same day as the price started to take off. In all they bought one fifth of the £52 million trust for a little more than seven million, much of that the profits from Laing's drug operations though the shares were in the name of Kyle's company, Property and Financial Services. They'd been buying SCOT shares for about £1.18 compared with a net asset value of £1.51, and Kyle made a cash offer of £1.42 for the rest with the backing of a consortium of merchant banks who recognized a good thing when they saw it.

If the deal came off Kyle and Laing would get their hands on a £52 million portfolio for about £46 million, which meant a profit of six million once they'd liquidated it. Not bad for a couple of months' work, and it would be a hundred per cent legal and above board. Well, it would have been if they'd played it by the book, which of course they didn't. What Laing and Kyle wanted was a quick settlement, they wanted the directors of the trust to agree the bid and recommend that shareholders accept the PAFS offer before another predator started sniffing around.

One of the second ranking merchant banks prepared the bid document. Their fee of £120,000 would come off PAFS's profits, but Laing and Kyle reckoned it was worth it, image was everything, but behind the scenes they played dirtier than anyone in the City had ever played before. They took the vicious techniques of Laing's world into the sedate Edinburgh financial sector and the effect was similar to dropping a piranha into a tank of goldfish.

In the space of just four days one of the directors found that his £15,000 chestnut hunter had gone lame, not surprising with a six-inch nail rammed up its hoof as far as it would go; another received black and white photographs of his twin daughters stepping off the school bus. They'd been taken with a long lens and were slightly fuzzy, and they didn't come with a message because one wasn't necessary. Another opened his front door to find a bottle of sulphuric acid standing next to the early morning milk delivery and a carton of raspberry yoghurt. All three received phone calls on the same evening and at a board meeting two days later they told my father they'd decided to accept the PAFS offer, had already agreed to sell their shares to Kyle and would be recommending that shareholders did the same.

My father told them not to be so soft, that he was looking for a higher offer which would mean a better deal for the shareholders. That night he got a phone call and the next day his wife, my mother, got into the family Volvo and drove down the hill to the local shops and smashed headlong into a lamp post when the brakes failed. It wouldn't have been so bad if she'd been wearing her seat belt but she wasn't, and she ripped through the windscreen in a shower of glass cubes and crumpled onto the pavement where she died of a ruptured spleen and pierced lung three minutes later, in the arms of a passing postman, bleeding heavily over his grey slacks.

The following week she was buried in the pretty local churchyard and control of SCOT passed to Kyle and Laing.

Two days after the funeral I drove to the office. It was a Sunday and I wanted to get my desk straight, I knew that I had to keep working, keep my mind occupied, to do something to blot out the memory of how she'd died, an ugly freakish accident in a two-year-old car that had just been serviced. I stayed until after dusk, then threw my briefcase into the passenger seat of my Porsche and drove slowly back to the family home on the outskirts of Edinburgh, indicating at every turn, stopping on amber, checking the mirror at every opportunity and keeping both hands firmly on the wheel. My mother had named the rambling stone house in three acres of well-tended gardens Stonehaven, and she'd stamped her personality on it like an adopted child.

The house was quiet as I unlocked the front door, stepped into the oak panelled hall and rested the case next to the umbrella stand. I headed for the kitchen, I wanted a coffee, but I heard Bach through the study door so I changed direction and went in to see my father.

He was lying on his back by the side of his huge Victorian desk, a wedding present from a distant cousin, a black walking stick by his side. The damp weather always gave him trouble with his back and it had been drizzling steadily all day. I heard a sniff and a sigh and I turned to see David sitting behind the door, back ramrod straight against the hand-printed wallpaper, chin up, tears streaming from unseeing eyes down sodden cheeks.

He shuddered and sighed again, his lips tight together and his nose running and mixing with the tears. His fists were clenched and his arms clutched across his chest and he started to rock backwards and forwards, banging himself against the wall and wailing, a mournful moan of pain that shocked me to the core.

'David, what's wrong? What's the matter?' I asked. I knelt beside him, one knee either side of his outstretched legs, and held him close, his chin on my shoulder as he cried and cried. 'Stop crying,' I said.

I turned my head towards where my father was lying. 'What's the matter with David?' I asked, but my father hadn't moved and it wasn't a stick lying by his side, it was his favourite shotgun and the blue and white wallpaper behind the desk was speckled with red. As I stood and walked towards his feet I could see that the top of his head was missing, and fragments of brain and skin and blood and shot covered the top of the desk. I noticed then the smell of cordite and shit in the room and I didn't have to kneel by the body to see that he was dead.

I took David by the hand and led him from the room, sitting him in an armchair next to the telephone table in the hall as I rang Shona, Tony and the police, in that order. Then I brought a thick blanket down from a bedroom and wrapped it around David and I went back into the study and picked up the letter lying on the desk, and I sat next to David and waited and read the letter again and again and then I folded it up and put it in the inside pocket of my jacket and waited.

By then I was into my fourth tumbler of whisky and Sammy had leant her cool unlined forehead on my shoulder, breathing gently while her hand rested on my arm, her drink on the coffee table untouched.

I continued. 'The coroner was sympathetic, and without a suicide note he was willing to accept that my father had shot himself accidentally while cleaning his gun. There was the usual warning always to check that guns weren't loaded indoors but he wasn't fooling anybody.'

'What was in the letter?' she asked, so quietly that at first I hadn't realized she'd spoken.

'It was rambling, the ramblings of a man who'd lost everything, almost everything, I don't know, maybe everything. His job, his wife, what else was there for him to live for? Two sons, maybe, and a big empty house that would always remind him of her. He felt he didn't belong in a world where gangsters like Kyle and Laing could get away with murder. The phone call he'd received before she died was from Laing, telling him to forget any ideas of master-minding a counter bid for SCOT, to let sleeping dogs lie, to keep out of it, old man, or you'll be even more of a cripple, old man, and wouldn't it be a pity if anyone else in your family had to use a stick to get around, old man.

'He said in the letter that he didn't want to live any more, not in a world where that could happen, he wanted to be with her and he said he was sorry, very sorry, and the notepaper was stained with tears and the handwriting shaky, the scrawl of an old, dying man. Christ, Sammy, he was only fifty-nine. He didn't have to die. Neither of them did.'

'Hush,' she said, and put her arm around my shoulder. 'They couldn't have known what would happen. They couldn't have known that your mother would be in the car or that she wouldn't be wearing her seat belt. It was just a terrible, terrible mistake.'

'No,' I said, harshly enough to startle her and wake up the cat. 'No. They might not have meant to kill my parents but they did. Maybe indirectly, but they were responsible. They were responsible.'

She stood up and held out her hand to me, and I took it and she pulled me up and took me into the bedroom still carrying my glass. The bedroom wasn't white, it was blue, blue patterned wallpaper, a thick blue fur bedspread, blue velvet curtains half drawn, a wardrobe and dressing table of blue-stained wood. A picture above the double bed showed a sea scene, white-tipped waves whisked up by a strong wind.

She slipped the dress down over her shoulders, she was

wearing nothing underneath, and she said nothing until she'd undressed me. 'Tell me what you want me to do,' she asked, so I made love to her under the waves and then I told her.

It was light when I left her flat, rubbing my chin because I needed a shave. McKinley was asleep in the car, head resting between the seat and the window, chest rising and falling as he snored loud enough to be heard a hundred yards away. I rapped on the window just behind his ear and he woke with a start.

'OK boss?' he asked.

'Sure, Get-Up. Let's go.'

'To the flat?'

'To the flat. And don't spare the horses.'

He started the car on the fourth attempt, which was good going for him, though to be fair we'd only had the Granada a week. He pulled away from the kerb, gently scraping a yellow VW and grinning sheepishly.

'Sorry, boss,' he said and crashed into second gear.

'Forget it. Just get me home.'

The courtship of McKinley had started the week after I'd seen him get knocked senseless in Kelly's Bar. I'd gone back to the pub and bought him a bottle of whisky in sixth of a gill measures, matching him drink for drink. I'd eaten a full plate of pasta and lined my stomach with milk and twice in the Gents I'd forced my fingers down my throat and thrown up as much of the whisky as I could. My head was swimming by the end of the evening but I was still on my feet. McKinley was impressed. So was I.

I told him I was a dealer, motors, stolen goods, drugs, anything I could make money from. I told him I needed extra muscle, I told him I could do with a driver. What about me? he asked, giving me a friendly nudge in the ribs and shooting me three feet along the bar, I've got muscle and I can drive. Like a lamb to the slaughter.

I told him I'd pay him £300 a week and he took my hand in his giant paw, looked me in the bloodshot eyes and thanked me from the bottom of his heart. I'd never regret it, he said, and apart from a few near misses in the Granada he'd been right. I had installed him in a cheap hotel around the corner from my flat and paid his bill one month in advance. Now he was a constant companion, though the main problem was finding him enough to do.

To back up my cover story I got him to drive me to various hotels (business meetings), casinos (poker games) and restaurants (can't tell you what's going on, Get-Up, but it's big), and more often than not I'd leave him outside in the car while I had a quiet drink or a meal alone.

Once I left him waiting outside the Hilton for four hours while I slipped out the back way and wandered around the shops in Oxford Street looking for a present for David. It was important for Get-Up to think that I was wheeling and dealing, though putting on an act was a hell of a lot more tiring than the real thing.

Gradually I spoke to him about his past, about the work he did for Laing, the people he'd met, the places he'd been to, teasing out the information I needed like a splinter from a septic thumb, careful not to arouse his suspicions, never pressing too hard, changing tack if it looked as if I was touching a sore place.

The information was obviously old, he'd been in prison for seven years after all. A few of the names he mentioned had passed on or gone inside, but most were still in business, one had recently been featured in one of the more sensational tabloids under the headline 'Drugs King In Sex Bribe Shocker'.

I told Get-Up that one of my major interests was dealing in drugs, particularly hard drugs, north of the border, but that I'd run into problems with a supplier up in Glasgow and was lying low in London until tempers had cooled.

The probing usually took place late at night in pubs or clubs after a great deal of drinking and several self-induced Technicolor yawns. I was starting to get anorexic, but Laing's involvement in the drugs world was falling into place. Background that I couldn't get from McKinley I managed to dig up in the *Daily Express* cuttings library.

British customs officers seize more than a hundred million pounds' worth of drugs each year – it breaks down into something like forty-six million pounds of cannabis, forty-eight million pounds of heroin and seven million pounds of cocaine, and that's just the tip of a mind-blowing iceberg. There are less than three hundred Customs and Excise officers and about twelve hundred policemen working on drugs and their batting average is roughly one for one

– one smuggler arrested for each officer per year. And that's with the help of CEDRIC, a £1.2 million computer based on a couple of Honeywell DPS 8/20s which is even more sophisticated than the hardware used by MI5. It's hidden away in a nondescript building in Shoeburyness, near Southend, and it replaced the old card index system which was scrapped in the spring of 1983.

Its top secret data base can cross-check all information collated by the various anti-drug agencies.

Suppose a one-eyed midget with a wooden leg gets caught trying to drive his Morris Minor off the Channel ferry with a boot full of cannabis. At the touch of a button CEDRIC will spill the beans on how many midgets are involved in smuggling, how many have only one eye, if any are dead ringers for Long John Silver and if any are to be found sitting on a pile of cushions at the wheel of a Morris Minor. You get the picture? But CEDRIC is a victim of the truism faced by all the miracles of silicon chip technology – garbage in, garbage out. The information that comes out is only as good as the facts that are fed into it. And nowhere within CEDRIC's memory banks was the name Laing, Ronnie, and there was no mention of a blue Rolls-Royce Corniche with a white soft top and personalized number plates. Tap in a description of a tall, willowy, middle-aged man with blond hair, deep set blue eyes, green-rimmed glasses, a wide gold band on his wedding finger, maybe include his passion for young girls, and CEDRIC might give you a handful of near misses but the one thing he wouldn't give you is Laing, Ronnie, because Laing, Ronnie, had never been caught with so much as an aspirin in his possession, in fact Laing, Ronnie, had never been caught period.

He arranged to bring drugs into the country, he financed

drug deals, he sold drugs on to wholesalers, but he never came within sniffing distance of anything that would raise the eyebrows of a lab assistant in a police forensic laboratory. Most of the cash he made went straight into Channel Island banks and was then laundered through Kyle's expanding business empire, so he didn't even have to account for suitcasefuls of fifty-pound notes in his Hampstead home. Ronnie Laing was now way past the stage where he had to finance supermarket robberies to make a quick killing.

The chances of the long arm of the law grabbing Laing by the silk collar were slimmer than a turkey's of surviving Christmas. He was insulated at two levels: a courier brought the drugs in and a middle-man, either trusted or scared witless, would handle the arrangements, never ringing Laing, only speaking when spoken to. On the few occasions a deal had gone sour it was only the couriers who ended up getting caught, and they knew it was more than their lives were worth to talk.

Getting drugs into Britain is a lot easier than most people think. From the simple trick of using false-bottomed suitcases to swallowing condoms full of heroin, much of it simply walks through the green 'nothing to declare' channel with throngs of sunburnt holidaymakers.

The customs can't and don't search everybody and a professional courier at work is harder to spot than a Herpes carrier. A sniffer dog is only good for fifteen minutes before getting bored, or stoned, or both. The West German police reckon they can train a wild boar to do the job all day long, but the British depend on the services of just twenty-nine dogs, which equals about seven hours concentrated sniffing a day. Not much of a deterrent.

Getting the drugs over on the Channel ferries is even easier, which is why undercover drugs police officers pose as passengers, hoping that couriers will relax their guard while in the ship's bars and restaurants. No, they don't catch many, which is hardly surprising. If your car's sills were packed with heroin you're hardly likely to offer the barman a few grams in exchange for a double vodka and tonic and a packet of pork scratchings.

There's always the possibility that a zealous customs officer might take it into his head to drill a hole in the sills, just on the off chance, so a better way is to dissolve the drug, especially cocaine, in warm alcohol and soak it into the carpets of the car, maybe into the upholstery and the car blanket as well for good measure. Dry them out, drive through customs and then extract the drug with more warm alcohol. Filter, evaporate off the alcohol and you're left with pretty pure cocaine. And for the non drivers, it works just as well soaking the clothes in your suitcase.

Some of the more inventive car couriers have come up with a nifty variation – before driving out of the country they take out an AA five star insurance policy. After picking up the drugs in Spain or Holland or wherever and packing them away in any one of a dozen hard to find places, they nobble the motor, call in the AA and fly home. A few days later the car, and the drugs, are delivered. And what customs officer is going to search a family car on an AA Relay truck? Well, they all do now, actually, after an undercover Customs officer overheard a husband and wife courier team discussing the scam while celebrating in advance on the ferry to Calais.

Ultra cautious smugglers can remove themselves even further from the dirty end of the business, by shipping drugs into the country in hollowed-out wooden elephants from India, inside drums from Africa, or even by impregnating postcards and airmail letters with LSD microdots.

But Ronnie Laing had progressed way beyond such ruses, and when he wanted a delivery he had heroin or cocaine or cannabis or any combination of the three shipped in from the Continent and collected at any of a thousand possible landing places scattered around Britain's 7,000 miles of coastline and driven back to London.

Customs and Excise have seven coastal cutters to patrol those 7,000 miles of beaches, coves and cliffs so a smuggler has more chance of winning the pools than he has of bumping into the boys in blue, and chances are that the drugs ship can outperform the cutter and its volunteer crew without breaking into a sweat.

Any captures are usually the result of intelligence work rather than diligent patrolling, so a professional team has few problems in getting through. And if the smugglers are unlucky enough to meet a cutter they can't run away from, then the consignment is simply pitched overboard and collected later. Ronnie Laing was sitting pretty, or at least he was until he was hit on two fronts, from North and South America.

The land of the brave and the home of the free has a drugs business worth some hundred billion dollars a year, about the same as the whole Federal budget. Cocaine is now a growth industry with twelve million men and women using it regularly and 5,000 new addicts created every day. Supplies were rushed into the country to meet the ever-increasing demand but, as usual, the free market system created a surplus.

If it were wheat, or oil, or Coke with a big 'C', then it

would probably have been sold off cheaply to the Russians, but they wouldn't touch capitalist drugs with a cattle prod. So with the North American market pretty well saturated, in fact stoned out of its twelve million tiny minds, and with street prices falling, it wasn't too long before the drugs bosses looked towards Europe, and to Britain in particular.

In America drugs mean Mafia, and in Britain Mafia means trouble and Ronnie Laing was gradually squeezed out. And just to prove that it's always darkest just before it goes pitch black, the villains who actually export the drug, the South American cocaine barons, mostly Colombians, decided they would deal directly with Britain and cut out the middle-men and they make the Mafia look like disorganized boy scouts. The Mafia might issue a contract for a killing, the Colombians don't even bother to write a memo. They just get the job done and worry about the paperwork later.

They're highly organized and, with the South American's disregard for human life other than his own, frantically vicious. Laing found himself with a smaller and smaller share of the London drugs cake and eventually he was left with the crumbs, which is about the time he met up with Kyle and decided to put his not inconsiderable fortune to a more, but only slightly more, legitimate use.

The phone call from Tony was short and to the point, the conversation of a man used to speaking on lines which are bugged. He told me where and when he wanted to meet, but gave no hint as to the why. 'Just be there,' he'd said. 'And come alone.'

The where was St James's Park, the when was five minutes after I climbed out of the Granada opposite Horse Guards Parade, the wind tugging at the coats of the two policemen stopping non-permit-holders from parking outside the barracks. The coming alone was no problem because I gave McKinley the rest of the day off and told him to meet me at the flat the following morning.

Big Ben chimed in the background as I walked along the path to the lake which bisects the park, past the concrete snack bar that's a scaled down version of Liverpool Cathedral, the modern one, not the pretty one. Pigeons, geese and ducks were taking bread from tame tourists, waddling from hand to hand, too gorged or too lazy to fly, waiting until positively the last minute before getting the hell out of my way.

Stand in the middle of the footbridge, Tony had said, and wait for me. He was late, walking from the direction of The Mall across the grass under the towering horse chestnuts, giving a wide berth to a game of football between white overalled painters and carpenters who were blasting a muddy ball at goalposts made of dropped pullovers.

We both leant on the faded blue-green railings, facing towards Buckingham Palace. The flag wasn't flying so the Queen wasn't at home, but if she had been, and if she'd been standing on the balcony with a pair of powerful binoculars, then maybe she'd have wondered what we were talking about, and if she'd had a supersensitive directional microphone and had been able to pick up what we were saying, maybe she'd have wondered why two grown men were verbally fencing like a couple of nervous interviewees.

'What's going on, sport? What are you up to?' he asked.

'What are you talking about, Tony?'

'Just listen to him,' he said, more to himself than to me. 'When I give you the word I want you to turn round very slowly and look at the fountain at the other end of the lake. Pretend you're deep in thought, listening to what I'm saying, then turn your head to two o'clock and tell me if you recognize the man sitting on the bench there. Do it now.'

I followed his instructions, not sure what to expect but knowing something was wrong. It was Iwanek, dressed just the way he was when I met him in the Savoy, except that he'd added a dark brown raincoat with the collar turned up. Shit, shit, shit. Tony hadn't turned but I knew he was waiting for me to speak, to explain.

Two men, both with hands thrust deep into the pockets of dark overcoats, approached Iwanek, one from behind, one walking along the duck-strewn path, and simultaneously sat down on either side of him. It looked like something out of a George Raft movie and I smiled. Tony had always had a taste for the melodramatic. Iwanek got up to go, I could feel the tension from a hundred yards away, and one of the men laid a restraining hand on his arm and spoke to him. He settled back down, resigned but with the air of an animal that realizes it's trapped but is still looking for a way out.

'Well?' said Tony, and this time he turned and we both looked at Iwanek like a couple of used car dealers at an auction, assessing the merchandise.

'What makes you think I know him?' I said.

'Just listen to him,' he whispered again. 'Playing with fire, playing with the big boys.' He sighed and looked at me, eyes hard and cold. Like his voice.

'Three reasons, sport. One, he was waiting for you outside the wine bar when we met two days ago. Two, he followed you here today. Three, he can't take his eyes off you. There's either something very wrong here or he's in love with you. Talk to me.'

'I hired him.'

'To do what? To follow you? Is that what he is, protection?'

'No, I guess he's checking me out, the equivalent of you or me asking for references or getting a credit check done. It's not a problem.' A lie, that one. Iwanek was a problem, a real humdinger, and one that I wasn't sure how to deal with. Hell, hell, hell.

'What's going on?' he pressed. 'What in God's name would you want to hire a man like that for?'

I suppose lying is like eating raw oysters, the first one is the hardest, you've got a psychological barrier to cross, but once it's done you never look back, it just gets easier and easier. I had no trouble with lie number two but if I'd had a life-size portrait of myself in the attic, done in oils and framed in gilt, then the face would have started to blemish, the skin to wrinkle and age.

'This client I wanted a girl for is going to need looking after while he's in London. That guy there was recommended to me, and I asked him to recruit another two. There's quite a bit of money involved, I suppose he just wants to confirm who he's working for.' That sounded about as solid as a self-assembly kitchen unit, because if it was bodyguards I'd wanted then I would obviously have gone to Tony, but he let that pass.

'What do you want to do with him?' he asked.

'Let me talk to him. I'll point out the error of his ways.'

'I could get my two friends there to give him the good news.'

'No, I don't want him hurt, he was just a little over-enthusiastic. Can I borrow them for a few minutes, though?'

'Sure. They won't break.'

I walked over the bridge and down to the path where the three of them sat like a row of brass monkeys. I stood in front of Iwanek and he looked up at me, unsmiling.

'Satisfied?' I asked, and I knew I had to be careful because everything I said would be relayed back to Tony and I was in enough trouble already. He just kept looking at me, curious rather than afraid.

'Are you satisfied?' I repeated. I had to convince him that I was in control, a hard man who could cause him a lot of grief if I chose to. The two men sitting like a couple of bookends would go a long way to persuading him, and if the worst came to the worst I knew they could hurt him badly. But then I'd run the risk of losing him.

'You wouldn't have expected me to accept the sort of job you offered without knowing what I was getting into,' he said, and the tone left me in no doubt that he was the hard man, not me.

'You've already accepted the job and you took my money. It's too late to be checking up on me. You're hired and there's no going back. You've given me a dilemma, Jim. I can't have you following me all over London, now can I? You'll get in my way. But if I break your legs, correction, if I get these two to break your legs, then you'll be no use to me. What shall I do, Jim? Advise me.'

'These two don't worry me,' he said, and I believed him. 'But I've got the message. I wanted to know who you are, what you do, and the sort of circles you move in. I still don't know what you're up to, but I've an idea now of the sort of business you're in. I won't bother you again. Give me a call when you're ready.'

He got to his feet and walked off without a backward look, leaving me to escort the two heavies back to Tony.

'I don't suppose you'd tell me what you're up to even if I asked,' he said. 'So I won't.'

'I'll be all right,' I replied. 'I know what I'm doing.'

I didn't hear a cock crow and the sky didn't split open to unleash a bolt of lightning, but I knew I'd lied three times and that the third lie had slipped off my tongue like butter off a hot knife. I left Tony behind and went off in search of a cab, having added years to the hypothetical portrait in my hypothetical attic.

The evening sky was threatening rain as McKinley braked sharply in front of Sammy's flat, sharply enough to throw me forward but not sharply enough to snap the seat belt and send me tumbling over the bonnet. Not quite. The taxi driver who'd managed to slam on his brakes and squeal to a halt three inches from our rear bumper hit his horn angrily, reversed his cab and drove past glaring at McKinley who took not a blind bit of notice.

'I'll wait here, boss,' he said.

'You're double parked, Get-Up, but we won't be long,' I replied, but I was only halfway out of the Granada as she came through the front door and down the steps.

She'd curled her red hair and it bounced and shimmered

as she walked, the ends stroking her bare shoulders. Her dress was long and black and could have been worn to a funeral if she'd wanted to be gang-raped by the pall bearers. It was slashed from the ground to just below her waist on both sides and her long brown legs flashed in and out as she clicked down the steps on high heels. Three things held the dress up, two thread-like silver chains across each shoulder and the swell of her breasts. Around her perfect neck was a single strand of pearls matched by a smaller group on her left wrist. It was all the jewellery she was wearing and Sammy didn't even need that.

'You look delicious,' I said as I reached for her hand.

'Don't I just?' she laughed, and I helped her into the back seat and slid in beside her. 'I hope you appreciate all the effort that went into creating this work of art.'

'You'll be telling me next that bodies like yours don't grow on trees.'

'They don't grow like this at all without a great deal of work. A lot of exercise, a lot of care and attention, and a lot of money.'

'You make it sound like owning an expensive car, looking after the bodywork and keeping the engine in good running order.' She crossed her legs as I spoke and her slender foot brushed against my trouser leg.

'That's a fair comparison,' she said, and already her hand had found its way to my knee, circling it thoughtfully. 'But some collectors' cars are more than a hundred years old. I'll be lucky if I stay in concours condition for another five. And it's not as if I've only had one careful owner.'

Now she was laughing, eyes sparkling as she tilted her head to one side and looked my face over. She reached up and stroked my right ear, nipping the lobe between finger and thumb. 'Where are we going?' she asked.

We weren't going anywhere because McKinley was twisted round in the driver's seat, mouth agape, eyes eating up Sammy and what the hell, who could blame him? She'd turn more heads than a road accident dressed like this.

'Let's go, Get-Up,' I said, and as he turned back in his seat his eyes were the last thing to move. He sighed, deeply and sorrowfully, like a poodle being asked to leave the bed of his mistress. He put the car into second gear and drove away from the kerb in jerks and jumps before switching the wrong indicator light on.

It took thirty minutes of McKinley's stop-start driving before he dropped us in front of the four-storey grey stone building in Berkeley Square which houses Spencers, a restaurant used mainly by advertising executives and media salesmen and anyone else on no-questions-asked expense accounts.

The square was clogged up with traffic and any nightingale brave or stupid enough to venture there to sing would be coughing up phlegm for a month. Several horns honked as McKinley leant over and asked what time he should pick us up.

'Just hang around, Get-Up. I won't be long,' I told him. 'Find a parking space nearby and keep your eyes on the front door.'

I took Sammy by the arm and together we walked up the stone steps, past the twin bay trees standing guard duty either side of the door and through the bar.

The food in Spencers tended to be overcooked and overpriced and the decor completely over the top: vivid flock wallpaper, cheap paintings in expensive gilded frames, and huge ornate chandeliers with electric candles flickering annoyingly. But it did have one advantage over any of a dozen other places I would quite happily have taken Sammy to – Ronnie Laing could be found there three or four evenings a week, often dining alone. He used Spencers as his canteen, always had the same table, was treated like a long-lost relative every time he crossed the threshold and knew the menu by heart. He tipped well, usually took the maître d's advice on food and let the wine waiter choose his drink. They couldn't have loved him more if he'd rolled up his sleeves and pitched in with the washing up.

A phone call earlier in the evening had confirmed that Laing had booked a table, and as Sammy and I were shown to a booth I saw him sitting in a corner facing the entrance, on his own and halfway through a plate of mussels, either a large starter or a small main course.

'We'll sit here, if you don't mind,' I said, as the waiter tried to steer us away from Laing, and I pointed to one of the small circular tables about twelve feet from where he was sitting. I recognized him from the photographs that had appeared at the time of the takeover but he wouldn't have known me from Adam. He didn't go to the funeral. He didn't go to either of them.

'Not at all, sir,' said the waiter through clenched teeth, and the 'sir' was very much an afterthought as he pulled out the chair for Sammy. Unfortunately it was the chair facing away from Laing and the waiter barely concealed his disdain as I slid into it myself and motioned her to take the other one. He rushed round to pull out the second chair and was rewarded with a toe-curling smile from Sammy and a long lingering look down the front of her dress.

I wondered if it would be enough to make him forget my breach of etiquette but he handed Sammy a menu as if he were passing her a love letter and pushed one at me as if he were serving me with a summons, so I guessed it would take more than Sammy's superb figure to wipe that one out. What the hell, tonight I wasn't going to be winning any prizes for good manners so I might as well start as I meant to go on.

'A double whisky, a malt, and you'd better make it a good one,' I said in the sort of voice you'd use to tell an Alsatian to walk to heel. Then I stuck my head into the menu until he tapped his pencil on his notepad, coughed, and asked, 'And for the lady?' with the accent heavily on 'lady' as if offering Sammy his sympathy for being with a lout like me.

'Good Lord, she's got a tongue in her head, man. Ask her yourself.'

Sammy kept looking at the table, her head down as if in prayer and her hands in her lap. 'I'll have a white wine,' she said, then looked up at the waiter through lowered lashes and moistened her lips and added 'please'. She turned her head to look at me and then looked past me over my left shoulder and smiled and I knew she'd seen Laing and that he'd seen her.

'Not bored already, are you?' I asked and her eyes snapped back to meet mine and she caught her breath.

'No, no, I'm fine.'

'Well, what do you want to eat?'

'I'll have whatever you're having.'

'God, you're such a doormat.' The waiter returned with the drinks and I reached up and took my whisky off his tray while he was placing Sammy's white wine in front of her. I drank it in one swallow and handed it back. 'Get me another.' Sammy was looking at Laing again and nervously fingering her hair so that from where he was sitting he'd see she wasn't wearing a ring.

'How was work today?' she asked.

'Same as it always is, boring but well paid, and the last thing I want to talk about is how boring and well paid it is. I don't take you out to go over my business problems – that's what I pay an accountant for. I just want you to look pretty and smooth my feathers. Sometimes I wonder how I've managed to put up with you for so long. And where did you get that dress?'

'A boutique in Chelsea, I thought you'd like it.'

'You thought wrong. It doesn't suit you at all, it's not your colour. How many times have I told you not to wear black?'

My second drink arrived as she bit her bottom lip and said in a quiet voice: 'I can't seem to do anything right today.'

I slammed the empty glass down hard enough to shake the candles on the table.

'Perhaps you'd better just keep quiet then,' I said and waved the waiter over, ordering for us both without consulting her and demanding another double whisky.

'And another white wine,' I added.

'I'm fine, thank you,' she whispered and there were tears in her eyes.

'You're not fine, now drink that up,' I said. 'You're more fun when you've had a few drinks. In bed and out of it.' Now she was crying silently, hands playing with her serviette, screwing it up into a tight knot.

'I'm going to the toilet,' I said and stood up unsteadily,

pushing the chair back so violently that it fell over with a crash and the waiter scurried over to pick it up. 'Don't fuss, man,' I said and headed for the gents, managing to bump into two tables on the way. As I barged through the door I saw Laing get to his feet and move towards Sammy.

I stayed in the white-tiled room long enough for Sammy to spill her tale of woe to Laing, to tell him of a relationship that had gone sour but which she was too frightened to end, of the verbal and physical batterings I'd given her, of the times I had humiliated her and abused her. Then she would dab her reddening eyes and sniff and he'd put his hand on hers and tell her gently that everything was going to be all right and that if she really wanted to get rid of the bullying bastard he was just the man to do it, and she would flutter those long, curling eyelashes and say that she'd be so grateful, so very grateful, but to take care because she had seen me put two men in hospital because they'd taken too much of an interest in her. She would dry her eyes and smile bravely and tell him her name was Amanda, that she was a model and that she lived in Islington, and she would give him the address of the furnished two-bedroomed first-floor flat that we'd rented in the name of Amanda Pearson a week earlier.

I walked back to Sammy's table and stood looking down at her, hands on hips, glaring and demanding to know just what the hell was going on, spraying her with spittle as I spoke, every inch the drunken bore who deserved everything that was coming to him. Please God don't let him break anything, bones, teeth or nose.

'I think you'd better go,' said Laing as he got to his feet, and it was the voice of a man used to getting his own way. He put a warning hand on my shoulder and two waiters hovered anxiously behind him, unwilling to interfere between a drunk and their favourite customer playing white knight.

'Keep out of this,' I said without turning. To Sammy I said: 'Get up, we're leaving.'

'She's staying. With me. You're the one that's going,' he said and the grip tightened. I took a deep breath and turned and pulled back my fist, and he hit me once about an inch above my solar plexus and my legs collapsed, the contents of my lungs exploded out of my mouth and I tasted bitter bile at the back of my throat, and then I was on my knees, hands clutched to my chest, coughing and choking. At least he hadn't hit me in the face, but even that was no consolation as I fought to breathe. I looked up at him and tried to speak and he stepped forward and thrust his knee into my face. I went backwards and the bile was replaced with the warm, salty taste of blood as my head hit the floor.

The two waiters stepped forward and picked me up and half led, half carried me to the manager's office where they wiped the blood from my mouth and told me that they wouldn't call the police this time, but I was never to darken their doorstep again and then they half carried, half pushed me out of the front door and down the steps to Berkeley Square.

'Jesus, boss, what happened?' asked McKinley, as I opened the car door and lowered myself painfully into the passenger seat.

'Just take me home, Get-Up. Slowly and carefully.' I could just about breathe but it was an effort and my mouth and chin were on fire. Two of my front teeth felt loose, my lip was still bleeding and spots of blood fell onto my trousers until I held my handkerchief to my aching face.

'What about Miss Darvell?' he asked as he shoved the gear stick forward and hauled the steering wheel round. 'Are you sure you don't want me to deal with this, boss?' he said before I could answer his first question. 'It won't do your reputation any good letting somebody hit you and get away with it. Tell me who it was and let me sort them out for you.'

'It's all right, Get-Up, honestly. Miss Darvell and I have just decided to part company for a while, that's all. Take me home. And if you see an all-night chemist on the way, stop off and get me some antiseptic. And some aspirin.'

Then I closed my eyes and leaned back in the seat and stretched my legs forward. McKinley muttered under his breath as the car picked up speed. I'm not sure what he said but it sounded like 'Jesus, she must pack a helluva punch.'

'So Laing doesn't do much in the way of drugs now?' I asked, lying back in the armchair and putting my feet on the glass coffee table between the chrome ice bucket and the three-quarters empty bottle of malt that McKinley and I were working our way through.

It was one o'clock in the morning, two days after I'd introduced Laing to Sammy, and we'd spent the evening at the Eve Club in Regent Street. The lip was healing nicely. If I was lucky it wouldn't leave a scar. I'd been plying McKinley with drink for more than five hours, and now his eyes were bleary and his voice slurred and I was once again asking him about his past. It was a bit like mining for gold, you had to sort through tens of tons of worthless crushed rock to come up with an ounce of the yellow stuff.

'Don't forget I haven't seen him for seven years or so, boss, but from what I hear he still does a bit to keep his hand in, but he's up against the big boys now,' McKinley said as he leant over for the bottle, shoulders straining through the dark blue suit I'd bought him two weeks earlier which was already soiled and stained with everything from spirits to engine oil and a few other substances I couldn't have identified even if I'd wanted to. He emptied the bottle into the glass, splashed in a handful of melting ice cubes and drank noisily as he wiped his wet hand on his trouser leg.

'Why did you never go back and work for him when you came out?' I asked. 'You all went down quietly enough.'

'Jesus, boss, what do you expect? If we'd grassed we'd have lost our kneecaps, our balls and anything else that hadn't been nailed to the floor. That's why we kept our mouths shut. I tried to see him my second day out but the message passed to me was that he didn't want anyone with a record on the payroll, so thanks but no thanks. All I got was a lousy five-hundred pound pay off – for seven years. Bastard.' His glass was empty now and he looked at me expectantly, and I nodded towards the sideboard from where he liberated another bottle.

We drank in silence for a while, or at least McKinley drank while I remained almost horizontal and watched the brass light fitting in the centre of the plaster ceiling rose through half-closed eyes, making light patterns with my eyelashes as I listened to the sound of my own breathing.

'Do you think I'm stupid, boss?' he asked eventually.

'What?' I replied, opening my eyes and raising my head

so I could see him slumped in the chair opposite mine and running his hand through his unkempt hair.

'I said, do you think I'm stupid?'

I leant back and looked at the ceiling again. 'That's a tough one, Get-Up. I mean, if I were to ask you who Don Giovanni was, would you think that he was an Italian Godfather?'

His forehead creased in a frown but he saw by the look on my face that I wasn't taking him seriously and he didn't ask 'Don who?' Whatever had been irritating his scalp had now crawled down to his beard which he scratched vigorously like a dog worrying its nether regions. 'Don't take the piss, I'm serious, boss.'

'I can see that, Get-Up. Come on, get it off your chest. What's worrying you?'

The irritation had migrated to his right ear and he was wiggling his index finger up and down and in and out furiously, screwing his eyes up as he concentrated and spilling whisky over his knees as his glass trembled.

If I'd been a psychologist I would probably have marked it down as acute displacement behaviour, but knowing McKinley it was more likely something with six legs and dirty feet.

I was sitting up now, holding my glass with both hands and trying to read this strange, big and possibly dangerous man mountain because any problem he had could quite easily and quickly become my headache.

'Well, it's like this,' he said. 'You've given me a job, and you pay me well, and you treat me with respect, though sometimes I don't understand what you're saying to me and sometimes I think you're taking the Michael, but generally you're OK and I like working for you.'

'That's nice to know – if ever I need a reference I'll come to you. What is it you're after, a raise?' I knew it wasn't money he was after, it was an explanation, but I had to let him ask for it in his own sweet time.

'No, it's not that, boss. It's just that, well, it's as if . . .' He fell silent, staring at my shoelaces like Sammy's cat, deep in thought. Then, as if he'd finally made up his mind about something, he raised his eyes sharply. 'It's all these questions you keep asking me. It's worse than being collared by the law. You keep pumping me about Ronnie Laing and his connections, how does he do this, how does he do that, who does he know, where does he live, where does he eat? Jesus, boss, I don't owe Laing no favours but I'd like to know what it is you're up to.'

He'd stopped fidgeting with his hands but he chewed his lower lip as he waited for my answer.

'Fair enough, Get-Up, but there's nothing sinister happening, believe me. I used to do a fair bit of drugs dealing up in Glasgow, mainly cocaine – I've told you that already. I had contacts going all the way from the ice-cream vans that tour the housing schemes up to the guys who service the universities and I made a good living out of it, but eventually I ran into the same problem as your ex-boss. A gang of neds who used to specialize in armed robbery decided to go into the drugs business in a big way at my expense. They didn't have my contacts but they found out where I was getting my supplies from and after a bit of persuasion those supplies dried up, and once I couldn't come up with the goods my customers moved on. That's why I moved to London.'

This was starting to sound like something Hans Christian Andersen might have written on an off day, but from the way McKinley was nodding his head it looked as if he believed me. I refilled his glass with whisky and leant back in the chair.

'I need a new supply of coke, Get-Up, and when I discovered you used to work for Laing I figured he might be able to help. But from what you've been saying that's a non-starter.'

'Too true,' he said. 'And anyway I'm yesterday's news as far as that bastard's concerned. He wouldn't do me any favours.' He went quiet and looked at my shoelaces again. 'I might be able to put you in touch with someone who could help, though.'

I knew then how the Klondyke prospectors must have felt when they first found a small nugget of gold glinting in the dross, because at last I was going to get what I wanted from McKinley.

'I thought you'd be out of touch after seven years.'

'Most of the old faces are still in the business, give or take the few who've moved on or been sent down. What is it you want, exactly?'

'You sound like a genie from a bottle, Get-Up. OK, I'll tell you what I want. I've got £250,000 in cash that I want to turn into white powder. What I need is someone to arrange the deal for me, to fix up a time and a place where I can hand over the cash in exchange for the drugs. After what happened to me in Glasgow I want to keep as low a profile as possible, so whoever I get will have to have the right contacts and be the sort who'll keep his mouth shut about my involvement. I need a middle-man, not so close to the streets that he can't think bigger than a few grams, but not so big that he isn't hungry. Well genie, can you grant me this boon, or should I uncork another bottle?'

'I think I can help, boss,' he said. 'And, yes, I would like another drink.' I poured him a refill before he continued. 'One of the guys Laing used to arrange shipments through went down soon after me for a three-year stretch, Davie Read. When he came out he was in the same boat as me, Laing wouldn't give him the time of day, so he's been doing some freelance dealing. He's got the contacts but he doesn't have the money to set up anything big himself, he's strictly small time.

'I reckon he'd jump at the chance if you'd cut him in for a percentage. Do you want me to arrange a meet?'

'Sure, he sounds perfect. In fact he sounds too good to be true. Can you trust him?'

'I don't see why not, boss. I'll tell him you're the front man for some very heavy characters and that if he steps out of line you'll have both of his legs broken.'

'You mean you'll appeal to the more sensitive side of his nature?' At that McKinley roared with laughter, he tossed his head back and I could have counted the fillings in the teeth he had left if I'd wanted to get a bit closer to his open mouth, but that had about as much attraction as inspecting a blocked drain.

'I've got a better cover story, Get-Up. This is what I want you to tell him,' and I gave him a story on a par with Snow White and the Seven Dwarfs. Hi ho, hi ho, it's off to work we go.

Kyle's office was on the first floor of a refurbished building, in a narrow street a grapefruit's throw from Spitalfields

Market. It was early evening and I waited near the carpark where Kyle's Mercedes was parked, sleek and shiny new and as green as the lettuce leaves blown up against the tyres by a light breeze.

The market had been closed for several hours and scavenging down and outs were sifting through the roadside rubbish, picking out bruised and rotting apples and potatoes and carefully placing them in old carrier bags or in the pockets of tired, worn overcoats.

Two rooks cawed and coughed and dived on a discarded banana, and pecked it apart until one of the last few delivery trucks roared round the corner and made them hop angrily on to the pavement. They were soon back in the road, pulling and eating, feathers as black and glossy as the leather briefcase I was carrying, which along with the Burberry and dark pinstripe suit branded me as one of the many office workers who'd moved into the area around Liverpool Street station as the overcrowded City pushed relentlessly east, upgrading buildings and filling them full of word processors, designer furniture and anti-static carpet tiles.

I was sitting on the low, red railing which surrounded the carpark, briefcase balanced on my knees, and from there I could see the door to Kyle's office, though I was too far away to see the small brass plate which read 'Property and Financial Services'.

On either side of the black panelled door, fixed to the wall about ten feet above the cobbled pavement, were two wicker cages, each containing a single songbird singing its heart out.

Maybe they were singing because they were happy, maybe because they wouldn't get fed if they didn't sing, maybe they were calling to each other and professing undying love, but

I reckoned they were crying to be let out, to be allowed to fly free above the stonecleaned offices and reslated roofs and join the crows and down and outs foraging for food instead of singing for their bird seed supper.

The door opened, and the birds redoubled their efforts as Kyle stepped onto the pavement and started walking towards the car. I was already up and moving quickly, anxiously looking at my watch, a man in a hurry with a train to catch. I crossed the road ahead of him, looked at my watch again, thirty feet, twenty feet, and then I was falling, tripping over my feet and losing the case as I pitched forward, hands outstretched to break my fall.

I hit the ground at the same time as the briefcase caught Kyle below the knees, scuffing my gloves on the cobbles and feeling my trousers tear. As I cursed and swore and pulled myself to my feet Kyle picked up my briefcase by the handle, then held it by either end as he handed it back to me.

'Not hurt?' he asked and I said no, thanks for helping me and whose bloody idea was it to have a cobbled pavement in the first place? And then he was gone, on his way to the shiny green Mercedes leaving me with three perfect sets of fingerprints on the case, which I was careful not to smudge with my gloved hands and which was going straight into a polythene bag when I got back to the flat.

'I'd like to meet him,' Sammy had said, and I knew without a shadow of a doubt that David would love to meet her. It was a nuisance to arrange, to explain to McKinley that I'd be out of circulation for a day, to fix up the Shuttle tickets and a hire car, to ring Shankland Hall and tell them I was taking David out.

It was a nuisance but it was worth it, worth it to see David hug Sammy and stroke her flowing hair, to see her talk to him and kiss him softly on the forehead. They clicked and I was overjoyed, she wasn't awkward with him, or pitying, she was just warm and tender, like a big sister. I loved her for it.

'The zoo,' I told David when he asked where we were going. I drove while he and Sammy sat in the back and we played word games, calling out animals in alphabetical order. Sammy made an appalling attempt to cheat by claiming that asparagus and aubergine were types of mammals and got a gentle cuff from David.

The Highland Wildlife Park, near Kincraig in Inverness-shire, is about forty miles due north of Pitlochry, and though I'd told David we were going to the zoo, it wasn't to see elephants, tigers and giraffes. All the animals there are native to Scotland, though many of them are long since extinct in the wild. Driving safari-park style along a wild and rugged road there are deer and cattle in something approaching their natural environment, and you can see brown bears, lynxes and Scottish wild cats close up. David and I were regular visitors, mainly I guess because he loved the Pets Corner where he could touch and hold and feed and play with animals who didn't care who or what he was, just that he was gentle and had food for them.

It was a chilly day despite a watery sun, so I made sure his old sheepskin jacket was buttoned up high over his thick red polo-neck sweater before we tramped around the enclosures. David was inexhaustible, running from cage to cage while Sammy and I walked after him, arms linked.

'What's your favourite animal?' I asked her.

'Easy,' she said. 'Polar bears.'

'You'll have to explain that one.'

'Purely visual, I suppose. Big and white and furry, friendly faces. They give the impression you could cuddle up next to them and be safe and warm and protected, but when they move you're left in no doubt about their immense strength and power, muscles rippling under the fur, paws big enough to rip a man's head off. Protective of their mates, gentle with their young, afraid of nothing. I love them. I'd take one home with me if I could.'

'They're killers, you know?'

'I know that, and in a way that's part of the attraction. To be that close to something that could kill if it wanted to, and yet to be safe and comfortable. Do you think I need a father figure?'

'Sammy, that's the last thing I think you need,' I said and she giggled.

'What's your favourite?' she asked.

'I knew as soon as the question left my lips that you'd ask it right back,' I said, and slipped my arm around her waist. 'I'll have to think.'

Together we followed David towards the otter pool. It was just after three pm and it was feeding time. There are some questions that reveal a lot about a person. Sammy's answer had told me something about her, it had shown me a side of her I wouldn't otherwise have seen, and my answer would do the same, unless I lied. But I wouldn't lie, I decided.

'My favourite isn't here either,' I said. 'And I'm glad, I

feel uneasy seeing any animal in captivity, but I feel most for the dolphins.'

She was listening closely, head tilted, brushing the hair away from her eyes, watching my face. She didn't have to ask why because she knew I'd explain.

'They're so bright, so intelligent, so perfectly adapted to their environment. Have you ever seen them close up?'

'I went to a dolphinarium once, but it made me feel sad.'

'I know. They do tricks, but at least they're not like sealions. Sealions are clowns, clapping, balancing balls and walking on their flippers, doing tricks for food. Nature's buskers. I hate to see that.'

A keeper was throwing small dead silvery fish to the otters with a minimum of fuss, and once the glossy animals had tired of chasing their food he tipped the contents of his red plastic bucket into the greenish water and walked away, leaving them to eat in peace, nervously eyeing each other as they chewed noisily like dossers in a soup kitchen.

'Dolphins are different,' I continued. 'They are much more intelligent. In the wild they're something else. Friendly, sociable, playful, gentle. They don't interfere with anyone else and they're completely non-aggressive, no claws, no sharp teeth, no spikes. But they'll kill to protect themselves, and they'll band together to fight off an enemy. God help the shark that tries to attack a dolphin.'

We stood together, watching David watching the otters feed until they'd finished. Then he romped over and forced his way between us, holding our hands and bouncing up and down as we walked back to the car. He asked if we could come back and I said yes, of course and he said what about Sammy and I said yes, she'd come too and he said what about Shona and I had to think about that one.

She was waiting for us when we arrived back at Shankland Hall, leaning against her Rover, smiling the smile of the wounded.

'You might have said you'd be taking David out today,' she said, looking Sammy up and down as we got out of the car. She stepped forward and kissed me on the cheek, and then hugged David before wiping saliva off his chin with a handkerchief. 'Hiya, kid,' she said to him and he laughed uncontrollably. The sister came out and David went inside with her, still laughing as he waved goodbye. This time there were no 'don't go's', the parting was easier, and I think that was because Sammy had been there and he knew he had another friend.

The three of us drove to a small country pub three miles from the nursing home, taking the two cars which was a problem because I had to choose but it was no choice really, I had to go with Sammy. Strike that, I wanted to go with Sammy.

The pub was a weathered stone building amid a clump of grey houses, probably the only source of live entertainment for miles around, but it was virtually empty, just a few red-veined locals standing by the bar and downing whisky as if the licensing laws had never been relaxed north of the border.

An untidy tower of roughly-hewn logs burned in a large brick fireplace, filling the room with warmth and smoke. To the left was a small bench seat, in front of it a round knee-high table made from the same dark wood, with two comfortable old chairs on either side. Shona and Sammy each flopped down into one. That left the bench seat for me, and when I'd put the drinks on the table and sat down they were facing me like a pair of temple dogs.

'Well, this is nice,' said Shona. 'Cheers.' It wasn't like her to be so bitchy but she was right, I should have let her know I was going to see David and I shouldn't have sprung Sammy on her like an unfavourable diagnosis.

'Did you enjoy yourselves?' she asked me, and I nodded and told her where we'd been.

'He's a lovely boy,' said Sammy, and Shona smiled at her, the smile of a predator ready to pounce. I'd never have to ask Shona what her favourite animal was, it would have to be the tiger, sleek and beautiful, quick to purr and quick to kill. I'd seen her in action many times, and admired her for it, but this was different. This was Sammy, and Sammy was a friend on unfamiliar territory.

'Yes, he is,' said Shona. 'Have you been to Scotland before?'

'No, this is my first time,' Sammy replied. 'But I love it, the air is so fresh, the hills have a rugged beauty that you simply don't see down south, and the people are so friendly. I'll be back.'

'I'm sure you will,' said Shona. 'I'm sure you will,' she repeated, quietly and thoughtfully. I felt like a sick pigeon being fought over by a couple of alley cats, but I couldn't understand why their claws were out, they weren't a threat to each other and I wasn't playing favourites. Or maybe I was, perhaps that was the problem.

'Sammy's a friend of Tony's,' I said, and Shona raised an eyebrow as if to say, 'I just bet she is.'

'Do you work together?' she asked.

'You mean Tony and I? Yes, sort of. I'm in public relations.' Which was, of course, absolutely true but I still grinned and stopped worrying. She was a big girl and could take care of herself. They fenced for a while but Sammy had the edge because I'd talked to her so often about Shona, and after half an hour or so the conversation eased and they discussed clothes and shops, diverting the rivalry into a friendly argument about the merits of their two cities, a dispute about cultures and not personalities. They parted as almost friends and I knew that next time they met they'd peck cheeks like old school chums but they'd never be close, never have heart-to hearts or cry on each other's shoulders. I could live with that.

'You'll be back soon?' Shona asked me in the pub carpark and I said yes, a couple of weeks at the most, I promise, maybe sooner. We took the same road back to Edinburgh but Shona had her foot hard on the accelerator and she soon left us far behind.

A couple of days after Sammy and I got back from Scotland McKinley fixed up the meeting with Davie Read. To fit in with the cover story, we arranged an appointment at Salisbury House in Finsbury Circus, the London headquarters of the National Bank of Detroit. One of the biggest blocks in the area, its face of light brown sandstone and window boxes bursting with purple and white flowers looked down on four games of bowls being played by shirt-sleeved office workers on a tiny green in the centre of the Circus gardens.

I waited close to the polished granite steps leading up to the main entrance foyer until I saw McKinley and Read arrive in the Granada, the rear wheels catching the kerb as they turned into the Circus looking for an empty parking meter. I walked quickly up to the reception desk and asked to speak to Mr Kolacowosky and hoped to God they didn't actually have anyone of that name in the building. I kept one eye on the glass doors as the girl behind the desk looked through her internal telephone directory, shaking her head and saying yes, she had heard me say the name but how on earth did you spell it?

As McKinley and Read started up the steps I told her not to bother and that Mr Kolacowosky had obviously moved on to better things and I headed for the door. I met them halfway down and steered Read round, my arm on his shoulder, thanking him for coming and saying to Get-Up that, with the sensitive nature of the arrangements, it might be better if we spoke in the open air and not in my office where we never knew who might be next door with his ear pressed against a glass tumbler.

McKinley nodded and said he understood and Read said what a good idea, and all three of us were nodding like those little dogs you see in the back of resprayed Ford Cortinas with large fluffy dice hanging from the driver's mirror.

I herded them over the road to the Circus gardens like a collie with a couple of wayward sheep, encouraged them past the bicycles chained to the black railings, through the gateway and down the tarmac path which circled the bowling green.

It was two-thirty pm so most of the lunching office workers had gone back to their desks and computer terminals, but several of the wooden benches were still occupied by men in suits and women in smart summer dresses eating Marks and Spencer sandwiches, salads from

Tupperware containers and doughnuts from brown paper bags as they stretched out their legs and enjoyed the waning warmth of the afternoon sun.

The air buzzed with the sound of traffic and the two-way radios of the motorcycle messengers. Through the trees came the sound of drilling and cutting and hammering from the repair and refurbishment that's always a part of the City background noise, standards and rents leapfrogging each other madly behind miles of dust-covered scaffolding.

Davie Read was about forty years old and a similar build to McKinley – as I walked between them I felt like a slice of corned beef in a roll. He was clean shaven and sweating slightly, either through nervousness or the heat, and in his large brown checked jacket and beige trousers he could have passed for a middle-ranking insurance salesman with a three-bedroomed semi in Ealing and a two-year-old Sierra in the drive. He wore a pair of gold-rimmed glasses and as we walked he pulled out a green handkerchief from his top pocket, mopped his wet forehead and blew his bulbous, slightly red nose. With his nose and girth he could have been a heavy drinker, but his breath smelt fresh so he was either a gin and tonic or vodka man or he was on his best behaviour. Whatever, he was all I had and McKinley said he could be trusted.

We passed four building workers lying shirtless on the grass, sunning themselves and looking up the skirts of anything aged between twelve and fifty that walked by.

'Get-Up's told you what I'm after?' I asked, as Read returned the damp handkerchief to his pocket, the sweat already reappearing on his mopped brow.

'Cocaine, a quarter of a million pounds' worth. That shouldn't be a problem, but he was a bit vague about why you wanted it – that's one hell of a lot of sniffing.' The glasses slipped slightly down his nose and he looked over the top of them like an admonishing professor. Hurry up, boy, explain yourself, except if I did this professor would be off like a scalded rabbit. My feet tingled as a Tube train ran through the tunnel below us from Liverpool Street to Moorgate, and the back of my neck tingled because if he didn't believe me I could end up buried beneath the earth at a similar depth to the train.

'I need to make a lot of money, and fast,' I said. 'I represent a group of investors who borrowed heavily to invest in the commodity markets, coffee in particular. We were banking on a heavy frost this year but it never materialized and instead there was a bumper crop and prices fell like a stone. We weren't alone, a lot of people have got their fingers burnt, it took everybody by surprise. Unfortunately we're not in a position to pay back the money we borrowed and we've only got a few weeks to make good the loss.

'We've decided that the most effective use we could make of our remaining capital is to go back into the commodity market, but in a different way. If we import £250,000 of cocaine we can realize it for close to two million pounds and recoup our losses.'

I spoke slowly and clearly, like a marketing director revealing his strategy for the forthcoming financial year and hoping that nobody would spot any flaws. From where we were standing we could just see the top of the National Westminster Tower, rising a head and shoulders above the rest of the City office blocks. If you could find a very large lumberjack with an axe the size of a bus and persuade him to hack away at the base of the tower long and hard, and if he pushed it in our direction and it began to topple then the top two floors would crash down onto the three remaining games of bowls being played on the green. My mind was wandering, tension does that sometimes, and I brought myself back to reality. This was no time to be daydreaming. McKinley had already told Read the tale of woe, how a group of would-be City whizz kids had got their fingers burned gambling on the commodities market with other people's money and how those singed digits would be caught firmly in the till when the auditors came a-calling next month. And to make the cheese in the trap look even more tempting he'd told Read that I was so desperate that he'd be able to cut himself a slice of the action.

Read started to nibble. 'How do you plan to get rid of it?' he asked.

Down boy, don't get too greedy. 'That's my problem – you can leave the distribution to me. All I want from you is the stuff wholesale. I suppose I'm not telling you anything you don't already know if I point out that coke is a rich man's drug. It's served up at all the best dinner parties instead of liqueurs, it's used widely in the City, everyone from advertising executives to merchant bankers is trying and enjoying it. And it isn't bought on street corners. The middle classes have their own distribution system and it's very well protected, believe me. It's not heroin, after all.'

We walked on in silence, Read with his brow furrowed as if he had a difficult decision to make but he'd already decided to bite. The only thought in his mind now was how much of the cheese he could grab before the trap clamped shut.

'What's in it for me?' he asked, and he looked across

at McKinley who was busy trying to scratch the middle of his back, shoving his left arm down his shirt collar and grunting. McKinley had already told him he could stick out for ten per cent of the gross if everything went smoothly, so when I offered him three thousand expenses up front and five per cent he sucked air in through his front teeth as if he was testing for cavities.

'Not enough,' he said. I pressed him.

'I'm offering almost sixteen grand for setting up one deal. I put up all the cash, McKinley and I will collect the coke, you don't even have to be there. All you have to do is make a few phone calls.'

He gave me the sort of look the wolf gave Little Red Riding Hood and he damn near started rubbing his hands together, pound signs rolling up behind the gold-rimmed glasses.

'Look, squire, if it's that easy you don't need me. And if it isn't that easy, and you can take it from me that it isn't, then I want more than a lousy five per cent.'

'I could find somebody else.'

'Sure you could, sure you could,' he said. 'Except we both know you're running out of time, don't we?'

I gave McKinley a withering glare for Read's benefit and fingered my watch. 'I suppose I can go as high as ten per cent.'

He positively beamed. 'That's more like it. But I'm still going to want the three grand expenses.'

I had the money ready and I handed it to him. 'You're quite happy taking the rest of your fee in cocaine?'

'I wouldn't have it any other way,' he laughed, because

twenty-five thousand pounds in white powder would be worth ten times as much on the streets. He wouldn't be pushing it to estate agents and record company A and R men, he'd be selling it in little plastic packets diluted to a fraction of its original strength.

'I'd like to talk specifics,' I said. 'How do you plan to make the delivery?'

He took the handkerchief out of his pocket again, and snapped it open with a flourish as we started our second circuit of the garden.

'The people I have in mind usually bring it over from Ireland by sea, and I'll arrange to collect it, probably somewhere on the west coast of Scotland. I'll let you know where. But if you like I'll bring it right to your door. At no extra cost.' He smiled, just sign on the dotted line, sir, you won't regret it.

'I want to be there when the stuff is handed over and when my cash is counted. And when you take your percentage.'

'That's fine by me,' he said. 'I'll ring Get-Up with the arrangements.'

'Don't leave it too long,' I replied. 'I'd like to get this over with as soon as possible.' And that was that. Easier than ordering a three-piece suite from Harrods.

We turned back and walked out through the main entrance and threaded our way in and out of the Circus traffic. At the bottom of the steps to the bank I shook Read by the hand and said I looked forward to doing business with him. As he and McKinley returned to the Granada I went up the steps, through the double glass doors and back into the reception area. The girl's face fell as I gave her a cheery smile, put my palms down on the teak-veneered desk and asked her if, by any chance, Mr Kolacowosky had left a forwarding address?

Read got back to McKinley two days later, on the Wednesday. Yes, the deal was on, the cocaine would be brought over from Ireland in ten days' time on a fishing boat which would be anchored in the Firth of Lorn, a few miles off Minard Point on the west coast of Scotland. The delivery would be taken the rest of the way in a dinghy which would cut into Loch Feochan (McKinley pronounced it 'Lock Fuckin') and land a couple of miles from a small village called Cleigh.

The drop would be at night and there was a complicated series of signal light sequences so that both sides could recognize each other, but McKinley and I wouldn't have to learn them because Read would be with us to make sure the handover went smoothly and to make equally certain that he got his cut. We arranged to meet at a hotel in Oban, about five miles from Loch Feochan, on the Saturday evening two hours before the drop.

Later that evening, with McKinley back in his hotel room, I made two telephone calls, one to Dinah telling him where and when I'd need him, the other to Iwanek for almost thirty minutes during which time his fee doubled. Yes he had the gun, yes he understood exactly what I wanted him to do, yes he would be in Oban to meet me, yes he was sure it would all go smoothly and yes he wanted his fee in cash. Always be careful of yes-men, my father had told me. Yes, dad, I remember.

The blue velvet curtains billowed gently into the room and through the open window I could hear the neighbourhood thrush telling me what a glorious evening it was, and how the one thing he really wanted in all the world was a lady thrush and how he'd be prepared to fight and die for her because he was the bravest and strongest bird around. Maybe I was taking a liberty with the lyrics but you couldn't fault the tune.

'She sounds happy,' said Sammy as she moved onto her front, red hair falling over her face and spreading across the mascara-marked pillow.

'He,' I said as I stroked the back of her neck. 'The males always have the sweetest songs.'

She lay by my side, face turned towards mine. With one arm above her pillow and the other underneath it, she looked as if she was embracing it the way she'd held me minutes before. I rolled on top of her, legs either side of hers, and kissed her cheek.

'Don't they just,' she laughed, pressing herself against me and then lying still, her breathing quiet and even. I'd been meeting Sammy three or four times a week, usually in the afternoons, usually to check on how she was getting on with Laing and usually ending up in bed under the painting of the storm-tossed sea.

'It's time you had a holiday,' I told her.

'By the "you" I take it you mean me and not us,' she giggled.

'And Laing. Somewhere abroad, somewhere sunny, somewhere French.'

'How about Paris?' The one eye I could see glinted with mischief.

'How very astute of you. The tickets are in my jacket pocket – you'll be flying out a week on Friday from Heathrow, and you're booked into a four-star hotel in the centre of Paris.'

'Who says Father Christmas always wears a red suit and a white beard?' she asked and then, don't ask me how she did it, I was flipped three feet across the bed and found myself lying flat on my back. Then she was on top of me and kissing me through a tangle of hair. I lifted her head and smiled.

'Will he go with you?' I said.

'Do zebras have stripey legs? Of course he will, and he'll have the time of his life. He'll have to make the usual excuses to his wife but he's used to that. And so is she. He'll get such a kick out of the fact that I'm paying, too. I take it I'm only getting a weekend, Santa?'

'Friday night and Saturday night, flying British Airways at half four and coming back late Sunday evening. What you do while you're over there is your own business. If you get my drift.'

Her eyes flashed fire but her lips smiled as she grabbed my wrists, held them above my head and kissed me full on the mouth, gripping me tightly with her legs. 'Come with me,' she said. 'Forget Laing and Kyle.'

'Next time. I promise. And then it'll be pleasure, not business.' And I meant it.

'Business can be a pleasure,' she said, then kissed me again, hard enough to bruise my lips. 'Tell me what to do.'

And I told her about carparks, a Rolls-Royce with a personalized number plate and an American Express card, and then I made love to her again. Or she made love to me. Whatever.

Dinah fingered the studs in his ear as we waited for Laing and Sammy to arrive at the short term carpark at Heathrow Airport. It was a bright, sunny afternoon and we were both in shirtsleeves sitting in the front seats of a black Transit van with 'Kleen Karparts' stencilled in white on the sides. We were tucked away in the far corner on the ground floor giving us a clear view of all the vehicles entering and leaving carpark 1A. Two spaces along was the Granada and I had the parking ticket for it in my chest shirt pocket.

Even with both windows wide open we were sweating, but that was probably nervousness and anxiety because we'd been parked for almost an hour. Twice Dinah had asked to go to the toilet. 'No can do,' I'd told him, 'they could be here any moment,' and now he was sulking.

'There they are now,' I said, and nodded towards the entrance where Laing was leaning out of the driver's side of the Corniche for his ticket. He drove up to the first level and Dinah followed as I stepped over the seat into the back of the van and sat down next to a rattling blue metal toolbox. Dinah pulled up next to the parked Rolls and I peered over his shoulder. I was wearing sunglasses and a floppy white hat with 'Arsenal' on the front and Laing had only seen me once but even so there was no point in taking any chances.

Sammy was stunning, hair tied back with a scarlet bow and wearing a beige boiler suit, a brown pullover knotted across her shoulders. Laing took two small suitcases out of the boot of the Rolls, slammed it shut and together they walked to the departure terminal, my stomach going cold as she slipped her arm through his and rested her head on his shoulder, then I mentally kicked myself because she was only playing a part. She was doing it for me. But that didn't make me feel any better.

'Nice bit of stuff,' said Dinah. 'Lucky bastard.'

'Watch yourself, Dinah,' I said. 'Keep your mind on the job.'

We gave them a full fifteen minutes, then I moved back into the passenger seat to keep watch as Dinah climbed down and stood alongside the driver's window of the Rolls.

I expected subtlety, a skeleton key or a complicated mechanical device that Dinah would wiggle and jiggle until he worked his way past the Corniche's sophisticated central locking system. Dinah was about as subtle as a brass knuckleduster. He took a sheet of sticky-backed plastic and covered the window with it, smoothing out the air bubbles with the back of his hand. From the back pocket of his black leather trousers he took a metal punch, looked right and left, gave me a curt nod and then banged it against the glass which cracked and shattered into a thousand cubes, most of them sticking to the plastic. He rolled it up and handed it to me through the window of the Transit van.

'Oh, nice one, Dinah. If I'd known it was that simple I'd

have done it myself,' I said, and dropped it into the back of the van.

'That was the easy part,' he laughed. 'It's the next bit you're paying me for. Keep your eyes peeled.' He lay across the front seat of the Rolls, head under the dashboard, and it was a full ten minutes before the engine burst into life.

'Right, that's us,' he said, wiping his hands on his blue T-shirt. He opened the back door of the Transit and took out a plastic brush and pan, sweeping up the glass cubes on the floor while I sat in the driving seat of the Rolls and ran my eyes over the controls.

'Follow me back to the garage, and for God's sake don't stall it,' he said. We drove out of the multi-storey carpark and I handed over the Granada's ticket to get the Rolls through.

An hour later we were in the Karparts yard where Dinah fitted a new window – getting spares was obviously not a problem for him. He went to work with a couple of Rolls keys and a file and after two hours handed them to me with a flourish.

'Your car, sir,' he said, and grinned. 'When will you be back with it?'

'Sunday morning, early afternoon at the latest. Will you be here?'

'Ready and waiting,' he said. 'Ready for the car and waiting for my money. Take care with those keys, by the way. They're good but they're not perfect so don't force them. Be gentle.'

He paused, then added: 'What are you up to?'

'Best you don't know, Dinah.' I slid into the plush blue leather seat and put the makeshift key in and turned it.

The Rolls started first time and I winked at him. 'See you Sunday,' I said.

He walked over to the double gates, and while he was opening them I reached under the passenger seat and groped around until I found a small white envelope. Inside was Laing's American Express card and a note from Sammy, short and to the point. 'Be careful. See you soon. S.'

I drove through the gates waving to Dinah as I passed him, and collected my case from Earl's Court and McKinley from his hotel. Laing had bought the car only six months previously so McKinley hadn't seen it before.

'This yours, boss?' he asked.

'It's borrowed, Get-Up. And if you're very good I'll let you share the driving. Settle back, we've a long way to go.'

The Rolls was a dream to drive and it swallowed up the miles to Glasgow like a ravenous schoolboy. I let McKinley take over the wheel after we passed Birmingham and told him I'd sit in the back and try to get some sleep. I'd left a clipboard and a sheaf of notepaper on the seat, and I placed Laing's American Express card under the bulldog clip and studied it while McKinley sat in the outside lane of the M6, foot down to the floor.

A dab of brake fluid would have removed the biro signature and I could have replaced it with 'R. Laing' in my own handwriting, but I had plenty of time to practise so I thought I might as well do it the hard way. Most people don't examine signatures all that closely anyway, especially overworked receptionists. They just pick on a few obvious features, a tall loop on the 'l', the way the 'a' was almost circular and the lower part of the 'g' curved back under the signature in a flamboyant underlining loop. If they match then the signature is OK.

I studied the way Laing signed his name and then I copied it over and over, using up sheet after sheet of paper, and by the time we got to Preston I could do a perfect imitation so long as I had the original in front of me.

It took me until we'd reached Carlisle and the M6 turned into the A74 before I could sign myself 'R. Laing' without checking.

I took over the driving again after we'd stopped for a break at Gretna Green service station, and I'd dropped the sheets of counterfeit signatures into a rubbish bin after ripping them up into a hundred pieces while McKinley was in the toilet.

The road was busy and I played chicken with the speeding lorries on their way north, and tapped the wheel in frustration at the numerous roadworks and single file traffic jams. It's a bitch of a road. Whenever I had to go to London on business I always took the Shuttle, even in a Rolls it's a tiring journey, playing havoc with blood pressures and brakes.

The two of us spent the night at the Central Hotel in Glasgow, courtesy of Laing's Amex card, and first thing Saturday morning I picked up a BMW from an up-market car hire company in the shadow of the Daily Record building at Anderston Quay.

Before the blonde receptionist handed me the keys she rang up the credit card company to check it was valid but that wasn't a problem, Laing was in Paris (God, my heart ached when I thought of him with Sammy), and he wouldn't know it was missing. If he should realize it had gone astray then I'd arranged for Sammy to say that she thought she'd seen it on the floor of the Rolls.

I drove the BMW back to the city centre, McKinley following in the Rolls, and we took the A82 out of Glasgow and headed for Oban.

McKinley and I were booked into the Caledonian Hotel, an imposing brown stone building with slated turrets and white sash windows peering over Oban Bay towards the Isle of Mull.

We had adjoining rooms at the front of the hotel, and from my window I looked down on the battered fishing boats bumping gently into each other in the swell as seagulls glided and cried, every now and again dipping down and diving into the sea for a piece of rotting fish or hunks of bread thrown by tourists.

It was about five pm and we'd arranged to meet Read in the bar at seven, so I told McKinley I was going for a walk and headed along the harbour wall to the modern, cream-painted Park Hotel. It too had magnificent sea views and I could taste the salt on my lips as I walked through the reception doors and asked to speak to Simon Fraser. The pretty brunette in tartan jacket and skirt smiled and rang his room and told me to go up to one two three, and Iwanek had the door open to greet me as I stepped out of the lift.

He was in a single room at the back of the hotel, the

colour TV was flickering in the corner with the sound off and on the small but neat bed was an unopened bottle of whisky and a small black leather suitcase.

In his hand was an empty tumbler, and he asked me if I fancied a drink and told me to help myself to a glass from the bathroom. He poured me a decent measure and we clinked glasses.

'To crime,' he said, and laughed. 'And to not getting caught.'

'Here's hoping we have a quiet night,' I said and drank deeply. He sat on the edge of the bed and waved me over to a comfortable green easy chair in the corner of the room opposite the television.

'Take a seat,' he said. 'I take it everything is set?'

'No problems at all,' I said, taking a large scale map of the area from my inside pocket and spreading it on the floor. I pointed midway down Loch Feochan.

'This is where the dinghy should be coming ashore at about eleven o'clock tonight. That's where I'll be with two other men. Our cars will be parked off the road, within sight of the shore. One of them will have a powerful torch to signal the boat and the handover should take place at the water's edge. It'll be dark, so as long as you keep away from the torch beam you should be able to get up close without being seen. There are no street lights that far away from civilization so leave your car on the road.'

Iwanek moved back on the bed and leant against the wall. He was dressed like a polytechnic lecturer, brown corduroy jacket and trousers and a green sweater, a pair of scuffed desert boots and brown socks with black squares on them, but no polytechnic lecturer had eyes like his, and they studied me through half-closed lids like a sleepy lizard about to ensnare an unwary insect with its long and very sticky tongue.

'They'll be armed, I suppose?' He had the knack of making every question sound like a statement of fact.

'Almost certainly, but they won't be expecting trouble, they're dealing with somebody they know. And you'll have the advantage because they'll have the boat to worry about and you will be on dry land.'

He brought out a packet of Silk Cut and lit one with an old gunmetal petrol lighter. He didn't offer me one which meant he'd been observant enough to notice that I didn't smoke or he just didn't care. He angled his head back and blew a smoke ring towards the pale green ceiling, but his eyes never left my face and he weighed me up through the wreaths of smoke.

'There'll be three of us, myself and two big guys. One is my bodyguard, the other is the man who set the deal up. I'll be carrying the briefcase with the money. For God's sake be careful, I don't want anyone killed.'

'Not yet you don't,' he said and laughed quietly, but it was only his mouth that smiled, there were no crease lines around the pale blue eyes and no spark of humour in them.

'Do either of your two friends know what you've got planned?' he asked.

'No,' I said. 'This is just between the two of us. So be careful. They're as likely to take a swing at you as the men in the boat are.

'I'll come back here to pick up the drugs and the money sometime within the following forty-eight hours. You just stay put and order whatever you want from room service. Then I give you the rest of your money and we part company for good.'

He'd emptied his tumbler but made no move to refill it. I wasn't surprised because Iwanek was a pro and pros don't drink while they're working, not to excess anyway.

'Have you got the gun?' I asked, and he patted the suitcase next to him.

'A Fabarm Eight Shot Slugster, though you'd be hard put to recognize it now,' he said. 'Matt black anti-glare finish, three inch magnum, lightweight and fast operating.' He didn't open the case but ran his fingers up and down the leather, smoothing it gently.

'The barrels are normally twenty-four and a half inches long but I've cut off more than half that and taken off the stock and the recoil pad and just left the walnut semi pistol grip. It'll fire eight shots and it's one of the sweetest pump actions around.'

'Pity you won't get to fire it,' I said and pushed myself out of the easy chair. 'I'll leave the map with you.'

Iwanek didn't get up, and he was still looking at the case and toying with the handle as I left the room, walked out of the hotel and turned along the harbour wall. It was starting to rain, drops splattering on the pavement, and I turned up the collar of my brown tweed jacket.

Before I reached the Caledonian I went into a small newsagent which was just about to close for the night and bought copies of all the national newspapers along with a *Glasgow Herald, Scotsman, Daily Record* and *Oban Times* and a packet of elastic bands.

The ruddy faced man behind the counter rang up the till and took my money. 'You'll be doing a lot of reading, then?' he asked. 'Or is it something in particular you're after?'

'What else is there to do in Oban on a wet Saturday

night?' I asked. He followed me to the door and reached for the bolt as I stepped onto the pavement.

'Aye, you've a point there,' he agreed and wished me a good night. I pushed the papers under my jacket and kept my head down as I walked back to the Caledonian. It was raining heavily now, and I started to run as water began to trickle down the back of my neck.

I borrowed a large pair of scissors from reception and spent the next half hour in my room cutting the papers into ten-pound note size pieces and bundling them together with elastic bands. On the top and bottom of each pile I put a real note, and by the time I'd finished I had sore fingers and what would hopefully pass for £250,000 in used tenners in a poor light. I packed them into the old brown leather attache case I'd brought with me and pushed it under the bed. Right on cue McKinley knocked on the door and said it was time to go down to the bar to meet Read.

We found him sitting on a high stool at the far end of the polished oak bar nursing a lager. He'd dressed for the occasion and looked every inch a Scottish landowner with his green tweed suit and heavy brown brogues.

On the back of his head was perched a shapeless hat of some unidentifiable material and I swear there was a fishing fly pinned to the brown band. I half expected him to tell us it was 'a braw bricht moonlit nicht the noo,' but he just smiled and asked us what we were having.

We took our drinks over to a table in the corner furthest from the bar, and McKinley attacked a bowl of peanuts while Read and I got down to business.

'You've got the money, squire?' he asked.

'Upstairs,' I said. 'Is everything still on?'

'It will be once I've made one phone call.'

'It's a bit late for that, isn't it? Surely the boat will have left by now?'

'You've heard of ship-to-shore radios, haven't you? I call Ireland and they contact the boat. Then, and only then, will the dingy head for the loch. You're not dealing with amateurs, you know.' He took his glasses off and began to polish them meticulously with a bright red handkerchief.

'I should hope not,' I said. 'Not for the sort of commission you're getting, anyway. I hope you're worth it.'

'Take it from me, squire, I am. There's no way you could have arranged this without me, just remember that.'

He removed his hat and placed it on the seat next to him and scratched the back of his head. That encouraged McKinley to delve into his beard again and pretty soon the two of them were scratching away like flea infested puppies.

'There isn't anything that could go wrong, is there?' I asked, and Read narrowed his eyes.

'Not getting cold feet, are we?' he asked. 'It's too late to back out now. That would be about as smart as auditioning for the lead role in a snuff movie. Not to be recommended, squire. The sort of people we're dealing with won't stand for that, believe me.'

'Hell, of course I'm not getting cold feet, you know just how badly I need this deal. It's just that a quarter of a million pounds is one hell of a lot of money and it's not cash I can afford to lose.'

'No, I suppose it isn't.' He turned and looked at McKinley. 'Not on top of the money you've already lost,' he added and laughed, shoulders jiggling up and down in time with his bellowing laughter.

McKinley smiled and helped himself to more salted

peanuts. Read took a swallow from his glass and wiped his mouth with the back of his hand. For the first time I noticed how hairy it was, only the finger joints were clear of thick, black curly hair.

'They're using a fishing boat to cross the sea, and then the stuff'll be transferred to a small rubber dinghy with a large outboard motor. If it looks like they've been spotted they'll make a run for it, but there's as much chance of that as there is of Get-Up here passing the Institute of Advanced Motorists driving test.' He laughed uproàriously at his own joke, mouth wide open and a couple of gold fillings glinting somewhere at the back.

'But what about the dinghy? Surely that's vulnerable?'

'Let's get something straight, squire,' he replied. 'The coastline,' he gestured with his drink, 'out there isn't exactly crawling with customs men, you know. Don't you read the papers? They're more understaffed than the Moscow branch of the CND. It's a chance in a million that they'll bump into anybody. If they do they'll run for it. And if they can't run for it they'll dump it over the side and go back for it later. Don't worry, it's easier than delivering milk.'

'Will you be armed?' I asked.

'God, you are nervous. No, I won't be carrying a gun, but the men delivering almost certainly will be.'

'I don't like the sound of that.'

'Don't let it worry you. Remember, they're the ones who are taking all the risks. They'll be coming in with the drugs, you'll just be a guy on the lochside.'

'With a quarter of a million pounds in his briefcase.'

'Yes, there's always that, isn't there?' He laughed again. He hadn't been drinking much and it wasn't that funny so I guess he was more nervous than he was letting on, but I believed him when he said he wouldn't be armed. I also believed him when he said the delivery boys would be. Still, how good a shot could they be from a rubber boat tossing around in the loch? I would have touched wood but the table our drinks were on had never been near a tree. Anyway, the whole point of the operation was that I wasn't depending on luck. Luck is for amateurs.

'What's the time, now?' he asked, finishing his drink with a noisy slurp.

'Ten past seven,' I replied.

'Time I was ringing Ireland. Can you lend me a ten-pence piece for the phone?' He roared at the look of surprise on my face and slapped me on the back.

'Come on, you can take a joke, can't you, squire?' He stood up, running his fingers along non-existent creases in his rumpled tweed trousers. 'I'll see you back here at nine o'clock. Everything is going ahead exactly as I explained to Get-Up last week. Stop worrying. Just be ready at nine, we'll take both cars. What are you driving?'

'BMW. It's parked outside.'

'Nice. Wrap up warm in case we're stuck outside for a couple of hours. See you.' Then he was off out of the bar, picking up a huge green, yellow and red golfing umbrella from the cloakroom and tossing a coin into a white china saucer on the counter.

'He means well, boss,' said McKinley, almost apologetically.

'I know, Get-Up, I know. You hungry?'

'I'm always hungry, boss, you know that.'

'Go and get yourself something from the restaurant. I'm going for a walk.'

I stood at the side of the hotel entrance and saw Read by

the BMW, examining the tyres, looking through the window and checking the speedometer like a hesitant buyer on a used car lot. Any moment now a young chap in a sheepskin jacket would come along and tell him it had one lady owner and had been treated just like one of the family and did he have a trade-in, sir, or would he be interested in an HP deal? Read took a pen and notebook from his jacket pocket and wrote down the registration number and then began to walk away, glancing at the Rolls as he passed it.

He stopped and took a closer look at the registration number, then walked around to the back, running his hand along the white soft top and down the rear wing. He scratched his ear thoughtfully. Unlike McKinley he had kept in touch with Laing's drug scene and he was sure to know what car Laing was driving.

He began scribbling in his notebook again, and I knew his telephone call to Ireland wouldn't just be to arrange the delivery, that he'd mention the Rolls and suggest that maybe, just maybe, Laing was around or involved. It wouldn't be enough for them to abandon the delivery but alarm bells would start to ring. I waited until Read got into a brown Range-Rover and drove off before I walked out of the hotel.

I rang Iwanek from a call box along the harbour wall to say that Read wouldn't be armed, and to confirm that there had been no changes to the original plan.

'Don't worry,' he said. 'I'll be there.' Suddenly everybody was telling me not to worry. That worried me. It had stopped raining but the wind was strong enough to whip up ripples in the pavement puddles as I wandered aimlessly towards the docks, shoulders hunched against the cold, fingers clenched tight in the pockets of my tweed jacket as I mentally ticked off the various stages of the plan.

I went over and over it in my mind and I couldn't find any faults. But they said the Titanic was unsinkable so I went over it again but it still seemed OK, and I relaxed a little and even started to whistle to myself but then I thought of McKinley and the whistle died on my lips.

If there was one weak link in the chain of events I'd set up then it was McKinley. He was like an affectionate Old English sheepdog, I trusted him completely and I only had to call and he'd come. He was faithful and loyal but I was using him, and if he ever found out he'd have every reason to turn on me, snapping and biting and going for my throat.

Several times I'd come close to telling him the truth, but I still wasn't sure how he would react or whether he'd use the information as a way of getting back on Laing's team. I trusted him, but not that much, and I couldn't take the risk. But that meant he would be at Loch Feochan tonight under the impression that he was taking part in a straightforward drugs buy, and when Iwanek turned up as the Lone Ranger he might take it into his head to go charging in like a head-strong rhino.

I couldn't tell him beforehand but maybe afterwards, after Iwanek had made off with the drugs and the money, maybe I'd tell McKinley the background, help him get away and start a new life. Then I thought of my parents and why I was doing this, and that what I really should do was to throw him to the dogs, another signpost pointing towards Laing.

McKinley was a bridge I would cross when I got to it. Until then I'd have to treat him like a mushroom – keep him in the dark and feed him bullshit. What the hell, he was a petty criminal and a violent one at that. I didn't owe him anything, he was being well paid, and if I started feeling sorry for him then it wouldn't be too long before I started wondering if Laing and Kyle deserved what was coming to them, and then I really might as well pack up and go home.

'Shit,' I said out loud to the grey sea, and a wee Scottish wifey wrapped up in a dark wool coat and fur boots tut-tutted like a minister and gave me a filthy look. Hell, it wasn't the Sabbath. I sat on the harbour wall, feet dangling over the edge, and looked across the water towards mist-shrouded Mull.

A seagull swooped past, then curved around and landed on the wall next to me, feet clicking against the wet stones, wings flapping for balance. Head on one side he looked me over. A tourist with a bread roll pinched from the dinner table? A teatime piece of cake? Anything? Nothing? He gave me a look more disdainful than the wifey's and pitched beak first off the wall before pulling up into a graceful glide, wings outstretched but motionless. I was impressed but I still hadn't anything for him to eat so he was wasting his time.

Back at the Caledonian the black-suited undermanager handed me Laing's American Express card as I walked into reception, practically tugging his forelock. I guess they didn't see too many gold cards in Oban. I had signed the chit earlier and he'd held on to the card to call up and check Laing's credit rating.

'We'll fill the figures in when you check out, Mr Laing,' he said, and I realized I was going to have to be careful going in and out of the hotel with McKinley. All it needed was for one of the staff to come haring after me calling 'Mr Laing, Mr Laing, you've forgotten your bill,' and I'd have some pretty heavy explaining to do.

McKinley had checked in under his own name and was paying in cash. Other than our meeting with Read in the bar we'd kept apart, so there was no reason for the staff to connect us and I'd have to make sure it stayed that way.

I saw McKinley through the glass partition leading to the restaurant, tucking into steak and chips and diving into extra portions of mushrooms, onion rings, peas, cauliflower and green beans scattered around the table, a large white napkin tucked into his shirt collar. His table manners were much the same as his driving, erratic, messy and a positive danger to anyone in the vicinity.

I left him to it and lay on the double bed in my room, gazing at the ceiling and feeling like a cigarette for the first time in twelve years.

I didn't sleep but the hour passed without my noticing and McKinley's knock on the door made me jump.

'Come in, Get-Up,' I said, and he sidled into the room wearing a huge black duffel coat and green wellington boots like an overgrown Paddington Bear. Under the coat was a thick fisherman's sweater and grey wool trousers. He looked as if he'd just come out of a sauna, sweat pouring from his skin. I couldn't help but laugh and he smiled.

'It'll be better when I'm outside, boss. It's pissing down and the wind's getting up.'

'Well, you can always shelter under Read's umbrella,' I said, and he grinned wider and sat on the bed, wiping his forehead with the back of his hand. I went over to the bathroom to swill the bad taste from my mouth and splash cold water onto my tired eyes. I came out rubbing a towel over my wet face to find him playing with the bedside radio and television controls.

'Could you get Radio Four on yours, boss?' he asked. 'Mine's on the blink.'

'I'm not one for listening to the radio, Get-Up. I didn't realize you were.'

'I used to listen to it a lot in prison. You get into the habit.'

I stripped off my shirt and jeans and it was McKinley's turn to laugh as I pulled out a pair of thermal underwear from my suitcase. 'Jesus, boss, Long Johns. My father used to wear those.'

'Yeah, well they're coming back into fashion. Especially for men about town standing on the side of a sea loch late at night.' Back on went the jeans and shirt, a woollen Pringle sweater from my golfing days and a pair of brown leather hiking boots. A Burberry scarf and the tweed jacket and I was ready, not exactly the best dressed man in Oban but there were no hard and fast sartorial rules about getting togged up for a drugs deal. Kneeling by the bed I reached for the briefcase and flipped it onto the chair by the door.

'I've never seen a quarter of a million pounds in one place, boss, do you mind if I take a look?'

'It'd only upset you, Get-Up. Come on, it's nine o'clock, we'd best get moving. Pop down and see if Read's there already. I'll see you outside.' He closed the door behind him and I opened the case. It looked like £250,000 so long as you didn't pull out one of the bundles and flick through it. If all went according to plan the case wouldn't even be opened at Loch Feochan, but if Iwanek was just a few minutes late and they got their hands on the money, or rather the cut up pieces of newspaper, then they were likely to shoot first and not bother asking questions.

The case had two locks and the key was in one of the leather pockets inside. I clicked the locks shut and left the key in the wastepaper basket. If we got to the stage where they wanted to look inside then it would give me a few extra minutes while I went through the motions of checking all the pockets in my clothing and asking McKinley if he had the key, and then if Iwanek still hadn't turned up maybe I'd get away with telling them the key must be in the car and if I was really lucky maybe I'd get to the BMW before they opened fire, and if the gods were smiling on me and no black cats crossed my path and if I hadn't broken any mirrors in the last seven years then maybe, just maybe, I'd get away without losing my kneecaps or worse. Now I really was starting to worry.

'He'll be there, he'll be there,' I said to myself, and that worried me even more because I hadn't talked to myself since I was nine years old.

I locked the bedroom door and left the key at reception. Read and McKinley were standing by the BMW in the hotel carpark, sheltering under the colourful golfing umbrella. Read had added a green waterproof coat to his laird's outfit and he waved cheerily as I walked up.

'Ready for the off?' he asked, handing me a powerful electric torch. 'You'll be needing that. There's a quarter moon tonight but it's cloudy enough to black it out every now and again. I'll be in the Range-Rover,' he nodded towards the four-wheel drive vehicle next to the Rolls. 'Don't get too close to me. These roads are bad enough at the best of times, on a wet night like this they can be treacherous.'

He climbed into the Range-Rover as McKinley and I seated ourselves in the BMW. Tonight I would be driving and McKinley didn't argue. The briefcase lay on the back seat next to Read's torch, and the two banged together as I put the car into gear and followed Read out of the carpark.

'Don't forget your lights, boss,' McKinley reminded me and I gave him a withering look.

'Just keep your eyes on Read,' I told him. 'I'll worry about the car.' I left it a full two minutes before I switched the headlights on but he still grinned like an intoxicated Cheshire cat.

'Nobody likes a smart arse, Get-Up,' I told him, but then my face cracked into a smile and I thumped his shoulder. 'You take care tonight, hear?'

Read drove like a pensioner at the wheel of a Morris Minor, slowly, infuriatingly slowly, and carefully, decelerating before every bend, his brake lights on more often than off, and the BMW never got beyond third gear.

If it had been midday at the height of summer then we'd have had a convoy of impatient traffic behind us, but we didn't see a single other car until we reached Cleigh and even then it was a farmer in a mud-splattered Land-Rover heading for Oban.

Once he stopped completely and the internal light came on as he opened the door and stepped into the road. He began running up and down in front of the Range-Rover, flapping his arms like a demented penguin. In and out of the long shadows he was casting along the tarmac road ran a handful of panicking pheasant chicks, speeding in circles and bumping into each other as they scurried and searched for their mother who was clucking anxiously on the grass verge.

Eventually the family was reunited and Read gave us the thumbs up in our headlights like a vaudeville star taking a bow on stage before getting back into the Rover and driving off again.

It took half an hour of Read's driving before we reached the tip of the loch and followed the A816 as it curved gently round to the right and along the southern shore towards the sea. We drove for about four miles until the loch narrowed and then widened again, then the Rover's hazard warning lights went on and it came to a dead stop beside a wooden five-bar gate. I pulled in behind as Read climbed out, opened the gate and drove through.

'Get out and shut the gate after I've driven through,' I told McKinley and followed Read, bumping and bouncing down a narrow dirt track leading to the loch side. A small flock of black and white sheep, startled by the unusual nocturnal activity, broke into a run and disappeared out of sight behind a hillock, bleating with annoyance. Read switched off his lights and I followed his example, blinking until my eyes grew used to the shadowy gloom.

He walked over to the BMW with a large red plastic flashlight in his hand as McKinley ambled down the path, and I pressed the button to wind the window down. Read leant forward, elbows on the car door, eye to eye.

'We're early,' he said. 'Best we wait by the water, though. The distance they've come means that their timing is unlikely to be spot on. Bring the money with you, squire.'

'I'd rather leave it here until I've seen the consignment.'

For a moment Read's good-natured smile slipped and his eyes hardened, and I realized that behind the laird's clothing and the hat with a fly in it there was still a criminal, a man used to dealing in a world where the weak were quickly fleeced by the strong and where only the hard men survived.

'Bring it with you,' he said again, and then he turned away as I got out of the BMW and leant into the back to pick up the case.

'OK, boss?' asked McKinley.

'Sure, Get-Up. I just forgot my manners,' I said, because it did make sense, if the money was obviously not in sight when the delivery men arrived it would put them on the defensive. The fact that Read had seen Laing's Rolls was enough to put them on edge, and I wanted it all to be all sweetness and light until Iwanek appeared.

We stood together on the shore, scanning the wild waters of the loch through the gloom and listening for any sounds other than the bleating of sheep and the occasional hoot of a hunting owl.

McKinley noticed it first. 'Listen,' he said, and sure enough in the distance I could hear a low pitched growl like a far-off motorcycle which grew louder and louder and then suddenly stopped.

A light flashed from the middle of the loch, on, off, on, off.

Read pointed his flashlight and flicked it on and off, long, long, short, long, short, long, short, long, long. Out on the water the light replied, on, off, on, off, on, off. Another complicated series of dots and dashes from Read and then the outboard motor started up again as they headed for the shore.

I saw them first as a dark blur against the blackened water, a smudge heading for where we were standing, more conscious of the movement than its shape. As they drew closer I could make out three figures in an inflatable boat, one at the back with his hand on the tiller, two others in the prow, tossing with the motion of the waves. The engine cut out about twenty feet from the water's edge and the boat turned sharply side on, running silently parallel to the shore until it coasted to a stop.

One of the men at the front jumped out of the boat into the water and held it steady as the second climbed out carrying a green holdall, spotlighted in the beams of the two torches, twin circles of light that followed them as they splashed unsteadily to the shore.

They moved apart as they waded knee deep through the water and simultaneously reached inside their jackets and came out with pistols. My stomach tensed, apprehension rather than fear, Read had said they'd be armed but even so the sight of the guns brought home just how dangerous this was going to be. The one with the holdall stepped forward onto the beach while his partner stayed up to his ankles in the loch.

Read passed me his torch and held out his hand for the briefcase and I handed it to him under the watchful eyes of the gunmen. He walked towards the man with the holdall and held out his free hand for it. The man in the water dropped down into a crouch, both hands on the butt of his gun as the waves lapped against his legs. Iwanek, where are you?

Read took the holdall then the night exploded in a burst

of light and noise and the man in the water flew backward, a gaping hole in his chest. There was a second explosion from somewhere behind me and Read pitched forward onto his face, the back of his green suit a mass of red, the briefcase still in one hand, the holdall in the other. His hat rolled off his head and the wind took it and whisked it away along the beach. Through the buzzing in my ears I heard the click clack of a third cartridge being thrust home as the gunman on the shore raised his pistol, but before he could fire there was another blast and he screamed and dropped the gun from his shattered hand. He flopped into the loch and threshed about in an imitation of swimming, dog-paddling his way back to the boat past the body of his colleague who was now floating face down.

I turned to see Iwanek, shotgun held across his chest, face streaked with black like a commando under a woollen balaclava helmet.

'Put your hands above your head,' he hissed and pointed the gun at McKinley's groin. 'Now.'

We both raised our arms and Iwanek moved around us, picking up the briefcase and the bag with his left hand, the right keeping the shotgun level, covering us both. I wanted to say no, this isn't what's supposed to happen, you don't understand, nobody is supposed to get hurt, that's why you said you'd use a shotgun.

I wanted to say that there'd been a mistake, go back, start again, but Iwanek knew exactly what he was doing, there was no mistake. I'd hired a killer and now he was killing.

Over his shoulder I saw the swimmer helped aboard by the man in the boat, pulled over the side by the back of his trousers, legs flicking up and over. Then the boatman leant forward and picked up a gun, maybe it was a rifle or a shotgun, it was too far away to see clearly, but I saw him aim it and I flinched as Iwanek grinned and tightened his finger on the trigger. The boatman fired first, the bullet whined and kicked up a shower of stones by Iwanek's foot and he cursed. He dropped both bags and fired two shots in quick succession at the inflatable which was now about fifty feet from the shore.

Then he turned back to us and pointed the shotgun at McKinley and fired as I threw myself sideways into McKinley, sending him sprawling as the shot tore into my left shoulder and arm, burning and biting into the flesh through the layers of clothing.

A burst of gunfire from the boat made Iwanek drop to the ground, arms and legs outstretched, then he rolled and was back on his feet, the shotgun still safe in his grasp. He gathered up the dropped bags and zig-zagged back to the road, keeping his head well down.

Through a cloud of pain I heard the outboard motor kick into life and subside as the boat headed back up the loch at full throttle, towards the sea. Then McKinley was looking down at me, asking me if I was OK, could I hear him?

The pain deepened and I felt myself slipping. I gripped his arm, hard, and he put his ear close to my mouth, beard rasping against my lips as I told him what he had to do and then his face blurred and spun and I passed out.

PART TWO

There was a fine mist in the room, the sort of drizzly veil that rolls down rivers on autumn days, blurring and blending the banks into a grey mass of misshapen lumps. River mists are cold and clammy and make the back of your neck crawl and arthritic joints ache, but this mist was warm and sticky like the inside of a sauna and the ceiling floated in and out of focus so I closed my eyes and concentrated on my breathing. I opened them again and the mist was finer and I could see a three-stranded brass light fitting, and the pink and white striped wallpaper seemed to jump into my vision and then Shona's face appeared, looking down at me side on which made my stomach queasy so I closed my eyes again and concentrated on not being sick.

The room felt hot and airless and my head rang with a cacophony of dull thuds and bumps, out of time with my breathing and my heart, and then I heard Shona say 'he's coming to' and the next time I opened my eyes the mist had disappeared but so had the light because it was night and it was dark, but I could still hear the muffled bangs and thumps in my head, my throat felt raw and my right shoulder ached, and when I tried to sit up pure pain lanced through my arm and I lay back and closed my eyes and concentrated on not dying.

At some point during the night I woke up on my side with someone poking and prodding my shoulder and back, then I felt a sharp pain in my arm and I slept.

It was light again when my head finally cleared and I could open my eyes without feeling sick, or passing out or wishing I was dead. The first thing I saw was Shona, the second was the worried look on her face, then I felt her cool hand on my forehead.

'How do you feel?' she asked.

'Like I was dead,' I tried to say, playing the wounded soldier, but my throat was so dry it sounded like a sea lion coughing. A glass of water appeared before me and I winced as she helped lift my head to drink. Sod the wounded soldier act, it hurt like hell.

'Thanks,' I managed. 'How am I doing?'

'The shot's all out, though some of it was very deep and you're going to be sore for a few weeks. A couple of inches to the right and it would have been a different story – you could have died.'

The bedroom door opened behind her and Tony walked in and sat on the bed. She sat down next to him and said; 'You should be in hospital. But after what your strange friend Get-Up told me I thought you'd want to keep this quiet. One of my father's friends is a surgeon at Glasgow's Royal Infirmary and he drove over to do the honours. He's well aware that it wasn't an accident but he won't say anything.

'He gave you an injection to make you sleep last night and he'll be back to check on you later this evening. You've been very lucky.'

I knew that. 'Where is Get-Up?' I asked.

'I don't know,' she replied. 'He dropped you off late on Saturday night, gave me a very cryptic breakdown of what had happened and then sped off in a Rolls-Royce saying he had to get to London.'

At least he'd managed to drive the BMW to the hotel and pick up the Rolls. I didn't remember the switch but that was hardly surprising because I remembered nothing after being shot. 'What time is it?' I asked.

'It's two-thirty, Monday afternoon. You've been asleep for more than thirty-six hours.'

'Is he coming back? Did he say he'd be back? If he is, he should be here by now. Damn.' Now I was talking to myself, had McKinley got the Rolls back to Heathrow in time? If so, where was he? Damn, damn.

'What is going on?' she asked, which was fair enough because up until now I'd been asking all the questions. Then Tony joined in. 'Who is he? And who the hell shot you? Where has he gone?' Three questions from him fired one after the other like an over-zealous TV quizmaster without waiting for an answer. They both looked at me, concern mixed with anger in about equal amounts. They wouldn't exactly twist my injured arm to extract the information but if I didn't tell them I would badly damage two friendships, two friendships that were very, very precious to me.

'You aren't going to like this,' I said, and tried to force a smile.

'Try us,' said Shona, and she placed another pillow behind my head. 'Just try us.'

'What's that banging noise?' I asked. 'It's been going on ever since I woke up.'

'The Tattoo,' said Shona. 'They're putting up the seating and stuff, it'll go on pretty much non-stop for the next few weeks.'

I remembered then that Shona's flat on the Mound over-looking Edinburgh was close to the Castle, home of the Edinburgh Tattoo, and every year about this time she and her neighbours had to put up with the preparations for the famous show. It was a small price to pay for the breathtaking views of the city, especially as the workmen now had to use specially-silenced tools, hammers and spanners all wrapped in cloth to cut the noise down to a minimum. I was just glad that the clinking and banging was coming from outside the window and not inside my head.

Tony stood up and walked around the bed, sitting opposite Shona so that I had to turn my head from side to side to see them both. That hurt so I looked between them while I talked. The fact that I didn't have to look at them helped. A little.

'Remember the two men that took over SCOT? Laing and Kyle?' They nodded. 'They killed my parents, no ifs, buts or maybes. My father left a note explaining what had happened. I found it on the desk by his body. In it he said that Laing had phoned him, warned him not to put up a fight to keep SCOT and that if he did try to thwart the takeover he'd get hurt. That was the day before my mother died when the brakes of the Volvo failed.'

Tony and Shona looked at each other in horror, and then back to me. I closed my eyes and Shona held my hand, tightly.

'Her death and the loss of his life's work were too much for him. He was depressed, lonely and afraid, and though it was his own hand on the trigger it was Laing and Kyle who killed him.'

'You should have gone to the police,' whispered Shona.

'I couldn't,' I said, and opened my eyes. 'There was no evidence, a letter from a man disturbed enough to kill himself wouldn't carry enough weight in court. There was no record of the phone call, and the brake fluid had leaked from the Volvo, or had been drained. It's not as if the brake lines had been cut. There was no evidence, nothing tangible.'

'Then you should have come to me. I could have dealt with them,' said Tony.

'How, Tony? What would you have done? Put out a contract on them? Just how long would it have been before it was traced back to you? Or to me? Neither of us are in the business of hiring assassins. And there were more practical considerations. I don't expect either of you to understand but I didn't want their deaths on my conscience, not directly. I couldn't kill them myself, even if I had the necessary skills. And I couldn't pay someone to do the job for me. I knew that if I did, it would always come back to haunt me and I'd wake up at night in a sweat with the sound of the gunshot echoing through my head and that one day I'd have to confess.'

'So what did you do?' asked Tony.

'I sat down with David a couple of days after we buried Dad and worked out a way of getting someone else to do the job for me. I'd already made a few phone calls to London and got some background info on Laing and Kyle, and Laing's drugs connections seemed to be the obvious solution.

'I figured that all I'd have to do was to set up some sort of drugs deal and make it look as if Laing had double-crossed them. The sort of gangsters in that business would act first and ask questions later, so if I could set them up they'd tear him apart.

'Five steps were necessary. First I had to arrange to buy a large quantity of drugs. Then I had to get Laing out of the country. With him out of the way I'd get someone to steal the drugs, that was step three. Step four was to leave as many signs as possible pointing to Laing. Step five was to plant the drugs on Kyle, in the boot of his car.

'It was like setting up a line of dominoes, once the first

one was pushed they'd all fall down, one after the other. The drugs dealers would hunt Laing down, and either they or the police would get to Kyle. And I'd be in the clear.'

Tony and Shona looked at each other across the bed again, Tony shaking his head slowly while Shona squeezed my hand.

'It's a long way from a threadbare plan like that to pulling it off,' said Tony. 'How did you manage it?'

'I rented a flat in London and spoke to as many people who knew Laing as I could, carefully so as not to set off any alarms. I've an old schoolfriend who's now a crime reporter on one of the nationals and he told me the story of Get-Up McKinley, the guy who dropped me here. He told me how he'd just come out of prison after serving time for an armed robbery that went wrong. He used to work for Laing. I traced McKinley and offered him a job as my minder. He jumped at it. Through him I arranged to buy quarter of a million pounds of cocaine. The deal was set up for Saturday night so I fixed up a weekend in Paris for Sammy and Laing.'

'Sammy?' said Shona, turning towards Tony. 'The girl you took to see David? You were using her, too?'

'Did she know what she was getting into?' asked Tony, ignoring Shona's question. 'And what about Carol?'

'I told Sammy everything. We used a rented flat and an assumed name – there's no way anyone will be able to trace her. She's my friend now, Tony. I won't let anything happen to her. And Carol knows nothing, except that Sammy was helping me.

'I hired an ex-soldier to steal the drugs, told him when and where they'd be arriving. That was Iwanek, the man you caught following me. He wasn't supposed to hurt anyone, just to take the cocaine and run, handing it back to me later. But he obviously had plans of his own. He killed at least one of the drug couriers and the guy who'd fixed up the deal for us. Then he turned the gun on McKinley and I got shot.'

'He took the drugs?' asked Tony. I nodded. 'And the money?'

At that I smiled, thinking of Iwanek opening the briefcase and finding stacks of newspaper cuttings.

'No,' I replied. 'Just a couple of hundred pounds and a lot of waste paper.'

'And how were you going to point the finger at Laing and Kyle?'

'McKinley was the first signpost, the fact that he was involved would trigger off Laing's name. To make it even more definite I borrowed Laing's Rolls-Royce and made sure that it was seen in Oban, close to where the drugs were due to arrive. And I paid for a hire car and the hotel bills with his American Express card.

'His trip to Paris was a complete secret because he didn't want his wife to find out. What can he say against all that evidence? He'd been pushed out of the drugs business and this was his way of getting his own back – the evidence is circumstantial but overwhelming. And it's not as if I had to convince twelve good men and true. Circumstantial evidence would be more than enough for the sort of people I've been dealing with.'

'So that's why Get-Up drove off in such a hurry,' said Shona.

'Sure, I asked him to put the Rolls back in the carpark at Heathrow, with the credit card under the passenger seat for Sammy to find. I just hope he did and that he didn't decide to keep the car and make a run for it. Laing will never know that his beloved car was up in Scotland, and he'll never see Sammy again.

'We left a hire car from Glasgow in Oban, and it won't take them long to find it and check that it was hired in his name and paid for with his Amex card. Laing won't know what's hit him when they catch up with him.'

'They'll kill him,' said Tony, and his voice was tinged with sadness as if a doctor had just told him I had a terminal illness. But it was sadness at what I'd done, not pity for Laing and Kyle.

'He killed my parents,' I replied defensively. 'Don't forget that.'

'What about Kyle?' asked Shona. 'What will happen to him?'

I was tired now and my throat was burning from the effort of talking but I had to finish it, I had to tell them everything, even though the fine mist had started to come back into the room and the banging in my head seemed to be getting louder and louder.

'I managed to get Kyle's fingerprints on a briefcase, and the idea was to put the drugs in it and plant the case in his car. It could have gone two ways then. Either I tipped off the police and he went to prison for a long time, or the suppliers would trace him through Laing. I didn't care much what happened. But that's all off now. No drugs, no plant. He's in the clear, for the moment. But if they catch up with Laing they might still get to Kyle.' Despite everything that had happened the prospect still pleased me. I wanted them dead.

'If they're that dangerous you shouldn't have got involved with them,' said Shona, concern showing in her eyes.

'You can't deal with filth like Laing and Kyle without getting your hands dirty,' I said, and I was surprised at the venom in my voice and the way she recoiled from me. 'It's all right, Shona, believe me.' She looked at me disbelievingly. 'OK, I know this looks bad but it'll soon heal,' I added.

Tears filled her eyes and she shook her head. 'You just don't understand what you've done, do you?' she asked, but she ran out of the room before I could answer. I tried to raise my head, to call after her, but the pain in my shoulder made me wince and I lay back, gasping.

Tony sat silently by my side, and it was some minutes before he spoke again.

'You've been an absolute prat, you know that. You've let us all down, you've betrayed our trust. You haven't only been messing with the lives of a few London thugs, you realize that? You've put your friends and your family at risk through your stupidity. I expected more from you than that.' He was looking through the window as he talked, down the Mound and across to Princes Street where afternoon shoppers mixed with office workers on late lunches. He walked over to the window and put his hands on the sill, resting his forehead against the glass. It steamed up from his breath as he sighed deeply, a depressing sigh that said as much as the verbal lashing he'd just given me. He stood upright and with his index finger drew a question mark in the condensed vapour, and as he pressed the dot under the curve he turned and folded his arms across his chest.

There was nothing I could say because he was right, and the fact that he had put it into words made it hurt all the more.

'What's done is done,' he said, and now he was business-like, Tony the negotiator, the wheeler-dealer, the salesman who wouldn't take no for an answer. 'Let's take this from the top. Is there any way you can be traced through this madman Iwanek?'

'None, I used a false name and I contacted him, not the other way round.'

'Always?'

'Since the first time.' He raised his eyebrows. 'I answered an advert, he used a box number so I wrote to him and he telephoned me.'

'Telephoned you where?'

'A flat I'd rented in Earl's Court – under a false name. The rent's paid until the end of the month and there's nothing in it that will identify me.'

'Fingerprints?'

'I wiped it clean before I left for Oban. Thoroughly.'

'What about the car thief?'

'False name again, and he never got in touch with me. I paid him in cash and he's no idea what I was up to. He didn't care so long as he got his money. I can't be traced through him.'

'What about this guy, the one who fixed up the drugs deal?'

'Davie Read? He thought I was a London banker who'd been dipping into the firm's funds for a spot of gambling on the commodity market. Get-Up fed him the cover story and I used another false name. Anyway, Read's dead.'

'Dead now, but he could have spoken to any number of people before you met him in Oban.'

'There's nothing he could have told anyone. Besides,

if he'd suspected anything he would have stopped the deal cold.'

'True,' he said and fell silent again, biting the inside of his cheek as he always did when deep in thought. He came over and sat on the right-hand side of the bed.

'How much does Get-Up know?'

'He doesn't know who I really am, or at least he didn't until he dropped me here. He thought he'd arranged a straightforward drugs buy, that I was a dealer who'd been elbowed out of Glasgow and was looking for an alternative supply. He thought he was doing me a favour.'

'He thought you were going to hand over the money?' I nodded. 'And he didn't know about Iwanek?' I shook my head. 'And what the hell were you going to do afterwards?'

'Pay him off, tell him I was skint and that I was going back to Glasgow. I'd never have seen him again.'

'And what do you think would have happened to him?'

I couldn't answer that, because we both knew the main reason for using McKinley was his connection with Laing and that the two of them would be in the frame together.

'You were sentencing him to death, you bastard,' he shouted and thumped the pillow next to my head. 'You callous, unthinking, cynical bastard. He probably saved your life, bringing you back here. He could have driven off and left you bleeding on the ground. And you were setting him up like a clay pipe at a shooting gallery.'

I wanted to say that McKinley was just a foot soldier in the drugs war, that they probably wouldn't have hurt him, that they'd have gone for Laing first and probably got their cocaine back from Kyle and then they'd have called off the dogs, but I didn't believe it so I didn't say anything. I just nodded.

'You'll have to tell him everything now,' he continued. 'If he ever comes back. And if he doesn't, sport, we're all in trouble, you, me and Shona. He might not know who you are but he definitely knows Shona now and where she lives. You'll have to tell him everything and offer him a darn sight more than a payoff. He can't go back to London, you realize that?'

I nodded again. 'I know.' Read knew McKinley so the people who brought the drugs in,would be looking for him. Besides Laing he was the one lead they had.

'The signpost you hoped would send them to Laing is now pointing right in your direction. Your only hope is to uproot it and bring it up here. Offer him a job, anything, but he has to stay close to you. It'll be a form of symbiosis, he'll need you to protect him, you'll need him to keep out of trouble. You'd better stick together like Siamese twins.'

'I guess you're right, Tony. I'll speak to him when he gets back.'

'If he gets back.' He stood up and walked over to the window again.

'That leaves only one character in your sordid little drama.'

'Sammy,' I said.

'Sammy,' he repeated thoughtfully, as if it was the first time he'd heard the name. He was chewing the inside of his cheek again and the arms were folded across his chest.

'I can't keep saying I'm sorry, Tony.'

He ignored me. 'How much does she know?' he asked. My heart soared then because his question meant that Sammy hadn't told Tony anything, she'd kept my secret to herself.

Because she loved me? Then I flushed as I remembered how I'd used her.

'Everything.'

'Everything?'

'She knows who I am, who I really am, she knows what happened to my parents, she knows exactly what I planned to do and she was prepared to help me.' I was proud of that, proud that she was my friend, my lover, and ashamed that I'd abused her trust.

'Then she's a lot dumber than I thought,' he said. 'Did you explain everything, she knew what she was getting into?'

I didn't have to answer that one because he could tell from my shamefaced expression that I hadn't. I hadn't told anyone the full story. I take that back, there was one person, David. 'She's not in any danger, Tony. I promise.'

'That's not a promise you can make, sport. What makes you think they won't track her down once Laing tells them where he was?'

'She didn't use her own name and I rented a separate flat for her. A short-term let, paid in advance. She'd never met Laing before, and all she has to do is to lie low for a few weeks.'

'Until he's killed? Is that what you mean?'

'Yes, if you like. There's precious little chance of Laing ever bumping into Sammy again, and once he's dead she'll be one hundred per cent in the clear. That still stands, Tony, whatever might have gone wrong she will be all right. I'll call her and tell her what's happened and that she's to take care, but it's hardly necessary. She knew that once she got back from Paris she was never to see him again. She knew what she was getting into.'

'You'd better be right. You had no right to use people

the way you did. I'm tempted to say that what has happened is all your own fault, but there's no point rubbing your nose in it. I just hope you've learned your lesson, that's all. Fight your own battles in future and don't play God.'

Then he patted me on the shoulder and left me alone. Later Shona brought me a drink of water, her face tearstained and her eyes red from crying. She got on the bed, leant alongside me and hugged me and kissed me on the cheek, and then left the room without saying anything.

I slept fitfully, I dreamt of suitcases full of cocaine and shotguns exploding and dinghies full of men in black waving guns and shouting. They were chasing me and I was running through water, it dragged at my feet and held me back and the men in black were catching up with me, closer and closer, because they were running on top of the water, skating along the surface. I looked up, gasping for breath, pains in my chest, and I saw Sammy on the loch side and she was screaming, and then her face melted into Shona's and David was standing next to her, crying, and then the men in black had them, surrounded and held them. I kept on running in slow motion but I looked over my shoulder and they weren't chasing me any more, they were carrying Shona and David off into separate dinghies, and then the outboard motors kicked into life and I waded out into the water after them, waving my arms as they roared off into the darkness. Then I was alone and the freezing water was up to my neck, numbing my body, and then it was over my head and I lost consciousness.

I woke with a raging thirst. It was morning and the sun streamed in through the window where Shona was standing, her hands holding the cord which she'd pulled to open the curtains and thrown light onto my face.

She came over and helped me to sit up, pushing a pillow behind my back and fluffing up the duvet, fussing like a broody hen. 'There's a mug of tea next to you,' she said, smoothing the quilt professionally like a nurse with a difficult patient.

'Shona,' I said, and waited until she'd stopped moving and stood by the bed, hands by her side.

'Yes?' she said in a low, quiet voice, looking through me with the lifeless eyes of a sleepwalker.

I wanted to say 'sorry' again, to explain why I'd done what I did, to explain how special she was to me, how the only people I'd meant to hurt were Laing and Kyle, but I knew there was nothing I could say, that she'd always love me and be my friend but that it would take a long time before she'd trust and respect me again. Maybe she never would, maybe I'd blown it for good. Talking now would only sound like I was making excuses, the tail-wagging of a guilty dog.

'Thanks,' I said, and she smiled and tossed her head.

'All part of the service,' she said and left me on my own with my thoughts.

I dozed, drifting in and out of sleep until she came back with the telephone in her hand, one of those remote jobs that you can use in the car, the garden or the toilet.

'It's McKinley,' she said. 'For you.'

'If he starts using bad language I'll call for help,' I said and grinned. It felt like a snarl.

'Not funny,' she said and turned on her heel and walked

out of the room, and what the hell she was right, it wasn't funny.

'How are you getting on?' he asked and it sounded as if he meant it, but the voice lacked warmth.

'I'm fine,' I replied. 'The shoulder still hurts but I'm on the mend.' If we had been in the same room we'd have been looking at each other warily, a couple of prizefighters who'd shaken hands and were ready to come out fighting. I couldn't tell from his silence how he felt.

'Did you get the car back?' I asked eventually.

'Let's get one thing straight, boss. You shouldn't have used me the way you did. You used me and you'd have thrown me to the wolves. I could have died, you know.' The words were tumbling out, running into each other like rushhour commuters pouring off a packed bus.

'When the bastard pointed his shooter at me I honestly thought that I'd had it. If you hadn't pushed me to one side he'd have blown me apart. I'd frozen, I couldn't move.' He dried up, an engine running out of steam.

He broke the silence after a few seconds, and this time his voice was bitter and angry.

'I'm not coming back. You'll never see me again. I can't trust you, not after what you did to me. I don't know what I'm going to do, but I'll do it on my own.' The sentences came out in short, sharp bursts like bullets from a gun.

'Get-Up, listen to me. I can't take back what I did, but I can try to make it right, if you'll let me,' I said, remembering Tony's words. Symbiosis. I needed this man.

'No,' he said, with a finality that left me in no doubt that I would never see him again. But there was one thing I had to know before he cut the connection and disappeared from my life forever. Had he finished the job?

He continued. 'If you hadn't saved my life I wouldn't even have phoned,' he said and then ground to a halt, realizing what a daft thing he'd said, then blustering on regardless. 'I would just have told Read's mates what you'd been up to. But you did, so the car's back where you wanted it. I rang Dancer like you said and he collected it from me. I said you'd send the rest of the money to him. Now we're even.'

'Get-Up, listen to what I say. Keep away from Laing, right away. Keep your head down. And if you need any help you can come to me.'

'No, I'm on my own now. You won't ever see me again.'

'Good luck, Get-Up. I mean it.'

'Go to hell.' Click, and he was gone.

Later Tony came and sat on the bed and laid down the law. Shona was to move out of the flat, soonest. She'd go and stay with her parents. That way if McKinley went back on his word – I began to interrupt, to say that Get-Up wouldn't let me down, but Tony steamrollered over me – then nobody could get to her. Sammy was to be told to lie low, I certainly wasn't to go near her for a while, at least until we knew what had happened to Laing and Kyle. I was to keep out of the way, Tony would be my eyes and ears in London. Yes sir, no sir, three bags full sir. Tony made me feel small, small and vulnerable, but I accepted the sanctuary he offered, the safe cool sanctuary of the strong, and I remembered Sammy and the polar bear.

Shona and Tony wanted me to go somewhere warm, to lie in the sun for a couple of weeks, to come back suntanned and rested and ready to go back into harness. I agreed.

I telephoned Sammy and told her I'd be out of the country for a while.

'How was Paris?' I asked.

'Don't ask,' she said.

'Good, I'm glad,' I replied, and I was. My stomach had been churning at the thought that she might have enjoyed herself with him. She broke the silence by asking what had gone wrong and I told her, warning her to keep a low profile and to have no further contact with Laing.

'You don't have to worry on that score,' she said, and I could picture her white teeth and easy smile as she brushed her long hair behind her ear. 'How's Get-Up?' she asked.

'Vanished. I doubt we'll see him again.'

'Where are you going?'

'I don't know yet, but I'll be in touch, I promise.' I paused, unsure of how to pose the question. 'Sammy?' I asked.

'I'm here.'

'When I get back, will you come up to be with me in Edinburgh?' Hell, that didn't sound right.

'On the payroll, you mean?' she asked.

'You know what I mean.'

'Yes, I know.'

'Well?'

'Well what?'

'If I was with you, young lady, I'd put you over my knee and give you a good spanking.'

'And if you were with me, I'd let you.'

'Stop teasing, Sammy. Will you?'

'I think I might.'

'Is that a yes?'

'It's a yes. But you knew that before you asked. Now away you go and enjoy your holiday – send me a card.'

'I might.'

'Rat. I love you,' and that one caught me with my guard down, right under the chin, and it sent me reeling onto the ropes.

'Must go. See you soon,' I said and fumbled the receiver back on the hook, cursing myself for becoming so awkward with her, and wondering how three words could so quickly turn me back into a gauche schoolboy. And I hadn't even told her that I loved her.

I rang her back. 'I love you,' I said.

'I know that, stupid,' she said, and hung up.

The first package holiday Shona could arrange was a fortnight in Malta, and she flew with me to London and put me on the plane at Gatwick, partly out of concern but mainly to check that I actually went.

I asked her if she wanted to come with me but it wasn't on, because I'd done enough damage to the firm over the past few months and someone had to mind the shop.

Shona had booked me into a modern, comfortable hotel overlooking St Paul's Bay, just a couple of minutes' walk through its gardens and across the road to the seafront.

The resort had grown up around a picturesque fishing village on the north-east coast, and it reminded me a little of Oban with its work-worn boats bobbing in the sea.

I spent most of my time walking around the harbour, stopping off at the dozens of friendly bars and cafés, eating at the local restaurants, resting and exercising my shoulder. The stiffness was going and the scars healing, but it would still catch me unawares every now and again and the pain would make me wince.

I did all the touristy things, went on trips around the capital, Valletta, took a boat trip to the island of Gozo where I bought a lace shawl for Shona, and cruised around the Blue Grotto, but most of the time I just lay on a towel on one of the huge flat rocks by the sea and turned brown like a lamb chop under a grill.

At the start of the second week the young nephew of the hotel owner came running up and stood over me, blotting the sun from my burning face, bare chested and panting, his cut-off blue jeans several sizes too big and held up with a piece of grubby string knotted at the front.

'Telephone for you,' he gasped. 'Come quickly.'

I gave him a handful of Maltese cents and patted his dark curly hair, jogged with him back to the hotel and took the call at the reception desk.

'Shona,' I said, it couldn't have been anyone else, she was the only person who knew where I was. 'What's wrong?'

The line was crackling and buzzing and it sounded as if she was talking with a mouthful of potato crisps, but I heard her say: 'My God, what have you done? All hell's broken loose here.' And then she explained what had happened, repeating herself when the line got so bad that I couldn't make out what she was saying.

They'd found McKinley first, in a disused warehouse on the Isle of Dogs. He was naked and covered with cigarette burns and quite dead. The little finger of his right hand had been severed with bolt cutters or something, and he'd been kicked and beaten hard enough and long enough to break most of his ribs and his hip.

He'd been chained by the hands to a metal girder running sideways across the warehouse, and his wrists were chafed to the bone where he'd struggled and fought to free himself but there was nothing he could have done because his legs were also chained, to the rusting back axle of a long-scrapped truck and his ankles too were bloody and frayed.

At some point he'd been hit repeatedly with a long metal bar and there were weals across his back and stomach, but they were nothing compared with the patches of burnt flesh where lighted cigarettes had been pushed and gouged into the soft, vulnerable parts of his body.

It had taken him several hours to die, and he must have begged and pleaded for them to stop every second of every minute of every hour because he'd told them everything he knew and he hadn't done anything, he'd been used from the start, and please God why didn't they believe him?

There hadn't been a single thing he could have said to stop them.

Whoever had tortured and killed McKinley caught up with Iwanek two days later in Spain, where he'd rented a villa about half an hour's drive inland from Alicante airport.

It was a white-painted building around a cool courtyard that would normally sleep six people but Iwanek lived there on his own, high on a sun-bleached hill surrounded by groves of orange trees.

From the side of his private pool he could sit and watch planeloads of pale tourists arriving for their two weeks in nearby Benidorm and then departing with brown skins and suitcases full of sandy clothing and cheap presents.

He drank a lot, invited local girls and holidaymakers back to his villa and his bedroom and began to put out feelers, tentatively probing the market for the briefcase of white powder he'd hidden under one of the flagstones in the kitchen.

There were plenty of wealthy people in the villas around the east coast of Spain, many of them British villains on the run, and he reckoned they'd be keen to buy and he hoped to make contact with dealers in the Benidorm resort.

He thought he would be able to make six figures without trying, but that's not how it worked out, and the middle-aged woman who cycled up the hill to cook for him each evening found his body tied to the large oak bed in the main bedroom, spreadeagled like a stranded starfish on a white sandy beach, only the sheet she'd so carefully washed and ironed wasn't white anymore, it was stained with blood and sweat and shit, the flies buzzed around the burns all over his body and the mouth was wide open in a silent scream of agony. When she staggered to the kitchen to get to the phone, she nearly tripped over the stone floor which had been ripped up to get at the hidden drugs.

McKinley's death, macabre as it was, had at first merited only a few paragraphs in the London editions of the nationals, and the discovery of Read's body at Loch Feochan became a seven-day wonder of the 'Police Probe Mystery Slaying' variety, but an enterprising reporter on one of the more sensational tabloid Sundays linked all three murders, cobbled together some spurious background on drugs smuggling between Spain and Britain and the paper splashed it.

The story spread north of the border, the *Herald* and the *Scotsman* both following it up and doing extended features on the influx of drugs along the Scottish coastline, and the *Daily Record* did a colour piece on the men who man the coastal cutters. The media's like that, feeding on itself ad infinitum, one reporter's throwaway line becoming another's page lead.

'What about Laing?' I asked.

'There's no sign of him. Tony thinks he's either been killed as well or gone to ground. Either way he says you'll probably never see him again. What are we going to do?'

'Don't worry,' I said, trying to soothe her. 'It's OK, that's the end of it. It's over.'

'I can't hear you,' she said through the crackling and buzzing. 'Are you still there? Hello? Hello?'

'It's all right,' I shouted, cupping my hand between the receiver and my mouth, trying to focus my voice and the reassurance in it. 'It won't go any further. It can't. Nobody knows I was involved, Shona, and as far as anyone else is concerned the trail stops cold at Laing and Iwanek.

'From what you've said, it looks as if they've got the cocaine back and that's all they wanted. It's over, Shona.'

'I'm frightened, I didn't realize it would end like this. Two people have been murdered, horribly murdered, and you're to blame. What have you done? Was it worth it? Are you proud of yourself?'

She was becoming hysterical now, hyperventilating and I was too far away to help, to hold her until the panic left her. 'Do you want me to come straight back?' I asked. 'I can probably get an earlier flight.'

'No, stay where you are, you need the rest. I'll be all right, I just worked myself up into a panic, that's all. Be careful.'

'There's no need to be careful, don't you understand?' I said. 'It's over, finished. I'll be back in a week anyway. How's David?' I asked, trying to change the subject.

'He's fine, but we're both missing you. Take care.'

'And you. And don't worry, it is finished. I promise. I'll see you soon.'

Then she was gone, my link with home broken, but I couldn't stop smiling as I replaced the receiver because it was over, or at least it soon would be.

I walked down to the harbour and went along to one of the small bars with pretty white tables and blue and white striped umbrellas outside on the pavement. Inside it was cool and in semi-darkness, and I sat on a wooden stool at the corner of the bar furthest from the door and ordered a bottle of champagne. I filled a glass and raised it in front of me, towards the shaft of bright sunlight that sliced through the doorway, spearing the gloom and illuminating a black and white mongrel lying on the stone floor. The light had a religious look as it poured in, as if I was on hallowed ground, back in the church where I'd said goodbye to both my parents. I nodded towards the doorway.

'Rest easy, Dad, I got the bastards.' I drank to him, and to my mother, then I drank for drinking's sake and then I ordered another bottle. Soon I was laughing out loud and drinking toasts to David, to Shona, to Sammy, to Tony, and to Ronnie Laing, missing believed tortured and killed. They'd catch up with him eventually, if they hadn't already. They wouldn't believe his protestations of innocence any more than they'd have trusted McKinley's version of events. Laing couldn't prove he'd been out of the country because passports aren't stamped for visits to France, a bonus of being in the EEC. Sammy had taken the receipt from the carpark at Heathrow along with anything else that could show Laing had been in France, and Amanda Pearson had long ceased to exist.

His car had been seen near the drugs snatch and the hotel bills in Oban and Glasgow had been paid for with his American Express card, along with a hire car that had been dumped in the hotel carpark. Guilty as charged and sentenced to die by torture, screaming, crying and begging them to stop.

Then I drank to Jim Iwanek, who'd died in agony on a bed in Spain, begging them to leave him alone and telling them everything he knew.

He'd told them where the cocaine was, and he'd told them who I was except that the name I'd given him was Alan Kyle, and before long Kyle would be dead and then the circle would be well and truly closed.

The second week passed quickly. I worked on the tan and spent the afternoons skindiving and I even went waterskiing, the shoulder giving me no problems at all. I managed to get the FT and the *Wall Street Journal* at a local shop, usually two days late and costing five times the cover price, but I read them from front to back as I lay on the rocks, water lapping at my feet.

I was looking forward to getting back to work, to the technicalities of handling a takeover or a share issue, the high-level discussions with board members and bankers, raising capital and restructuring contracts. I loved the job and for the foreseeable future I was going to give

Scottish Corporate Advisors, and Sammy, my undivided attention.

The memory of Laing and Kyle would soon fade, an episode that I'd keep locked away in the dark recesses of my mind, along with McKinley's tortured corpse. It would return from time to time to haunt me, I knew that, and there would be times when I'd wake at night sweating and shaking after dreaming of burning cigarettes and scorched flesh, but in my heart of hearts I felt that my hands were clean and that it had been their own fault. It was behind me. It was over.

The plane touched down at Gatwick at eleven o'clock on a chilly autumn morning, the change in temperature a shock to my system after two weeks in Malta. I zipped up the linen bomber jacket that had been too warm to wear in the sun but which wasn't thick enough for Surrey with Christmas only a few months away.

I went straight through the Nothing to Declare customs hall, I had just one battered leather suitcase and a duty free carrier bag with two bottles of Glenfiddich, and I was eager to get back to Edinburgh where Shona had promised to put me up until I was ready to move back into Stonehaven. On the way to the taxi rank I bought an early edition of the *Standard* and I opened it as the driver pulled away from the terminal building.

Her picture was on page five under the forty-two point headline 'Police Hunt Call-Girl Killer' and she was smiling. Her hair was longer than when I'd seen her rushing out of the door, and it wasn't as curly. It was an old photograph but the pouting lips and large almond eyes were the same. It was Carol.

The story said she'd been found naked in a bath full of water with her arms tied behind her back, and that she hadn't been raped but the police suspected it was a sex killing because of the cigarette burns on her breasts and thighs, and they were working their way through her client book which the *Standard* understood contained a host of top people including MPs, showbusiness and City names. Blood tests had shown that she'd taken a cocaine and heroin cocktail some time before she died and police were also investigating the drugs link.

Carol was dead and it was my fault and it was far from over because if they had found Carol they would find Sammy, and Sammy knew who I was because I'd told her everything and before they were through with her she'd tell them everything, too.

My mouth was dry and my hands were shaking and I felt like I was falling, a sick emptiness in the pit of my stomach and all I could hear in my head was Shona's voice saying 'What have you done?' over and over again, and all I could see was Sammy's face and her eyes as she held me and told me it was going to be OK. The empty feeling became a cold hardness inside, and gradually my hands stopped trembling and I breathed deeply and locked her out of my mind and tried to work out what the hell I was going to do.

I rapped on the glass partition behind the cab driver's head and asked him to drive back to the airport, and he shrugged and hauled the cab round with a screech of tyres against the tarmac.

Back at the terminal I ran to the bank of payphones,

rummaging through my pockets for change, sorting out the ten and fifty-pence coins.

I called Sammy first. There had been no mention of her in the *Standard* and there was an outside chance that she wasn't involved. Sure. And maybe pigs might fly. As it happened she wasn't in the flat and I did speak to a flying pig.

'She's in the bathroom, who shall I say is calling?' asked a male voice which was obviously more used to cautioning suspects than taking telephone messages.

'Just a friend,' I said.

'Actually, she's busy at the moment. Give me your name and number and I'll have her call you back.' At least he hadn't called me Sir.

'Good afternoon, inspector,' I said, taking a pot shot at his rank, and slammed the phone down. Damn. Sammy was missing, and the chances were that she'd been there when Carol had been tortured. Tell us what you know, look what we're doing to your friend. Listen to her scream. Tell us everything about this man, Sammy. Where does he live? What does he do? Tell us about his family, Sammy. Oh my God, no. David. David?

I could feel the clammy fingers of panic clutching at my heart as I rang Shankland Hall, closing my eyes and praying until the sister came to the phone.

I fought to keep my voice steady as I asked: 'Is David all right?'

'Yes of course,' she said. 'You've just missed him. Miss Darvell was here to collect him earlier this morning.'

The sense of relief was overwhelming and I leant forward and rested my forehead against the cool plaster of the wall, allowing the tension to escape in a long drawn-out sigh. Sammy had got away, maybe she hadn't even been there when Carol was killed. And she'd gone up to Scotland to get David out of harm's way.

'They said you'd be ringing,' continued the sister.

They? They? The panic was back now, a hundred times worse than before. I took a deep breath but my lungs still felt empty and hollow. It was as if my brain had been starved of oxygen, going under for the third time, drowning.

'Who was with Sammy?' I asked eventually.

'I rather assumed he was a friend of the family, or a relative of Miss Darvell. He seemed very close and took her by the arm several times.' She paused and I could almost hear her thinking. 'There's nothing wrong is there?' she asked.

'No, no, nothing's wrong,' I managed. 'I'm just back from a holiday and I'd forgotten that Sammy was taking David out. And the man will have been her brother. Did they say when they'd be back?'

I was sweating, the trembling had returned and I closed my eyes tightly. Please God let them be all right.

'No they didn't, I'm sorry. But it won't be tonight for certain, that I do know. They were going on a trip, I seem to remember Miss Darvell saying. She did say I was to give you a message, though. It was about work, I think. Let me see, I have it written down somewhere. Yes, here it is. She said you were to arrange the transfer of the funds and that she would call you at your home at seven o'clock with the details.'

I thanked her and hung up but God knows how I kept the despair out of my voice, because now they had Sammy and David and I thought about the cigarette burns and this I couldn't bury in my subconscious. My eyes stung with tears because it was all going wrong and I'd lost control, and I could still hear Shona saying 'What have you done? All hell's broken loose here.'

I wanted to run, but there was nowhere to run to, and I wanted to hide but I couldn't because I was the only hope that Sammy and David had, without me they were dead and please God don't let them be dead already.

I was to arrange the transfer of the funds, Sammy had said, which meant that whether or not they'd got their hands on the drugs they wanted their money as well, all £250,000 of it.

I didn't have the cash, but if push came to shove I would be able to get hold of quarter of a million pounds by seven o'clock. It would mean pulling a few strings and twisting a few arms but I was in the money business so it wasn't a major problem. But I was under no illusions about the message Sammy had left. There was no way on earth that the men who had killed McKinley, Iwanek and Carol, and probably Laing and Kyle too, were going to swap a suitcase of money for Sammy and David and let us all ride off into the sunset.

The money was secondary, what they really wanted was revenge and a warning to others that there had to be honour among thieves. They wanted me dead and that meant killing Sammy and David, too. Please God don't let them be dead already.

I rang Tony's office. His secretary said he was in a meeting and wouldn't be available until late in the afternoon, but when I told her who I was she said that yes, Tony had been expecting my call and that if I would hold the line she'd go into his office and get him.

Tony was on the phone within seconds, and if I'd expected tea and sympathy then he soon put me right. This wasn't the friendly back-slapping Tony I knew, he was bitter and angry and for a moment I was glad he was on the end of the phone and not standing in front of me.

'You've seen the *Standard*?' he roared.

'I'm sorry, Tony, I'm really sorry. If I'd—'

'It's too late for sorry,' he interrupted. 'Christ, did you read how she died? And it's all your fault. You stupid, stupid bastard. Do you have any idea at all where this is going to end?'

'Tony, listen to me. We don't have time for this. Argue with me later, hit me if you want, ignore me, hate me, but first help me. I need your help now more than ever before. Just do this one thing for me.' There was silence, and I closed my eyes and willed him not to hang up on me.

'Where are you?' he asked eventually.

'Gatwick Airport. I've just arrived back from Malta.'

'Wait there. I'll be with you within the hour. And you've got some explaining to do.'

'Don't hang up, Tony. I haven't finished yet. You have to do something for me.'

I told him the two things I wanted and God bless him he didn't ask why, he just said yes, he could get them both and I was to wait where I was.

If he'd been my fairy godmother and granted me three wishes, and if I didn't have to go through a metal detector before catching the plane to Edinburgh then I'd have asked for a semi-automatic handgun as well, something small enough to hide in a coat pocket but big enough to kill at a distance. But Tony wasn't my fairy godmother and the only way to get up to Stonehaven in time was to fly, and anyway I couldn't risk using a gun that could be traced back to him. If Sammy had told them what she knew then Tony was in enough trouble already.

He arrived before twelve-thirty in his blue Lagonda and helped me load my suitcase into the boot without saying a word. It was only after we'd fastened our seat belts and my shoes had settled into the pale blue sheepskin carpeting that he turned to me, raising his eyebrows without a trace of a smile and asked: 'Well?'

'Did you get what I asked for?'

He gestured with his thumb. 'On the back seat.'

I turned and looked over my shoulder and saw a green and yellow Harrods carrier bag. 'Thanks,' I said. 'Were they easy to get?'

'I'm in the business, you know that. I had them both in stock. Where are we going?' Still no smile.

'I have to get to Edinburgh within the next few hours. The Heathrow to Edinburgh Shuttle is the best bet. Do you mind?'

'It doesn't look as if I've any choice, does it?' He started the car. 'Tell me what's happening. And what do you want with the gear in the back?'

Tony was one of those drivers who got other motorists grinding their teeth and gripping their steering wheels, cursing and hitting their horns and brakes. I'd never seen him check his mirror before manoeuvring, his eyes were always on the car in front. He treated his Lagonda like a racing car, which in effect it was with its souped-up engine and specially modified steering and suspension. He weaved in and out of the traffic as we headed north towards

Heathrow, hands light on the wheel and foot heavy on the accelerator, driving the way the manufacturers intended and the police frowned upon. It wasn't the most relaxing way of travelling and the atmosphere in the luxurious car was already tense.

'You know as much as I do, Tony. I told you last time I saw you, up in Edinburgh, what I'd planned, that I'd set up Laing and Kyle and got someone else to do my dirty work. I thought I'd got every angle covered but the whole bloody thing's gone wrong. Shona rang me in Malta to tell me that McKinley was killed last week, and it won't be long before they catch up with Kyle . . .'

He looked at me as he passed a Jaguar on the inside at eighty. 'They already have done,' he said. 'He died three days before they got to Carol. I suppose the news didn't reach as far as Scotland. And Laing still hasn't surfaced.'

So at least something had gone as planned, Kyle had been killed and Laing was dead or running scared. But there was no feeling of satisfaction, no warm glow of a job well done, just a gut-wrenching panic at yet another sign that the men I was up against would kill and keep on killing until everyone they thought was involved had been removed. It was a cold-blooded hunt which was a thousand times worse than the revenge I'd planned. This was business with no element of personal hatred. People were being killed solely as a warning to others, coolly, calmly and professionally. No hard feelings, business is business. They'd caught Sammy and David and I was next on the agenda.

'They have killed Kyle and I thought it would end there, I swear it. They caught up with Iwanek in Spain but that was his own fault. He'd barely arrived in Benidorm before he started trying to flog the stuff. It must have been like a bluebottle flying smack bang into the middle of a spider's web, setting off all sorts of trip wires.'

'Trip wires stretching back to where?' he asked, and that was the £250,000 question and this time he deserved a straight answer because now he was in as much danger as I was. I took a deep breath to prepare myself because the shit was really going to hit the fan.

'Ireland,' I said and turned to look at him. We didn't accelerate and he didn't slam hard on the brakes but the temperature in the air-conditioned Lagonda dropped at least ten degrees. It was a full thirty seconds before he spoke, and only after he'd softly rubbed the scar where the ridge of white skin merged into his moustache.

'Jesus Christ, what have you done?' he asked quietly, and it reminded me of Shona's words, except this time it was well and truly rhetorical because he knew exactly what I'd done. 'I assumed it was a few London hoods you'd got involved with, that I could have dealt with. But the IR bloody A? You must have been mad. They'll never stop, you know that don't you? They'll keep on coming until we're all dead.'

'It shouldn't have happened this way, the circle should have been closed once Laing and Kyle were killed,' I said. 'That should have ended it, Tony. I can't understand how Carol got involved.'

'Carol got involved, you stupid, inconsiderate bastard, because you involved her. If you'd been straight with me from the start I'd never have let you within a million miles of her. She didn't deserve to die the way she did. Alone and screaming and blaming you and probably me too.'

'It's too late for what might have been, Tony,' I said. 'We can't go back. God, I don't want to spout a load of clichés but what's done is done. If I could turn time back I would, believe me, but she's dead and McKinley's dead and I can't change that. I've got to look after myself, and Shona and David, and you've got to protect yourself. If Carol gave them your name then you're in as much danger as I am.'

'You think I don't know that?' Tony replied. 'That I hadn't worked that out for myself? I'm scared shitless, more frightened than I've ever been in my life. And you know how well protected I am.'

I did, too. The Lagonda Tony was flinging around the A217 was enough to turn heads in its own right, but he'd spent another twenty thousand having numerous refinements installed. He'd got the car from a South American dictator as part payment for an arms deal and it came complete with an ultra-sophisticated alarm system. A pigeon landing on the bonnet was enough to set off a howling siren and a personal radio bleeper which Tony always carried. Most of the money had gone on structural refinements, armouring the body panels and reinforcing the underside making it virtually bombproof, armour-plated glass replacing the original windows, a petrol tank that you could fire a bullet through without causing an explosion, if you could find a bullet large enough and with enough velocity to penetrate the armoured tank in the first place.

The tyres were practically invulnerable, you could drive them through fire or over broken glass without any problems, and a blow-out at ninety mph wouldn't even be noticed. The car had a common or garden radio telephone, but it was also equipped with a short-wave transmitter operating on a frequency used by diplomats and terrorist targets and constantly monitored by the Metropolitan Police.

At the touch of a button he could release five gallons of oil from the armoured boot which sounded like something only James Bond would need, but Tony swore he'd once had to use it and I believed him. There were other safety features he hadn't told me about, and as far as he was concerned it was money well spent.

His home was even more secure. It was a turn of the century five-bedroomed detached house on three floors in Notting Hill, standing alone in half an acre and surrounded by an eight-foot wall. From the outside it looked like a highly desirable residence, which it was, the sort of house you'd expect to be occupied by a Channel Four film producer. It was also a fortress, and inside Tony was safer than the Crown Jewels. Anything larger than a cat moving across the lawn would set lights flashing on a console within the house and in the police station a mile away. The front and back gardens were covered by closed circuit television cameras. Just like the Lagonda all the windows were of toughened glass, and the outside doors were reinforced with steel. Tony had no household insurance. He didn't need it.

Underground was a wine cellar which doubled as an inner sanctum, lined with concrete and entered through a three-inch thick steel door. Once locked it was airtight with a self-contained oxygen supply and virtually bomb-proof. There was a separate and well-protected telephone link with the local police station, and more than a few guests had remarked on the mauve telephone on the wall behind the chateau-bottled claret.

At home, in his office and in his car, Tony was safe, but we both knew that he was vulnerable when he moved between the three and we also knew that the sort of men we were dealing with now were fanatics with very long memories. If they decided that Tony was a target then it might be days, weeks, months, even years, but eventually they would come for him. Maybe while he was on holiday, playing squash, walking his Labrador, in his local pub, anytime, anywhere. No wonder he was frightened.

'But it's not myself I'm worried about, it's you, and those close to you,' he said. 'I got hold of Shona at the office today so at least she's safe. But there's no sign of Sammy. Where is she?'

I'd been honest with him up to this point, but if I had any chance of getting Sammy and David out of this then I had to work alone. The last thing I wanted to do was to lie to Tony but I had no choice, if I could handle it myself and quickly then perhaps I could close the circle once and for all.

'She's safe, out of harm's way,' I lied, as casually as possible. Another stain on my hypothetical painting.

'If that's the case, sport, what do you need those for?' and he glanced at the Harrods carrier bag.

'I'm going to take them on at their own game, Tony. And it's best you don't know the details. Either way you'll be OK. If I win then it'll be over, if I lose then perhaps they'll let it die with me. Whatever, I have to try. And you can't help me, nobody can. It's best you don't know.'

'I might be able to help. I have friends. And don't forget that Laing could still be on the loose.'

'God, Tony, I know that. If anyone could help it would be you, believe me. But I have to do this myself.'

'A man's got to do what a man's got to do? Very macho. I'm your friend, let me help.'

'I can't, Tony. I'm sorry.'

He drove on in silence, burning up the miles along the M25 towards Heathrow at a steady ninety mph, flashing his headlights at anyone impertinent enough to stay in the outside lane and several times overtaking on the inside. 'Where are you going?' he asked after a while.

'Stonehaven,' I said. 'There is one thing you can do for me.'

'What's that?'

'You can order a hire car for me at Edinburgh Airport. Something big and powerful. I've got my Access card and a cheque book so there's no problem in paying but it'll save time if you book it for me.'

'So Shona won't be there to collect you?'

'No. I'd rather she kept out of the way until this is over. And I'd feel safer if you did the same.'

'Don't worry about me, sport. Just be careful. And if I can help, let me know. I'll be there like a shot.'

'I know, Tony, I know. You've done more than enough already, more than I deserve. I won't ever forget this.' I put my hand on his shoulder and squeezed gently but he didn't look at me and he didn't speak again until we arrived at Heathrow. He waved me goodbye and good luck as I walked into the terminal with the case in one hand and the carrier bag in the other. I'd left the duty free with Tony. I wouldn't be drinking for a while.

'The car will be waiting for you at the airport,' he shouted after me, and it was when I arrived in Edinburgh two hours later. It was bitterly cold and the wind tugged at my hair as I loaded the luggage into the red Cavalier.

My watch said 2.55 and in just a little over four hours I'd know when and where this was going to end, one way or another. The Cavalier started first time, it had a full tank of petrol and it kicked me in the back as I put the accelerator pedal to the floor and headed for Stonehaven.

I stopped off at a hardware store on the outskirts of Edinburgh, one of those tiny shops that have been in the same family for years, where they'll sell you fifty different types of nails, a brown paper bag of assorted screws and the sort of tools that Spear and Jackson no longer bother to make.

It smelt of wet string and candle wax and oil and the old man behind the counter in a stained brown overall called me Sir. I bought a hacksaw, a small wood saw and a strong carpenter's file. I couldn't see any packets of sandpaper but the old man asked what I wanted, dived under the polished wooden counter and came up with four single sheets of large grain paper.

'Anything else?' he asked eagerly, like an old Spaniel begging for a stick to be thrown.

'I don't suppose you've got any foam rubber, about so big and so thick?' I said, marking out the size with my hands.

'I think I have, in the back,' he said, and scurried off. I wandered round the little shop, running my fingers through barrels of bulbs, a huge cardboard box full of assorted bundles of string, and racks and racks of screwdrivers, spanners, hammers and things for getting boy scouts out of horses' hooves. Before long he was back, a piece of yellow foam rubber clutched to his chest which he carefully rolled up, tied with string and placed in a carrier bag with the rest of the purchases.

I paid him and drove the rest of the way to Stonehaven trying to work out exactly what I had to do and the order in which it had to be done.

The day after my father's funeral the house had been closed, I had driven David to the nursing home and then gone straight to London in the Porsche. A lady from the village came in twice a week to air the rooms and dust the furniture, but other than that the house had been left alone, deserted. That's exactly how it looked as I drove up the drive and parked in front of the stone porch. It wasn't a home any more, it was a building waiting for a family. It had no heart, no soul. The leaves had started to fall from the sycamores that marked the boundary with the road and they swirled around my feet as I groped in my jacket for the keys.

It was early afternoon but the house seemed gloomy inside and it felt and smelt damp. I'd planned to bring David back to the house when this was all over, bring in a housekeeper to clean and cook for us, but now I was having second thoughts. Without our parents as a focus it was just a collection of stones and slates and wood and we'd be better off starting afresh.

I opened the door to the study and walked over to the green velvet curtains which had been drawn since the police forensic team had left. The room had been dusted once or twice, certainly not as thoroughly as the rest of the house, and though somebody had tried to wash the blood off the wallpaper there was still a speck or two there, and on the bookcase I could see a piece of lead shot looking no more sinister than the stuff anglers use to weigh down their lines. I found the key to the security cabinet in the bottom left-hand drawer of the desk.

From the outside the cabinet appeared to be a simple mahogany box, about five feet high and three feet wide with double opening doors. It could have held drinks or files but it was lined with steel and the lock was better than the one on the front door, and inside was a rack with spaces for a dozen shotguns including the one my father had used to kill himself.

The key turned easily and silently and I drew back the doors. The guns gleamed and light glinted off the engraved plates. There was a pair of Denton and Kennell Number Ones, walnut stocks and delicate engravings, and three Midland over and under shotguns my father used to give guests who fancied a little rough shooting. There was a Winchester over and under and a couple of Beretta Sporting Multichokes that he lent to more serious shots, but my father's pride and joy was a pair of Purdeys that he'd bought for nigh on £12,000 six years ago at a Sotheby's auction at Pulborough.

They used to belong to one of the best game shots of all time, the second Marquis of Rippon, who was reckoned to have blown apart something like half a million birds in his lifetime. They had a history and my father loved them.

He'd spent hours polishing and cleaning the pair, but it was only one of them that he'd used to blow his brains out and that was the one I took from the cabinet and tucked under my arm as I grabbed a handful of cartridges and relocked the doors. I picked up the carrier bag of tools and foam rubber, walked down the hall and unbolted the door leading to the back garden.

At the end of the garden next to the grey stone boundary

wall was an old brick building that in years gone by had been a stable but which was now used as a tool shed, a place to store gardening equipment during the winter months and the place where we went to look for anything that had gone missing from the house. It was filthy and the wooden door was covered in cobwebs. It wasn't locked because there was nothing inside worth stealing, but it had the one thing I wanted which was a solid oak workbench with a huge steel vice, made like they don't make them any more.

The light switch wouldn't work or maybe the bulb had gone, but there was still enough light coming in through the cracked and dirty window panes to see by. I opened the vice as far as it would go, placed the shotgun between the heavy metal plates and clamped it as tightly as I could. The hacksaw cut easily, surprisingly easily, through the barrels, but I was still sweating by the time they clanked noisily onto the stone floor.

The stock was a lot harder. I tried to remember the shape of the gun Iwanek had used but he'd moved so quickly once the shooting had started that I'd barely caught a glimpse of it. I decided to try to cut it into the general shape of a pistol grip and I scratched into the walnut with a rusty six-inch nail I'd found on the bench, marking out the lines where I would use the wood saw. I had three or four goes but it still didn't look right. Eventually I attacked it with the saw, hoping that once I'd got started the shape would become obvious, like a sculptor chiselling away at a block of stone, allowing the material to define its own form rather than having one imposed on it.

It took half an hour of solid sawing to take off the bottom eight inches of the stock, the wood was hard and compact, more like metal than the product of a tree and

I'd really worked up a sweat by the time I had finished. I used the hacksaw to cut the remaining bit of the stock into something approaching a grip but it was very uneven and wouldn't sit in my hand. The balance was completely gone and it was going to need both hands and a lot of concentration to fire accurately, but I planned to follow Iwanek's advice and get in close so maybe that wasn't too important.

It was starting to cloud over and I could hardly see what I was doing inside the shed so I picked up what was left of the shotgun and the sandpaper and went back to the study.

I sat in my father's captain's chair in front of the desk and rubbed and sanded the grip until it was smooth and slid into my hand and my finger could reach the trigger without straining. I loaded two cartridges into the breech and went into the garden again carrying a thick blanket from one of the spare bedrooms, down the crazy paving path to the stable building.

It wasn't overlooked; behind the boundary wall was a field of yellow oil-seed rape and in this part of the country a shotgun going off at dusk wouldn't worry anybody, local farmers were forever taking potshots at rooks and rabbits. The stable wall furthest away from the house was bare brick with no windows or doors, and I hung the blanket over it by tying two of the corners to the old rusting guttering.

I stood about twelve feet away and let go with both barrels, one at a time, the shot ripping through the blanket, shredding and tearing it and kicking up puffs of brick dust from the wall. At that distance the shot spread out in a seven-foot wide circle, much wider than a standard shotgun but that's why the barrels are normally so long, to focus the energy and the destructive power. Shorten the barrel and the range is drastically reduced, but close up that didn't matter and judging by the state of the blanket there wouldn't be much left of the target from twelve feet away.

The gun had kicked in my hands and pulled to the left when the first barrel exploded, but when I fired the second I was ready for it and steered the gun round, held it steady and firm and hit the already tattered blanket dead centre.

Back in the study I cleaned and polished the Purdey, much as my father used to, carefully, lovingly, but above all efficiently. When I had finished I tried to fit it into my brown, metal-framed leather briefcase, a present from Shona, but it was too narrow and the lid wouldn't close.

Then I remembered my father's old briefcase, a black plastic one, scuffed and grubby with a thick plastic handle with indentations for the fingers. The reason he'd always used it was that it was a good five inches deep and held twice as much paperwork as any other case he'd ever had.

I found it in the cloakroom under the stairs and by its weight it was obviously full of papers. It was locked with two gilt combination locks at either end, the gilt finish long since worn away. The numbers were my father's birthday, 611, and my mother's, 129, and I tipped out the papers onto the floor, took the empty case through into the study and heaved it onto the desk. The gun fitted diagonally, plenty of space above and below and at least an inch and a half to spare at either end.

I took the shotgun out and untied the rolled up piece of foam rubber which was about half as big again as the case but about the right thickness. All I needed was a pair of scissors or a sharp knife to cut a hole for the gun, and I found the former in one of the drawers under the kitchen sink and I hacked and cut the foam rubber so that it fitted tightly around the gun with a couple of gaps where my fingers could grip the barrel and the butt and pull it out smoothly.

It was six-thirty pm and I spent a full thirty minutes practising walking with the case, swinging it onto the desk in one fluid motion, then flicking the locks open, lifting the lid and bringing the gun out.

I did it again and again, until the actions felt right and I could get the shotgun into my hands while looking perfectly calm and relaxed, until I could do the whole operation blindfold, doing it all by touch while my eyes looked straight ahead. I did it with my eyes closed, I recited poetry with a fixed grin on my face and eventually it came naturally, one moment I was placing the case on the desk, the next the gun was in my hands, cocked and ready to fire. Bang, bang, you're dead. Maybe.

The call came at seven, exactly as promised, and it was a girl. At first I thought it was Sammy, and half a sentence had passed before what she was saying registered and I realized the voice was slightly softer and younger than Sammy's and that it came with a warm, Irish brogue.

It was a voice J. Walter Thompson could have used to sell Guinness, Irish whiskey, or holidays in tinkers' caravans, a voice that was mellow and sweet, that you felt was ready to break into an infectious laugh and tease you and scold you.

'. . . but I suppose there was no way you wouldn't be there, now was there? You have the money with you?' There was a slight intake of breath as she asked the question, a startled gasp as if she'd just been kissed unexpectedly on the cheek.

'I have it here,' I said. 'I want to speak to Sammy.'

'Well now, you'll just have to be wanting, for a while at least. They're quite safe, and they'll stay that way as long as you do as you're told, and you are going to do as you're told, aren't you?' A pause. 'Aren't you?'

'Yes. Don't hurt them. Please.'

'Do you have a pen and paper? I'll say this once, and only once. Drive from Edinburgh, across the Forth Bridge to Perth and from there take the A9 to Pitlochry, exactly as if you were going to Shankland Hall to see your darling brother.

'This time, though, you'll continue along the A9 for another forty-five miles or so until you reach Kingussie. Then you'll leave the A9 and take the B9152 to Kincraig, on the northern shore of Loch Inch.

'Go through Kincraig and drive for exactly 2.4 miles from the last streetlight in the town. Then you'll see a signpost on the right for Inshriach Distillery, down a single track road. The distillery has been shut down so we won't be disturbed.

'Follow the track to the end, you'll pass a terrace of cottages on the right, and then you'll come to the carpark in front of the distillery building. It's E-shaped and on the left you'll see a large black door. Immediately to the right of it are metal steps leading to another door on the first floor. You'll be met there.

'Now, I want to make one thing clear to you. You will be watched, and if we should for one minute think you are trying to double-cross us again your lady friend and your brother will be dead. If you don't come alone they're dead. If you don't have the money with you they're dead. The drive will take you four hours if you're lucky, four and a half if you're not. If you are not here by midnight then they're dead. And once they are dead we'll come for you. I suggest you hurry.'

Then the line was dead, and the message was all the more chilling coming from such a provocatively sexy voice. In the bookcase behind the desk was a leather-bound atlas and I turned the pages until I came across a large-scale map of the Scottish Highlands. The distillery would be close to the River Spey and by the look of the map it was in the middle of nowhere which is why they had chosen it. To the west was Loch Ness and south west was Loch Ericht. To the east were the Cairngorm Mountains and the whole area around the distillery seemed to be thickly wooded so there'd be no problems if they had to make a run for it. But at least it would be dark when I arrived, and tonight the weather forecast was cloudy and there wouldn't be much in the way of a moon.

Four hours sounded about right for the drive so I sat for a while, head in my hands and elbows on either side of the atlas, thinking harder than I had ever thought before because this time it was my life that depended on the decisions I made now. My life and Sammy's and David's.

Fight your own battles, Tony had said. How? With a gun I'd fired twice? Against professional killers? My conscience was in cold storage now because I had already accepted that this time it was going to be my finger on the trigger. The luxury of getting somebody else to do the killing, of removing myself mentally and physically from the end result, was something I couldn't afford now.

As I studied the map and tried to put together a workable plan I felt no guilt for what had happened or for what was about to happen. That would come later, and I'd try to deal with it then. For the moment the part of my brain that solved problems and worked out strategies was insulated from the part that decided morality and apportioned blame. Friends and enemies were just pieces on a chessboard, taking part in a game I had to win.

There were three points in my favour. They were professionals dealing with an amateur, which meant there would be an element of surprise on my side. They wouldn't expect me to be armed, but I would have a shotgun and I was prepared to use it. And it would be dark. They were my strong suits and however I played it I'd have to maximize those advantages.

In the kitchen I found a pile of large, black plastic bags and a ball of thick string. In the stable building I dug out an old inflatable dinghy in which my father had taken me fishing before the pain in his back became too much to bear. It had been deflated and carefully packed into a green nylon bag with rope handles, and I loaded that onto the back seat of the car along with a foot pump and two plastic oars.

All I needed now was something heavy, and under a trellis table I discovered four long rusty chains made up of half-inch diameter steel links. Each was about fifteen feet long and I could only lift them one at a time into the boot and the car sagged on its back axle. A helicopter buzzed over the distant fields like an angry wasp as I slammed the boot lid shut.

Back in the house I raced up the stairs three at a time and rushed through my wardrobe, picking out the darkest pullover and trousers I could find, and choosing a pair of dark brown walking shoes. In the cloakroom I grabbed a green Barbour jacket and hurtled through the front door as a tall figure in a fawn raincoat came around the side of the house. I fumbled for the locks on the briefcase, cursing loudly, as the man broke into a run, coat flapping against his legs as his feet crunched into the gravel.

'Whoa, sport, it's me,' shouted Tony, and for the first time I heard the high-pitched whirring whine of a grounded helicopter as the blades came to rest. I'd been so caught up with my own thoughts that I hadn't noticed it land in the field behind Stonehaven.

'Thanks for dropping in, Tony,' I said, trying to clear my head. He still wasn't smiling, and neither was I. What the hell did he want? I thought, but I already knew the answer. I didn't offer to shake his hand, this wasn't a social visit.

'Who's the chauffeur?' I asked.

'A friend. A good friend and somebody who's done me a great many favours in the past. I didn't like having to ask him again. And be careful what you say, you're skating on very thin ice at the moment. His name is Joel Riker. He learnt to fly in Vietnam, Hueys, H-23 Hilliers and Chinooks, but now he can fly anything with a rotor blade. That's a Sikorsky we picked up at Edinburgh. I'd cut out the cracks about him being a chauffeur, too. A year before the war ended he was flying a gunship near Pleiku in South Vietnam when he was shot down. The gunner was killed and Joel and his co-pilot were on their own for six days. They had to fight their way through thirty miles of Viet Cong infested jungle before they were picked up. Between them they killed sixteen VC, most of them with their knives.'

Over Tony's shoulder I could see Riker climbing down from the white helicopter and walking towards us, head bowed under the slowly-turning blades. He was tall, thin and wiry, three inches of wrist sticking out of the sleeves of a tatty old sheepskin flying jacket, a gaunt face topped with a shock of prematurely grey hair.

'How do you know they weren't exaggerating?' I asked. 'These Yanks are all the same.'

'They came back with sixteen sets of ears,' said Tony quietly, and there wasn't a lot I could say after that.

I shook Riker's outstretched hand, his grip was soft and gentle, the handshake of a dowager duchess. His voice, too, was effeminate, a nasal, slightly out of breath purr. He sounded a bit like Bambi.

'What's the game plan?' he asked Tony.

'Give me a chance, Joel. I haven't even found out what the rules are yet. Come on, inside.'

'Tony, I don't have time. I have to go. Now.'

'You're not going anywhere, sport. Inside.'

The two of them bundled me back through the front door, along the hall and into the study.

'Sit,' said Tony, and as I opened my mouth to speak he placed a finger across my lips. 'Be silent.'

Riker leant against the desk, legs crossed at the ankles, arms folded across his chest as Tony paced slowly up and down in front of me, thoughtfully chewing the inside of his cheek.

'I rang up Shona from London and got the number of David's nursing home. So I know he's missing. And Sammy's disappeared, too. And you raced up here like a dog with its tail on fire. I want to know where they are and what you plan to do. Come on, Rover, give.'

I gave. I had no choice, I didn't have the time to mess Tony about, and even if I ran out on him all they would have to do was to follow in the helicopter. I gave. Where, when and how. The lot. When I had finished Tony looked at Riker and raised his eyebrows.

'It could work,' said Riker, answering Tony's unspoken question.

'There's no alternative,' I said. 'I have to go in alone. They'll be watching me.'

'I agree,' Riker said to Tony. 'If we had enough time and manpower, then we'd stand a chance of storming the place, but as it is . . .' He dropped his hands to his sides, palms out. 'I think we should let him do it.'

'OK,' nodded Tony. 'You're the expert.' He turned to me, rocking gently back on his heels. 'We're coming with you.'

'No,' I said, and stood up. 'I have to go alone. Haven't you been listening?'

'You will be going alone,' he said patiently. 'We'll take the high road.'

'They'll hear you coming for miles in that thing.'

'Give me credit, sport. Have you got a map of the area?'

I pointed towards the atlas on the desk behind Riker. Tony picked it up and stood with the pilot as he ran his finger across the page.

Riker spoke quietly. 'It'll be dark so we won't be seen, but the noise will carry for at least two miles, possibly three even if I come in low. Let's say three and a half to be on the safe side. Here.' He jabbed at the map. 'Then we move through the woods on foot. That could take two hours, say two and a half at most if we don't get lost. We can do it. But we'll have to leave soon. Like now.'

'Me too,' I said, but they weren't listening to me.

'Fuel?' asked Tony.

'Enough.'

'Anything else?'

'Artillery,' said Riker, and I realized that they had also flown up from London and passed through the metal detectors. I unlocked the gun cabinet and pulled open the doors like a magician producing a rabbit from a hat.

'Gentlemen,' I said. 'Choose your weapons.'

Riker took the Winchester and Tony chose one of the Berettas. I handed out cartridges and felt better, I felt part of it.

'OK?' Tony asked Riker.

'Sure. Let's do it.'

'Now listen to me, sport,' Tony said to me, laying his hand on my shoulder. 'Do exactly what you planned to do. We won't make a move until you go inside and we hear shooting. Just forget we're around.'

'We have to go,' Riker interrupted, checking his watch.

'Right,' said Tony, looking at me long and hard. 'One more thing. Laing still hasn't surfaced, which could mean he's dead, or on the run, or that he's behind the killings. Be careful.'

Then they turned and I followed them into the evening gloom and watched as they walked down the side of the house, vaulted cleanly over the dry stone wall and waded through the yellow flowers to the helicopter. I locked the front door and pocketed the keys.

It was 7.45 pm when I slid into the driving seat of the Cavalier, next to the attache case and the Harrods carrier bag, and pulled out of the drive and pointed the car towards the Forth Bridge as the helicopter clattered into the air.

* * *

About ten months before all this had started, before I'd even heard of Kyle and Laing, I had helped one of the few remaining independent whisky firms in Scotland raise cash through a rights issue, and I'd been their guest at a weekend 'fact-finding exercise' visiting distilleries in and around Moray and sampling large quantities of the amber fluid.

The tours of the distilleries had been very much like a school trip, lectures by serious-faced men with ruddy complexions and tweed jackets who had been in the industry all their working lives and for whom whisky really was Uisge Beatha, the water of life.

I remembered very little about the individual distilleries because they all looked basically the same, but a few facts had stuck in my mind like midges to flypaper.

Each year, Scotch whisky earns more than £700 million in markets all around the world. A bottle of Scotch is drunk every tenth of a second in the United States, a bottle a second in Venezuela, a bottle every seven seconds in Norway and a bottle every twenty seconds in the Philippines or Malaya or somewhere, and it all comes from about 130 distilleries in Scotland, each making a whisky with its own distinctive taste. Perhaps the weekend whisky binge hadn't been a complete waste of time, after all. It was only when I began to pull the facts out of my memory that I appreciated just how much I had learnt about the industry.

Most of the whisky they make goes for blending, producing brands like Bell's or Famous Grouse, but some are just bottled as single whiskies, malt or grain. Blends account for about ninety-eight per cent of sales and it can take up to fifty individual malt and grain whiskies to make one blend.

At each distillery someone in the party had asked: 'But what gives Scotch its flavour? Where does the taste come from?' The question would always be greeted with a knowing smile and a load of Highland waffle about that being one of the great mysteries of distilling, and if everyone knew the secret then the Japanese would be able to produce the real thing instead of the paint stripper they mixed with imported malt to make something that a true Scot wouldn't dream of allowing past his lips.

The most honest answer we had been given came from the export director of the host company, a tall, thin greying man with a bushy handlebar moustache who wore the kilt for the whole trip but who was never out of a dark pinstripe suit when in the firm's Edinburgh head office. The simple answer, he said, is that we just don't know.

One of the folk laws surrounding Malaysia's national drink is that it's the old stills that produce the spirit's flavour and bouquet, and that when new stills are needed the old ones are faithfully copied, knocks, bashes, dents and all. There seems to be an element of truth in that, all the tweed jackets agreed, but research scientists with PhDs can drink the stuff all night and still not decide why that is. Or why cheaper whiskies result in harsher hangovers than a good single malt.

What they can tell you is that whisky, when it has been distilled, is a mixture of ethanol and a host of other minor constituents, essential oils from the malted barley and other cereals and chemicals from the peat, which do depend on the type of still, its shape and even the way it's operated.

Going over in my mind the way whisky is made triggered off memories of the four or five distilleries we'd visited and I tried to picture their layout. All were sited near streams or rivers or pools and most were well away from towns and cities. That meant the men and women who worked there were supplied with cottages, usually in terraces close to the distillery with pretty gardens front and back.

The girl on the phone said the distillery had been abandoned, so the cottages would be empty. Mothballed distilleries are pretty common in Scotland now as gin, vodka and white rum become more popular, and their design and isolation means the buildings aren't good for anything other than whisky production. The big whisky firms just close them down and move the workers out, sometimes keeping a token staff on a care and maintenance basis.

One of the distilleries we went to had its own malting room where the barley was screened and soaked in huge tanks of water called steeps, before being poured into revolving mechanical maltings about three times the height of a man where the barley germinates and the starch turns into sugar.

Then it's dried in a peat-fired kiln, the air thick with smoke, before being ground up to form grist. Most distilleries miss out this stage, though, preferring to have the malt delivered from a central malting firm – it's more economical and means they always have a regular supply. If Inshriach had one, the chances were it would be on the ground floor or in a separate building.

The handover of the cash was going to take place on the first floor which meant it would be in one of three places, the mashing room, the fermentation room or the stillhouse.

The floors in all three would be of thick wire mesh running the whole length of the building with steel staircases climbing up and down to link the various levels.

The mashing room is where the grist is mixed with hot water in large metal barrels with gleaming domed copper lids about twenty feet across. Much of the mash tuns is below floor level with about six to eight feet sticking through, and inspection hatches set into the lids along with temperature sensors. The wort, the thick sugary liquid, is drawn off from the tuns and the crud that's left is sold for cattle food. 'Which is why the Highland coo always has a wee smile on its face,' we were told on four separate occasions. The whisky might vary from distillery to distillery but the jokes remain the same.

The wort is cooled and pumped into even bigger vessels, fermentation vats, this time made of wood and holding up to 45,000 litres. Yeast is thrown in and this converts the sugar into crude alcohol.

The fermentation rooms always smelled like breweries, the air heavy and sweet as the wort bubbled and frothed. 'One chap fell in and took four hours to drown. He wouldn't have lasted so long if he hadn't had to get out and go to the toilet twice.' That one we heard three times.

Again, the bulk of the fermentation vats is below floor level. About twelve feet in diameter, they would come up to a man's stomach, and unlike the mash tuns the lids are flat and made of wooden sections which can be removed one by one.

There could be as many as a dozen vats in the fermentation room. A good place to hide, and to fight.

Somewhere close to the fermentation vats would be the stills, tall copper cones, rounded and bulbous at the bottom like an onion and stretching up to five, six, maybe seven times the height of a man, thinning out until just a few feet thick and then bending over so that the evaporating alcohol pours off and down towards the spirit safe, where the still-man can check the quality and proof of the whisky without being able to touch it.

There would be at least two stills, probably more, larger wash stills for the first distillation and smaller spirit stills for the second time around. The spirit that's eventually sold in shops and pubs and bars is the middle cut of the second distillation, but even that is barely drinkable until it's been allowed to mature for several years under lock and key and the watchful eye of HM Customs and Excise.

The casks would be stored in long, narrow, bonded warehouses, probably wooden with pitched roofs and likely to be found at the side of the distillery. If the distillery was in mothballs then chances were the warehouses would be empty too, except for the smell of maturing spirit and whisky-soaked wood, but they'd be kept secure and without windows so that's where David and Sammy could be kept out of the way. Maybe.

Thinking of the two of them added a good fifteen mph to the speed of the Cavalier, but I didn't ease back because Tony and Riker had delayed me and the roads were good as I passed through Perth and headed for Pitlochry.

It was starting to rain and I switched on the windscreen wipers and turned up the heater, then turned it down again as I realized I couldn't be cold because my palms on the steering wheel were sweating.

* * *

It was dark by the time I reached Kingussie following the route Sammy, David and I had taken to visit the Highland Wildlife Park. God, it seemed a lifetime ago. I turned into the B9152, driving to Kincraig parallel to the shore of Loch Inch. The Cavalier headlights carved out tunnels of light through the blackness, the road speckled with raindrops, the windscreen wipers whirring quietly. The effect was almost hypnotic and twice I braked too late and too hard when an insomniac sheep wandered in front of the car.

The inhabitants of Kincraig were all indoors out of the rain when I passed through the town, and it had been more than an hour since I'd seen another car on the road. I felt like the last man alive, the only occupant of a dead world, a ghost planet. When I crossed the last streetlight, plunging into the dark and leaving the glow of the town behind me, I pressed the trip counter on the speedometer and watched it count off the tenth-mile segments as the road twisted and turned through the hillside.

I saw the signpost just before it clicked up 2.4. It leant to the right, the wood was cracked and gnarled and the lettering was obscured by green moss, but I could just make out the 'Insh' of 'Inshriach' and I pulled the wheel round sharply to the right and drove into the woods.

The track was just wide enough for one vehicle with passing places every hundred yards or so. It was rutted and potholed and the car bucked and swayed as it bounced from hole to hole.

The soaking tree trunks glistened under the headlights,

branches whipping to and fro in the wind. The windscreen wipers began to clog up with fallen leaves, and the car skidded as I followed the track to the right and guided the car uneasily alongside a line of stone terraced cottages, gardens overgrown behind white picket fences, windows blank like the eyes of a blind man, washing lines bare, rainwater cascading over blocked gutters. On the downstairs window sill of the middle house sat a brown and white cat, its eyes glowing brightly, tail twitching as it turned to watch the Cavalier go past.

The track opened up into a large tarmac carpark in front of the distillery itself, a two-storey whitewashed building, E-shaped with the three prongs of the E pointing towards the cottages. On the left of the building was a white Ford Sierra and I parked by the side of it, three yards away from the black door the girl had described. I switched the lights off and allowed my eyes time to get used to the watery moonlight which faded and flickered as rain clouds passed overhead, then stepped out of the warmth of the car with the briefcase.

My footsteps echoed around the courtyard as I climbed the metal steps. At the top I wiped my soaking hands on the Barbour jacket and seized the brass door handle.

The door opened easily and silently and I crossed the threshold into the mashing room, moonlight reflecting off the copper-topped tuns.

Down the left-hand side of the whitewashed stone wall were a series of small, circular windows, five times the width of a ship's portholes. Through them I could see clouds passing over the dulled stars in the night sky and then the moon was blotted out and I was in complete darkness.

At the far end of the room was an oddly-squeezed

goal-post of light, and as my eyes became accustomed to the dark I could see it was a closed door with light shining through from whatever lay beyond. Then the moon reappeared from behind a cloud like a scolded child putting its head around a door and I moved across the room, the thick wire mesh floor rattling under my feet with each step, briefcase handle gripped firmly in my right hand, left hand forward to open the red-painted wooden door in front of me.

I felt like a latecomer to a party as the door opened and I stepped into the light, blinking. All conversation, if there had been any, stopped and everyone was looking at me as if I'd arrived at a black tie reception dressed in a blazer and slacks. But this wasn't a party and there was no smiling host to step forward and cover my embarrassment and offer to introduce me to everybody.

The light came from a battery-powered lantern which was hanging from one of the steel girders that criss-crossed the high roof above the fermentation vessels. There were no windows in the fermentation room and the lamp suggested that all power had been cut off to the mothballed distillery.

I could see four people in the room, spread among a dozen wooden circular tubs which came up to just above stomach height, ranged in three lines of four, two lines close to the walls and the third running down the middle. With the red door behind me I was standing in a corridor between the central line of four vats and the right-hand batch.

At the end of the room and to the left were David and Sammy, David sitting with his back to one of the vats with his legs pulled up against his chest, Sammy standing by his side, ruffling his hair. David beamed as he saw me and tried to get up, but Sammy crouched down beside him and whispered into his ear. He settled back down but watched me carefully with wide eyes. I smiled and waved with my free hand.

'It's all right, David, you'll soon be home,' I said loudly, still walking, now passing the first vat, the hand holding the briefcase clamped tightly shut, eyes taking in as much as I could.

The girl was standing six feet to the right of David and Sammy, in the space between the left and centre lines of vats. She was about five feet two with close-cropped red hair and an elfin face with a crop of freckles around her pert nose. In thigh-length boots and green jerkin she could have passed for Peter Pan, but she was wearing a green waterproof anorak zipped up to the neck and blue jeans and in her right hand hanging by her side was a large black handgun.

She took a cigarette from her lips with her left hand, dropped it to the ground and moved to stamp it out, but it fell through the wire mesh in a shower of sparks to the room below. 'Well now, just in time,' she said, glancing at her wristwatch. 'And with the money, too.' Hers was the voice on the phone.

She smiled and turned to her partner, tall, thin with a mane of black curly hair and a long, hooked nose. He was standing at the end of the corridor I was walking along, but slightly to the right so that the lower part of his body was obscured by the last wooden vat in the right-hand line.

He was wearing a similar anorak, but his was open to the waist showing a white crew-necked pullover underneath and he had on grey herringbone trousers instead of jeans. They both wore blue and grey training shoes and could have passed for students hitching around Europe, if they'd had a couple of rucksacks and if they hadn't both been carrying guns.

His was black and seemed bigger than hers and from sixty feet away it looked like a revolver, but the lamp was tied with a piece of wire to the girder which crossed the room directly over their heads so it shone straight down on them, and it was hard to judge exactly what they had in their hands other than to see quite clearly that his was pointing at my stomach.

The door clicked shut behind me and I whirled round in a panic because I'd left it open. Ronnie Laing was there, leaning against the wall, arm across the door, a lazy smile on his suntanned face, every strand of his blond hair in place, blue eyes watching my every move with cold amusement.

He wasn't carrying a gun, with two professional killers on tap he didn't need one. He rubbed his long tapered hands together, smoothing them like a concert pianist about to play to a packed Albert Hall. The smile grew wider.

'So glad you could make it,' he said softly, the spider to the fly. 'I was almost hoping you wouldn't come and I'd be able to play with Sammy.' The eyes behind the green-framed glasses blazed with evil intent and I knew full well that unless I came out on top he would get to play with her and that she'd die screaming while he stood over her, smiling his lazy smile.

I was surrounded, but two had guns and one didn't so it was no contest. Laing would have to wait.

I turned my back on him and began walking again. I swung the case slowly backwards and forwards in time with my feet and started talking, not concerned with the words or the sense, just trying to keep their minds off the case and what it contained and my mind off what was going to happen and what could happen if it all went wrong. Mouth in overdrive, brain on auto-pilot, I was back in my father's study in front of his desk, reciting poetry.

'The money's all here,' I said, and I was surprised at how steady my voice was. My throat was dry and my tongue felt twice its normal size and I couldn't swallow. 'Just keep calm,' I said. 'There's no need for anybody to get hurt.'

The girl smiled at that and she moved to the right, away from David and Sammy, and stood behind the penultimate vat in the middle line about six paces away from her partner who moved to his right and stood in the corridor facing me.

She raised her gun in both hands and pointed it at my chest and my skin crawled as I saw that she was still smiling, eyes flashing like a flirtatious teenager.

Now I'd passed the second vessel and the third was only three steps away, left, right, left and then I was swinging the briefcase up in a relaxed, fluid motion across my body and onto the wooden lid of the vat in front of me.

The man's gun was pointing down towards the floor and I hadn't seen him take off the safety catch but that didn't mean anything because the chances were it was already cocked and ready to fire. They'd both moved forward and their faces were in shadow, the lamp shining behind them giving them halos around their hair like two wayward angels.

The case came down on the lid with a dull reverberating thud and I saw Sammy jump. She stayed low beside David and put her arms protectively around his shoulder, hugging him to her. Our eyes met and instinctively I realized that she knew exactly what was going to happen next. She half smiled, a brief flash of her perfect teeth, and she nervously reached up to brush a strand of loose hair away from her face. As my hands moved towards the case she shifted her body, putting herself between David and the two killers, watching me over her shoulder, muscles tensed, a cat ready to spring.

I could feel Laing's eyes boring into my back and I fought the urge to turn and look at him. If I did I knew for sure that I'd be lost. The man and the girl were moving again, she walked round to the right and into the corridor next to him, he then shuffled across to give her room and the bottom half of his body was once more hidden by the last vat in the right-hand line.

I wanted to scream at them, to tell them to stand where they were. Stay calm. Stay cool.

'I suppose you'll want to count it but I'd be grateful if you'd get a move on because I want to get David home as soon as possible,' I said, as my hands moved to operate the locks on the case. I'd already set the combinations and the locks flew open as I pushed the gilt buttons either side, the two clicks sounding like one.

The girl's gun was still aimed at my chest, the man's down at the ground. They turned to smile at each other as I raised the lid.

'You've no idea the problems I had getting the money together at such short notice,' I said. 'I almost didn't make it. And you didn't give me nearly enough time to drive up from Edinburgh, the roads can be vile at this time of night . . .'

I was talking too much but it didn't matter any more because the shotgun was in my hands and I stepped away from the open case. In one movement Sammy pushed David sideways onto the wire mesh floor and threw herself on top of him, using herself as a shield, a tigress protecting her young. But David wasn't her offspring, he was my brother, and she was still risking her life to keep him out of harm's way. Whatever happened I promised myself I'd never let Sammy down again, no way would I ever disregard the loyalty she'd shown, a loyalty I knew I didn't deserve. I held onto that one thought, blocking all else from my mind.

The girl turned first, her eyes opened wide and her mouth formed a perfect circle of surprise as she fought to unscramble the messages from her retina.

The man saw the look of confusion on her face and he stepped forward towards her and then began to turn. Her gun was pointing at my groin but she made no move to pull the trigger, and she frowned in confusion like a little girl trying to remember her nine times table and then I fired.

The shot ripped through her anorak and jeans the way it had shredded the blanket tied against the outbuilding back at Stonehaven, and the green and blue of her clothing was stained with red as she lurched backwards and slammed into the wooden vat behind her, mouth still open, face untouched because I'd aimed low. Behind me I heard Laing curse and scrabble for the door handle. I ignored him, he wasn't armed.

The gun dropped from the girl's fingers and rattled onto the metal floor and she groaned and pitched forward with her hands clutching her bloodstained stomach.

I turned the shotgun towards her partner but I knew I wouldn't make it because his gun was already levelled at my chest and the finger was tightening on the trigger and I still had to move through ninety degrees to stand a chance of hitting him, so I angled it upwards instead and fired at the lamp above his head.

The two bangs were simultaneous and the lamp went out. I heard it shatter and the pieces slam against the roof as the bullet from his gun caught me in the chest, lifted me off my feet and threw me backwards down the corridor. I hit the floor shoulders first and then my head crashed back and I felt it open and bleed, but the pain was nowhere as bad as the crippling numbness in my chest. The door behind me opened and closed as Laing fled the scene, footsteps clattering and echoing.

I could breathe only in short, halting gasps, like an engine starved of petrol, shuddering and juddering. My ribs felt as if they'd been hit with a sledgehammer and at least two were cracked or broken, but I was lucky that he'd gone for the chest and not tried a head shot or hit me in the legs because then the lightweight bulletproof vest that Tony had given me at Heathrow wouldn't have saved my life, and I'd be lying bleeding to death on the floor like the girl and not inching backwards to rest against one of the empty oak vats and groping around to find the shotgun in the blackness.

David started screaming and then his piercing yell was muffled as Sammy put her hand over his mouth and comforted him. 'Are you all right?' she called. 'My God, are you all right?' But I couldn't answer, I was still recovering my breath and, anyway, to have replied would have given away my position – horizontal, hurt and, for the moment at least, helpless. Sammy didn't call out again, though I could hear her whispering softly to David.

Somewhere in front of me the man moved, slowly and carefully because he was as blind as I was in the pitch-dark room, but he was fit and healthy while I was lying winded on the floor and feeling as if an elephant had sat on my chest. And he had a gun in his hand.

He had seen where I'd fallen so all he had to do was to inch forward in the dark until he found me and then it would be over. I managed to pull myself sideways, dragging myself to one side and out of his way but stopped when he heard me moving, and then there was a flash and a bang about fifteen feet from me and a bullet tore a chunk out of the vat to my right so he knew I wasn't dead, but at the very least he must have thought I was in a bad way because he'd seen the first bullet slam into my chest.

A second shot hit the floor and the bullet screeched off the metal and ricocheted into the blackness. Then there was only silence and I tried to steady my breathing because in my ears it sounded like a steam engine puffing and blowing, and I could hear my heart pounding but there was nothing I could do about that.

I screwed up my eyes and then opened them wide but it made no difference, the darkness was absolute, no light at all in the room. Then my eyes started to play tricks and I saw greenish circles and spots of red which twisted and rolled, and white whirlpools swirling above my head as my information-starved brain produced its own signals to make up for the lack of stimulation from the optic nerves.

He moved again and this time he was creeping sideways, to my right, but I wasn't used to relying solely on my ears so I couldn't tell if he was ten feet away or twenty as the perspiration dripped down the back of my arms like blood from an open wound.

I reached into the pocket of the Barbour jacket and pulled out Tony's second going away present. They smelled of rubber as I pulled them over my eyes and pressed the ridged button on the right-hand side. The light intensifiers flickered once and then I could see again, the goggles picking out details of the room and its contents in a greenish-grey hue.

They came from a consignment Tony was in the process of selling to a West African state. Manufactured by Ferranti, powered by a small nickel-cadmium battery, they were the perfect issue for infantry fighting at night.

Worn like a pair of ski goggles, they didn't have to be fixed to a rifle like the Nato night sight, and they allowed soldiers to move easily in the darkness with their hands free to shoot and fight.

From where I was sitting I couldn't see Sammy or David but the man was there, about fifteen feet away to the right, facing in my direction and creeping stealthily towards me, right arm holding his gun at waist height and his left waving in front of his chest.

He was pushing one foot forward, slowly, feeling along the metal floor so that as soon as he touched my body he'd know where to pump in the bullets. He stopped moving his left foot, transferred his weight over and then began moving his right. Two feet ahead of him was my shotgun and he was heading straight for it.

Reaching for it was out of the question, I could barely breathe never mind crawl to the gun before his probing feet found it, and once I had started moving he'd have a good idea where I was, and it wouldn't take more than a few random shots in my direction to hit me and this time I might not be so lucky.

My ribs felt on fire as I took a lungful of air and spoke. 'You're standing two feet to the right of a vat, your right foot is forward and you're holding your left hand out in front of your body. Unless you drop your gun I'm going to blow your balls off.'

Immediately the words left my mouth I rolled over twice, wincing with the pain as I got out of his line of fire.

He stopped dead in his tracks and in the grey-green image intensifiers he looked like a zombie with his arms outstretched, his mouth open so that he could breathe shallowly with the minimum of noise and his eyes wide and staring, trying to pick out any details in the dark and wondering how it was that I could see him when he couldn't make out his own hand in front of his face.

He pointed the gun at where I'd been lying and then what I had said sunk in and he dived to his left, thudding into the vat and falling to the floor where he scampered off in a panic on all fours towards the wall.

He disappeared from view but I heard another dull thud as he collided with something in his rush to get away. I managed to crawl to the shotgun on hands and knees, the metal mesh biting into my skin. I knelt with the gun between my thighs as I fumbled for a couple of fresh cartridges from my pocket, and as I slotted them into the breech I saw the man again, this time standing upright in the far corner of the fermentation room, face towards the wall with his arms outstretched, palms touching the whitewashed bricks. He was moving quickly crabwise, legs moving together and then apart, like a rock climber traversing a cliff face. He was heading for a door at the end of the corridor I was in, the twin of the entrance I'd come through from the mashing room.

He reached for the handle with searching fingers as I brought up the shotgun, still kneeling, but he tore open the door just before I pulled the trigger and moonlight flooded in and the goggles went opaque. I fired anyway, but when I ripped off the goggles the door was open and a cloud of white powder was billowing down from the pockmarked wall above it.

I staggered to my feet and lumbered to the door, the goggles bouncing around my neck, bending double because of the pain but also to keep myself as small a target as possible. I peered around the door frame and saw a row of four stills, copper gleaming in the moonlight. At the far end of the stillhouse long, thin windows stretched from the ceiling to the floor below as if in a church, and they rattled eerily as the wind outside buffeted and pushed and threw squalls of rain against them.

A shot cracked through the air, whistled past my ear and into the roof behind me and I pulled back my head. Footsteps clanged as he ran down metal steps to the ground floor and then it was quiet again.

Still bent double I went over to Sammy and David, crouched together on the floor, David crying and Sammy holding him in her arms, whispering gently into his ear, kissing away the tears. I knelt beside them and stroked the base of David's neck.

'Stay here,' I whispered. 'Whatever happens, stay here.'

Sammy seemed too shocked to speak and she just nodded dumbly and carried on petting David. Neither of them was dressed for a night in an unheated Highland distillery. David was wearing old brown cord trousers and an American baseball jacket I'd brought back as a present from a business trip to Baltimore last year. Sammy wore a light-weight blue linen trouser suit, and they were both shivering.

I took off my jacket and put it round her shoulders, but it didn't stop her trembling because it was fear and anger that were making her muscles shake and spasm, not the cold.

The girl's gun was lying three feet in front of her and the butt was dotted with blood. She was moaning softly, almost purring like a contented cat. There was a dripping sound, plop, plop, plop, like water from a tap, but it wasn't water it was blood running through the metal grille and onto the concrete floor below.

I didn't feel sorry for her and I didn't move to help her, because she'd been the only one smoking and that meant it had been her who tortured Carol and it had been her that Carol had begged to stop. But she hadn't stopped and Carol had died in her bath, burnt and bleeding.

I picked up the gun, wiped off the congealed blood and handed it to Sammy, who looked at it as if I'd given her a dead mouse. I checked the safety catch was off and that there was a bullet in the chamber as the gun trembled in her elegant hand. It looked out of place, like an air raid shelter in a pretty country garden. Would she use it? Probably not, but it made me feel a little easier knowing it was there.

'I'm going to shut the door again and then I'm going outside,' I said to her. 'No matter what happens, stay here. It'll be pitch dark so don't move around. Do you understand?'

She nodded and hugged David tightly, her eyes wide and afraid and fixed on the girl's body.

'Listen to me, Sammy,' I said, and she looked up and forced a half smile.

'If that door opens when I'm gone, fire the gun.' I pointed to the doorway leading to the stillhouse. 'It won't be me, I'll come back the way I leave, through the door at the end,' and I gestured towards the door where I had walked in only minutes before, swinging the briefcase and telling everybody to keep calm.

'And make sure it's me. Laing's still around. Do you understand?'

'Yes,' she answered, her voice dull and flat, but at least she was looking at me when she said it and not through me. I kissed her on the forehead, and as I ducked back to the door I heard her say 'Take care.'

I fired the shotgun's second barrel through the doorway then slammed the door shut, plunging the room into darkness once more. After pulling the goggles back over my eyes I ran to the opposite end of the fermentation room, the way Laing had gone, through the door and to the top of the stairs at the entrance to the mashing room, footsteps ringing on the metal floor.

The clouds were thicker now and they completely covered the moon so I kept the goggles on as I took the stairs two at a time, reloading as I went.

I was so busy looking out for Laing that I lost my footing on the wet metal at the bottom and pitched forward, going down on one knee and cursing, but the noise wasn't a problem because I wanted them both to know I was coming.

The courtyard was deserted save for the two cars, no sign of Laing or of Tony or Riker. Maybe they'd had mechanical trouble, or maybe it was just taking longer than they had planned to get through the dense forest. Whatever the reason for them not showing up, I was alone. It was to be one against two but one of them was a professional and well used to killing and I was an amateur, fighting because I was hurt and angry and in a corner. Place your bets, gentlemen. Evens the hired killer from Ireland, thirty-three to one the corporate financier from Edinburgh.

'Where are you, Tony, now that I need you?' I asked of

no-one in particular. But the plan from the start had been to end this myself and it was too late to call time now.

At least if I did fail then there was still a chance that Tony and Riker would arrive to clear up the mess and save Sammy and David, the cavalry arriving in the final reel, in time to save the day but too late to rescue the hero.

The door at the base of the staircase was locked so I moved back and fired at the wood just below the lock. It splintered and cracked and some of the shot ricocheted off the brass fittings, but the door sagged on its hinges and the second explosion knocked it back completely, throwing it through the doorway and onto the concrete beyond.

My ears roared with the echo of the shots as I went back up the steps, quietly, on tiptoe, but moving quickly, free hand on the rail so that this time I wouldn't trip and give my position away.

I waited until I reached the top before reloading, and then stepped inside the mashing room and silently closed the door. I tiptoed between the stainless steel mashing vessels, grey-green in the goggles, and stood in the middle of the room, shallow breathing, completely still, shotgun pointing down.

I started counting in my head, slowly ticking off the seconds, more to calm my breathing and racing pulse than to keep track of time.

The floor below was clearly visible in the image intensifiers, the metal grille acting as a veil, and after a short while I could forget it was there, moving my head from side to side to keep the whole of the concrete area in vision.

A block of weak moonlight fell on the floor in front of the shattered oak door and my heart stopped as something moved, but it was coming from the wrong direction and it was furry with four legs, the brown and white cat come to investigate the noise and see if there were any rats or mice poking around for stray malt pellets.

It stood stock still in the moonlit square, tail twitching as it sniffed the peaty air, and then it gently lifted its head upwards and stared straight at me through the grille. Fifty-five, fifty-six, fifty-seven, and then there was the rasp of a shoe against concrete and the cat turned and ran in one movement, back into the night.

He was down in a crouch, about thirty feet from the fallen door where I would be silhouetted against the moonlight and he'd get a clear shot. He licked his lower lip, and if he'd had a tail he would have twitched it. Ninety-three, ninety-four and he was moving again, still crouched, into the centre of the room below.

It must have been a storage area at some time but now it was bare and he was as unprotected as a beetle on a Formica kitchen top. He took the gun in both hands, steadied his feet shoulder-width apart and held the weapon out in front of him like a cop in an American TV movie.

He was five feet to my right and I didn't want to risk firing the shotgun at an angle, but if I moved he was bound to hear me so I stayed where I was and counted, one hundred and ten, one hundred and eleven.

Something clattered in the courtyard outside, probably the cat but he thought it was me and he tensed, moved two steps to the left to get a clearer view and then he was right underneath my feet.

I pressed the open barrels of the Purdey against the metal grille and fired, the gun kicking in my hands as the shot funnelled through the gaps. The floor rattled and shook and the top of his head disappeared in a shower of crimson, a scarlet rain that blew across the concrete.

He stayed upright, the gun still levelled at the doorway, one hundred and twenty-five, one hundred and twenty-six, and then the arms started to rise upward, pointing to the ceiling above his bloodsoaked head which turned up to reveal a pulpy mess where the face had been, strips of flesh hanging down over the chin and the lips, what was left of them, drawn back in a grimace of a smile. His eyes, untouched by the shot, were white circles in the red and they looked into mine as the arms moved higher, one hundred and thirty-three, one hundred and thirty-four, and they went right over his bloody head and he fell back onto the concrete like a sack of malt tumbling from a conveyor belt, a lifeless thud followed by a ringing echo as the gun rolled along the floor.

One hundred and fifty-nine, one hundred and sixty, I couldn't stop counting, my brain fixed on the numbers so that it wouldn't have to dwell on the man twelve feet below me, eyes wide open and staring as his legs and arms twitched, nervous spasms because there wasn't enough brain intact for conscious movements.

He had stopped moving by the time I reached one hundred and eighty, only three minutes since I'd waited for him to investigate the wrecked door. I went back down the steps and stood over the body, kicking it gently, just in case, but it wasn't necessary. I didn't have to hold a mirror against his mouth or check for a pulse because the sightless eyes showed that he was dead.

I knelt by the corpse and went through the pockets of the anorak, loose change, a cigarette lighter (so maybe he was a smoker too and maybe he was the one who'd used the lighted cigarettes), a box of cartridges and the keys to the Sierra. There was no wallet, no driving licence, no identification, but that was to be expected. They were professionals, and professionals don't wear labels.

As I took the keys I heard a footfall in the doorway behind me and I swivelled around still in a crouch, ready to fire the shotgun with one hand which would have snapped my wrist like a damp Twiglet if the hammers hadn't clunked down on two empty chambers.

'What a fucking pity,' said Laing, and this time he did have a gun in his hand. 'What a fucking pity,' he repeated.

I stayed down, hunched low but ready to dive to one side, left or right, like a goalkeeper preparing himself for a penalty. One chance, sudden death. Please God let him shoot me in the chest.

'They were going to kill me,' he said. 'They'd already killed Alan and that bastard of a mercenary you used to double-cross them, and then they came after me.' He shook his head slowly from side to side. 'You almost made it. You were that close.' He held up his left hand, index finger and thumb an inch apart.

'Do you want to know why they didn't kill me?' he asked. I nodded. Keep him talking, pray that Tony and Riker would get here.

'A postcard,' he said, grinning boyishly. 'A fucking postcard that I'd sent to Alan, care of his office. All it said was "Having a time here. Wish you were lovely", but it was posted in Paris and the date showed when I was there. That postcard and that stupid joke saved my life. But it was too late to save Alan. They found it in his office after they killed him.'

He was toying with the revolver, slowly scratching the barrel along his cheek. I tensed, ready to leap.

'I like the idea of the bulletproof vest,' he said. 'But it won't work again. The next one goes right through your fucking head.'

I relaxed, sagging down onto the concrete floor, cradling the useless shotgun, beaten.

'Sammy told me why you did it, you know. She told me everything before we killed Carol. They let me help, they wanted me to help, to involve me, I suppose. But I'm going to have Sammy to myself. Completely and utterly to myself. Shall I tell you what I'm going to do to her?' And he did, carefully and precisely, missing out none of the details, while tears of rage, of shame, of frustration, of pure helplessness, welled up in my eyes because there was nothing, absolutely nothing I could do now. I'd lost the edge. I'd lost control. I'd lost.

'You must have really loved your old man to go through all this,' he said thoughtfully. 'I didn't exactly shed a tear when my dad shuffled off this mortal coil. Mind you, he didn't top himself.'

'I'm going to kill you,' I whispered.

'You're not, you know,' he said, and levelled the gun at my head. 'I'm afraid it's going to be the other way around. Give my regards to your parents.'

Time stopped. You know how it is when they show the film of the assassination of President Kennedy, the black and white grainy frames played in slow motion, his head whipping forward and backward and then forward again, so you can't tell how many shots there were, or where they came from, whether the only shots came from Oswald in the Dallas book warehouse or if there was someone else to the side or behind the motorcade, firing at the same time. You can't tell, no matter how many times you see the film, and no matter how often I reran Laing's death in my head I still couldn't get it right, I couldn't work out if his head erupted first or if his chest turned red and wet, whether there were two shots or three, whether he fell forward towards me or just crumpled in a heap. I didn't even hear the shots. He was dead, that was all that mattered, and I was splattered with his blood.

Then I heard Bambi say 'Easy, son,' and I saw Riker and Tony in silhouette, guns at the ready.

'Jesus, where have you been?' I asked, struggling to my feet and breaking the shotgun, ejecting the spent cartridges.

Riker stepped over Laing, walked past me and then looked down at the body of the man I'd shot. He surveyed the metal grille above our heads. 'Nice shot,' he said approvingly. 'Very nice.'

For some reason his approval made me swell with pride, praise from a pro, so I bit back the remark I was going to make about it being no wonder America had lost the war in Vietnam if that was an example of their time-keeping. I was starting to get cocky, and it was overconfidence that killed the cat as my grandmother used to tell me. Sweet old lady, but she could never get her proverbs straight. If the cat fits, wear it, was another of hers. It was years before I found out what that one meant. My mind was wandering, I suppose shock and panic does that, so I fought to steady my thoughts, concentrate on the job.

'What kept you?' I asked Tony, and he shrugged. I noticed then that his raincoat was dirty and torn and that his trousers and shoes were covered in mud. His face was criss-crossed with scratches, several still bleeding. It couldn't have been a picnic clawing their way through thick woods at night.

'Forget it,' I said. 'I'm just glad you're here.' Riker, too, looked abashed as he joined us in the doorway.

'What's the position?' he asked, shouldering his shotgun.

'I've killed two of them,' I said. 'The other's upstairs.' For some reason I added 'She's a girl' but there was no reaction. 'Sammy's upstairs with David. Could you get them away, now? Not back to Stonehaven, to Shona's parents, maybe. Stonehaven's in a bit of a mess,' I finished lamely.

'Sure,' said Tony. 'What are you going to do?'

'I'll clear up here and join you later.'

'We'll help,' said Riker.

'No, it's my mess. I'll clean it up. There's no point in all of us taking any more risks. I want to see this through to the end. And it won't be over until the bodies are buried.' I handed him the keys to the Sierra. 'Where's the helicopter?' I asked.

'In a clearing about three miles away,' said Riker.

'That's a point,' interrupted Tony. 'What are we going to do about the chopper?'

'Leave it where it is tonight,' said Riker. 'There's no way I'm going through those woods again. I'll come back to Edinburgh with you and then pick it up tomorrow. Assuming I can find it.' He smiled. 'Hey, what would I tell the guys we hired it from? "Sorry guys, I've lost your Sikorsky somewhere in the Highlands." Do you think we'll lose the deposit?'

Tony slapped him on the back and together we walked up the steps to the first floor. When we got to the door of the fermentation room I held up my hand, motioning them to wait.

I banged on the door hard and shouted, 'It's me, Sammy. It's OK. I'm coming in.' But I needn't have bothered because when I knelt beside the two of them the gun was lying by her side and both her arms were around David.

Riker and I walked David through the mashing room and down the steps after Tony and Sammy, and together we eased him into the rear of the Sierra. There was an old tartan blanket in the back and Riker tucked it around David, for warmth and for comfort.

'He'll be OK,' he said. 'By the look of him he's been drugged, Librium or Valium, something to keep him calm and sedated. I don't think he'll remember much of what's happened.' He sat next to him and closed the door.

'They made him take some white tablets soon after we picked him up at Shankland Hall,' Sammy said as she got into the front passenger seat.

'What about you?' I asked as I bent down to get level with her.

'They didn't give me anything, but it might have been better if they had. I've seen a lot of things tonight that I'd sooner forget.'

'Did Laing hurt you?'

'No, but I saw what he did to Carol and he took great delight in telling me what he planned to do.' She started to cry, softly.

'I'm sorry.'

'Hey lover, it's not your fault, I don't blame you.' She reached out and gently punched me under the chin. 'The man had to do what the man had to do,' she said, echoing Tony's words. She smiled. My heart fell every time she gave me one of her forced smiles, and this was one of them.

'Bullshit,' I said.

She leant forward and kissed me on the lips, her long red hair brushing against my cheek. 'I understand,' she said. 'That's why I wanted to help.' Then she smiled and this time my heart didn't fall.

She reached for my right hand and played with my fingers. 'I don't think the girl's dead, she was still moaning,' she said. She shuddered and then slipped the Barbour off her shoulders. 'Here, you'll catch cold,' and dropped it over my arm before closing the door.

I walked over to David's side of the car as Tony switched on the engine and flooded the courtyard with light.

I wiped his tearstained moon face with my handkerchief through the open window until I realized I was smearing him with blood. He didn't notice and tried to touch my cheek. He looked like a Red Indian covered with warpaint.

'All for one?' he said in a halting voice.

'And one for all,' I finished, and ruffled his untidy, greasy hair. 'You're going home with Sammy and Tony. They're going to take you to see Shona. Be good.' Tears started to brim in his eyes so I quickly added: 'I won't be long, I promise. I've just got a few things to do here. I'll see you soon.'

Riker leant across and wound the window up and I stood back and waved them off. As the sound of the Sierra faded into the distance my eyes grew used to the darkness once more, and with the quarter moon reappearing from behind a cloud and the stars starting to twinkle in the sky again, I didn't need the goggles to find my way back up the stairs to the first floor.

The girl had stopped moaning, but as I rolled her onto her back the eyes flickered open and her tongue gently moistened her lips through small white teeth.

Enough light came in through the open door to illuminate her torn apart chest and legs. Rivulets of blood were collecting in the folds of the tattered nylon anorak, she was bleeding from so many places that there was nothing I could do to stem the flow. Plop, plop, plop.

'I'm cold,' she whispered. I put the jacket around her and gently stroked her hair.

'I'm so cold,' she said in a voice that was scarcely more than a whimper. I knelt next to her and took her hand.

'Can you hear me?' I asked, and squeezed. It was the hand of a small, frightened child and it went with the voice. Her eyes opened again, halfway at first and then fully, a slight smile on her lips.

'Of course I can hear you, boy,' she said, and shivered as if someone had walked over her grave.

'What's your name, love?' I asked.

'Maggie.' Her eyes closed again.

'Listen to me, Maggie. Listen carefully. You're dying, Maggie, and there's not a thing I can do about it. You've lost a lot of blood and there's no way I can get an ambulance out here, we're hours from anywhere even if I could get to a phone. I can't move you. Do you understand? There's nothing I can do.'

Her grip tightened, and then relaxed. 'And what's the good news, doctor?' she whispered.

Her chest had stopped rising and falling but she wasn't dead, not yet.

'Can you hear me still?' I said, lips close to her ear, and she squeezed again. 'There's something I have to know,

Maggie. Does anyone else know about me? Did the two of you report back to Ireland or were you working alone? I have to know.'

Her eyes opened again, the pupils wide and black in a circle of pale green. 'James,' she said. 'Where's James? Where's James?'

'He's dead, Maggie. I'm sorry. Listen to me, Maggie, please. Does anyone else know about me? Is anyone else going to be coming after me?'

She began shivering again, tremors running right along her body. I put my free hand on her forehead and she was cool to the touch.

'Maggie, I must know. Not just for me but for my family, too. And my friends. Are we safe?'

'You're safe,' she whispered at last. 'You're safe, boy. We were to get in touch only when the job was finished.' She coughed and blood trickled down one side of her pretty mouth, bright red against the whiteness of her skin.

'Oh, James,' she moaned softly. 'James.' Then her grip tightened, so hard that her nails bit into my flesh. 'Don't leave me, not yet,' she said urgently. 'Stay with me. Please stay with me.' I was back at Shankland Hall saying goodbye to David, frightened of being left on his own, needing to be with someone who loved him.

'It's OK, Maggie. I'm not going anywhere,' I said gently. She lay quietly until another spasm of coughing wracked her body and she sighed, a long moan that came from somewhere deep within her.

She lay still with her eyes closed and I thought she was dead. When she spoke again, even though it was just a faint purr, she startled me. 'You'll be hearing my confession?' she asked, and I held her in my arms, listening and forgiving until she died.

I lifted her easily and carried her down to the Cavalier, laying her down on the tarmac as I opened the boot and wrapped her in two of the black plastic bags, sealing them with tape, winding it around and around like a child doing up a Christmas present.

She was easier to handle when completely covered. I didn't have to look at the tousled red hair, the pert nose or the blood on her lips, she became just a parcel to be disposed of, not a pretty young girl that I'd killed with a shotgun. Out of sight, out of mind.

Laing was surprisingly light and I tossed him into the boot with Maggie, sheathed in plastic. James was heavier but I was still able to carry him draped over one shoulder after I'd put the bags round him. I lowered him onto the front seat, clipped the belt across him and closed the passenger door before going back for the shotgun, lying where I'd left it, next to a pool of his blood.

The water would have been cut off as well as the electricity, so I just left the blood to soak into the concrete. Besides, there was no way I could repair the damaged door or collect all the spent cartridges and bullets from around the distillery so I'd have to leave it, another mystery to lie unsolved on the files of the Highland police. That and the Loch Ness monster.

I put the goggles on and thoroughly checked all the rooms, looking for anything I might have left that could point to my having been there. Not that I thought I had dropped something incriminating because I'd left all identification back at the house. It was my conscience getting to work already, niggling and probing like a tongue worrying a loose filling. You won't get away with it, you've done wrong and you'll get caught, you'll pay for this. My father telling me that it didn't matter what I'd done so long as I told the truth.

I gave the area around the car a going over, too. It was all clear but it didn't make me worry any less. I was about to slip on the Barbour jacket I'd taken from Maggie's body until I noticed the blood on the lining, so I threw it into the boot with the shotgun on top of the two bodies. God help me if I was stopped by the police tonight, three bodies, a sawn-off shotgun and a bloodstained jacket. Calling that circumstantial would be on a par with claiming that Hitler had a bit of a temper.

I pulled away from the distillery, lights raking the terraced cottages as I headed for the tunnel of trees. The cat was back on its perch, head turning to watch me drive away, as the plastic wrapped body strapped into the passenger seat bobbed back and forth each time the car hit a pothole.

I thought of driving with the lights off and using the image intensifiers but decided against it. With the headlights switched on any oncoming traffic would be dazzled and unable to see inside the Cavalier, but at this time of night the roads would almost certainly be deserted anyway.

The car felt leaden, weighed down as it was by four occupants and the inflatable dingy, and I kept it at a steady forty-five mph as I followed the A9 over the River Spey and back towards Pitlochry. I left the main road after passing the village of Etteridge and drove along a little-used track to Dalwhinnie, close to the northern tip of Loch Ericht, sticking to the route I'd planned earlier in the evening in my father's study after Maggie's phone call.

Shown on the map as a thin line linking the A9 with the

A889, it was a short cut across the bleak Glen Truim, barely wide enough for two vehicles in places, wires strung between EEC-funded fence posts to keep sheep from wandering in front of what little traffic there was.

When I reached the sleepy granite village of Dalwhinnie I turned the Cavalier right onto an even narrower track which wound along the northern shore of the loch through the thickly-wooded Loch Ericht forest. On the map it appeared as a dotted line which petered out after Benalder Lodge, but I'd no intention of going that far.

Two miles down the track I stopped the car and switched off the engine, listening to it crackle and clunk as it cooled in the frosty night air. The tree tops whipped to and fro as the wind tried to pluck them from the black, gritty soil, and I shivered as I opened the car door but I still couldn't bring myself to wear the jacket.

There was no convenient gate as there had been at Loch Feochan when McKinley and I had driven down to the shore with Read, but the track was less than fifty feet from the water's edge so I reckoned I'd be able to carry everything without too much trouble.

I took Laing first. He seemed to have got heavier and I had to manhandle him out of the boot and drag him through the fence and half roll, half pull him over the rough grass and heather. James was next and I dragged him, too. Maggie I carried, carefully, tenderly, head against my chest as if I were taking her over the threshold, and I put her down gently where the water lapped on the ribbon of stony beach.

The chains and inflatable boat I dropped over the wire fence and then I drove the car half a mile back down the track towards Dalwhinnie, just to be on the safe side, in case a passing poacher got curious or a courting couple decided to drive along for a lovemaking session in the woods. Both were unlikely in the extreme, logically I knew that, but the maggots of unease and guilt were already gnawing away at my mind and the inner voice that was my conscience was telling me that I wouldn't get away with it, that somebody would catch me, somehow, somewhere.

I walked back in the darkness, jacket in one hand and shotgun in the other. My heart missed a couple of beats when I thought I'd gone too far but then I saw a hump in the grass by the fence. It was the boat in its bag, and I stepped through the wires and pulled it, and the chains, down to the lochside.

Clouds passed over the moon but they were thin and wispy, no heavier than a veil across a bride's face, so I didn't need the goggles as I unpacked the canvas bag, tipped out the deflated boat and unwrapped it on the beach. I connected up the plastic foot pump and it took four or five minutes to inflate the boat, my legs ached and I was breathing heavily by the time it lay on the stones, rocking in the wind. The plastic oars were each in two halves and I screwed them together and pushed them through the rowlocks.

I pulled the boat half into the water and weighed it down with one of the lengths of chain while I hauled the parcel that was Laing along the beach and heaved it in, knocking one of the oars out as the inflatable distorted and bent with the added weight. I pushed it into deeper water and climbed in, my legs soaking from the struggle.

I rowed slowly but powerfully through the choppy water until I was about a hundred yards from the shore. Making certain the oars were secure, I tied the chain around the body and rolled it over the side. It cut cleanly through the water and disappeared without a sound leaving the inflatable bouncing up and down, freed of its heavy load. A few seconds later a small stream of bubbles trickled to the surface and then they too were gone.

The journey back to the shore was easier than the hard slog out, but the wind pushed me to one side and rather than exhaust myself pulling against it I went along with it, beached the boat some fifty yards further along from my setting off point and carried it back to where Maggie and James lay side by side.

By now the adrenaline was flowing and the pain in my ribs had been replaced by a dull ache so I dragged James to the boat with little difficulty.

The black plastic around his feet tore on the rocky beach as his shoes scraped along the ground, and as I pulled him through the shallow water one fell off and I had to go back for it. I pitched him into the boat and then ran back for the chain that would hold him on the bottom of the loch until he rotted.

Water flooded into the inflatable as I pulled myself in and lay for a few moments gasping for breath, my head resting on his stomach, before I rowed out into the middle of the loch for the second time and pushed him overboard.

Back on the shore, I carried Maggie in my arms and placed her in the boat as it bucked and rolled in the water like a floundering porpoise. The chain, and the shotgun I'd used to kill her, I put by her side.

I thought of her confession as I rowed out into the loch for the third and final time, of the things she'd done in her short life, the people she'd killed and the way she'd killed them.

She had killed for money, she'd killed for her beliefs and

she'd killed for information. There had been no regrets during her confession, just a baring of her tarnished soul before she went to meet her Maker. She'd died without apologizing and with the name James on her lips.

I sat with her as the boat drifted in the wind, oars at rest. I wanted to tell her I was sorry, that I would turn time back if I could, that I was sorry that she'd died, sorry I'd killed her, that revenge wasn't sweet, it was poisonous and bitter, a taste not to be savoured and enjoyed but to be spat out in disgust.

I needed to tell her what I'd done, to bare my soul the way she had to me before she died. So I spoke to Maggie for the best part of an hour as we tossed in the loch, in a quiet voice that she couldn't have heard even if she'd been alive, the wind taking my words and dispersing them over the water like dead leaves scattering down from autumn trees. I didn't feel any better, I didn't feel any easier. I'd confessed, but confessions to the dead don't count.

After wrapping the chain around her and tying the bloodstained jacket to her legs I tried to drop her over the side as close to James as possible, but there were no reference points to guide me and it was impossible to judge distances in the dark. Still, I tried. It was important, to me if not to them.

With a grunt I rolled her over into the loch, but unlike James and Laing she floated, spinning slowly in the dark water until I prodded and pushed with one of the oars and the air trapped in the bags belched out and she sank slowly beneath the waves.

As the black shrouded parcel went under I remembered her pale green eyes, her pert nose and her mischievous smile. Then I blotted her out of my mind though I knew she would surface eventually, like a corpse rising from a hastily-dug shallow grave.

Now I was alone in the boat except for the sawn-off shotgun. I picked it up by the shortened barrels and caressed it, the metal ice-cold but the polished wood smooth and warm to the touch.

'I'm sorry, Dad,' I said. 'It wasn't worth it.'

I threw it high and far, and as it spun through the air the breech opened and the gun formed a 'v' like an unwieldly boomerang. It bounced along the water with a splash of spray and then was gone.

My brain registered movement at the periphery of my vision and I turned to watch a hunting owl swoop down and land in a clump of heather, wings outstretched and talons open.

Then, with a flurry and a flapping it was up again, climbing into the night sky and crossing the moon as it flew silently over my head towards the far side of the loch. In its claws a brown fieldmouse twitched once and was still. I gripped the oars tightly and pulled for the shore.